praise for HUNGER'S BRIDE

THE INTERNATIONAL LITERARY EVENT
OF THE YEAR

In the United States

"This is an extraordinary debut, with depth of detail and narrative skill presented effortlessly throughout its staggering length. Highly recommended."

—David A. Berona, *Library Journal* (starred review)

"Creates not just a single world, but worlds overlapping and interpenetrating . . . Serious readers take note."

—James Leigh, *San Diego Union-Tribune*

"Remarkable . . . mystery tethered to the life of Sor Juana Inés de la Cruz, the spectacularly evocative 17th-century Mexican nun and poet."

—Carlin Romano, *Philadelphia Inquirer*

"An extraordinary debut, with depth of detail and narrative skill presented. . . . Highly recommended."

—*Kirkus* (starred review)

In Canada

"There are marvels here . . . a work of massive scope and grand ambition. . . . What the author does . . . is let language loose, and the result is startling, at times frightening and often beautiful. . . . The greatest achievement of Anderson's novel . . . is in the evocation of the teeming, sordid pageant of Mesoamerica: its mythic, blood-soaked history, its geography of extremes, the holocaust of its cities and its people."

—*The Globe & Mail*

"An instant collector's item."

—Susan Walker, *The Toronto Star*

"Like Molly Bloom on peyote. Anderson has an uncanny knack for writing believable female characters filled with both self-love and self-loathing. . . . Anderson writes as the best painters paint—with clarity, finesse and infinite suggestion . . . all this beauty is worth the trip."

—*Vancouver Sun*

"One of the most remarkable books in recent memory . . . a taut, challenging novel of ideas . . . Anderson's debut stands proudly alongside such works as Gabriel García Márquez's *One Hundred Years of Solitude* and Eduardo Galeano's *Memory of Fire* trilogy."

—*Quill & Quire* (starred review)

"Richly imagined and rendered . . . Gertrude Stein-meets-William Gass . . . *Hunger's Brides* is a beautiful monster. . . . See for yourself."

—*Calgary Herald*

In Britain

"We must ask how this extraordinary masterpiece came to be left off the Booker shortlist."

—A. N. Wilson, *Daily Telegraph*

"One of the longest literary novels in popular memory since Vikram Seth's *A Suitable Boy*. . . . Fortunately, it's not a case of never mind the quality, feel the width. *Hunger's Brides* realizes its ambitions, taking the reader on a journey spanning 350 years and bringing to life one of the greatest literary figures of the 17th century."

—*Publishing News*

Paul Anderson

Sor Juana, or the Breath of Heaven

THE ESSENTIAL STORY FROM THE EPIC, *Hunger's Brides*

CARROLL & GRAF PUBLISHERS
NEW YORK

SOR JUANA, OR THE BREATH OF HEAVEN:
The Essential Story from the Epic, Hunger's Brides

Carroll & Graf Publishers
An Imprint of Avalon Publishing Group, Inc.
245 West 17th Street, 11th Floor
New York, NY 10011

AVALON
publishing group incorporated

First Carroll & Graf edition of *Hunger's Brides* 2005
First Carroll & Graf edition of *Sor Juana, or the Breath of Heaven* 2006
Published in the U.S. by arrangement with Random House Canada, a division of Random House of
Canada Limited.

Library of Congress Cataloging-in-Publication Data is available.

ISBN-13: 978-0-78671-778-1
ISBN-10: 0-78671-778-5

9 8 7 6 5 4 3 2 1

Printed in the United States of America
Distributed by Publishers Group West

for Satsuki

Contents

CONTENTS

17th day of April, in the year of Our Lord 1695

A NUN OF THE HIERONYMITE ORDER slips out of the room to inform the Prioress, who will notify the Archbishop of Mexico. Who will in turn send word to the Viceroy of New Spain, and he finally to his monarch in Madrid. While I just stand by—raging, as Juana Inés de la Cruz lies stricken with plague. And I, Antonia Mora—betrayer, forger, *whore*—know exactly who to blame. Let the official record show that in these last, darkest days, Sor Juana Inés de la Cruz emerged from the safety of her seclusion and toiled unstintingly, impervious to the swelling pandemonium—with me, her oh-so-loyal secretary and companion at her side—ministering to the sick of this convent, even down to its servants and slaves.

The end began two months ago. Late February, 1695. It is become now a year to remember.

The first whispers sifted in like smoke: a strange pestilence, burning like a brushfire through the Indian population of nearby Xochimilco. Soon neighbours all across Mexico City were reminding each other of a terrible plague said to have reached the coast on a slave ship in from Africa last year. Killing hundreds, then vanishing. Leaving villages without a living soul. Fathers and husbands gone mad: home from a week's hunting to find their thresholds strewn with bloated bodies lying in the sun where dogs had turned away from them. Buzzards too sated to fly . . . rumours too horrible to be anything but true.

Here in the capital it has always started among the poor. This time is no different. Out of every ten Indians, it strikes nine and kills eight, depopulating an overcrowded slum in as little as a week. Among the Europeans, our city's densely packed religious communities offer up the ripest pickings. By the time the sickness takes hold in the convent of Jesús María, a few short blocks away, our own cloister is ablaze with tales—not so wild, it turns out—of nuns vomiting fire, of bodies swollen black, hunched, horridly misshapen.

All but a few here have succumbed to the rising hysteria, and I have felt it in me, in the pit of my stomach, a fluttering like young love. I have seen it wavering like firelight in my neighbours' eyes . . . and it is a temptation difficult to resist. I resist another day or two by writing this.

I write as she taught me, I write because she no longer can.

Three separate strains of disease, shipmates now ashore and travelling the same road.

Sometimes they attack simultaneously, but more often each culls its own prey—wolves dividing up a flock. The first favours the body's hollows and joints, spawning grotesque swellings at the neck, under the arms, between the legs. Death is slow but survival, if in a greatly diminished state, is at least a possibility.

The second—*el Dragón*, or so we in whispers now call it—covets the lungs, drawing from its tortured interlocutors carmine flames of arterial blood that scorch the air for several feet about the deathbed. *Llamas de carmina* everyone says, never red, never vermilion or scarlet. Carmine. What is it we sense in this tint just short of purple—the dye of the cloak that protects, or the mantle that none may resist?

How I wish I could ask her . . . this, and *trescientas cosas mas.*

The third killer, the deadliest, we call *la Flojera*. The Lazy One. A name that chills me to my very soul. *La Flojera* fancies her meat predigested, liquefied. Savaging its victim's moist linings, her softest tissues . . . within hours a friend, a woman, is reduced to a moaning sac of overripe fruit leaking thin blood from her body's every opening.

Three nights ago, dark rites of propitiation for the deadly sins that surely brought on this plague flared into orgies of frenzied mortification. Chanting, flickering tapers, the swaying glow of censers . . . hairshirts black with blood and moonlight. Thirty nuns crawled that night on flayed knees over the convent patio, and with excoriated tongues licked its paving stones clean in the shape of a glistening cross.

We are the Brides of Christ, heads teeming with dreams of a lover resurrected as the plague claims us in our bloodied beds one by one.

It has been a consummation of appalling violence.

In this place of women, men now are everywhere, scuttling stooped and harried through the rooms and passageways, shovelling lime into now-vacant cells. Litter bearers and gravediggers, priests bending reluctantly to hear gasped confessions, handkerchiefs pressed to pale faces against the meaty stench. Any servants not yet stricken stay away. So few able-bodied women now remain that surgeons and priests do double duty supervising the labourers as they burn the dead women's garments.

Any man caught fondling a corpse or looting it of jewellery will be, by order of the Viceroy, drawn and quartered in the public square; and by order of the Archbishop, excommunicated from God. But we have discovered that neither decree is necessary. From best to worst, all of us have at last been delivered from sin.

It seems we have gone dead inside. Emotions, appetites, even the senses.

The screams echoing through these stone corridors are horror-filled and agonized—children's voices crying out for Lord and mother in equal measure, while we the living communicate in brief shouts, as though to the deaf.

We move, day and night, through a kind of roaring twilight welling up from the corners of our eyes. And *everywhere* now this sullen smudge of smoke fed on sodden cloth. In some insidious way it is indistinguishable from the drone of bottle flies buzzing above the jumble of unburied bodies beside the bonfires. Few of us notice anymore that everything, every surface—plaster, porcelain, stone, skin—glistens with a fatty sheen of suet and ash. Until the evenings, when by lamplight we all scrub furiously and wonder if the oily clinging of it will ever leave us.

Yesterday morning I struck an Indian full in the face for handling a body too roughly. Convent discipline verged on total breakdown. Mass hysteria, even violent madness, hovered about us, very near. . . .

Then, after the blackest night of all, just when it seems every last one of us must be taken, a clear morning breaks. An hour of eerie calm settles over this place. Though we cannot know it yet, the plague has withdrawn just as suddenly as it came.

There will be only one death today.

The stench too has lifted—and the flies, scattered now on a breeze that wafts the delicate fragrance of tangerines into Juana's cell. The nuns and novices who have assembled here, as though at a summons, exchange looks hungry for miracles. It is already beginning. They will say your body smelled of tangerines.

Oh yes, Juana, you've scripted your little dialogue with Greatness but do you know how I feel? To sit by and watch you—all these days and weeks. It didn't have to happen this way. This is my fault, my doing.

And now you watch me watching you play the sainted martyr. Ever the valiant sister: "Burning my body won't be so bad," you murmur. "Better here than on the Other Side. . . ."

Each time your beautiful eyes close, my heart leaps into my throat. Then they open once more.

"So, Antonia, it seems I won't have to lie next to Concepción after all, and listen to an eternity of her gossip."

You could have held back, not leaned so near—taken even a few hours' rest. The chaplain offered you his plague mask, and you just smiled.

I will not say good-bye to you. I will not be part of your chorus.

Oh, Juanita . . . look at you.

 Leaf shadows play over the far wall as though reflecting off water. Juana turns her face towards the low window above her bed of planks. Rust-red daubs and handprints, violent smears along the whitewashed wall and windowsill above the bed. They appear to me now—in this one insane instant—grim as hieroglyphs, gay as a child's finger paints.

"Would you like me to bring your telescope?" I ask. Stupidly. I will either speak or lose my mind. "Mother Superior has kept it in her chambers." Juana shakes her head weakly, no, but I persist. "You were never forbidden to use it. Not officially."

"Yes, 'Tonia, that's true," she answers softly. Some of the novices in this vault-like room have never heard her voice. "And Galileo Galilei was never forbidden to write poetry. . . ."

To those who have known Juana the longest, to one who has just bathed her lingeringly . . . she has never been more beautiful. Pale as parchment, her body like a girl's, disincarnate, feather-light, unadulterated . . . purely and completely her own. The fever has left her now, its work done. Gone from her face are the lines these past days had etched there.

Through the low window, sunlight streams into her unflinching black eyes. Only now do I understand she is blind.

"I feel the sun. Is it a clear morning?" Juana asks.

"Yes it's clear . . . very clear."

"What can you see—can you see the volcanoes?"

"Yes, *mi amor*," I answer finally. "They are white and splendid. If I were that bird, that eagle soaring up there . . ."

I am not sure how to go on.

" . . . I could see your mother's hacienda."

"Others?" she asks.

"Can't you hear them, the *urracas?* And *there,* a parrot . . ." *You are doing this for me, to distract me.*

"And flowers?"

"Juanita, *hundreds!* The jacaranda trees are still blooming in the streets. *Y las flores de mandarín*—you must smell *them* at least. There are roses, too. . . ."

I look up at the women gathered about the bed. I think every last one—some weeping openly now—must know by heart Juana's lyric on the rose. Sister Eugenia looks decidedly unsteady, one of the few to be nursed back to health, and by Juana herself.

Then the Mother Prioress, our desiccated paragon of gravity, enters the cell. We make way as she approaches the bed.

"Sor Juana? Can you hear?" The Prioress leans nearer, putting out a hand to steady herself. "I've just received word. From the *Archbishop.* Juana . . . ? He says he wants you to leave the convent. For your own safety . . ."

Sor Juana Inés de la Cruz lies unmoving, eyes closed, her breath a stuttered rustling in her chest . . . then stirs, as the faintest hint of a smile caresses her dark lips.

JUANA INÉS
DE LA CRUZ

B. Limosneros, trans.[1]

Rosa divina que en gentil cultura
eres, con tu fragrante sutileza,
magisterio purpureo en la belleza,
enseñanza nevada a la hermosura.

Amago de la humana arquitectura,
ejemplo de la vana gentileza,
en cuyo ser unió naturaleza
la cuna alegre y triste sepultura.

¡Cuán altiva en tu pompa, presumida,
soberbia, el riesgo de morir desdeñas,
y luego desmayada y encogida
de tu caduco ser das mustias señas,
con que con docta muerte y necia vida,
viviendo engañas y muriendo enseñas!

Rose, heaven's flower versed in grace,
from your subtle censers you dispense
on beauty, scarlet homilies,
snowy lessons in loveliness.

Frail emblem of our human framing,
prophetess of cultivation's ruin,
in whose chambers nature beds
the cradle's joys in sepulchral gloom.

So haughty in your youth, presumptuous bloom,
so archly death's approaches you disdained.
Yet even as blossoms fade and fray
to the tattered copes of our noon's collapse—
so through life's low masquerades and death's high craft,
your living veils all that your dying unmasks.

took her maiden name, Ramirez de Santillana. She gave me *Juana* and *Inés*. The year was 1648: Isabel was beautiful, spectacularly pregnant again and still defiantly unwed. She took her confinement in what everyone called the cell, a hut of dry-laid fieldstone serving as tool shed and sometime way-station to any Dominicans stopping the night on their missions among the Indians. And so it was that even at my life's beginning, my cell was haunted by the Dominicans and their good works.

Of course I've heard it described. Gables thatched with dried agave spikes . . . in a child's imagination they loll like leathern tongues. From the ridgepole, the cane-stalk bassinet hangs just inside the door, at eye level set beyond the reach of snakes and scorpions. Walls left unmortared for ventilation, and in the evening breeze the slight basculations of the bassinet. If I have a memory all my own it's a modest one: of loose-chinked stone . . . a wall of shells pale as canvas, pegged in place by wands of light. And beyond, panes of jade vegetation and turquoise sky.

The shed stood at the upper reaches of Grandfather's hacienda in Nepantla. In the poetry of the ancient Mexicans, Nepantla means 'the unstable margins of things,' and according to family legend I'd surely have been raised there, in my shaky palace of shells, had not Grandfather, who was riding the fence line on a tour of inspection, glimpsed my seraphic head through the doorway. Naturally he relented, and ended his daughter's exile.

I'd one day learn that my mother's exile had been largely self-imposed, a dramatic gesture directed at my father because he was not there. Adults, it seemed, were complicated. And none more than she.

The chief thing, for me and for our *Siglo de Oro's* latter, better half, was that she did emerge from our cell—either by Grandfather's leave or at his beseeching. Whereupon she refused first the offer of his horse, then the offer of his help with the hollow-boned bundle of cherub she held.

She stalked down (here I imagine Grandfather riding meekly behind), little moved by the view. Just above the ranch house the path bends north over a hill. Straight ahead lay the city on the lake, its far shore a frail glitter in the distance. The bearish shoulders of Ajusco Hill would have blocked her view of the island where Mexico rests on the charred stones of the city it supplanted. For that is the custom of this place, to build on the ruins of the vanquished.

Below her lay the ranch house, a one-storey horseshoe barred to the west by a high corral of *ocotillo* thorns. Once down, she returned to running the hacienda, having handed me over ("fastened me," as she put it) to a wet nurse she called Sochee. In my version it was to preserve her figure; in Isabel's, to preserve her nipples from the predations of an infant cannibal. I once ventured to ask, If I was so much worse than my sisters, why was it that Xochitl never once complained? A question answered with the barest shrug, leaving me to conclude all on my own that a descendant of the Mexicas[†] could have no objection to nursing an infant of my sort.

[†]Meh-SHEE-ka(s)— the dominant nation of the people loosely called Aztecs, whence 'Mexican' and 'Mexico'

From about that time, the frequency of Father's visits dwindled to roughly once a year. He still came faithfully for the breaking of the yearlings but only on rare occasions now for the breeding of the mares. It seemed attending the birth of daughters was no longer in his routine. My sister Josefa told me, with malign satisfaction, that he used to come *much* more often before I was born. This only made it all the more like a royal visit for me, and not just because of his family's remote and lofty origins. There was the unmistakeable nobility of his bearing, there was the civility of his manners—and he was so *handsome*. With black, black hair, and a manly chin, and big soft brown eyes like a horse's—no wonder even the wildest ones bent to his wishes.

And tall, taller than Grandfather, even. When he stooped from the saddle to scoop us each up for a hug good-bye, it was like being lifted into heaven.

Then he was gone.

We caught our breath.

The seasons resumed their turning.

 It was harvest time—I would have been nearly two—when I discovered the roof. I was in the courtyard confecting mud delicacies in the flower beds when there began a faint but incessant knocking at the great double doors. Eventually Xochitl hobbled over to open them for a dozen or so fieldworkers saddled under immense baskets of maize. Very quietly the first worker asked if *la patrona* was in, and when Xochitl shook her head, their faces brightened.

I had edged closer to determine for sure that these baskets, higher than each man's head and tapering to a point behind his knees, were indeed attached by straps—or was this some sort of centaur of the fields?

Xochitl waved them in. The baskets must have been crushingly heavy, to judge by how the straps cut into each brown shoulder. And still the men lingered at the door, asking after her, and very respectfully. Her health, her hip, her daughter Amanda, who was sleeping in the *rebozo* strapped to Xochitl's back.

Xochitl said to hurry up, before doña Isabel returned to find them all standing around.

"Yes, hurry up," I parroted, eager to see what might happen next with those baskets.

"You have taught her our tongue?" one asked.

"She learned. Same as Amanda."

"Doña Isabel does not mind?"

The first few men through the doors were all looking at me now.

"Go on up," Xochitl said more sternly, and drew the screen aside.

For over a year I had played in that courtyard with only a folding screen of woven straw between me and the sacred science of the stair. I had seen the ascending rectangles begin halfway up the wall and had— to the extent I noticed at all—thought them ornaments. It seemed my older sisters had not been interested; but then, they could go *outside* and wrestle for their lives with the coyotes and eagles and panthers and jaguars—and who knew what else—that we heard at night.

One by one the corn men lumbered up. Then, from down below where I swayed in wonder, I watched them turn and, from the topmost rectangle, step straight into the sky.

Xochitl shifted to block my ascent and redrew the screen, but the next day at siesta, I clambered up—with all the grace of a turtle, an indignity foisted on me by the thoughtless wretch who had built the steps so high.

At first all I took in was a wobbly carpet of cobs baking in the sun, and the hot, moist smell of the world as a drying oven. All I had known was the compound. I was splendidly unprepared for what I now saw.

Even a very short girl could see for nearly ten leagues[†] all around.   [†] twenty-five miles

To the southeast was a jumbled crust of sharp hills and spent craters like heaps of burnt sugar subsiding in a pan of caramel. To the south-west, as though warped on a loom, rough-woven panels of sugar cane stretched, and all through them the silver threading of irrigation ditch-es. An Aztec feather-cape of greens fanned west and north—deep groves of limes and oranges, and blue-green plantations of what I even-tually learned were Peruvian pineapple. Closer in, ranks of spindly papaya and the oily green oars of banana trees transplanted from the Philippines.

It may have been then that I had my earliest intimation of the links running from form to knowledge to power, for it was not long afterwards I began to draw. Maybe if I drew a thing I might learn to look for what I had not yet seen. And no sooner had I taken up my first piece of char-coal, than my eye found the pyramid in Popocatepetl. It took longer for my mind to trace the paradox hidden underneath: that volcanoes should mimic the simplest, stablest polyhedron, the pyramid—five sides to the cube's six. To picture that smouldering mass up there as *stable* was like a gentle tickling right behind the eyes.

For the next year I went up to the *azotea* every day, once I'd endured the first few spankings and then the dire injunctions to stay well back from the ledges.

Out onto the plain—as day after day I sketched their progress—the long dun caterpillars of aqueducts edged forth on their tiny arches . . . and on cold winter mornings I traced the little teapots of hot springs that riddled the join of plain and hill. Farther off stood a lonely tableland, and on it what Grandfather felt was certainly the ruined city of the House of Flowers. If only I looked hard enough I might make out the huge stained stones through the tangle of overgrowth . . . and then I would draw them for him.

I had discovered a world!—entire and new.

And now my old world was about to discover me. For I'd started trail-ing after my sister Josefa, who was not going out each day to wrestle jaguars after all, but to attend a school for girls. Though her teacher, Sister Ada, would not at first let me into the classroom, as I was only three, she indulged me, allowing me to look on through the window at their lessons of reading and writing. On the third day, as though by magic, a small bench of fresh white pine, sticky still with fragrant resins, stood under the low window. It was tranquil there beneath the arches, bees whirring among the bougainvillaea and geraniums, the gurgle of a little fountain echoing as from within a cave. . . . But I felt a great mystery about to be revealed. Far from nodding off as Sister Ada must have expected, I fairly bristled with concentration. The way my mouth was watering, one would have thought I was observing a lesson in cookery.

"I *must* learn to read," I pleaded that third day. "Please don't tell my mother—please?" Sister Ada consented not to tell for a little while, versed as she was in the attention span of three-year-olds. But when two more weeks had passed she insisted I ask my mother's permission, and in exchange she would find me a seat in the classroom, where I might learn a little of the alphabet. And what good would a seat inside do anyone spanked by Isabel? "No, no," I said, "I like your classes very well, but I can read now." She laughed—no, *brayed*. Which annoyed me, so I proceeded to treat her to samplings from the many little mottoes pinned up about the classroom walls. I had just the rudiments of reading but my memory was prodigious, and in combination these were enough to make her cross herself and go quite pallid. In our region, when one learns swiftly it's said, *The sorcerer has passed there.* Anyway, her gesture was to me a very satisfactory form of applause. I thanked her for the lessons and left.

Grandfather was away in Mexico City visiting my aunt and her rich husband. A day or two later he returned with his latest trove of books and a few childish texts to serve me as primers, but he found it was too late for these.

That same week the parish priest made a rare visit to my mother. At its conclusion Padre Luis, himself a man of scant education, confided, "Your Juanita has much promise. God must have designed her for great exploits."

Isabel had little time for either priests or the Church. "Well then," she replied, "he should have *designed* her as a man."

From that day forward, Padre Luis went about suggesting, to anyone who would listen, that there was an unholy character to my hunger for learning. Priests.

I stopped eating cheese, though the *queso de campo* of the region— stringy and sharp and sour smelling—was a great favourite of mine. It was said that cheese made one stupid, and I already learned too slowly to appease my appetite. Though I missed the cheese sometimes, I did find that within a few months I could read nearly anything. Now when I needed to ask the meaning of an unfamiliar word, often only Grandfather could give it. If he was away for more than a week, we might spend an hour or two like this, with him helping me vanquish my collection of strange new foes.

First among the cherished memories of my childhood is that big sun face, round and tan, a thick red-grey ruff lining his jaw and tufting his chin. My *abuelo's* was the first serious portrait I sketched. His hair was reddish brown, the hairline high and well back from his temples, which lent a further roundness to the cheeks and forehead. His eyes were green, and clear as gems. After seeing him next to Father, I could no longer confidently call him tall; he was thick-set, with rounded shoulders. And down the years, to line up my sketches of him side by side was as if to chart the progress of ageing in the cinnamon bear.

Grandfather rented two haciendas from the Church. Ours in Nepantla, which Isabel ran, and another he looked after, higher up, just below the pass. In that house was a library I had only heard him speak of, but that shimmered in my mind as the real and true El Dorado. And it was from that great larder of books that Grandfather regularly restocked his shelf in Nepantla. Architectural studies, treatises on Euclid and Galen, and—still maddeningly inaccessible—the Latin poets. Virgil and Lucretius, Lucan and Catullus, Seneca and Juvenal. The names alone were as the metres of a mighty epic.

By the time I was five I had sworn an oath on the little ruby pricked from my thumb to learn Latin without delay. This was to be the first of my great failures, for as it turned out I would not master the godlike speech of Romans for almost ten years.

In translation, mercifully, was Ovid's *Metamorphoses*, and of course Grandfather's beloved *Iliad* and *Odyssey*. And the great classic of our Castilian tongue, Baltasar de Vitoria's *The Theatre of the Pagan Gods*. But the book he perhaps treasured most was by a soldier who fought under Cortés. *The True History of the Conquest of New Spain* is an old man's chronicle of the campaign, a story of the sufferings and deceptions inflicted on the common soldiers the author had fought beside as a youth.

"Books are powerful," Abuelo said. "This single book is why, *en mi opinión*, the many generations of us who followed Cortés have raised not a single monument to him."

Books *were* powerful, irresistible even: the scent of mildew they brought down from the mountains was for me like fresh bread, a bakery laid out between each set of covers.

Grandfather was a capable if reluctant farmer, but how he loved riding out over the land. Sometimes it was to El Dorado, or the land of Quivira, or the Seven Golden Cities of Cíbola, and then he would return to share out some of that fabled hoard: a legend, a rumour, a report he'd just read or heard.

"We live, Angelita, in the El Dorado of legends. *Sabes,* not so many years ago, on his way to a city on a lake, a man named Hernán Cortés—"

"Because he was courteous?" I asked, eager to show off.

"I doubt he was called Cortés for his courtesy. With his soldiers and a few horses, this Cortés was coming from the east, up from the sea. Sometimes they had to hack their way through the densest jungles they had ever seen. But as they worked their way upwards, he and his men began to climb through a cool forest of cedar and pine. Huge trees with growths hanging from them, like the beards of prophets. Yes, *feel*—but much longer than mine. Once at the pass, Cortés stood gasping in the thin air, satisfied he was now higher than any man had stood in Europe. Yet the peaks soared still a thousand *varas*[†] above their heads. He was surer than ever that it was indeed snow up there—though it was beyond belief, in such steamy latitudes as these. Can you see it, Juanita, the stubble on those lean wolf jaws of his? To confirm the marvel, he sent up ten men to fetch down ice."

[† each roughly a yard]

Grandfather neglected to add that they went also to fetch sulphur for their cannon; nor did he mention that Xochitl was from the pass and was his source for the story of the ice. She would one day tell me her people were greatly reassured by such a display of human curiosity from one rumoured to be the god FeatherSerpent returning from the East.

But they had never seen a curiosity quite like this.

"Just a few leagues from this hacienda—just there, beyond that next hill—Cortés came down from our sacred mountain to meet the Mexican Emperor. They met on the south shore of the lake that circled the imperial city . . . *great Tenochtitlan.*"

"Mexico," I said gravely.

"Yes, Angel, and here everything begins. See them: Cortés and Moctezuma[†] stand in the shadows of late afternoon, beside the longest of the stone causeways connecting the island to the land. This one, which we have now renamed the Calzada de San Antonio, is as straight as the horizon at sea on a still day. And wide enough to accommodate

[† the variants Moctezuma, Montezuma and Moctehuzoma are standardized to Moctezuma here]

six carriages abreast! Before this day, the emperor's feet have never been allowed to touch the earth. Now, he stands ankle-deep in soft black mud. Into that mud he inserts the full length of his index finger. And what comes next stuns his attendants. He places it in his mouth. . . . "

Here was a gesture of grace, of surrender to *charys*, that Grandfather considered worthy of an Athenian—of old Pericles himself.

In a few weeks the great Moctezuma II, Regent of the Fifth Sun, incarnation of the war god BlueHummingbird who commanded a million men, would be taken prisoner in his own palace by a ragtag band of mercenaries. Iron clad, gold crazed, famished, reeking from the purulence of their wounds. Or so, listening to my grandfather, I imagined them. Locatable by their smell even through the stench of the dread Black Room, its every surface tarred in blood. There, stunned by their success, uncanny in its suddenness, they hold Moctezuma captive. Though captained by a lawyer (¡un abogado!—¡imagínate, Juanita!) they are in truth led and guided by a woman the Mexicas had sold to the Mayans as a slave. Now she has returned to bring her people, the chosen ones, a very different destiny.

"The unstable margins of things, indeed—eh, Angelina?"

The unstable margins of things. . . . The feature that gives Nepantla its name stands to the east: across the entire east, where the ground is heaved and rutted as by a titan's wheel of quakes and slides and lava floes. The country of my birth lies across the foothills of two white-tipped volcanoes. Iztaccihuatl and Popocatépetl. WhiteLady and SmokingStone. One dormant, the other murderously active. As the legend goes, they are lovers from rival tribes. She lies in a drowse of stone—struck down by a wizard's curse—while he, distraught, stands fuming over her, in a tower of ice and the black rock the Egyptians first called basalt.

Their slopes are the dark green of pine and cedar. After a rain in the afternoon, which falls as snow at the peaks, the fresh-glazed ice dazzles in the sun's decline, as the rains drift beyond them like a blue-black scrim. The effect is theatrical yet they are real—one deadly real—and from real stuff fashioned: rock, rain, ice, the very earth. Two immense actors up on the East's solitary dais. There in the setting sun they blaze up as if footlit by colossal lanterns. In autumn, when the rains come daily, rainbows are commonplace, prosaic as the tremors. And so it is not uncommon for them to be framed, quite perfectly, quite implausibly, under an immense rainbow. As though she has fallen in a bower of shimmering iris . . .

Ever since I can remember, ever since making a childish pledge to always live within sight of them, they *are* those lovers, more than they are mountains; they *are* that play, and the play can only be reality itself. This theatre has been my grandfather's gift to me.

I craved more time with him. But he took any excuse to be out, away from the place in Nepantla, which he conceded his daughter ran more ably than he ran the hacienda up in the pass. She could outwork any man, as Grandfather sometimes said to reassure himself. She was a force of nature, everywhere at once, startlingly so, like the first burgeoning of spring. Giving orders to Xochitl in the kitchen, riding out to the orchards and cornfields, butchering calves, fretting over lambs, shouting instructions to the *charros* as they bred the horses. All this, the work of a day.

Father's company, on the other hand, was too rare a delicacy to crave, which did not keep me from brooding on his absences. Grandfather one day referred to him as an adventurer, and this struck me as a calling of the highest sort. He was like a handsome ghost, a restless paladin of old whose occasional visits were so very vivid and memorable that all the rest seemed a fabrication. One spring day—I might have been four—felt particularly real. He had thrown open the portals and called in to all the girls to come out for horseback rides. They ran happily after him, but I'd been watching from the roof as he had put a fiery roan stallion, stamping and backing and screaming, through its paces. It was that horse he would now have us ride.

Josefa, and even María who was almost an adult, balked at being hoisted into a saddle that bore every sign of becoming a catapult. Though frightened I sprinted down from the roof, but by then there was Amanda, in my place, looking tiny and demure and being led about so placidly she might as well have been on the back of an enormous roan lamb.

I felt someone behind me at the door, and turned to find Isabel. In that proud face I thought I'd seen every variation on anger, but this one shaded swiftly into hurt. Which on her I had never seen and did not see for long before she turned away and walked across the courtyard to her room.

Father had seen her face too. So ended the children's rides, before my turn, as he thundered off on a long ride of his own.

Abuelo, for his part, stayed away for weeks sometimes. I came to think of men as a variety of migratory bird. Father on his noble and secret missions. Grandfather, reading, riding between the two haciendas, mending fences, tinkering with his little hydraulic projects—windmills, watering ponds, catchment basins.

It must have been the next spring, during one of those rare planetary conjunctions that brought Father and Abuelo to the hacienda at the same time. On the hill above the house Grandfather had recently installed a millpond to be replenished on windy days by the small wind-mill he'd had the workers build to his specifications. One morning he took me out with him right after breakfast. Though the ground in Nepantla was dry, he explained, the real problem was not the scarcity of water but rather the swiftness of its drainage. For this I must be wary of dry streambeds.

I knew this already.

"Imagine, Juanita, flash floods from a blue sky! Boulders, trunks and mud all washed down in massive swipes." This was dramatic even for him. "And so, in a way—no?—Time itself has gouged these ravines. As with an adze—there—in its fist. See how, between the arroyos, the high ground runs like roots? Are they not like the buttress roots of cypresses?"

I felt strangely anxious to know what he was leading up to.

Did I know that the people of this place once believed our volcano held up the sky? Here he included the heavens in the generous sweep of his arm. "They saw SmokingStone as a tree, rooted in the earth, its plumes of smoke and steam as branches supporting the heavens." His eyes met mine.

"We live, Angelina, in the Manoa of legends and—"

"I know, Abuelo, and you are its El Dorado."

He put his arm around me then. We looked out over the world he had helped me to see, that I still see as if through his eyes. The stage of the horizon and the forms beyond. The dry, grassy hills, the blond camber of their narrow spines. The orchards rising up from the ravines. Intersecting diagonals of deep green lemon trees and avocados. Volcanoes that were lovers, who were really cypresses. . . .

"*Abuelito!*" I cried, eager to please him. "See how the hills are like snakes now?—see the diamonds on their backs, their green bellies."

He looked down at me as if surprised, and with a sober nod of that great head replied, "Why no, Juana Inés, I had not, until now."

And then he began to explain that we would be leaving Nepantla. The land was even richer up at the other hacienda. With my mother tending it, we would earn nearly as much as the two places combined.

"Abuelito, you're not leaving us?"

"No, no, child, not I." I should have guessed, then. "You'll like it up there. Just as much as here."

The message in all this was clear enough, I thought, with his parables of the tree, the mountain that changes yet abides: Permanence in change. I would soon read as much in Heraclitus. I wanted to shout, Of course I will love the other place, Abuelo—it has your library. Touched by his concern, I kept this to myself.

But that wasn't what he was trying to say at all.

Abuelo and I were looking back down at the ranch house. He was quiet a moment. A thread of mesquite smoke rose from the clay chimney pipe. A loose tissue of other such threads trailed up from the plain. Ewes bleated in the high corral of *ocotillo*; little red flowers budded among the thorns. There was the sweet scent of mesquite, and also of sage. And in the big laurel spreading its shade over the south wall a flock of *urracas* raised a castanet racket of the usual chatter. . . .

It was one of the rare times Abuelo talked to me of my father. "Did you know, child, that I was the one to introduce him to my daughter? With you here beside me now, how could I regret that miracle? I was up in the pass riding on a narrow trail when I met him. A natural horseman!" This was a thing Grandfather knew how to admire. "Your father is descended from the great Basque whalers. They crossed many times, you know, before Columbus ever thought of it." He found it deeply honourable that Father had come to America to restore his family's noble fortunes.

"It was always my great hope that they would marry. The love at first was obvious. But when your father did not come back for Isabel's lying-in this last time . . ."

Was that the time when Abuelo came to bring us down from the cell? Yes it was, and yes, my head was *very* angelic.

"I am not sure my daughter has yet abandoned her hopes. But never mention this. She would rather die than confess it."

The great current of his talk faltered then. Isabel called, and for once I skipped gladly down to the house. All that day I was in high spirits, playing on the patio with the others—my sisters and Amanda, and the younger children of some of the field hands. Usually I found such play difficult, though I loved to observe the others from the roof, admiring their capacity to invent new games on the spot, then enjoy those games well past the point when I might have stopped.

That day, Father was sitting at a table under the arches in the shade of the laurel. Beside his hand on the table rested a little *cántaro* of cool water, its top covered by a lace mantilla, its clay sides sweating in the heat. He himself had brought it from a journey to a land called Guadalajara. The flask was made of *barro comestible*, the speciality of potters in a village far to the west. One could *eat* the clay when the water was gone, a notion that enchanted me.

Even slouched in a chair, he seemed coiled to spring onto the back of a horse. He had a quick mind and was often amused by my little offerings, but the trick was holding his attention. I thought to ask him how the *cántaro* was able to keep the water so much cooler than the surrounding air. The thing was somehow to connect this to horses. Did he think, as I did, that by allowing the sides to sweat, like a horse, it dispensed its heat faster than the air could replace it? Or was there something about evaporation itself that cools? Since dogs didn't sweat in the heat but panted, were they panting sweat?

I was an idiot—what did he care about dogs?

But phantoms were perhaps formed of vapour after all, as was sometimes said. For when one entered a room did not everyone feel cold? So why oh why did I now stand before this one, flushed and sweating and babbling? I was about to ask, but my paladin of smoke was so *absorbed* in watching Josefa and Amanda playing with spinning tops beside me at the well. And yet I had no sooner observed the patterns being traced on the flagstones than—impelled by this madness of mine for hidden forms[2] —I called for some flour to be scattered there in order to better apprehend the effortless *motus* of the spherical form; whose impulse, persisting even when free and independent of its cause, should—it seemed to me then—be mathematically describable. . . .

Exactly how I conveyed all this, I can't recall. He only blinked those great brown eyes at me and shook his head a little, like a horse adjusting to a bridle.

But later that day he did take me out for a short ride on his big roan. So I supposed I was partly successful. When he swung me down, I curtsied. "*Gracias, señor caballero.*"

"Oh, but it was my pleasure," he said and bowed. "And anyway, *señorita*, I owed you a ride. . . ."

He remembered. He remembered.

That night I lay awake well into the night, sitting up finally to watch the slopes of the volcano glisten in the moonlight and thinking about the geometry of pyramids. *We were going to the mountain. We were going to the library*. Perhaps Father would like it there. Enough to stay.

A wind was blowing from the west. A shutter was banging somewhere. I suppose I didn't realize how late it was. . . . All at once I had a sort of childish revelation about the addition of pyramidal angles and rushed out of bed to share it with him. Rather than take the long way round through the arcades, I ran barefoot across the windy courtyard to their room, in which I could see a light, and blundered in on a scene not meant for my eyes. It was the first time I'd seen my mother that way, yet I felt a shock of recognition as though finally seeing her as she was. I couldn't have explained how, but I knew then that some of the sounds I'd associated with the night were not from the fields or hills but from her.

She was like a panther, beautiful and carnal and wild eyed. She was not ashamed, but this was no time for my nonsense. "Child!" she rasped, "will you *never* learn your place?"

Will you never learn your place.

He reached out an arm to restrain her. It is my last image of him: sweat drenched and lean, his eyes deep and blackened by lamplight, his hair atangle, and even as he withdrew from her grasp his movements were all fluid grace. He smiled gently, and shot me through with a look I will never to my last day forget—a farrago of melancholy and regret. Was there still a trace of that look in his eyes the next morning as he turned in the saddle to cast one last glance over the slopes of the Smoking Mountain? I like to imagine he was regretting bitterly even then that he would not see me grown up. He was leaving, my phantom pursuing a fantasy—wealth, glory, some goddess of Fortune. To be a hidalgo in Spain, a latter-day *Conquistador* back from the New World, and eligible at last to marry up to the station his family had fallen from—with one of the stale and pasty virgins of his dusty Basque village.

He'd made up his mind. And looking into those rich, dark eyes, I knew. I knew, and my mother did not; even as her soul merged with his, she did not know. Even as it shattered like glass beneath the blows of a hammer, she did not know. But I did, in that instant. And for this my mother never quite forgave me.

After that night I ceased being a little girl in her eyes.

**I**n leaving Nepantla I lost a father. During the slow, jolting journey up to our new home in the pass I recovered the twin I'd all but forgotten. Amanda and I were wordlessly skirmishing over who was to get the preferred seat, nearest the back of the mule cart. To settle this, naturally we needed to know who was older.

"Same," Xochitl said, ever the peacemaker.

"Not roughly," I insisted, *"exactly."*

"Same day."

No one had thought to mention this. There were so many more interesting things to talk about around our house.

The same *day*—I a month early, and Amanda, who was Xochitl's first, a week late.

"We're twins?" Amanda asked, excited, for many of the old stories Xochitl told involved twins.

No, there was more to it than that, which I at least knew. But it was typical of Xochitl's kindness that she seemed to share our regret.

So we alternated at the seat of choice. And within a day or two we were calling each other twin. It was our special joke but it expressed, too, all the wonder of a rediscovery that might never have happened at all. What if I'd ridden instead with María and Josefa up ahead in the first mule cart? What might my life have come to then?

Isabel drove the lead cart, a mantilla over her chestnut hair to shield it from the dust. My sisters rode next to her. Grandfather ranged back from their cart to circle ours before riding way up ahead, then back again. Our cavalry escort was looking nervous, I thought. Or else guilty about being the most comfortable among us: he sat a horse as easily as a rocking chair. Maybe he didn't want us to notice his delight to be bringing Isabel to take over his obligations at the hacienda up in the pass.

It must have been March when Father left, for the *ocotillo* corral wore a crest of red blossoms. By the time the rest of us were ready to leave Nepantla, it was already late fall.

All criss-crossed and scored, the road looked like a big ball of twine as it rolled and bumped away under us. To roll over it was to grapple with an unseen wrestler. The awning's noise and light and sudden shadow as it flopped and flapped were stunning, like being tossed in a blanket. But at least it fanned us. Closing my eyes, I tried to see myself lazing under an ostrich fan, on the deck of a barge on the Nile. The Nile in flood. The Nile in spate, the Nile in cataract . . .

This was clearly not working. At any other time I'd have been content to look for menageries in the clouds, as I often did up on the roof in Nepantla, but at least a roof consented to stand still. Grandfather, riding by, said I looked seasick. *Seasick*—I hadn't even been on a lake yet.

The seat next to the muleteer was heaped high with Isabel's dining room treasures—chairs, cutlery, lacquered sideboards. . . . So there was no room to ride on our little barge's upper decks—and anyway the driver was increasingly drunk on *pulque,* a ferment of the sweet sap of the maguey cactus.

To distract us, to distract me, for Amanda could sit still for hours, Xochitl had us trying to play a finger game with string. I was willing enough, but we had to reach out one hand or both to steady ourselves so often that the game fell apart. Just then the cart pitched, and a wheel dropped sickeningly into a hole before lurching out again. A small cry escaped Xochitl's lips. As soon as she could breathe, she called up to the driver, "Are you even awake, you idiot?" Her hip had never knitted properly after the accident, a fall from a horse, and the pain must have been awful.

However bad, the accident could not have been worse than the agony of birthing Amanda after it. It took *two days,* and had Xochitl not herself been a midwife, who can say how it might have turned out? But it did spell an end to her work in the fields and her life up in the pass. After the fall and the agonizing delivery, her hair had turned all but white. She wore it in a single lustrous plait, sometimes down her back, but when she worked in the kitchen, behind her head in a coil. Her face was the hue of oiled mahogany. To sketch it, I thought, one must begin with an arrangement of triangles: of her cheekbones, and chin; the black triangles of her eyes when she smiled; the sharp taper of her brows. Two triangles, base to base, formed her lips—the upper smaller, the lower quite full.

Isabel called her Sochee, but the X was a 'sh' and the end was like 'kettle,' only lighter. Like 'rattle'—it *was* a rattle, a faint rattling at the end. sho-CHITL. Since I could first speak I had been calling her Xochita.

The driver was now garrulously singing away.

"Xochita, what's *wrong* with him?"

"*Ye iuhqui itoch.*"

" . . . his rabbit . . . ?" I said. Amanda nodded expectantly. I knew the words but what did they mean?

"*Pulque,*" Xochitl said, "once was a sacred drink, offered to the Rabbit."

"God was a *rabbit?*"

"A double . . . a mask . . ."

And so it was said, sarcastically, that each drunkard had his own way of making the rabbit sacred. Some fight, some sing, some cry and quarrel. And some vomit, as this one had just now done.

Such is his rabbit. I was enchanted. And so, distracting me in a way the finger game never could have, Xochitl set Amanda and me to guessing at riddles and the meanings of old proverbs.

"What is a great blue-green jar scattered with popcorn?"

"The sky!" I said. But Amanda had called it out too, maybe a little ahead of me. "Another!"

"It is good to see you take an interest, Ixpetz. We should travel together more often."

"*Ixpetz?*"

"PolishedEye," Amanda answered.

"I *know,* but—"

"It is used," Xochitl said, "for someone quick to see into the turnings of things." By the light dancing in her eyes I could see she really *had* intended it to rhyme with Inés. My second name came from the Latin for 'lamb,' but Isabel used it whenever she was vexed. Which was usually. From then on Xochitl often said Ixpetz as a balm for the rasp in Inés.

"What about Amanda?" I said.

"That little one? *Cuicuitlauilli in tlalticpac.*"

"Nibbler . . . of earth . . . ?"

"A person who takes pains," Amanda said, "to learn a thing well."

Who learns by nibbling at the world. How lovely! NibbleTooth, that would be my name for her. And so, from that day forward we were to become PolishedEye and NibbleTooth, twins and riddlers and best friends.

She had blue-black hair, just like mine. Her skin was darker than mine, though paler than her mother's. Pale lips and a square little chin. Brown eyes, while mine were black like Isabel's. Always near her mother's side, Amanda had seemed so still I had thought her passive. But now I remembered times when at a nod from Xochitl she burst into a run across the courtyard with an explosive joy, like a foal frisking in new grass. As into a wind she ran, and as she ran the mask of her reserve tipped back like a little hat on a strap.

It now seemed to me that those times of play were always when Isabel had gone out. Grave, still, poised . . . Amanda was *watchful*, not passive.

"I have one," I said. "What dresses like a tree, is spiny, and leaves traces like a frightened squid?"

"What?"

"Books!" I felt my face flush. This one was not so successful as theirs. "Another, Xochita. Please?"

But instead it was Amanda who asked, grave and ominous, "Something seized in a black stone forest that dies on a white stone slab."

"Tell us. . . ." I shivered, expecting the worst.

"A head-louse we crush on our nail!"

"This one is nicer," said Xochitl, making a wry face. "What goes along the foothills, patting out tortillas with its palms?"

"A butterfly?"

Amanda nodded and smiled. She had known, and let me answer.

Blinking, Xochitl looked from Amanda to me, to Amanda again. "Daughters," she said gently, "you make my face wide."

"It means she's proud," said Amanda quietly. Indeed Xochitl's face was wide and smiling, and her eyes were very bright. And what else did I see there—relief?—but how could Amanda and I have been anything but the greatest of friends?

Amanda spoke our tongue hesitantly. In her mother's tongue she was another person—she had come to speak Nahuatl with a fluidity I now lacked. Our family's language, Castilian, was a sweet deep river of breath, clear water over a streambed of smooth even stones. Nahuatl in the ear was all soft clicks and snicks and collidings of teeth and tongue, like the secret language of sibyls. In the mouth, the canals of the cheeks, Nahuatl was rich, like *atole*—and thick like *pozole!*—yes, that was it, a thick stew. With chunks of the world bobbing in it like meat, and you wanted to *chew* it—but gingerly—anticipating a hardness, a stone or bone shard, against the molars, and . . .

But no, that wasn't quite it either. Until I had tasted *pulque* I would never quite find it. *Pulque*, which wrapped itself like a film, clinging, viscous, to the palate and molars and tongue. That was the sensation of Nahuatl in the mouth. Finding this new love right under my nose was like finding Amanda again.

More proverbs, more riddles.

If I was PolishedEye and Amanda NibbleTooth, what was Grandfather?

Xochitl barely hesitated. *He had achieved the four hundred,* he had accomplished many things.

And Xochitl herself? She shook her head. What about Isabel, then? *WoodenLips.*

What did that mean?—*one of firm words, who cannot be refuted.* Ah. Well. And Father?

No.

Please? No, it was not her place. But Amanda and I badgered her relentlessly. All right, enough.

Aca icuitlaxcoltzin quitlatalmachica.

What?

Aca icuitlaxcoltzin quitlatalmachica.

One who arranges his intestines artistically. I suspected she had used it ironically but I would put this away as a keepsake, in a quiet place, and work out its meaning myself one day.

Most of the heat had gone out of the afternoon. I watched the horizon for a while, the colour slowly draining back into the sky. I had glimpsed that a people's riddles were roads into its world, and our language the mask our face wears. And I now knew riddles to cure seasickness. It was a secret I wondered if the old Basque whalers knew, and if there was hidden somewhere a riddle in my father's leaving us.

The road rose and fell more steeply now. I caught a glimpse of two farmhands at the top of the last rise. "What about them?" I said to Xochitl. "Is there a saying for them?"

She thought for a moment. "*Ompa onquiza'n tlalticpac.*"

"The world . . . spills out."

"For the poor, yes. Spills. From their pockets. And from the rags they wear, they themselves spill. . . ."

At nightfall we halted in the churchyard in Chimalhuacan. Everything in the carts was caked in a fard of fine white dust, including us, as though we had been made up for a play or some ceremony. Grandfather was on friendly terms with the priest here, which was surprising enough since he was always fuming about the priests he rented the haciendas from. But directly after he finished his fulmination, he would cast a guilty eye my way to add, "Do not let that keep you from reading your Bible, Juanita. It is another El Dorado." The priest, Father

Juan, was a distant relative and had baptized me. *Natural daughter of the Church*. That's what he put on my baptismal certificate, just as he had for María and Josefa.

We stayed a day to rest a little and bathe. Amanda and I set off exploring, leaving Josefa and María to wail about the state of their hair. We ducked into the church. It was built of a pinkish-brown *tezontle* cut from lava and rough as a file. Inside, it was dark and cold, with just a few candles shimmering on altars beneath shocks of fresh-cut flowers. As our eyes adjusted in the gloom, I saw the font where I was baptized. Above it a painting of John the Baptist.

We got as far as the *crucero*† when Amanda tugged hard at my sleeve—

"Cinteotl . . ." she whispered, backing away and pulling me with her. Seated on a rough wooden throne, not crucified but bleeding from scores of wounds—as from volleys of arrows—was a black Christ. Not black—the blood was black, the skin stained a deep mahogany like Xochitl's. His head was lowered, and in a gesture of great weariness the fingers of his left hand ran through a dust-brown wig of what must have been human hair.

But what Amanda stared at—almost *through*—was the ear of corn held upright in his other hand: as of a king, bloodied, with a sceptre of corn.

I let her drag me back up the aisle, and once she knew I would follow she ran like a deer. Only the stone wall at the west end of the churchyard made her stop and wait for me. The moment passed like the shadow of a cloud, and we burst into nervous laughter. Later we helped Father Juan plant some pine seedlings along the fence. One day, he said, they would grow and shelter the church from the wind. As we worked he told us of his plans to raise funds for a statue of Our Mother Coatlalocpeuh to stand guard at the church entrance.

Later that afternoon as Father Juan continued to work in the churchyard, Xochitl told us Cinteotl was the son of the Mother of the Corn. So was that Cinteotl or Christ all bloody in there?

"Maybe a double," she said, the triangles of her eyes narrowing as she watched Father Juan still digging in the churchyard. "Maybe ask *him*."

 We set out again the next day. From Chimalhuacan the road got smoother and rose only gradually. We were moving across the lower slopes of Popocatepetl and heading north towards Iztaccihuatl. The

†transept

air was cooler, and we travelled mostly in the shade of the enormous pines and cedars that flanked the road, thicker at the base than our little cart was long. We persuaded Xochitl to let us take down the awning.

Leaning back against the corn sacks, Amanda and I rode quietly for a while, a little stunned by the great white peaks leaning in over the trees. From Nepantla they had been actors alone up on the stage of the horizon. Now they loomed like enormous attendants bent over three small creatures in a crate, or so it felt as we rolled along.

We had crossed over into a land of giants. Everything towered far above. The axis of this new country was the two volcanoes, so still as to make the sky around them race with clouds and wheeling birds. There were more birds here. Hawks and vultures, as there were back in Nepantla, but also falcons and eagles. Xochitl said we were just big enough now not to be carried off by one. She looked into my wide eyes and laughed. "And tomorrow, Ixpetz, you will have a sunburn on your chin from so much looking up." Her laugh—hup!—came out in a little swoop, pulling up. It made you want to laugh too. She was almost chatty, a real swallow's beak, maybe because the road was smoother, less painful for her hip.

Did I know the story about the volcanoes as lovers?

Muchi oquicac in nacel! I said. *Every one of my nits knows that one!* Even this earned a smile, and she looked younger by years. Amanda was just as wide eyed as I was at the change in her. But this was Xochitl's land.

"Is it true, Xochita, what Grandfather said about Cortés sending men up there for ice?"

"The Speaker himself sent relays of runners every day."

"The Speaker?"

"Lord Moctezuma."

"Did they see each other, you think?"

"Who?"

"Cortés's men and Moctezuma's. Going for ice."

"Our people saw *them*. The Speaker was watching from the day their ships landed. He sent his artists to paint them. From hiding places all along the road."

"Someone told you?"

"I saw it. The ships and men. The horses . . ."

"You're not *that* old, Xochita."

She smiled again. "No, bold-tongue, in a book."

"You read *books*?"

"Ours, not yours. It was my family's place to keep the painted books. *Intlil, intlapal in ueuetque. . . .* [†] My ancestor was the wizard Ocelotl."

†the Red and Black,
the ancient ways,
'knowledge and death,'
and the insignia of the
keeper of its books

"Your ancestor was a *jaguar?*"

"There are limits, Ixpetz, even for the young."

"I'm sorry. . . ." I felt a flush rushing to my cheeks.

From the way she smiled I could tell she was not angry. "And *your* ancestor also, daughter," she said, squinting one eye at Amanda. "One bold tongue is enough."

Xochitl talked lightly on, her face mobile and relaxed, its triangles tilting this way and that. I snuggled in against Amanda to watch the mountains as we listened. The keeper of the painted books, it seemed, was himself part of that book, and in speaking it the keeper kindled a fire in the hearer's mind. Whereas the book itself was only the ashes of the fire the morning after, cool and delicate and precious, but not the same. To one who loved to sketch, how beautiful this notion of a book not written but painted.

"Up there—you see, near that big rock? There is a hidden opening. Some of the old wizards escaped through it and under the volcanoes, when the sea and fire descended on our people."[†] Her eyes scanned the

†Nahuatl metaphor
for the Conquest

hills. "Every few years now, early morning or dusk, one of the old ones is seen, wearing the ancient dress and speaking words of jade, the old songs of heart and blood. . . ."

She glanced around to get her bearings. As she looked away, my eyes followed the windings of the braid coiled tightly at her nape. The strands of grey and black through the thick white coils were like the graving lines of fine chisels in soft stone.

"Here the ground is holy," she said quietly. "The words are simple but we lose what it is like. . . ." She seemed reluctant to go on.

"What is it like, Mother?"

Her eyes had not left the mountains. I thought she wouldn't answer. I wondered where exactly she had fallen from the horse and if maybe she was remembering this.

"Here, Amanda, every step you take, you walk in halls of jade."

We lay back quietly, propped against each other and the sacks of maize. I was getting drowsy. The road wove in and out among those trees that had been too large to cut down and uproot. We watched the sky pivoting on its axis. Once, these volcanoes had *been* the East; now they could be in any direction at all.

I slept. And dreamed of being carried off on enormous wings . . . by a bird with an eagle's head and talons, and the long white neck of a swan.

I awoke just before Amanda did. A light rain tickled my face. The sun, not far above the western hills, seemed lower than we were, as if the last light rose past us to strike the peaks far above, still radiantly lit. Quietly we watched the soft rain beat traces of silver through the sunbeams where they slanted up among the boughs.

The trees were thinning. We were entering the town of Amecameca, less than a league from Grandfather's hacienda. María and Josefa were standing up in the lead cart, gawping shamelessly at the refinements of the largest settlement we had ever seen, and would traverse in under five minutes. Xochitl pointed out the school. "For girls like you." She looked at me with a crooked smile.

Then we were off the main road. The track bent sharply east. A gold light poured over our shoulders and cast ahead of us the shadow of a giant with two tiny heads—for Amanda and I were standing now, behind the driver. As we clung to his backrest, Xochitl clung grimly to our skirts to keep us from pitching headlong out. Across the ditch on the left and beyond a windbreak of oaks were orchard rows of apple and peach and pomegranate converging in the distance as they ran. Workers stopped and doffed their hats as Grandfather cantered grandly past. Close to the road, one woman squinted at Xochitl and waved with a little flutter.

I looked back. She stood there still, the sun setting red beside her through folds of road dust.

Closer to the house were plots of squash, and beans and tomatoes. We crossed a small stone bridge over a brook that fed the irrigation ditches. At the far end of the bridge stood a little guard post, empty now, as was the watchtower that topped the house. The house itself was framed by two tall African tulip trees, and in each orange blossom glowed the sunset's radiant echo.

As in Nepantla, the house was laid out on one floor. Here, though, the roof was not flat but shingled and pitched to shed rain—and, Grandfather promised, sometimes snow.

The western wall above the veranda was a pocked grey-white. The watchtower and the chapel belfry still blushed the softest rose in the faltering light. Workmen in white cotton breeches and shirts took form round the carts as if exhalations risen of the dusk. We heard the quiet murmurs, ". . . don Pedro . . . doña Isabel . . ." They formed a brigade to relay the sacks and tools to the sheds. No one questioned that Isabel should work beside the men. A woman went with a taper and lit the lanterns strung along the veranda. Amanda and I chafed to explore the house, which was still dark. We were not to go in until Josefa and María had safely swept it out, and they looked in no hurry even to start.

Grandfather was soon relinquishing his burdens to the men, but when one tried to help Xochitl she refused—a tight urgency in the shake of her head. I distinctly heard one man call her Mother in Nahuatl. I wanted to call out to them—She's not as old as she looks!— then bethought myself. It looked more like respect than consideration of her age. And I noticed the workers themselves were careful not to let this regard be noticed by don Pedro or his daughter.

It was full dark now, and enthusiastically supported by my sisters, who were sick already of sweeping (though they'd hardly started), we begged to sleep around the firepit. Xochitl was in the kitchen struggling to bring enough order for breakfast in the morning. Isabel was back from the sheds and briskly sweeping out Grandfather's room.

Grandfather helped us light the fire, a fragrant heap of pine and mesquite, a waver of flame soon reflecting in eight black beady eyes over blankets pulled up to our chins—how chilly the nights were up here.

"A story please, Abuelo. *Please?*" He obliged us grandly and continued even after my sisters had nodded off, though weariness crumpled his great round face and bedraggled his big mane. In repayment for his putting my sisters to sleep, I offered to tell him about the wizard Ocelotl. But as I quickly realized that he knew much more than I, I asked instead the difference between priests and wizards. It was complicated, he said, but a priest has words and laws, and a wizard has visions. I wanted to go get Xochitl so they might tell us together about Ocelotl.

"It's late," Grandfather said. I didn't think she would mind. "*Mira, Angelita, que te lo cuenta.*" A warning in his tone stopped me. "This Martín Ocelotl, and his twin—"

"*Twin?*"

"And his twin, Andrés Mixcoatl, led an Indian uprising. It began right here in these mountains." The brothers were incarnations of the gods MirrorSmoke and FeatherSerpent, or so people here claimed. For this they fell afoul, Grandfather said, of a horror called the Inquisition and were finally condemned. Mixcoatl burned. "But Ocelotl . . ." he concluded mysteriously, "Ocelotl disappeared into the night."

He had his second wind. The firelight glowed softly on his face. Now there came tale after tale of golden cities and fiery mountains, blue hummingbirds and eagle knights, wizards and jaguars, curses and troths. Of the magic traps the Mexica wizards set for the Conquistadors, but who, not knowing Mexica magic, rode right on as if through gossamer.

Through half-lidded eyes I saw Amanda's eyes blinking, slow . . . close—flutter, stop. Then the threads unravelled and we were lofted up and up towards the mountains, Amanda and I, and softly stretched on sleep's stone ledges. By hummingbirds.

The next day we ran everywhere together, exploring. We scrambled up to the watchtower, and to our delight found a little bronze cannon, battered and so long out of use there was a nest in it. To the south, beyond the belfry of our chapel, faint blue smoke smudged up from the town. Beyond the house to the east bristled fields of maize, then what might be the grey-green of *agave*, and then a glimmer of water. From there, deep forest rose in ranks of pikes sharply up to the snow line. It felt like mid-morning, yet the sun had still not cleared the volcanoes. They were right there, right over us. That first day we must have stared up at them for an hour.

We had come up to get a commanding (even superior) view over the house, towards which our eyes finally condescended. I kept the sketch I made during those early days when it all seemed so new. The firepit around which we had slept stood near the centre, and next to it a well. A wide, shady arcade ran right around the courtyard, except for the main portal on the eastern side, between the kitchen and the library. At the four corners, full rain barrels bulged beneath waterspouts set in the eaves. On the north, near the kitchen, was a tiled basin in the shape of a cross.

The flower beds—roses, calla lilies, hyacinths—had run wild, and now nodded and buzzed and beamed along the colonnade from kitchen to dining room to what was now my bedroom, next to the watchtower steps at the northwest corner. From my bed, which Amanda and I had dragged under the window, I could see all but the tips of the volcanoes, so high were they, so close by.

I had expected a hard fight from my sisters for that room. But María found the volcanoes oppressive; Josefa *just shuddered* to imagine the sight of them at night. So instead they made a great show of their maturity by choosing to share the only room left. I applauded this. And, yes, it was the largest—fractionally. To one side of them was our mother's room, on the southwest corner next to the entrance to the chapel. To the other side was Grandfather's room, in the southeast corner next to the library.

The library, I resolved, would later be reconnoitred from every possible angle. Chins propped on our forearms, forearms on the sill, we had been kneeling on my bed under the window onto the courtyard.

"But Amanda," I said, "where do you and Xochita sleep?"

She led me at a dead run past the dining room and into the kitchen: beyond it hung two hammocks in the pantry's back corner. It seemed unprepossessing to me, cramped even. She was thrilled that she and Xochitl each had a window, and that the two afforded a cross-breeze (designed not for their pleasure but to keep the pantry cool and dry).

I kept this last observation to myself but resolved to take the matter up with Grandfather. "Let it alone, Angel. Amanda is happy."

And so I did. There was so much else to do.

 Once we had settled in, the next order of business was to thwart the movement to put me in school. I had missed the first two months, and was certain to be made the butt of the cruellest pranks and jokes. Isabel surprised me by taking this seriously. Besides, I told Grandfather once she was out of earshot, there was not much chance of falling behind in only a year since apparently my classmates could not yet *read*. Here I let my head loll about like a boggled newborn, at which Grandfather laughed wheezily.

"I've been reading for *three years* already, Abuelo, did you know that?" My average was a book a week, and lately more like two. So that made over two hundred now, and I began to recite them for him in alphabetical order. Thus was the matter quickly settled.

And next fall was an eternity away. . . .

I was not quite as confident of my advantage as I let on. Through each siesta I read furiously while the others slept. Beside me, Grandfather snored his bliss for an hour in a hammock strung between the arcade's columns before the library door. I sat at a small table, his hammock beside me, an armspan away. Under one window, on the inside table, was a chess set. Reaching through the wrought-iron bars we could have played, my imaginary opponent and I, like contented prisoners whiling away the years. But I had a library to conquer, book by book. And so at the little table crowding the door, I sat—*stuck*. For this was the threshold I had not yet won Isabel's permission to cross.

"I said no, Inés. The library is a man's place. It is not for little girls too accustomed already to having their way." She had said this not even looking down, with me trotting alongside her on the way to the paddocks. "I don't care what he said. He spoils you." She was splendid, I had to admit, striding out in the sun, tucking that thick chestnut hair under her sombrero. In her riding boots she was almost as tall as I remembered Father, taller than Abuelo. I hadn't known anyone could cover so much ground just walking—it was a wonder she bothered with horses at all. She walked the way I talked—would she stop for a minute, wouldn't she care to explain?—we could negotiate. She laughed, then. A laugh deep like a man's. Warm. Brief. I couldn't remember ever making her laugh. I would try to be funnier the next time. But she still didn't stop or even look down.

Nevertheless, that day and the next and until she stopped bothering to reply, I got some inkling of her reasons. Women and books had no place in this country; a woman's place was out in the world, in the fields and grain exchanges and stock markets, if she was prepared to fight for it. And if she wasn't, she would be at the mercy of men all her life. Not all the wishing or fighting in the world put women in libraries.

We would see about that. Time, I thought, was on my side. And since she had been so obliging about school, I laboured mightily at patience.

In the meantime, Grandfather brought me out each day a heaping tray of books to choose from—and a fine, adult selection, too. Each afternoon he shuffled through that doorway, and in his face was the quiet pride of a baker with a tray. In just that way did he place the books before me.

And through those days and weeks, it was as though I had broken open a vast garner. But I was no granary mouse. I ate like a calf, like a goat—everything at once. Herodotus, Sophocles, Aeschylus, Thucydides—here, at last I had reached the source of all learning. Our great poets, Lope de Vega and Góngora—the *early* Góngora, Grandfather stressed with a certain severity. Our Bible, of course, and now Juan de la Cruz[†] and his love lyrics to Christ.

[†]St. John of the Cross (canonized 1726)

And tales—of hungry picaroons erring through the Spanish countryside. While reading *Don Quixote*, I woke *mi abuelito* in the Hammock of the Sacred Nap almost every afternoon to protest the cruelties of

Cervantes, who, Grandfather conceded, had suffered sufficient indignities himself to know better.

This is probably why, the day I reached for Homer's *Iliad*, Grandfather placed his hand over mine. There was something we should talk about first. An attack by Apollo—*¡la emboscada más cobarde!*[†]—against Achilles' noble friend Patroklos. Though Abuelo sketched out for me just the barest outlines of that craven blow to the back—and from a *god*—his voice grew husky and tottery under the burden of Apollo's disgrace. So when the dark day again fell across those pages, I prodded his shoulder till he woke, and shared with him my outrage. No, Abuelo, you were right, this was not at all a thing for a god to do.

[†] the most cowardly ambush

For a week or two that first winter we puzzled together over a volume by an Italian, Pico della Mirandola, which I thought a marvellous sort of name. It was a treatise, Grandfather believed, on updating the hexachord to the octave, which he was very keen to read. This splendidly named *musicus* had written it in Latin, which my *abuelo* read easily. The trouble was that by inadvertence he'd purchased an Italian translation of an Italian who wrote in Latin.

At one point, we had fairly run the gamut when Grandfather sounded a note not far from fury. "Ut!" he sputtered. "This . . . this is finally and completely enough!"

I responded with a great severity of my own. "A terrible translation, no, Abuelo? That it should give two such scholars so much trouble?"

At this he coughed and patted my hand. "Yes, Angelita, a bad translation. That must be so."

By then an eternity had translated itself into a year. It was autumn and time to enrol in school, which brought me crashing to earth. I sat— dazed, in a sort of horological horror—in the forecourt of the school, under the motto Charity, Chastity and Grace. Just inside, Grandfather was arguing that I should be placed if not with the teenagers then in the third year at the very lowest.

Yes, don Pedro, but grandfathers were, after all, *expected* to think their little *nietas*[†] *very* precocious. "*Más, fiad, señor,* in our long experience with children." Since this would be my first year, I must of course begin with the beginners, but—*but*—they, the reverend sister teachers, would know just how to bring me along at a satisfactory pace.

[†] granddaughters

The fourth week ended prematurely, on the Wednesday afternoon, though it began exactly as had the others, and that was the problem.

With our ABCs. As ever, Sister Paula stood before the class and led us in the most maddening singsong sham of question and answer—this was the Socratic method she was playing with. How marvellous that we had somehow divined in under a month that A should stand for . . . Avocado! And were we sure? Oh yes, very.

So stubby were her legs, and arms to match, that she was forever treading on her rosary and then dipping her head to check herself, as though the beads were slung not at her waist but round her neck. And how she *exclaimed* over our sham right answers. My mind was invaded by the sketch of a pullet—pacing and bobbing and rearing back to crow, and stuntedly flapping and clapping over our great successes.

For weeks now, to quell the need to scream I would chant along under my breath. The chant ran on and on like this. Hard and quickly:

A is for Aleph in Hebrew; it comes from Chaldaean. *B* is for Beta in Greek, a borrowing from Phoenician. *C* is for—can we name the capital of Chaldaea . . . ?

This question of the sorcerer's passing through Sister Paula's class-room that day, the precise wording of the hex I threw, has been taken up by those whose qualifications are beyond reproach. And I do not dispute that by the Wednesday of week four my ABCs had spiralled and rami-fied within me until I had perfected a whole new gamut. As an alterna-tive to Sister Paula's version, my solo began at *M*, for '*mi*,' of course, and for 'Mem' in Hebrew . . .

Well M̲em *is* interesting. Does it not look to you like the horns of an owl? Which is after all the al̲most universal symbol of *muerte y mortali-dad.*[†] Now, the Reverend Athanasius Kircher believes the alphabet is m̲odelled after for̲ms in nature, and yes, just like the hieroglyphs of Egypt—of which one of the clearest is—*precisely*, an owl! But a M̲ister Herodotus says a gentle̲man na̲med Cad̲mus introduced the *entire alpha-bet* to Greece fro̲m Phoenicia. And we know the Phoenicians were m̲ariners and?—no?—why, *merchants* too. Yet this Cadmus brought back not only our *abecedario*[†] but also the *boustrophedon*, the lovely flow of our script fro̲m left to right, and down and back again—m̲uch like the tilling of your father's fields, is it not? And if we trace this now in ink, see all the little "m̲'s" lying on their sides—hm̲m̲m̲? Well, why *not* indeed?—m̲aybe

[†]death and mortality

[†]Spanish for the ABCs and also for the primer that teaches them

it *was* the same field in which Cadmus had sown the dragon's teeth. The very teeth which then sprouted up as men, if memory serves. Yes as enemies, unfortunately. And the Greeks—well, yes, right after Cadmus's funeral maybe, *quien sabe*—called this new marvel of the alphabet *stoicheia*. And surely felt it was minted expressly to convey *stoicism*—an invention the God of the Hebrews only imparted to Adam *after* the Fall. And here is the best part now: God still denied the *stoicheia* even to the seraphim, for after all—*angels never had to sit in school with so many SIX-YEAR-OLDS.*

I did not go on to the letter N. Sister Paula was in such a flap of crossing herself that she had come within one stub pinion of her own miraculous assumption.

My hexachord may not have run to exactly these words and notes that day, but whose childhood recollections are not coloured by the perceptions of others? Elders, adults like Sister Paula, should know to be more careful about exaggeration and its effects on children, and on the truly credulous. Her version of how the sorceress hexed her classroom has followed me for years, and it is greatly vexing that I can do so little against it.

When Grandfather brought me home that day, he described for Isabel the little Inquisition the sisters had held before releasing me. He was scandalized that their chief concern should be whether the others had been infected by my polluted lips.

"Infected?" he snorted. "Such a disease we should all hope to catch...."

So that's what an Inquisition was. To calm Grandfather I told him I thought it might have been much worse. Still, this idea of pollution, infection, was unsettling. Just from my being near the younger girls? I was not so very different. I was good with facts, never forgot what things were or where they came from, and sometimes grasped even the whys. But I knew so little about *how* things were, how they *felt*.

And then, there were the books Grandfather had not let me see.

he nuns had sent up a whirlwind of prayer as Grand-father escorted me home from school. *Hail Mary, full of grace, the Lord is with thee . . . Virgin serene, holy, pure and immaculate . . .*[3] Or so I recall, if not to the letter. Well, I might be different from the others in some ways, even if I was a little confused about how, but I *wasn't* polluted and I wasn't infected. Abuelo promised me I was not con-fused about that.

And I'd hardly begun to appreciate all the things the other children and I shared. They had a mother, for instance. And like me, they were subject to the arbitrary exercise of her power. I had won the good sisters' agreement to an early matriculation, only to discover I was still denied access to Abuelo's library.

"If you're quitting school," said Isabel, "it's because you're learning enough here. Are you or are you not learning enough here?"

Not that the argument was flawless. But what impressed me was that she had bothered to reason with me at all. And she didn't just sail off either, as if to say she had more important things to do than remonstrate with someone my size. She stood planted there, and under those long arching brows her black eyes beheld me evenly. This was important enough to settle here and now. What unnerved me was that I knew I had not yet understood *why.* She never went into the library. And as she stood facing me down, whatever her reason, it felt bigger than I was.

I flinched. Retreated. Gave way to her—*yet again.*

But there were other arrangements to try and titles to sample, laid out on Grandfather's book trays. Lycophron and Pythagoras; commentaries on the Cabbalists and their codes, on Galileo and other such 'moon-starers.' And, especially now, *novels:* tempting *picarescas* of young children running away from cruel mothers, of spurned knights throwing rings into reflecting wells, of wrongly accused brides vindicating their honour before the pitiful, shamed accusers, whom it took little effort to picture wearing nuns' habits. . . .

Sometimes I would close my eyes and choose at random from Grandfather's book tray. Once my hand fell upon a manual on the making of suits of armour, which, when ornamented with jewels and pearls and precious metals, Grandfather said were among the most beautiful things ever fashioned by man's ingenuity or in his image. Among the great European armourers were the Colmans and the legendary Jacobi Topf. So icily beautiful were his designs, I had soon devoured the manual front to back.

How darkly fastidious, these black arts—all the intricacies in the fluting, the roped and scalloped edges, the treatment of the surfaces—acid-etched and russeted, blued and blacked. For the warhorse, the buff armour of ox hide, and the chanfrons and crinnets without which its lovely head might be severed at a single blow of an obsidian axe. So impressed were the Conquistadors with the quilted Mexican armour, they adopted it themselves. Though they did still cling to the kite-shaped bucklers as if to the thread on which swung their lives.

Yet nothing prepared me for the annihilation of Melos.

Did Grandfather not see me reading Thucydides? How could anyone forget *this*, Abuelo least of all. Yet he had forgotten, as he was beginning to do, as I should have seen if I had been attentive enough to notice. Then he did remember. He sat with me for over an hour, at first patting me awkwardly on the shoulder, then pressing his forehead to mine.

These are old stories of course, but who among us may claim never to have been wounded by one such as this, and a little changed inside? It is that chapter in *The Peloponnesian War* when the mighty Athenian navy stops at the small island of Melos to dictate terms. Terms the Melians so gracefully contest in their final hours.

Each fine point, they turn this way and that, pleasantly—on both sides, for the Athenian envoy too is a man of high reason. They are all men like Thucydides, who stood by and watched, and was once an admiral himself. The fine, precise minds, the superb learning, these precious things they shared.

"And all *for what?*" I asked Abuelo angrily. But I felt confusion too, that a book by a historian two thousand years dead could loose such a flood of feelings in me—wonder, fury and grief; the channels scored then have never quite silted in. I know that chapter as though I'd written it, as the one who watched them fall.

ATHENS: You know and we know, as practical men, that the question of justice arises only between parties equal in strength, and that the strong do what they can, and the weak submit.

MELOS: As you ignore justice and have made self-interest the basis of discussion, we must take the same ground, and we say that in our opinion it is in your interest to maintain a principle which is for the good of all—that anyone in danger should have just and equitable treatment and any advantage, even if not strictly his due, which he can secure by persuasion. This is your interest as much as ours, for your own fall would involve you in a crushing punishment that would be a lesson to the world.

ATHENS: Leave that danger to us to face. . . . We wish you to become our subjects with least trouble to ourselves, and we would like you to survive, in our interests as well as your own.

MELOS: It may be your interest to be our masters: how can it be ours to be your slaves?

ATHENS: By submitting you would avoid a terrible fate, and we should gain by not destroying you.

MELOS: Would you not agree to an arrangement under which we should keep out of the war, and be your friends instead of your enemies, but neutral?

ATHENS: No: your hostility injures us less than your friendship. That, to our subjects, is an illustration of weakness, while your hatred exhibits our power. . . .

MELOS: Surely then, if you are ready to risk so much to maintain your empire, and the enslaved peoples so much to escape from it, it would be criminal cowardice in us, who are still free, not to take any and every measure before submitting to slavery? . . . We trust that Heaven will not allow us to be worsted by Fortune, for in this quarrel we are right and you are wrong. . . .

Thus spoke the last Melian emissary, before every man of Melos was slaughtered, every woman and child sold into bondage. Before every stone sacred to Melos was pulled to the ground. It was *terrible*—stupid and pitiless, the exercise of beautiful minds in a mindless, fatal cause. And then for trusting to heaven, for their faith in *right*, the Melians are held up to the scorn of all practical men. What real choice was left them? In the left hand, Athens holds slavery and criminal cowardice. In the right, annihilation.

"Yes, you are right, Angel, the Melians were very reasonable. But they were not realistic. There is no shame in surrender to a greatly superior force, or to Fortune, or God. There can be a kind of grace in this. Pericles saw this. Moctezuma saw. . . ."

I was sitting in the same chair as always, looking towards the library door, with the kitchen at my back. He had dragged the other chair to sit beside me now, so as to be able to look into my eyes and reason with me. His thin old leg, though not quite touching, felt warm next to mine. My face was hidden in my hands. I knew it was childish to cry like this. Gently he coaxed them down to the table, letting his big bony hand rest lightly across my wrists.

"But Socrates was an Athenian too, wasn't he, Abuelo? What about Plato's *Republic*—he proved to Thrasymachus that honour was necessary even among thieves. Socrates *proved* it."

"Yes. Yes he did. And resoundingly. But the Athenians had not read it."

"*Why?*"

"Because, Angelina, it would not be written for thirty more years."

"But Socrates was alive, he was a teacher. He and Thucydides both lived in Athens."

"It may be they never met."

"How big was Athens, then—bigger than Tenochtitlan?"

"No, no."

"Bigger than Mexico City now, or Seville?"

"Even smaller."

"Then how . . . ?"

They *had* to know each other. Aeschylus, Sophocles, Socrates, Pericles, Thucydides. These were Grandfather's heroes. They *were* Athens. How could they have become great all alone, all together, all at the same time? No. They influenced, *learned* from one another, as I learned from Abuelo. Athens made them, but they made each other great. Or else what was a city *for*? On Melos, Thucydides had somehow failed Athens. I sensed this, I knew this. But if he and Socrates had never had the chance to meet, or walk together, or know each other's hearts, then I must feel that their city had failed them first.

I could not have expressed it then, I was so hurt and shocked by something in it. Troubling enough that the envoys were so like-minded, so *gracious*. It would take years to understand, of course—yet how much more disturbing that in their golden age they were so much like us in ours. I wasn't ready to accept that they truly felt as we feel, but they spoke and thought like the very finest of us. This was not some wild-bearded tribe in Canaan—they could have been sitting at our table. Graciously, amiably. Terrible things happened, I knew. Earthquakes, floods . . . But here was the first, most terrible sense of a wrongness in the machinery of the world. A thing out of true. A bent cog that might be turning now in me.

The most bloodthirsty general of all the Tartars could have given the order to exterminate the Melians. But this was Thucydides, a *stratēgos*, one of the Ten. This was no earthquake, no eruption, no flood, such as we had here in this valley—our volcanoes were Necessity. *This* was only strategy. Navies do not inspire loyalty, though they might command it. . . .

"It was the greatness of Athens that inspired the states to follow her, wasn't it Abuelo?"

As I spoke, I kept my head bowed, ashamed of my hot, sticky face. I watched instead Grandfather's big hand where it lay over my wrists. Of vague surprise was that such a knobby, knuckly hand as his should be as pale as my wrists and palms. The skin was faintly spotted like an old pelt, and between the knuckles a pale, purplish-blue. The knuckle and index finger bulged out beyond the normal width, as if the finger of a bigger hand were sewn on and wrapped in a dressing. Much of the time his hand hovered a little, trembling, a soft patting that only occasionally brushed my skin—an ungainly bird uncertain where to light.

One thing above all others had badly shaken me. Even though Thucydides did not give that order, he would still have counselled it. Even if he did not counsel it, he had given orders like it during his own time as an admiral. *He knew.* Yet by the time he wrote, so many years later, he had seen in that hour not just the end of all that was Melos: for by then the great poets, the beautiful minds, were dead and Athens was broken. Euripedes in 406, Sophocles in 405. Socrates executed in 399, and Thucydides himself soon to be assassinated. Athens killed them both in a year, but not before he had seen his failure. He wrote with the same unsparing eyes, even then.

In all that time, he had still not learned mercy, even toward himself.

I saw an old man seeing this in exile, who had still not surrendered to grace, made peace with his lack of charity, and who used it to wound himself, knowingly. Mercilessly. And so wounded us.

"*He knew,*" I blubbered out. But for the first time in my life, words had failed me. I had not cried like this since my father left. "Abuelo, he knew it was wrong. *He* was—and still he didn't feel sorry."

Isabel had stopped on the way to the kitchen. She stood just behind Grandfather and asked what the fuss was about.

"Thucydides," he mumbled.

From the corner of my eye, I could see her shake her head. "I told you, the child is too young." Then she walked swiftly past us to the kitchen.

"Then I am too, Isabel," he called after her. "Too young."

I had been staring at that pale *salchicha*† of a finger and trying not to look up at her. I fancied I saw a haplessness in it . . . like a little elephant trunk, that blank expanse just below the elephant's eyes where the trunk seems grafted on.

Grandfather's tone is what finally made me look up at him. His face was turned towards the light out in the courtyard. His head was tipped a little back, as if to keep the world from spilling from the delicate chalices of his eyes. I had never seen an adult cry, or even near to it. Amanda cried easily. Her chin would pull her upper lip down, which got all long over her teeth and rolled under them a little. This wasn't like that at all. It was quiet, and still.

After a moment he turned to me that big face of a medieval lion. I must not blame my mother, he said. *I must not, but I did.* There was something now I must never mention to anyone. Did I swear? he asked. His eyes were so beautiful then, green as wet grass. I'd have promised anything.

"Your mother has never learned to read."

"But . . . Abuelo . . ."

This seemed incredible. This was utterly mystifying. She was intelligent—that much I knew.

"Yes, Angelita, very intelligent. You are right. Something in the letters made her furious—physically sick, and furious. We tried for years. She jumbled everything. It was the most painful thing between us. Some of the worst moments of her life were at that desk in there. So try, *señorita*, to be more understanding. And a little thankful for what you have."

I have returned to Melos and Thucydides a dozen times at least since that day. And each time they reveal something new to me. The war ended in the defeat of Athens, and as the Melian envoy had foreseen, her fall served as a lesson to the world. For if right is only a question between equals, so also is loyalty. In the hour when Fortune ever so lightly tips the scales to Sparta, the confederacy under Athens must dissolve as if built upon a pedestal of sugar. The Spartan confederacy had held precisely when the Athenian did not: when the scales were tipped against them;

whereas Athens sued for peace at the first reversal. Six years after that, they violated, being practical men, the terms and principles of the treaty they had asked for. In 404 they surrendered completely. Sparta broke Athens, and the war broke Greece.

I have read the Athenian poets many times since then. I believe that the Athenian emissary, a practical man, was wrong about loyalty and right, and wrong about the message that sparing Melos would have sent the confederate states. For already the greatest poets and dramatists of Athens had prepared the states to follow her in a show of mercy to Melos. Homer, they would have followed precisely *for* love of honour. Euripedes, in repugnance for savagery. Aristophanes, towards the pleasures of peace. Aeschylus, through the awe of suffering. Most of all they would have followed Sophocles, who was already eighty, and had shown all Greece that to know the mind of any god, most especially Ananke,[†]was to earn her undying hatred.

[†]sometimes translated as Necessity

The Melians insisted on seeing right; Thucydides refused to see things as they might be. Athens betrayed herself by surrendering to expediency; Thucydides betrayed her by making it pass for necessity. He had made his sacrifices to an impostor. This is what I felt but could not find the words to say. Thucydides, more than anyone else except perhaps Grandfather, made a poet of me. How furious I was with him, so clear eyed when I was not, so unsentimental where I could not be. So bent was he on opposing the *Iliad*'s cant of honour and glory—*he* would be the one to unmask it; he, for one, would not be gulled.

It seemed to me that day he was a kind of priest, with terrible, clear eyes. Eyes that had seen plagues and holocausts and exile, eyes that had watched Athens die and, themselves dying, had calmly watched his own executioner smile. . . .

So, in truth, I was not so very different from any child in each of the ages since the last ABCs were taught on Melos. After the last die had been shaken loose from the last pedestal, after the last Melian bone had been made dice, we learned our ABCs from Athens. Yes, we had learned also in the infancy of the world, but Athens was our first school.

To each generation since, the little building blocks, the dies, the primers.

And since that day at the little table outside Grandfather's library, I have had the most maddening time keeping it all straight: when a die is cast, is it to Fortune, or in the mould of Necessity? Keeping straight what

came first, the roll of chance or the press of the stamp. And how it is that
to set the dice upon someone is to oppress and tyrannize; and if it is our
fate or only ill fortune to worship miscalculation and ignorance as
imperatives.

Must this now forever be—*un dado, un datum, un desafio?*† Is it such
good strategy to call these things pragmatism? And who are these prag-
matists and men of action who follow *might* as noun, but will not hear of
it as verb?

†'a given, a datum,
a dare'—Spanish
synonyms for 'die'

What is that moment in which a world conceives its own end? *When
its inner poetry gives way to prose.* That must be what a poet is, I thought,
what poets do. And this was another way for a child, not quite so young
thereafter, to reverse the losses of that day. Of course these were childish
things—of letters and blocks, and wizards and puzzles. But if priests had
words and wizards had visions, *poets must be wizards with words.*

Real poets would never just find the might in *is*, but seek their being
in 'might.' To make a place for vision here, for words of might—this
seemed a fine thing then to do.

Here was the lesson Melos foresaw in Athens's fall, but since
Thucydides we had lost the heart of it. This loss has been like a flaw
pressed into a die, an error in type, that reproduces itself—inked and re-
inked for each new run of primers. It is as one letter disfigured in the
press, a die miscast by hazard so that never in the hundred generations
since Melos have we read 'mercy' spelled aright.

Not long after, I sat down to be a poet.

> Yet in 'mercy?' and 'right!' combined,
> but for a miscast die,
> might one not rightly find
> (and who if not 'I')
> the anagram of a 'mightier cry!?' . . . 4

hough I might find the wizardry of poetry a very fine thing, it had not yet spelled my entrance to the library. Eventually I grasped that I was jeopardizing a territorial agreement, delicately arrived at, wherein Grandfather had ceded to his daughter full sovereignty over the hacienda in exchange for remaining in perpetuity the library's uncontested patriarch and sole subject. What was extraordinary in this was that it appeared to have been arrived at in complete silence. As though a stern Jehovah had chiselled—neatly, so even a child could read—the new order onto tablets for us. No one was to enter there but he, not even to dust or tidy. Inwardly I could mock the rule, but for a time the silence cowed me.

Adults were becoming mystifying, more abstruse and difficult to read than any book. My father had been mystery itself, and Isabel was always elementally Isabel, but there was now Xochita and even Abuelo.

As in the case of our game of being twins: the morning after our arrival in Panoayan, Amanda and I'd swooped through the courtyard—PolishedEye and NibbleTooth, Ocelotl and Mixcoatl—shouting, "*Mellizas, mellizas! Cocoas, cocoas!*"† It was a joke no one else appreciated, but for us it was not mirth that made us laugh so, but rather purest delight. Xochitl told us to hush, which was startling enough. Around Isabel we never did much shouting, but when I caught sight of Grandfather glaring darkly at us—a thing I'd never seen him do—we fell silent. Which only made me all the more determined to make them see it one day for themselves, for instinctively I felt that anything that could give us so much joy must be true in some way more essential than fact.

Sometimes it seemed the adults barely talked of anything consequential at all, except *to* us or *through* us, or in glares. Here we had been endowed (some of us prodigally) with speech, and yet they insisted on making everyone around them read the garble in their silences. Why wasn't Amanda allowed to sit with us around the firepit? Xochitl would not say whose idea it had been—only that she didn't want Amanda 'bumblebeeing around.' And then there was school. No one had asked, let alone insisted, that *Amanda* go to school. This troubled me more than I let on, even to her. Some shape was sleeping there, something mute I

†*melliza,* Spanish for twin; *cocoa,* twin, snake or dragon in Nahuatl

did not want to disturb—during my month at school I'd found that what I missed most, felt most in danger of losing, was not the library at all. It was Amanda. The day Abuelo brought me home from Sister Paula's class, I swore a sacred oath that Amanda and I would make a school together in the fields and woods and hills. And I would tell her every little thing that was said at the firepit. As for the library, each day we would take with us one of the books I happened to be reading.

We always stayed out till the very last minute, till they took to ringing the chapel bell to call us in to lunch. When we did come in, it was through the kitchen, where we drank enormous quantities of cordials— beet, hibiscus or tamarind—or *agua de horchata*. After lunch Amanda would stay with Xochitl, while I went on to the little table outside the library door. There I would begin to read, and the pain of separation ebbed so quickly I had barely the time to feel guilty over it.

But each morning I awoke anxious to find her again. Days began early—often before dawn, with Amanda in my bedroom doorway, shifting her weight impatiently from foot to foot. We would stand a minute in the gathering light, nose to nose, knee to knee—and lock our hands hard, just for an instant. Then it was a sprint (I lost, I always lost) across the flagstones—icy under our bare soles—and up to the watchtower.

First we checked the bird's nest in the cannon barrel for eggs. But that year there was only the most delicate little cup of grass lined with blue-green down. Where had its architects gone? Next we snuggled under an old horse blanket up there that Father had used with the yearlings. By flapping it and waving it under their noses, he would gradually teach them not to shy. I was sure it still smelled of horses.

We waited.

On a clear morning it is as though the sun rising far to the east chisels WhiteLady's fall from a block of purest indigo. *Head thrown back—chin upthrust—soft heave of breast—knees demure . . .* I squinted up to see how a true poet would see her. Though SmokingStone was more spectacular, its white flint tip edged in keen fire, she was the one we watched, right above us.

The very instant the last pale rose had drained from El Popo's cone, we slapped and clattered barefoot down to the kitchen to find Xochitl grinding corn for tortillas. Soon we waited even that long only on the clearest mornings, for we were dawn's *cognoscentae* now. If the sky was at all cloudy, we were in the kitchen early enough to help with the cooking fire. Once the flames licked up, Amanda and I each took a kindling stick and with a little tremble of fire lit the lamps. Next we huffed and heaved in an armload of firewood, never forgetting to check the woodpile for scorpions first. Now we made a great show of helping Xochitl with the tortillas, so she might be free to make for us—Xochita, hurry *please*—a breakfast basket to take out into the fields.

We might go north then, through the orchards, or south past the paddocks. Very rarely west to the road. But almost always these days east through the cornfields, out along the river and past the little plot of maguey cactus. Though now it grew wild, it had been planted, Xochitl said, long before Cortés camped there—yes, right there—safe on open ground by the river. It is from this place that Panoayan takes its name: *Place of Maguey by Water.* That first night at the firepit Grandfather had been so excited to hear this, but when I made to call Xochitl out of the kitchen, I got another of those silences that made me—if just for a minute—never want to tell him anything again. But I couldn't stay quiet long. I was beginning to tell my own stories by the fire, constructed of the countless things I'd learned that day in the fields—rhymes and songs and plants and dances with Amanda. She had only to go through a dance once to remember it. From her mother, Amanda had to learn the dances mostly by ear—Xochitl's hip let her do little more than talk Amanda through the steps. She had the most wonderful grace with a gesture—the turn of a wrist, the tilt of her head. Amanda didn't talk much, at least compared with me. She didn't run on and on. She was quick with a story she'd learned, or a riddle. Dance was her great talent, but where she spoke most clearly was in the secret language of gifts. . . .

During a month of nights she made us each a heavy cotton satchel for the plants and flowers and rocks we collected in the woods. On each bag she had beaded a rabbit, mine green, hers blue. Some nights a flower on my pillow. Little dolls and polished stones, abandoned bird's nests—once, crickets in a cup.

A gift could be like a vision, a conjury delicate as glass. A gesture was like a magical symbol, like the corn, or a crown, but not stuck to an old hairpiece—a gesture was alive. And even, a little dangerous. Had I yet written a single poem like that?

All *I* knew were things from books. There were Grandfather's legends, but few new ones anymore. He seemed not to tell so many these days. Amanda did like the ones I made up. This intrigued her, that stories were not just learned but invented. And if I helped a bit, we could even write little songs together. To make it more interesting, she would have to find a line in Castilian[5] and a line in Nahuatl. This one was for Xochitl.

> There are diamonds in the grass.
> There are serpents in the clouds.
> In the earth are halls of jade,
> and feathers in the temple.[6]

The next morning we recited it for her, and flushed with our great success went back to write another. For our reading and our poetry there was a shady place just beyond the cornfields, which were then in full bloom with the blue flowers that grow among the corn rows. It was like wading through the blue of the open sea, and we were giants whose feet touched bottom. A strip of trees ran between the corn and the plot of maguey, and there we would sit just above where the river ran closest. One of Abuelo's windmills perched on the riverbank near us, another at the far end of the field. Carrying out over the river and the cactus, the view to the mountains was clear and unbroken. After two years it still was hard not to stare at them.

To get us started I read her a page of verse I had laboured over that night. It began . . .

> In soft echoes are heard,
> > the bird;
> in flowing waters that sing,
> > the spring;
> in phrases' sweet shower,
> > the flower;
> in green-throated salute,
> > the shoot . . . [7]

I told her I had written it for her. What I meant was that I was *giving* it to her. She sat blinking at me for a moment. And then, as was our custom, she gave me something in return. She announced she was to learn to be a midwife, as her mother had been. The song she sang so gravely then she could not have learned overnight. I was struck by what a serious and grown-up affair this was, and that my tall swift twin was almost

a grown-up too. And if I didn't try very, very hard, I would never keep up
with her. . . .

My beloved child, my precious one,
here are the precepts, the principles
your father, your mother, Yohualtecutli, Yohualticitl, have laid down.
From your body, the middle of your body, I remove, I cut the
umbilical cord.

Know this, understand this:
Your home is not here.
You are the eagle, you are the jaguar,
you are the precious scarlet bird,
you are the precious golden bird of Tloque Nahuaque;†   †the Lord of Near
you are his serpent, you are his bird.   and Far
Only your nest is here.
Here you only break out of your shell,
here you only arrive, you only alight,
here you only come into the world.
Here like a plant, you sprout, you burst into bloom, you blossom.
Here like a fragment struck from a stone, chipped from a stone, you
are born.
Here you only have your cradle, your blanket, your pillow where you
lay your head.
This is only the place of arrival.

Where you belong is elsewhere:
You are pledged, you are promised, you are sent to the field of battle.
War is your destiny, your calling.
You shall provide drink,
you shall provide food,
you shall provide nourishment for the Sun, for the Lord of the Earth.
Your true home, your domain, your patrimony is the House of the
Sun in heaven where you shall shout the praises of, where you shall
amuse, the Everlastingly Resplendent One.
Perhaps you shall merit, perhaps you shall earn,
death by the obsidian knife in battle,
death by the obsidian knife in sacrifice . . . [8]

It was terrifying, and beautiful, like Aeschylus. This was the song for the newborn boy. The midwife first removes the cord. She takes the afterbirth and buries it in the earth in a corner of the house. She lays the cord out to dry in the sun. Later, if the boy is a warrior, he will carry it with him onto the field of battle. And if he falls it will be buried there.

I asked her the song for a girl. But Xochitl had said Amanda was not yet ready to learn it.

Amanda gave more, but that wasn't why I began to feel guilty. Jealousy I'd felt before. Of losing what I had. I'd felt it sometimes when Isabel would call Grandfather away from me for some reason. But this was new, this was envy. . . . The things Amanda could share with me seemed so much finer than mine—even *poetry* now. The only other thing I had left to offer was teaching Amanda to read. But books were *hard*—she had better understand that. Harder still was reading aloud before an auditor so very stern of late. I had been making her read Plutarch. Plutarch is a Greek who wrote a lot about Greece, which I had been trying so very patiently to teach her about. Plutarch is hard, even in Castilian. (And I was in no mood now to tell her how much trouble *he* had had learning to read Latin.)

There was a passage she kept stumbling over, right at the bottom of the page. Over and over, trying harder and harder to please me, her eyes almost as round and wide, for once, as mine. "No, don't look at me— *read*—no, you're trying too hard." She was almost *nine*. I was so frustrated because something delightful awaited, if only we could reach the top of the very next page. I had made a crown for her to wear, to mark the end of this difficult and profound and beautiful passage. And the crown was a very grand gesture—a wizardly conjury of my own, if she would only, please, *get there*.

†Bee-OH-shuh

"I *know* the names are Greek, but if you can't say 'Boeotia,'† how are we ever to read Hesiod?" It was as though she didn't even understand anymore what was coming out of her mouth. *Did* she?

"*Nympheutria—anakalypteria*—tell me, Amanda: which is the bride's attendant, which is the unveiling gift?"

Would *I* have known, had I not just read it myself the night before? Well, today was not the day, either, for telling her I had no Greek at all.

"No, Amanda. *Nympheutria!* That's what they'd call *you*, if *I* were getting married. The unveiling thing is the—oh never mind, the *other* one."

Amanda cried easily. Silently, no sobs. Her neat head bent; then her eyes just gushed. She was quick to tears of tenderness, quick to tears of pity, or love—watching them netted one day like bright fish in her soft black hair was a moment of fascination. But she would never, *ever* be made to cry by something like this.

Over her face had fallen a mask of cold wood. How square the chin, how pale the lips, how very hard the wood.

It was the first day in two years I walked home alone.

As I approached the house, I saw two horsemen down by the paddocks and between them a long-horned black bull. It was almost as tall as the horses themselves and chafing at the tight tethers—two ropes bound to each rider's pommel. Isabel was sitting on the top rail of the corral and Abuelo had forgone his nap to stand with her and watch. The bull had been brought from Chimalhuacan. "Is he ours now?" I asked.

Isabel surprised me by answering first. "No, only for a week or two."

The bulls I'd seen were sullen, sluggish things. Freed of its tethers, this one moved swiftly around the corral, then stopped to hook one of its horns—lightly, now left, now right—against an upright, as if to test the firmness of its anchor. The older horseman glanced at Isabel then. The younger one had been stealing glances at her for a while. After a minute she climbed down and called to one of the workers to bring poles for braces.

Abuelo had held his silence until now. "This one," he told me proudly, first glancing at his daughter, "would be worthy of the finest corridas of Spain, not these butcheries here. True, the calves will be a little wild. . . ."

Just before dawn I awoke—and *there she was,* as always. But now Amanda waved over me a large white square of fine muslin, the sort Xochitl used for squeezing water from curd.

"Is this a truce?" Friends such as I did not deserve peace offerings.

"No, Ixpetz—I thought *you* would guess. Mother didn't know either. Look—*now* see? It's a *veil.*"

Yes, Amanda, I saw. I did see at last.

We slipped out through the kitchen without even waiting for Xochitl to put food in our satchels.

On our way out to the fields, we went by the corral. Seeing us, the new arrival began to cut powerfully, quickly, back and forth across the enclosure. The bull still looked as if it could come right through the braced fence—or even over—if it saw something it wanted.

Amanda had already started towards our reading place. She hesitated, seemed about to say something, but then quietly came with me. As we picked flowers, she told me a little more of what she'd learned about midwifery from Xochitl. As the morning wore on, she grew more distracted. Soon it would be time to go in for lunch. She led me back to the shady spot past the cornfield. We sat. She was quiet, her eyes downcast. We sat. She looked up at me. Finally she said, "Have you given up?"

What an idiot I was—of course that's what she would think. I dug Plutarch out from under all that day's flowers and the wilted ones farther down. She must have seen my relief. She read, and for the first time in a while I was not stern at all. And she read *beautifully*, the whole of the lovely passage I had marked, which ends,

> After veiling the bride they put on her head a crown of asparagus, for this plant yields the sweetest fruit from the harshest thorns . . . 9

"The veil!" she said, delighted. "Wait . . ." She started digging in her own satchel for the muslin. "Wait, wait, I'll be your *attendant*, your . . . *Nympheutria!* Was that right?" She had closed her eyes to concentrate and opening them, looked up, the question in her eyes.

But as she opened them she saw that I, for once, had been the quicker. The crown was in my hands. It did look strange, I supposed. We didn't have asparagus, so I had taken agave spikes, cut them into long triangles and woven them into a slim crown. It was the best I could do. I had wanted *nopal.*†

†prickly pear

She looked at it a long while. "It's for you," I said. She nodded. She had understood all right. "Let me be *your* attendant for once, Nibble Tooth."

And I was. We plaited her hair. She wore a muslin veil, and an almost-asparagus crown. And I thought the bride, at her unveiling, very beautiful.

As I turned her around and pulled back her veil, her big almond eyes were full and danced like the light in a birdbath.

We missed lunch. As the bell tolled on, we chattered like *urracas* about crowns. "In Greece this could have been a laurel crown, for great feats of letters. You can read now, Amanda, really *read*. Plutarch is hard—but good, no?" The Greeks used crowns for everything. The crown of obsidion for generals raising sieges. "And no Greek woman not a virgin would be caught dead without her headpiece, also a kind of crown, like this—"

With my hands I showed her how it was—like a plane of holiness settled over the brow. Was it not like a rising into loveliness? Not quite an ascent into the sky but a surfacing . . .

"And the most beautiful thing—when the nuns in Mexico City take their vows, do you know they wear tall crowns of wildflowers? Wedding crowns like the asparagus—but for marrying *Christ*."

"Cinteotl?" she said, wide eyed.

"Maybe, maybe not," I said, mysterious. "But listen to *this*, when a nun dies, she's buried wearing the same crown she wore as a girl, Nibble Tooth, as a bride. Isn't that lovely? Of course, the flowers would be a bit dry. . . ."

And as though the day were indeed blessed, Isabel had been busy with the cattle and had missed lunch herself.

The next morning at dawn, Amanda woke me wordlessly, an index finger to my lips. She led me out by the hand in my nightgown. It was a cold spring morning in the mountains. We weren't even dressed—we could see our breath. She was leading me towards the corral. A little nervously my eyes sought out the bull in the chill half light. I wanted to be sure it hadn't come through the fence. "Amanda . . ." I said, half complaining and chilly, in my bare feet. But Amanda wasn't looking at the bull, was almost casually looking *away* from him. Then I saw. My heart stopped.

The bull stood stock-still in the centre of the corral. Silent, solid, puffing gouts of steam, like the mountain itself. It shook its head now, wreathed in smoke, and glared at us with its small black eyes as through a green-wood fire. And around its horns was wound, in a long figure eight, a

    dark

        blue

            cornflower

                crown.

Green had been the colour of my envy that spring. Dark blue, the shade of its leaving.

My princess of the corn. She spoke to me in dance, in her love of swiftness, in the laughter she was so quick to cover with her hands. In the way the mask of all her wariness dropped away as she taught me a step.

We ran into the fields that day, and I could almost keep up with her. She stopped and waited for me. As always.

It was the next day that Xochitl told us about the special place.

 How indignant we were. How could she have waited almost three years to tell us of it?

"Because you are almost women now." Xochitl smiled, her eyes a tilt of triangles. How easily we were mollified. But then perhaps she also knew how close Amanda truly was. Xochitl had waited "because the earth up there is jade. And because there are certain dangers. . . ."

I had come to think the word *danger* much abused by adults. There were, for example, the wild animals Isabel had once hinted that my sisters wrestled each day just beyond the portals in Nepantla. In the opposite sense, Abuelo was known to backtrack if he felt that his true tales of dangerous bandits or werewolves had brought them too vividly near our firepit. But this was not Xochitl's way, not the way among women. The special place was safe, but there were precautions to take along the path.

"To look big, walk close together."

As if Amanda and I might walk in any other fashion. "And make noise as you walk." She spoke now to me directly, and when I saw her eyes twinkling with this, I knew it really would be all right.

†pumas

Though *miztli*† often hunted during the day, jaguars rarely did, and there was a much better place for them, where the deer and the pigs came for salt. "Which is why—listen carefully now—you follow the south bank of the river, and do not follow the first stream up or the second. The third. Where it joins the river is a deep pool. There is a place to cross over. Then look to Iztaccihuatl. You see straight above you a line of waterfalls. The highest is at the snow line." We were to repeat it now for her. First me, then Amanda.

"It was a place for the women of our family," said Xochitl. "It is the Heart of the Earth, of the goddess of the earthquake. And of our grandmother, Toci. Among the men, only Ocelotl knew the way."

"His mist has not scattered," said Amanda, which meant he was respected. Xochitl nodded in approval and told us the Heart of the Earth was the jaguar's tutor. His pelt is on her throne.

"Did Ocelotl go there for visions?" I asked, casually.

She wasn't easily fooled.

"Could be, Ixpetz. But I think mostly he slept. Beside the spring you will see the stones he used for his *temazcal.*[†] It is for my daughters now, who have made my hair white and my face very wide."

Just as we were turning to go, Xochitl called to us. "Here . . . There is enough for breakfast and lunch. But when you look down to the hills and the sun is two palm-widths above—start down. Never later."

We set out at a fast walk, which threatened at every step to break into a trot. I held Amanda's hand tight to keep her from breaking away altogether.

"Did you hear, Amanda? She didn't even tell us to keep it to ourselves!" Amanda nodded proudly. But if she had, I asked, wouldn't we have been right to take it as a grievous insult? And wasn't it beautiful about the Heart of the Earth, and . . .

And so we went as we would each time, to what became *our* special place. East through the corn, shooing deer, which would cheekily stop again after clearing the fence—a high fence whose lowest rails we ducked through—in one soaring, effortless bound. So calmly they hung at the top of their arc that it seemed they might nod off up there in the air. They were like her, tense in stillness and in flight utterly at peace.

Ten minutes above the river, the path reared up more steeply. The stream by which we had found our way slowly fell away to the left. For half an hour we climbed a long incline of uniform width, pitched as steeply as the stairs up to the hacienda's watchtower. On either side sloped away banks of shale and what seemed almost to be coal but with a glassy sheen. To our fancy, this incline appeared as a nose, one we followed to the place Amanda named *Ixayac.* Its Face.

The top of the incline ended in a sheer wall five times our height, but up the surface of which a zigzag of handholds and footholds stood out as clearly as rungs. Amanda scrambled up without hesitation, and I clambered gratefully after her. This climb, I saw, was what would keep us safe from anything on four legs following us.

We stood on a deep bench, the lower of two. Each of its brows sprouted a score or so of stunted pines. The stream ran out of a thicket in front of us and dropped away a little distance to the left. Amanda walked right up to the edge where the stream fell. I inched up cautiously behind her. It smashed and frayed and tumbled its way into a deep hollow of rubble and shale. From there it ran more smoothly along the north cheek of the incline before disappearing into the trees.

We sat down on the ledge. A stone's throw out from us, three grey rock doves flapped a broad arc across our field of view. Eventually I let my feet swing out into space, though not quite so freely as Amanda did. The world we looked out upon could have been another continent. But this *was* the other continent fixed in the imagination of the Europeans I had read. This was the great glittering lake they had seen or heard or dreamt about. It snaked its way north up the valley until it lost itself in the blue-grey of distance. And there was the white city on the lake, plotted, unlike any city in Europe, on a grid perfectly aligned to the cardinal directions and without defensive walls. Grandfather said Cortés's soldiers wept—as if they had had been overtaken by a dream of death and now stared out upon a warriors' heaven. A city without walls to defend or overcome . . . imagine it.

Just then, Amanda pointed out the small wedge of a falcon stooping on the doves. In three heartbeats it fell through them—an axe head splitting a block. In a tangle of esses, two doves flew on.

I had thought it far off, this place I'd read so much about. Before the Conquest, Tenochtitlan was a vast island city, an ivory eye—or, with its grid of streets, a white sunflower framed in leaves of an iridescent green. These were the *chinampas,* or floating gardens. The island was tethered to the shore by the mooring cables of long causeways running through shades of blue. The city was bone white, but its temples were painted in the gaudy hues of parrot plumes and jewels. And the pyramids of ruby and emerald and sapphire were as the flower's jewelled nectary. The pyramids were gone now and the *chinampas* much reduced, but the air was still clear enough to see the bell tower of what could only be the cathedral, and beside it the Viceroy's palace.

We sat on the ledge, swinging our feet, attempting little verses on what we saw. We decided there and then, like children nursing a candy, to make no further explorations until our next visit, so as to draw out the pleasure of discovery. After just an hour, we were ready to start down.

At the river we stopped to watch in wonder the enormous trout that converged at the bottom of the pool. There seemed to be a vent, some kind of spring at which they jostled and fed. And then it was dusk, which fell swiftly up the mountain. Amanda and I hurried through the cactus field, the richness of the day steeping quietly in us.

Near the hacienda stood a small enclosure, just back from the river where it winds through the cactus plot. Four bare poles under a thatch of maguey spikes, and a killing floor of smooth stone slabs. Incised in the floor was a channel to run blood straight into the water, which could be sluiced clean with just a bucket or two. The floor had always been here, and on it may once have stood an altar. It was useful now for slaughtering livestock so as not to attract scavengers to the house.

My heart sank to see Isabel look up as she and a workman butchered a lamb. This might befall a lamb if it were to break a leg, or perhaps come home late.

Isabel sent Amanda on to the house. I stood silently as they finished in the gloom. She had fetched up her skirts and tucked them between her thighs, and was plastered to her elbows in a black mud. I saw finally that it was blood, as she squatted there like some vengeful idol to the beauty of dusk.

She washed up, sending the workman ahead with the meat. She had not asked, and seemed not to listen to my mumbled evasions as to where we had been till such an hour. After administering a spanking with her customary efficiency and power she asked if I remembered yet. Grandfather's seventieth birthday. Which I must have known he attached significance to, and today of all days to leave him alone when he counted on me. . . .

I blurted, "If I was so late, why didn't *you* read for him?"

My ear rang and buzzed for an hour from a slap more impulsively delivered than the spanking.

"Come in when you've stopped."

That night I tossed and turned and ground my teeth—to be gone again, up to Ixayac—or anywhere. The place where my true life was. Not this, not here. This was not *my* life.

What kept me for so many hours so close to tears was not the ringing in my ear or even the humiliation. It was shame—scalding and caustic and vile. He *did* count on me.

"Angel, will you . . . ? My eyes are tired." And I would read for him— enchantingly, as any great actress would. That was our game. I had never thought of it as his needing me. Even though now, no matter how stunningly I read, how emphatically—how *loud,* I could never quite wake one of his eyes. The right. The one he kept turned away from me at the firepit. The truth was, he often just listened now, nodding sagely at the flames as I spoke.

That night dealt me a succession of confused dreams, and on each card the emblem of my guilt. Snake, horse, lion, falcon, *manatí.* Each appearance brief, each somehow me—a fugitive, a figure like Proteus wriggling through a thousand shapes to flee to Egypt with his sea calves. Or the daughter of Erysichthon—always unclean, no matter how many her guises.

I was still close to tears when I saw Xochitl the next morning.

"Two palm-widths above the horizon. Just like you told us, Xochita."

"Tell me about the trout."

I knew she asked this by way of consoling me. But how did she know they'd be there?

"As a girl I watched them," she said. "Just like you two. We had to practice a lot to spear them."

"You *speared* them?"

Amanda nodded. "They're quick."

"Yes, NibbleTooth, but also because they are not there."

"*After*, you mean?" I still didn't see.

"No—*then*. You see a fish. And there is a fish. But not there . . . over *here*." As she said this, she had turned up her right palm, now the left. "Not yet, eh, Ixpetz? Next time take a long stick. Our spears were higher than our arms could reach and straight. Put the stick in—"

"It bends!"

"Near the bottom, where the hot water comes, it bends more. The stick is straight. But not always. The fish is. But not there."

"Xochita, this is just *refraction*," I said, eager to explain.

"No, this is god."

"It's only *light*."

"Look more, Ixpetz. You will see the double you keep asking about."

She had never once given me a straight answer about any of this, nor had she ever been the one to bring it up.

"Sometimes we say *ixiptla*, sometimes mask. Or double. *Or* . . . twins."

"Why so many, Xochita, so many words?"

She made a funny face, the face of an insatiable child pleading for one more treat—a face just such as mine. "Maybe we were never sure we understood. Twins, doubles . . . Who can say, Ixpetz—*one* of them might be right."

How did she always manage it? She could make me want to laugh in the blink of an eye.

"Sometimes we say they are a couple. Like those two mountains."

"Maybe," I said, "the lovers are also between the fish."

"Maybe very good, Ixpetz."

"Fish," I said, trying not to smile.

"Fish."

"Not one fish."

"No."

"Not two."

"No."

"Here and there."

"Yes, Ixpetz. Near and far."

"Many masks—one face."

"Not one."

"Faceness—*face*. Only 'face.'"

"Ahh . . ."

"And we're needed, somehow."

"*We* bend the stick!" Amanda said.

"Very good, NibbleTooth."

"But, Xochita, if you stand directly over the water," I said, "the stick . . ."

She shook her head sadly. "You think too much."

"That's no answer, Xochitita," I crooned. "Please?"

She thought about this. "In the world there is no such place. To stand."

"Above god," I added, hoping she might say more.

"Help me grind the corn—both of you. I am late again."

"I have a question."

"Grind."

Not even the poetry of Xochitl's reticence prepared us for this place beyond the trout pool that she had bequeathed to us. By the time we had started down I knew, and for once kept it to myself, that it was not to our maturity she had trusted. Such beauty kept its own secrets. We never told anyone.

We planned to go the very next day. But so many things, it seemed, had to happen before we could make our way back up to Ixayac, to discover the hot spring, the falcon nest, the plunge pool below the little waterfall. It seemed like years.

FOUR-YEAR
FAST

A year later, as the cart lurched up the track and away from Panoayan, a last shred of pride kept me from turning back and begging to be allowed to stay. I rode beside the muleteer, my back straight, my front crumbling.

One driver, three mules, a burro and a girl. I hardly recall a single feature of the roadside. Knowing I spoke Nahuatl, the driver asked me a polite question or two, to which I replied in monosyllables, hard as these had been for me to manage lately.

The one ray of light to reach through the clouds and down to me on that cart seat was that it was not the same muleskinner, drunk on *pulque,* who had driven us from Nepantla five years back, madly bawling away and singing. And vomiting. He had his way of making the Rabbit sacred. Mine was to work myself into an unholy fury: I was homesick. *I'd been away less than an hour.*

Away an hour and already so much to be thankful for. It was a different driver. No one saw me cry. And I didn't vomit. But then, riddles were a cure for seasickness, weren't they, and I now had a riddle to cross *oceans* with. For what a sight my ungrateful tears would have made—hadn't I demanded this very thing? Had I not vowed to Isabel that I would disguise myself as a boy and go to the Royal University? I would find my own teacher. Take classes! And among the towering racks of the New World's greatest library, stroll forever. This was what adventurers did— pursued their destiny, defied the risks, strove towards high exploits like giants storming heaven. But with Amanda.

Not like this.

How I wanted to let Panoayan go now. Place of thorns, this El Dorado of loss—of pasts and precious jades, of tongues and riddles and *friends.* Josefa and María were right: these mountains were oppressive— suffocating. They might be the Heart of the Earth, a place of women's secrets, but that heart was cold now, and still. Or so I wanted mine to be in me. I was on my way to the city of Mexico, seat of empires. This was to be my life. I must make myself hard as iron and full of briars.

At the eastern shore the late sun loured on the lake with a light dulled to pewter. In the shallows, mats of flotsam heaved in a dance of woodblocks, reeds and corn husks. Up and down the shore, mounds of refuse stood slumped in squat pyramids—rags, cobs, potsherds and rinds, glass glints, strips of hide—as if built on the trash of an earlier tribe. That was the custom of this place, to build on what remains, and never, ever be free of it.

Back from the flat shore sprawled a midden of wattle huts and mud, endless mud and lurking dogs. In one hovel a woman in a greyish *huip-il* nursed a dirty-cheeked infant while squatting and poking at a brazier. As if in its smoke she sought some small help in driving the flies away from the infant's mouth and eyes. This was a blouse such as Xochitl and Amanda wore. I had never seen one dirty. Outside, *mace-huales*[†] lurched about drunk . . . dogs fought. For this, I was not yet hard enough.

[†]Nahuatl term for the lowborn

Was this really the lake I—and how many others—had dreamt of and conjured? It was not enough to leave home. Now I had to give up even my illusions of what we had seen from up at Ixayac. And everything Grandfather had taught me to see. . . .

This was not that blue-green eye into which *los conquistadores* had stared, and I had too—as down through the *oculus* of a vast underground cathedral. Over there, crouched beneath that rust sunset, was most certainly not the city of the white sunflower, its nectaries tall pyramids of cut gems. I had seen it *myself*, from Ixayac—seen this shore I now stood on. But then again, my eyes were not so very clear after all, and no longer was I his ray of pure white light.

I saw this shore become still more hideous as the light failed and a thick darkness gathered. For a few minutes more I could still have looked back to the volcanoes—the white chisel-tip edged in fire, her lover standing over her.

I would not. That beauty was behind me now.

But I would *never*—not dragged by four hundred mules—enter Mexico over this *calzada*. The old causeways the Mexica had built were as straight as dies—not these corruptions, as full of crooks and sags as an old stick. I would find a boat. The driver glared but said nothing. I guessed that he'd been planning to stop at a *pulquería*, and that a weakness for drink must surely be the chief hazard of mule-driving. Well, he might as soon talk sense to his mules as stop me getting down.

It was cold that night alone on the shore. But I was eleven now, and after all the brave talk, here was a thing the intrepid would never fear to do. I dragged my trunk down the beach. Any villager sober enough to see could have followed my trail to where I hid in a thicket. All that night I clutched tight to my chest a purse containing the fifty pesos Grandfather had left to me. It was a lot of money, and it was still his.

It was for our books.

Never had I imagined so many mosquitoes might exist in the world. Nor that all at once they would converge on me. At first light I was of a more subdued cast of mind. I climbed into the cargo canoe and went where the man gestured, up into the bow. He wrestled aboard the cedar trunk that carried my earthly attachments. There *were* books, quite a lot. By the time we had taken on two more passengers, weavers from Puebla and their huge bundles, the canoe seemed more awallow than afloat.

The boatman pushed off. Seeing the European girl in her one presentable dress and perched at the prow on her cedar trunk, they must have thought her the daughter of some Iberian grandee. One weaver whispered, glaring pointedly at my well-ballasted trunk, "*Aicnopilpan nemitiliztli. . . .*"

Among the poor is no life for kings.

To which I could not help but retort, "I'm not so rich, friends, but I hear my uncle over *there* is."

They were not much older than I, a couple already, or brother and sister. And once they had recovered from their embarrassment we laughed a little about their surprise and my rich uncle. They did not ask me how I had learned their tongue, and I liked this restraint and saw its dignity, and I liked them as they talked about their hopes for sales and how many days they might have to stay, and whether they would go back at all. Something passed between them then, and I surprised myself in resisting the impulse to ask about it.

We advanced alongside the causeway, though as the boatman paddled steadily on I was pleased to see us pulling away. I asked why there were even canoes *on* this shore anymore. He said the canals were still preferred for moving cargo within the city as long as the water was high. Few of the streets were paved, and after just two days of rain most became bogs to the heavy carriages.

As we talked, my eyes strayed once or twice to the white peaks behind the boatman. The sun had risen between them. I watched it go from gold to red and back to gold as it rose through the smoke plume of Popocatepetl. I decided there could be no real harm in speaking the language of that country once in a while, though all of that was behind me now. The weavers were excited and nervous, and glanced up past me too: for what was behind me, in truth, was the city. As the conversation died out, I turned to look, thinking I might as well get my bearings, since I knew more about the canals of Venice than those of Mexico. I suppose I was a little nervous too.

Again Mexico was closer than I knew. It filled the horizon—a canvas stretched wide as a painted sail. The scene had just that quality of grandeur and poise, of all the business of the world in suspension, stilled in its detail and brushing. The sweep of streets, built up twice my height above the water—hundreds, all running in parallels to the shore; the gold light striking the blocks of the great houses, as if crates stacked for off-loading from a single enormous wharf; smoky blue shadows between the buildings; grey-black threads ravelling up into a coppice above the chimneys. . . .

Right beside us, to the south, were the floating gardens, faintly undulating. Around and amidst them worked scores of canoes, their sides flashing like the wet bills of cormorants in the morning sun. These were the farmers at their floating crops.

And all the furious activity at the entrance to the canal! Banging and shouts, the clank of iron, and ringing steel. Horses and mules, the clatter of carriages, a swarm of men and bundles. And half of these men were black.

Africans . . .

Close now to the entrance, I saw that the Indians were ferrying bundles up from canal to cart, and the Africans down from cart to canal. They were as two colonies, red and black, in a teeming mercantile exchange of ant wares and formic delicacies. And I—I was bringing, high in the holds of my belly, a whole colony of butterflies. . . .

We entered the canal.

My uncle was rich, one of New Spain's richest men; and he had half the slaves in his charge out looking for me. The driver had not rushed to a *pulquería*, after all, but had prudently gone to give Aunt María my views on causeways. It was Aunt María herself who was waiting at the dock.

She stood looking very tall atop a flight of broad, shallow steps. She stood tall, too, as the only woman in her generation of our family to have conceived a child in wedlock, or to have achieved marriage at all. I had met her just once, but there was no mistaking her. Hers was the cultivated pallor of one whom luxury permits to evade the sun; her hair was a shade lighter than Isabel's deep chestnut, with glints of copper at her temples. And yet they were unmistakably sisters. Like Isabel's, her brows were black, but not so long, nor wide-spaced, nor arched. It was Aunt María's nose that was long and arched.

Isabel was beautiful. And her beauty was for me an annihilation—no matter how I held the mirror, all I could see were *her* traits. As a way to ward off that beauty, I had once in a poem made her nose 'aquaductile' in its straightness and strength of line.

But María's was truly aquiline and she, quite striking. In the prepossession of her nose, her pallor and the heavy blackness of her brows, there was the handsome brooding of a crow.

To see better, no doubt, for she seemed a little short-sighted, she had drawn back her white veil—veils were fashionable again, I learned, if only among gentlewomen recently landed from Europe. Which, of course, María was not. Around her neck hung a heavy silver chain and a thick crucifix inlaid with onyx. Otherwise she was dressed chin to heel in black shimmering silk.

She looked calm amidst the bustle of porters, and well she might: many of these men were her husband's slaves. But with a dozen running thither and yon looking for me, she had known exactly where to come. She had come alone, and she had driven herself in a light phaeton just right for two, hitched to a charcoal-grey horse. The carriage was spotless, unlike every other carriage or cart in sight. Uncle Juan, largely at his own expense, saw to it that at least one street running from his house to each of the southern and eastern canals was paved. And though the *tenayuca*[†]

†a paving of ovoid stones

was rough, I think I could have enjoyed that first ride; as, in other circumstances, I think I could have liked her. But this was my jailer conducting me into exile.

And so began the first year of captivity. At least I was not made to walk to the gates.

"Isabel warned me you were willful."

That was all either of us said on the ride.

I had never seen before that day a house with three storeys, nor could I have imagined wanting one. The doors were tall and impressively carved, the grillwork at the windows heavy and elaborate. The frames of doors and windows alike were of a blond limestone, as was the lintel, whose ends were scrolls carved like the capital of Ionic columns. And in each of the scrolls' *oculi* I noted with grim satisfaction the ugly little face of a gargoyle.

The house itself stood as if cut from a quarry of dark grey slate. The grey was relieved only by a thin strip of blue and white tiles between each of the storeys, and another strip of tiling running under the eaves, with three more gargoyles as waterspouts. The way the sky was lowering, I wouldn't have to wait long to see them retching water.

In Panoayan I'd never thought much about the rain. There was always a big tree to sit beneath, and it was dry under the arcades. Here, the rain would add one more wall to those already keeping me in. Certainly I'd never associated rain with *moods*.

The first rule of this new life: we were never to go out alone.

Since Aunt María dragged poor Magda everywhere, this injunction was of little concern to my cousin. She was five years my senior, and with so little natural sparkle that her mother had undertaken to vigorously fossick the New World's largest city for marriage prospects. In my years in that house, and in a city thick with the scions of mining magnates, not a single one panned out.

I would never have imagined such an enormous house could so quickly become insufferably small. First, because it was only half a house. Uncle Juan's parents, a wizened little pair glimpsed only on the rarest occasions, had the whole of the opposing half. Which is to say that halfway to the back, on each floor, the corridor was blocked by a locked door built into a wooden divider. What's more, the courtyard was sectioned neatly in two by a heavy canvas, lashed at the sides to the handrails and columns of each storey's inner corridor and fastened at the top to a metal mesh, whose original purpose had been to keep out intruders and doves. So although the courtyard was technically open to the sky, the rain and light fell in tiny, cramped squares.

At ground level all this oppressive cloistering gave way to farce, for the canvas was tied down to buckles not only set in the flagstones but sunk even into the bottom of what must once have been a lovely fountain. I came to see in all this the letter of some arcane covenant on the sharing of family property, or the judgement of Solomon to halve the child. But not at first, when it just seemed laughable. At least once a week, one of the Indian servants was down scrubbing the greenish growth from our side of the canvas, and there were moments of true hilarity in watching her try to co-ordinate scrubbing motions with her counterpart—giggling and shouting instructions—on the other side of the bulging, bumping sheet. I had read of wedding nights in distant countries that might look thus.

And if all this were not enough to make me run for the doors, *our* half was a warehouse. The courtyard was choked with crates and bales, and the end of each corridor was stacked to the ceiling with inventories that seemed never to turn over. The secret path to vast fortunes was indeed perplexed and tortuous.

The next rule: we were to go to Mass twice a day, bent like porters under the heavy crucifixes assigned for the excursion. It was as if Aunt María hoped the three of us might be called from the pews to assist in the ceremonies. In churchly company, she would go to awkward lengths to trot out a near-complete store of the idioms of divine praise and favour, very much as I had done to practise Nahuatl. *God willing . . . Heaven be praised . . . If it be His will.* But in the cathedral itself she often freshened them, as if to prove her usage no mere formula: *Jesus be praised; if it be the will of Jesus Our Saviour; may the Son of God, Redeemer and Messiah, forbid . . .*

We were never to have friends over without notice.

In my case, this could never be anything but hypothetical, since I met no one on my own.

We were never to dress up as boys and go to the Royal University.

Never. It was not to be.

The Royal University was a preposterous idea for a girl. And dressing up as a boy . . . just this year someone in lascivious dress had been caught walking in the main square after curfew and discovered to be a man. After the trial, he was hanged in the square before a jeering mob.

And there would be a special penalty for sneaking out. Any domestics in a position to prevent me would be let go, nor would they find a place elsewhere if Aunt María had any say, and of course she had a very great deal of say.

This was coercion—*extortion.*

Good, we understood each other.

It was no hollow threat. Maybe this is why I never sought to know the servants, though we sometimes exchanged a word or two in Nahuatl. The better I knew them, the more I cared, and the more inescapable became my prison.

While most of the great houses used Africans, our house employed only Indians, and it was widely acknowledged that slaves were much better off than serfs. The Africans were hardier, more resistant to disease, less numerous and often learned a trade. There were standards of fair treatment and there was a commission to appeal to. There was competition for their services, and they could at least hope to save enough to one day purchase their freedom. Some could hope to be freed by their holder.

An Indian was the property of the conquistadors. Or so it was at first. The Conquest was privately financed. *Los conquistadores* had taken enormous risks and expected a return. "Return?" Abuelo had snorted. "Cortés had all but stolen his ships! Was honour not a return, or service to the Crown—was the greater glory of God not return enough?" A sneer was not something that rode easily on Abuelo's broad face, but there it had sat, like a moustache on a calf. From his lip the sneer had faded quickly but not from his voice. Five hundred conquerors had been made *encomenderos* by the Crown. The *encomienda* was the return on a capital investment—New Spain divided among five hundred shareholders. But they had not the faintest interest in land. Dumbfounded, I had asked if I'd heard him right.

The conquerors of America had not the faintest interest in land.

Unless it was in Spain, of course. And even there, no peninsular gentleman would ever let himself be seen at manual labour of any kind. Horses, bulls and swords stood as the allowable exceptions. "Transportable wealth. Liquid capital. Gold, Angelina." Gold and rents.

Every village in New Spain was for rent. Villagers from Panama to Florida to California were subject to pay tribute as serfs and could be rented like a house. A block of houses, rather, for they were rented out together.

Their nickname, though, was *burritos*. Little beasts of burden. This part Abuelo didn't teach me. I had to learn it in the city.

"Of course, Juanita, matters could not stand this way for long. Even allowing for the depreciation of disease and death, let us say four percent a year, the resource yielded a return out of all proportion to the outlay." The conquistador's lease was redrafted to expire at death and the property reverted to the commonwealth. These days wealthy businessmen rented villages from the Crown, or from landholders such as the Church. The Church cared about land.

Paid a wage now, the Indians could be sent home at night to their own districts, so did not even have to be fed and housed. For the past hundred years, the city administration had struggled to contain them in five barrios, five blocks of rental properties. The Europeans were to live in the centre and, above all, to keep the Indians away from the Africans, whose cults and superstitions were almost incurable.

So, too, proved the epidemic of *mestizaje*.† Passion leapt the barriers, life drove roots beneath them, opportunity sifted through every crack, and all made a mockery of the prophylaxis.

In but one respect were the Indians envied by the other races: they were exempt from the jurisdiction of the Inquisition. So highly prized was the exemption that many of the light-skinned castes learned Nahuatl or the Mayan language so, if the need arose, they could pretend to be serfs.

The Inquisition had fetched a poor return on its investment in the Indians. Loving persuasion had proved so much more effective an evangelist, and harshness the very thing the Indians best resisted. Here was the first lesson Cortés learned, and at the urging of his translator he befriended Moctezuma. Indian resistance, on the other hand, was a fearsome thing. And here was Cortés's second lesson, taught in the siege of Tenochtitlan, where tens of thousands starved rather than surrender, where the women fought like Saracens, where the starving died with war axes in their hands.

The lake, too, had been a friend once, before the caravels and cannon. Yes there was steel, yes there was cavalry, but the single decisive engagement of the Conquest was a naval assault, on a white city on an island on a lake.

Now, there were sixty thousand *burritos* dredging out the canals and drainage ditches around the valley on any given day. But not the same sixty thousand. Many died too quickly to learn a trade or to acquire special skills. Many from the mountains had not learned to swim.

Water was not their element. But then, the lake was being drained.

As it was with the labourers, so it was with our house servants. It was not so much that they belonged nowhere else—they belonged *to* nowhere else. In Nepantla and Panoayan our field hands were rented from the Church; they came with the land. Yet I had never seen my mother, for all her faults, treat a field hand unfairly or speak to him cruelly. María, who on the canal dock had so clearly been Isabel's sister, was not like her at all.

This was Injustice.

I was permitted one monthly excursion of a personal nature, though never alone. I was allowed to buy books. This one right was never questioned, never threatened. So, whenever Uncle Juan requested my presence in the salon, I tried to go less grudgingly. Abuelo's fifty pesos were so much more money than I'd understood. And when the book-sellers learned whose granddaughter I was, fifty pesos became a hundred. I had known the bookmen's names for years, heard them listed many times in a roll call of thieves, and no doubt many were, but thieves with sentiments. Their sentimental gestures began to fill my shelves. My prison would have a library.

My room was on the third floor and was larger than mine in Panoayan. During the day at least, it was quiet on the third floor. The room faced east, with a view of the mountains, though I permitted myself only glimpses. The mornings were full of light and warmth and the afternoons dim and cool. But the most splendid feature by far was the bookshelves. They made almost the full circuit of the room. Though not ornate, they were well made, of a hardwood I didn't know, and built for this space. When I arrived they were also entirely bare of books.

The prisoner hadn't expected to find her cell so agreeable. Nor had I expected such a good first impression of Uncle Juan. I remembered imagining, years before and on no evidence whatever, that he and my grandfather had quarrelled. That was why Abuelo was making fewer visits to Mexico.

The day I arrived, Uncle Juan himself supervised my cedar trunk's precarious ascent, directing the porters to set their burden down next to the bookshelves. He seemed to have guessed about the books. His brusqueness with the porters bespoke a habit of command, but he thanked them—casually and very badly—in Nahuatl. The phrase he so blithely dismantled was *Tlazohcamati huel miac*. I looked hard to see if this was supposed to impress me, but though painful to my ear it tripped off his tongue like a stone worn smooth from a very long journey in one's shoe.

He said *Tasoca*, he had said it often, and I was impressed.

At the door he nodded, a little shyly. "The shelves will look better with books in them again." At that, he turned to go.

"I hope you didn't give up your office, Uncle."

His smile seemed faintly perplexed. "No, Juanita. We have offices near the palace. It's where I have to spend most of my time now."

And so it was. Not a month went by, it seemed, in which I saw him more than once—usually in the salon with his business associates, some of whom had literary tastes. For their entertainment I might be asked to improvise verses on a theme or rhyme scheme of their choosing. One or two of his regular visitors displayed a genuine interest. I eventually let them hear poems I was writing. Though it was not quite a pleasure, neither could I make the salon out to be a torture. Still, at the first opportunity I would excuse myself and go up to my room.

If I stood—at first, on a chair under my window, or then a small stack of books, or soon just stood—I could see down into the street. Once it happened that a neighbourhood urchin spotted my face up there, and we would exchange a sign or two from time to time. Over the years the faces changed and the number of urchins grew, as if the window had become a landmark; I came to believe their knowledge of the city was as intimate as ours had been of our woods.

Finally a small gang of more prosperous boys noticed me, and my window became the target of their affections. There were spectacular, manly throws of rotting fruit: the best results came with tomatoes. One time, for my entertainment, using fireworks I imagine, they blew up a watermelon in the street, an early instalment on the day they would find a catapult, or a cannon. I tried not to take umbrage—perhaps they were only practising for the theatre, which I hoped to visit one day too.

The nights were altogether different from the day's calm. The house was in the southeast barrio, and though land was indeed scarce in the centre, Uncle Juan had built here by choice, to be closer to the canals. It was an Indian barrio, well supplied with *pulque* concessions. Carefully supervised by Church and Crown, the trade in *pulque* remained one of Uncle Juan's more profitable businesses. Two thousand *arrobas*† a day, every day.

†fourteen thousand gallons

Eventually I grasped that some *pulquerías* also served as houses of prostitution. At daybreak, when the sun struck the wall above my bed well before there was brightness in the streets, the poor harlots could be seen doubled up against a wall—sleeping, I hoped, and not badly hurt. Sometimes there was more than one, sometimes they fought among themselves, or over clients—once over a little package that I couldn't make out, but which seemed precious to them. I could not keep from looking.

It must have been the starkest horror down in the beds of those canyons for someone with nowhere to turn, for even at the height of my room, the stillness was often rent by shouts and shrieks. The most brutal, grisly scenes of knives and cudgels and helplessness played themselves out under my lids. I could not keep from seeing myself huddled against just such a wall.

The night floated up on a tide of loneliness.

In that first year I was often terrified. Not so much of the streets themselves but of having nowhere to go.

I have become a light sleeper, I think from that time. When I did drift off, it was usually by snuffling my pillow, letting myself imagine it was Abuelo's shoulder. Drowsy, I could smell him. Mesquite from the firepit, and leather . . . warm wool, and the most delicious, very faint scent of rising dough.

It was only natural that I should wake in the night, having dreamt of him. Often the same dream: of him riding away on what I finally understood was Amanda's roan lamb. But he went west from Nepantla, not east, the direction my father had taken. Abuelo swaying on the back of a lamb as large as a camel didn't seem comical at all in a dream. When I awoke it felt as if he had just left the room.

One night something happened to make me wonder if as a young child I had often been afraid of the dark. I woke to screams. Coming from the streets three storeys down was a shrieking so terrible I couldn't get back to sleep at all. Lying there looking out at a quarter moon, I thought of a song we had learned from Xochitl. And of the time I first remembered hearing it. I was lying against her in a hammock, at night, in the storeroom behind the kitchen. . . .

There had been a jaguar killing cattle. It had come closer to the house than anyone expected, into the corral, with the horses. I have never forgotten the screaming of the horses. Abuelo awoke in great confusion, and in his undergarments had started up to the watchtower to load the cannon. "Father, come down!" shouted Isabel. She'd taken an instant to throw on a cloak, and had an arquebus in her hands. She fired into the night above the courtyard.

The sound was shattering, coming without warning over the terror in the corral. Grandfather teetered on the steps as though he might fall. I froze, and my sisters, too—they huddled together just outside their room, their nightgowns a pale smudge of starlight. Isabel went inside to reload and before we could rouse ourselves Xochitl had brought Abuelo a lantern. As she helped him down the steps, she whispered something to him. I had never seen them speak. Returned to his senses, he rushed—lantern high—after Isabel, who was already through the portals. Xochitl scooped me up, told María and Josefa to go back to bed, and took me to sleep with her. Amanda was already there in Xochitl's hammock.

Xochitl sang to us. We lay on either side of her, clutching at her breast, as we had at the beginning. She sang the song of the magical sleeping mat. A mat against the jaguar, Night, who mocks and taunts our vision, who is the mirror that multiplies each shadow until our eyes are filled with giants. She sang a charm against the giant wizards and bandits who wait at the crossroads under the cover of night.

> *Nomatca nehuatl*
> *niQuetzalcoatl,*
> *niMatl,*
> *ca nehuatl niyaotl*
> *nimoquequeloatzin*
> *Ye axcan yez:*
> *niquinmaahuiltiz nohueltihuan . . .*
> > Even I,
> > I, Quetzalcoatl,
> > I, Matl,
> > even as I am War,
> > who mocks all,
> > so it shall be now:
> > I will mock my sisters . . .

She sang us the song FeatherSerpent sang out to his sister, PreciousFeatherMat, where she fasted the four-year fast of penance with the mountain priests. The screaming had stopped, the shouts died out, and the gunshots. There was only Xochitl's voice now, its soft rattle and sway in our ears, its purr against our cheeks. Quetzalcoatl called to Quetzalpetlatl:

> *auh in ipan catca*
> *chalchiuhpetlatl,*
> *quetzalpetlatl,*
> *teocuitlapetlatl.*
> > There was he found,
> > on the mat of jade,
> > on the mat of quetzal,
> > on the mat of gold.

FeatherSerpent called out to his sister for protection and comfort, for he had been sickened and tricked by the jaguar, his adversary and twin. He had tasted now four times of the sacred *octli*,[†] and was intoxicated. In his vision, in his confusion he called his sister to his side, and she spent the night of intoxication with him, and brought him great comfort.

[†]*pulque*

And next to Xochitl in the hammock I slept. But before I fell asleep I knew she'd sung that song to me before. It felt as if I had heard it many times.

I remembered the song and the desolation of that night from our first weeks in Panoayan. I remembered it all those years later in Mexico City in a still unfamiliar room walled in by dark bookshelves, with screaming coming up from the streets.

The next night I sang the song to myself, and slept deeply. I dreamt I woke. Abuelo was sitting beside the bed, not discomforted by the absence of a chair there and amused that this should worry me. I saw him as clearly as when we sat together at the little table by the library. "Angelina, think . . . what do you really want with all your heart? Only ask it."

There was something in this, too, I had heard or felt before, and a few days later I found it in Kings. Solomon was in Gibeon making sacrifices to the God of his father, David. Well pleased, the God of David came to Solomon and asked him to name whatever he wanted.

Solomon asked neither riches nor honour but a wise and understanding heart, if he was to be given sovereignty over so great a people. He was granted what he asked, but also the riches and honour he did not seek.

I hadn't the faintest interest in riches, a good deal in honour, more still in understanding. What was the wisdom here that Abuelo was offering me? I read the passage again many times. It hurt—finally, in a good way—to be reminded of him, but I couldn't find it. I read all of Kings and Proverbs again, and the Song of Solomon. A mountain of wisdom was there, and passages of great beauty, but no special message that felt expressly for me. For the next several days I tried to be attentive to everything around me, which after all was only books, the household and the street. I thought again about Xochitl's song, the four-year fast, the four sips of *pulque*—had they got drunk on the fourth sip or the fifth? I remembered that FeatherSerpent had once travelled four years through the underworld with a big red dog. The two struggled together against giants and dragons, crossed deserts, brought back the bones of a lost race of men. But I couldn't find the wisdom there, and after a few weeks I slept better. And thought less about my dreams.

I found other escapes. A frequent one during those years was *The Nun-Ensign*. It was the most awful play, based on the true history of Catalina de Erauso, a nun who broke out of a convent and, disguised as a man, fled to South America to gamble, duel, court ladies and battle Indians. For her valour in the field, she was decorated with the military commission of ensign. She met the Pope as a woman (Catalina, that is), and eventually returned to Mexico, once again a man, and finished out her days as a muleskinner. Given my special experiences with them, I felt I might one day aspire to something similar. Skinning one could not be that difficult, once you let the *pulque* out.

If my destiny was to live out my life in a prison of books, I was equal to it. And much better books than *The Nun-Ensign* lay all around me, but fewer and fewer still unread, at least in Castilian. Teaching myself Latin now was urgent. I had sworn to learn it years ago—all the way back in Nepantla. My vow so fervently renewed, I became infuriated by my slow progress. The feature that most distinguished me from Isabel was a rather beautiful head of blue-black hair. It had been the envy of my sisters and now my cousin Magda, too. I remember Magda standing at the door to my room to watch me, as for the second time I cut a good length of it off. She found the experience satisfying, apparently, for I remember how she made a point of letting me see. Pausing dramatically until I looked at her, she glanced about the room, finally at the shelves, half filled almost with books. Her face was bloated like an invalid's, and gloating was its sickness.

She hated me. After that, I never doubted it.

I saw nothing in her life to gloat about. Well, she could stare however hideously she liked, but I pledged that if I hadn't learned Latin by such and such a date, I would crop it back farther still. *Better to have a head shorn of hair than one empty of learning.*[10] It took twenty sessions and three haircuts before I pronounced myself satisfied. Next, I vowed, would come Italian, then Greek, then Portuguese, then French. . . . At least one language a year. At such a rate, by the time I was eighteen I might be ready to contemplate learning Arabic. Ready to contemplate anything at all except the birthdays themselves, which were exactly twice as bad as they might have been. I only knew how to celebrate birthdays for two.

November twelfth.

And this next one, my fifteenth, would be incomparably worse. A girl's *Quinceañera* is her coming-out, our fondest tradition. It is when a woman begins to fulfil her destiny, takes her first soft step into womanhood.

I had been here four years.

María said she was willing to organize a *Quinceañera* for me. She was sure many of Magda's friends would come. Had I been willing to go to even a few *tertulias*† with Magda over the years, I might have had friends of my own to invite. María said this without evident malice, as if stating a fact, and it was. One that contained only part of the truth. Truer was the generosity of the offer. When I refused it, María said nothing. She stood just inside my room, her colour rising. I expected rage. What I saw was the wounding of her pride. And if it hadn't been for Amanda, if it hadn't been four years, if it hadn't been the *Quinceañera,* I might have accepted—apologized and thanked her for her offer.

†parties, 'mixers'

Birthdays were the days I could not keep from looking at the mountains.

I knew that if Amanda and I were able to see the city from Ixayac, she could see me now. From here, if I let myself, I could see its face—and in it, hers—staring down at me. . . .

We had run together every day to Ixayac and never told a soul. It was a holy place, our sacred place. And if I am ever to speak of it, there are things that must be said first. It was a year of pleasures so intense, I ached with them. And I had only to place my palm below Amanda's ribs and then my own to feel the same fluster of wings, settling there.

Then it ended. When I was not careful, when something slid. And then Xochitl finally said no to me, for the first time in my life. *No, Ixpetz,* that city is no place for Amanda, no place for any of her people—no. And even as she began to shake her head, I knew it to be true. I had not seen it before because I did not want to. Amanda, though, had. She had been watching the day come for years, drawing nearer—ever since the firepit. That was what Xochitl had meant by bumble-beeing around.

But Xochitl would have had to explain to Amanda *why,* and feel under her own palm, then, the fluster of her daughter's heart . . . settling.

I knew the exact moment Xochitl talked to her, about the firepit, about bumblebees: the afternoon of our first full day in Panoayan, when Amanda and I came in dazed and excited from exploring. When we had each drunk two glasses of lime cordial. When I had gone off to the library.

Amanda knew from then on, and came with me anyway, ran with me everywhere, while I could afford to be blind. It was her most perfect gesture.

She let me have our childhood.

For four years now it had often been too painful even to think of her—the face of Ixayac or the mask of her hurt. I had made of it a hole in my memory but felt it now in my chest. In the weeks leading up to my *Quinceañera,* there opened in me a blackness I had never guessed at. It welled up from this hole in my chest, in a black tide leagues deep. It felt like the cries from the street, but the sounds were coming from me.

I could only just manage loneliness, not this. This floated up as mockery.

It mocked me to my face.

Didn't want to see? I hadn't seen because it was *inconvenient.* I must find—must *have* my destiny, so everything else must just fall into place as if preordained.

No, even this was too easy.

Exactly what hadn't I seen? Just what was it I didn't know? I did know that the Indians were not from the Indies. I knew about the Mexica. And I knew Xochitl was descended from the great Ocelotl. I knew he had dared to challenge Moctezuma with the truth, and had survived his prisons. I knew their empire was unbearably cruel, and I knew they had been lied to and starved and massacred. And I knew about the diseases that killed a million not-Indians a year for a hundred years. And I saw they were serfs now. I knew sixty thousand laboured without pay, or purpose or benefit or rest, or hope for release. And I saw to be a slave was to be better off. I knew what liberty was—it was what every Athenian had an inviolable right to. Unless he was a slave. And so I knew a little about justice—I knew at least this, I knew everything I needed to. And I knew better than Thucydides about necessity and false sacrifices and false goddesses like destiny and fortune. I knew Xochitl worked for us, and was wise and funny and had nursed me and sung for me in the night many times and raised me and taught me and was my mother. And I knew Amanda was Xochitl's daughter and my best friend and my twin—and this I knew with all my heart. I saw she was the best part of me, the part

I could never be. I knew her gifts, I saw her grace. I knew she had let me stay a child for a little while longer, one day at a time. And I knew that although she had so much less time left and could run so much faster, she would always wait for me. This I saw every day we ran to Ixayac and never told a soul.

So what exactly couldn't I see? What didn't I know? What great night had so blinded my eyes and mocked me now?

I couldn't *see* Amanda was an Indian.

I didn't *know* she was my burro.

And now four years later how it mocked me to my face. All day, as my *Quinceañera* approached, and would not stop.

Give her a wise and understanding heart, to have sovereignty over a great people.

I tried to think of the other things I had learned and known and seen, and done—some of them fine, even in this place.

But they meant nothing to me.

And I thought, *How do I defend myself from this, make learning my shining shield?* Because it's *what* I know, my knowledge—my mind—my great *gift* that mocks. She was the best part of me—*my enemy is inside.* She does not know, she does not see?—she knows too much! She knows of the four-year fast, she knows of PreciousFeatherMat, she knows of the road of shame into the underworld, the nine levels of hell, knows about the wisdom of proverbs and the sacredness of a rabbit satchel. She knows all about rates of return and rates of depreciation, and loving persuasion and friendship. She knows of the harlots down in the street with nowhere to turn, she knows of Solomon's sword and his judgements. She knows too much. Divide the child.

She knows now what Amanda knew. She sees what Xochitl saw. Twins who could not both have a childhood—one could or neither. Two lifeless halves, one living whole. Decide. Divide.

And Xochitl allowed this out of love and the terrible purity of a wise and understanding heart. And Amanda heard Xochitl and gave herself up to this love, out of the most perfect and incomprehensible grace.

Then, when I thought I could bear no more, my *abuelo* came, the night of my fifteenth birthday.

He came twice in that month. Not in a shining vision, not as an apparition from the beyond, but as a warmth and a voice so natural that I knew both came from within. This, more than anything that he said, helped close the hole in my chest. *My friend is inside me too.*

Twice that month he sat with me, and though he has never yet come back except in dreams, I've always felt I knew where to find him. Both times he said very little, which was a little unlike him. The first time he began with a simple question. The second time he insulted me.

Who has the eyes of Thucydides now?

Hugeous jolt-head.

It was a month when things changed. Mercy was a beginning.

Uncle Juan came the morning after my birthday. As he glanced discreetly around at the books and papers scattered over the floor, I realized he had not come fully into the room in four years.

"We may have to build you another bookshelf."

I didn't know what to say. I just stood by the window looking at him.

"Now that you're a woman of the world"—his smile held a trace of irony but kindness too—"I have a business proposition for you." He was a big man, soberly dressed, with a long, serious face. The forehead was high, the jaw heavy and long. His hair was a pale, papery brown, singed grey at the temples.

"Does it have to do with *pulque?*"

"Palaces."

"Palaces . . ."

"A competition of poetry. The incoming viceroy is its patron, I am its sponsor. And still I have not been able to meet him. My friends think you could do well. You don't have to win, just be among the last ten or so. Be on the platform. The judges pick the last three, he picks the winner. I want him to see you."

"A business proposition."

"The finalists get a private audience with the Viceroy and his wife."

"Is that your prize or mine?"

"If you're a finalist, anything you ask."

Anything I ask . . . a little child who knows not how to go out or come in.

"Uncle Juan . . . you've been kind. Generous. But I don't want anything. Thank you. I don't want this."

He shrugged, his face showing no trace of irritation. "I just thought you might enjoy the day. I know your grandfather would have. These tourneys are quite an affair."

I saw how good my uncle was at his business. "And how would you know that, Uncle?"

"How? I knew the man."

"*Oh.* How well did you?"

"It may be hard for you to imagine a time before your birth, but he came here often then. María *is* his daughter. You haven't forgotten."

"No."

"I'm sorry to say this, Juana, but I think you have. He was a friend to me and a friend to my parents, who have few. He always tried very hard with María. He was always welcome in my house. He used to stay for weeks. Consulting archives . . . special collections at the Royal University. *There* was a man to talk with. You remember that, of course."

I remember.

"As soon as you could read, whenever he came to buy books it was always for the two of you. You were all he talked about. His best new stories were all about you. Your reading, your sketches. It wasn't always easy for María. Your mother of course had sketched as a child. There was a story he loved to tell about the two of you translating musical theories from—Italian, was it? Portuguese?"

"He told you?"

It was Italian, Uncle.

"You seem also to forget how you answered María when she tried to speak to you of him. You were not the only one hurt by his passing. Does it never enter your mind that some people are afraid of you? But no, never mind that. We're talking of him now. Don Pedro told me himself about your month at school with the nuns, the day of your ABCs."

"Sister Paula? You've known . . ." *Even this.*

"Yes, Juana, all this time. In his last few years it was obvious the books were no longer for him at all. He stayed only a few days. And very near the end he came for a single book. Do you remember what it was?"

"On falcons."

"He wasn't well. He left the next morning." After a moment Uncle Juan's face brightened. "But I know he liked it in here. So we were happy to give you this room, of course."

"What?"

"His room, Juanita, his bed. Only he ever slept here—how could you not know? María said she told you."

"No, she . . . I didn't."

"That woman of mine—what goes through her mind?" His features hardened. He turned and moved swiftly to the door.

"Uncle Juan?"

"Yes."

"Why do you think Abuelo would have liked the day?"

"We went to many bullfights together, Juanita."

"But . . ."

"Of course—I didn't say. Our poetry joust, it's in a bullring."

fter Uncle Juan left my room, *Abuelo's room*, it was several hours before I could bring myself to look for María. I had never felt such a violence—of four lonely years—massed black like cliffs of hail. But she was his daughter. The thought, however fleeting, had only ever brought me displeasure. Now it was all I could find to temper the cruelty of what she'd done—keeping Abuelo from me, withholding the one small kindness that would have brought comfort in that house. I might have had him with me through all those nights, through that first year of sleeping afraid.

How the kind stroke withheld whets the edge of rage.

"Why?"

I found her in the salon where the light was good for the reading of Bibles in mid-afternoon. A room of crucifixes, upholstered sofas—sculpted, crested, inlaid, moulded—and one farthingale chair with the upholstery removed for her holy lectures.

"Come in."

"What brings anyone to this?"

"Juan just left. Ask him."

"Nothing in the world dishonours Grandfather so much as pettiness—*Why?*"

The Bible lay open in her lap. Her right hand kept the page. Clutched at the base, the onyx cross snapped left and right, spun in the fingers of her left hand. Into her face had come a strange expression, almost of reverie.

"Why . . . why . . . why," she asked.

"Petty cruelty and injustice."

At that, the cross stopped and her head swung to me. "Why?—because you think you're *better*. Why?—because you're so much like her. Why?—because having you in his room thinking you're better is like seeing them in the library all over again."

"Isabel?"

"Yes, Isabel."

"You're *envious*—still?"

"I could read."

"I see that, yes."

"Leaving so soon?"

"I'm nothing *like* her."

"More than you know. Much more like her than him."

"Why would I listen to *you?*"

"Don't go. I'll tell you, if you like."

"Give me one reason—"

"Give you? *Give?* You live in this house—all you do is take from us. What do you ever give in return? Juan asks one small thing of you."

"He *asks.* You hold the lives of your servants over my head."

"Wait—so clever, and still you haven't found the right question."

"Why take me in the first place? Why not send me back? Why the hideous threats? *And why put me in that room?*—if it's just to shame your-self and the man who gave you *life.*"

"Closer, Juana Inés, you're getting closer. . . . Ask why we never ques-tioned a single purchase of yours, when each book brings us closer to ruin."

"Whatever are you talking about? I've bought nothing on the Index."

"'The Index.' It's not just banned books, it's how *many.* What do you think attracts their suspicion in the first place? *Private collections,* Juana."

"Then why—"

"At last a question from you, Niece, I want to answer." She released her cross and placed her hand beside the other, on the Bible in her lap.

"Yes, we said nothing, Juana Inés. Because my father *was* better. Better than any of us. . . ."

I opened my mouth to answer. But all I wanted now was to be away from her, from here.

"And you, Niece, are not the only one around here with questions. Like the one I had for your uncle."

I paused at the door but did not look back.

"Can anyone in this house—I asked my dear noble husband—please tell me what they will make, when the day comes, of a creature like you?"

A creature like me.

I had started the fight but had no stomach to finish it. I sat at the edge of Abuelo's bed and stared at the bookshelves, more than half full again. And in each book was a face, filled with what I had not seen. I saw every-one around me knowing more about my life than I did. And what I did know was already sickening enough, the things and the people I seemed prepared to sacrifice.

Now came the discoveries of these past few hours, appalling me even as I quarrelled with María. How jealous I had been to keep Abuelo's memory for myself. And there were little things that wounded me in ways I couldn't understand at all. Isabel had sketched as a girl? I had been told this years ago and pushed it out of my mind. And how unaccountably painful it was to see her and Grandfather in the library through Aunt María's envious eyes. And to know, or know so late, that Abuelo had friends in this house, that he and Uncle Juan had gone to bull-fights—many—together. And then to see my trips to the book shops in a new light. For it was dawning on me that Uncle Juan might have an arrangement with the booksellers to cover my purchases. I had been so proud of my haggling.

The day and the month after my fifteenth birthday were not always easier than the weeks before it, as I saw still more of what I had failed to see—here was a knowledge I did not seek—of the shapes and silences that lay among and between us, and that I had always shied from. These too were forms, with secret geometric formulas, with their own dark knowledge and power.

And there was a silence and secret shape in this grim half-house that I had never wanted to know about. It had nothing to do with me, I'd told myself. Let it be their affair. But their affairs and mine were not so separate as I liked to think, and if I, for the thousandth time, had been just a little more attentive to anyone other than myself, I would have seen that María (née Ramírez de Santillana), proud wife of the rich and powerful Juan de Mata, was afraid. The signs lay silently all about her, only waiting to be read. The crosses, the Masses, the bizarre formulas of piety, the endless reading of just one book.

Uncle Juan asked if I had never thought people might be afraid of me. I hadn't, and if this thought were not enormous enough, there was the mystery of *why*. That María might be one of those people hadn't occurred to me either. But it was true—she *was* afraid. With so many enormities to grapple with at once, I missed the obvious. She, at least, was not afraid of me for myself but because she feared something much more dangerous.

That night after our quarrel, when the house was quiet, I stood at the railing along the third-floor colonnade. Over the courtyard the stars were mapped in a mesh of fine-drawn wire, and as through a sieve darkness poured down over the flagstones.

After a time a servant went to the well to fill a bucket. She staggered with it back into the kitchen. The surface grew still again. Between kitchen and fountain, splashes gleamed dully on the flags. As I watched, it seemed as though each stone rested on the face of a gargoyle smiling into the earth as if behind a hand. As I walked back to my room, the voice of the blackness and mockery felt nearer by the instant. Inside, the charm of Abuelo's presence, fading like a scent, seemed frail magic against an enemy whose echoes had slipped in behind me. Frail magic, but it came from within and felt like all I had, these few words he had left me.

Who has the eyes of Thucydides now . . . ? he'd asked, smiling gently and sitting where there was no chair. And what he said next, I knew I had heard something like it before, but from my mother's lips. *You have the most wonderful eyes, Angelina, for seeing far. But none of us sees everything at once, no one can see near and far at the same time. Try for yourself. Hold up your finger. Like this . . .*

This was the month when my four years of confinement ended. But no, things were not always easier. For there came to me next a remembrance of a day not long after Abuelo and I had talked about Melos. . . .

Grandfather awoke from his afternoon nap tremendously refreshed— beaming. He climbed like a small bear down from the hammock and came to sit at the table. He glanced at the manual I had open before me—gave the impression it could have been on any topic at all, so keen was he to exercise his faculties. "Ah, Jacobi Topf. The very greatest of the armourers, Juanita. Greater even than the Colmans, without a doubt. Grace without ostentation, ornament but never at the cost of effectiveness." It gave him pleasure to see me looking into this again. And what, did I think, was the work of the great armourers—true art or mere craft? For in the armourer's *fabrica,*[†] who can fail to hear the echo of the Creation, feel the Hand that turned and piped our clays . . . ?

[†]workshop

The late-afternoon light slipped in through the columns and lit the wall beside us. Xochitl had swabbed out the courtyard; the wet slate cast up a soft glow into the library, warming the ceiling and tops of the shelves. His great sun face was washed clear as the first dawn. Even the tired right eye looked less bleared—if not emerald clear, then of gold-green marble.

The first few birds were coming for their evening bath in the stone basin. I had heard Isabel's horse canter by not long before. She would be coming in any minute.

"And is the armourer's art"—he was growing, by the minute, more passionate—"not the very echo of God's highest handiwork, for did not Jacobi Topf forge even the hardest metals in the image of Man?" Grandfather had turned towards the brightness in the courtyard and was fashioning, with those bony hands, some visor or knee-cop or pauldron of light.

"And is this art, Juanita, not a vessel of Man, even as the body is a vessel of the soul? And does not this armour, in shielding his flesh, act like our Church in guarding his soul?"

But no, not at all. I thought it a skill more like pottery. It was so *finicky*. All the plodding and plotting, the stickling—the *fussing*.

I had said this with a vehemence that surprised me and in a tone I would never normally take with him. Needing now to justify myself, I took pains over the next two days, went to lengths great even for me, to marshal my arguments. Yes, this was a craft, a trade like any other. I distilled for him its essential qualities. In the armourer's anxious measurements, he is like a tailor with his tape. And is he not the very image of a tinker with his tools and tins? His obedience to contour likens him to the upholsterer as much as to the sculptor. In his concerns with joints and articulations who can fail to see the maker of toys or the wright of mills and carts? Over the gussets see how he frets like a *sastra!*† In all the padding and plasters and unguents for blisters, why, he is like a nurse brawling with a cobbler.

†dressmaker

At any other time in my life then or since I would have deferred to him, for the sheer pleasure of hearing him again, to feel that river of his talk washing over me as it had so rarely done of late. But it was so soon after Melos, and I could find no beauty in the work of the armourers, not even Jacobi Topf.

"Then what is an artist, Angelina?" he said thoughtfully, a little crestfallen.

"But Abuelito," I replied, "an artist is like a wizard, like *Ocelotl*. Have you not told me as much yourself?"

He gave me a gentle smile. "And the craftsman . . . ?"

These years later, while I sat in the room I at last knew had been his, each detail of that afternoon returned to me with the force of a blow.

How gracelessly I had argued with him. He was only feeling fresh, he was only happy to be alive, he had only come to talk to me. And his vision was by far the more beautiful.

To be with him again in some way, I started a verse on the armourer's art—my own craft of make-believe. I had taken a view against his not from belief but because it *comforted me*. It made the icy beauty and power of the engravings before me less troubling.

I sat at the desk and wondered how to begin. I tried for the tone he himself might have taken.

> Such forgers of forges and foundries,
> Of tomes and poems such marvels!
> Of tottery pottery such prodigies
> we cobblers and scribblers and artisans are!
>   With truth, ourselves to arm and furnish,
> we solace seek in arm'ry furnaces.
> For our eyes the visor of blinding burnish,
> for our minds the blade of glancing surfaces.
>   Therewith at chinks in the ramparts
> we pry—all the keyholes of iron artifice
> try; so as by these lights to detect (at a glance!)
> —in art the highest or arts most black—
> the fussy craftsman's homely hand . . . [II]

I began the verse as a penance, but it came to me that this could be a prayer, as from a warrior on the eve of battle. He would have liked that. *But enough, Angelita, of all this shriving.* That's what he would have said. It is not such a crime to fail, though it is a sin if you cannot forgive yourself.

No, this was not the poem for him. I did not finish it. I should be drafting the lines that would win the poetry tourney—a *joust*, Uncle Juan had said, in a bullring. And how proud Abuelo would be if I did, I would make his face so *wide*, and wipe away a little of my thoughtlessness. Uncle Juan was right. Abuelo would have so enjoyed the day: coaching me on strategy, assessing the challengers, reading the judges' sober miens. Such a game he would have made of it, to make me feel safe. We would be knights of old, vying heart and soul for a handkerchief.

Since gaps in this account will not be tolerated by those whose offices are holy, I cannot forestall his dying much longer. But not yet, not . . . *yet.*

We had a bullring to visit. And I had a battle to join, under the standard of El Dorado, and an old lion as my counsellor.

He had been there before.

I'd have my shield of learning, my shining corselet of wit, and for sheer grace and quickness in the ring I'd have my twin with me: *Amanda, Princess of the Cornflowers.*

And only she, only she would lift my veil.

BULLFIGHTER  had so wanted a spectacle.

To prepare for it, I let my mind turn to everything I had read about the sacrificing of bulls, bullocks, heifers, fatted calves, sea calves—oxen, bison even, and any and all contests against them. Herakles wrestling the white bull Phaëthon, forcing its mighty horns to the earth. And the white bull of Poseidon, father of the Minotaur—the Apis bull of Memphis, the bull hunts of ancient Iberia—there was so much to know! I did know our Iberian bulls would rather die than run—even from armoured horses and knights keen for jousting. First lesson: *die rather than run.* Well, maybe for the knight but surely not the bull. And which was I to be?

I saw how things would have to go. Down in the sand, pairs of combatants locked in mortal struggle. The last line of the contestant's poem rings out; all eyes turn to the Emperor. Thumb up, thumb down. The fanfares to rival Jericho, jugglers and jesters in the intermezzos. The day wears on, crowd favourites distinguish themselves—side bets, punters and touts. Fisticuffs in the aisles. The Maid battles on—quickness, grace, strategy, her arms . . .

The final pairing, the equal contest of noble adversaries—the bow, the curtsy—lord to lady, lady to lord. Acrostics and anagrams, reversible verses, triple echoes and *dobles entendidos.* Sonnet and gloss, eclogue and elegy, pyrotechnical panegyrics!

And then fireworks bursting across the sky like a thousand pomegranates launched by wild urchins—the booming of mortars now—for *there had been a tie.*

A tie.

Both are spared, both crowned—an unprecedented double laurel, and yet the bloodthirsty crowd *roars its approval down.* Then, soon, too soon . . . the lamentations at her early retirement from life in the ring. The encomiastic farewells, the tribute from her greatest adversary.

A quiet life, a lifelong friendship. People salute her in the street. She is allowed to walk in the street. She is walking with a friend.

She has a friend.

By the time the day came, I knew the tourney would not be as my imagination had painted it. Still, I told myself, it would be the most interesting thing to happen to me in years. The only thing. I might as well have been in my room for four years. Born of a vestal. Raised by wolves.

It turned out the bullring was available only because the Archbishop decided bullfights were not to be held during the festival of Guadalupe this year. The lake was high. It was the end of the rainy season and she was supposed to be our island city's protectress against the Flood. The Archbishop may have thought she needed to concentrate.

It wasn't even a real bullring.

Well, it was real, but not permanent, not an arena like the Roman Coliseum, but a rickety assemblage of wooden bleachers and scaffolding that could be dismantled in sections and stacked, then remounted at a day's notice. The carpenters had honed this to a fine art—indeed, many also built theatrical sets.

The contest was not decided on the sand, in pairings and jousts. There were four hundred contestants, an unheard-of number. I had only to do the arithmetic. It would have taken days. The poems were not improvised on the spot, on some whimsy of the Viceroy's—a theme, a metre, a style. Instead, we'd had two weeks to prepare. Two weeks?—I could have filled a book. And the theme was no noble fancy but rather Our Lady of Guadalupe. Now *there* was a surprise. The whole city was obsessed with Guadalupe, Guadalupe. . . .

But at least it was to be held in the Plaza del Volador. It was right next to the palace, but I didn't care so much about courtiers. No, I hoped I might see the Indian fliers who each day spun outwards on long ropes from a great whirling wheel five storeys in the air.

There *was* pageantry for our poetry joust. On the day of the city-wide invitation to contend in the tourney, we could hear the parade coming towards us, since ours was one of the few paved streets in our barrio. Sumptuous silver-trimmed carriages rumbled over the stones. There was even a sedan chair (I had never actually seen one) got up as Apollo's chariot, its sides emblazoned with gold and copper suns.

And such a dizzy cacophony! An intoxicate musical mob marched (out-of-step) drummed (off-beat) and intermittently blared (off-key)—effortless masters of this most intricate musical counterpoint. There were carriage bells and fifty church bells and a boys' choir. Up and down the block rose laughter and murmurs of wonder, exclamations and shouts of recognition as the menagerie passed: figures dressed head to foot as wild animals and unicorns and other fabulous beasts, spattered with mud to the knees. And as though driving them from the realm, there followed on his white charger a knight in a full suit of plate burnished black and gold-chased. As he passed abreast of me in the doorway, a smudged and weary-looking woman knelt in the street. Her male companion brusquely pulled her up—*it isn't really real.* Her face wore a quizzical look as she puzzled over the paradox. And somehow she did not look quite so tired.

A phalanx of soldiers now, brandishing halberds behind a troupe of Indian dancers, forty or so.

They shushed.

All the dancers wore bracelets and anklets thick with countless little shells, and as each *danzante* swished and whirled and bounded, the sound rose two-score multiplied. Swiftly there mounted among us the susurrus of a wind that surges and gusts along the oaks on a windy night at the hacienda. And to remember this I felt a kind of hush falling in me.

On they went with crowns of turquoises and bobbing quetzal plumes, precious cloaks embroidered in hieroglyphs, and feather capes of quetzal and heron. . . .

Next walked envoys of the religious orders and the Inquisition. A company of mummers and jesters scampered about with toy wands behind a knot of university scholars holding up True Learning's shining silver sceptres. Garish allegorical floats, and the indispensable dragon—*No hay procesión sin tarasca.*[†] Or that's what everybody said. This was my first one.

[†]No procession without a dragon or monster

Then came the parade marshal, the bearer of so great a burden of dignity it bowed his legs. He carried the silver mace of his office, and on a staff of solid silver *THE PLACARD.* For Saturday, twelve o'clock noon, on the eighth day of December, in the year of Our Lord sixteen hundred and sixty-three, the Placard announced the grand theme . . .

LITERARY PALAESTRA
AND POETICAL JOUST
IN WHICH
THE IMPERIAL, PONTIFICAL AND EVER AUGUST
MEXICAN ATHENS
proposes a design of the triumph of the
Most Holy Virgin of Guadalupe
to be sketched on a versical canvas in imperishable colours,
in which she treads upon the Dragon of sin, heresy and idolatry
and thereby abates the Great Flood sent to the Dragon's annihilation . . .[12]

As the marshal with the placard passed, it began lightly to rain, which served to remind us of the gravity of the theme. When the judging began two weeks later, a light rain was still falling. The Plaza del Volador seemed the sagest of choices now, since during the floods of 1629, it was one of only three plazas not to go under. Some of the lowest streets lay ankle-deep for five years thereafter. We all might hope Guadalupe was concentrating now.

I approached the plaza with Uncle Juan. We had to go the last four blocks on foot through streets so crowded as to be impassable by coach. I was peevish and glum, knowing this was not to be a real joust at all. But I was cheered to see a shop selling nothing but bullfighting gear, and the streets so festive. And there at the plaza entrance, beside the university gates and just above a little flight of steps, towered a massive bulletin:

SEGURO: AZAR DEL TOREO[†]

†CAUTION: BULLFIGHT IN PROGRESS

I laughed outright. Some wit had scratched in an *n* to make *TOREO* into *TORnEO*. They wanted a real tourney too. Caution: poetry hazard.

The bullring looked impressively large. The plaza itself seemed more riot than festival. Hundreds of vendors had spread out their wares with no hint of order or pattern. Thousands, now, milled through a square littered with trampled fruit, pottery and crushed straw hats.

The only clear route was in the shadow of the palace walls, where the guards permitted no commerce. Uncle Juan took me firmly by the arm; there was a great deal of intimate jostling and more than one impertinently placed hand before we reached the wall. This was becoming a very adult affair. Well, it's a borrowed dress anyway, I thought, but this was bravado, for however adult my body might look from the outside, I did not feel entirely sure of myself in a plaza full of unwashed men.

Exotic tapestries had been hung from the palace balconies, and I noticed something curious: running from the corner of our plaza to the main square was a narrow street with nothing but barber stalls, with their lancets and leeches and bloodletting basins, their whetstones and razors, their brushes and soaps.

Then we were inside the bullring and there *was* blood in the sand.

It was thrilling and disconcerting. For an instant I wondered if it might turn out as I'd imagined after all.

But as we were seated on the platform with all the luminaries to await the Viceroy's arrival, we were treated to a farce. Anticipating His Excellency's Excellent Lateness, the tournament secretary had thought to provide us with the same sort of diversion that preceded the bull-fights. It was that adventure of don Quixote in which the indomitable knight jousts with the furiously valiant Rinaldo for the legendary golden helmet of Mambrino. The great helm is, alas, a bronze barber's basin worn on a rainy day just such as this to preserve the hat of a barber not furiously valiant but today floridly fat. The barber's 'grey-dappled steed' was the most abject ass, infinitely worse than Sancho's, indeed of a class with the Knight of the Woeful Figure's own charger, Rozinante, the sad-dest *rozin*† ever bestrid. And this gave me a quiet moment. This was a wound barely closed. And as the ancient Rozinante lurched about drunkenly under the weight of don Quixote, I remembered this was just the sort of horse expended nowadays on fighting bulls. There came then into my mind the most heart-sickening image of that old jade swung up on the curved horns of a bull the size of a windmill, and with all the wind's irresistible power unstrung and gutted and slung to the ground.

†jade

So when I was given, next, a chance to laugh I took it gratefully. Enter don Quixote's Lady Dulcinea, a hairy-chested serving wench played by a bearded dwarf. Even Uncle Juan had tears running from his eyes. And now came the mighty Rinaldo, unhorsed and japing about under his barber basin as the old knight tried to run him through with a lance. Sancho, the realist, who fancied he saw a barber and no fighting knight, was trying anxiously to restrain his master.

"Leave hold, Sancho—hugeous jolt-head—thou eternal disbeliever . . ."

Hugeous jolt-head . . . eternal disbeliever . . .

I had woken Grandfather during this very section. I wanted to protest the cruel treatment Cervantes had yet again served up to the old Quixote. Why didn't Cervantes just let him go home? After only a hundred pages don Quixote already had so many fine stories, and true friends to tell them to.

"Read again, Angelina. Maybe you were too angry with Cervantes. Not every windmill is a giant, I know. And what looks like a funny adventure sometimes isn't, it's true. But as we look back, the same may sometimes be said of a disaster. Tell me when you've found it, and come and read. It has been too long since I read this myself. Now let me sleep another minute or two. . . ."

He didn't go back to sleep but, pretending to, watched me with a green squinty eye under the arm flung across his brow. So I found it, and nudged him. And as I read for him he lay back in the hammock and looked off into the west. Some while after I finished, he nodded and smiled. "There. Thank you, Angel—for do you know, I had forgotten the proverb, which is of course the very best part."

> . . . Let me tell thee, Sancho, it is the part of noble and generous spirits to pass by trifles. . . . '*Where one door shuts, another opens. . . .*' Thus fortune, which last night deceived us with the false prospect of an adventure, this morning offers us a real one to make amends.[13]

I had not believed in the magic of this day, and had been only too ready to slide back into the gloom emanating from me as much as from that dark house. Unlike my great hero the nun-ensign, I had never even tried to free myself. I was the hugeous jolt-head. In that moment I felt Grandfather's presence for the second time, and the last—heard the husk of emotion in his voice, saw the big beaming face. And I was delighted to be in a crowd just like this, laughing till I cried like them.

The new Viceroy did look splendid riding into the ring and up to the platform on a jet-black stallion caparisoned in pale green silks. The triumphal entry had been the Viceroy's idea, as an advent far more dramatic than in a university lecture theatre. For the first time, the finalists were all on the podium and the Viceroy himself read their poems aloud—then decided on the spot. Still . . . the ceremony I had in mind involved me in at least a *vuelta*[†] or two on that black stallion. I could ride him. I sat a horse passably well—I am my father's daughter after all.

[†]victory lap

Ten thousand people turned out, and three bishops. It was a lot, more than I could ever have imagined. Did one city really need three?

And never had I seen such an array of brilliant university gowns as on the platform that day, with its unsteady pulpit and the carved judges' chairs, each under its own canopy. I watched them all watching me up there along with them on the dais, and thought, *Today the Royal University has come to me.*

I took first place—and I did make a friend. Second prize went to a boy three or four years older than I. It created a sensation that 'children' should take the first two places, and the University's professor of poetry only the third. But the professor seemed so genuinely pleased for us that I liked him instantly. The boy, Carlos,† was vaguely descended from Góngora, the greatest poet of our language. Grandfather would have said the 'two greatest poets'—the greatest being the early Góngora, with the late as distant a second as all others came a distant third to him.

We were at a reception at the parade marshal's house when I saw the other prize-winners again. It must have taken a cargo ship to supply textiles enough for all the dresses: velvets and satins and silks in crimson and violet and lemon. Jewels and pearls by the hod and barrow, and silver more plentiful than tin. Capes and plumed hats, jewelled swords—and spurs—silver spurs half the length of a man's forearm. The risk of a goring on a dance floor surely exceeded the rigours of the ring.

The courtyard was a delirious polyhedral arrangement of waist-high hedges, benches under fruit trees, stone paths in diagonals through flower beds. We were led in stately pomp towards the platform on the north side. Above us for three full storeys was a living green drapery of creepers abloom in fiery pinks and peach. I had no idea such a place might exist in this stone desert of a city. Like ours, this was another of the great houses with three tiers of colonnades running around a patio—but open to the sky, not barred like a prison window. *Here* was a courtyard and a fountain. Not a warehouse, not a half-fountain crushed like a tin prison cup.

I was standing on the dais with the officials and other finalists—of course, all men—and I wondered at the water pressure. This fountain squirted and gushed and sported and rolled as if the sprite of a fountain bathing in itself. We were, it was true, on the Alameda, just at the end of the aqueduct, but was there maybe a little wind-assisted pump somewhere? Such reflections on hydraulics soon lead me to notice that the soft jostle on the dais was just as intimate as in the plaza, and less impertinent only to the extent that similarly placed collisions were passed off here as accidents.

Moorish rugs were spread over that half of the dais protected by a canvas pavilion, open across the front and patterned upon the tents of distant Arabia. From the pavilion's corners, indeed from most of the courtyard columns, rich pennants, paper streamers and bunting drooped prettily. Throughout the patio, people posed studiedly under a fine, warm *llovizna*.† The evening sky had reached the palest blue edge of grey. In that soft light the ladies gloried in their lambent fabrics; the men stood in quiet counterpoise in soft browns and blacks—charcoals and glosses and mattes. Among us at elbow height wobbled trays of chocolate and nutmeats borne by proud, puffing nymphs with beribboned hair. We were all at least half-aware of the beauty of the scene, and ennobled in a small way by our role in it. The rainfall blessed the women round the dais with sparkling curls and a hint of glaze on our lips, our cheeks, our wrists.

The glazing of our eyes was next effected by the speech makers.

When at last the quartet started up, I turned to Carlos, who had maintained a geometrically fixed distance from me all this time, and asked if the composer was Zarlino. I was quick to admit that I'd read a good deal of orchestral music but had heard next to nothing actually performed. Indeed it was, he said. Perhaps he might be permitted to escort me to a concert or two this month? He was home for all of December from the Jesuit seminary in Puebla.

This was all very quick. I would have to learn to be more careful about such easy openings. Coming up from just behind me was the other prize-winner (and to think I'd assumed the competition had ended), asking if I agreed with Zarlino, against Galilei, that music should have its own voice and not imitate the spoken word.

"My agreement, sir, might depend on the words spoken. In this past hour I find myself quite vehemently swayed towards Zarlino."

The conversation, as it must, turned to the competition. Carlos briefly feigned shock that a girl should be chosen, let alone a *doncella* of such tender years. (He was so much older.) But the professor remained so gracious that Carlos soon confided he was relieved not to have embarrassed the family and the name of Góngora, entirely. His true love was mathematics, and he would have the Chair of Mathematics one day.

To repay their grace I reminded them of what the Knight of the Woeful Figure had said about poetry prizes. "Always strive to carry off the second prize, for the first is forever awarded as a favour . . . the second going to the one who should have placed first—"

"Making third place, second," said the professor, smiling.

"And the first place, third," I continued.

"Which, as we know," Carlos said, "is in actuality second. . . ."

But such an unholy fuss was made when it became known that I had been born in the very year Miguel Sánchez published the first great work on our Virgin of Guadalupe. And had I not just won a great tourney taking her glory as its theme? Surely, said one fellow, this was a sign she had blessed the outcome herself.

It was Carlos who made the discovery. Just how old *was* I? he'd asked, that is, if he might presume. . . . So I was born in 1648! (Truly mathematics was his gift.) But what of it, don Carlos?

"Does the lady think it mere *coincidencia?*" he asked.

Here was an interesting word, I said (because it was new to me—and just as new was the sensation of being caught at a disadvantage). Had he meant the *coincidentia oppositorum?* But no, obviously he did not mean Guadalupe and I were opposites. Indeed he seemed to mean the reverse—but then what was the reverse of a union of opposites? A disunion of opposites, or a union of dissimilarities—or a complete non-relation of perfect irrelevancies? Well, I couldn't stand there gaping forever, so I played for time.

"And where on earth, don Carlos, did you hear—"

"It has been newly employed," he said brusquely, "by a distinguished English scientist, Tomás Browne."

Fortunately he now went on to laboriously define it, which gained me the time I needed.

"But don Carlos, what can this new term possibly mean? To bring two events into conjunction precisely to say there is none? To say that what appears to mean something means nothing at all? Does your Englishman not offer to refute Superstition only at the cost of making Hazard his cult?"

Just such a conversation as I had dreamt of having one day in the capital . . .

I went on now rather eagerly—according to my information, English was a mere dialect, a gumbo of German and French, possessing a simplified lexicon improvised to communicate the rudimentary sentiments of global trade and the terse niceties of piracy.

"Which would make it, would it not, gentlemen, akin to the pidgin the Spanish use in the Philippines?"

England, its manners, its mercantile impulse, its rough tongue, creeps into many heated discussions here, for many of my fellow citizens are nervous about privateering, and about being cut off from Spain. Since the rout of our Armada, we spoke of the English, I imagined, much as the Romans had of the pirate fleets of the Vandals.

At this point we had attracted a small audience. It was the best part of the day, a real piratical free-for-all. People jumping in, flailing about, and whenever some fool or parlour wit would take my side, I'd change tacks, for the sheer fun of it. So thick was the spread of confusion that only Carlos seemed to notice, and smiled, I thought, a little wickedly.

"And after all," I said, on just such a tack, "there is our own debt to Latin. Few would think our Castilian the poorer for it."

"No great poetry," thundered some bluff wit in return, "has ever come from any *Protestant* country!"

"Was there not once word," I asked, "of a great flourishing on their stages at the same time as Spain's own best day?" I had heard of at least one great play—on the wizard Faustus, no less—and was distracted by a thought: how curious it was that such a character should take the name of 'one favoured by the augurs.'

"But *señorita*, what notice should we take of their dramatists," Carlos said slyly, recalling me from my reverie, "when the English have closed their own theatres down?"

"*Señor*, do the Iberians not consider our Mexican culture to be a pidgin of like kind, precisely when they themselves have not produced a great poet for, what, a generation now? We should not be similarly complacent." He seemed prepared to agree so I tacked instead into rougher waters, arguing that any country capable of producing a great queen might just be ready to make one decent poet.

"Perhaps you'd care to amplify—"

"Well, yes, don Carlos, happily. Imagine, if you will, a great *pidgin* poet."

There was a gratifying moment of silence. Carlos nodded, appearing to consider this seriously. Then a thick-whiskered fellow said, "*Señorita*, you have the mind of a man."

"Ah, the mind of a man." I eyed them each in turn, taking my time. "A man, perhaps, *caballeros*. But *which* man . . ."

We were interrupted then, and I felt sorry Carlos was going back so soon to the seminary in Puebla. But we still had a month and there would be other receptions.

I did get to take home a glittering prize. A jewelled snuff box I couldn't wait to use.

As for the winning poem, I'm sorry it was not so good. Better than Carlos's but not much. Here in the city, craftiness and the contrivances of fashion counted for more than substance—*Art takes form, form takes substance, substance takes craft.* Or so it was said. How they worshipped at the shrines of their subtle framing devices. And at lines ending in unexpected rhymes, such as *urraca / saque / triquitraque / matraca.* . . . I would do many like this to earn my keep.

I was already a little sick of hearing about Guadalupe, but I owed her something better. One day I would write a poem for Carlos, for he had been truly passionate about her. If his poem had displayed slightly less skill, so also had it used less trickery than mine.

After just a few such experiences in the arena, I would come to feel that poetry written for the tastes of its time could almost never be great. We must write through our time, or even to it, but never *for* it. Poets must concern themselves with neither fashion nor even what people want, but with vision—raw and immediate—of what lies beyond our eyes. Beneath this, our great Dream of Common Sense.

But a poetry competition was not the place for such concerns, and this not quite the day for leaving the last childish things behind.

People were kind. "The Poetess, the Poetess!" they had cried as I left the ring, and again on my way to the carriage from the parade marshal's house. At the receptions that month, the gentlemen proved very attentive. Having Isabel's features and increasingly her form no longer seemed so terrible.

And I was out of my cave.

†probable reference to Pandora

The boulder had been rolled back—the jar unsealed and Hope† broken free. I was determined Aunt María would never seal me in again.

There were receptions and luncheons and balls for the Poetess to go to, and she would no longer be denied. In another fortnight the prizewinners were to have an audience with their majesties, the Viceroy and his German wife. A German. Here was a people that *elected* its emperors.

Her hair, they said, was of spun gold.

So much the better—but I was to meet my first *Goth.*

. . . tiende la vista a cuanto
alcanza a divisarse
desde este monte excelso
que es injuria de Atlante.
Mira aquestos ganados
que, inundando los valles,
de los prados fecundos
las esmeraldas pacen.

Mira en cándidos copos
la leche, que al cuajarse,
afrenta los jazmines
de la Aurora que nace.

Mira, de espigas rojas,
en los campos formarse
pajizos chamelotes
a las olas del aire.

Mira de esas montañas
los ricos minerales,
cuya preñez es oro,
rubíes y diamantes.

Mira, en el mar soberbio,
en conchas congelarse
el llanto de la Aurora
en perlas orientales.

Mira de esos jardines
los fecundos frutales,
de especies diferentes
dar frutos admirables.

Mira con verdes pinos
los montes coronarse:

con árboles que intentan
del Cielo ser Gigantes.

Escucha la armonía
de las canoras aves
que en coros diferentes
forman dulces discantes.

Mira de uno a otro Polo
los Reinos dilatarse,
dividiendo regiones
los brazos de los mares,

y mira cómo surcan
de las veleras naves
las ambiciosas proas
sus cerúleos cristales.

Mira entre aquellas grutas
diversos animales:
a unos, salir feroces;
a otros, huir cobardes.

Todo, bello Narciso,
sujeto a mi dictamen,
son posesiones mías,
son mis bienes dotales.

Y todo será Tuyo,
si Tú con pecho afable
depones lo severo
y llegas a adorarme.

JUANA INÉS
DE LA CRUZ,

"Echo, finding
Narcissus on a
mountaintop"

THE DIVINE
NARCISSUS

Alan Trueblood, trans.

. . . so let your gaze take in
all the land it surveys
from this lofty summit
that leaves Atlas in the shade.

    See, into the valleys
those streams of cattle pour
to graze on the emeralds
that stud each valley floor.

    See, like drifts of snow,
the curdled milk in jars
puts the jasmine to shame
with which dawn snuffs out stars.

    See red-gold ears of grain
sending billows everywhere
like waves of watered silk
stirred by waves of the air.

    Behold the rich ores
those swelling mountains hold:
how they teem with diamonds,
glow with rubies and gold.

    See the leaping ocean
how the dawn's welling tears
are congealed in conch shells
and turn into pearls.

    See, in those gardens,
how the fruit trees flourish;
behold the broad range
of rich fruits they nourish.

    See how green crowns of pine
on high summits endeavour

to repeat the exploit
of the giants storming heaven.

    Listen to the music
of all those singing birds.
In all of their choirs
sweet descants are heard.

    See from pole to pole
realms spread far and wide.
Behold the many regions
which arms of sea divide,

    and see the ambitious prows
of those swift-sailing ships—
how they cleave in their passage
the azure's crystal drift.

    See amid those grottoes
creatures of every sort,
some timidly fleeing,
some bursting fiercely forth.

    All this, fair Narcissus,
is mine to dispose of;
these are my possessions,
they accompany my love.

    All is yours to enjoy
if you cease to be cold,
put severity aside
and love me heart and soul. . . .

t had turned out to be a fine day of jousting, after all, but what I missed in the bullring that day was spectacle, high drama. There was low comedy, and the high comedy of our English-pirate free-for-all. And low drama, for the two full minutes it took the Viceroy to look over every part of me before awarding his prize. No, I wanted colours and costumes and light—fireworks, fine voices and much finer poetry. *Ceremony*. I was not so very different from everyone else here. Juvenal was not mistaken in prescribing bread and circuses as the philtre for enthralling us.

Uncle Juan had largely financed the tournament, so as we rode back home from the parade marshal's house I gave him back the snuff box. I couldn't help asking if my victory had been paid for, since he'd paid for everything else. The carriage drew up before the house.

"You have done more for my standing with the new Viceroy in one day, Juana Inés, than my underwriting a dozen of these affairs."

He helped me down from the carriage, then walked quickly to the door. But once there, he paused to hold it open for me. There he stood: big and stocky, earnest and calm. And for no particular reason he struck me as brave, not in bluster and brandish of steel, but quietly, steadily brave. I liked him. As I brushed past, he held up a hand to detain me. "Oh—and Juana Inés, whatever else I may do," he said with a wry quirk of a smile, "I never tell a viceroy what poets he should like."

He did not posture or pretend. This was a business proposition, and while business was obviously good, I sensed it was also precarious. His network of alliances went to the top of both the *Cabildo* and the *Audiencia,* and into the lower echelons of the court. But one does not approach a viceroy with money. I was an asset now. I found I didn't mind. I had met a few of his associates at the house. Serious, earnest ... if anything, a little preoccupied. Since they were much like him, I guessed that these were not just associates but friends. No posturers or hypocrites. I'm sure Uncle Juan knew these, too, and saw to their handling and care. What I liked is that he didn't have them at his house.

But he was not much of a family man. He seemed no more interested in poor Magda than he had been in me up till now. And there was something strained between him and Aunt María, who seemed more anxious with secrets all the time. His parents we hardly saw. I did have an intuition that the canvas dam across the courtyard and fountain had been more their idea than his, and that they might have preferred to get their water elsewhere. It arrived in the city all the way from Chapultepec springs via the aqueduct to the Alameda. The mains had been clay, then lead for a while; then someone somewhere in the city administration read a book of Roman history, and they were clay again (whose almost weekly repairs, in our neighbourhood at least, Uncle Juan paid for).

He also paid his debts, and he knew just what to get me. The Poetess and her escorts had been reserved a private box at the theatre. I *loved* the theatre—I just knew it, even though I'd never been. But I had read a hundred plays, made them burn like fire in my mind—*these* were our painted books.

He wouldn't come with us, being too serious for such things, but he did insist Aunt María and Magda go. It would do them good to get out. It would do Magda good.

They squeezed—parts of me—into another of Magda's old gowns. But it was of a lovely, sky-blue satin, which set off to advantage, I supposed, my black hair and black eyes. And then we were in the carriage, as the three of us had been on so many trips to the cathedral. I could not ride even a short way facing backwards without feeling ill, so as always María and Magda sat facing me. The ride was mercifully brief.

It was the single greatest thrill of my life to arrive for the first time at the theatre, ablaze with light, in a gleaming coach drawn by matched horses, steel tack flashing silver. As I stepped down I could hear the orchestra warming up above the shouts and cries of the coachmen jostling for position.

Inside, we met a group of Magda's friends, a girl and three young gentlemen. "Magda, why haven't we met your cousin before? You didn't tell us she was so beautiful . . . and that dress, what a splendid hue! You should try that colour yourself." Magda's evening was proving visibly less transcendent than mine.

Although the vicinity of the private boxes was perfectly dignified, looking down into the pit I could see why the public theatres were called *corrales*, and this one, El Coliseo, no less. I had not expected so much hooting. The idea of calling out to the players, warning them of an intrigue or ambush, well, that was perhaps the best part of the show. The *entractos* were also popular affairs and in parts delightful. There was a Mexica *mitote*† with ancient instruments, but I was glad it ended quickly as I had no intention of being homesick. Between acts one and two was a farcical skit that went over well, and a later interlude of ballads. The play itself was a local production stealing shamelessly from Ovid's version of the tale of Narcissus, and yet I was strangely fascinated.

†a traditional dance

Afterwards, in the milling and stir in the forecourt, I spotted a poster for last week's show: *The Nun-Ensign.* The awful play I had read a hundred times. This was my fellow prisoner and hero—fugitive nun, duellist and lady muleskinner. How I would have loved to see her just once outside my head.

On the way home all I could find to talk about was the play. Though I knew it to be no masterpiece, I was thrilled to hear for the first time poetic texts from the lips of trained actors, to see passions so nakedly expressed. On and on I chattered like a songbird between two ravens—countenances growing ever darker—about how certain lines seemed to weaken this effect or that, how the themes had been muddied, the symbols clumsily worked. I was talking now to work this out for myself, for during the slower moments in the theatre I'd had an idea for my own version of Echo and Narcissus. There'd be a prologue featuring two couples, one European, the other native Mexican. The Mexicans would be America and Occident. . . .

I would make Echo the brilliant angel who had fallen from Paradise—*then* rebelled. That was important. And at first sight of Narcissus it's as if she's always known him, who is after all as beautiful as any angel. In love, she takes him to a mountaintop and offers him a new paradise, a new world, if only she can tempt him to stay with her. . . .

I didn't have it all worked out. What little I did manage to say probably didn't make much sense to Magda and María anyway. But instead of looking bored or annoyed, they were watching me carefully. Thus encouraged, I even managed to find fault with Ovid's own vision of Narcissus, which had always seemed too harsh, simplistic. I saw Narcissus more as the victim of his yearnings for perfection, as Christlike—

"What?" croaked Aunt María, across from me. "What did you just say?" She leaned forward till her nose nearly touched my face.

"I said—"

"Is that what they teach young girls out in that godless countryside—to *blaspheme?*"

"I'm sorry, *Tia*," I stammered, "but I didn't blas—"

"The Son of God, narcissistic! You heard her, Magda."

"She said it."

"I did *not*."

"Did Isabel teach you to call your elders liars, too?"

"I was only trying to correct—I did *not* call Christ narcissistic. Narcissus, in his pain, was Christlike—there's nothing wrong with *saying* this. The teachings of the Greeks anticipate His Gospel. The Church has accepted—"

"What the Church teaches—at least here in this city, Juana Inés, is humility. Here, what we expect of ourselves is only the most careful soul-searching. Here in *our* city, we would never allow a child, still less a female child, to run riot through the pagan texts of antiquity *spouting blasphemies on the Passion!* Evidently you are one of those who have no respect for the Holy Office—"

"Have you ever *seen* an *auto*, Juana?" asked Magda suddenly.

"No," I said, grateful for what I thought was a change of subject. We had pulled up in front of the house but Aunt María, resting her hand on the handle, made no move to get down.

"We *have*. Several," she said coolly. "The effect has been lasting." She glanced at Magda. "Perhaps we may still broaden your marvellous education in some small way. You seem to enjoy riding in our carriage. Tomorrow I think we shall take you on a little tour. Magda has been a very enthusiastic student of our local history. There is much in this city you have yet to see. . . ."

In the morning, Aunt María wore her usual black silk, and a black veil. We all had on our heavy crosses. Magda's dress was of a purple velvet and suited her slight frame. Over her crucifix she wore a string of warped pearls of a fashion called *barruecas*, much prized in the city.

She was almost pretty. Her hair was a dark, flat brown. Her profile was not so prepossessing as her mother's. Her one unfortunate feature was her eyes: very small and deep-set, the irises so large as to leave scant room between her lids for the whites. The colour was an attractive one, a nut brown, but one could not help thinking of the polished pips of small, soft fruit, the cherimoya, perhaps, or the lychee from Cathay. Her

nose was of a normal size but—between those tiny, beady eyes—
betrayed a certain thickness at the bridge.

Sundays we usually ate little before mid-afternoon, but this day's breakfast was whipped chocolate, pork hocks and eggs fried in lard. As we left
the house my escorts each carried a small assortment of fresh roses, out of
season now and brought in at great expense from the south each year for
Guadalupe's festival. Whites and yellows and reds . . . the effect was quite
gay. In the coach they insisted on sitting on my bench, on either side of
me. It was my first inkling that this was not to be a ride like the others.

What they'd said was true: I liked the coach rides. I loved the horses,
the rasp and chiselling of silver-shod hoofs over the flags. María had
once confided her belief that their collection of coaches, gigs and carriages was the finest in the New World. "We choose our things," she'd
announced then, "on the basis of elegance, not vain show." The carriage
cab was small and of a hardwood finished in black lacquer. The spokes
were a lacquered grey. Inside, there *was* opulence: the walls were surfaced
in the finest Chinese silk, deep brown and embroidered with gold dragons.
The seats were thickly upholstered in velvet of a matching brown. The
door handles, painted black outside, revealed themselves to be of bronze,
as were the door bolts, gleaming and heavy. Fore and aft were sliding
panels. The rear one was bolted shut, the one forward was open to allow
communication with the driver. The heavy wooden side panels were
drawn back for our tour.

We were not going to church.

When this dawned on me I was stunned, unable to imagine what
might deflect Aunt María from the cathedral on a Sunday morning.

Aunt María and Cousin Magda were taking me over the route and to
the stations of the last great *auto de fe* of 1649. Thirteen people burned at
the stake, a hundred more in effigy.

Magda could only have been five or six at the time of the *auto*, yet fifteen years later the sheer volume of ghastly detail she'd retained or had
since learned was appalling. While I was to learn that to hear a story told
can be more terrible than seeing the horror itself.

Our carriage had barely reached the corner when Aunt María said, "It
started here. A neighbour came to tell us the Proclamation was being
read through the streets. We rushed out of the house, Magda beside me,
running on her chubby legs to keep up. Everyone was moving towards
the *casas de la Inquisición*, where the processions began."

"I *remember* them," said Magda, in a tone of reminiscence. "Minstrels coming down the street in bright colours, trumpets blaring, fifes piping . . ."

"Every block or two," said Aunt María, "the procession would pause for the chief constable to dictate the Proclamation to the crier." He called out to all the nobles and their families an invitation to attend, wearing their finest, a general *auto de fe* on the eleventh of April.

Since I was now a noted Poetess, it might interest me to know that María had always preferred the Portuguese 'auto-<u>da</u>-fé.'

"Our Castilian phrase means simply 'act of faith.' But for the Portuguese, Juana Inés, it means 'the act that *gives* faith.' We will give you some help with this today."

The coach clattered towards the Monastery of Santo Domingo. A light rain fell. The streets were quiet, with everyone at Mass at one of the fifty churches throughout the city. My aunt and cousin began to describe the days leading up to the *auto*, when at least thirty thousand celebrants made their way to the capital, swelling its population to four hundred thousand. The city's fifteen thousand carriages, most now in use at once, found room to pass only with difficulty even at three in the morning. All the plazas stood brightly lit, packed with people come to refresh themselves with glasses of *atole* or chocolate or *pulque*. On almost every corner Indian ladies were selling tortillas and tamales. Every inn in the capital was full. Each morning found thousands of revellers rolled up in blankets, asleep in the plazas and under the arcades, or in doorways and alleys.

Our carriage lurched to a halt beside the canal—we had nearly run down a beggar, a man of about fifty, with the aspect of a Gypsy or a Moor. Barefoot, in grimy rags, he carried a little bundle slung over his shoulder as if he were travelling, yet with nowhere to go, as he wandered back and forth across the road. The stench from the canal was overpowering. A carcass must be floating there, and the canal silted in. Magda and María had not brought the roses for colour or cheer but as nosegays. They fed at them now like ghastly hummingbirds.

Magda asked if I ever heard from my father, if I thought he might ever come back. It was the first word anyone in that house had ever spoken of him. I could not meet her gleaming, hateful eyes as she then turned to me and recounted the stories that were in circulation all that year of 1649—tales of new and hideously effective tortures and of the vast sums wasted on bribes to Inquisition officials . . . who were of course utterly incorruptible.

"Some of the accused had been turned in by their own children," said Magda, glancing past me at her mother. "Others by neighbours or in-laws or friends. They said the familiars of the Inquisition were every-where gathering testimony."

Aunt María spoke, not turning from the window. "One neighbour whispered that the *proveedor general* of the Windward Fleet had been arrested for Judaizing. His wife had grown so arrogant as to demand that all requests for appointments with her be made in writing."

"Mother even knew her a little, didn't you, Mother?" Before María could answer Magda exclaimed, "One woman was arrested—you know what for? Just smiling at the mention of the blessed Virgin!"

I remembered then that my cousin had been the one to serve me breakfast, and the pleasure she had taken. I felt my stomach lift as we lurched through a pothole. The closeness in the cab was becoming unbearable.

I caught a glimpse of the cathedral. We jarred over the rough paving for another two blocks, then turned east and came to a little square. María called for the driver to stop—we were getting out. *Gracias a Dios.* Aunt María held the door as I stepped down. Opposite us on the north side of the square was a small pink church built of the rough *tezontle* blocks I knew from the mountains. Early Mass had just let out, and over the heads of those streaming through the tall doors I could see a rose-coloured altar and pillars of pink marble spirals. The windows must have been stained in the same colour, for pale rose diagonals fell through the smoke in the nave.

The square looked festive at first. Indian musicians with their pipes and drums. A company of mummers calling to the passersby to gather round. Running the full length of the plaza's west side was a string of workshops, which I was surprised to see open. But then with Guadalupe's feast day coming on Wednesday, perhaps they were rushing to finish a special commission from the temple. Out in the open air, I looked about for the courage to tell María I'd had enough.

Occupying the entire block across the street to the east was an aus-tere building with none of the flourishes for which the city's masons are noted. And it was towards that building we now walked. The iron gates were on the southwest corner. Two girls my age were giggling and flirting with the guards stiffly standing one to each side of the entrance. Overhead hung a banner on a silver staff, but angled in such a way that I could not read it until we were at the gates.

I had thought the building had three storeys; it was two—each no less than four times our height. I could see the banner's emblem now. It was a wooden cross, rough and unplaned, knots like the swellings of lesions all down its sides. Just inside the gates were several counters and offices arranged around a small patio, achingly bright in the sun. Running east and north were two long corridors. There was an impression of coolness. A cool draft of air flowed past my ankles. I thought of a deserted hospital.

A scribe scuttled by with an armload of heavy cases. Aunt María pointed out the warder with his keys heading down the eastern corridor. He had a blanket rolled under his arm.

Here were the Palaces of the Inquisition. In these palaces there were many rooms. He went to prepare a place in one.

I backed away.

They made no move to stop me. I walked blindly into the plaza. I could feel Magda and María close behind, one to each side. An Indian lady was selling herbs and cures, her white hair coiled at her nape just as Xochitl wore hers. This *curandera* clearly had faith in her exemption from the Holy Office's jurisdiction, and I was afraid for her. The mummers looked to be university students and though I did not stop, by the direction they were facing and by the twisting and clowning and groans, I knew their skit to parody what happened across the street. And I was afraid for them, too, but did not stop until I had passed the musicians and reached the workshops and stalls.

There was a little apothecary, with his stoppers and funnels, alembics and spouts. A printing press and bindery, its stamps and dies. Then a shop with inks, quills and papers for scribes. A candlemaker, and the smell of fats reducing in the back, and on tables his candles in ranks of white, black and green. Next door was the engraver, his vitriols and acids and etching tools in neat ranks on a shelf. Standing at a high bench with his heavy needles was the maker of awnings and sacks. Then a carpentry, with all the planks and rigging, screws and vises. Here was a supplier of surgical equipment: scalpels, forceps and specula, beaked masks.

Next door a Sunday crowd had gathered to watch a smith at his forge.

Behind me the music drummed and piped jarringly to the hammering at the anvil. I could feel María and Magda standing close.

A row of humble craftsmen at their shops. Scents of pine and glue, solvents and printers' inks. I thought of Grandfather, tried to summon the feelings that being with him brought. I so wanted to lose myself in them now, to make an escape in my mind. Watching the farrier at his forge, it seemed he was indeed a prince among these journeymen. Young and narrow-hipped, bent to his anvil, he was cased in sweat like a warhorse, his naked torso armoured against flame and shards by a scorched apron of ox hide.

I took in all the terrible power of shoulder and veined forearm and yet the delicacy in his wrists as he angled the tongs and banked and rolled the hammer. *The art is in the wrists, Angelina.* Yes Grandfather, you were so very right, for smiths and armourers and the *jinete-matador*[†]—a kind of empathy in the wrist, to capture the very image of life. It is a craftsmanship of temper and temperance and temperature. Of edges, brittleness and breaking points, of heating, folding and collapse. A building up, a grasping, a hammering at stresses—relief, release, relaxation.

[†]knight-matador

Such a flurry of enterprise on a Sunday, special commissions for the Church. And now I understood, and knew what this place was. These were the busy, fussy craftsmen who forged the pears and branks and gags, who built the gambrils and gibbets and gallows, who raised the bleachers and rigged the scaffolding. Supplied the inks and quills, laid out the instruments and the restraints, saw meekly to the fit.

I knew all about this—for Grandfather I had distilled all the essential qualities. I wanted very much to find again comfort in these: measurement, contour, surface, articulation. . . . I tried hard to picture Abuelo's face, any face at all—even the mask of Amanda's features when she was hurt. I tried to make my thoughts fly straight, my eyes bend neither right nor left, to hold to all the faces I had lost, to solve the riddle hidden there. Fear was the riddle now, the thing I had not known.

Subdued, I took my place next to Magda in the cab, with María coming in after me. I made no protest. Only to be away from that music, that ringing, that craft. The horses' hooves rasped and chiselled over the flags.

Five companies of the Soldiers of the Bramble were picketed all night around the square, to guard the Green Cross and the Palaces of the

Inquisition. The streets around them for once were bright with torch-light. The eleventh day of April, 1649.

The drama starts in the darkness two hours before dawn, as the Archbishop's carriage approaches the Holy Offices. The night's revellers, both afoot and in the many well-stocked carriages, pause in their debauches to cross themselves as the black carriage passes. Whispers of the Archbishop's arrival fly like startled swallows through the cells of the Inquisition's secret prison.

His Illustriousness, the Archbishop don Juan de Mañozca, *is* the Inquisition—forty years' service in the tribunals of the Holy and General Office, member in perpetuity of its Supreme Council and sec-ond only in rank to the Inquisitor General in Spain. It was Juan de Mañozca who in his younger days had brought the Holy Office to the wild slave port of Cartagena. It was the then famous don Juan de Mañozca who detected and grimly prosecuted the Great Complicity in Perú. And it is his nephew, Juan Sáenz de Mañozca, who under his famed tutor has risen to become the Inquisitor of this *auto*.

At the southwest corner the gates swing open. A young monk rushes to open the carriage door. The Archbishop, a lean and vigorous man of seventy, steps lightly out. He walks into the courtyard and down the eastern corridor. All is in readiness. The antiphon and hymns have been sung in the pink chapel, where a special Mass has been held for the Inquisitors before this final battle. The rosary was said at Prime. For the fourteen prisoners condemned to the stake, fourteen pairs of Jesuits have been sworn in. *For confession, a Dominican, for contrition, a Jesuit.*

In shifts they have begun to attend to the prisoners, exhorting the condemned to repent so as to receive absolution before death.

All the prisoners have been given breakfast. At the mouth of a pas-sageway joining the prison to its outermost patio, the young Inquisitor, Sáenz de Mañozca, takes up position under his uncle's watchful eye. In the dim courtyard, lit by one or two torches and the first glow of a false dawn, the Inquisitor orders that the prisoners be brought out in single file. He reads out each sentence, and hands to the prisoners the costumes they are to wear in the coming day's production: for the condemned, the short *corozas*† and black *sambenitos* of sackcloth; for the reconciled, the tall *corozas* and yellow *sambenitos* with the double cross of Saint Andrew. To the penanced, he hands the same yellow sacks, but bearing a single cross.

†a stiff, peaked cap; a dunce cap

Those prisoners who will not stop protesting their innocence, the Archbishop orders gagged.

The vigilants out in the little plaza know it has begun when the bells of the cathedral begin to toll. And after them, all the bells of all the churches in the capital. A carillon—of discordant timbre and pitch and period—a tolling to make the hottest blood run cold. Sixteen familiars of the Inquisition come out first, ahead of three parish crosses draped in black. Next come the Indians with the exhumed remains of heretics who've fraudulently received a Christian burial and are now found out at last.

Behind them, others carry painted effigies. Father de Moedano's effigies are revered as the most lifelike. Some of his faces are of people dead for years, yet all who knew them see. His memory for heretics is remarkable.

Out into the bright morning stumble the condemned, sad jesters in their black sacking emblazoned with flames and devils, in their dunce caps painted with serpents. The women hold little green crosses.

But the onlookers have been expecting to see fourteen condemned prisoners, not thirteen.

During the night, Isabel Núñez has confessed and repented of her Judaizing. But this will not be known until ten days later, when she and another whore of Babylon—stripped to the waist—are each tied to the back of an ass and whipped through the streets. Two hundred lashes each.

Thirteen prisoners . . . The number raises a perplexed murmur all along the procession route to the amphitheatre. Scores of bleachers and platforms have been built and rented out along the way. By eight o'clock, the Procession of the Green Cross is within a few blocks of the plaza of the Indian fliers, the Plaza del Volador. The bullfights have been cancelled, the barbershops shuttered, the market stalls boarded.

The amphitheatre has been built to hold eighteen thousand. It covers the south, east and west; to the north it is open to the palace balconies and to a ructious mass of spectators unable to get seats. The total number in the square would exceed thirty thousand but for a hastily delivered order forbidding, on pain of excommunication, further entry into the desperately crowded square.

To the left, on the west side, is a grandstand constructed to accommodate the noble families of the realm and the officers of the Church, the most eminent being seated at the base. The various dignitaries, families and Inquisition officials can be seen retiring, throughout a long, hot day

of sentencing, to comfortable lounges under the grandstand for the taking of rest and refreshments. The prisoners' dock is pyramidal, and the
prisoners are distributed equitably. No side of the square is favoured.
Between the dock and the grandstand is a large mahogany table to
record the proceedings upon. The secretaries of the Holy Office sit in a
row of heavy, carved chairs, each with its own canopy. Across from the
table rise two pulpits for sermons and the reading of the edicts. Between
these is a massive scaffold for the prisoners' sentences to be read from.

For the past hour, the armies of Christ Triumphant have driven the
squadrons of Satan through the Plazuela del Marquez, then down the
Calle de Mercaderes de San Agustín and up to the corner of the Calle del
Arco. The Green Cross has at last reached the approaches of the square.
Close behind the file of the condemned, and surrounded by the
University's rectors, the warden of the Inquisition's prisons leads a white
mule. On its back sways a lacquered chest inlaid with mother-of-pearl. It
contains the charges against the condemned.

Here the situation gets out of hand.

Throughout the course of the procession, Tomas Trebino de
Sobremonte has never ceased to trumpet his guiltlessness. Even knowing he is to burn alive, as the one unrepentant Judaizer, defiantly he
swears through his metal gag to practise the law of Moses to the death.
Wildly gesticulating, violently shaking his head, Trebino roars back his
insolence to a crowd hurling fierce insults and exhortations to repent.
As he makes his way through the streets, a hard-pressed company of
infantry struggles to protect him from the incensed mob armed with
paving stones and staves.

But when, still mouthing abominations, he nears the entrance to the
square where thousands have been kneeling in hushed adoration of the
Green Cross, the crowd closes in to silence him.

The soldiers panic, unwilling to die protecting a heretic. Yet the mob
is so dense that they cannot get out of the way, and they fight back to
save themselves. Before wading into the fray, the Archbishop sends
someone through the empty back streets to the cathedral, with an order
to silence the massive bells. The Archbishop waits. Each contingency
and response has been anticipated—for the rigour of his forethought,
the providence of his planning, he is rightly famed. Before long all the
bells of the city fall silent and a languid stillness blankets the square,
damping the fires of Christian fury.

The Archbishop, mounted on the back of his little mule, enters the sea of men and the waters part. At nine o'clock that morning, calmly, slowly, the Archbishop's venerable mule rounds the corner of the University with both troops and prisoners in tow. . . . Combatants in the everlasting war between God and Nature, Spirit and Flesh, they shuffle awkwardly down the little flight of steps and into the throng in the now silent plaza.

In reverence the crowd kneels until the Archbishop has taken up his station atop the scaffold. He sits under a black velvet baldachin, its coping adorned with gold brocade and golden fringes. The Inquisitors file in behind him.

By now the prisoners have occupied the dock. On the lowermost benches, Indians hold the effigies. Next, those prisoners to be penanced; above them, those to be reconciled. At the tip of the pyramid, and all around the uppermost rung, huddle the condemned, each between two Jesuits ceaselessly whispering.

Cloaked in shame in their sackcloth and dunce caps they sit, the bedraggled crew of a foundered ship, faces drained by insomnia, white with terror or fury.

The accused are prodded to stand. The crowd rises from its knees as the Archbishop sits—erect, without reclining—in a great white throne of marble. Behind him, the exchequer plants the Standard of the Faith. Before him stands an ebony table. Upon it a great book and a little brass bell. Visible beneath the table are glimpses of the Archbishop's sandalled feet.

Feet like fine brass.

All through the day of judgement he will toy absent-mindedly with a great key. It hangs on a thick golden chain in his left hand. From time to time his right hand reaches out and rings the little bell to accelerate the proceedings: time is short.

The Inquisitors settle onto cushions around his table, and throughout the proceedings are seen lounging like Persians, leonine eyes alert.

After the adoration of the Green Cross, still draped in black, after the reading of the Proclamation of the Faith, after the Bull conferring papal authority on the Holy Office of the Inquisition, the most profound silence reigns over the expectant multitude.

Each slow step rings out as the Dean of the Cathedral labours up to the pulpit. He salutes the Tribunal on his right, and glancing up at the Archbishop begins his sermon.

. . . Come hither; I will shew unto thee the judgement of the great whore that sitteth upon many waters . . .

The lacquered chest bearing the suits against the accused is brought forward. Four secretaries scuttle to and fro, conveying the heavy briefs to the pulpits, from which the charges are read in slow, rhythmic alternation. Three secretaries at a table sit scrabbling intently, quill hands lightly convulsed, to capture every nuance of the proceedings, just as they have done at interrogations.

. . . And I saw the dead, small and great, stand before God; and the books were opened . . .

Over the hushed plaza a little bell rings out with the sound of glass cracking in a flame. Then from a rostrum on the high scaffold at the centre of the amphitheatre, the sentences for each case are called out. Clasping the ceremonial black staff in front of his chest, the warden of the secret prisons brings each prisoner in turn to stand alone at the foot of the scaffold.

All eyes are on the Archbishop as he cants slightly forward to consult his notebook.

. . . And whosoever was not found written in the book of life was cast into the lake of fire . . .

First to be judged are the dead. Among them an eighty-year-old woman who lasted a full six months in prison. Her remains and effigy are consigned to the flames.

Now it is the turn of the living.

An exultant roar goes up as Tomas Trebino is sentenced first—to burn alive. Merciful, the Tribunal orders that the other twelve, before burning, be garrotted. From the prisoners' dock to the scaffold, the warden weaves back and forth like a shuttle.

. . . And upon her forehead was a name written, Mystery, <u>Babylon the Great</u>, the mother of harlots and abominations of the earth . . .

Among those condemned to die, it may be that one face at least, that of an old woman, is suffused with the peace of a loving god. The warden brings her, the last of the condemned, forward to hear her judgement. Ana de Carvajal staggers to the base of the scaffold. She is sixty-seven. Her breast cancer is so advanced, and she so wraithlike, that the heart-shaped tumour is visible beneath her *sambenito*.

She, too, is the Inquisition. In the *auto* of 1590, her father was burned in effigy. In 1596, her mother burned garrotted, her brother Luís burned alive. In the *auto* of 1601, when Ana was nineteen, the Holy Office reconciled her: but to lapse into the cult of the Pharisees was to be condemned to the flames.

Now, forty-eight years later, the Inquisition finds she has relapsed. At last her long wait is over.

. . . How much she hath glorified herself, and lived deliciously, so much torment and sorrow give her: for she saith in her heart, I sit a queen and am no widow, and shall see no sorrow . . .

Again the little bell rings. The warden brings forward the scores of the reconciled one by one. Since reconciliation comes at the price of confiscation of property, many in this group are wealthy. Among them are several women, and chief among these is Juana Enriquez, widely resented for the refinement of her manners and dress, for the luxury and glamour of her parties and balls, for her coaches and the bevies of servants that once followed her wherever she went.

Gone now the servants.

In yellow sackcloth before the scaffold she stands alone. She hears her fate read. Two hundred lashes. Confiscation of all estates. Banishment from the realm. Shrill cries of satisfaction rise from the crowd. Babylon, the Great, is fallen.

. . . And the kings of the earth, who have committed fornication and lived deliciously with her, shall bewail her, and lament for her, when they shall see the smoke of her burning . . .

Next, Simón Váez Sevilla: the richest man in the New World. At the foot of the scaffold, he stands in sackcloth, a green candle in his soft hands, a noose around his white neck: all behold the arrogant kingpin of a mercantile network of false converts spanning both oceans—*the whole globe*—from Malta to Manila.

Two hundred lashes. Confiscation. Banishment. Perpetual and irremissible prison. The crowd bellows another note in its paean to Apollo.

. . . For true and righteous are his judgements: for he hath judged the great whore, which did corrupt the earth with her fornication, and hath avenged the blood of his servants at her hand . . .

The condemned are led away through the jeering crowd to the *quemadero*, the burning ground. From the chapel, the last terrible strains of *De Miserere* die out.

The reconciled and the penanced are made to abjure their errors once more, to swear not to relapse, and to kiss a little iron cross thrust against their lips. The tension mounts; teasingly the black baize draped over the Green Cross falls away inch by inch in little tugs, as each sinner submits and returns to the bosom of the Church.

When at last the Green Cross stands clear of its black cloak of mourning, a great clamour of joy and triumph goes up, like the sound of many waters. Kettledrums, trumpet blasts, shouts—*Long live the Faith!*—the choir singing *Te Deum* now like larks, soldiers firing volleys into the air. . . .

The Archbishop's eyes are as a sheet of flame.

. . . And I saw an angel standing in the sun; and he cried with a loud voice, saying to all the fowls that fly in the midst of heaven, Come and gather yourselves together unto the supper of the great God . . . that ye may eat the flesh of kings . . .

An uncanny scene surrounds Tomas Trebino as they attempt to strap him to the back of an ass for the procession to the *quemadero*. The creature goes mad the instant it feels Trebino's weight. Braying wildly, it charges into the other animals brought to carry the condemned. One beast after another balks. The animals, normally docile, are so restive now that the prisoners, many of them aged, will have to walk to meet their death. It is an outrage to all aficionados, who for months to come, in taverns all over New Spain, will denounce this breach.

Only by firing repeatedly over the heads of the maddened crowd can Captain Mendoza's escort prevent the wildly ranting Trebino from being torn apart along the route.

He will not walk at all unless permitted to walk backwards. For a few steps he does, until his Jesuits call out for him to be carried.

The rest of the condemned, some silent, others crying or ceaselessly muttering—the satanic, half-mad citizens of Gog and Magog—crawl along the Alameda. For hours, hundreds of watchers have been clustering like pine cones in the branches of the giant trees that line the boulevard. Thousands more have scrambled up onto the piping of the aqueduct and squat like sagging rows of buzzards above the newly renovated Plaza de San Diego.

The stakes on scaffolds above the pyres are arranged over a rectangular area covered with lime. The shoddy construction also scandalizes many: the steps are narrow and unsteady; the arrangement of ropes and pegs on each stake does not allow the condemned to sit comfortably. It is a disgrace.

Eleven chests are stopped, eleven breaths. Eleven pairs of Jesuits may rest.

The last to mount and be strangled is Símon Montero. Hands bound behind his back, he does a little dance of contempt and clowns for the crowd, then feigns a stumble on the narrow steps to force his confessors to keep him from falling to his death.

"The carpentry," he cries out in the instant before his garrotting, "is better in Seville—"

The order is given to light the pyres. Silent Indians work the bellows.

. . . And he laid hold on the dragon, that old serpent, which is the Devil, and Satan, and bound him a thousand years . . . And cast him into the bottomless pit . . .

Tomas Trebino has also reached the terminus.

He falls silent, watching everything set alight around him. Effigies, chests of bones, strangled companions. Ana de Carvajal. Perhaps he has read Dante, and the scene is not without the slim comfort of some small precedent. His confessors mistake his silence for mortal terror. They remove his gag that he might repent. Instead the blasphemer launches into an attack on the poet of Revelations. Trebino exhorts John the Witness to join him in the fire, that the great saint might repent and confess his own crimes.

The executioner holds Tomas Trebino's head steady as they light his beard on fire.

Trebino struggles to look down through the flame. With his foot he drags a block of wood to the stake as if to say, *begin.*

On that day Nature in all her elements is forced to submit. Fire consumes him. Air receives the smoke. His charred bones are wrestled from the jaws of street curs and buried in shallow earth. His suet is scattered over the waters of a reeking canal.

His quintessence is consigned to oblivion.

In the suffocating closeness of the coach, our mingled perfumes ill mask the fetor of our bodies: María, Magda and I ride slowly home through the alleys of the New Jerusalem, covered in silence and ash.

Since I am not yet in a position of open defiance, soon enough I will oblige and give them an accounting of sorts. Gaps will not be tolerated. It is why the repeated questions, it is why the careful notes. It is a kind of fussiness, after all.

But the Inquisition is no conclave of rattled nuns. And it is not the want of charity, chastity and grace that the holy officers so fear and loathe but the slattern of Incontinence. Against her they are bulwark and bung, caisson and closter, dike and dam. This is the craft of clots and clods, of pears and branks and the surgeon's beaked mask.

These officers and learned doctors, these are the humble stop-gaps. Craft is enough, all is craft. The meekness that inherits the earth.

And who is their Jacobi Topf? Is he born, have we met somewhere, will we yet?

But gaps are everywhere . . . and lie in silent shapes just where there seems no gap at all. Their shrine and studio is memory. And how they shift and gape at this latest charge: that Uncle Juan's parents were secret Jews.

So differently now those days echo in my memory. For then, what Aunt María feared more even than my recklessness was her own daughter. Magda, the one who served the breakfast. And how unfathomably wise it was to dam the fountain, not comical at all. And the whimsy of finding Uncle Juan brave was not at all whimsical: for however sincere his efforts to be a good New Christian, he could never quite turn his back on the parents who would not abandon an older faith.

And is it true, as the holy officers now suggest, that my own father was one too? For it is among the Basques and Portuguese that the Inquisition finds so very many of its secret Judaizers. And indeed was there not a faint echo, in the *auto-da-fé* of 1656, of that great spectacle of 1649? The arrests began the following year and took place throughout the early 1650s. When Father rode away from us for the last time, I was five years old. It was the spring of 1654.

Did he stay away from us, so often, so long—and then abandon us— to keep us from harm? The Inquisition brought my childhood to an end during a carriage ride. It remains for me to know if they had already taken my father.

So many questions they have. I too have questions now. If it's an accounting they want, I too seek a settling of our accounts.

Magda asked about him. Did I think he was ever coming back? To be cruel, I thought, but perhaps to be doubly cruel. If she knew. And if she knew, it was because Aunt María did also. Grandfather had introduced my father to Isabel. But who introduced María to Uncle Juan? Were Juan and my father friends? My eldest sister and Magda were about the same age. . . .

How painful it can be to see where one has not looked, into places one has not dreamt of. How very differently I might have looked upon my aunt María, if I had grasped the worst of her fears. And what if I had known from the beginning that Uncle Juan had been my grandfather's friend? I liked him already—he might have become a second father to me. How I needed one then. And I would have feared, not pitied, Magda, had I known what she was. It is from her stock that the Inquisition's familiars are drawn.

Gaps will not be tolerated by the holy officers—gaps are all around us. I too was once frightened of them. But no longer. Yes, I will give them a reckoning of sorts. But for this, let there be another art, with eyes to see the gaps through lenses of clemency. With ears to hear their music, and hands to turn the instrument that plays it. Let there be others, too, for this work.

We will play on drums and spinets, on barrels and pins, on time's very axle. We march under the Ensign of the Trout with trident tongue. When they hear our chiming, jingling tune of links and the gaps between, the holy armourers may find, as others have, that mail is lighter, suppler, stronger than plate. That each of us carries part of the score, and that we are all linked in surprising ways and strong. Strong despite ourselves, surprising in spite.

And even as night is the lace around each star, yet there is nothing frail in that dark. Of this night lace now may we fashion a shimmering net and cast it. And let us see if not a few fishers of souls are caught.

LUÍS DE
CARVAJAL

"Heretic's Song"

B. Limosneros, trans.

The brother of Ana
de Carvajal, a
woman condemned
to the stake after a
forty-eight-year stay
of execution, wrote
at least one sonnet
while awaiting his
own sentence in the
Inquisition's secret
prisons. It is not
known whether the
heretic Luís de
Carvajal was
already a poet
before his trials, or
became one.

I sinned, Lord, but not because I have sinned
do I your clemency and love relinquish.
For my wrongs I tremble at being punished,
yet dream of being through your goodness pardoned.

I accuse myself, even as You have waited on me,
of being abhorrent in my ingratitude,
and so my sin of being all the viler,
for your being so worthy of all love.

Were it not for You, what would become of me?
And from myself, without You, who would deliver me
if your hand withheld its grace from me?
And but for me, my Lord, who would fail to love You?
And but for You, God, who would suffer me?
And to You, without You, my Lord, who would carry me?

Isis BOOK TWO

CONTENTS

Este, que ves, engaño colorido,
que del arte ostentando los primores,
con falso silogismos de colores
es cauteloso engaño del sentido;
  este, en quien la lisonja ha pretendido
excusar de los años los horrores,
y venciendo del tiempo los rigores
triunfar de la vejez y del olvido,
    es un vano artificio del cuidado,
es una flor al viento delicada,
es un resguardo inútil para el hado:
    es una necia diligencia errada,
es un afán caduco y, bien mirado,
es cadáver, es polvo, es sombra, es nada.

JUANA INÉS
DE LA CRUZ

B. Limonsneros, trans.

She rejects the flattery visible in a portrait of herself

This painted semblance you so admire,
of an art flaunting its mastery
with false syllogisms of colour,
that smoothly mocks the eye;
    this face—in which flattery pretends
to still the horror of the racing hours,
to stay the hand of ravishing time,
and spare us ageing and oblivion—
    is only panic's thin disguise,
is a garland to bar the hurricane,
is a cry in the wilderness,
is a token gesture made in vain,
is wasted toil and—through these eyes—
is Corpse. Dust. Shade. Nothingness.

THE
CONFESSIONS

had forgotten this. Now the memory brings no pleasure.

Even here, he said, even in America, we serve the Sovereign of Two Worlds.

We were at the firepit, just the two of us, and had spent the day together reading. The air was crisp and cold that night—up from our lips drifted curls and waves of mist but we stayed late by the fire. There were too few such days, such nights.

Abuelo rarely spoke about the war. The House of Austria, stretched thin between Vienna and Madrid . . . Turks and Moors to east and south, Bourbons and Protestants to west and north. Three hundred dukedoms and principalities tangled up in an impossible snarl of loyalties and betrayals. Catholic France sponsoring the Protestant Union, Lutheran Saxony fighting alongside the Catholic League. . . . Four hundred armies swarming over Europe like locusts, like packs of dogs turning on each other. The populations of Europe slashed by a third in barely a generation, thirty years of war . . .

"Three times as long as Troy, Angelina. And we fought for no better reasons . . . every duke craving a kingdom, every king an empire. No wonder Homer went blind, straining to see to the end of it."

My grandfather volunteered in 1618. The truce with the low countries was expiring. Losing Portugal seemed just a matter of time. Everyone remembered that year, he said, for the comets. Three in the span of a few months, swords of flame over the horizon. This would be the Armageddon, the war to end the world. The important thing was to be fighting for the right side. They were just boys.

"No sooner had I survived the first campaign but I was *praying* for the war to end. The death, the rotting bread, the pestilence . . . Each Horseman had a season. Summers of war and fire—the cities went up like torches. Autumns of plague. And winters, winters were the harvest of the famine sown each spring, when the farmers were plucked from their planting and pressed into uniform.

"The land was exhausted anyway, not at all like here. Even when a field was sown, for every seed planted you were lucky to harvest six. One to replant, one to save, one to trade, the rest to armies and kings."

It grew worse.

He had always dreamt of travelling. He travelled, now. Through the Spanish possessions of Italy to Vienna they rode, thence to Bohemia, across Bavaria and through the Palatine. Then up the Spanish Road towards the low countries, the United Provinces. In Westphalia he had watched mobs begging offal from the slaughterhouses. In Prague thousands had simply starved . . . tens of thousands more dying on battlefields and in *lazaretos*[†] all across the continent.

[†] 'lazarets,' stations of quarantine

"In '21 we thought it might be over, after White Mountain. There were such high hopes for the new king, though he was himself just a boy. I left in '24. Almost an old man already at thirty-five. And even then I was lucky . . . Lucky not to have seen a thing like Magdeburg, where twenty thousand townspeople were massacred in a day."

What he said next surprised me, for I knew he considered it his great good fortune just to have survived.

"And yet, Angel . . . I never fought under Spínola."[†] He lifted his chin just a little. "It would have been good to have served a prince in the field. But had I stayed for Breda, how many Magdeburgs might I have witnessed?"

[†] the ablest Spanish general, who laid siege to Breda and later pardoned its defenders

With the tip of his traveller's staff he raked at the embers. I was not sure I'd understood him, and went hunting for the lines of Sarpedon, Zeus's mortal son, to Glaucus.

> Glaucus, say why are we honor'd more
> Than other men of Lycia . . .
> The shores of Xanthus ring of this: and shall we not exceed
> As much in merit as in noise? Come, be we great in deed
> As well as look, shine not in gold but in the flames of fight,
> That so our neat-arm'd Lycians may say: "See, these are right
> Our Kings, our Rulers: these deserve to eat and drink the best;
> These govern not ingloriously; these thus exceed the rest.
> Do more than they command to do. . . . [1]

When I had found this and read it for him, I saw I'd understood him well enough. He didn't speak for a moment, but I knew he would go on now.

"The whole way back I walked with a bloodied bandage around my head, and when I think of that walk I still hear the flies buzzing at one ear. Ahh," he said, "I see you hear them too. I walked back to my village, but the want and the sickness were too terrible there. Everyone was gone. I kept on, following the south bank down to the mouth of the Guadalquivir, stood up to my hips where the brown of the river ran to brine. My boots were more like sandals by then, but upside down, so worn were they at the soles. I went barefoot down the shore all the way to land's end, walking and thinking and arguing with the flies. I looked across the straits to Africa, past *el peñón de Calpe* to Mount Hacho, and past that one to where I was sure I glimpsed the Atlas range.

"I stared at those mountains and thought hard about walking right down through Africa to land's end *there*. Angelina, I was standing at the pillars of Calpe and Abyla! Hardly a hundred years before, and for the two thousand before that, this had *been* the end of the world. But it felt in that instant as if its end lay not ahead but at my back—and I had escaped it.

"I unwrapped the bandage, and tossed it into the sea. I was not ready to be an old man quite yet. No, I would come to America and see for myself if the New World had an end *at all*. *Los Portugueses* were evasive as always. '*Tierra del fuego*' . . . ice and fire, seas of fog, earth disappearing into thin air. What was anyone to make of that, eh? But when a Portuguese[†] tells a Spaniard about the sea," Abuelo bent forward confidingly, his elbows on his knees, "you can be sure he is keeping the best parts to himself."

[†]Magellan

Nodding assent, I fed another stick to the fire as he talked. The flames roared up.

"Then I met my Beatriz on the boat across," he said, brightening, "a girl from the south bank, the village right next to mine. There was the end of one dream, but the beginning of a happier one. . . . And yet, and yet, who could ever have imagined it? That the horror I had volunteered for as a young man would not end until the year a certain granddaughter of mine was born."

"Me?"

"You, *mi hijita*, you. . . ."

 How proud he was to have served, even an empire bankrupt and broken. Of all the epithets attaching to the Spanish king—Catholic Monarch, Planet King, &c.—the one my grandfather pronounced most proudly was this, *Soberano de los Dos Mundos*. So yes, proud, and sad, and with a fascination for the death of empires that stayed with him to the last day of his life.

Sovereign of the Two Worlds.

When I moved from my uncle's house to the Viceroy's court, so eager to serve, I wrote an elegy for a king, the young king my grandfather had served under. Courtiers who had known that king sniggered behind their handkerchiefs—even those who had been with him at the Alcázar[†] as he died. Even my friends smiled and thought me naïve, made excuses for me. *She is only seventeen.*

[†]the Royal Palace in Madrid

At the hour of his death, it is said, every eye in Madrid was dry. It is also said that just three people cried—Queen Mariana, and no one could name with any certainty the other two. One wag at our court averred that it was not three people but three *eyes:* the last shopkeeper in Madrid to extend the palace credit, and his one-eyed wife.

I weep for the king who dies unmourned, I wept for that one, Philip IV—to have presided at the ruin of Europe's greatest throne. I wept for the prince born to lead but never shown how, an Alexander without an Aristotle, unable to unravel the knot in the thread of his greatness. For the dying empire does not prepare its princes for this. Olivares did everything to keep him from the field, built for him a country pleasure palace, the envy of all Europe until Versailles. *El Palacio del Buen Retiro.*[†] A palace fit for our century of ten thousand comedies. Such merriments the comedians made on his retreats.

[†]Palace of the Good Retreat

Quevedo, for one. *Our king is like a hole. The more land they take from him, the greater he becomes.* I could never quite forgive Quevedo this one.

Philip was just sixteen when he ascended the throne. Planet King! they proclaimed him, that centrepiece about which all lesser bodies revolve like hungry courtiers tabled in their epicycles. Lesser bodies such as his future son-in-law, the young French Sun King, Louis XIV.

As I sat to write his elegy I thought of how he had been mocked, by history and by the stars. Forty years on, he must have seen this himself, as death approached, so elliptically. And seen also how he had been mocked by his own courtiers from the start. For, just a few years before the western Hapsburgs had acclaimed him Planet King, centre of the universe, the Hapsburg Emperor in Vienna had been studying astronomy. With Kepler.

Such a gift I have for seeing the emblems woven into other lives.

I could not forgive Quevedo, and yet within a year or two at court I was doing it also. I said things like this: *Louis did more for Copernicus than Galileo ever did—while Philip did for Ptolemy. Single-handedly.*

Did I really tell myself it made any difference that I was more than half in earnest—all the while knowing they would laugh twice as hard?

Philip IV. Who kept his dwarves like princes; kept by his princes a dwarf.

This was how I had come to serve the servants of the sovereign. Having forgotten all about my elegy and about the service of princes.

I may have forgotten this, but there is nothing wrong with my memory. Even to those closest to me I say the little that I can. It seems I have only to meet someone to find myself asked about my past. Yet I do not like to look back. Still less to have my childhood made the subject of my confessions.

 Who is this Jesuit, Antonio Núñez de Miranda? Who comes to the palace yet is not of the palace, who does not live among us, yet is never far. Who confesses us all: the Vice-Queen, the Vice-King and most of his administration. All are a little afraid of him. He is not old, being of a generation hardly older than my father's. Small bones, small head, the skin dry as parchment, the stooped nodding walk . . . Maybe this is why so many say he seems ancient. They speak of his hatred of pride, of his humility . . . of the grey eyes meekly downcast, the thick lids heavy, as if in mirth—until opened wide the eyes blaze with rage, staring into yours. They speak of how it takes some getting used to.

This subtle man, among the most brilliant I have yet met, whose memory is uncanny, perfect, better even than my own. He has urged me to meditate on the past, and has listened to my confessions attentively. This soldier who bears no arms, yet is commanded by a general in Rome for whom he would gladly die. And yet with me, Father Núñez begins with none of the harshness and choler for which he is so well known. With not a little poetry, he speaks to me of Loyola, founder of the Company, son of a Basque nobleman born in the ancestral castle. Father Núñez speaks of how the young Loyola loved music, how he won his knighthood in the service of Antonio Manrique de Lara, Duke of Nájera and Viceroy of Navarre.

Ignatius Loyola, first General of the Company of Jesus, who wrote so movingly of his spiritual awakening, a man who until then cared only about martial exercises, with a *great and vain desire to win renown.*

Crippled in battle, Loyola lay for months on a convalescent's bed in an empty castle. Among the few works accessible to him were the writings of a certain monk. Over and over Loyola read them, absorbing the vision of this Cistercian who depicted the service of Christ as a holy order of chivalry and saw, in the lover of Christ, a chevalier plighted to the service of his liege.

Of course I am not told all of this at once. Father Núñez works patiently, over the weeks and months. In fact his greatest skill lies in what he does not say. He does not mention that the Manriques are Spain's greatest military family, nor that Rodrigo Manrique was Queen Isabela's great defender and first grandmaster of the Order of Santiago. My spiritual adviser gives no sign of knowing that the grandmaster's son wrote perhaps the finest poem of our language, at the death of his father. And so, only obliquely, does he remind me of my grandfather and what I have forgotten about service.

From his own purse, Father Núñez pays for my instruction in theology, since certain of my ideas in this area he deems dangerously inventive. The tutor he provides is merely the Dean of Theology at the Royal University. Father Núñez does this for me. He knows not a little about my childish dreams.

Who is this man who puts at my service his perfect memory of *my* memories? Of a past of which it seems I've begun to speak so very freely? And asks me now, Who is it, Juana, *you* would serve, and how? Thus am I brought to ask myself a most curious question: *where* best to serve, where to serve *best*—from a palace or a convent cell?

It would not have come to me of itself. And yet the question seems the sum of all the questions I have been asking myself. Have I come all this way from little Panoayan just to be a rhyming servant? What did I come so far to do? Write *comedies*? Is this truly *all*? he asks. What might a girl with such gifts not accomplish? Might she not also compose simple carols to console the hurt and the hungry?

Palace or convent. Solve the riddle, untangle the knot. Of course I do not use such childish terms, not openly, not at nineteen. But from what I remember of riddles, the solution often consists in finding false oppositions. Palace or convent—why it is hardly a choice at all. For each contains a library, does it not? Father Núñez only nods. Fate has fashioned for me a keeper who knows also how to turn the keys of silence.

He sits quietly across from me, as I tell myself we spend most of our days here cloistered from the men anyway, entertaining ourselves with plays and books and convent gossip. We knew that the Empress María lived in a convent in Madrid, a situation which nonetheless could not keep her from visiting half the capitals of Europe. Philip's true spiritual adviser was an abbess. His sister had entered a convent. He took half his meals there, the Queen almost all of hers. And it was common knowledge that the King's lovers—married or single, mothers or barren, it mattered not—were to enter a cloister as soon as he had finished with them. Just as a horse ridden by Philip was never to be ridden by another.

We women talked frequently of someone else as well. Christina of Sweden. Who had abdicated her throne for the Spanish Ambassador, the Count de Pimentel. Of course, the lover I still prefer to imagine at her side is Descartes. She travelled all over Europe, often dressed as a man, went anywhere, said anything she pleased—in eleven languages. Every year or so there was a new rumour that she planned to tour America. When she announced her intention to visit Madrid, every convent in Spain was put on alert, for Christina never failed to visit all the convents in her path, and liked nothing better than to lodge there, with all her train and baggage, parrots and monkeys. Female monkeys only. At first I thought this curious, but how else was one to lodge in convents, after all?

Her library in Sweden once exceeded fifty thousand volumes, but the number she took into exile to travel with was not inconsiderable.

Fourteen thousand.

Christina was the great sponsor of Descartes, Bernini, Scarlatti, Corelli; Christina was the Learned Queen, founder of the Arcadian Academy; but more, I see that Christina was the nun-ensign, my favourite heroine, one who embodied every fantasy I'd ever had, had lived adventures I'd not yet *dreamt* of having—

Nun-Empress.

It is Father Núñez himself who points this out to me.

He knows a good deal about our late King, too. He has come to know what I know, and a few things of his own. Of Philip, slave of lust, and his abiding fantasy to seduce a nun. The King grew so desperate to possess one sister in particular, he commanded her abbess to arrange an assignation. When she let him into the convent by a secret subterranean passageway, the King rushed in to find his prey awaiting him, stretched out on a slab, bled white, to all appearances dead by her own hand. Philip staggered out, horrified, whereupon she was revived and spirited to a new convent at the far frontiers of Spain. To protect her daughters, so far will Mother Church go. Yet is there a Lord to whom even she is but a handmaiden.

And so, again obliquely, am I reminded of more recent incidents at the palace. Things I would give anything to forget. Head or heart, heart or soul, soul or flesh. Palace or convent.

At this point I might have noticed my tendencies running away with me, for I decided now that really, for a woman, palace was to convent as *gallinero*[2] was to *caballerizo*[†]—cote to stall. Hardly a choice at all. Truly I had come far. From false opposition to false comparison to a choice between illusions. Perhaps what I was running away from was myself. Or perhaps I only thought myself an empress.

No, he insisted, the choice is real.

Who is this man to ask me to choose? I have dreaded just such choices all my life.

Choose—I chose, to reduce my choices to *which* convent, and even this was no choice at all. The convent of San José of the Discalced Carmelites. The most rigorous, of course. Teresa de Ávila's Order. He casually suggested one more lenient. This I chose to take as a challenge. And when I came to see that my choice was in fact a house of torment, I fought my way out again and came back to the palace, only to walk among the courtiers and ambassadors as if back from the dead. And it is true that I have returned from a place few return from. More strange even than the giant, is her revenant. If I felt monstrous in their eyes before, their scrutiny has become for me a purgatory.

Father Núñez admits to having made mistakes with me . . . such as letting me enter a convent too harsh for my temperament. While I may doubt this, he has become in other respects disarmingly candid. Father Núñez calls my position, now, untenable.

"The essential was to draw you out of the palace. Your friendship with the Vice-Queen will go on, but not as before."

He says this with such authority I cannot decide if I am being given my instructions or if he is conveying something the Vice-Queen has told him in confession. "Your haste in leaving her protection has embarrassed her. . . ."

He has manipulated me, allowed me to deceive myself, and makes no apologies.

[†] as henhouse was to equerry

"It is your soul I am concerned with."

"Only this?"

His eyes are no longer downcast, no longer heavy-lidded, not veiled and meek. He despises coquetry, I see. Fears it, perhaps. Now am I invited to find his candour chivalrous. "I am here, Juana Ramírez, to make war on you. To make war on the Evil in you and against the Enemy, for the dominion of your soul. And if only because I now consider you a house divided in all you do, I am optimistic of victory."

I thank him for the *mise en garde*.

To want the best for my soul *is* to want what is best for me. He says this very sincerely. There will be times ahead when I do not know whom to trust—this need in him, I can always trust. He means this, and I believe him. Thus am I encouraged to believe he loves me. And looking into his face I do believe. *He loves my soul.* Is this a small difference, I wonder, or an abyss?

"Should this seem harsh, Juana Inés, try to remember: once I have beaten you, I will carry your soul to God. And if it helps, you may think, child, of a bright angel and a dark. . . ."

I am beginning to see that Father Núñez may one day be capable of cruelty.

"Only believe that it is not the bright one that I detest."

Quite openly he explains my options to me, which are few . . . for a penniless bastard from the hills with so few friends at the palace. Or, apparently, in any other quarter of our city. He observes that I entered the first convent with a certain urgency. Since I am soon to be out on the streets again, I should make a more practical choice this time. That is, if I am really so disinclined to the institution of marriage as seem the other women in my family. Were I prepared to alter my disposition, there are men whom he might persuade that a spotless virtue is not everything in an obedient wife.

Choose. How desperately I did not want to, and confessed to him instead. Until he knew enough of me to shape his questions perfectly, like a key.

Marriage in the world, or marriage *to* the world.

Sincerely, he asks how he may next serve my soul. He arranges for me to visit other, more lenient convents, assures me the problem of a nun's dowry might just be surmounted again.

The day goes agreeably, with cakes and teas. Everywhere he is well known, everywhere he is revered. I see that he confesses many of the prioresses. He sings to high heaven the praises of the nunnery of San Lorenzo as we leave. Towards the end of the day, he takes me to San Jerónimo, under the patronage of the widow Santa Paula and the learned virgins of the Holy Land, under the protection of Saint Jerome and the rule of Saint Augustine. It is a convent renowned for its programs of music and theatre, and for the quality of its library.

On the way back to the palace he takes me to a *recogimiento*. A place for prostitutes, a place of personal reflection and recollection, where the windows are bricked shut. To enhance concentration. Not just those on the outside, but those giving onto the courtyards, too. And the doors barred. My next step I really should take carefully. I will not be able to return to the palace after another fiasco. There are countries one does not return from twice.

He has to go away for a time. To Zacatecas. No, he does not know for how long. Not days, months maybe, at least a few weeks. He looks forward to hearing what my choice has been.

But I look so surprised. I need not. He leaves me in the hands of another. There is a book he has treasured since the days of his youth. . . . He looks, for an instant—it's almost embarrassment. Reverend Father Antonio Núñez de Miranda claims to find a greatness in me. A beauty of the soul that for all his searching he does not find in himself. He brings out a book, but does not pass it to me. He says he leaves me to the care of a great companion, one who has also read the words of Sarpedon to Glaucus, for he has written that *with great gifts come the greatest responsibilities.*

Augustine. Our Holy Mother Church's greatest writer, greater even than Jerome. There is a saying. Who claims to have read all of Augustine . . . lies. But this, Juana Inés, I *have* read.

And these were the dishes wherein to me, hunger-starven for thee, they served up the sun and the moon. . . .

This book I have read many times, child, and offer it to you now as a guide. With chapped hands trembling as with ague, Father Núñez opens my fingers and places *The Confessions* in my hands.

I open the cover. And under his eyes take in the chapter titles as the parched take water, as the famished, bread. Adult Cruelty and Folly, The Attraction of Shows, A Twofold Prize, A Passion to Shine, A Year of Idleness, The Two Wills, The Anatomy of Evil, A Soul in Waste, The Wreckers, Faustus the Manichee, The Teacher as Seducer, The Death of a Friend, The Problem of Forgetting . . .

All the helpful titles, the edifying rubrics. But I had not read it yet. They were as the chapters of my own life. And as I read, the thirst only grew.

Here was a companion who had journeyed far. From the lands beyond the pillars of Calpe and Abyla. Who had lived a life in the world, yet married *to* the world. With his voice a secret in my ear I read of his boyhood among the Afri in Numidia, on the shores of Africa. His studies and dissipations in Carthage, capital of Roman Africa. His lusts. His lusts. Foaming over with lust in Rome and Milan. His years defending the heretical Manichees, his conversion to the Lord of *totus ubique.*[3] After the ransom of Rome, enemies on every side, for thirteen years he sat writing *City of God*. . . . To shore up the faith of the world *in* the world.

His mission and destiny were no less than this. I read of his reluctant accession to the bishopric, and even as the Vandals gathered at the walls of Hippo I watched as the Bishop sat quietly in the library, writing against time, writing to Saint Jerome in the desert in Egypt, putting the finishing touches upon *City of God, On Nature and Grace, On the Spirit and the Letter*. . . .

Here was someone who had humour—*give me chastity and constancy— but not yet!* Who had discovered in the intimate connection of physical love the very source and wellspring of friendship. Who knew beauty— *too late I came to love thee, O thou Beauty both so ancient and so fresh* . . . who had tasted of the sweet joys of the secret mouth in the heart, probed the narrow entrance to the soul, who saw what it is to be in love with love, to know the horrors of going too far—and yet be unwilling to turn back.

Whence this monstrous state . . . ?

At the age of nineteen Augustine found and was forever changed by a single book, a pagan book since lost. Cicero's *Hortensius*, an exhortation to search for wisdom. And so in Augustine I had found someone who understood, as no one else, this craving for wisdom. Even wisdom in loss.

For the bare search for wisdom, even when it is not actually found, was preferable to finding treasures and earthly kingdoms. . . .

Here *is* a friend, to turn to when I no longer know whom to trust, a companion for a path in the desert on the road to *City of God*. Here is a soul that has greatness. A heart to serve, a spirit to sing praises, a hand to write them. *The Confessions*. The greatest of books. A meditation on greatness itself.

Had anyone delved more deeply into the mysteries of the mind? Struggled more greatly to resist his greatness? Surrendered to passion so utterly? Remembered so completely—and survived it?

My infancy is dead long ago, yet I still live. . . .

Father Antonio Núñez de Miranda is a subtle man. And though I shall never know for certain how he intended to serve in giving it, this gift to a lonely spirit I do not forget, nor ever shall. To have such a friend, to swim in such intimate waters, to learn of even distant events and episodes in the life of our friend, these we do not simply hear or read, but know and feel and live as once before. To be given a great book is to be given a second life.

So a question now for the subtle man. To give, even in evil intent, a great book to one's enemy—so that he may see the truth of himself, so that the walls of his life may be pulled to the ground . . . can this truly be called an evil at all?

Tolle lege, tolle lege.[4] Augustine heard it spoken in the voice of a child. Take up and read. . . .

Perhaps, one day, I may yet hear it answered, in the small voice of a man.

JUANA INÉS
DE LA CRUZ

B. Limosneros, trans.

Prolix memory,
grant me surcease,
one instant's forgetting,
let these sufferings ease.

 Slacken the bonds
of all that is past,
lest one more twist
force them to snap.

 Surely you must see
how an end to my days
only liberates me
from all your tyrannies.

 Yet I seek not pity
in begging a respite,
but some other species
of torment in its stead.

 For can you think me
so brutal a beast
as to ask no more of life
than not to cease?

 You know too well,
as one to me so near,
that what I hold most dear
is what this life gives me to feel;

and know too that forfeiting this,
I surrender all hope
of that love, that bliss
that for all eternity lives.

 For this alone, your clemency
do I kneel to implore:
not so that I survive—
but that hope's lease not expire.

 Is it not enough
that so long as you are near,
my absent Heaven's every trait
returns to flood my mind?

 A torrent of reminiscences—
her noble finesses,
her tongue's sweet cadences,
her tenderness . . .

 And is it not enough,
that you extract,
 from glory's seasons past,
the present's draughts of agony . . . ?

manda and I were planning to climb back to Ixayac
that morning. We woke especially early, well before
dawn. It was windy. There were no stars and no sign
of the moon I had fallen asleep to. I smelled the
smoke but half-asleep imagined it was Xochitl,
already grilling tortillas. And then I knew that it
wasn't, as Amanda and I climbed to the watchtower.

PROMETHEUS

A vast wildfire seethed up the far north slope of Iztaccihuatl. Already
it was turning the corner to the western face, not far from Ixayac. For a
long while we couldn't tear ourselves from the sight of a conflagration
rising over two thousand *varas* into the sky. Then Amanda shook my arm
and we rushed down to find Xochitl standing in the kitchen, speaking
rapidly in Nahuatl with three men, woodcutters on their way to warn the
people of the town.

"Go get your mother," she said, which I did at a dead run but when I
banged her door open I found her almost dressed.

"Wake your *abuelo*, Inés," Isabel said, without even glancing up. "And
knock first." She looked at me now as she reached for her cloak. "Don't
frighten him. Can you do that?"

I heard the evenness in her voice.

"*Sí, claro,*" I said, and walked steadily to his room feeling very grown up.

When I brought Abuelo to the kitchen, everyone else was there. The
workers were just outside, all crowded around the door. Isabel had gotten Amanda to translate as many of the details as the woodcutters
seemed to possess. There had been lightning, but the men were not
denying the possibility that they had sparked the fire themselves. Seeing
Abuelo come in properly dressed, his hair neatly combed, Isabel seemed
very close to giving me a smile.

"*Papá, buenos dias.* It's good you've come," Isabel said. "With this wind,
your *molinos*† can be a great help to us now. The men will dig the trenches
where you say. The woodsmen will stay and help. I'll ride in to warn the
town and be back in two hours."

†windmills

Grandfather was a colossus.

He set two men to fashioning leather buckets and two more men,
extra mattocks. He directed the remaining workers, with such picks and

mattocks as we already had, towards the places to start digging. Amanda stepped forward and I did too, though there were not yet implements enough to go around. "No, no," he said, "for you two I have the most important job of all. We need you up in the watchtower to look for spot fires, and any cinders on the roof—call out right away." Amanda and I would not have let ourselves be coddled. The spot fires I might have thought a ruse to keep us out of the way, but with almost no rain in a month, surely the shingles of the house and outbuildings really could catch fire. And from the tower, it was soon clear how true this was: the shingles were cracked like kindling beneath moss tinder-dry.

And there we spent the rest of the day, Ixayac close yet out of sight above us in the smoke. In the ochre light we could see both windmills where they stood above the river, one at each end of the maguey. Blades spinning dizzily in the rising wind, the nearer of the two stood just past the stand of evergreens where Amanda and I often went to read in the shade of a giant cedar. From the base of the windmill a ditch ran through our little strip of trees, then along the north side of the corn-fields and out to the orchards. Grandfather was fixing something at the far *molino*. From right beside him, a second ditch cut across the maguey, along the south side of the cornfields and into the watering troughs next to the paddocks. The air was increasingly thick with ash, smoke, and now dust.

The field hands worked in three parties, a half-dozen men in each—and so quickly that I realized the ditches they were excavating had already been there, filled with loose gravel and overgrown with grass or corn. This was not the first fire Grandfather had found a way to master here—and with the volcano smoking away above us, how could it be otherwise? By the time his daughter was back, a trench encircling the house had been linked up to the water troughs and was filling with water. From the well in the courtyard, workers were filling the leather buckets and passing them up to two men soaking down the roof.

Once the ditches had been scraped out, half the men set to work cut-ting down the fields of corn. With so little rain this spring, the stalks and leaves were too dry, so near the house. The remaining men set up a brigade to relay up buckets of freshly dug earth for spreading over the rooftops—first of the house and chapel, then of the outbuildings. Now, a few splashes from a bucket every hour would be enough to keep things moist.

Maybe luck did come first to the well prepared, or some days were simply luckier than others, for by nightfall it had begun to drizzle, then rain, then pour. But no one seemed to think the day's work wasted.

For three days straight the rain came down. During the hours when Amanda and I were normally out exploring, we did little else but read—at first from a frustrating volume of selections translated from Plutarch's *Moralia*. His other book, the parallel lives of Greek and Roman heroes, had been a great success with Amanda. And this new one started well enough with its wicked diatribes in the style of Menippus, and with fine touches in his advice to brides, but his dialogues on morals were mostly dull and though he'd been a priest at Delphi, his famous essay on the failure of the Oracles was left *out*. At least in the afternoons alone at the table outside the library—and evenings now, with the firepit rained out—I was free to pore over Reverend Athanasius Kircher's *Oedipus Aegyptiacus*. Egyptian Oedipus. I knew of the Greek Oedipus who had solved the deadly riddle of the Sphinx—and reading I found myself returning to something that had always puzzled me. How a riddle in Egypt had somehow become a monster in Greece. Had the other monsters, like the Chimera, begun as riddles too . . . ?

Ancient Egypt of the enigmatic forms . . . priests and priestesses with the heads of dogs or bulls or birds, like ibis-headed Thoth, inventor of writing and guide of souls into the western deserts. Avidly now I read about the teachings of a great sage who lived in the Egyptian desert at the time of Moses: Hermes Trismegistus, divine messenger! His secret texts had been only recently rediscovered but surely the riddles veiled therein contained great natural magic and the highest wisdom. If my excitement was burgeoning, Magister Kircher's was truly palpable. Reading him now was almost to be present as the greatest scholar of the modern world hailed his great forerunner: *I, Athanasius Kircher, and the new sages of Europe salute you from afar.* He was hopeful—on the verge, one could feel it—of recovering the most powerful Hermetic formulas. Light from darkness . . . attraction at a distance . . . a jar so tightly sealed as to exclude even air. . . . Was it really true that the Reverend Kircher had had himself lowered into Vesuvius to study its crater right after an eruption? How he would love Panoayan. Such marvels he could teach us. And what a master of decorum he must be to preserve the dignity of the cassock amidst such updrafts.

Clearly, great new discoveries were imminent: for to the classical instruments and faculties of mind, the new sages of Europe were now learning to couple close observation and measurement. And by the great Jesuit's shining example I was learning that the most powerful instrument of all, as Aristotle himself had said, was *admiratio*, the faculty of marvelling at the world—and surely I was acquiring some of this myself. From the Reverend's description it was child's play to construct a magic lantern, and through it project not just light but forms and likenesses. And what a sensation it created in our dining room when, after dinner one night, I projected my first image onto a sheet draped over the *aparador*.[†] I did not much care for Kircher's own first choice: a painted devil for terrifying sinners. An image of our volcano gouting beet juice turned out to be quite startling enough.

†sideboard, credenza

The best thing was, Reverend Kircher wasn't even dead, according to Abuelo. I had never read a living writer before—as far as I knew, but then I was fairly sure one couldn't tell the living from the dead just by reading them. How I would love to visit him one day.

The only trouble in imagining any such journey would be in keeping its real purpose from Amanda, who in the afternoons and evenings had Xochitl teaching her all the ancient songs and dances and medicines, and secrets only to be handed down directly from mother to daughter and never otherwise spoken of—potions, perhaps, or incantations and who knew what else. Whatever Amanda might feel about my afternoons and evenings, I was not the only one with a parallel life. I was determined at least to keep Egypt for myself. But somewhere on the road to Reverend Kircher's Rome I was bound to let something slip—for if building the lantern had been easy, leaving Amanda out of it had not been easy at all. Harder still to work at the harsh riddles of Hermes alone. She was good at riddles. We had always worked at them together.

And now the Greek had turned against me—as they will even when bringing gifts—for it was almost as if the Plutarch of the dull but harmless selections we had been reading had now forgotten Greece entirely, such was his new-found passion for *Egypt*. Suddenly this new Plutarch was running on—without the slightest discretion—about the proverbs of the Alexandrines and, worst of all, about Isis, *she who weeps*, a deity so august as to seem the sum of all the goddesses of Greece. I would have to find something else for us to read. Quickly.

It had been raining since dawn. The light was soft and grey, the air crisp. Snug under blankets and in rough woollen cloaks Amanda and I sat under the eaves, but in front of my room instead of the library, so as not to disturb Abuelo. Casually I mentioned that, like Plutarch, Hesiod was also from Boeotia.

"Place of Wild Oxen," Amanda said, instantly. After this auspicious beginning it would only be a matter of time before I persuaded her to try *Works and Days*.

When she agreed—reluctantly—to the change I ran for the book. Instead of walking the full circuit of the arcade I sprinted through the rain—not wanting to give her time to change her mind. The courtyard already lay mostly under water. The rain barrels were frothing and fulminating as if they themselves had been dunked. I knew Amanda was watching, and to make her laugh I ran right under a waterspout to the library door, where I called in to ask Abuelo for the Hesiod. He didn't seem to be reading in there at all but was just sitting, chin propped on a hand, staring out the window at the rain. He turned to see me standing there dripping water.

"*Escuintle*," he chided, shaking his head. "You will catch your death."

He found *Works and Days* so quickly that I wondered if Hesiod wasn't a favourite of his. Shuffling back to the door he glanced down at the book, and then up at me with a sad little half-smile. "An excellent choice, Angelita. Your author would be at home in this weather." As I reached out, he straightened a little and stuck out his belly.

"*Espérate.* Dry off those hands first. Here, on my shirt. Now don't you dare run back across."

"*Sí, Abuelito,*" I said and for him I ran, chill and wet, the long way around.

"And dry yourself off before you start reading!" he called across the courtyard. "You're liable to be sitting out there all day."

I read to Amanda for a while, for the sheer pleasure of the words. The text was plain and strong, about hard work in the fields, about the calendar and crops and when to plant. It felt like a book about surviving hardship itself. Crops failing, and weather, and debt.

Just then, as a thunderclap stole the breath from my chest and the hail erupted, it happened I was reading—my voice rising more each instant— Hesiod's lines on surVIVING WINTER. North winds, frost, and hardship enough to *curve an old man like a wheel*. A hail of stones fell as big as avocado pits bounding crazily all about us like whole fields of grasshoppers startled underfoot. Then the hail and the rain just stopped.

The courtyard lay like a case of slate beneath a slurry of pearls, and in the air moved scents of tree sap and hail-mown grass. Clouds hung from the hills just as the breath did from our lips. Ice! We played in the hail like besotted jewellers, letting pearls stream from our fingers.

When we could no longer feel them, we skittered back to our rocking chairs and books and burrowed under the blankets. Amanda was clearly touched by Hesiod's plain words for life on the land, and intrigued, as I was, by the idea of the four ages and races of Man. But we needed to read something warmer. And yet if I were to switch books on her again . . .

I knew exactly how to do it.

"Wait now, NibbleTooth. Hesiod keeps talking about the gods' gift of good crops and bread, and he's told us twice about Pandora—which means what again?"

"Gift . . ."

"'*Universal* gift,' and yet he blames her for dragging Man down to the Age of Iron. The first Woman—*again*. But even so, that still meant Man had managed to drag himself down from Gold to Silver to Bronze without any help from her. And she was only created for this fellow Epimetheus[†] because Zeus'd ordered it. Looks to me like *this* was the afterthought. And now Hesiod has the gall to call her a plague on men who eat bread, which are like *tortillas* here—and what men eat those?"

"All men."

"She did not ask for that old jar, anyway, and who put the Spites in there in the first place? And she was the one who found the gift of Hope in a jar the men had thought empty. That reminds me, Helen is so famous for starting the Trojan War, but a certain poet was struck blind till he finally admitted she was never *in* Troy. Now Achilles, he made trouble without anyone's help, but he gets called a great warrior and Pandora a plague on men. Thetis wouldn't even have *had* Achilles if she hadn't been ravished by Peleus. What desperate tricks didn't she try, to stay out of trouble—fire, water, lion, snake, squid she changed into, anything to get away from him. Pandora, Helen, Thetis, Isi—I ask you, NibbleTooth, what of *their* hardship and grief, and what of poor Penelope, so many years without Odysseus? Well I'll tell you: *grief* is a plague on the women who bake bread *for* men. Or tortillas. . . ."

[†] 'afterthought,' brother of Prometheus, 'forethought'

For some moments Amanda had been eyeing me suspiciously as I plunged on.

"Are these not like the stories your mother tells of CloudSerpent pursuing his sister? And did you know that Thetis rode dolphins?—which swim fast and chase really fast fish, very much as otters do, which reminds me of the seals of King Proteus of Egy—and amazing sea journeys and of another *great* book by Homer . . ."

Amanda sat angled toward me in the rocking chair. Under a mound of blankets all that could be seen were her hands holding Hesiod and—in the shortening intervals between the clouds of her breath—the grimace of exasperation pulling at a corner of her mouth as I myself ran out of steam.

"You want to read something else now?"

Disapproval, exasperation, but not anger. *Splendid.*

"Yes, NibbleTooth—the *Odyssey.*"

The weather cleared enough to see WhiteLady again, white as we had never seen her. She and Popocatepetl rose into the sky entirely cloaked in a light shawl of snow. Up one flank the fire track was an immense scald—steaming still from valley to treeline. It stopped at the northernmost edge of the western face. Ixayac was safe.

Surely we could go now.

As the weather cleared, Isabel rode out to inspect the damage. We had lost half the apple crop and all the vegetables to the hail, and the corn that we ourselves had cut down in the field nearest the house. Worse, Isabel had seen not one but two pumas. She made me promise to stay close to the house for another day or two.

Amanda and I did not get to the *Odyssey.* Even as the weather improved, I grew ill. I lay in my room, fussed and hovered over by Amanda, nursed by Xochitl on bitter infusions of herbs and a chicken stock seasoned with purplish *chipotle* peppers and lime. Of the first day I remember little but dreams and the lusty bawling of cattle pent close to the house. We seemed closer to Ithaca than Ixayac, so with a sigh I asked Xochitl, would she at least tell us something more about this place it seemed we would never get back to? Amanda was sitting at the end of the bed, Xochitl on a chair next to me, the bowl of broth in her lap. The shutters were closed. The whiteness of her hair glowed softly in the dim light.

"What have I told you two already?" she asked, testing us.

"It is a place for women," Amanda said. "The Heart of the Earth, Toci—"

"Goddess of the earthquake," I chimed in, "our grandmother."

"Good. You have not forgotten quite everything. But I did not tell you how."

"How . . . ?"

"It is as the moon, who waxes and wanes, that Toci instructs the Night. As she who is reborn in blood each month, she teaches the jaguar. As the warrior in childbirth, she wears his pelt on her throne. And in this she is also called Tlaelcuani, in licking the gore of birth from the child, and of love from the father."

"Filth . . ."

"Sip. There . . . Yes, Ixpetz. But the filth she eats is rarely her own. And it is she who gave women the *temazcal*. And tell me, did you find its walls still standing?"

"Xochita, we don't *know*," I said.

"How is that, did you not go up?"

"Yes, Mother," Amanda said, "but we didn't want to see everything at once."

The triangles of Xochita's eyes unfolded like little boxes.

"Hup!" There was that laugh we so rarely heard. Like a bird with a hiccup.

"You girls. I had forgotten how it is, to be so young. . . ." Though she'd said this with a smile, we were wounded. Xochita had told us about the special place only because we were almost women. Reading our expressions she added, "No, what you did was good, a sign of respect. Or am I mistaken?"

"But it's been days and we still haven't seen anything!"

"You will soon, so lie back. Sip. More . . . good. Next to the hot spring you will see the walls of the sweat bath, where the midwife once went for her instruction. When I was a girl, two women of our village and the midwife climbed up there together at the full moon. They waited there almost a month, until their time."

Amanda nodded. What else had she already been told?

"But what did they do up there, Xochi, for all that time?"

There were baths to take, and medicines. Prayers and songs, for the midwife and the mother to offer to Cihuacoatl and Tlazolteotl, guardians of childbirth. There were readings to make of the baby's luck in the grains of thrown corn.

"Prophecy!—Tlazolteotl was a *wizard*."

"As the jaguar's tutor, she wears the skirt of black and red," Xochi answered, not exactly disagreeing. "It is why Ocelotl made the journey often. This climb, I made many times as a midwife. I was planning to go again for myself. For Amanda. But my luck was not so good. Something slid . . . then I fell and could not climb."

For a moment her gaze went to the bowl cooling in her lap. As she looked up her voice was firm. "It is a place of cleansing, a place for thought and care. A woman born under the sign 1 Ocelotl, as I was, goes to Tlazolteotl for steadfastness. She wears a crown such as you once gave to Amanda. But not of maguey—hers was of CottonFlower. Like me."

Her face was playful and almost shy.

"You?" I said.

"Ichcaxochitl," Amanda said. *CottonFlower*. She might at least have told me.

"You did not know my full name, did you Ixpetz. . .?"

On the third day I was able to get up and walk about a bit. All morning Amanda was helping her mother prepare a feast for a mystery guest the following night.

But what an uproar had been coming from the corrals since yesterday. Finally I wobbled out to see.

What had sounded the day before like the cattle of Peleus being savaged by a sea wolf was in fact only slightly less dramatic—our cows being bred to the black bull from Chimalhuacan. This normally took place in the far paddock but with the pumas about and the jaguar attack some time back, mother had brought the bull nearer the house. Two days in bed and already life had passed me by.

Abuelo intercepted me between the library and the kitchen. "Are you sure you're strong enough to be up? I should have dried you off properly myself."

"I'm feeling much better, Abuelito."

He didn't say anything for a minute. Normally he would have had his arm around my shoulders by now. "Maybe you should stay inside, Juanita. We've been seeing a lot of snakes in the yard since the fire."

Snakes. Was there to be a plague of snakes now? All this time Amanda and I should have been reading Exodus! Standing next to Abuelo, with the portal so excruciatingly near, I had visions of our captivity here being drawn out by spiders next, then scorpions. Vicious termites, butterflies . . .

"Angelina, would you mind coming to read something for me? There are some pages in bad repair. With all the smoke in the air and the dust, my eyes . . ."

I saw, finally, that he'd come out expressly to keep me from the corral, yet his green eyes were indeed red and bleary, as though he'd been the one ill. Titanic on the day of the fire, he had seemed subdued since.

Cancionero general. A waterlogged and mouldered copy of an anthology of lyrics. It looked three centuries old, but proved to be scarcely half that. The selection truly *was* hard to read, but as much for its beauty as for the damage to its pages. Verses by Jorge Manrique. In time, I would come to know this, his most famous poem, as if it were my own—the one, when the day came, it was a mercy not to have to write.

> *Recuerde el alma dormida,*
> *avive el seso e despierte*
> *contemplando*
> *cómo se passa la vida,*
> *cómo se viene la muerte*
> *tan callando . . .*

It was this poem Grandfather asked me to read now at the little table under the library window. After the fourth stanza he held up his hand. "There. That was the part I had been wanting to hear again." We sat quietly a moment afterwards. "I must have told you. Manrique's father, the Count of Paredes, was an Iberian hero. The second Cid, they called him, so great was his glory. Founder of the Order of Santiago, our highest military order. And fighting at his side was his son, our great poet." As Abuelo added this, his chest was big with emotion. He rested a trembling hand on my arm as was his habit, while for a moment his eyes wandered into the empty space above the courtyard. "Then the father would die, then the son—both defending Queen Isabela."

"But Abuelo, we live in America."

"One does not cease to be a loyal subject of the Crown. Not by mere accident of geography. Without *los Manrique*, truly there would be no Spain today."

I asked Grandfather to tell me about tomorrow night's dinner guest. I knew he was a military officer. Yes, of the rank of lance-captain. Isabel had met him while chaperoning Josefa and María at the ball in Amecameca. A *ball?* Yes, Juanita, two nights ago.

At the courtyard's centre stood the well, a small turret of mortared field-stone. On the east side of it, a big armspan away, lay the firepit, bounded by squared blocks of the same origin and shape as the flagstones but thicker. Within that ring the flags had been pulled up; outside it, lengths of log lay in a gnarled circlet girdling the pit. Stripped of their bark, they were otherwise indistinguishable from those around a real explorer's campfire. And this was exactly how Abuelo had made it feel for us, from the very first night of our arrival from our old home in Nepantla.

On a clear evening, if we went there straight after dinner, from behind the hills to the west a good deal of light would still be coming up, the stories flowing as the light ebbed, infused, in that fading, with a loneliness. It would be just the two of us now. My sisters had lost interest. Amanda was not allowed.

In that silence I would sometimes think about our first night in Panoayan, the only time Amanda had ever been there with us. María and Josefa were swinging at cobwebs with brooms. Xochitl was in the kitchen. It was full dark. Abuelo emerged from his room with a lantern and, tucked under his arm, a rectangular board. I caught sight of something else in his left hand. It was the first fire-bow I had seen.

"*You* know what this is, Amanda," he said, "do you not?"

She nodded shyly.

"Can you show me the Fire-Bow?" he asked her, swinging the lantern behind his back. What was this about? The thing was right there in his left hand.

But Amanda had not misunderstood him. She pointed up at the sky, and though it was a mass of stars, I was fairly sure she was pointing out Orion.

"Not those two?" Abuelo asked, pointing towards the constellation of Gemini. She shook her head. There spread across his face an immense smile of satisfaction. He turned to me excitedly. "As I thought, Angelina. There has been a confusion. Many have written that the Fire-Bow for the Mexica was in *los astillejos,* which we know today as Castor and Pollux. But the confusion was ours, since none other than Nebrija translates *los astillejos* directly from the Latin to mean not Gemini but Orion. And can you not see it there, clearly, a fire-bow in Orion's belt and sword?"

He held up the little bow and drill as if to impose them on the stars.

Still smiling with pleasure he offered her the bow. "You know how," he said without a doubt in the world. He produced from a pocket in his vest a bit of paper in a tight fan-fold between his thumb and forefinger. As if it were a delicacy to eat he offered it to me, which eased the sting I'd felt at being passed over for the main honour. He explained that, in days gone by, papers folded just so had served as the ceremonial tinder. "And to drill this first fire, *señoritas*, was once the very greatest of occasions."

And so we bent to the task as he guided us in how to work, very ceremoniously, together. By then my sisters had left off their sweeping and come to join us at the fire and together we prevailed upon Abuelo to let us sleep around the firepit, just this one night. The stories began. His first, as I recall, he left unfinished. And for this I blame my sisters' wide eyes and gasps of horror. For, pointing confidently at Orion now, Abuelo invited us to see the sky as he believed the first people here had—sitting perhaps on this very spot—as a chest cavity, a great carcass of night, the shell of its darkness cracked open, and at its heart the fire-bow drilling the first sparks of light and—

And that was all. He'd decided we were too young to hear the rest.

I was speechless the next day to hear Xochitl tell me Amanda wouldn't be coming to the firepit again. She would say no more. I simply could not imagine it was Abuelo, who had singled Amanda out for the honours just the night before. I ran to him to protest. He looked very grim. I believe he was hearing of it for the first time himself. He would say only that it hadn't been his idea. So it must have been Isabel—who didn't answer me at all. But why should she care?

The truth was that she didn't. Keeping Amanda from the firepit, keeping Amanda from being hurt, was not her concern.

WALKING
FISH

I tilted my face to the morning sky. Up from the pale thread that limned the peaks there fanned overhead a gradient of soft hues, and in its velvets and peacock plumes glinted brilliants of ruby and crystal, glimmers of ice blue and apple green . . . But I had no time to waste on sunrises. I ran to meet Amanda in the kitchen.

And then we did go. No earthly power could hold us, nor unearthly frog plagues, nor blood-spate, nor vicious cattle lice. We passed the first two streams that boiled and battered down the mountain. A little farther along and just before the third, the string of boulders where we crossed the river was wet and slippery with muddy brown water roaring and seething in places over the rocks. A day or two earlier we couldn't have crossed. At the trout pool we had a twinge of disappointment, but also what I took to be our first good omen. The water was too muddy to renew our acquaintance with the trout, but we did see an otter trundling off up the bank, and sideways in its mouth a big fish bobbing like a trout moustache. Amanda ran ahead of me up the long bridge of Ixayac's nose, each steep step a grimace in the muscles of her calves.

The face we saw in the features of the place—the nose and forehead, the eye-hollows and pine-topped brows—only emerged when we were far enough along the bridge to have left the surrounding trees behind. I finally caught up to her at the *umbral*. After three days in bed I felt faint, eyeing the handholds to the first bench.

"I'll follow you . . . up . . . in a minute."

"We go together," she said, puffing but pacing still in her eagerness to go on. She waited with me a moment, then picked up both our satchels. She slung them over her back, their straps crossed like bandoleers, and climbed ahead of me to the top. . . .

Back at last.

The sky was not so cloudless as on our first day up. In arroyos and valleys all the way along the east side of the lake, mist hung in wisps and shrouds like a row of tars in winding sheets tipped for committal to the deep. Through cloud rifts, quicksilver beads fell in showers. White birds, brilliant in the sun, sailed against storm clouds of blue-black and charcoal. Yet for all the beauty of the scene, we didn't sit, didn't bounce our heels against the ledge, didn't scan the valley for more than a minute. The anticipation of exploring, which we had once thought to prolong for a day, had become an agony.

The bench was as deep as our courtyard was across . . . maybe thirty *varas*, I thought, gauging one against the length of my arm. Amanda pronounced its depth to be twelve *matl*,[†] making its width thirty on each side. Popocatepetl smouldered sullenly across from us—*next* to us—way up yet just to the right. Straight overhead, from the snow line, thin plumes of waterfalls stepped like cloud ladders down the face of Iztaccihuatl. One chute would stop and disappear, to be relieved by another a little over and farther down—until the last plunged into a cleft of rock ten times our height above us, to re-emerge as a small, calm stream from the thicket directly at our feet.

The only way in was to wade up, ducking under the bushes over-arching the stream. The water had been ice not an hour ago, yet the shock we expected did not come. It was not at all cold. We waded swiftly in to our knees and then, to get under the thicket, frog-walked over large smooth stones.

We might so easily have been disappointed. After ten days of frantic anticipation, what place could live up to such feverish visions?

Ixayac could.

So many first impressions we never discussed. The splash and sparkle of water, the shelter and hush, as if from the rasp and rush of breaths—indrawn, checked, endlessly prolonged. Blackberry bushes in bloom, and among them a hummingbird's soft throstling. Tiny frogs creaked, shy yet urgent. From the upper bench down, a fine spray of mist drifted, fog from a cauldron of rainbows. The faintest echo whispered from the rock wall behind the waterfall—did she murmur something, a word . . . did I? We straightened, searched each other's eyes in disbelief. A minute ago we had been high on the open flank of two great mountains, yet now we crouched, enclosed, in a nest of calm. Ixayac *was* the heart of the earth. It throbbed. Soft as a bird in the palm of god.

Amanda's almond eyes welled for an instant but then she smiled like a maniac, and hugged me hard. I felt the strength in her.

Up on the right was the old *temazcal*. A few grey stones had tumbled from its sides. We set to work restacking them. The largest were too

[†] 'armspans'—units of measure close to the Spanish *braza* or fathom

heavy to lift alone. When we were done the walls came to our shoulders. We plastered the chinks with reddish mud and laid pine boughs across. I streaked her cheek and wheeled away with no hope of outrunning her. By the time she had thoroughly smeared my hair and dragged me into the pool, the sun was barely two palm-widths above the horizon. As soon as Amanda noticed, still wet we started packing up. It was hard to leave.

Just before taking the handholds back down we stopped at the edge and gazed out, like emperors come to a balcony to gratify the fawning multitudes. The mists had burned clear. After the heavy rains, the lake's expanses of blues and greens were hedged at each river mouth with frail blooms of mud. Yet in the pale blue around the city, its floating gardens still gleamed an emerald green. The air was clearer than ever, and I was sure I could see the cathedral tower, and even the scaffolding of the corrupt construction works that so scandalized Abuelo and never seemed to cease.

And there, the falcon again—two! One hovered, while the other folded into a dive on a flight of rock doves wobbling along like paper ash on the warm afternoon air. The dive scattered them—a blow struck through smoke—sending them to ground. The two falcons swept overhead screaming, talons empty, caught a draft above us and—wings motionless—went soaring up the face.

The stream at our feet tumbled over the precipice, then reappeared briefly where it glided into the stand of pine well below. The river Panoaya emerged from the far side of the woods and began a long muddy arc, bending past the maguey and our reading spot and out into the valley beyond. At this height the maguey field was a scatter of pineapple tops across a chopping block, the vanes of the windmills spinning like the wheels of small sleepy toys. We were looking toward the hacienda, yet though we had a sweeping view to the south and west and north, our view of the house itself was blocked by a little rise. It dawned on us what this meant: even here on the upper bench no one could see us from the hacienda, even had they ten Galilean telescopes.

It meant Ixayac was ours.

Next morning, we lit the lamps then made a tremendous commotion grinding corn and mixing paste for the day's tortillas. Performing with incomparable industry, we pretended not to notice Xochitl limping sleepily in from the pantry where the hammocks were slung. At the end of the counter she stood with her arms crossed until we acknowledged her.

She took her time assembling our lunch, an especially large one. Then instead of letting us bolt off, she wanted to talk. Placing her hands over Amanda's satchel, Xochitl made us both sit across the narrow table from her. She asked if we had stuck close together, as she had warned us to do. She asked about the trout pool. She asked about the *temazcal*. We answered proudly that we had replaced the stones and made a roof with fresh pine boughs. We told her how we had sealed the walls with mud.

So had we remembered to bring materials to make a fire today in the bath? "Mother, I packed them last *night*." I'd rarely seen Amanda impatient. Palms flat on the table she leaned as if to get up.

"Look at you two," Xochitl chided, "panting to go. Like you had drunk a potion of jimsonweed." Had we even seen the *axolotl?*[5]

"The what?"

"Walking fish," Amanda said. It had legs like a dog but also fins.

This was like guessing at proverbs again in the mule cart from Nepantla. A *salamander*. Xochitl looked doubtful. There were many kinds; this was a special one that breathed water but also air.

"Xochita, they *all* do that."

If she was going to be such a sceptic, I could be difficult too.

"They are not all *sacred*. And," she added, less sharply, "they are not all gold."

Was it just loneliness, or that she would have liked to come with us? With her hip, clearly it was impossible. Even to get across the river meant leaping from rock to rock. It felt cruel even to consider offering.

"Normally, Ixpetz, they are in lakes, not streams," Xochitl continued. "Ocelotl brought them there."

"Why did he, Mother?"

The walking fish was a double, but a double of water and sky.

"It is a favourite of the god Xolotl. . . . But no, you are impatient to go."

"Xochita!"

Her smile showed in all the triangles of her face except her lips, pressed together in a firm, straight line.

"We'll look for them, Mother," Amanda said. "How do they look?"

"Big."

"How big—as a dog?" Amanda asked, excited.

"As your forearm, sometimes, but also hard to see. They hide well in a marsh. But up there you will find them before long."

They could be of many different colours. Pure white with red eyes, or black and white like our Spanish clowns, by which I took her to mean a harlequin, or blue or grey-green. Or gold. Ocelotl had brought them up to our special place, to the Heart of the Earth, but only the golden ones. For among the *axolotl* of this colour some went on to become spotted, like the jaguar himself. Then, a very few of these transformed yet again. They lost their fins and walked out on the land like *lizards*. I searched Xochitl's face for the slightest sign she was teasing us and could find none.

But all colours, she added, had the one quality sacred to Xolotl. God of twins and strange births.

"Twins?"

"Ssh, Ixpetz—what quality, Mother?"

I hadn't been shushed by Amanda much and was sure I wouldn't grow to like it. But what Xochitl told us next made me forget my annoyance. She wasn't joking now.

"It is timid, but has a magic even Ocelotl lacks, a power even the jaguar cannot match."

"Xochi, *please.*"

"Axolotl has the power to remake itself. If I cut off its tail, it makes another. Or a leg, or a claw. I have seen this myself. Ocelotl believed even a heart or a head, if the stars were right, but this I am not sure I believe. . . ."

We lifted the pine boughs from the roof of the *temazcal* and laid them aside, thinking to replace them once the fire burned down—if we could ever get it lit. But after striking flint to fire-stone about four hundred times the tinder finally caught. We fed it dried branches and ringed the fire with large smooth stones. Tomorrow we'd leave nothing to chance—bringing not just *pirita* and flint but steel, and a lens for the sun and even a fire-bow. We were half-frantic with so many things to do at once—light a fire, explore, search for the axolotl . . . and I had a surprise of my own for Amanda, but it had to wait till after our bath.

What first? We scouted the perimeter of the pool in case axolotls had been everywhere under our noses yesterday. We found only frogs.

Then to make sure more treasures were not just waiting out there for us—yet other pools teeming with axolotls, schools of them basking like otters on the banks—we set off, each of us, to explore our own side of the bench. I quickly gave this up. If there was treasure on my side, it was buried deep under any one of a hundred stunted pines, which, aside from a huge wasp's nest on a branch overhanging the blackberry bushes, was all I found. No other pools, no golden salamanders.

On the far side Amanda staggered out of the trees, the belly of her *huipil* bursting with pine cones.

"For the fire," she called, pointing to the *temazcal* with her chin.

"Like *copalli!*" I called back, delighted, and rushed to help her.

We tossed the cones beside the fire, which had begun to burn down, then hardly breaking stride we went up to the hot spring. We had thought we might jump in for a minute on our way up to the second bench, but so hot was the steaming water that it was taking us forever to ease in. I was sweating like mad and sticky all over, though standing only ankle deep, the hem of my dress in my hands, ready to pull it over my head. And yet I couldn't force myself any deeper. Amanda, naked beside me, was not sweating half so much but she couldn't get in either.

"*Ya!*—*estoy harta.* Let's go up and see. We can do this later."

"We shouldn't be running everywhere, Ixpetz."

"What do we *do*, then?"

All of a sudden I felt drained.

"We sweat," she said. With her *huipil* and skirt in one hand, she led me down to the *temazcal*. We replaced the pine boughs and threw in the pine cones one by one like incense. We squatted naked on the dirt, soon slicked to mud with sweat. Standing now and then, heads bent beneath the boughs, we smoothed the sweat down our own thighs and belly, and across each other's back as if smoothing out a dress for ironing. We made mud masks and with them still on made forays into the hot spring, eventually immersing ourselves almost to our hips. Any higher and the heat seemed so thick we couldn't breathe with it. Each time we returned to the *temazcal* we brought water cupped in our palms and threw it on the hot stones. The steam started up at us in searing waves. Tomorrow we must bring a bowl up for this, and something to drink from.

We tried the spring one last time, but unable to bear it a minute more we waded on half-scalded legs into the pool below the icy waterfall. At the shallow end, where the hot spring ran in, the water was warmest, but step by step we pushed a little deeper, colder, farther up. How very similar then were the sensations of ice and fire.

At the deep end of the pool, beside the little waterfall, was a black slate ledge warmed by the sun. We lay on it to dry off, our chins propped on the edge, and peered into the water. We could just reach the surface with our fingertips. In the lee of a heap of rocks the water eddied softly, disturbed only by the trickles running from our hair. We babbled mindlessly about this or that, almost as though talking to ourselves, while keeping a weather eye out for axolotls.

"Sacred to Xolotl," said Amanda, digging an elbow into my ribs.

"Prized by Ocelotl," I muttered back.

Soon we were setting each other *trebalenguas.*†   †tongue-twisters

"The salamanders Xochitl says are sacred to Xolotl, and brought to Ixayac from Xochimilco by the wizard Ocelotl, are they striped, spotted or speckled?"

"Are they walking fish or water dogs?" Amanda shot back in Nahuatl. "Or are they otter?"

"Ixpetz now asks NibbleTooth if the axolotls—speckled, striped or sometimes spotted, salamanders sacred to Xochitl—were sent by sorcery to Ixayac from Xochimilco by the wizard Ocelotl—"

"You said sacred to Xochitl—sacred to *Xolotl.*"

"Alright but say it *faster* now, NibbleTooth. Like this . . ." Here was something I could do with a quickness even Amanda could not match.

Eventually the surface of the water grew still, and a pair of explorers very much like we two looked up at us from under high cowls of stiff, dark hair. But what struck me then, aside from their exotic head-dress, was not how like us they were, but how like each other—the one's eyes larger and rounder, the other's chin a little squarer. Only natural that I knew Amanda's face better than my own—I saw mine only when hazard brought me before a mirror. It was a station I rarely took up willingly since I had always found Isabel's features there, in a sense, before my own. Now, as we stared down, the strange thing was that Amanda could look so much like me, yet not at all like Isabel. Here was another gift from Amanda for me to treasure—

"Wait," I said, leaping up. *My surprise.* I had almost forgotten.

A specialty of our region has become all but indispensable to the women of Mexico. It is a cream made from a butter of avocado and wild honey, widely thought to stay the ravages of time, or at least those of our sun and the high mountain air. We of course cared for nothing of this yet—but oh the glorious feel and fragrance on the skin. Seeing what I'd brought, Amanda's almond eyes grew round as owls'.

Giggling we smeared it over each other, an aromatic lard. Scarcely had I finished Amanda but we were batting away the first wasps. In no time at all, we stood aswirl in them.

"Spin," I yelled, spinning like a top to keep them from landing. We ran up to our thighs into the water but still they buzzed around. One landed now on her.

The only thing left to do was plunge headlong into the coldest water we had ever felt. And yet we waited: the game began. . . .

From that day forward, after the *temazcal*, after the masks and the hip-deep dip in the hot spring, we would bring out the honey cream and slather each other as fast as we could. Then as the wasps swirled we held still, held still, there at the edge by the most supremely icy spot, beneath a waterfall not half an hour old, so recently was it snow. Nothing but a peltful of wasps could ever have persuaded us to jump—and there we stood until we imagined—or did it?—it did it did it did, the first one began to sting

      and

         we

            leapt!

               and came up gasping shock and squealing laughter.

Afterwards, exhausted, we would lie splayed out on our backs beside the big pool. Now was the time for listening to the water plunge, for watching the clouds over at the tip of Popocatepetl smouldering there across from us. Eventually, when we could bring ourselves to stir again we would peer down, on hands and knees, to the bottom of the pool and point out to each other with our noses the locations of crayfish and frogs. And in a certain light with the surface of the pool slightly wavering, I could not have distinguished her reflection from my own.

But that day we still had a mystery to solve. From the lower bench we had seen the last of the high cataracts laddering down from the snow line to vanish into a crevice a good way up the bare, dry wall that formed the forehead of Ixayac. And yet there was this stream here beside us.

The holds for hands and feet were not at all easy to make out, and the rocks, continuously wet, were slimy and treacherous. But the climb proved worth the risk. The upper bench was as wide as the first but less deep, the bare rock wall vertical, soaring hundreds of *varas* above us.

But what we were ecstatic to discover was a single jet of water, waist high, bursting from the dry stone in a long rooster tail.

"Let's stand in there!" Amanda cried, dragging me in. We tried to hold out against the force of water but anywhere near the opening was impossible. The horizontal surge had scalloped out a shallow teardrop from the smooth bedrock. There in the pool where the jet fell to our shins we could just hold on, clutching desperately at each other's arms for fear of being swept down to the lower bench. The water—a liquid snow—sent an ache like a deep bruise through our knees and shins. When we could take no more we staggered out to come and sit sideways at the ledge, stretching our legs out on warm stone worn smooth as a hide.

I came to see that the skin cream of our region did have magical properties, in the delicate spell of stopped time. For the next year we ran past the trout pool to Ixayac, and never told a soul. Perhaps we kept the secret for Xochitl, who could not go up and had told only us. It was a time of searching—it was only a game—for rituals and visions and secret ceremonies.

I have been instructed to meditate upon all the crimes of my life, to overlook none, no matter how seemingly small, and truly who can tell which sins are great, which insignificant? I return to this time and find they are not few.

Yet there is so much here I find difficult to regret. It was a year of pleasures so intense I ached with them, and do still some nights. We woke so fresh each dawn, ready to use our hearts again, ready to make them run. In this manner the circuit of our childhood quietly crossed its equinox, and into a season of lengthening shadows, where, if anything, the air was brighter, clearer. I feel that year still as a memory in my legs, my knees, my thighs, for we ran everywhere—we ran in delight, we ran to joy, and it turned and waited. For one more year. Childhood, the purest part of it, was drawing to a close.

For the Greeks, whose language I have still not learned, the word for this particular excellence I think is not *aretē* but *átē*, which some call 'ruin.' Once, though, it meant divine infatuation. Sophocles must have preferred this sense, for it was he who said mortal life can have no true greatness or excellence without the special infatuation that is *átē*.[6]

But while we were at Ixayac, the heart of the earth beat only for us, and time seemed to stop.

A los triunfos de Egipto
con dulces ecos
concurren festivos
la Tierra y el Cielo,
pues están obligados
ambos a hacerlo;
y acuden alegres
a tanto festejo,
el golpe del agua
y el silbo del viento,
el son de las hojas
y el ruido del eco.

Coplas

Ya fuese vanidad, ya Providencia,
el Filadelfo invicto, Tolomeo,
tradujo por Setenta y Dos varones
la Ley Sagrada en el idioma Griego.
    Quiso Dios que debiese a su cuidado
la pureza del Viejo Testamento
la Iglesia, y que enmendase por sus libros
lo que en su original vició el Hebreo.
Mas ¿por qué (¡oh Cielos!), por qué a un Rey Pagano
concedió Dios tan alto privilegio,
como hacerlo custodio soberano
de la profundidad de sus secretos?
. . . .

JUANA INÉS
DE LA CRUZ

B. Limonsneros, trans.

The triumphs of Egypt
in dulcet strains
the Earth and Heavens
in concert hymn,
since neither can
refrain;
while upon such festivity
joyously attend
the purling of streams
and whistle of the wind,
the rustle of leaves
and the echo's lament.

Coplas

Be it vanity or Providence,
the indomitable Ptolemy Philadelphus[7]
assigned seventy-two sages to the translation
of the Holy Scriptures into Greek.
    God so ordained that to his care
our Church should owe the Old Testament's purity,
and that by his hand be corrected
wherein the Hebrew original erred.
But why (O Heaven!), why to a Pagan King
did God grant so exalted a privilege
as to make him sovereign Guardian
of His deepest mysteries?

. . . .

fter the decline of Athens and before the rise of Constantinople there was the city Alexander founded on the ruins of ancient Egypt, at the mouth of the Nile. In Alexandria's harbour stood the island of Pharos, its lighthouse a wonder to all the ancient world. Fifty fathoms high, and in its curved mirror the whole world stood reflected, as in the panoptic eye of God. A promontory shaped like an hourglass lay between Pharos and Alexandria, and behind the city spread a lake, Mareotis.

City of the suicides Cleopatra and Marc Antony, site of Alexander's tomb, built by his viceroys the Ptolemies. From Ethiopia and Upper Egypt, Persia and Palestine, Rome and Athens the settlers came. The Ptolemies constructed a museum and gave orders that every ship entering port surrender its books so that copies could be made, and so to collect a knowledge that came and went on the winds. Books from everywhere—not just in Greek but in Persian, Hebrew, the holy languages of the Indies, and in the hieroglyphics.

At the firepit I exclaimed over the great works inspired by the liberal patronage of the Ptolemies. Troubled by my first doubts as to the vastness of our holdings, I asked Abuelo how was it he'd never brought out books on Alexandria before. And might not the generous collections of Mexico City have a similarly inspirational effect here? Which was my way of asking when he had last been to Mexico for new books.

Since, he ventured in reply, Alexandria was my current area of scholarly interest—with, evidently, a sub-specialization in the romances of Cleopatra—did I perhaps recall reading that the Serapeum had housed also the Nile-gauge, sacred controller of floods? Geometry too was a gauge. The Alexandrians became great geometers precisely because the flooding forced them to revise their land surveys so often.

"You see, they *practised*." He let the word hang a moment in the air. "So, *señorita*, perhaps we might soon be seeing a revival of your own studies in geometry. . . ."

On Grandfather's book tray the next afternoon was just such a work. All of them, in fact, had to do with geometry, as if he'd simply lifted an entire section onto the tray. The topmost volume was the most appetizing, with quite beautiful engravings. It was in Latin, which he of course read and I still could not without guessing at every second word. Finding me still there frowning over the figures at suppertime, Abuelo said he was happy to see me working at my mathematics again. He said this gently, not reproachfully at all. I studied his face closely for the irony I expected there and found none. What he had chided me for on one day he seemed to have forgotten the next. That is what came to my attention at the time. But how painful to wonder if he had been hoping I would ask his help. I'd been neglecting so much more than mathematics and Latin. This would come to me in time.

Alexandria's was a revival that would have made even Alexander's strict tutor proud. There was Euclid, and Heron, master of the triangle, who invented a water wheel driven by *steam* alone. Apollonius of Perga—the Great Geometer they called him. Even Archimedes had come to Alexandria as a boy, had absorbed its passions as he walked beside the Nile and visited the lighthouse at Pharos. For did he not invent a screw for raising and lowering water levels, did he not install a great curved mirror in the lighthouse of Syracuse to set fire to the Roman fleet, did he not die trying to keep a Centurion from carrying off the very diagrams now before me? Well, if he died to preserve them, surely it would not kill me to study them carefully, even in Latin and Greek. For this was precisely what the natural philosophers of our century were doing. Ours was a revival of the Alexandrian revival, a rebirth raised to the second power. Galileo, of course, but others too in Italy and France, divining and reformulating the forgotten geometric techniques of the ancients, as laid out in the *Conics* and the legendary *Plane Loci*, a lost work that had raised endless speculations for the past thousand years. I worked with great speed. If I was to be of any help there was no time to lose.

The Nile may have made the Alexandrians great geometers, but it was into the conic sections that their greatest passion was channelled. The cone in itself was intriguing enough: in outline a triangle, in surface curved like a sphere. But where transected by a plane, precisely there at its edge, like a broadsword's swipe through a gorgon's neck, the joining spawns the most marvellous hybrid brood: parables made of mind and number, planes *and* solids both, the straight and the curved, intersecting there at order's edge in the cut that does not stop, time itself turned to stone. . . . At last, *there it was*. For through the conic sections and with

Alexandria's help I had finally seen it: geometry as the swordhand of Perseus raising the Gorgon's head aloft.

As I read and worked, the sum of books in the library of Alexandria was mounting towards seven hundred thousand. A staggering number, and more flowing in every day. There came to me late, well into the night, an image of the Nile itself as that river of knowledge, and the beginnings of a verse.

> *Soothe, sinuous Nile,*
> *your liquid swells . . .*

I saw knowledge in a river, libraries in the sea—one blue sea as the library of the Nile, and all the rivers of the world that verse there, collected, catalogued, held. I saw a city in an hourglass, the eye of God in a lighthouse . . . and it came to me that the bright geometric figures, these and the arcane equations that represented them, were themselves so like hieroglyphs. For if hieroglyphs were symbols drawn from nature, might not Nature herself be distilled in formulas just such as these?

Long after I put out the lamp, behind my closed lids danced traces of light—triangles and parallelograms, spheres and cones, shapes called tetrahedron, dodecahedron . . . secret formulae, $r=a\theta$, $A=\pi r^2$ . . .

Early in our explorations at Ixayac we had been forced to concede that the axolotls were gone from the pool or we would have seen one, no matter how cunning its camouflage. But we had found enchantments enough as the days and months passed. In the shallows scuttled crayfish, and tiny snails. Little frogs that heaved and leaned at each croak as if crooning to a duet partner. And as in a gathering of the very highest aerial society, we decided, red-trimmed butterflies danced minuets devised by dryads, while blue dragonflies shuffled and snapped and skimmed over the water. One day we carried two small turtles up from the river to keep them all company. The turtles grew as the snails disappeared, but there were a few tadpoles left that we decided were very much like salamanders.

There was a kind of solemnity in our nakedness now as we bathed or swam or lay on the dark slate by the waterfall to dry off. Amanda no longer lay splayed to the sun but kept her ankles joined and her arms crossed over the slight swelling of her breasts.

"Have mine changed?" I'd asked anxiously a few days before. I didn't think so at all, whereas her nipples stuck up like raw little chessmen.

"They *have*, I think," she not-quite insisted. "A little. . . ."

Lunch was almost always on the upper bench, next to the teardrop pool. It was cooler with the mist and more comfortable to sit, where the stone was worn smooth. And when we did grow too warm we made dashes through the icy jet of water bursting from the dry rock face. The game had been Amanda's invention, as the game with the honey cream had been mine. But today she didn't want to play. She said she wasn't feeling well, though she'd been eating like a goat. Yesterday she'd had a nose bleed that wouldn't stop for half an hour. Still, we did not lack for things to do—the falcons from last year were back. We had been watching them for hours each day. Their nest was in a niche above the upper bench, three or four times our height up the face. Soon there came a batch of chicks. We could hear them— even over the crash of water the clamour was riotous whenever one of the parents would swoop back with lunch. A dove, a grouse, a crow, occasionally a water bird. Once, we thought, a kingfisher. What a sight it would have been to see a falcon take a kingfisher as it swiftly skimmed the river.

At first one of the parents would perch at the lip of the rock niche and tear its catch apart for the other, which brooded almost constantly over the nest. We were sure this must be the female, even if falcons didn't seem much like chickens. From the rock she would gather with a precise delicacy gobbets of rent flesh or guts and feed them down into the nest. After a few weeks we could see the chicks, their beaks at least, reach up to take the meat. We thought there were three, and once they were bigger we could see we'd been right. How curious to discover they were entirely white, as though tarred and dipped in fluffy clumps of cotton. Which lent them the most tender, confused expression. They looked like lambs—we had to laugh. But what savage lambs these must grow to be.

By now both adults were constantly bringing these lambs their meat. More than once over the course of our own lunch we'd see each of the parents swing by the niche with a crumpled bird and simply drop it whole into the nest, then fly off again. Within a few more weeks the young presented a reasonable likeness of their parents. Their faces grew fierce and barred, and but for some cottony tufts on their heads, they were real falcons. They took turns now leaping up to the lip of the niche and spreading their wings in great shows of falcon daring and vainglory. . . .

Amanda and I were almost eleven. María was sixteen, Josefa fourteen. Isabel was spending more time with them now, evenings of sewing and embroidery. As for this guest of ours, Diego Ruíz had been reaching the hacienda a little earlier each time, often now before Isabel was back from the fields. The lance-captain would let his dog run out with him from the garrison for exercise, a heavy-headed mastiff. If we happened to come in not through the kitchen but through the main portal, the dog's yellow eyes did not stray from us, though the thing never stirred from its master's side unless released.

Our mother took Josefa and María off to Chalco in the morning. We could stay up at Ixayac as long as we liked. After failing to spear a fish in six tries each we generally agreed to return our spear to its hiding place and move on. But today something was holding me there.

"Ixpetz, come *on*."

For the second time in less than a day here was Amanda tugging at my arm. My shoulder ached, my whole arm in fact. I must have thrown the spear twenty times and not given her a turn at all. But two throws back I was sure I had nicked one.

By noon Amanda and I were already on the upper bench, sitting on the dry stone on the south side of the teardrop pool. The view to the west was clear. We could see to the lake's north shore and to the villages beyond. The parent falcons had returned, but rather than bringing food they had been roosting quietly atop one of the pines rising from the lower bench. Aside from the crash of water, which we hardly heard anymore, it was quiet. A cool spray drifted around and between us as we picked at the great mass of tamales *con rajas* we had brought all this way up for lunch.

Amanda wasn't a bit hungry. What was *wrong*? We were very close to quarrelling. She hadn't wanted to swim in the lower pool for two days now. Or take a *temazcal*.

I was reading the *Pinakes* by Callimachus. So I'd brought her the *Argonautica*, a book by his student. But I could see she wasn't really reading. It couldn't be that she was bored—not now, with the falcons. We had everything we needed here. And what could be more fascinating than Jason and the Argonauts? And yet I felt it. High in my stomach a nettled sensation.

Alexandria was making it next to impossible to keep Greece and Egypt safely apart—the forms and the riddles, the now and then, the parallel lines of our mornings and my afternoons—to keep them from converging. It had even crept into the books I was picking for us to read. Callimachus and Apollonius, though they wrote in Greek, were librarians of Alexandria. I so wanted to tell Amanda of this white hunger that had awoken in my heart, this thing like hope, pushing to be born in me, to join in the great work of deciphering the emblems of universal knowledge, tracing its forms, charting its equations, its infinitesimal changes. In Alexandria the signs had been so hopeful, a revival that was like a foretelling of our own: Galileo, Descartes, Pascal, Bernouilli, Torricelli. Even now, this very day perhaps, Magister Kircher in Rome was adding new wonders to a universal museum not unlike Alexandria's, and so resurrecting the dream of the Ptolemies. The great work was happening right now and yet an ocean away, in the studios of the artists and physicists of Italy, the mathematicians and philosophers of France. How could I even begin to tell Amanda of this, and yet how could I not?

Very casually I started in with Alexandria's librarians, the poets Callimachus and Apollonius, the grammarian Aristarchus. Already Amanda was wrinkling her nose. Grammar was her least favourite subject.

"Seven hundred thousand *volumes*," I put in hastily. Could it even be imagined, such a sum? What was our library here, next to that? With so many books coming in, another library was set up in the temple of Serapis. This new repository, they named the Serapiana—*the daughter library*. I asked Amanda if she did not find this lovely. She made no comment. Scholars began streaming in from all over the world to Alexandria, so the Academy of Athens founded a daughter Academy there too, under a librarian named Theon. Not a poet, this one, but a powerful mathematician, who taught astronomy and divination.

"Magic, Amanda. He must have been a wizard, like Pythagoras, like Ocelotl—"

She suggested we go down.

Was she even listening? Because this was the best part—this Theon had a *daughter*, Hypatia. He believed she could become a perfect being—a *girl*, NibbleTooth. Barely eight and she was already helping her father study an eclipse of the sun. I knew I'd caught Amanda's interest, yet she was adamant about not staying. I felt a flush of anger but tried to calm myself by thinking thoughts that, if not altogether wise themselves, were about wisdom.

And then as she started to her feet there erupted a din of screeching falcons such as we had never heard. On the lip of the niche two fledglings were jostling to spread their wings and wildly crying out as if their wingtips were raw nerves in agony. An even greater commotion came echoing back from the uppermost branches of the pine opposite—swaying under the weight of two—but no *three* screeching falcons. A second of the fledglings vaulted now from the niche and came crashing awkwardly into the boughs. Only by clutching desperately at the branch with its talons did it keep from toppling backwards to the ground. The third, still back at the niche, flapped and lunged without letting go until at last overwhelmed by the sheer pitch of urgency of the other four beckoning with shrieks. No sooner had it leapt off the ledge but the parents launched themselves, soon followed by one, then two, then all three.

Amanda and I had come to a crouch, breathless, stunned and all but deafened as they wobbled then swooped screaming back and forth over the bench.

It was dusk when we came down.

In the morning I took the lead and kept it all the way up, with her straggling behind. We worked our way along the river towards the bracelet of stones where we crossed over. A flock of white pelicans was wheeling and diving at the trout pool ahead. From a trot I broke into a run. Each pelican following the next, they dove and rose again, dripping like the paddles of a waterwheel. Gaining height they merged a moment against the snowfields, then broke into the blue just in time to fold again and plunge to the water like spatulas after their handles.

I spotted an otter where it stood on the pool's far bank, one forepaw raised delicately, muzzle uplifted to sniff the air. I could not have said whether in contempt of their proficiency—for not one pelican in five ever needed to break formation to actually swallow a fish—or in resentment of these interlopers fouling his larder on their way from the lake back to the sea.

By early afternoon we were close to quarrelling once more.

With Amanda refusing yet again to swim or take a *temazcal*, we'd spent the whole morning on the upper bench at flying lessons. She sat, distracted, hardly watching at all as the adults hovered above the fledglings, dipping and turning at the merest tremble of those beautiful wings. Wings the very shape of loveliness and power, tips tapering to an archer's bow, to a single pinion of grace. I watched them now as if to save my life. I watched them with falcon's eyes. As the adults led, all five soon dove and swooped and swept in widening relays and volleys. Wild shrieks like the clash of steel. What were they feeling? Was it joy? If so, how wild the heart to give such voice to joy. Shrieks and shrieking echoes—one after the other—terror, terror to wild exuberance, fierce exultation, to a joy like rage. Their echoes crashed against the face, careened off the water. Tears started from my eyes. I blinked the chill into my lashes. I was the one exalted, exulting in these echoes.

And what had been that terror if not the fear they might never fly at all?

By mid-afternoon Amanda wanted to start down.

We still had at least an *hour*. How could we leave even a minute early, with so much for us here? Two benches, two pools—*five falcons*. With her face so closed off from me, it felt as if all the secret shapes and silent tides of the world were trying to divide us. I began to tell her more about Hypatia, whose father had been teaching her about mathematics and stars, divinations in the flights of birds. But there were things even he did not know, so he let her go off to study in Athens, at the Academy, under the direction of Plutarch himself. . . .

Amanda had collected her things in her satchel yet stood hesitating at the ledge where we climbed back down to the lower bench. I stood close behind her, looking out into the valley. Imagine that journey, Amanda. See, that was the Aegean down there—the near shore was Egypt, the city on the island was Athens. And see that canoe just entering the *chinampas?*—the galley taking her away from home. We had each other, Amanda, but Hypatia was *alone*. She missed her father terribly, but she was following her destiny. And did Amanda not think I missed Grandfather sometimes up here? Did she think I'd never felt bad about always being here, with her?

Still she wouldn't look at me, as if convinced everything I said was only another trick to delay her. Which was true, but it wasn't because of the falcons and it wasn't just so we could stay late. It was because I was afraid. Could it be we no longer loved the same things—or no longer loved what we shared? This was my punishment for wanting to keep Egypt for myself, concealing it from her.

When she started down without another word I wasn't even angry. I only followed her to the next bench, talking all the while, talking as we gathered up our things, and as we walked down the little stream and under the overarching bushes. I slipped ahead of her to slow her down.

"You know, Amanda, Hypatia became a teacher so famous that men came to her from everywhere, and so beautiful half of them grew sick with love of her. But she was a healer like Ocelotl. Like your mother." Since I could not stop her I was walking backwards, talking quickly, unsure of the remaining distance to the ledge. "She cured one of these men with a therapy of *music,* a medicine of harmony—do you see? And to another of these lovesick men she showed her soiled undergarments—"

Amanda stopped. Suddenly, mystifyingly, I had her full, angry attention. Her eyes narrowed.

"Why would she do that, Juana?"

Were things so bad between us? She seemed suspicious of everything I said or did.

"Tell me why you said that," she demanded.

"I said it because she did it, that's why! To show him his idea of beauty was not where true beauty lies."

I stood facing her, my heels at the ledge, the whole Valley of Mexico—Athens and Alexandria—falling away behind me. I was desperate to talk to her and could not find a single thing she wanted to listen to. And now the tears did come.

Amanda looked at me for a long moment. Her eyes shimmered. But when she still said nothing I turned, embarrassed, to start down.

"Wait, Ixpetz," she said. I felt her fingertips on my shoulder. "The other song. For the girl. Mother is teaching me. . . ."

I turned back, watched her pause an instant to collect herself. On a ledge overlooking the city on a lake she sang me the song for the newborn girl. And still I did not understand yet why.

> My beloved daughter, my little girl, you have wearied
>   yourself, you have fatigued yourself.
> Our lord, Tloque Nahuaque, has sent you here.

You have come to a place of hardship, a place of affliction,
    a place of tribulation.
A place that is cold, a place that is windy.
Listen now:
From your body, from the middle of your body, I remove,
    I cut the umbilical cord.
Your father, your mother, Yohualtecutli, Yohualticitl, have
    ordered, have ordained
that you shall be the heart of the house.
You shall go nowhere,
you shall not be a wanderer.
You shall be the covering of ashes that banks the fire,
you shall be the three stones on which the cooking pot
    rests.
Here our lord buries you, inters you,
and you shall become worn, you shall become weary.
You are to prepare drink, you are to grind corn,
you are to toil, you are to sweat, beside the ashes, beside
    the hearth.[8]

When she had finished she told me how the midwife takes the girl's umbilical cord and buries it in the earth next to the hearth. The girl does not take the cord with her to the fields of battle. A girl goes nowhere.

"No Amanda—it's what my mother says too but it won't happen to us. Look at Hypatia." Canoes flashed in the sun on the lake and by the landings where we had always discerned vestals going to their altars. "See, she's already reached the dock. Our city is right there. We've *seen* it—it's too late to keep us here. Somewhere down there is the greatest library of the New World, as hers was of the Old. Our Academy will be the Royal University and—"

"*No, Ixpetz. It's not that.*"

She hadn't told me about the song to talk to me about our destinies. Or our umbilical cords. There was something else. Well then *what?*

Le había llegado su luna . . . Amanda's cycles had begun.

"But. Let me *see,*" I said stupidly.

She shook her head, and in her shyness I saw suddenly that *this* was why—all this time. She hadn't been bored with us or me at all, or with Ixayac.

She confided that Xochitl had known it was coming even before it happened.

"If *I* didn't know, how . . ."

"Mother wouldn't say." Amanda shrugged. "You know what she's like. But she had the cloth ready for me."

What cloth?—and why hadn't I known? Why couldn't I see? I wanted to ask again—but no. Tomorrow.

Once again Amanda was the faster one, I thought, as we walked ever more quickly back down to the hacienda. So far ahead I might never catch up. I was the only one left. The only one at the hacienda not quite—still and ever almost—a woman.

As we came through the kitchen door, I asked Xochitl, wasn't ten terribly early?

"I'm almost eleven," Amanda said.

Xochitl didn't pretend not to understand what I meant. "Early, yes. Only by a year or two."

"Will my time be soon?"

"Maybe, maybe not. Your sister Josefa was twelve."

"Xochita, how do you know these things?"

"This sorcery, Ixpetz, is called doing laundry."

"What about María, then?"

Xochitl shook her head. "I should not have told you Josefa's secret."

"Xochita, please. Don't make all the secrets here from *me*."

Her eyes widened slightly at this—she looked not so much startled as stung. "There is no reasoning with you when you are like this."

"Like what?"

"*Moyollo yitzaya.*"

Your heart turns white with hunger.

I told her I didn't need another proverb, I wanted an answer.

"Three months."

"*Ago?*" María was *sixteen*. I might be five years away?

It was unthinkable.

HEART OF
THE EARTH

And in those days there appeared in Alexandria a female philosopher, a pagan named Hypatia, and she was devoted at all times to magic, astrolabes and instruments of music, and she beguiled many people through Satanic wiles. And the governor of the city honoured her exceedingly; for she had beguiled him through her magic. And he ceased attending church as had been his custom. . . .

BISHOP JOHN OF NIKIU, *Chronicles*

hat night I read until tears of rage streamed from my eyes. I had hardly slept in days and yet as I read now, it felt more like dreaming.

Heresy. This new thing was in some way that still escaped me the collision of Egypt and Rome, and Alexandria was where they met. I thought I understood that in Rome treason had become heresy, but now in Alexandria heresy was being made treason. Of all places, *Alexandria*, a crossroads for all the faiths of the ancient world, a city much like Mexico. Heresy—it made no *sense*, for what could Xochitl's parable of the trout have meant but that all faiths, all visions of god, were only the masks of what cannot be known?

I could not understand this hateful book, much less how it was making me feel. But perhaps I had begun, in some small way, to blame Ixayac. There, too, everything was changing, everything verged on transformation. Coming upon us so swiftly, it had overtaken even Amanda. It shimmered all about us, and the magic of stopped time no longer felt so sovereign. Late that night there came to me the idea of making some ritual to mark the changes. I knew a lot about rites and initiations into secret ceremonies but I didn't *know* any, or they wouldn't be secret after all. I did know that the Eleusinian mysteries had five levels. Purification was the first, knowledge was only the second. Next came the riddles of a third level, then a fourth, where there was nothing more to know except through silence. And that was all I knew.

Well, then Amanda and I would have to make up our own ritual. Surely that was better anyway. It should be like a coronation, a rising into loveliness through holy fire, a secret theatre of sacred gestures. In the hours before dawn the magic lantern of my mind swirled and smoked with the possibilities—rites of the Maenads and Corybantes, ox blood and *hippo-manes*. I would bring the *Metamorphoses* and mark all the transforma-tions—but no, that would be the whole book. We'd read just the stories of Thetis and Proteus who changed bodies as naturally as the flooding Nile redrew the shapes of the fields. Indeed this was the message of the Egyptian Hermes: that the flow of god's truth plunged all around us in a swift flood, and that to bind its meanings into a single form was to dam that flood and incur the most terrible violence. Such a torrent must be touched only in tangents—riddles, enigmas, proverbs and chants. Secret initiations.

We didn't have seven hundred thousand volumes to choose from, or the painted books of Ocelotl, but I had Exodus and Proverbs. In Proverbs I found lovely lines.

Doth not wisdom cry? and understanding put forth her voice? She standeth at the top of high places, by the way in the places of the paths . . .

. . . hear the instruction of thy father, and forsake not the law of thy mother: For they shall be an ornament of grace unto thy head. . . .

Surely in vain the net is spread in the sight of any bird.

With just such incantations as these might Amanda and I deflect the tides of events into channels of our design, just as we had done all around our house the day of the forest fire. At first light, I marked the passages with green strips of ribbon to show Amanda. I went to meet her, and there coursed through me a tremendous flood of energy. As we reached the far end of the cornfield a half-dozen deer leapt the fence just ahead of us. I chased them a little way up the path shaking a fist in mock threat, then turned and waited for Amanda. I began talking about our ritual, and tried not to take her silence for disapproval. It wasn't so unusual for her to be quiet. But how very awkward talking was while in the lead—on narrow paths, head turned to trail a kite-tail of ceaseless patter, glancing back every so often to gauge the effect only to lurch over some tree root risen up to trip me.

Today she truly looked tired. Had she slept? I asked. No, not very much.

We were sitting quietly on the flat rock beside the little waterfall. "Aren't you going to swim?" she said after a while.

"Not if you're not," I said. She shook her head just perceptibly. "Did Xochita tell you, you shouldn't when . . . ?"

"No, she said it would be all right to."

"Well, if you don't want to that's fine."

She looked down a moment and smoothed her skirt over her knees.

Then she glanced up slyly and asked if I still wanted to see the cloth. For a moment I thought she meant the one she was wearing, so I tried not to look disappointed when she brought three out of her satchel instead. They were pretty much as I might have imagined, but three?—four, counting the one she wore.

"Mother said today there'd be a lot."

We decided to climb to the upper bench to check on the falcons. She had always been swift, always graceful, but had rarely seemed delicate—and clumsy, never. As we probed next to the waterfall for our handholds and footholds, I heard from below me a sandal scuff as her foot slipped. When she reached the top after me, her right knee was scraped.

We set down our satchels and took up station at the lower end of the teardrop pool. The sky was a pale, clear blue. The first wisps of cloud gathered at the lip of the volcano. The falcons, all five of them, far, far above us, gyred at their leashes like slow-swung lures. From time to time the faintest cry reached our ears.

We picked a little at our lunches. For the second day in a row I'd lost my appetite, not from annoyance this time but from excitement, though I tried not to let on. Since getting the idea for a secret ritual I could hardly contain myself—within me I could all but feel the ingredients stirring, churning, as in the mortars of the Moorish alchemists.

"And NibbleTooth you can make a dance for us and I'll try hard to learn it. *I know*—we'll throw the corn grains to read our destinies. What else . . . no need of holy water—we have that here. We'll take an extra long *temazcal*, then hold ourselves in the hot spring longer, deeper, than we ever have. We can even cook some eggs in the spring for luck. What do you think of that?" *Still no answer.* "Then we dip ourselves three times under water, like people do against the evil eye." I realized that I knew so many of these things from lists of practices banned by the Inquisition. What else had they banned? *Chickens*—the drawing of spirits with hens. The African *curanderos* only ever used a black hen, which they would then rub hard on the victim's body. If the bird didn't die right there from the influx of spirits, its throat had to be slit. So maybe a chicken. "We don't really have any caiman's teeth, either, or stag's eyes. But we can check under the falcon's nest for bird bones and claws—come on! Or . . . all right. Later if you like."

She just sat there, her legs folded under her, looking out over the valley, not joining in at all. I so wanted to offer her the perfect gesture.

"What should we *do*, NibbleTooth? This is the place of women's secrets, isn't it, for the women of your family? *This is the Heart of the Earth.* We'll be doing it for Xochita too—I'll bet she told you she would have liked to bring you here herself. Didn't she."

"Yes."

She had picked up a pine cone, was studying it intently as she turned it in her hands.

"We'll bring chocolate, and tobacco, and flowers. What else?"

She shrugged.

"Should we stay the night? Should we bring *peyotl*?" I was not entirely sure what *peyotl* was—she glanced away from me now—but one needed rare ingredients for secret potions. She was always picking herbs for Xochita, so why shouldn't she do it for us? "That's it—jimsonweed!"

Staring vacantly down at the lake she had begun plucking bits from the pine cone. After a moment she said, "Mother's teaching me, already."

"Teaching you what?"

"The ceremony."

The ceremony. The real one.

My frustration chased my temper through bright spirals behind my eyes. I waited until I could trust myself to speak. "No, Amanda, we need something of our *own*. Or do you just want to sit around up here all day doing nothing all the time? No wonder it's become boring."

"It's boring for you?" she asked, startled.

"We hardly read anymore. We don't swim." I knew I was being unfair now. "You're not even interested in the falcons. You just sit around staring off into the sky."

"That's not true."

"So we'll get jimsonweed, no? We could go down right now, try to find some." I started to wrap our tamales back up. "What does it look like?"

"I can't say."

"You don't know or you won't say?"

"I can't."

"So you do know."

"I can't Ixpetz. I promised."

I was getting sick of Amanda's secret knowledge. Had I not been telling her all about Alexandria? Did she care nothing for finding a destiny all our own?

The fledglings had come back to the niche. The adults were nowhere in sight. A chill mist of tiny prisms drifted round us. Without our swim the sun was especially hot.

"I'll learn your dance. I'll work hard to learn it quickly. And I'm writing a poem to teach you. I've already started. Listen . . ."

I recited what I had written. She gave no sign of having heard my little verse, not nearly so impressive as the one for the newborn girl.

"Of course, it's not finished yet. . . ."

Her eyes had settled on the city on the lake. Something in her face then looked defeated and helpless, unbearably sad. I thought I was the one who was sad. At work in Alexandria now was something that I could not quite grasp and yet that could not be stopped. The Christians had begun destroying the temples of Mithra and then the synagogues. By the command of a Bishop named Theophilus the temple of Dionysus was pulled down, and after it the Serapeum in Memphis—though he dared not touch the temple of Isis there. When the other peoples of Egypt still did not rise against him, he sacked the temple of Serapis and the daughter library in Alexandria and took control of the Nile-gauge. And when he died, the new Patriarch, Saint Cyril, the nephew of Theophilus, carried on his uncle's heart-sickening work. *Saint* Cyril? These barbarians were *Christians*. Theophilus meant *beloved of god*, but how could that be? What sort of god was this?

Flying back with a teal in its talons, one of the adults hovered now and tumbled the body into the nest. The young falcons set to quarrelling over their meal with the most terrible screeches. For some reason their squabbling made me furious. I was on my feet, casting about for a stone to throw at the nest. There were only a few pine cones.

"Ixpetz, you can tell me what's wrong."

Amanda sat there watching me, her hands still, shards of pine cone patterned on her skirt. There was such a chord of resignation in her throat, it was almost as if she'd been afraid too, was asking even now to hear anything save what I needed to tell her. But I was no longer sure what that was—what was it I was afraid to say? Or was I more afraid there was nothing left to say?

Hypatia's private classes were banned now by Cyril the Patriarch, and only her Academy lectures on mathematics were to be tolerated—no more classes at the homes of leading citizens. And then something happened that I could not bear. The details were few, and horrible. I could tell her in the hateful words of John of Nikiu. No, for us, I had to find words of my own. . . .

Hypatia began to take long rides south along the Nile by chariot, making short forays into the desert. South of Alexandria were the Natron lakes, whose salt waters had since the most ancient times been used for embalming. In the desert lived five thousand warlike hermits, assembled now by Cyril and roused to a fury against Hypatia. One day as she had almost regained the safety of the city, the monks of the salt marshes pulled her down from her chariot and carried her to a church called Caesarion.

The Nitrian monks stripped her, tore off her philosopher's robes, then battered her to death with heavy pottery jars. To her chariot they hitched the naked body and dragged it through the streets to a place called Cinaron. There the monks took the one who had been Hypatia and scraped the flesh from her bones with oyster shells and pottery shards.

These were the details.

That day at Ixayac, I had just these few incidents to offer, and endless questions. For all their horror, they danced and japed about like tantalizing clues to a riddle whose answer I felt must seem one day, as in all the best riddles, obvious once found. Why had Hypatia in a time of such danger been out alone, driving her chariot through the salt marshes of Wadi n' Natrun? How could it be that the warlike men of God were led by an illiterate named Peter the Reader, that the manner of her death was in Alexandria the penalty for witchcraft—inflicted now on superstition's great opponent . . . ?

Hypatia's murder was the end of Alexandria as a great centre of learning as the students and scholars and mathematicians and librarians began to drift apart and leave for other places. And as the Dark Ages began, the pages of seven hundred thousand books heated Caliph Omar's baths for six months. Six months of heat and light for a thousand years of darkness. What sort of equation was this?

And yet, despite my confusion, from the expression in Amanda's eyes I was convinced she *had* understood—everything, even why I was telling her. And seeing this I was so sure the silence, this new, dark shape between us, would just dissolve and we could talk about everything, and my fears for us—

"We should go down now."

She'd said it not unkindly, but infuriatingly all the same.

I led all the way, not once looking back. Down the ridge of Ixayac's nose, through the woods, past the trout pool and across the river. I skirted the maguey plot and then, instead of cutting through the cornfields for home, I waved her on and turned for the far paddock. Baggy grey clouds hid El Popo's tip, and through them rose a plume of brownish smoke and steam. The sky was otherwise clear, the deep blue of late afternoon. Hummingbirds and bees wavered and mumbled over sprays of wild-flowers. The pastures were a furnace, moist as the *temazcal,* the air a bellows—the cows' heavy calls, the cicadas' eddy and pulse, a bright grist of sound milled in its intervals and ratios. . . . To walk in that air was to eat, to feel it fill my mouth with moist earth, life.

I walked to the fence of the far paddock where we had watched the black bull among the cows. The bull on whose sharp horns Amanda had hung for me a cornflower crown. Just a year ago, but so much was now different. My twin had had the change that would make her a woman. My own time floated near like an intimation. I felt my breaths shorten, a diffuse, liquid sensation in my knees and in the soles of my feet. It was like standing barefoot in warm shallow mud.

here was a mild earthquake just before dawn. I found the kitchen door open and Amanda already outside, her black hair plaited with blue ribbons. She wore her best *huipil.* In the dim light her knees and shins were dark against the whiteness of her cotton skirt. She had cleaned and oiled the leather of her *huaraches.* I glanced down at my own, the sandal straps dusty and spattered.

"Where have you been?" Now she was eager to go—would I ever truly know her? Maybe she had understood after all what I'd been trying to tell her, or maybe Xochitl had said it would be all right. "It's *late* already."

It *was* late, but I had been up for an hour packing my satchel with magnets, pyrite, flint, a fire-bow just in case, the *Metamorphoses,* the Bible, a block of oily black chocolate, a knife to cut it with, our lunch, then, on top, cornflowers, *cempasuches* and agave spikes.

We spoke very little, having decided to run almost all the way up to give ourselves more time. She took the lead easily. I was carrying the heavier satchel but I didn't mind at all and didn't once ask her help. Though I was not quite out of breath, my knees felt weak as we reached the lower bench. We made our way up the stream then clambered up to the *temazcal.*

"Let's go see the falcons first," Amanda said.

We usually went there last but I did want the day to be different. Still, I wouldn't leave until we had started the fire so that the coals would be ready when we came down. I laid fresh pine boughs to one side as a covering for the roof. Then I refilled the clay jar we used to splash water over the stones and drink from. We'd just reached the upper bench when the falcons launched themselves out into the valley in single file, up and up, far above a long vee of ducks arrowing towards the lake in the distance below them. Today was to be a hunting lesson.

I was anxious to come down and get started. I laid the bundle of *cempasuche* flowers at the threshold of the *temazcal,* so as to have to step over them going in and coming out. But Amanda wanted to swim first, though that too we usually did afterwards. I saw how the cloth was attached as she undressed. It was of the same dark, tightly woven cotton we used for *rebozos,* folded half a dozen times and tied front and back to a sash around her waist. She undid the sash. She looked at me anxiously, as though I might laugh or even be repelled. But as she stood, otherwise naked, half turned from me—her breasts like little barrels, small spigots at the tips—my breath caught in my throat.

"You look like a warrior, now, NibbleTooth."

At that her head dipped, a little nod of modesty, as in surprise, as if to check: *Was it true . . . ?* And I remembered how just last year we used to stand on the slate rock above the pool and stick our bellies out like the women with child who had once come here to await their time. Now she could *have* a child. For a moment we were both serious, a little shy. But she grew more animated as we smeared ourselves with the honey-avocado cream. Almost immediately the wasps began to circle and her quickness made a spectacular game of it as she dodged and whirled, squealing madly, away from them. I had already leapt into the pool.

"Amanda, hurry!"

She faltered then and had to launch herself in a long running leap into the pool to keep from being badly stung. As we stood in the sun to dry off, I noticed our two turtles sunning themselves too, as they often did, on a small rock next to the waterfall.

"Do you do your dance first or should I do my poem?"

Her eyes wavered and I had the distinct impression she'd forgotten about the dance she was to prepare.

"Your poem."

It still wasn't finished but I gave what I had so far, the refrain, two verses. When she said nothing, I asked her to teach me her dance. She improvised the most dispirited little shuffle, hardly better than I could have come up with myself, and I knew I was right. She had forgotten all about it.

We'd put this off long enough.

"The *temazcal*," I said, and stalked off ahead of her. Brusquely I laid the pine boughs overtop, grabbed my satchel, stepped over the flowers at the threshold and squatted in the heat. A full minute later she ducked in after me. She really didn't seem to care about this at all. Well, I did care, and I knew how we had to do this, and with great seriousness. The heat was intense. Taking the knife from the satchel, I reached up and pried little beads of dried sap from the branches, then threw them into the fire for incense. From beyond the walls the little waterfall plashed and a smoky light fell through the doorway. Once I had tipped all the water from the clay jar onto the stones, the air was too hot to breathe through our noses. As we squatted there, heads bowed, our breaths came in little gasps through our lips. Runnels of sweat puddled under us. Through the pine smoke and steam and the sweat blinking into my eyes it was hard to say how much blood was under her but it didn't seem like much.

"Listen carefully. What we do next is daub ourselves in blood. You do me, I do you. We draw signs. On me: sun, hourglass, quarter moon, pyramid. On you: lighthouse, quarter moon, jaguar, cotton flower. All right?" She nodded without looking up. "Then, when we're ready to come out, we each dip a finger into the mud and place it in our mouth." There was a formula I had heard somewhere that came to me now. *Dare Terram Deo.* Render the earth unto god. "That's it, we say this first, *then* we put our fingers with the mud into our mouths." This was the Heart of the Earth after all.

"Repeat it."

"*Dare Terram Deo.*"

That was better. She'd said it just right. Once outside, we would stand by the pool while I read from Proverbs. After that we'd dry off on the slate rock and weave crowns of cornflowers and agave. We'd put them on and it would be like rising through a plane of loveliness, *ornaments of grace* upon our heads. Then, solemnly, we'd take each other by the hand and plunge into the pool—head first, for once. "Okay?"

"Okay."

"Then we eat the chocolate. *Yollotl, eztli,* right?" *Heart and blood.*

"Yes," she said. "Heart and blood."

And last of all, when we were ready to go down we'd leave the lunch we'd brought as an offering. Was she ready?

A stillness settled around us.

She was facing the door. I edged next to her, facing the back of the hut, and turned slightly towards her, my right shoulder to hers. The coals glowed red in the shadows. I dipped my finger into the puddle under her. She started nervously when I touched her back with my fingertip. It left only a dirty little track, with hardly any blood at all. I dipped again and scooped but with all four fingers now. Again, sweat, a little mud, the faintest hint of blood.

"Is that *all?*" I said.

"There was more yesterday."

"But this is the most important *part.*" Blood was for the mixing of the secret salts and balms, blood was the essential agent, blood was for binding the spirits and resins. *Blood*. Wasn't that obvious?

"I—I'm sorry."

It must have been the way we were squatting, facing past each other, my shoulder to her side, but I had the idea it might be like milking a cow. You didn't just wait for the milk to fall, after all. So I put my fingers there. She flinched, then held still and quiet. There wasn't anything really to squeeze but I did a kind of kneading with my fingers, as we did with the cornmeal, or when squeezing water through the muslin for the curd. I raised my fingers to my face to see better. Just plain dirt on the knuckles, and on the tips was nothing like paint at all, only the thinnest smears of rust. I shook my head, disgusted, furious.

"What should we do?" she asked, her eyes wide.

"We need blood."

I picked up the knife where it lay next to the green rabbit satchel.

Slowly, gravely, Amanda offered her arm.

I looked into her eyes.

"Not you," I said, mollified. "We need something to collect it in." And then I remembered. "Wait here, I'll be back."

The turtles were still there sunning themselves on the far side of the pool. I snatched one up and sprinted back to the *temazcal*, ducking in out of breath and suddenly dizzy. For a moment I knelt, bent double, my elbows in the mud. When the dizzy spell passed I looked up at Amanda still huddling where I'd left her. I settled back on my heels, the knife still in my left hand, the turtle waggling his legs in the other.

"Why do you want to hurt it?"

"I don't, but we *need* to now."

"But *why* do we need to?"

"If you'd warned me there'd be so little blood we could have brought a jar of it—collected some from you yesterday, if there was as much as you said."

"But why our turtle?"

Why was she making such a fuss? We could get another. There were dozens down by the river. How many chickens had I seen her plucking with Xochitl? How many lambs had we seen Isabel slice through the throats of? And we had *eaten* them. This was just for blood. "Where else are we going to get blood *and* a shell?"

"Why do you want to use his shell?"

"Are you so stupid or just pretending? Like a dish, like a mortar for alchemical elements, like a palette for paints. *Now* do you see?"

She stood suddenly, knocking the boughs away as she straightened up. The sudden light was bright. Her face was a hard mask with thin tracks through the grit beneath her eyes.

I squatted there, exasperated and a little embarrassed now.

"Aren't we just like them?" she said.

"The turtles?"

"The priests."

"What priests?"

"From the desert."

"*What* des—"

What desert.

She was asking me a question.

To this simple question, there must be an answer.

I could say they were not priests but monks. After all, I was very learned. All the correct words came to mind. Desert monks. Hermit, eremite, anchorite. How should I answer?

I set the knife down, carefully. And the turtle.

"We're *not* like them."

It bumped over my toes on its way out of the hut and began working its way through the tangle of *cempasuche* stalks strewn across the threshold. "We're not, Nibble Tooth. *You're* not."

She said nothing.

"Do you think *I* am? After everything I've told you? I wanted to do this for *us*. Something just for us and Ixayac. Weren't we doing this together?" Her eyes skimmed mountains we had looked at hundreds of times. "You're the one who talks about real rituals. I wanted this to be *real* for you. As real as Xochita's."

She was at least looking at me now.

"You have your mother, Amanda."

"Well you have your grandfather."

Abuelito . . . Yes, I had my grandfather. I remembered his face the day of the storm as he handed me Hesiod, the day he sat quietly waiting for me to ask for help with my geometry. And it felt then as if I hadn't seen him, truly talked to him in years.

"Why don't you go down to Xochitl now."

I wasn't angry. I felt the words coming from a long way away, from a desolate place. All my confusion and resentment and hurt and envy were a heaviness pulling, sagging down in me, at my guts and lungs and heart.

"Go on. I'll stay for a while. No. I want to. Be by myself, for a little while. Don't worry. Two palms," I said, and smiled weakly. It felt as if my lips were sliding off my face. And the truth was, she looked as I felt. Stricken. My twin. Her face pale as my white heart.

I slipped my shift back over my head while she dressed, then went with her to the edge of the bench and the holds. We stood a minute looking out over the city on the lake.

As I watched from above she started silently down, then hesitated at the bottom. She looked up. "Ixpetz. I'm so sorry." She said it too quietly to hear, but I could tell from her lips, from her chin, its edges crumpled like a leaf.

When I was sure she'd really gone I slipped the satchel strap over my shoulder and made my way to the upper bench. My limbs were so weak with trembling I was afraid I might slip. I sat for a while in the mist beside the water jet. I spread the contents of my satchel out. The cornflowers and agave strips for crowns. The *Metamorphoses*, green ribbons sprouting out of Proverbs.

I watched the falcons returning after another hunt. This marvel of falcon flight, such slender, trembling wings were these, to marshal the wildest legions of the air, to plummet as each wing folds itself as neatly as a letter. I listened to their voices, for what they might tell, but they had nothing to say that I could ever decipher. Through what mysteries had Egypt made the falcon the god of silence? Who was this child of Isis, and what mysteries did its silence hold, this speaker of such wild speech? Did the truth dwell in the pauses between its cries, as with the trout in the pool? Or between these echoes reverberating now—like blows from a shield—off rock and water? And what was the exultation in that throat and those wings but the talent of flight that resolves itself like a target in the archer's eye?

I wanted to run, to call after Amanda, but to say what?—that they cry after the knowledge of it, with the sudden wild joy of it, this talent in their wings. To know at last what those great bows are shaped for. *In vain the nets are spread for them*, before their sight, in those clear eyes. To have found the talent that will not betray them, never to surrender it again, and know to what high places they are bound.

I had wanted visions, I had wanted us to pant on jimsonweed like water dogs, like walking fish—for us to lie gasping on the bank, and wake as tigers—I had wanted to see into everything, all the mysteries and silences. But now something had slid, something had smashed. We hadn't stopped the Nile together, but we had stopped the running. I believe I already sensed this but refused to see the import of what I'd done. I spent the next month, then the next years explaining it away, why the year of running had stopped. And each time I did this, it felt a little worse. I had scratched the jade.

LIBRARY

All the way down from Ixayac, I thought of Abuelo, how badly I needed to hear his voice, to feel his big knobbly hand on my shoulder, his forehead against mine. Just to talk, as we used to, and to ask him to help me to understand friendship, and how and if and why it must end; to help me know my talent and my destiny, for I had come to know that they were not separate, these riddles and my life. While my life was rich and I had discovered a lot, if only I knew more, looked harder, opened my eyes still wider, I might yet see the wonder of secret meanings woven into everything, every word and gesture. This was Pandora, this was the universal gift.

I came in through the main portal. At the end of the passageway into the courtyard my steps faltered, stopped. The black mastiff crouched before the library door. His baleful yellow eyes fastened onto mine as I stepped over him. I could feel his breath on my ankles as I stopped short of the doorway and leaned in to call to Abuelo. Seeing the dog should have served as warning. I was caught completely off guard.

Standing behind Grandfather's chair and stooped indulgently to read what Abuelo was writing at his desk was lance-captain Diego Ruiz Lozano. Casually he turned—both of them turned—at my call. His face was utterly bare of the slightest guilt or gloating. Abuelo's face, though, fell, as he read the hurt and shock in mine.

Who was this popinjay in uniform, that he should stand in that library as if born to it, when I had only stopped at its threshold like a church beggar? I had read half the books *in* there. Abuelo opened his mouth to speak. Stepping back I turned, trod upon the mastiff's paw—a yelp, a bark of fury, Diego roaring at the dog—Abuelo calling *Angel, wait—*

My satchel thudded to the ground. I ran through the courtyard, past the well, the firepit, to my room, stopped at the door—turned back and ran furiously up the watchtower steps. And then I had nowhere left to run. I was trapped. Trapped by these mountains, this tower, trapped by this place. I turned away. My eyes went past the threads of smoke rising over the red roofs of the town, past the vegetable plots to the west—dust hanging like a shower of gold in the sun—past the orchards to the north—and finding peace in none of it. I collapsed sobbing fury in the shadow of the wall.

A few minutes or an hour passed, and hearing him labouring wheezily up the steps I dried my cheeks on my sleeve. Quietly he set the green rabbit satchel next to me on the yoke of the cannon carriage and leaned awkwardly between one wheel and the barrel to catch his breath.

"Angelina, I am sorry about this," he began. "A painful moment. For both of us. . . ." He seemed at a loss, and to see him struggle to apologize, I felt worse than ever. Because *I* should be the one.

"Abuelo, no—how could I blame you for wanting company?—but *Diego.*" He held up a hand to stop me. Maybe he would have said, then, exactly why the moment was particularly painful for him: for what Diego had been watching him sign was a promissory note for a hundred pesos. But I didn't let Abuelo finish. It was all tumbling out of me now in a rush. Not directly about Ixayac but about turtles and trout, about the falcons and how it felt to watch and hear them call. At first he was mystified, then stood, his hands hanging down helplessly, as I mumbled and rambled on about Amanda and friendship, about my selfishness and all my fury at the riddles I could never quite solve.

Did he see? But no, how could anybody understand any of it. Or me. Or my fears that I might do something truly terrible one day. His frown uncreased at this and he opened wide his arms. He patted my back as I cried against his belly for a while, blotching his shirt and the lacings of his doublet. Even then I did not think of what had happened at Ixayac as anything more than a horrible failure.

"How odd," Abuelo said, "that you should be speaking to me of falcons." He pulled me up to sit on the warm cannon barrel next to him.

"Did you know that in Andalusía hunting hawks were a kind of universal madness when I was your age? It was . . . either 1599 or 1600 . . . *y esas malditas escopetas*[†] had not yet ruined the hunting. In the streets of the towns anyone of substance had a hawk on his wrist—or hers. The Moors were the greatest masters, in hawking as in so many matters. Yes exactly, Angelina, in mathematics, too. Once on the banks of the Guadalquivir I held a gyrfalcon on my wrist. *Y te lo juro, Angel,* the power in that bird's talons could have crushed my arm. It came into my mind then that I had only to remove its leather hood to have it carry me—as if unfurling a sail—off across the Gulf, right over Cadiz, and home to Tangiers. For this was a falcon of *Africa.* What a moment that was. Of

[†]'these damnable fowling pieces'— shotguns

course a gyrfalcon was not for children, or even commoners. In many countries it was then an offence for anyone less than a king to own one. And if a child might possess nothing more than a kestrel, what bird, do you think, was exclusive to an emperor?

"An eagle?"

"An eagle—*exacto*. Or a vulture, though I know of no emperor who kept a vulture. But for hunting there is nothing like a falcon. Marco Polo's friend the Emperor of Cathay never went on a hunt with fewer than *ten thousand falconers*. What do you think of that?" he said, giving my knee a jocular tap. "Eh? Well yes, as you say . . . I've always thought ten thousand a lot myself. But you know, Pope Leo[†] was just as mad for falcons, as was only natural for one of his noble ancestry. And during his time, it is said, bishops all across Christendom wrote countless letters of admonishment: nuns were not to disrupt Mass—or come to confession either—with their falcons and bells. Letters uniformly ignored, for the ladies knew perfectly well that no mere bishop would stand against the Pope on this subject. Nun-falconers, Angelina. Imagine that!"

His arm around my shoulders, we sat silently for a moment watching the sun slump behind the hills, scanning the sky with the eyes of hawks. "And yours, Juanita, what kind were they, these five?" I didn't know what kind. I supposed there were a lot?

"A lot?—all *kinds*. Lanners, gyrfalcons, peregrines. And merlins—very game for their size. I have heard of them attacking even herons. There was a book . . . *Dios mio*, I'd almost forgotten. *El libro de la caza*. . . . The favourite book of all my boyhood after that day on the riverbank. Don Pedro López de Ayala wrote it out in a Lisbon prison after the fiasco at Aljubarrota. His and King Frederick's were the two greatest masterpieces ever drafted on the art of the falconers."

He glanced at me to see if the topic of books might still be a painful one, then rose stiffly to his feet, putting a hand to the small of his back. "And how is it, I ask myself, that I have neither of them now? Then you could have found for me an engraving, shown me these falcons of yours. You know, Angel, you were right after all. It is high time I made a little trip to Mexico City."

My stomach dropped. No, no, he assured me, he'd been meaning to go for some time, but I couldn't persuade myself that he was not going just for me. I felt the gentle yoke of his arm across my shoulders. . . . *Not now.* To be apart from him was the last thing I wanted. Not even at the

[†]Leo X, second son of Lorenzo de Medici

thought of him pulling into the courtyard with a whole wagonload of books. This grand notion only came briefly to me the next morning anyway, as I watched the wagon my grandfather drove disappearing up the road. For the first in all the times I had watched him leave, he was not on horseback.

What I was thinking now was *war*. Now—with Abuelo away. If a preening varlet in *charreteras*[†]—who I felt sure had hardly finished a book in his life—could just stroll into our library, now was very much the time. Grandfather would not be here to see me at my worst and be ashamed for me. Once I hit upon my strategy, I steeled myself to act very badly indeed.

[† epaulettes]

Our perennial dinner guest was not remotely like my father, had none of the qualities I might envy him on my father's part. Neither vital nor mysterious, not noble, nor in any discernible way intelligent. So it had not been long before I was back reading at the table. Isabel gave no sign of minding. It was not that she had grown so very flexible in her ideas of etiquette, however; it was that he was no longer quite a guest. He sat on my right, while on my left Abuelo would sit hunched at what I thought of as the head of the table. Very occasionally my grandfather might speak with Diego on some military question, rumours of a disturbance or unrest at one end of the territory or other. The lance-captain replied sparingly, as though invested with a chaste secret, or with what struck not just me but Abuelo too, I suspected, as an affectation of modesty.

Once Abuelo left for Mexico hostilities got underway. At supper Josefa fairly glistened in Diego's company, as she had ever since their return from Chalco—she and María both, like porcelain, though I had not yet found out why, eyes glazed, they so brightly basked in our guest's *proximidad varonil*,[†] in the radiant kiln of his smile. At least his teeth were straight. And he did have a thick head of wavy hair, almost black. The beard was of a rich oily black like a Moor's. I knew little of men's grooming, but those sweeping moustaches had always seemed not so much fashionable as the very locus of his vanity. Then there was the dashing uniform my sisters made so much of. Did no one notice him spilling food on it? Compared to the designs of Jacobi Topf, what a paltry thing that uniform was—all cloth, clusters and buttons. Less like a fighting soldier's armour than a court juggler's motley. As different as a pauldron was from an epaulette. And he may very well have danced

[† proximate virility]

splendidly, as Josefa insisted, but I'd have liked Amanda's opinion before conceding even that.

Tonight for *el plato principal* was a fiery *manchamanteles*.† Stew green chillies for a full two days. Mix with roasted sesame seeds. Grind in mortar. Fry with chicken, sliced banana, apple, sweet potato.

Season as necessary.

Not for the first time I watched our parlour warrior displaying now the most sweetly piquant delicacy of constitution: sinuses and pores that fairly gushed at the slightest spiciness—making, to be sure, the stores accumulating there in the pilose pantry of his upper lip all the more savoury, despite all the hapless daubing and wiping of his overmatched napkin.

Isabel had known I was up to something from the instant I took up my station—without a book—next to Diego. And as I started in, those huge black eyes fixed me with such a look, as I addressed our military attachment with the first words I had ever spoken to him other than in answer to a direct question. What did he think of our little library? Surely in his travels he had seen much finer. Did he find anything in there he liked yesterday, had he flipped perhaps through a book or two? What were his own favourites and beloved authors? Novels of adventure, I guessed, as was only natural for a gentleman of action, but surely too the epics of chivalry, the exploits of the great knights, must fairly course through his veins—El Cid, Orlando. Why, he must be able to recite whole reams by heart as easily as breathing. On a day, that is, when his nostrils were less burdened. His martial intelligence could no doubt call upon vast stores of verses with which to inspire his men before a campaign. Like this one, wasn't it fine?

> When to gather in the taxes went forth the Campeador,
> Many rich goods he garnered, but he only kept the best.
> Therefore this accusation against him was addressed.
> And now two mighty coffers full of pure gold hath he.
> Why he lost the King's favor a man may lightly see.
> He has left his halls and houses, his meadow and his field,
> And the chests he cannot bring you lest he should stand revealed.[9]

How did the next stanza go again, don Diego? No, but surely the simple soldier was only being modest. Even Cortés's captains had time for literature, and they actually fought real battles, faced constant, cruel, relentless death. And hadn't the odds against them been tremendous? To take the battlefield today must be so disappointing, against a foe so reduced—diseased, defenceless, starved. . . .

Exasperated to see me acting up at supper, Josefa came into my room afterwards with the marvellous news. Our mother was *pregnant* again. We would have a new brother or sister. They had known for ages already.

The next night, seeing that Isabel had said nothing so far, I felt my own valour fairly soaring, and with it my volubility. How could I fail?— I fought on the side of right. As Saint Teresa herself had once said, God moves even in cooking pots. And from there to our table through the transubstantiations of spinach purée, *pollas Portuguesas*, rice tortes, *clemole de Oaxaca, turco de maíz* . . .

After heaping my plate with food, I had not so much as touched the cutlery, so busy was I with chattering at our guest while maintaining a commanding view of the terrain. I sat in a superb position to inventory the contents of his moustaches, accumulating as he ate. Even had this last observation not come to me quite so vividly, I would not have been tempted to touch my food. The hungers of my body were as nothing compared to those of my mind. And yet I cannot say my thoughts ran yet to victory: rather, to the image of my dying unflinchingly in the attempt. Unlike my sisters, I had never seen our mother pregnant; but over these past few days and particularly since last night I'd divined something at once frightening and thrilling in her eyes. Something hooded and veiled, yet serene—the brooding of some great magic. But no, I told myself, this was only the mystery of life growing within her, and an everyday sort of magic that was.

Over the next few hours I found myself casting about for words more adequate to express the new sensations those eyes provoked. Naturally she was still annihilatingly beautiful, her eyes lustrous and black, enormous. But now there was something in the relentlessness of her focus, something pitiless. I saw a lioness stalking belly to ground, painfully, her milk pooling angrily in the dust . . . but no, hysteria would not do. Composing lines in my head as I watched her, caricature was what I reached for—some disarming conceit on architecture. Instead, what came crowding in were more like verses of incantation, propitiatory—a counterspell.

> Her tresses chestnut freshets;
> her front a banner's vellum
> scroll
> on capitals of temple columns;
> her brows an ogee archer's unstrung
> bows;
> the aquaductile nose:
> to rule and compass a triumph of compliance—
> a rose bulb on a seraph's wings declining;
>   while panther jaws (tabby's chin)
> gape like Night's own portals
> at her smile's pure radiance.
> But those two black moons in their orbits,
> scattering sable shards and glints—
> are they obsidian
> or flint?[10]

In such desperate fashion did I screw up my courage, and so it went for the next few nights as I waged my crusade against the Infidel.

Through it all Diego nodded, sweated, stanched his nostrils, smiled and took more roast chicken, nodded bemusedly as my contempt grew. Just as I thought. Here was nothing but an opportunist, thick as pudding, and plodding and utterly without pride. It went on until even I began to pity him. With Grandfather there, I could not have done it. On the eve of Abuelo's return, Isabel put an end to it.

"All right, Inés."

"All right what, Mother?"

"You *know* what." I did know to heed the warning in that tone. "But you'll have the courtesy to ask him first."

Ask Grandfather's permission, to enter *our* library?—it was the merest formality. It was over. It had been so easy. At first I was surprised that she hadn't intervened, if only to spare our guest. I had beaten him. But by now I knew my great ally had been neither valour nor righteousness but splendid timing. I had nature on my side, and Isabel had weightier concerns.

Within hours I would see by how much I had underestimated him. In my sisters' eyes now he would be nobler than ever. They would gaze upon him with something less like hunger than tenderness. As for our mother, from that night forward she stopped asking him to leave her bed before dawn. Before I dismissed it, the idea came that she'd been sending him back to the garrison, just perhaps, to spare not Abuelo's feelings but my own.

As far as I could tell, Diego never slept in town again.

Here, then, was a better strategist and actor, a mercenary more disciplined, than I had given him credit for. Never letting himself be angered, remaining to all appearances confused, too vain and dim to be anything but despised and dismissed by me.

I had worried only about my keys to the library, rather than his to our gates. I had talked loosely of war, but what I had won was only a skirmish.

What's more, I was to discover that he'd fooled not just our mother and my sisters, not just me, but somehow Abuelo, too. For in a manoeuvre worthy of *los contratistas milaneses,*[†] he'd persuaded my grandfather to accept a loan. Though I would not know it for some time yet, this had been the very business they were concluding when I first stumbled upon them in the library. I never found out precisely how he managed it. Would it have been a gesture of restitution for leaving—or rather not leaving—Abuelo's daughter with child without marrying her? Whatever the stratagem, he must, with the most superb delicacy, have left the merest suggestion in the air. . . .

[†]the condottieri of Milan; 'contractors,' soldiers of fortune

So it was not, no, the poetry of El Cid that coursed through his veins but the icy blood of the Sforzas. Here was the best investment a hundred pesos ever returned.

When Grandfather returned home he took the news of our great good fortune with admirable calm. I'd been looking out for him from the watchtower for hours. At a dead run I cut across the bean fields to meet him halfway up the track from the main road. He had brought the wagon back empty. Abuelo reined in the horses right there in the road and retrieved a single book from his *carpeta*.

"Here it is, Angel. *El libro de la caza de las aves.* . . . Now we shall find out about those falcons of yours."

But did he think I had run to him only for this?

Looking anxiously into my face he went on. "I mentioned it was written in prison, did I not?" Now he seemed to think my expression one of disappointment. Hastily I accepted the book he'd been holding out to me. "But did I remember to tell you that our author was also a kinsman of *los Manriques?* Queen Isabela's noblest defenders—the poet and his father? The founder of the Order of Santiago? You've not forgotten. . . ."

The beautiful verses in the mouldering book he had asked me to read for him last year. No I hadn't forgotten. And I was not disappointed; no, I was grateful for his safe return, but puzzled, and yet could find no way to frame the question without seeming to complain. All that way for one book? Why take the wagon, then?

Naturally we had a special dinner to celebrate Abuelo's homecoming. There was a beet and apple cordial to drink, and red wine for Diego and my grandfather. Even María had a little glass. As we sipped and dabbled at a *sopa de ajo,* our mother smiled and chatted easily with my sisters and Diego, while equally I avoided glancing at the moistening tip of his nose. There was such an air of occasion I was half expecting her to announce her condition to all, although it was ridiculous: this was not at all the way to break such news to one's own father. And yet it seemed suddenly mean and unfair that Grandfather should be the last to know. . . .

In fact, I had been the last to know. He had been the first she'd told. It had prompted his trip. Abuelo had gone to talk to Uncle Juan about my one day soon coming to Mexico.

After Amanda had cleared the soup bowls, Isabel encouraged Abuelo to tell us of his journey, which he did with surprising economy. Returned from such excursions in the past, he had treated us to accounts of hair-raising encounters with highwaymen and wild beasts never before seen outside of Africa, and to rousing denunciations of the grasping churchmen from whom we leased the hacienda. Tonight he mumbled only that it had gone well. Taking in his weariness, Mother asked gently for simpler news, of Aunt María and her husband; and as Isabel waited for a reply, the black eyes I had lately been composing apotropaic verses upon glanced an instant into mine. Just then Amanda came in with less than her usual grace as she strained under the weight of a great china platter almost her armspan wide.

I had managed to avoid *her* eyes for days now. I hadn't played—had hardly spoken with her since the disaster at Ixayac. If I had looked at her now I might have seen *she* was the one who thought she'd done something wrong up there, that she had let me down somehow, or hurt me.

Nor did I see that she had followed my lead and stopped eating too, just as I had while Abuelo was away, as evidence of my seriousness. It was a gesture Amanda had read instantly and answered in kind, in the language she understood better than anyone . . . and so much better than I, who took so long to read her reply.

And how like Amanda to speak as she spoke to me now.

Under a sprinkling of black olives and pine nuts, raisins and *chile chipotles* were two enormous trout, grilled whole and entirely filling the platter. One trout lay on its side, the other on its belly—they must have weighed five *libras*† each. They could only have come from one place, one way. And indeed the platter had been placed before me and turned to show the wound in each trout's side, where the spear had gone through.

†1 'libra' = 1 lb.

How could I avoid her eyes now? I couldn't, but for an instant I still tried, dreading what I might find there—triumph, vindication, scorn? Instead I found what looked like exhaustion, like Abuelo, as if she had carried that platter all the way from Mexico. And then she was gone.

The morning after my grandfather's return I was up early, and it was back to the watchtower I went now. Not to watch the sunrise, as Amanda and I had used to, but to keep an eye on Abuelo's room for the first signs of stirring. It took *hours* for him to wash up for breakfast then shuffle back after it from the dining room. By then I was freezing even under the heavy wool blankets I had dragged off my bed.

Beside the well a *pastilla*† of ice sealed the full bucket over, as if with wax. A light frost glittered on the slate flagstones. Grandfather rocked his way over them unsteadily, cautiously, as if his soles hurt. Heedless, I raced down the steps and across the courtyard after him.

†lozenge, troche

I caught up as he reached the library door. He looked surprised to see me—was he teasing or had he really forgotten? Then I noticed that despite the cold, the cloak he wore was not his heaviest but the formal one. And from the gentle smile spreading across that big face I felt sure he'd remembered all along.

"*Si la damisela sonriente* would do me the honour. . . ." He moved aside, and with a little bow invited me in ahead of him.

I stepped across that threshold for the first time. I couldn't help glancing down—half afraid that whatever force had prevented me all this while might even now reach out to trip me up.

And then I was inside.

He did not follow right away. Feeling him watching, I walked in a fashion I hoped sedate straight down the narrow aisle I had probed ten thousand times with my eyes. Right to the end, to the huge, broad desk where it sat edged in sunlight beneath the window. Beyond the bars I could see the mountaintops, but I had to stand on tiptoe now to see the roofs of the sheds above the window ledge.

According to my calculations—and depending on the thickness of the books, their arrangement and the height of the shelves, which after all ran almost to the ceiling—there just had to be space for three, perhaps four thousand volumes. I was sure I had read part or all of almost fifteen hundred books. So as I turned now from that first aisle—the only one I had seen all the way to the end of, no matter how I'd craned and stretched and crouched—I was nearly strangling in the anticipation of making *two or three thousand* new friends. Whom might I find at this next turn, what great teacher stood ready to meet me in the very next aisle?

It was the coolness in the room that struck me, as if the books still stored the night's chill within their covers. Then I noticed the smells, all familiar, and in a familiar combination, but until now never anything but faint. Leather, most of all, and glue, the mustiness of mildew and dust, tobacco from the pouch on the desk, the wool of Abuelo's cloak . . . together it was these that had smelled to me once like fresh dough rising in an oven.

I went down the next row. I ran a finger through the dust thick on the shelves—and along leather spines and over stamped titles, tapping hello to old friends. Though I could discern no particular system or order, a surprising number in these first rows were familiar.

All together, it was a lot of books. And yet as I crept along the aisles there could be no doubt: I had over-estimated. Gaps of varying sizes separated clusters of books. Not a single shelf was tightly filled. Towards the back on the north side, closest to the kitchen, some of the upper shelves were bare or with just a book or two at each end of a row. The idea of a theatrical set came to mind. Had there been more books once, perhaps while we were still in Nepantla? Or was it possible that in the years since, during each trip to Mexico, he had been taking more books away than he'd brought new ones back? Lost in thought I began to close the circuit of the room, coming back along the west wall, on whose outer side I had sat, so many times, beneath the arcades at the little table under the window. How curious the sensation to be standing at that window now, not peering furtively in but gazing out, at the Hammock of the Sacred Nap slung between the columns. As my eyes wandered out into the sunlit courtyard beyond, I tried not to think too much about what I might be feeling.

In the far corner was an armchair whose existence I should have guessed at before this. The little chess set, on this side of it, I had seen many times through the window.

I had read almost all of the books. I hadn't three hundred left.

After a moment I became aware of Abuelo at his desk sitting over an open book and was glad he hadn't been watching my face. I came up the aisle behind him and a little to one side. I was struck for the first time by his frailty. He was not much taller than Isabel now. From the front, his face was full and round, though no longer so brown, a little yellowed even. The bristling mane, once red-brown, was almost pure white, with just traces of cinnamon. In profile, his head if anything looked heavier— the heavy jowls and loose folds swung under his chin like a bull's. At the dinner table his dewlap hung like a small bib as he frowned over the slippery quarry on his plate. But from the back, his neck was frail as a stalk holding up the great head of a sunflower.

He turned in his chair and smiled as I drew near. "Welcome, Angelina," he said, holding out his hand, "I hope we have not left it too long. . . ."

I took his trembling hand between mine—resting my left in his palm, supporting both with my right as if to cradle a sprain. It was only as I opened my mouth to reply that I caught sight of something on the ceiling.

The construction was the same as elsewhere in the house: pitch-blackened oak rafters the width of my hand and spaced a little less than a *vara* apart. Perpendicular to these and cutting the room into three were two massive transverse beams propped on rough-hewn pillars as thick as my waist. Over the desk the rafters formed panels, a triptych, and spanning it—crudely painted, though skillfully drafted—there floated a host of angels. Mouth agape, head tipped back on the hinge of my jaw I just stood there staring as Abuelo proudly pointed out to me the angelic choirs, fashioned from jewels as man was from clay.

"Just as the genii are," he added, his eyes glowing, "from a fire of gemstones. Or so say the Moors." Craning up as he was, the loose dewlap drew almost taut, like the bib of a pelican bolting a fish.

There hovered the archangels Gabriel, the messenger, and Uriel, God's fire. Cherubs, seraphs—there in all their celestial orders, the thrones and principalities, the virtues and powers—all the angels in their seven choirs. Here, just beyond my outstretched arm, was a thing I'd never dreamt of: my grandfather loved angels, the sight, the very thought of them.

I was willing to admit there was much I didn't know about him, but his love of angels had been here all along—so close, just out of sight. How fine it was to see him excited again, to be there with him—*in*, not just looking in—standing together beneath the nine celestial orders. Silently I thanked each one for their heavenly intervention in conveying me here at last.

What he told me next was if anything a greater surprise. My mother had drawn these for him, when she was almost exactly my age.

"When she had finished it for me," he said, "she never came in again. Our classes of reading were over." Not long after, she stopped sketching too.

 For the next few days I was in the library at first light, anxious that no one intercept me, anxious, perhaps, not to see the image of Amanda standing at my bedside, her brown eyes brimming with accusation.

First I lit the lamp above his desk, then lit a lantern and went along ranks still in darkness shifting books, shifting shadows, from shelf to shelf. Piled on the left of the desk were the four titles he was working through. Jumbled over the other side were, he said with a shrug of excuse, the dozen or so he hadn't gotten to reshelving. But reshelve them where? If there was a system, he'd been quite at a loss to explain it, and so he consented to a minor tidying up—I wouldn't disturb him, would do whatever I could before he was even awake.

But as the work proceeded, he began grumbling at the sudden descent of a celestial order fanning now in ever-wider spirals from his desk. By way of reassurance I decided to recite the entire index of everything I'd reshelved so far—where I'd put each volume and why—as he sat dazed beneath the angels, his chair backed against the wall. After a minute of this he raised his hands. "If I need something—"

"Anything at all, Abuelito. I'll fetch it right away."

I collected all the books I had left to read and put them alone on three bare shelves at the far end of the room. One hundred seventy-four in all.

I would have to make them last. And no more skipping chapters—I would read everything, cover to cover, and go back over all the ones I had left unfinished.

In my eagerness to share our library I found myself, during Abuelo's naps, dipping into the books he was reading too. I had the idea of teasing him, by sketching things—objects, people, towns—mentioned in the first few pages beyond his bookmarks, where I then inserted the sketches for him to find. Into a work on the hydrology and drainage works in Mexico City, I slipped the picture of an aqueduct and a good likeness of Abuelo at the top standing next to me, each of us holding a mattock. In another book, an account of Magellan's explorations, I hid a simple map of Tierra del Fuego: at the tip, mountains and fog, and Abuelo and I dressed as tars, waving banners and holding up oars. And then there was a report by an early friar in America, and in that one was a drawing of the horse—rendered as a two-headed deer—that the Mexica spies had drawn for Moctezuma. I turned ahead a page or two and slipped my own rendering in for Abuelo to admire.

Much of the morning my grandfather would spend softly dozing in the armchair, or nodding over his desk . . . under his neck the folds and fine creases filling like a small bellows finely ribbed with whalebone. When after a week Abuelo still hadn't said anything, I began to wonder if he was reading at all.

Then one morning as I sat quietly in the armchair in the corner, a book in my lap, my elbows straight out in order to reach the armrests, a great roar burst from the general direction of the desk.

"Now she reads my *books!*"

I giggled nervously, no longer quite sure of my joke. "Juana Inés, come here—*¡ahorita mismo!*" Not Angelina, not even Angel. . . . As I edged toward him he turned—chin tucked, neck ruffed like an ancient grouse in display.

I thought he might really be furious.

Finally I saw the smile in his eyes. "You shelve my books, only *you* know where. Now you read them, what's next for me . . . examinations?"

Indispensable at last.

And so the rest of our mornings together passed. Eventually I returned to Reverend Kircher's Egyptian Oedipus and only with regret came to the end. For a long while I sat with the book in my lap. With a fingertip I traced the colophon: it presented an engraving of Harpocrates, the Greek

Horus, holding a finger to his lips. Was he saying, I wondered, that there were mysteries that went beyond speech, or else secrets that should not be spoken?

As for our afternoons they passed once again as they'd used to, *Abuelito* snoring away in the hammock while I worked at the table outside. Waking usually with a snort, he would clamber down from the hammock with little grunts and sighs, and we would sit talking things over until dinner. We spoke of the arts of falconry and armoury, of knights and wars and crusades. We consulted on the case of poor King Frederick II . . . it was very sad. A man utterly obsessed. Such was his passion for falconry he once abandoned a battle—during a *Crusade,* a siege of Jerusalem, no less; he simply left the field to go hawking. Abuelo thought probably he had captured some great falconer or other among the Saracens and was determined to learn his secrets before fate, Allah or God could cheat Frederick of his prize. How could one fail to feel a certain empathy, even kinship, for such an unfortunate? And as we talked of the Holy Land, Abuelo remembered the Pharaohs, who had been such keen hawkers they were often embalmed with their best falcons. . . . Egypt again, whether I looked for it or not. If all roads led to Rome, they led there through Egypt.

From the little table I looked through the window into our library. This was just the beginning of the great store Abuelo and I would one day have. *Here* would be my place of visions—*mi claustro,*[†] my magician's cave. Not Ixayac. Here I would build up a collection worthy of the *studiolo* of a princess. So much more than the cell on the hill in far off Nepantla, this felt like the place I had been born to, and wrenched from.[II] In here, I would find the missing part of me.

I hardly saw Amanda in that time, aside from at supper, and I had no answer for the platter of trout. From inside the library, when I thought of Ixayac, I thought only of the maddening riddles I could not solve and all the changes Amanda never wanted to hear of. But being here in the library was a change, too, wasn't it? A wonderful one. In the teachings of Thrice-Great Hermes, it said the acolyte's frustrations were to grow to such a violent pitch that he became *as a stranger to the world*—as surely mine had, but if things had gone slightly awry up at Ixayac, maybe it was for trying to say something that shouldn't be said. Maybe certain riddles were solved alone. Which is why I didn't really want to talk to Amanda right now. Or no, I told myself next, I had simply tried to fly too soon,

[†]in Spanish either 'cloister' or 'womb'

before I'd understood the simpler lessons all around me. Could it be said any better than Hypatia herself had?

Life is an unfoldment, and the further we travel the more truth we can comprehend. To understand the things that are at our door is the best preparation for understanding those that lie beyond.

When I had found wisdom in instruction, when I had solved the equations and deciphered the hermetic messages written in the heavens in living gemfire, when I had found at last my talent—then I would be ready to fly, too.

Or no . . . in searching for a magic ceremony I'd let myself forget the distinction Paracelsus made between magician and *magus,* for the true magus concerns himself not with the supernatural but with natural forces as yet unseen or misapprehended. Here was the work of discovery going on all over Europe, the great work I could be part of.

And yet this was also much like the great life and work Hypatia had led. Neither then nor later could I ever quite let go of the riddles in her death, in its savagery, in her nakedness and defilement.

FIRE-BOW

nce, we had sat under the stars, we two, through every phase of the moon: the snowfields above the court-yard glimmering in starlight or moonlight, or tower-ing blind in the darkness of new moons; and there Abuelito would spin out stories of the wilderness and of discovery, lost empires and lost knowledge, cities of gold and white cities of the sun. From the fire, sparks started up like fire-flies—and one night there were real fireflies—as we prodded the embers with our traveller's sticks. In that enchantment of lights hovering and blinking all about us, Abuelo told me he had seen our volcano answer one night with its own crimson shower the swarms of shooting stars falling all that August night, firefly-green, through the sky.

With the years, such flights of poetry from him had grown rarer, the evenings shorter, the silences longer. During the past year I had hardly spent any time by the fire. There were hardly any new stories, which wouldn't have been quite so bad if so much repetition had kept polish-ing the old ones. Instead, I heard him speaking now in a tired sort of blur, often trailing off. . . . Not only would he forget the details, he'd for-get he'd been talking at all. Many nights he stayed out there alone. But sometimes Josefa or María, or even our mother, would go out to sit with him for a little. Afterwards, he would go back to the library. When I got up in the night I could sometimes see the lantern casting its light from above his armchair deep in the corner.

But now the firepit was once again the indispensable end to our day in the library. And it was almost as before. After one of these new evenings together, when the fire had finally burned down, I lurched exhausted to my feet. I hugged him and kissed his dry white hair.

"Good-night, Abuelo."

"It was a good day, was it not?" he said softly, looking up at me. And I remembered. The many times, when I was just a young child, that he had carried me from the firepit and tucked me into bed. If I woke, he would kiss my hair, and ask if it was not just the finest of days. To which I would murmur in answer as I answered now.

"*Sí, Abuelito.* We had a wonderful time. . . ."

I could help him with his stories now since I knew most of them. More confident of finishing them, perhaps, he made more of an effort. And at last I began to sense that to keep the blur in his right eye and the blankness in his cheek from tripping up his tongue, the effort it cost him was not small.

He spoke of such things as the comet that hung like a sword over the hills of Rome for months after Caesar's death. Caesar had ruined the republic with his presumption. I was hoping to hear a word or two about Cleopatra next, but Abuelito wasn't finished with Julius Caesar just yet. "Pontifex Maximus, he appointed himself, Angelina. Infallible high priest, bridge to God! The comet, they called the Soul of Caesar, called it certain proof of his divinity. And a very neat trick it is to establish one's divinity by dying—do you not think? Dictator for Life, indeed."

Other stories, some I'd heard often, he no longer liked to tell. However much I asked about the Mexico of our day—the Royal University, its library, the city's drainage schemes and countless construction scandals— it had become for him an emblem of fallen greatness, of all the chances we, perhaps he, had lost.

But the Mexico of the Triple Alliance he would always happily talk about. Texcoco, Tenochtitlan, Tlacopan. The valley of the three capitals, three kings. Some things I could add to the telling. I knew that unlike the Athenian alliance at the time of Melos, Mexico's never dissolved. It held firm to the final hour. And I knew that Tenochtitlan was the greatest in power, as Texcoco was in learning. In Europe at that time, the only city to compare it with was Florence. Texcoco of the greatest poets, astronomers, historians. Texcoco of the archives, the painted books, the annals. For me, Texcoco was Athens, then Alexandria, and in the end, Florence.

Tenochtitlan was always Rome.

The last time Abuelo spoke of this was the last time we ever talked of the past. Both eyes were alive again that night with an emerald fire. He had just been telling me of his intention, as a young man, to explore to the very tip of *la tierra del fuego,* just to see for himself that the land did not simply trail away into smoke. Now he spoke with a passion I had not seen in so very long, and this night, three stories were new. Three. An unhoped-for bounty.

We had been in the library after dinner and were late lighting the fire. It was an hour or two before moonrise. On a night so clear, the skies above our mountains cannot be called dark at all. The darkness is in the land. Its dark rises up and through that sky of lights in finest tendrils . . . like shoots through the brilliant muslin of a bedding cloth. We walked out of the library together, out from under the arcades, and to move beneath that sky, to arrange the tinder and kindling then strike these tiny kindred sparks under the eyes of such multitudes, we were touched by a shyness . . . as perhaps of newlyweds before a vast and joyous wedding party. Or so it seems, looking back.

As Abuelo drilled sparks into the tinder I blew softly, then, as little pink and tangerine flames licked up, blew myself dizzy. It was like coaxing a flower into bloom. Once it took, I backed up, my bottom seeking out the smooth hollow I liked to sit in. Finding it I sat, facing east toward our mountains. Less trusting of his bottom, Abuelo reached out a tentative hand and settled stiffly into his place.

The first of Grandfather's three tales was about Nezahualcoyotl. FastingCoyote. Emperor of Texcoco and the greatest poet and philosopher of all the Mexica.

Abuelo turned and fixed me with his light green eyes. "This FastingCoyote founded a Council of Music—not just musicians but painters, astronomers, physicians. Poets and historians. This, at the exact moment the Medicis were founding their Academy. Can you imagine if they had known of the other's existence? Here was such a ruler as even Lorenzo the Magnificent would have been honoured to know. Such a synod that would have been!"

There came a time in the Triple Alliance when a particularly brutal general was to take the throne. To block his ascension, FastingCoyote offered to subject his people, the city of Texcoco, to the rule of Tenochtitlan. Forever. "This is the calibre of man we are dealing with, Angelina. A generation before the Conquest, FastingCoyote will give proof of his vision yet again. The leadership of the Mexica is now in the hands of one man, Moctezuma the First. FastingCoyote goes forth from Texcoco to warn him, as the poet's son will one day go to repeat his warning to Moctezuma the Second as Cortés approaches. Do you see, Angel? Disaster was near."

Sparks shot up like molten beads as Grandfather poked at the flames. I had never really seen the boyishness in him. The soft pelican pouch at his neck seemed almost to pout as his chin nodded and wagged at the fire. His thoughts turned to a temple that FastingCoyote had raised, a temple to the Unknown God. My grandfather praised the king's delicate poetry, regretted how many of his writings had been lost when the archives of Texcoco were burned by the friars. Abuelo recited a beautiful fragment in Castilian for me, and I decided to try to put it in Nahuatl again for him. I would ask for Xochitl's help with the translation and tomorrow night recite it. It did not occur to me that she knew it in the original.

> I, Nezahualcoyotl, ask this:
> Is it true one really lives on the earth?
> Not forever on earth,
> only a little while here.
> Though it be jade it falls apart,
> though it be gold it wears away,
> though it be quetzal plumage it is torn asunder.
> Not forever on earth,
> only a little while here.[12]

Abuelo grew quiet for a while. A three-quarter moon rose and shimmered through the plume of Popocatepetl. A few tongues of flame sputtered up. Once clear of the volcano, the moon bathed the courtyard in a creamy radiance. It softened the edges of everything, smoothed the lines and creases away as even our cream of avocado and honey could not do.

As Abuelo tried to tip the unburnt end of a log into the embers, I watched the big-knuckled hands grip and waggle his traveller's staff. From earliest memory my eyes had been drawn to those sausage fingers, and in that soft, milky light I thought of the blankness just below the elephant's eyes where its trunk seems grafted on. The thought seemed to come from such a long way back. . . .

After a while he began to talk of the last great sorcerer, who had no doubt sat at many campfires on this very spot. Now I learned that he had not lived all his life in the mountains. Just before the Conquest, Ocelotl had gone to live in Texcoco and study at the archives, for it was a time of restlessness. Then, great temples of sail were sighted off the coast. Moctezuma II, disturbed by the portents, summoned the seers and historians. But he imprisoned them. Their pronouncements displeased him. Next he summoned the sages and the sorcerers, and Ocelotl first among them.

"We do not know, Angelina, the precise words Ocelotl chose. But from what I have been able to learn of his character, I believe they ran to something like this: 'Lord Speaker, I can dispel certain mysteries for you. The auguries have become ever more evasive and strange because those who brought them were afraid and had no taste for prison. Whatever is coming is rooted in the past, and I have come from Texcoco just as others have in the past to say this: The Speaker has not listened. The levies have become excessive. Tenochtitlan is feared and detested far and wide. And this, for generations. Whatever advantage the Mexica might have gained from fear, we have lost to hatred, for a sufficient hatred overcomes much fear and caution.' And so Ocelotl spoke to an emperor. You know how Moctezuma thanked him for his troubles?"

"He threw him into prison!"

"*Eso, hijita.* As Ocelotl must have expected." Abuelo's smile was less rueful than wry. It was good to share such things. "And as far as I can tell, he was not released until some time after Moctezuma was himself Cortés's prisoner. . . ."

The moon had swung high into the south. The light fell slant on the rock faces and the snowfields, faintly purple now, like the milk in a bowl of *moras.*[†] The sloping cone of the volcano above Grandfather rose pale and featureless, like a tall Bedouin, I thought, in his flowing headdress, or a jinni, its face in shadows of amethyst.

[†]blackberries

The fire had burned down. Sleepy now, I looked up at the sky as I listened, the constellations just visible in the starry profusion. The Great Bear, Gemini . . . the Fire-Bow that Amanda had known how to find for Abuelo in Orion.

Grandfather's third tale too was about Ocelotl. It had to do with the Inquisition and Ocelotl's new friend the Bishop. We spoke of Ocelotl often here—Abuelo and Xochitl both. There was nothing strange in this. As she would say, *Truly his mist has not scattered.* And yet as Abuelo began, something was bothering me.

"The races of Man come and go, Angelina. This I understand. And I have seen enough of the rest of Europe to know no other nation would have done better than Las Casas, Sahagún—and Antonio Vieyra, today. . . ."

No, what bothered me was this: we never all of us spoke together— of Ocelotl or anything else.

"And Lord knows, Angel, an honest man expects no thanks, even from a Bishop. But God, O God, how we lied to them. . . ."

And then I asked, as if it were nothing, a question I had not asked for years.

"Abuelito, what happened between you and Xochita?"

Now that I had startled myself by asking it, I expected him to be angry. He was staring into the ember glow. Drafts played in shadows over the coals. The tip of his traveller's staff lay among them, smoking, motionless.

"Some things are better left unsaid, Juanita. It does not mean we were not friends."

After another moment or two he looked up and turned stiffly to face me. He did not look angry at all. "But it is good you ask about this. I have need of your help."

"With what Abuelo?—anything."

"Her."

"*Xochi?*"

"And Amanda, yes. Your mother is pregnant. . . . You knew."

"Josefa said."

"From now on, it will be harder for Amanda and her mother."

"*De acuerdo, Abuelito.* We'll watch over them *together.*"

At that, his frown eased. He scratched at the ruff under his chin.

"Yes we will. Now do you want to hear about our Ocelotl and his Bishop or not? Good. Well, you remember I once told you Ocelotl had a twin. . . ."

When I awoke, he had one arm still under me and was bending to pull back the sheets. He had not carried me to bed for years and I wouldn't have thought he still could. Moonlight flooded into the room through the doorway. Moonlight spilled under the eaves and in through the window. Pure white now . . . the tint of amethyst was gone, as if a trick of light from the fire. In that milky light his face was rinsed clear and clean of lines, as if the blankness had spread from his sausage finger to an eye, a cheek, finally to fill the room, the moon . . .

My arms were still around his neck. So close above me, the eyes in that big fine head were like opals, black yet clear, like smoke through lantern glass. Reluctantly I let go of him, regretted it. Over my forehead a big hand hovered ever so lightly now as if cupped to shield a candle. He smoothed my hair and kissed it.

His mouth was firm, resolute, an old lion's. The smile was only in his voice.

"Has it not been the finest of days, Angelina?"
Ah, sí, Abuelito. The very finest.
We had the most wonderful time.

I

Recuerde el alma dormida,
avive el seso e despierte
contemplando
cómo se passa la vida,
cómo se viene la muerte
tan callando;
    cuán presto se va el plazer,
cómo, después de acordado,
da dolor;
cómo, a nuestro parescer,
cualquiere tiempo passado
fue mejor.

I

Recall the soul from its sleep
kindle the slumb'ring brain and wake
to contemplate
how life passes by,
how death arrives
so quietly . . .
    How soon pleasure leaves—
how its memory
returns as pain;
how, it seems,
any past time
was better.

II

Pues si vemos lo presente
cómo en un punto s'es ido
e acabado,
si juzgamos sabiamente,
daremos lo non venido
por passado.
    Non se engañe nadi, no,
pensando que ha de durar
lo que espera
más que duró lo que vio,
pues que todo ha de passar
por tal manera.

II

When we see the present,
how in a heartbeat it is finished
and gone,
if we judge wisely
we shall wonder if what is past
has ever come.
    Let no one be deceived, no,
to think what is hoped for
shall last,
any more than what we've seen go,
since all things must pass
so.

JORGE
MANRIQUE

B. Limosneros, trans.

III

Nuestras vidas son los ríos
que van a dar en la mar,
qu'es el morir;
allí van los señoríos
derechos a se acabar
e consumir;
　allí los ríos caudales,
allí los otros medianos
e más chicos,
allegados, son iguales
los que viven por sus manos
e los ricos. . . .

IV

Dexo las invocaciones
de los famosos poetas
y oradores;
non curo de sus ficciones,
que traen yerbas secretas
sus sabores.
　Aquél sólo m'encomiendo,
Aquél sólo invoco yo
de verdad,
que en este mundo viviendo,
el mundo non conoció
su deidad . . .

III

Our lives are rivers
running to the sea
that is death;
there run all our dominions
straight to their end,
to be consumed;
　there, the mightiest streams,
there, the lesser
and small,
all lie together now, equals,
those who live by their hands,
those who command. . . .

IV

Here I let fall the invocations
of the famous poets
and orators;
I am not healed by their fictions,
though they bring secret herbs
strange flavours.
　To this alone do I commend me,
This alone do I invoke,
truly,
that in a world of living,
this world knew not
its deity . . .

manda was the one who brushed the damp earth from my knees and walked me back from the plot in the shady spot where she and I used to read. It was Amanda who sat close beside me at the table in the kitchen as Xochitl did her best to console me without ever quite speaking of him. It was Amanda who, for weeks, waited just inside my room each morning for me to rise, and waited near the library for me to come out again, just to walk me back to my room. Every day she brought each meal there. Was there anything else I needed, was there anything special Xochitl could make for me? Anxious, almost anguished, she wore an expression I saw often during that time but would not recognise, because she was the mirror I did not want to look into.

Diego moved in. My sisters went to live with my aunt in Chalco. I did not think to wonder if they'd asked to go. Yet even with Diego around, there came a time when I could no longer spend all my days alone in the library.

I had been sitting at the desk, a book open before me, staring out the window at the mountains, just as I had sometimes surprised him doing. When caught, he gave such a sheepish little smile. And at last, there it was in my mind, that little smile.

Abuelito, I'll put your books away now. And clear off your desk . . . ? If that will be all right.

The ones jumbled on the right were easier; these he had read. But four, he had not finished. It took a moment to touch them, a little longer to shelve. The last one dropped. Cursing my clumsy hands I bent to pick it up where it lay face down in the aisle, awkwardly folded. A little roof unevenly pitched. A small hawk covering a kill. It was like finding him all over again, turning that book face up. On the stone floor underneath lay a scrap of paper, a crude map. Mountains, sea, two stick figures dressed as tars with oars and banners. A girl and an old man with a sunflower face, waving grandly from Tierra del Fuego.

When I came out that day Amanda was there. It was early evening, the air already cool, the sun behind the hills. Her eyes looked searchingly into mine, her eyes big and full, colt's eyes of softest brown. She came to a decision, drew a little bundle wrapped in sacking from the folds of her *rebozo*.

She had made a doll. Body of hemp, arms of braided wool bound tight with cotton thread. Corncob head, cut cross-wise to make a round sun face. Cornsilk hair, faintly red. I was without a thought in my head but could not stop staring at the doll.

Numbly I asked what this was. She was afraid I did not like it. She said I could take him with me now, wherever I went. I could feel my face working as I tried to find the words. I should have hugged her, held her and never let go.

Just then, Isabel came in from the fields.

She looked so tired and dusty, and so pregnant, a giant egg lumped under her dress, a camel's hump come uncinched and slipped round to her stomach. Huge—hatted booted skirted—she grimaced, wrenching her chin back and forth as she tugged at a knot in the cord of her riding cloak. Hands high, chin high, head cocked to one side, a dangerous exasperation in her black eyes. Seeing us malingering at the library door she barked at Amanda to go help her mother.

Amanda's face went wooden. As she turned for the kitchen I clutched at her arm. Isabel brushed past. I remember shouting back, something about Isabel's touching concern for Xochita all of a sudden. For an instant her gait faltered, but her physical distress must have been such that she could not turn back. I led Amanda into the kitchen by the hand, showed the doll to Xochitl, railed against all my mother's injustices. After a few minutes of this, Xochitl broke in brusquely to tell me not to make such a stew of my chameleons, by which I took her to mean that I made too much of my travails, dressing them up in colours not their own. Even Xochita, now.

 Once the baby was born we started seeing a great deal of Diego, and of Diego's black mastiff. No matter how far up the river we walked or how deep into the woods, the dog found us. It clambered over us excitedly—panting, lolling, trembling—insolent snout, yellow eyes dead, corrupt, breath foul like an animal rotting in the brush. Though the mastiff smirched and pawed and slavered over both of us, it took special interest in Amanda. This was the breed so efficient against the Mexicans during the Conquest—to this in peacetime come the war dogs and warmongers. It could smell a difference between us.

I had never felt a hatred so intense for any living thing, and fury and disgust. It was not a difference of race it smelled, but that Amanda was a woman and I was not. Yet it was not only that it found difference where I wanted there to be none. And it was not that I was shocked. We had lived on ranches all our lives. These things were natural with animals. And this was not natural at all. It followed us with its nose, it followed us as Diego's eyes followed us at home—all of us, my sisters, Amanda, me, even Xochitl. And lo, after a while, on his big pied gelding, handsome Diego would come riding along to liberate us and let himself be gazed upon . . . the glossy hair kinked in the manner we call *chino* and drawn tight into a short pigtail of briars . . . the wide, full lips such as any woman might wish for herself, the thick gleaming brows, the fine pale forehead under the splendid sombrero, the eyes deep-set, a turbulent dark brown, and yet in their darkness a little dull. Dullish knots twisting in smooth white pine.

It was Amanda they watched. Each time he caught up with his dog he waited a little longer before calling him away: bad dog. But once he had, the thing came instantly, and we knew it had not wandered off. It had been sent, like a message. How I detested that animal. Amanda was afraid of it, I was not. And I was not afraid of its master either. Such a striking figure he cut—of the soldier clown, preening varlet in battle dress. Was there nowhere an uprising to put down, did he never go anymore in to the garrison?

He sat at the head of the table, the man of the household now, to whom all its appurtenances and comforts fell. I was not afraid, but then, it was not me he looked upon as property. Protecting her or hating the sight of him in that chair—what played the larger role in what I did next? It occurs to me that I may have hated him for something I had discovered in myself.

What I thought then was that if I had beaten him once, I could again. In one night. I was forgetting for an instant how limited the first victory had been, as I prepared a little parable and concealed it in a snare. Speaking to the dining room in general, I said they would never guess who Amanda and I had seen out in the woods. Diego's head shot up. He glanced down the table at Isabel. I said, though I lied, that Amanda and I had met the woodcutters, the ones from the forest fire last year, and had taken our lunch with them in the woods. A younger one had started to tell a story, but was hushed by an elder. I had, naturally, no idea why.

How frustrating that had been. Something about a bridegroom's promise to the Devil, and a wedding night that ended with an impalement on
a cedar tree.

The nursing blanket halfway down her shoulder, Isabel had been staring into the baby's little fox eyes as it grasped and sucked at its blue-
veined egg, but now she looked up.

In truth, this legend was so well known to everyone in our valley that
any large tree might be called a *wedding tree*. Diego, of course, was not
from our valley. I had come prepared to do more of the work myself, but
he proved all too eager to display his local knowledge now. And displayed, thereby, a good deal more. Isabel warned him that I already knew
his story but he pressed on, oblivious or unable to help himself. Yes, a
landowner, he said, granted enormous riches by Satan, in exchange for
one small promise. I did not ask what it was, making his eagerness to tell
me all the more plain. But Isabel was already watching him closely.

The promise was, he went on, that when the landowner should one
day take a woman to marry, Satan was to . . . *precede* the man on their
wedding night. *To speed the plough, so to speak.*

Saying this, he gave me a wide, slow smile. Such a promise—who
could blame the poor bridegroom for not wanting to follow such an
act . . . ?

Speed the plough.

This was more than I could have hoped for, this was providential,
pure gift. When his voice had quite trailed off to the stoniest silence
around the table, I thanked him for the story and—fair turnabout—
coldly offered the one I had prepared for him and for which he had so
admirably prepared the ground. An old story. Also about a woodcutter.
A man named Erysichthon, who had cut down a grove of oaks sacred
to Cybele.

For this sacrilege she visited upon him a hunger, such a hunger as was
in that country called the Wolf, and in other places the Ox. A hunger so
great and so foul as to make him eat anything, any sort of filth. And so
he did, until he had devoured all the bounty of his lands and bartered all
his wealth and property for the filthiest stuff, since his desperation was
obvious to all who had traded with him. And when he had lost everything to the Wolf, he reached out for his own daughter, who had a great
and precious gift—to change her bodily form, like Thetis who had shifted through so many shapes and yet failed to prevent her own rape. In his

sickness the man saw Fortune smiling upon him now, for thanks to this gift of hers he could offer his daughter—ever fresh and ever new—to every man for miles around.

At some point Amanda had come in to clear the plates. She was standing awkwardly by the table, hesitating over the half-eaten meals. Something in the scene kept her from interrupting to ask if we had finished. I asked Diego if it was not indeed a sad tale thus far. And here was its ending: such was this hunger that the accursed man, panting and slavering like the diseased dog he had become . . . devoured him*self*.

Oh and there was, I remembered, just this last detail. The man's name meant *earth tearer*. So what had his crime really been—did the lance-captain have an opinion? Was it in cutting down something sacred? Or in trying to speed the plough where he shouldn't?

As I finished, I was looking at Amanda. I had meant only to glance meaningfully in her direction, but I could not look at my mother and could not trust myself to look any longer into Diego's eyes. Amanda blushed furiously. All three of us now were looking at her. . . .

The most perfect silence settled over the table, for what felt like an hour. I could hardly breathe. I simply could not believe it had gone better than I had dared dream. I was first to find my voice. Nodding curtly toward his plate I asked if he had quite finished. Amanda would like to clear.

Isabel whisked me out of the room. I could not help thinking she was taking me to the killing floor, which I remembered vividly as the scene of my last great correction. Instead she announced I would be going away just as my sisters had, but to live with her sister in Mexico. *Mexico*—just like that. I told myself I should have humiliated our gallant defender weeks ago.

But in fact everything had already been arranged by my grandfather. Isabel had only been waiting for the moment.

The next morning, dishevelled from a long cold night garrisoned on the rocking chair outside my mother's door, Diego cast about calling for his mastiff, calling to it as he walked stiffly to the portal, calling awhile outside, coming back in and climbing the watchtower to bellow from up there like an unmilked cow. Isabel took over his chair and sat rocking while she nursed. How calmly she sat, and at an hour when she had always been out in the fields.

•

I went into the kitchen. Although Amanda had been mortified to have everyone at the table looking at her the night before, this morning she was all smiles to show me she understood I had been protecting her.

I was bursting to tell her our news, about how hereinafter our lives in Mexico would be like a storybook—but, smiling excitedly into my eyes, she said *she* had a surprise. She led me out through the corn and as we walked she stayed close, lightly touching my arm, brushing my shoulder, and finally took my hand. With the mastiff already outside, I expected it to find us any moment now, here in the tall corn. We threaded our way through the field. As we reached the fence I started again to tell her about what had happened after dinner and how I had been expecting the worst thrashing of my life. Yet now we had the most glorious news, she and I. Rather than asking what it was, she was pointing out a bucket leaking drops of water where it swung from a cedar branch just beyond the fence. I was trying to tell her we had *permission*, we were going to my aunt's in Mexico City at last, maybe even tomorrow—

Who was?

We were.

My first lesson on the world as storybook was long overdue, and yet so slow I still was. The pace of my classes was picking up: two questions she shot back in quick succession, the first, unthinking and innocent, the second, to cover her hurt and embarrassed pride.

Is your mother giving me away?

Am I going as your maid?

A minute ago she had been all smiles, now this bitterest sarcasm, this patient anger one has for a stupid child. Where had all this come from? What on earth had gotten into her? I'll never be your maid, Ixpetz. But Amanda you're *not*. I'll never go there. Why, Amanda, why *not*? Our people only go to that city for one thing—what thing?—and always have. Who says? My mother says. What *thing*?

To die.

I could find nothing to say to this.

So no matter what, I'm better off here, to let him have me, just like Mother when your—

Whole worlds flashed then in her eyes—fury, sadness. Then shame. I could not ever remember her ashamed. What could Amanda ever have to be ashamed of?

What, Amanda—when my *what?* Come back! Finish what you said— come back! She ran up the path through the trees, her white soles lifting like the tails of deer.

I was left standing there. I was left to read her language of signs.

I lowered the pail. Over each other and up the sides, two turtles clambered on a thick wet cloth. Surely not the same two as up at Ixayac. But they were the same size. . . .

A little water still sloshed in the bottom but their backs were already dry. I started back towards the house, the bucket banging away at my calf. I went in through the main portal thinking to get the turtles water from the well.

Xochitl stood just inside the kitchen door, wiping her hands with a kitchen rag. Her dark face seemed oddly youthful through the doorway. The sun lay like purest silver in her hair. Across the courtyard, Diego had the fieldhands lined up like a platoon for inspection. The scene that ensued caused an uproar that ended in Diego storming off for a day or two. The dog was still missing. Diego had roused himself to a towering fury and, until Isabel stopped him, had been bent on extracting a confession from one—any—of the bewildered men.

It was not until after supper that night, a delicious meat sauce of chilli and black chocolate, which Xochitl had served us herself, that I went, feeling strangely light, to have my talk with her. Chocolate had once been a sacred thing, and Xochitl had never cooked with it for us. It was a sign of great favour, though I did not know the reason for it tonight. And the turtles were surely a sign of Amanda's forgiveness for before. Now I would find out what Xochita had been telling her and clear up this misunderstanding about Mexico. I would reassure them both. I would promise to protect Amanda just as I had at dinner the night before. I felt proud. I had kept a promise to Abuelo, who had asked for my help. I was at peace. And I had even solved another riddle, from a previous evening of stunning insights into elliptical and hyperbolic statements during the *manzana* in Amecameca. Neither elliptical nor hyperbolic, the parabolic is not so much a truth as a parallel, such as when the attentions paid to a girl are of the sort only meant for a woman. Part parable, part parody.

Everything was falling into place, as I knew it must. I felt in my bones the time had come for us to find our destinies. . . .

"I said *no*, Ixpetz. That is final."

The kitchen was a shambles of unwashed dishes. Xochitl sat close beside me at the table, which was dusted at one end with corn flour. Insects tapped blindly at the lantern glass. The pantry door was closed, the door into the yard was open. A sallow panel of lamplight fell on the beaten earth pale with starlight. A breeze agitated the blades of the corn leaves . . . an army of spearmen on a night march.

I was so astonished. A flat no, the third. The words clear, the tone unmistakable. I had tried everything. But how could that be? When it really mattered I had always been able to persuade her. She wouldn't even let me go in to talk to Amanda.

"It is not just you she does not want to see. She is angrier at me."

"You?"

"For knowing this day would come."

"But *why* does it have to come, Xochita?"

Whenever I had cried before, cried hard, whether out of shame or heartache or rage, Xochita had always comforted me. Even now I could see she wanted to, but it was as if she couldn't raise her arms. When the scene ran through my mind again later that night it seemed that all the triangles of her face had been pulled out and down, as if a baby were pulling at her cheeks.

"It was not easy at first, Ixpetz, to take you to my breast. . . ."

She averted her face, looked into the empty dining room. Her hands on the table widened slightly—to take her weight as she rose or to keep themselves from slipping into her lap, I couldn't tell.

Helpfully, I asked if it hurt very much to nurse, if nursing me had been as bad as Isabel said. But this only seemed to make things worse. I put an arm about her shoulders, the other hand to her dark forearm, left small, pale prints as I patted her. I asked her not to feel badly. I knew why she could not entrust Amanda to me, because of something I had done.

"No, Ixpetz. It is something I have done. . . ."

She seemed unsure how to begin, was worried about what Abuelo might have been willing or unwilling to tell me. There was something that happened long ago. . . . But I knew all *about* it, the fall from the horse when she was almost ready to have Amanda. And to have turned her hair white almost overnight it must have been unendurably painful. *Of course* she couldn't work in the fields anymore with her hip . . . and though I was anxious to help, I could not help mentioning that surely she did not miss life in the fields so much, any more than I believed she regretted so very much coming to nurse me. And though my mother was sometimes harsh, I thought things would be better now, and Xochitl did not really think a life of fieldwork was for Amanda. Xochitl stopped me with something puzzling.

"But I did not work in the fields, Ixpetz."

She had first met my grandfather in her village. He had ridden up there more than once, interested to learn more about Ocelotl. She asked me something still more puzzling, if I had ever once seen any of her people on a horse. "Spaniards ride horses. We do not."

Then I saw it with perfect clarity. My mind recoiled from the thought. *It was Abuelo's horse.* He would never have forgiven himself—*of course. . . .* Though this was something that happened even to the finest horsemen.

"I always walked back down to the village alone." She could not look at me. "But we were late. The horse was going fast. The light . . ." So clearly then I saw her riding behind him, at dusk, her arms at his waist trying to hold on—with her so pregnant, as Isabel had just been—reaching around that great egg between them to cling to his coat—just as the horse stepped into a *toza* burrow.

Now she was talking about her village, her high standing among the villagers as the *curandero's* daughter, the blood of Ocelotl. Whose mist had not scattered. She had been a healer herself already, and almost a midwife—it was proper that she had never married. Old for a bride, they said, but young for a midwife. The joke had been gentle, and in it their approval. A fish of gold they called her, with pride.

"*Quen tehito. . . .* Can you understand, Ixpetz?"

"Regarded by the people."

"They said this of Pedro. I mean your grandfather." I had never heard her use his name, but who else could she mean? I felt a rush of pride.

"They say it also of your mother. The land is in her heart, the earth."

This, I did not want to hear. Heart of clay, more like it.

"They respect you, Xochita. I could always tell."

Slowly she shook her head. "They do not say fish of gold now, Ixpetz. *Tla alaui, tlapetzcaui in tlalticpac. Quen uel ximimatia in teteocuitlamichi.*"

Things slip, things slide in this world. Fish of gold, what happened to you?

"Did you know Abuelo asked for my help, Xochita?—to look after you and Amanda."

Again a moment of surprise, that I should feel better for trying to comfort her and yet that in trying to comfort, I should seem so to wound her.

Now, I thought, surely now with her face so tender. If I just asked her once more. Why else had she been telling me all this if not to convey her fears for Amanda, and how delicate a thing was destiny? But Amanda and I would be together, we would care for each other.

"For the last time, Ixpetz—No! Will you never open your eyes? Amanda will *never go to that place.*"

The words hung in the air as I fled—out through the dining room and into the courtyard and up the watchtower steps. She had never spoken to me like that. It stayed in my mind all that night.

I sensed it in Xochitl's voice if not her words. The more I thought about it, the more clearly I saw it in her face. She had scratched the jade, had torn the quetzal feather. *Xochita.* Who was wise and strong and good. Whose ancestor was Ocelotl. Even she could do something terrible.

And if she could, I could.

In the quiet of my room the tears came as a relief. So much had happened in the past two days. There was so much about the world I had never found in books. I saw Isabel's face, not gloating, but as if to say she had been telling me this all along.

There began, at about this time, two dreams that have recurred many times. Two nightmares, or perhaps they are one in two parts. A black dog at the killing floor skinned and bloated and swinging from a pole, and Amanda at Ixayac, naked beside the plunge pool. As she slathered our magic cream of honey and avocado all over, her eyes never left mine, never left them as the wasps began to land, never left them until she was furred in gold and they began to sting and sting all over her face, her breasts and thighs that purpled and swelled, her eyes that ran gold. . . .

By morning I was sure I knew what Xochita was telling me. *I had scratched the jade, too.* I had been afraid of this myself, the words had even come into my mind, though I had not truly understood what this could mean. Now it was clear. It *was* why she would not let Amanda go with me. Because Amanda had told her what had happened at Ixayac.

And if Amanda could not come to Mexico with me . . . ?

For eleven-year-olds, things need not be complicated. All reduced to this: what was my perfect gesture to be? How would I answer hers?— all her perfect gifts to me. Isabel was sending me away. Just as she had sent my sisters away. It was to protect them from their willingness, I saw that now. How I wanted to go, but Amanda could not come. How I wanted to stay with her but I could not stay. I did not want to go without her but she could not come. I can't stay, I can't leave.

I had only wanted to solve the riddle.

It was a game. Find the magic recipe to stop time, turn back the Nile, find a destiny in light. I was eleven now—so what would my perfect gesture be? All my great gifts were as nothing if they could not save Amanda now. Solve the riddle, dissolve the conundrum, resolve the dilemma. *Absolve my failure.* For until now it had only been a game with a marvellous prize. Solve the riddle and learn your destiny.

It was dawning on me that this was no game for children, and that failure had a price.

What is our punishment for failures such as these? And is it for failing to solve the mysteries or for shredding the fabric that veils them? What is a golden age, how does its end begin? What does it mean to lose a friend? The best part of myself.

There came into my mind images of that day up at Ixayac, of squatting in the smoke and the steam, of symbols and magic signs traced in mud, of black hens and turtle shells. Amanda never understood what I wanted. But she trusted me. And I saw then Sister Paula's face the day my grandfather came to take me home from school. Abuelo promised me I had not polluted the other girls. That I was not infected. That this hunger to know—*everything*—was not a disease. But now I knew differently, and he was no longer here.

We had climbed to the Heart of the Earth, we had walked in halls of jade. If I had not done something terrible at Ixayac, even had I not hurt her then, I could not deny I was hurting her now. What difference did it make whether I had scratched the jade or had done something that only *felt* like that? She is not safe with me, she is not safe if I go. What will my perfect gesture be?

And then I knew. I could not solve it. I knew I would fail, I knew I would leave.

During the next two days I could hardly bear to be near her. Each time came the shock of a horrified recognition: *this is your life*, I thought, over and over. *This will be your life.* There is a prize, there is a price. Solve the riddle, to save and keep her. I saw Amanda's face each day more drawn and gaunt.

The prize is to learn my destiny and join the great revival in Europe, a new golden age. The price is to end the race of gold, and stop the running to Ixayac.

The price is an age of iron when children are born already old.

The price was Amanda.

Pure waters of the Nile
recede, recede
and deny
thy tribute to the Sea,
for such bountiful
cargo she can only envy.
Cease, cease, roll on not one more mile,
For no greater joy awaits thee
than here . . . nigh.
Recede, recede . . .

Soothe, sinuous Nile,
thy liquid swells;
hold, hold fast,
to gaze in rapture
on what thy beauty brings to us,
from earth, from Heaven's Rose and Star,
whose lifeblood thou art . . .

JUANA INÉS
DE LA CRUZ

B. Limosneros, trans.

AGE OF IRON

†bundle, muddle

our years later, after my ride through the Sunday streets with Magda and María, I wanted to go home. The price had been too high, though I would not quite see how high until I had made the journey.

Uncle Juan had offered to send me by carriage, a different carriage, but understood when I declined. With a porter close behind us with my little *lío*,† he walked me himself all the way from the house. The bundle contained only a change of travelling clothes, but slung over my shoulder I carried for luck the green rabbit satchel Amanda had made for me, and in it some keepsakes. As we approached the canal there was just room to go two abreast alongside the file of wagons advancing still more slowly than we were.

"You were wise to want to walk, Juanita."

The wharf on the canal was a pandemonium. Landing here four years earlier from Panoayan, I'd thought it like an anthill. The anthill had been kicked over now. With *la Virgen de Guadalupe*'s festival in just two days' time, the waterway was as choked with canoes as the street and landing were with heavy carts. Jostling to land, the dugouts were backed all the way down the canal like a string of stewards serving at a cardinal's table. In one canoe, bunches of bananas each as big as a man. In the next, their feathers dusty from the trip, a half-dozen black *guajalotes* squabbling like curates with scarlet wattles and smoke-blue heads. Every third canoe all but overflowed with fresh-cut flowers and—out of season in our valley—roses rushed in relays of express post horses up from the south. I'd have no trouble finding passage to the eastern shore. An unbroken file of empty dugouts was heading there.

Something stirred in the air like a scent, faintly exhilarating. What I had taken for shouts of confusion I now heard as a kind of workmanly raillery. Near me a tall African took an armload of flowers from a snowy-haired Indian, who had the wildly bowed legs of some ancient cavalryman. I caught a snatch of something in a decent Nahuatl. The African was asking him if he hadn't maybe kept a few for a sweetheart. The old man laughed outright, then—glancing toward us—stopped. It occurred to me that all these men might in fact work for Uncle Juan.

"The northern canal, Juana, will be even worse, and the basilica itself—*olvídalo*. Ten times as many as at the poetry tourney on Saturday."

"A hundred thousand people?"

"You should go. I would take you," he said, still taking in the scene. "What your aunt and Magda did . . . it would never happen again."

"I have to go back, Uncle."

He glanced down at me. "I just wanted you to hear it."

"I know. . . . Thank you."

He went to find a boatman to take me. As he walked down I noticed a pink bald patch the size of my palm on the crown of his head. He found a boat in less than a minute. I met him halfway down. It was difficult to hear, to talk. To say good-bye to him.

"Say hello to your mother. Tell her it's been too long."

Afraid I might cry, I said nothing in answer. The boatman shoved off with a paddle blade. Uncle Juan called out. "If you do decide on just a short visit, consider being back for the audience with the Viceroy. Royalty can be a bit particular about their invitations. . . ." He began this with a shrug, but hearing him raise his voice awkwardly to bridge the distance gave me an inkling of what was at stake for him. First prize. Our first prize. I had forgotten it entirely. Before I could make an answer we were too far off with so much noise on the dock. I met his eyes, held them and nodded. He nodded back. The boatman manoeuvred us into a throng of dugouts bumping hollowly and angling towards open water.

With the mountains dead ahead I did have a little cry—the surfeit of an emotion I couldn't identify quite. Sorrow, regret . . . and something like relief. Foot traffic on the eastern causeway went at a crawl. Halfway along, a herd of cattle was broken into smaller clusters by pilgrims struggling to get past. Seven smaller herds, perhaps fifty cows in each, with five or six horsemen strung among them like sea serpents rearing above a flood. After a while I reached into my *lío* for a little lunch of dried figs tied up in a handkerchief. When I turned back to offer the boatman some, he smiled and shook his head. Sweat stood out on his brow; he was paddling smoothly but hard. Each stroke sent little whirlpools spinning away behind us.

I slept now, warmed by the sun, no screaming rising from the streets, no processions, no candles. No carriages, no forges, no hell. And dreamed of Ixayac.

The wharf behind us had been the picture of my own confusion, and yet I had left it strangely heartened. The feeling, or the word for it, had been not quite *relief* but *reprieve*. So much like the day of my arrival when Aunt María had met me at the landing, it was as if I were simply turning back and none of the intervening four years had happened. The dirty village on the lakeshore did not lack for mule teams. It took an extra hour to find an honest-looking young driver with a team of oxen.

On the morning of the second day, we entered the highest valley. Soon I knew that we could not be more than an hour away. In no time we had turned off the main road onto the track running up to the hacienda. I clutched tight in my lap to the satchel of keepsakes I had brought against the accusation that I had not written in all this time. How hollowly it rang in my mind to say that I had not looked back, or tried not to, because I was afraid I could not otherwise find the courage to stay away. I had not wanted to look back but had brought the things I had loved with me, because I could not bring the people. And I had never blamed Amanda for not coming out to say good-bye to me.

I knew that things could not be as they had once been but I understood now that Xochitl had been right, that the capital was no place for a daughter of hers. I knew something now about servants and Indians, and about all she and Amanda had kept from me and how much they had given by withholding it. And I wanted to tell her that I saw at last the enormous difference between having a fate and pursuing a destiny, and that if there was ever a problem for us to have tried hard to solve, it was not how I might find mine but how she might escape hers. We were fifteen now. Things could not be the same, but maybe in a few years, when we were older, we might find our own way in the world, together.

But above all that day, there was something I needed to say to Amanda about what had happened at Ixayac. I saw how much I had wronged her. And since then I had understood even something of why—though I must not let this sound like an excuse. It had taken years, but I had resolved the one mystery that I had allowed to drive us apart. How these things had consumed and bewildered me. That the Alexandrian renaissance died that day in the body of its most illustrious expositor, a rebirth ripped from the womb in a church called Caesarion. . . . That the heavy vessels used by the monks of the Natron lakes were certainly Canopic jars filled with embalming fluid, to make the dead last a thousand years. That the pottery shards and oyster shells the desert monks had used to scrape the flesh from Hypatia's bones would surely have formed the conic sections called parabola. That the commentaries on the *Conics* of Apollonius, the highest glory of the Alexandrian revival, were written by none other than Hypatia and her father.

A mystery called Cinaron, a riddle call Caesarion, a puzzle of broken pottery. But out of so many riddles, in all the years of my exile, there was one whose edges had never lost their sharpness. And this one I had solved. *Ostrakis aneilon*. Oyster shells . . . and also the roofing tiles on whose fragments the name of the one to be banished was inscribed. Hypatia had been ostracized, for ten centuries. But for this solution there was to be no prize.

Oyster shells, pottery tiles, parabola. . . . One other conic section is the turtle shell.

In the whiteness of my hunger I had sacked the Sarapeum, destroyed the Serapiana, violated all that was chaste in a time that has gone. Hypatia's role had not been mine to play at all. This part was for another. The best part of myself.

As the ox cart came to a stop behind the house, it was this I was remembering, and Ixayac. I had seen something of the world, and knew now that heresy was not just about books; neither were treason and betrayal only things of distant countries and pasts. And I had more yet to learn about the Inquisition, and from Magda. Even now I wonder what I might have found to say. I was not to get the chance, for not even Hypatia's banishment was truly mine to play. But I think I had already sensed this. A *campesino* I did not recognize was making his way toward us. I pointed out to the driver the water troughs for the oxen and promised to bring him water to drink from the house. My hand trembling a little, I gave him an extra centavo for the journey. I called to the farmhand to put 'good' corn into the feedbags. Good corn. I must have sounded even more foolish to him than I did to myself. He plainly had no idea who I was. Standing here talking nonsense—trembling hands— was this how I was to face Amanda?

I forced myself to think instead of Xochitl. How I had *missed* her. I rapped shyly, then a little louder. The kitchen door had never been locked. A young Indian woman opened now. She stood before me in the doorway, nursing an infant under her *rebozo*. "*¿Sí, señorita? A sus órdenes*," she added in a good Castilian. Perhaps seeing my distress, she stepped back and beckoned me in. "*Pásele*."

A pale, curly-haired boy of four or five was playing with wooden soldiers on the kitchen floor. Struggling for calm I went into the pantry. A single hammock was slung in the corner, where a cross-draft between the windows made sleeping more comfortable. I felt my blood turn to rust— a ball of iron in the pit of my stomach. "Where is Xochitl?" I could not even have formed Amanda's name. The young woman's eyes widened. She clutched the infant more tightly to her.

"Who?" she asked, and stepped between me and the boy. He reached up to where her hand fumbled to find his, this boy who was my half-brother. I rushed from the kitchen into the courtyard looking for Isabel, for anyone.

In the middle of the courtyard, where the firepit had once been, I stopped. Like a sentry, yet somehow broken now, a man sat in the rocking chair by Isabel's door, where he had often sat, our dinner guest waiting for her to come in from the fields. Lance-captain Diego Ruiz Lozano was much changed, much aged. The head of hair once so thick with curls lay lank. Lacklustre now the black beard, and from the upper lip hung limp tatters of black rag. A blanket covered his legs, his knees thinned as if by palsy.

"No, Juana, they have not been here for some time. . . . You've grown."

To be hearing this from his lips, how I rejoiced that the years had been so unkind, that the wellsprings of his life, its roots, had proved so shallow—that four years should sap them dry.

"How long?"

"We never did get to say good-bye."

"How *long*, Diego?"

"You look more like your mother than ever. . . ."

I said nothing. After a moment he looked away.

"She found a place for them on the far side of the pass. She went to a lot of trouble. Isabel should never have let Amanda have so much *money*. She should never have let them leave with it. I warned her, I warned them. . . ."

They never arrived. He had sent troops everywhere looking for them—to Nepantla, to Xochitl's old village, every village on the far slope of the volcanoes. The roads were dangerous. He blamed the fifty pesos. A ridiculous sum to give a child, to give any Indian.

I turned away from those eyes—walked unsteadily down the arcade, could not bring myself to enter the darkened library. Taking up the satchel I'd left by the kitchen door, I walked into the fields, through the dry corn, out towards the river. The shady spot where we used to read lay in a strip of trees between the maguey and the corn. At the foot of a cedar, a giant among the pines, stood a small granite cross. There I sank softly to the ground, sat mindless, empty, emptiness itself.

Then into the vessel of that abhorrent emptiness rushed such a violent swarm of faces, voices, memories. . . .

It had never occurred to me that she would not be here, that this life I had left was not simply waiting upon my return. For four years I had fought not to look back at these mountains and think of Amanda here, looking from Ixayac down over the city. I looked up to them now, the mist thinning . . . the cone of El Popo cut by a wedge of cloud, WhiteLady stretched out below him . . . chin, breast, knees. What was the use of straining to see the secret shapes hidden in the world if I could not see into myself?

On a patch of grass by the water troughs, the cart had been pulled up, the oxen unhitched. They had drunk their fill and were milling away at feedbags of the good corn I had called for. The young driver had slept his siesta under the cart and was stirring now. I watched him stretch, the languor of having no cargo to load or unload.

I spread my keepsakes out before me among the pine cones and rust-coloured needles. I had been right not to look back. It solved nothing. Worse, I'd had this truth right before me for years. Into my lap I took the *Cancionero general.* It fell open to the very page, so often had I read it.

> Let no one be deceived, no,
> to think what is hoped for
> shall last,
> any more than what we've seen go. . . .

In the shade of that tree, there came to me the idea that the thread of my life had been broken. Perhaps it was the sheer hazard of holding the battered copy of *El cancionero general*. Or something to do with pottery shards. Whatever remained of my childhood had ended during a ride in a beautiful carriage through the streets of Mexico; but though I might blame the Holy Office, it was a childhood that had no right to outlast Amanda's, just as I felt no right to grieve its loss. And that city was no place for a child. With these few things before me I would make a new start, not by looking back but by carrying my life forward with me. The poet must never look back.

I turned at the sound of the ox cart as it lumbered slowly past the house, felt something stirring within me to watch it leave. . . .

One last time in Panoayan I ran—I ran *from* Panoayan, as I had never run in four years in the city. I went with all my strength after the cart— a broken book in my left hand, my satchel flailing and flapping in my right. As I ran up the track between the orchards and the fields and as the rich bloom of damsons filled my mind I would have let myself see no similarities between the past and what I was doing now, no precedents or patterns at all, not even in the explorer's compulsion to abandon the known world, to discover the new. Yes, I had quit Ixayac for a library I had barely glimpsed, and yes I had abandoned Panoayan for a city I had only seen from afar and as if in a dream. But I had *seen* Mexico City now. The receptions, the poetry jousts, the prizes. I had met the Viceroy and was to have an audience and meet his blonde wife. So of course I knew that world, and ran toward it. There I would make a new thread and spin out my dream of a different destiny.

Too breathless to laugh at the young driver's confusion, I clambered up on aching legs to the cart seat. Such a whirl of seasons lay ahead of me, such episodes, such deep tones and bright hues, like the brilliant shadows of a magic lantern cast blindingly from a lonely darkness. Behind me lay the mountains, a painted pane of glass, a child's pyramid of ice gouting smoke and beet-juice fire.

Ahead, three commoners, three young poets, arriving at the most brilliant palace in a new world. The audience with a vice-king, the fascinations of a vice-queen—the most exotic creature I had ever seen, a princess in a dream.

Glass.

Afterwards, staying up all that first night with Carlos, reliving every detail. Pouring out my heart to him, all our hurts to each other, telling him things of Nepantla and Panoayan. Discovering our shared passion for the great work in train in Europe, so far away . . . his growing doubts about becoming a Jesuit.

The bastard country girl installed at the palace as the vice-queen's handmaiden. The thousand wagging tongues, the slights, the propositions, the rumours, the envy. The spectacle of a public examination by forty scholars of the Royal University to determine if the prodigy of my learning were divinely inspired, as in the case of the Angelic Doctor,[†] or inspired by an angel of an altogether different order. Red devils on glass.

[†]Aquinas

A night of masquerade. By now I was the practised one, the initiate of masques. And in our disguises Carlos and I stopping at every *pulquería* in the city. The harlots, the humble broken faces crudely painted . . . Watching the dawn together from a rooftop after a night of gazing for the first time through a fine telescope Carlos had built himself. Hearing his vow of undying friendship when I so needed a friend; the unspoken offer of much more, when I had hurt everyone I had ever loved. It was a night that changed his life far more than mine. His whole existence had been in the city, mine in the country, and now he wanted to know everything about that countryside—because of me, *for* me. But this was precisely what I had left so completely behind. Figures not so easily painted on glass.

These past years I have fancied that my ideas about the changeability of life were progressing—for of course metaphors for poets are very fine. From broken threads to broken books, from everlasting fire to an *hojarasca*, a scattering of leaves. From panes of crudely painted glass to the projections of a camera obscura as detailed and complete as anything a mirror receives. But I have had occasion to wonder if this is really the way to part the veil over one's destiny—to cut the threads of the past only to become tangled up in them, and perhaps stumble on someone else's path.

JUANA INÉS
DE LA CRUZ,

THE SCEPTRE OF
SAINT JOSEPH

B. Limosneros, trans.

INTELLIGENCE:
. . . that Woman, who but through sin
entered my dominions,
should then vanquish me,
and, a Slave, crush me beneath her heel. . . .[13]
What mystifying veil does God cast
over a secret so stupendous
as to outsoar my grasp,
yet not quite my awareness?

LUCERO:
Worse, so far from seizing it in your talons
you have it barely sighted,
as by your lights one descries
how distinct are the objects it symbolises:
since Philosophy has, by her various sciences,
assigned it the symbol for Innocence,
and for Liberty made it the most dread
hieroglyph in Egypt—while for Victory
no less, in other nations. Oh memory!
How it afflicts my Intelligence to divine
liberty, victory, and innocence,
in one glyph signified.
    Conjecture, what do you make of this?

CONJECTURE:
Much and nothing.

ENVY:
Whereas I, as is meet, quite outdo myself
in impugning its qualities. And thus to its undoing
let us hasten.

LUCERO:
This I do intend.
But so as to build its ruin on a solid foundation,
show me, Intelligence, another scene,
and let us see what new quarry your prowess takes in. . . .

11th day of July, 1667
Ixtapalapa, New Spain

My dearest Juana,

By now you know I have given up trying to persuade you and have left Mexico City. And if they have not told you already, you should also know I lied. I did not leave the Jesuit college willingly. I was expelled.

Seven and a half years ago voices—angelic voices, I thought—began flooding my mind, imploring me to study with the Jesuits, to enter into their service and care. But over the past few years another voice has come to haunt my sleep. It has returned almost every night. Indistinct yet imperious it leaves me no peace. Eventually the college had to find out that I'd taken to wandering the streets of Puebla, after everyone was asleep. It was not what they thought, what they tried to get me to confess, but it would have been too humiliating to try to explain. I said nothing in my own defence.

If I say now that I left because of you, Juana, it is not to lay blame. . . . But enough of this.

As you well know, the Viceroy's cousins are returning to Europe, speaking of nothing but you. You were a splendid success at their farewell party. They showed me the verses you composed for the occasion. You have done better work.

Tuesday, I came upon them in Mexicaltzingo just as they were having the last of their trunks hauled across the river. The girl is slightly more intelligent than her brother and the rest of their playmates. She remembered me as a friend of yours and has invited me to travel with them. How lucky to have had some of your fame rub off. I will grant it has been fascinating to journey with the lesser nobility. How many times have I made the trek between Mexico and Puebla and never once had an entire Indian village turn out to entertain me with dances and song.

It would have been uncivil and a little stupid to travel just ahead of them all the way to the coast. With my luck we would have ended up making the crossing to Havana, or even Cadiz, on the same small ship.

We in our position cannot afford the luxury of making enemies among the ruling classes, can we.

There. Go ahead and laugh. Here I am, travelling to Spain with the

THIS NEW EDEN[14]

Carlos writes to Juana at the Viceregal Palace. More than three years have passed since they met, at a poetry joust.

very class of Spaniard that is driving me from Mexico. Yet I know you can understand how much less painful it will be for me to watch these parasites sucking their own country dry. Well you know my feelings; and now you know my plan, which is to leave this strangling, benighted continent. I say it again, Juana. There is nothing here for us.

Enough for now. It has been a long, full day.

Your faithful servant, Carlos.

 16th day of July, 1667
Puebla de los Angeles, New Spain

Dear Juana Inés,

I have reached Puebla. My noble companions will be staying on a few days as guests of the Bishop. A Dominican, he has been known to me by reputation for some time now. The Jesuits here are convinced that without their intervention he is sure to become Archbishop one day. In the meantime, where you and I would do very well on two hundred pesos a year, he will have to make do with his Episcopal stipend of sixty thousand, raised from the blood of our soil.

I have been anxious to find myself free of the Viceroy's cousins. I tell you I could not have suffered their company a minute more. Nor, I would venture, could they mine.

The Indian dancing I wrote you about only whets their appetite for more. One day near nightfall we reach a river overflowing its banks. *Gracias a Dios* everyone sees the futility of risking their possessions, not to speak of lives, on that river, at that hour, for a capricious detour to see more dancing. Grudgingly our little raiding party turns back to a *casa de comunidad* about a mile from the river, near the village of San Martín. I had not known such houses existed, but my foreign companions delight in apprising me that almost every Indian village maintains at its own expense a guesthouse to lodge those on Crown business. Very loosely defined, this applies to almost anyone and perfectly to us. By the time the food is served everyone at table is in a foul humour (then, O calamity, too little salt). One of the gentlemen begins roundly abusing the *mesonero*, until, with the greatest reluctance, I have to intervene. Though the royals say nothing, our honeymoon has ended and we all know it.

Most infuriating of all is how, as league by league we draw closer to Spain, their farewell tour through America turns everything to an ever-sharpening derision. Yet at the same time they somehow manage to treat whatever we pass—farms, villages, orchards, ruined temples—as their own personal inheritance. How these peacocks boast of possessing a thing they claim to despise. It is the sleek who have inherited the earth.

By noon today we covered the remaining three leagues to Puebla. Making the trip to Veracruz alone, so desolate a prospect as I left you in Mexico, now seems truly splendid. Certainly travelling ahead of them will be infinitely better than trailing behind. At each stop I would have found both stores and servants exhausted.

On the other hand, the bandits who along this road run many of the taverns, such as that rat-trap in Chalco, will no longer metamorphose into paragóns of generous civility when I arrive without my nobles. Why is it that at the same inn, the rich are actually charged less and lodged better?

I hasten to add that we did not stay at the inn owned by your aunt's husband but I did walk up the street to see her. A delightful woman, and lovely. Hearing me speak perhaps at too-great length of our friendship, she gave me directions to your mother's hacienda, suggesting I go and make her acquaintance. It is too far to detour now, but I hope one day to make that journey. I imagine she will be beautiful.

Sitting here writing to you, I find my heart lighter than at any time since I decided to leave Mexico City. I think you are still friend enough to be glad of that.

Good-night Juanita. . . .

17th day of July, 1667

Mi querida,

Remember when we met, and later that month at the palace? Two children in a room full of European aristocrats. There we were, you and I, being awarded first and second place in the *certamen*†—teen prodigies, poor, and American-born to boot—with the Royal University's Professor of Poetics a red-faced third.

†poetry tournament

My first year at the college in Puebla, your first year at court. Who could have blamed us for turning to each other—then and during each college vacation?

But I hadn't fallen in love with you yet.

I've never spoken of this. The day it happened we were not even in the same city. I was in Puebla, poring over a letter about you from a professor who was there, who saw it all with his own eyes. The Viceroy himself said seeing you that day, besting all those professors in debate, was like watching a galleon fending off a handful of canoes.

Forty professors from the Royal University of the Imperial City of Mexico, the incomparable capital of New Spain—against one teenaged girl!

Whose idea had it been? The Viceroy's?—his wife's? They must have found it all so amusing. Was it done expressly to humiliate America's greatest university? Obviously the stated purpose was a sham: how could anyone hope to tell by examining you whether your learning was innate or acquired, diabolical or divinely inspired? Were you given the opportunity to decline the invitation? I doubt you would have anyway. How did you feel—elated, terrified? Did they tell you there would just be a professor or two? Surely not forty! Were you hoping to please the Vicereine, or to show *them?*

I think I know.

I have many times imagined the scene since then. Ah, to have been there!—noon in the palace's Hall of Realms . . . settling into their seats, the Viceregal couple—sleepy gestures, watchful eyes. . . . To their left, the ladies of the court taking their seats once again, murmuring wickedly behind wavering fans. To the right, the gentlemen still frenziedly wagering.

One girl, beautiful and pale, standing alone at the centre of the hall.

The sages begin to file in, puffed up in the colours of their respective faculties—mathematics, astronomy, music, law, theology, philosophy, poetics . . . I can just see them strutting in, the historians, the humanists, the scripturists, the rhetoricians, the astrologers—peacocks all. And a few parlour wits invited to leaven the proceedings.

Silence falls. A clever preamble by the Viceroy. The university rector receives the instruction to proceed. The first easy questions, dripping condescension. Cautious replies, indulgent applause. The queries longer now, more in earnest. You begin to relax, riposting with precision and wit yet the applause seems fainter now. Through narrowing eyes, the ladies are beginning vaguely to see in this performance a betrayal, the men, cause for disquiet. *Sotto voce* various gamblers curse each hapless professor for a fool as he is toppled by your lance. Yet somehow they envy him his chance at humiliation.

The ranking pundits look increasingly desperate now as their turn approaches. Questions bifurcating and ramifying into such complexities that even their posers seem to lose the thread. Others, you bring to stumble into the very snares they've laid. Spider-like, you reel them in one by one, many ceasing to struggle almost immediately, meekly sitting without even attempting a rebuttal. Those who do . . . manage to sound at once shrill and petty, their objections reduced to cavils.

Now in an attempt to confuse you they put their questions in tandem—history, then theology, then mathematics, then part two of the history question. But like a chess master playing on several boards at once you see their game at a glance, while *they* become distracted by the interruptions.

Finally one greybeard, whose local eminence has been for some minutes crumbling to a highly public rubble, starts to shout you down. The bettors who laid the longest odds rise indignant in your defence. The rector turns to the Viceroy to protest!

Shouting now on all sides.

The Viceroy inclines his head slightly: the Vice-Queen is whispering something in his ear. Suddenly he rises. The room falls quiet again. Smiling he thanks the Royal University for its participation and, suddenly solemn, bows to the red-cheeked girl.

How they must hate you, these wise men. Nothing left to do but paddle their canoes away across a sea of indignity. A rout of unimaginable proportions.

Is that how it was Juana?

And was that the exact moment of my fall?

No.

The precise instant was in the beginning . . . as the learned doctors swaggered in, when you stood alone, head bowed in concentration, unsure of the outcome. I fell in love with you then. In a scene described to me in a letter, from a casual friend.

Juana I've borrowed enough money to get us both passage to Europe. We'll never be free to exercise our talent here. Now that I've really left maybe you'll take me seriously and stop treating me like some impetuous boy.

Come away with me.

I will wait for you in Veracruz until you send me word.

Until you send me word . . . Carlos.

21st day of July, 1667
la hacienda de San Nicolás

Querida Juana Inés,

I could not quite bring myself to write these past few nights. Emotions too unstable to be wrestled into an envelope and commended to the void, only to be ferried across it by some stranger. By the time this packet of mercury wings its way to you I am sure everything will have slipped and shifted yet again.

It was dawn when I set out from Puebla, exhilarated. . . .

The roads are deserted—the sun rising grandly before me above the fog. But before I have ridden many leagues to the east, a kind of melancholy infiltrates my mood. The road has been climbing for the last couple of hours away from the boggy ground Puebla is anchored to. I dismount and look back over my trail.

The plain below is choked and blue with the smoke of a thousand fires. And looking out over this landscape for perhaps the last time I see a battle scene for one of your Florentines, Da Vinci . . . "War on Eden." A campaign giving no quarter and leaving in its wake an America of drained watercourses and scorched slopes from Quito to Mexico. New Spain indeed. This country will resemble arid Spain soon enough.

My cast of mind sombres to the point where even as I find myself at the first mountain pass, leaving the battlefield at least temporarily behind me, and surrounded by waterfalls and freshets, by the sound of water surging below, all I can permit myself to see pouring forth is the lifeblood of a great leviathan groaning under our assault. Here I spend my first night, cloaked in mist and dreaming of a sea battle sounding all around me. . . .

My aching joints wake me before dawn. My horse, tethered all night in the same mist, is not at all eager to be saddled with me, the mule still less so to be burdened with my affairs.

From here the trail twists its way over an ever-steeper series of grades. Two leagues up for every one down. Killing work for the animals. Negotiating even the lower trails exacts the utmost concentration, as bogs threaten to engulf the unwary at every turn. I have been remembering our talks and believe your grandfather to have been right: I now see for myself that without Moctezuma's help, his gifts of food and of course his unwillingness to attack the Spaniards as they walked their horses along these steep game trails and treacherous marshes, the conquest of America would have died right here.

Then there are these high-country rivers, most of them impossible to ford. What a miracle of water is our New World. I hear the roaring an hour before I reach it. Unthinkable to cross without that bridge. More spume than water, the river tumbles battered from the heights of a glowering volcano as high, I suspect, as our Popocatepetl. On the far side of the narrow bridge, which I must coax the animals across, stands the hacienda de San Nicolás and my first meal in nearly two days. *El terrateniente* receives me courteously, though he is too wary to lodge me at the main house. Only after I have paid an outrageous sum for a chicken, which his Indian cook prepares for me most deliciously, does he say I could have had, for a tenth the cost, one of the delicious fowl that abound in the surrounding woods. *Guajalotes,*[†] of course, but also large woodcocks and something the Indians here call a pheasant . . . he just assumed a city man would prefer chicken.

[†]turkeys

We sit over lunch in a lush garden beneath the blinding whiteness of this volcano, Orizaba, and securely above the inexhaustible source of fresh water it provides. My host is from Andalusía. A simple man of eminently good sense, he confides that this water is more precious to him than all the gold of the Indies. Many of the first *conquistadores* were poor men from his region. In Andalusía and Estramadura it is common knowledge most died paupers. Here, with a few fruit trees a man can feed his entire family, with more than enough left over to barter for necessities. The munificence of one fruit tree, Juana. I'd never really grasped it. With the land so rich, he says, why should there be so many starving on the plantations on the coast?

My belly full at last he offers to show me his Eden. Eden it seems is on everyone's mind. To move through these orchards, through these shoals of blossoms, seems less like walking than swimming through musk. To stop walking for more than an instant is to stand softly plumed in the bright slow wings of butterflies, some as large as my hand. Shuttling by are more kinds of hummingbirds than I ever guessed existed. And weaving among them, honeybees heavy with nectar rumble a short way to the dozens of beehives he has set up among the trees, whose branches droop beneath their burden of flowers. Cherimoyas, other species of anonas, lime and orange, and fruits I've never even seen in the markets. He has me taste something they call *sciochaco*: white fleshed, its flavour like cherry, but with spicy black seeds like peppercorns.

Farther back from the river, he has left wild the surrounding woods that peal and ring with bird calls, and against this carillon, green and blue volleys of parrots screech overhead . . .

Within a few hours he has invited me to stay as long as I like, and repeats the invitation as I am packing up early the next morning. Instead I find myself riding away up a trail through the healing green of a forest I am only truly seeing for the first time. It is as if the waters of the Flood have just receded and granted me, the last man on earth, the terrible privilege of experiencing this world for all humankind. Never have I seen such flowers. Yet they must have been all around me all along. It seems my eyes are become children, and must be taught all over again.

Would they see even now, were it not for our talks of your life in the country? We are city people, on both sides of my family. I would not even be here had you and I not met. One does mathematics perfectly well in a Jesuit college. Only poets need the land.

How I wish we two could share this. Every bird call, the wind across the valley, the rill and rustle of water on every side. In the late afternoon, I watch a jaguar fishing in a rocky stream below me. It looks up, sees us, and I know a moment of fear. But the slope is steep and the fishing good, so we are safe enough. My horse stands stock still and trembles, nonetheless. White-eyed, the mule looks ready to bolt with all my books and papers.

Books and papers. Pointless to imagine I could have stayed on at San Nicolás forever, but that is not what flashed through my mind as my host was inviting me to stay. I thought, *No books . . . there'd be no books here.* We are driven from Eden for the blood on our hands, yet prolong our exile only to plunge them in ink. What makes a man ride alone out of paradise for an insignificant pile of books not yet written? At this moment, Juana, I would give a lot to hear your answer.

I feel this little book growing inside me, an album of verses devoted to this gravid miracle of water . . . dedicated to the verdant destiny of this new continent, our occidental paradise—

The most extraordinary thing! Just as I am writing this, seated comfortably at my little fire—a violent earthquake. The ground heaves under me with power enough to raze a city. I may well arrive in Veracruz to discover it destroyed. Yet the sick terror of a man in the forest quickly passes, as he grasps that there stands over his head only a light canopy of leaves and stars.

It must also be so of flood. Out here the forest dweller only moves to higher ground, while the city man loses all his worldly goods.

The thought occurs just now that perhaps the great myths of cataclysm and flood needed in the end to build cities, in order to make themselves understood.

con cariño, Carlos

1st day of August, 1667
la Nueva Veracruz, New Spain
Juana,

The morning after the earthquake I awake more refreshed and rested than I have felt in months, only to find myself and all my belongings covered in snow. Now at least I know what it will take on this journey to get a good night's sleep. . . .

All day the trail falls steeply into hotter country. After six leagues or so I come upon the *hospedaría de San Campus,* the most abject excuse imaginable for a hostelry. Not a scrap to eat for man nor beast. So many starving dogs and rats skulking about the place you'd have to sleep with your boots on for fear of having them dragged off for food. The innkeeper was another fortune hunter, from Estramadura. One who came for gold but could not settle for water. He goes about the place unkempt and half naked, muttering. A recluse whose penance it has become to serve the passing public. It is my first contact with a breed I will be seeing a lot more of down here, one I should get comfortable among: the failed white man in the tropics.

After another few leagues over flat ground and through a fading light I come on a clean, well-ordered settlement in the sharpest possible contrast to the misery of San Campus. San Lorenzo de los Negros is populated exclusively by runaway slaves. *Cimarrones*—arrows that fly to freedom. Even they call themselves that.

Cimarrón . . . You, Juana, will feel all the pain and yearning in that word.

I decide to stay the night, with some trepidation, but find myself well treated and fed. The Governor at Veracruz allows these people to live here without fear of reprisals, as long as they supply the port with the surplus of their well-tended fields. But whatever dignity this should have permitted them has been stripped from these unfortunates by the one condition haunting their existence here: they must refuse to shelter—worse, must return to their owners—any new runaways who reach San Lorenzo.

The next day, I arrive with no little excitement at the outskirts of Veracruz, but find here little more than an outpost in sandblown squalor. Sand everywhere. Rotting houses half buried in it. Laughable city walls. Here some contractor has brazenly defrauded the Crown, for you could breach these pitiful defences without even getting off your horse. No point whatever in closing the city gates to pirates.

As I already knew, the sailing season for Europe is still months off, but the ship I was hoping to take to Havana, where the waiting is said to be much more comfortable, sailed without me. No room, said the Captain. Unless of course one is in a party of rich Spaniards getting an early start on their triumphal return from the Indies.

Incredibly there are no inns in the New Veracruz. And the Old, where Cortés first set foot on the shores of America, is just a collection of fishing huts. Standing on this infernal shore watching the only ship in port sail to Havana without me, I understand perfectly Cortés's decision to burn his ships to keep his men from deserting.

No other ships for a *month*. I simply have to get on the next one. In this season many fall prey to the fevers. The airs hereabouts, when still, are positively foetid. Or they blow a northerly gale, driving sand deep into every crack and crevice. Just a few weeks ago, Juana, I imagined us taking long walks at the seashore. However, the sea here is not the sparkling blue of our lakes but rather a sullen grey-green. Salt marshes and estuaries everywhere indent this coastline, and the crocodiles, which even on land can be swifter than a man, litter their banks exactly—and treacherously—like logs after a storm. No such thing as a carefree day at the sea, with sharks to one side and crocodiles to the other.

They are mad for dog meat apparently.

The contents of my purse have dwindled alarmingly. I've taken up hunting in order to pay for a cook (a recent widow with six children), who will work in exchange for the lion's share of whatever fresh meat I can bring in. You will probably laugh at the idea of me as a hunter, yet the turkeys stand thick on the ground and make easy targets.

On several of my jungle forays I have come across the overgrown ruins of one ancient temple site or another, but the mosquitoes here are so ferocious I am never able to stop long. Would it surprise you to learn that the part of America most proximate to Spain is infested with parasites? And not just of the two-legged sort. The jungle (and to a lesser extent the town) crawls with gnats, wood lice and mites. Nightly the remorseless hunter repairs to his lair only to find himself the mottled prey of more resourceful foragers—ticks and leeches grazing implacably on the flesh at my neck, wrists and ankles. Leeches enough for all the physicians of Europe. Certainly there should be no ill humours left in me. So after a week of this (and of eating turkey every day) I am ready to beg the fishermen in Old Veracruz for fishing lessons. At least there'd be just the sharks and the crocodiles.

your most faithful servant, Carlos

14th day of August, 1667

Juana,

I begin this having waited a fortnight to write you, hoping my mood would brighten. Yet how could it, when with each passing day I learn more about the workings of this place? The Inquisition's censors infest the port, crawling all over incoming book shipments in search of works by Las Casas, Erasmus, Descartes, anything on the new sciences. But since the royal seal was issued two years ago, they search also for anything touching on Indian cults and superstitions. Even Cortés's letters to his king may no longer be read here in America. A century and a half after the Conquest—what is it that the Crown fears so much more now than then? Or is it that Madrid now fears everything and everyone from Cuzco to Versailles? Truly I despair of ever seeing my own work in print if I remain on this continent. And yet even if publishing in Spain is not quite impossible, in order to be read in Mexico my texts will have to get past the censors in Seville, then here, only to find my fellow colonists preferring European writers.

For their part, the port authorities care nothing for books. Instead their tariffs and regulations are expressly framed to strike down anything that might impede the Crown as it deflowers this land and squanders our patrimony. Forbidding us to export finished timber, the Spaniards burn down leagues of forest for their cattle to overgraze. Then they tell the American he can do what he will with the meat but not only is he required to export his cow hides for the manufacture of Spanish shoes, the Crown forces us to repurchase those shoes by forbidding us to make our own. For over a century now the *gachupines* have run like wild horses through the verdant pastures of our America while we the Creoles, who are born here, lurch about under hobbles and trammels—formally denied key posts, and informally, the most lucrative opportunities.

This I have witnessed first-hand since my boyhood. In Spain my father tutored royalty, but born here his children are treated as foreigners in our own land. America is in every way richer, more abundant, more enterprising than Iberia and yet in what does the true scope of our enterprise here consist? This trading system benefits those who already have capital, and benefits most those nations that have already accumulated the most. It bleeds us dry while enriching the few stooges here who do the bidding of the merchants surrounding the court in Madrid. Meanwhile the Royal Treasury has been all but bankrupted by the importation of manufactured goods from northern Europe in exchange for—what else?—gold and silver, the only Spanish products that the northerners do not already produce more efficiently.

Spain has become Europe's laughingstock. And what does this make us? Surely our America deserves better. Castile has been given stewardship over a New World—a second chance for Spain and for Man—only to exhaust and despoil it so much more quickly than the Old. More damage has been done to our America in a hundred years than to Europe in five thousand. I am told it is worse out in the islands. Wherever the land was once the richest and most densely populated, the Indians are now completely gone and the land is worked to death by half-starved negroes. The yield steadily falls, but at the same time the acreage is expanding so rapidly that the price of sugar keeps slipping, such that the merchants are always looking for new ways to use sugar and so maintain its price. They will be building our city walls with it next.

This past fortnight I have found myself retracing the journey that brought me here, the route of the Conquest in reverse. And in a sense for me it has been a conquest reversed. I cannot claim to have liberated the lands I have crossed; instead they have conquered me. I have you to thank for this, for teaching me to see through your grandfather's eyes. The Conquest has entered into our past, but that other America is not dead. She lies as if in a fever dream while these foreign parasites feast on her prostrate body. This is my homeland. How can I bring myself to leave her? I may not go to Europe, after all—there is so much work to be done here. I know this now.

Made desperate by the infernal hunting and my wasting purse, I decided to give up the house and, with great reluctance, threw myself upon the mercies of a local monastery. The Jesuits were clearly out of the question for me. The Augustinians nearly destitute. After two days with the Dominicans (nearly as hard up as the Augustinians) a friar meekly asked if I had ever visited the lovely Franciscan monastery not a league south of town. . . .

I am only now getting the chance to finish, having arrived just this afternoon, but you can write me here if you care to. I will be staying on here as long as they will have me. They have invited me to collaborate with them, but more on that later.

Enough for now. It has been a long day . . .

Carlos.

17th day of September, 1667
Convento de Nuestra Señora de Dolores
Veracruz, New Spain

Juana,

I am sure you have been on tenterhooks to know about my new home. Some years back a rich patron donated a tract of fertile property to these Franciscans, which they have cleared and cultivate judiciously. The land reliably yields three crops yearly if properly rotated. The monastery itself is spacious, surrounded by trees, and constructed to take advantage of breezes from the sea.

My first impressions—of a place more concerned with cultivating the earth than the mind—were quite mistaken. Rather than giving way to luxury, the comfortable conditions here permit these men to carry on the admirable work of their great Franciscan father, Fray Bernardino de Sahagún. He has, I can confidently state, invented a new science of Man. It undertakes to map systematically the constellations of these American societies, the patterns of their superstitions and attendant practices. Without him and a few others (I am convinced your grandfather was one of them in spirit), the Conquest would have extinguished this alien sky, which may yet be blotted out by smoke from the Inquisition's fires. Sahagún's writings were twice confiscated as tending to mar the glorious portrait being painted of the Conquest back in Spain. Yet the Franciscans only chart these systems the better to guide the Indians to the safe harbour of our Catholic Faith, by the light of *their own innate reason* and not by the torchlight of fear.

Brother Manuel Cuadros, the most learned man here in the things of the New World, has himself only just arrived from the Indian college at Tlatelolco, where he claims to have learned more theology from his students than ever he taught them. He believes the native Americans to be natural Christians, and cites as an example Our Lady of Guadalupe's chapel on the Cerrito de Tepeyac, the same hill where the Mexican goddess Tonantzin was once worshipped. Tonantzin, *Our Mother*. Tepeyac, from the Mexican—*stone that crushes the serpent*.

Meanwhile, how often do we ourselves portray the Mother of Christ as a new Eve protecting her Child, crushing the Serpent beneath her heel? And did you yourself not tell me you have heard Guadalupe pronounced as Coatlalocpeuh?—*she who has dominion over serpents*.

My Franciscan friends now regard the fast-growing veneration of Guadalupe throughout New Spain as an illustration of how the natives can be led naturally to the worship of Christ. But our fellow Creole, Fray Cuadros, has made me see much more: Guadalupe shall be the mother of our liberation. As he puts it, the Spanish have made orphans and bastards of us all, *criollos*, *indios* and *mestizos* alike. Guadalupe is fast becoming—though we might be only beginning to grasp it—the Mother Protectoress of all America's peoples. The mother of our sorrows. And this is why Fray Cuadros and a few others fear the Church will try to discredit her: precisely because it is now widely held that Guadalupe *is* the new Eve, who has come to protect this new Eden. Imagine my excitement, after the journey I have just made, to take part in such work.

Interesting times here, and dangerous.

And you. Tell me you have finally quit the palace and I will be there to fetch you in a week, I will set a new record reaching you.

Juanita, good-night.

 25th day of October, 1667
Convento de Nuestra Señora de Dolores
la Nueva Veracruz

Dearest Juana Inés,

At last a letter! What a pleasure it is to read whatever flows from your agile quill, even if you disclose nothing of your life these days. If it is tact, do not worry, I no longer delude myself. Still, I cannot stop dreaming that you will one day tire of the palace and join us here. Brother Cuadros has complimented me on my knowledge of Indian customs, which I have been quick to explain are but scraps picked up from you. He has heard a great deal about you, of course, and has confided he hopes one day to meet you. If you were to come, I know you and I would find a way . . .

I am dismayed you find our project here so objectionable. Yes, it is dangerous, but in these benighted times what ideas are not? You are right to remind me the Church's greatest fear here in the New World is still that the ancient beliefs will be rekindled to ignite a revolt. The Indians still vastly outnumber us, after all. But the Church has no cause for suspicion: What these Franciscans are attempting is to restore the ancient bridge between our Mother Church and the native Christianity of America. Brother Cuadros assures me that among the Indians the conquered accept it as their duty to worship the stronger gods of their conquerors alongside their own. And what better evidence of God's strength and will, for both victors and vanquished, than the bloody miracle of a conquest against all human odds?

Clearly the policy of forced conversion, as prosecuted through our extermination of their gods and priests, has been a failure. Fray Cuadros has convinced me the Indians convert willingly once it is demonstrated that our Catholic faith is indeed universal and encompasses their own.

Rightly you warn against manipulating symbols to release forces we cannot possibly understand. But did not the early fathers of our Church run a similar risk at Ephesus, grafting the veneration of Mary onto the cult of Diana? And yes, the common people are bound to invent a lot of superstitious nonsense. Meanwhile others try to make the New World a repository for the unsolved mysteries of the Old—El Dorado, Atlantis, the Amazons . . .

And some of this nonsense is not so innocuous. Like the Beast of the Apocalypse etched in the terrain around Mexico City—the lake of Chalco its head and neck, its wings the rivers of Texcoco and Papalotla, four lakes formed from its spittle. Fie!

But you know how I despise this sort of thing. The Dominicans see devils everywhere as it is. Rightly do you remind me of the resemblances between our portrayals of Guadalupe and the woman of the Apocalypse, *a woman clothed with the sun, with the moon under her feet, and on her head a crown of twelve stars* . . . But this only shows how deeply these soul-sick and weary times of ours crave an Apocalypse. And in this the Indians are more like us than in any other thing. How our age yearns for the Kingdom of God to be restored in this New Eden.

And how the Spaniards fear and resent this American virgin who begins to escape their control! Guadalupe is the mother we orphans of America desperately pine for. Is it possible your objections to our project are of a more personal nature? The Viceroy's cousins told me that the aristocrats have taken to calling you Our Mexican Athena ...

I leave you, then, with a question.

Carlos.

Yes, she promised her protection—the protection of a monarch—yet what could I possibly need protecting from here? For surely there could be nothing left to fear as the favourite, the indispensable handmaiden to the Vice-Queen of the Imperial Court of New Spain. . . .

Every winter, elegant ambassadors from the capitals of Europe set sail, ears ringing with tales of New Spain—Mexico City!—streets paved with silver, its poorest beggar better fed than the King of France.

The story is well known: Cortés's men weeping at first glimpse of the city that now lies beneath these stones. These same men on the eve of the Conquest then toured as Moctezuma's guests the wondrous place they were about to sack. And though they had already seen many marvels in many lands, still more men wept to see the central market. For its variety and colour, its cleanliness and order, for the sheer generosity of a soft continent offering herself at their feet.

Today it cheers me to imagine those hard-handed conquerors sobbing like little children; for now, at the height of the shipping season from the Philippines, weekly mule trains from Acapulco totter into market under fragrant loads of pepper and clove from the Isles of Spice. Bolts of silk, crates of porcelain and bright lacquerwork from Cathay. From the south, the last delicate figurines of gold from Chile and silver from Perú. Then by December the first shipping sails in from the East. From Africa, ivory and diamonds, slaves and hides, Arabian incense, balsam and carpets. From Europe, wines and knives, fabrics and olive oil . . . All these distant wonders come now to contend with the local wares: here blankets, turquoise and walnuts, there cotton tapestries and quilted jackets, cloaks woven of iridescent quetzal plumes, jars of Yucatan honey—scented of orange, papaya, lemon—bubbling black chocolate, blazing bushels of flowers, broad baskets of spiced and roasted grasshoppers . . .

Scarcely can humankind have known such an intermingling of colours and flavours, scents and textures—and sounds. Today as I wander one last time lost and as though drunk through the winding alleys of plunder, the air fairly ripples with the soft murmur of Indian voices, the cries of hawkers, squawking parrots and caged songbirds, a donkey's bray, an aristocrat's mocking laugh, the tocsin of an anvil. . . .

Within weeks of crossing over from Spain some of our courtiers, accomplished veterans of the amatory combats of Europe, can be heard in public declaring—with a sincerity astonishing in professional flatterers, astonishing even to themselves—that nowhere are there women so beautiful as those of Mexico; and overheard in private lamenting that never again will they enjoy the same surfeit of sensation, never again the same intensity of desire as here, in America. They have known such hungers.

Here at court the new envoys marvel indulgently that the fashions of Mexico should lag so little behind those of Paris, even down to the cork-soled slippers with the half-moon buckles that were all the rage less than a year ago, and marvel that the necklines should dip deeper than in Madrid, that the lace should be so fine. But while our gallants flatter the Europeans with their evenings, their nights they consecrate to the negresses, the mulattas, and particularly to the *zambas*[†]—cinnamon-skinned, the most exotic of all. Through the shops and avenues they glide like dark swans, trailing scents of Nubian civet and Syrian spikenard, swans collared in jade and lapis, braceletted with garnets from Ormuz, rubies from Ceylon and Sicilian coral. Dark swans alighting from mahogany carriages they themselves have bought—along with their freedom—through the wicked application of their special virtues.

And so it is that here at the palace the emissaries of the Old World to the New consider it part miracle, part scandal, when the rare priest dies attestably a virgin.

So beautiful herself, and as exotic, with her pure white hair, her blue eyes of an Orient cat, the new vice-queen too is fascinated by these creatures. She acknowledges the most exquisite as we pass them in the street, on a whim summons one of the most elegantly attired to the palace for an audience. The vice-queen clears the reception hall.

She wonders—her curiosity does not seem entirely idle—if a titled courtesan might make her way here, as a certain down-at-heels Duchess has been able to do in Madrid. They talk, while I put in not so much as a word. Practical matters of prices and services, of domestic arrangements and security, now medicines . . . Leonor's smiling blue eyes never leave mine long—my face is hot, my head spins to hear the questions she matter-of-factly asks.

[†] 'zamba': woman of mixed Indian and African blood.

"Oh there is money enough," she yawns when the woman has been shown out, "but there are as yet too few gentlemen in your lovely Mexico with whom to consort not-too-dishonourably."

I do not know which to find more breathtaking, the questions or the cool calculus in her findings. But at fifteen I come too quickly to two conclusions of my own: that a palace exists precisely to be a place like no other on earth, and that I exist to live in one.

In the beginning everything fascinates her. And in her company, for the first time in so many years I am free to move through the streets. The Vice-Queen, twenty maids- and ladies-in-waiting, and her guard of cavalry and pikesmen. Our progress raises a furore wherever we pass, often afoot with the carriages in tow. San Francisco Street for gold, San Agustín for silk. The barrio of San Pablo for pottery, Tacuba for iron and steel. Weekly we stop in at the tobacco merchants of Jesús María and, just across the plaza from the palace, at the elegant shops of the Parian, which its Filipino merchants have so proudly styled after the famed Parian of Manila.

One area I do know, between Mercaderes and Calle Pensadores Mexicanos. The booksellers' district. Here too we go often, at first. Here, I lead.

Usually it is Teresa who guides us, the saucy daughter of a wealthy silver merchant of our city and engaged now to a gentleman of Castile. One day for the Vice-Queen's diversion Teresa takes us to the used clothing market, most of whose articles have been stripped from the dead. The day after, we go to El Baratillo, the market for stolen goods and contraband. At the entrance, the Captain of the Vice-Queen's guard balks. Teresa coaxes, flirts and finally cajoles him in but later, as we approach the zone of las Celestinas, the houses of the courtesans, his objections are not so easily overcome. The accounts of the good man's public dressing-down by our Vice-Queen swiftly make the rounds.

On the way back, we pass a convent where a *sopa boba*[†] is being ladled out before a long file of indigents circling the walls. Leonor stops and ladles soup for two hours, busies us handing out cups, sends kitchen scraps every day for a month.

[†]simpleton's soup

The people laugh to see, one Sunday at the cathedral, a servant fetching a flagon of wine back to her screened box. At her side I laugh, too— at the minor miracle of laughter in a cathedral. But not everyone finds this so delightful. For some, inviting a *zamba* to the palace was already the last straw—a prostitute, her crime punishable by death. The whispers of outraged civic virtue reach us even here now—whispers, Leonor remarks, from the thin lips of those women among the Creole gentry who got there through marrying up, and who give as little satisfaction at court as they are accustomed to giving in lower quarters. And so they have turned— dire and severe—to the Church: *These harlots of Babylon must have their wings clipped, lest Mexico become a modern Gomorrah . . . &c., &c.*

But for our good ladies, I've arrived at a dire prophecy of my own. That these, their pious petitions, clutched in bony hands better clasped in prayer, will be torn from them and scattered by the terrible energy of our times. By this bright whirlwind that leaves us all gasping and dazed. . . .

The Marquise Leonor Carreto. The most extravagant of our Vice-Queens, yet none has been so often seen in the streets, or so widely, even in the humblest barrios. The *vulgo*[†] take her curiosity for care and love her for it, grumble hardly at all at first as she spends enormous fortunes— mock naval battles on the lake; Roman baths and *placeres* on a certain ill-famed island; hunts and hawking on an imperial scale . . .

[†]commoners

Though each vice-queen renovates, Leonor's wing of the palace is all but entirely remade. Fondly known as the dovecotes, the *camaranchones* under the palace eaves must be expanded for the large number of ladies in her retinue. A hundred women in all, counting the servants of her servants. Her ladies from Madrid are entitled to a strict maximum of three. Those of us added to her company here in Mexico get no more than one—always assuming we can afford so many. The Vice-Queen's patio, the largest of the palace's three, eventually encloses a garden and fish pond in the Asiatic style, a small orchard, arbours of flowering trees, flower-beds, two fountains; yet there remains enough space free at the north end for official receptions and formal balls when the weather is fine. Around the patio, the great halls are renamed after those at the palace in Madrid. Hall of Comedies, Hall of Mirrors, Hall of Realms . . . She names the halls after the Alcázar, but she is determined to lead here in Mexico the court life Queen Mariana only dreamed of having, the life the enlightened are living in Versailles. It is Versailles we must follow now.

The season's fashions have just arrived on a last fast ship before the hurricane season. We are in the garderobe as her dressmaker studies the latest designs. Even on a bright day, little light infiltrates from the salon. Lamps burn at each end of the Vice-Queen's dressing table. She rests her hand on the dressmaker's shoulder as she bends to study the designs. Fuller skirts and tighter corsets are back, which can only bring Leonor's slenderness into even greater evidence. Necklines so wide and so low as to require the fuller figured among us to bow with a certain vigilance. A v-shaped stomacher—the jewelled and embroidered panel is to taper suggestively to the euphemism of a ribbon bow, well below the waist. Sleeves are to be shortened to the elbow. Falling bands and soft tassets are finally and definitively banished. Passable in embroidery, I know less about dresses than any of the others yet am singled out for the honour of dressing her on this special day. She stands in her silk underskirts, as if to exhort the dressmaker to work faster. "We have been at war with France for half a century, and this new peace, I assure you, is written in smoke, yet . . ." She takes the gowned doll from the dressmaker's hands, looks at it more closely, turns it over, as though to check the lady's bare shoulders. "One does not see the wings, Juanita, but though each book and post is examined for codes and Bourbon treachery, these dolls and fashion plates from Paris fairly fly to every capital in Europe. And now here, to me."

"To *us*," she adds, and gives my hand a little squeeze. Once her new dresses are finished, the best of her old ones will be altered for me. The honour is as unprecedented here as it is contemned by the wealthier ladies.

"Beauty, *mi amor,* is the empire that knows no borders."

And Beauty's proper consort is Laughter.

Her first act as Vice-Queen is to solemnly inaugurate the New World chapter of the Academy of Improvisation, modelled on that of Madrid, in which all the writers and court wits contend for prizes and for the favour of a monarch's laughter. But, for our Academy, a startling improvisation: here in Mexico, women shall participate. It is to the Academy that I owe my presence here. . . .

We had been summoned to the Hall of Mirrors, for an audience granted the three prize-winners of a poetry joust, and to my uncle, who had underwritten the whole affair. The Viceroy was again much taken with me, though with the Vice-Queen now at his side his interest was more clearly paternal than the first time we had met. But then, that was in a bullring. Uncle Juan had steered the conversation to the precariousness of commercial shipping and supply lines, to which the Viceroy responded by remarking upon the parlous state of the treasury just now, with so many silver ships being taken by privateers. The conversation was tailing off awkwardly, towards the parlous state of the empire itself.

"Excellency, Spain so briefly on her knees," I offered, "still stands taller than all Europe on its feet."

It was a little moment he was grateful for, from a fifteen-year-old. I have since learned few at court express such sentiments anymore. We went on to discuss the bright prospects for peace with the French, after fifty long years. I sensed her studying me, but we had been instructed to avoid looking at her—at either of them—directly, lest she yawn, perhaps, and we inadvertently penetrate with our commoner's eyebeams an aperture of the Royal Person. I still had no idea how contemptible she found such protocols. But though I'd gained her interest, she waited to see how I would fare at the Academy before inviting me to come and serve her at the palace.

At the north end of the west wing, the staircase has been removed to make room for the Vice-Queen's personal study and gallery. From atop the south staircase, then, the weak-kneed visitor is led through an antechamber and a smaller reception hall, spirited through the Vice-Queen's gallery—lest, perhaps, the plebeian gaze deface a painting—and shown into the salon, glittering home of the New World Academy. . . . In each chandelier burn a thousand candles, their lustre glowing in the gilded cornices and on walls panelled in white marble.

If the Academy is in session, it is evening, unless it is well into the night. In which case everyone is drunk. The Viceroy has long since taken to his bed. The Vice-Queen has left her rock-crystal chair and the dais to join the others on cushions on a stone floor softened with deep Moorish carpets. A fire is blazing in a fireplace wide enough, in a pinch, to spit a bullock in. It is a fire which never burns down before dawn, at least while the pages who feed it live.

If the visitor is young, she has smoked tobacco, maybe once, sipped wine once or twice, eaten chocolate much less often than she would have liked. But never all together, not like this. Under the steward's disapproving eye, pages liveried in silver and satin circulate a dozen argent platters heaped high with cigarettes, a dozen gold braziers to light them; while chocolate offers itself in every form imaginable—sculpted or blocked, bitter or spiced, whipped or spiked with brandy . . .

In deference to the Vice-Queen's Austrian tastes, somewhere out of sight someone brightly savages on a clavichord a turbulent organ piece, which Leonor, giggling beside me, says is by the Werkmeister-designate in Lübeck, who has secured his appointment by marrying the old Werkmeister's daughter.

I have done little more than taste each thing to please her. Brandies, sherries, ports . . . a wine from France that bubbles, hilariously, on caval-cades of trays that wobble past like upturned balustrades; and indeed within a few hours, the room entire is upturned and hilariously unsteady. Even without the fine tobacco smoke too thick now to see quite through, I might have been drunk on the perfumes alone. Yet I am far from the most intoxicated in the room. No, holding that distinction is poor don Alfeo, of a highly distinguished family in Seville.

It is the last round of the night. I have won everything so far. Hiding my condition is so far beyond me that I'm inspired to take things in the other direction and, as the incumbent, propose a round on drunkenness itself. Slurring very deftly, I improvise a ditty on don Alfeo who lies mel-lifluously snoring now behind a drape.

> PORQUE *tu sangre se sepa,*
> *cuentas a todos, Alfeo,*
> *que eres de Reyes. Yo creo*
> *que eres de muy buena cepa;*
> *y que, pues a cuentos topas*
> *con esos Reyes enfadas,*
> *que, más que Reyes de Espadas,*
> *debieron de ser de Copas.*[†]

Falling in worship to my knees, I then finish with a flourish.

> *Mis amigos, os presento,*[15]
> *Don Alfeo de la Espada,*
> *¡de la capa drape-ada,*
> *de la gloria remojada,*
> *del aguardiente empapada!*[††]

It is, I am told the next morning and to my great horror, not so much the verse as the besotted delivery that carries the final round. To close the session, the cleverest of the Vice-King's *sabandijas,*[‡] the dwarf Perico, cheekily christens me *la Giganta,* and placing a coronet of salad greens on my head, proclaims me the evening's Mistress of Wit. I am especially honoured, for Perico was a fixture at the Academy in Madrid. He becomes my first true friend at the palace. He was once a great favourite of the Sovereign himself, but with death approaching, King Philip sent

[†] Because your lineage is so broadly known, you profess to all, Alfeo, that through your veins runs the blood of kings, and yes it must be of purest vintage, methinks; for it is said you outdo the best of those prickly potentates, who vexed by being merely Kings in Arms, yearn to be Titans of the Tankard.

[††] Dear friends, I give you Don Alfeo of the Dagger!— steeped in glory, soaked in brandy, cloaked in drapery.

[‡] *hombres de placer*— the human menagerie assembled to divert the sovereign: dwarves, jesters, the misshapen, the insane

his most beloved *sabandijas* to accompany the Viceroy to the New World. Land of prodigies.

"Our promised land," Perico adds with a wry pout. "He thought he was sending us home."

Perico has never used any other name for me, but says it with such warmth and open admiration, even now I wear *la Giganta* as a badge of honour.

New rhythms and new music, cultivated palates and clever tongues. The dangerous new ideas of Europe in free circulation and we, *amazed* by our daring. So many new friends, in my new home. Perico. Carlos, of course, who comes whenever he is back from Puebla. I make a few fast friends among the courtiers too. Fabio I help to devise a betting system for roulette, based on the new theories of probability of my dear friend the monk Pascal. Fabio is decent and light-hearted, nothing troubles him. Fabio I can learn from. He is in love with the Vice-Queen, I know, yet he finds the strength to love her from afar, knowing it is impossible. And among the handmaidens, there is Teresa, who for all her wealth and spirit will only ever be a Creole, as I am, and never accepted by the others.

And yet the Vice-Queen calls me her literary lady-in-waiting. I should call her *Leonor* whenever we are alone. Leonor comes to find me every afternoon down in her library, devouring the contents of each aromatic page like a glutton over a new dish. Hers are the intrusions I never resent. The times spent with her are an extension of my education. Her judgement is flawless, and yet she flatters me by asking my opinion of this or that writer, about the plausibility or structure of a given philosopher's arguments. Our impassioned conversations spill into her bedchamber, where we are more assured of privacy, and where, as we talk, I spend what seems like hours brushing her shimmering hair before a mirror. Sometimes she reaches back over her shoulder and fans my hair across hers, blue-black over palest blond. "Almost the same, don't you think?" Leonor says, laughing sometimes, her blue eyes looking into mine—mine, black and round with disbelief as I see us in the glass. I am not quite so blind as to fail to see, the contrast could not be more complete. Her nakedness is at first a shock to me, but she explains that the body of the Royal Person belongs not to her but to the Realm. All her most intimate acts are open for inspection by physicians and counsellors. In the Queen's case, notaries may be called to stand at the midwife's shoulder as the heir is delivered, to warrant the integrity of succession. It was rumoured that Olivares[†] oversaw even the royal conceptions.

[†]adviser to King Philip IV

"Perhaps this is why so many were botched."

She says this lightly. I tell myself the joke is aimed at the malignancy of Olivares.

A small brazier stands beside the dressing table to keep her warm. We begin with the unguents and pastes, working up from her feet, finishing with a lotion made with almonds. She has heard of a miraculous cream made with avocados in the mountains, wonders how it is I haven't heard of it. Her hair is next. By now her skin has absorbed the creams. I kneel and begin to apply the perfumes and powders with a feather brush. She stands, to assist me, steadies herself with two fingertips on my shoulder or the crown of my head, arches an arm gracefully over her head, then the other, lifts one foot to rest a toe on the chair, then the other. Finally her makeup.

If there are no distractions it takes an hour to finish dressing her for the evening. Leonor says it is important to be discreet: some of the other handmaidens, with duties less exalted, are from rich and powerful families. There is resentment enough, now that I am so often called to dress her.

Flashing eyes, a Tartar's wide cheekbones and high—a ripe, smiling mouth, and yet her features are strangely delicate. Her figure is full and womanly yet so finely boned she is as small as a girl. Who dominates every room from the moment she wades lightly in, skirts flowing like a river. Playful and teasing, clever and intuitive. Sophisticated, in politics a subtle strategist. The Viceroy never comes to a decision without seeking her advice. Though descended from the House of Austria and married now to a Spanish Marquis, Leonor Carreto was a handmaiden too once, in the service of Queen Mariana. "*Exáctamente como tú, mi alma.*" Exactly as I am. The Marquise says this more than once.

She has decided I must accompany her to Spain when it is time for her to return, so I must learn all about the life there. Mariana was just my age when she came from Vienna to marry her uncle Philip. The palace protocol was odious, is still. The stories are legend. Once, Philip's first wife took a bad fall, and though badly injured, Queen Isabela de Borbón lay in the road for hours while the one man other than the King permitted to touch her person was fetched from the palace. Some time later, a quite dashing Count had the temerity to sweep her up and out to safety during a fire at a theatre. A few days afterwards, he was murdered in the street.

"But then," Leonor says, her eyes glittering, "they say he set the fire...."

She has known the greatest artists and writers of the empire. She met Lope when she was only five, Quevedo at fifteen, Tirso at eighteen. She grew to know Calderón intimately, and met with him frequently after he was made King Philip's chaplain. And while Quevedo was often crowned the Master of Wit in Madrid, she is not at all sure he would have such an easy time of it here in Mexico. Not that my gifts caught her completely by surprise. The greatest improviser the Spanish court has ever seen was from the Indies, too. The poet Atillano could make up the most astounding verses—learned or salacious, or both at once—according to the whimsies of his audience.

And so it is in this that I am keenest to impress her. She can recite the wittiest passages from dozens of comedies, to which, when we are alone, I improvise new speeches and dialogues to divert her from her loneliness.

Finally the court life she and Mariana dreamt of. Mariana, she says, would envy her now.

Leonor confesses to having dreamt of coming to New Spain ever since meeting the great American Ruiz de Alarcón, when she was only nine. We should go one day to his birthplace. Is this Taxco far? She is casually proud of her gift for languages—German, French, two dialects of northern Italy. The Castilian spoken here in the New World enchants her, the pleasant turns of phrase, the warmth and charm of our terms of endearment. *Mi alma, mi espejo, mi conquistador* . . . She delights in finding in my speech some expression or other that had been Alarcón's. I do recall that she had only been nine, but am nonetheless flattered. The seductions of the powerful are seduction to a second power.

 Now that the renovations are quite done, Leonor is rarely seen outside the Vice-Queen's wing of the palace but is everywhere within it. For two more years the *hojarasca* whirls harder, as if by the hour. Every day a saint's day, a prince's birthday, a wedding, a confirmation. Rousing displays of horsemanship and jousting with cane lances beneath her balcony. So many occasions to be commemorated with poetry, so many gifts and prizes to be accompanied with a verse. Nights of masquerades, carnival processions, mock battles in the square with flaming arrows, Roman candles. The dances. I have so many dances to learn I am grateful for each single one of the dozen I know. The dignified pavanes, la Chacona, la Capona, and others less decorous—none less so than the Canary and the Folly. But now there are dances to be sung to, and even a few to improvise poetry to. The best by far for poetry is the Rattlesnake. But the revels cannot really be said to be in full swing until the shocking and shockingly popular *bailes bacanales* are announced—the sarabande from India, for one, and an African dance so lascivious it has never been danced at court. Until now.

So much laughter—Beauty's consort too is everywhere. And knows no borders either, it would seem. Leonor has the idea of releasing a crate of snakes into the Hall of Comedies one night during a play. Only with the greatest difficulty do I dissuade her. No?—not even harmless ones?

Parties at the merest pretext or, of late, the rarest: the celebration of a Spanish military triumph. We celebrate, one whole night, the forty-sixth anniversary of the famous surrender of Breda; the women play the Spanish, the men the beaten Netherlanders. Not long after the King's death, there is a party with a secret theme, only later confided to me in greatest secrecy. We fête the loss of Portugal, eight thousand Spanish soldiers lost in eight hours. It is only once Philip dies that I understand how much she has despised him.

But she forgives me my elegy on the King. Because it is beautiful, she says, because I am beautiful, because I am seventeen.

There are some things it is time for me to understand about our late sovereign. His infidelities, his actresses, his obsession with nuns. Even in the Queen's company he made no effort to keep it to himself. The fortunes of a nation rise and fall on the spirit of its queens, and it is the married queen who bears the most terrible burden of all—supreme responsibility without power. So it is the duty of the Queen's ladies to cheer her, minister to her spirits. Mariana arrived at fifteen but each month thereafter aged her a year. Leonor did everything in her power. How terrible to stand by, to watch Mariana's spirit broken.

Our salons of jests and jousts only gain in ferocity, and at first I glory in it. And how it unnerves these men to listen to the verses the cavalier owes to the lady of the Hall—verses of a refined passion—but written by a woman now. Ah, to see their faces. To see hers.

> . . . On your most hallowed altars
> no Sheban gums are burnt,
> no human blood is spilt,
> no throat of beast is slit,
>   for even warring desires
> within the human breast
> are a sacrifice unclean,
> a tie to things material,
>   and only when the soul
> is afire with holiness
> does sacrifice grow pure,
> is adoration mute . . .
>   I, like the hapless lover
> who, blindly circling and circling,
> on reaching the glowing core . . . [16]

Such was the shock, one might have heard a pin drop.

More ferocious, too, the rumours and speculations about this *person* winning almost every night at rhymes; and even the laurels for learned discourses go to almost no one else, unless the topic is mathematics, which I avoid, or is astronomy and Carlos has come. Carlos too is brilliant but a man. Carlos too is poor but has a distinguished name, if not exactly noble. Yes, great things are expected of Carlos. Just not at the palace.

And Carlos at least has a father's name that is his to use.

But this other one, *la Monstrua*—I've heard them whisper it—how can anyone, a girl so young, acquire such learning in the wilds of that demonic countryside? No, there is something too uncanny about it. Nepantla? *Is* there such a town—and what must it be like, if *los nepantlas* are the local word for rabble? This bit of local intelligence comes courtesy of Teresa.

It is just a matter of time. Late one evening a cultured gentleman makes bold to impugn in rhyme an unnamed maiden's paternity—to which, before striding from the room, she rhymes something to this effect: not being born of an honourable father would indeed be a defect, but only if she'd given him his being, rather than receiving hers *from* him. Whereas the cultivated gentleman's mother was much the more magnanimous (in having him follow such multitudes) so that he might just as freely follow the suit and choose the father who best suits him. . . .

Have I gone too far? But not at all. Leonor is all assurances afterwards. In Madrid, the rough and tumble is more savage by half. I should have heard Quevedo's squibs on Alarcón's hunched back. Truly?—she hadn't mentioned his deformity before? But *no*, Alarcón was not wounded by the cut, any more than my Perico would be. And in administering it, Quevedo had no more dishonoured himself than Velázquez had by frequenting dwarves. No watcher of this curious compendium that is Man must ever close her eyes to this—this is life, life in its entirety. These were geniuses. It may hurt the man, but life nourishes the genius. I, more than anyone, must learn to see this.

The next night she sets the opening topic: the intellectual superiority of the white European born in the New World. In a salon full of gentle-born Castilians she herself takes the affirmative, taking me, Carlos, and the new Jesuit confessor at the palace as her prime examples. Relentless, she chooses for our second topic the effect of African breast milk on the Creole male. Carlos is stewing, has come to talk with me about something. I see him regretting it.

Is it true, she muses, as is held, that the Creole's affection for the source long outlives his infancy? And is this hardy milk, dispensed in such charming vessels and in such abundance, not perhaps the secret source of the greater potency and vigour of his body and mind?—

But Juanita was raised on Indian *breastmilk.*

Teresa.

I see them all watching me. Carlos, Fabio, Perico, the courtiers. Leonor. I have not told her this. Teresa is trying to cause a rift between us.

"The Academy would now hear," Perico leaps onto a chair, "how *la Giganta* answers the charge. Indian milk—*is it true?*" He has said this gently. I know it is in jest, and an opportunity to respond in kind. He'd be the last to care.

I could have spared her. A friend. Is it even true, what I say next? Rumours like this make the rounds about all of us. She is impulsive by nature and not a little giddy at the approach of her wedding. I know in my heart there is no malice in it. I see the ropes of pearl glowing in her hair, her hopes glowing at her cheek. Things will not be the same for her.

Teresilla, you may be a slip of a thing
but you've given your poor Camacho quite a whirl . . .
Those branches on his brow've grown so towering,
he stoops to enter even a vestibule . . . [17]

 Carlos comes the next day, under the pretext of taking his leave yet again, and in truth Puebla de los Angeles has not been graced with his presence for a while. He gives himself airs, as though he were above the Academy, but he comes often enough—verily does one wonder if the seminary is ever *in* session. I know he has come to admonish me, as he does so often lately. From no one else do I take this, and from him it has begun to pall. But I am dreading today—could anyone find recriminations more bitter than those I found for myself during the night?

I am afraid he might.

In the Vice-Queen's patio I wait for him where we are least likely to be overheard. Under the trees runs a chain of bowers—flowering hedges, head high, cut in interlocking els all along the bottom of the garden, from the Hall of Comedies to the palace library. Twice I catch sight of Carlos wending his way towards me. I have no particular affection for the new French fashions for men. The tiny jackets as though shrunken up the rib cage, the beribboned shoes and canes, the petticoat breeches, the fur muffs. And I am not so finally reconciled to Paris's latest rulings on what is divine in women's beauty—Heaven knows, they caused trouble enough in Troy. As we women put on our livery, with its *décolleté frôle aréole*, the latitude of our neckline makes it very hard not feel like pages, platter, and peaches all trussed up in an expedient parcel.

But any particular style has to be preferable to this new outfit of his.

Carlos has never needed a riding habit to go to Puebla before, a leisurely ride of thirty leagues. It occurs to me to be grateful: else I might not be able to face him at all. Bucket-top calfskin boots, netherstocks and leather breeches, a basque short-skirt with points at the waist, over which a short sword has been belted. Unfortunate, assuredly . . . calamitous is barely adequate. Apocalyptic might do—not Elysian, not Parisian, but a mix of all the sins of style of all the ages brought to stand together and be judged. A lace falling band *and* a lace cravat, both frayed to a hoary fringe, and both plainly second hand. Which only makes sense—the Plains of Judgement being evidently at the used clothing market, and how much easier to strip the dead where you find them standing. I see fashions from the eras of at least three Spanish kings, a French one, and perhaps a Caesar. Has Perico helped him shop?

By now I am happy Carlos has come. The velvet of his dark green doublet is bare enough in patches to pass for black satin. Across his frail chest a faded orange baldric and over one thin shoulder a heavy buff coat. The ensemble is capped off with an ostrich plume so bedraggled on a wide-brimmed beaver hat so battered I wonder if the ostrich was not captured wearing it during one of its cerebral inquisitions into a dune. As for how the beaver was taken . . . it does not bear thinking about.

He is twenty-two now—and even in a travelling outfit, this is no way to make one's way in the world. The overall effect is like a vision from Isaiah, where the beaver and the buffalo, the ostrich and the goat, the lion and the fatling lie down together. I have not quite lost the last of my nervousness, yet at this range I can no longer ignore his poverty, his unworldliness . . . and am flooded with the strangest emotion, equal parts pity and tenderness. He is so dear. A small frail military adventurer.

I rise to greet him, a little taller in my heels than he in his. He struggles manfully to hold my eyes. We learn here to wield the hourglass, as it were, like a rapier. At times it amuses me to observe the power this simple geometrical figure has over men, this body I have inherited from Isabel. But when I am alone with Carlos, when we are truly free to speak, it is as if we had no bodies at all . . . two spirits entirely free to jouney to any country, to fly anywhere the mind may go. How furious he is when he first hears this from me, and refuses to see in any part of it a compliment. Why?

He stands before me—the eyes made enormous by his thick glasses, bleary from too much reading, and angry, obviously, at the mere sight of me. I notice finally that he has cut his hair. He has left a little hank, a lovelock pulled forward over his shoulder like a chipmunk's tail, bound in a small black ribbon.

This good-bye does not feel like the others. He does not stay long. He has been reading my face, no doubt. But I no longer know how I am feeling. I think to ask him if the sword is a genuine original of the Roman Empire. I think to ask what sort of weather he is expecting on the road to Puebla. . . . I can think of nothing to say at all. I know he is in love with me.

He is in no mood for preliminaries.

"I simply cannot see how you can bear this snakepit another day."

The first harsh words he has spoken to me—no, we have disagreed. It is the tone that is new. How can I, he demands to know, have remained for so long blind to the jeering cruelty of this place—to the racist sneers, this fanatical obsession of theirs with pure blood? Have I not heard them whispering, 'Was her grandfather a *salta atrás*[†]?'

'backslider,' who sets back the cause of racial purity by breeding with one of the inferior castes

I have told only Carlos anything about him, and have begun to regret it. "And what other place is there," I ask, "for a poet *but* here? Quevedo, Góngora, Calderón. Secretaries, chaplains, chamberlains all."

"Is *she* the one poisoning you?"

This is so like him.

"What point is there for people like us to be envious of someone like Leonor?"

"Lope, Quevedo, Alarcón never had this kind of rival. They never had to be beautiful. I always believed it was *her*, but seeing you last night . . . I'm afraid what may ruin you, Juana, is not her beauty but your own."

He has taken his glasses off and—strange sensation—he seems nearer, as if I were the one having problems with my vision. His face wears the oddest look. As his lips part, I have the panicky feeling he is about to kiss me . . .

"Even as you have ruined Teresa."

 Now these letters.

He judges me from afar just as when he was here. Surely he does not imagine a woman could simply go to him—wherever he is now—even if I wanted to. *Why didn't he tell me he was really going away?* Does it have to be love—does friendship mean so little to him? One long perfect night gazing through a telescope together—pouring out our hearts, our souls, into the vessels of the other's eyes—were those hours not marvel enough without bringing Love into it? Was our time together not enough as it was?

And these outlandish projects of his. What business would he have seeing Isabel? Impertinent. Of course she is beautiful. What would he expect? And this great new enthusiasm for the countryside, for what is past. I write Carlos sonnets to tell him I'm sorry—he accuses me of insincerity! Then of disloyalty, even while he writes letters filled with sedition to me, *here*.

And through what strange geometries he pursues me, this future holder of the Chair of Mathematics. Running from the arms of the

Jesuits towards me, then right past me to a monastery. Then from one Indian village to another, where—ledger propped on bended knee—he composes arguments desperate to persuade where they cannot seduce. He asks me to contract to a life of charming escort, intellectual helpmeet, mother to a litter of children poor as church mice and nearsighted like a thin-skinned father whose talent merits rewards reserved for the *gachupines*. A father whose indignation renders him unfit for any lesser employment. He asks me to share a lifetime of slights.

Yet though he offers it to me, he doesn't even see it's not this existence he wants for himself. The respectable lot of a Jesuit scholar is all Carlos really wants. Not me.

And this other fantasy he conjures—my great Examination before the Scholars.

Forty scholars—why does everyone say forty? Even Carlos. Does he so need to see a Catherine against the forty sages of Maxentius, a Christ before the forty learned Pharisees? Can it not just be me?

When the Viceroy calls a halt, his face does not beam with triumph as Carlos imagines it. Replies like mine will do nothing but fire the very rumours the Viceroy wants quelled. He has called for this examination to put an end to the speculations about my learning's origin, which are becoming worrisome. The last thing the palace needs is the Inquisition sniffing about.

Not forty, not sages. A handful learned, none too well prepared. And no one is at all prepared to be answered in verse.

"Now would *la docta doncella*," asks the Professor of Music, "care to share with us her views on the relation of harmony to beauty?"

I begin by proposing that the limits of the senses mean that each, obviously, measures properties in different registers: touch, taste, &c. But not the soul. The soul knows there is but one true proportion. Sirs . . .

Here's an everyday example:

> Place along a line
> a half, a third,
> a quarter, fifth, and sixth—
> fractions geometry uses.
> Convert these into solids
> and proceed to weigh them

Choose an object of some weight
and in like fashion
to the line's divisions,
set out the counterweights.
These may be made to sound in harmony
as in that very common
experiment with the hammer.

Thus Beauty is not only
surpassing loveliness
in each single part
but also proportion kept
by each to every other.
Hence nothing represents
Beauty half so well
as Music . . . [18]

As its import sinks in, he sinks to his seat, his lips working slightly, like gills. In answer to the question in his eyes, I press on . . . *And as you, sir, so plainly see, Pythagoras calculated the harmony of the celestial spheres to be a circle of fifths, the music of a silence of such perfection we hear the voice of God in it.*
Sing.
Yet what if, gentlemen, this circle were instead a spiral—picture a figure winding up a cone poised upon its apex, a staircase if you will. Let us imagine a music of not spheres but spirals, whose section is not the circle of fifths but the cutting plane of an ellipse, as in the new studies of planetary motion. . . . A new notation, then, for a new vision of the heavens. A measure not closed, but spiralling like a staircase from the realm of man, up through those of Nature, thence to God. And yet as we climb, so small and so frightful, up that vast winding stair built to such a titan's foot, we find ourselves rising up the scale of that silent concord within which, could we but hear it, the soul finds its rest. . . . [19]

The Viceroy frowns, his mien darkening, and it is on this flattened note that the grand examination ends. But does it occur to none of them that many of my answers were in verses already written? Why doesn't it—because I am so young, or so female, or because one does not, in one's spare time, compose poetry on questions of speculative music?

And since that day, the mill and mongery of rumours grows ever worse. The Viceroy is more to blame than anyone. *After* the fact he is pleased enough with my replies, because the day makes for a good story. He tells the new ambassador from Milan that watching me dealing with my questioners was *like watching a galleon fending off a fleet of canoes.* Greatly pleased with his analogy, he repeats it too often. Too sure of my place, I complain of this to Leonor, of being foisted on the Milanese Ambassador like the Viceroy's favourite talking toy. She answers curtly that my gifts are an asset of the Crown. Velázquez understood this perfectly, without needing anyone to explain it to him.

Wounded, I take it out on the Viceroy, though of course I am not quite fool enough to say any of this aloud. *'Galleon'?—our chocolate-loving Viceroy has become a bit of one himself, comfortably in port, portly now in comfort. El gran galeón de la Mancerina. Does the Marquis de Mancera not see the satire in our naming a chocolate platter after him?*

Sweet Carlos, loyal, honest friend . . . the fruits of the victory he recalls to me contain the seeds of the bitterest defeat. There were Pharisees enough to spare, *but no temple this.* Christ in the temple didn't debate with a heart puffed up with vanity, with this insane need of mine to hold up my learning like a fist and shake it in their faces. . . . What Carlos does not understand is the *desengaño*[†] I discovered that day, and which invades me now. The University had been my most cherished hope—hope for a theatre of universal ideas nobly declaimed and defended, hope for a place where I would at last find my teacher. When that afternoon ended, I knew not on this side of the Atlantic, nor perhaps on the other, would I find a teacher to guide me, to trust enough to follow . . . to one day hope to walk beside.

[†]disenchantment, disillusionment

Faithfully the letters come. To gently shame me, remind me of our talks. Of Panoayan, of my dream of seeing Tuscany, of the Academy of Florence—*Academy,* what a mockery. Botticelli, Da Vinci . . . I have heard them snicker at even Leonardo here, at how he squandered his talent on trifles. *He,* on trifles! Accused by such as these. . . .

But the day I read Carlos's version of the examination, I see the question the Chair of Music should have put to me. And I do not know how I am to answer. *Answer.* I am called but I do not know how. No less then than now. Answer. If I am called, how do I answer? *If* I am called, I do not know *how.* Answer now.

'Why, señorita—if you are beautiful—is there so little harmony in you?'
'And why, Soul, dost thou know so little peace?'

PALACE
GAMES

t a turn in the hallway I come upon the three of them, brought up hard against the door of his chamber. The Ambassador of Milan and two of the hand-maidens, in a wing of the palace no woman should visit. He dangles a cluster of black grapes—obscenely plump—above red mouths gaping with the blind hunger of new-hatched birds, bids them suck each grape whole—one passes from mouth to mouth to mouth. A crush of silks, a thigh wedged between two thighs spread wide, a knee lifts . . . Teresa. He turns to kiss Imelda, cups hard her breast, presses the tip clear of the bodice, pinches, a hard dark grape . . . Bites down and splits it, grape juice running down. Chafes it with a fingernail.

Women's hands meet, fingers over wrists as vipers mating twine. He turns his face to me, smiles, as I stand frozen there.

You wanted to see me . . .

Yes, I have come for more.

 Leonor is not like the rest. Does she not tell me how much she and I are alike?—and I am not like them. We spend hours together in her gallery, just we two, sitting at different benches, sketching. Hardly a word passes between us over whole afternoons. What need have we for talk, when all around us such brushes speak? Originals by Murillo, Rubens, and one name new to me, of a Greek living in Toledo. Superb copies of Gracian, Botticelli, Titian. She has devoted an entire wall to Velázquez. He brought her to her love of art. They saw each other almost every day near the end. She, the Queen's most trusted lady-in-waiting; he, the King's chamberlain. She loved him like a father, grieves him still. In these half-dozen years since his death, his reputation has not ceased to grow. Madrid talks of no one else. Rubens, they have quite forgotten. Everyone sees his greatness, now.

No one loves art more than she does.

Leonor leads me into her study. I follow willingly. I love this room, try always to see it as for the first time: four unsteady herons stopped mid-stride—precarious stepladders running along shelves that line each wall to vertiginous altitudes; books, maps, illuminated manuscripts . . . the shelves fairly founder beneath their burdens. This is the room I have always dreamt of having. Near the tall windows a whole cabinet of curious animal skulls vacantly ogling. Thrown together in a walnut case, a precious cornelian vase, potash, verdigris, bits of rock and statuary. On brass carriages huge magnifying glasses stand ready for inspections. Leonor dismisses the attendant and herself fetches down folders that bulge with prints and engravings. Two folders for Velázquez alone, virtually everything he has done. Even sketches Leonor has made of some of his sketches from Italy. For the third time this month she brings them out, spreads dozens over the lacquered table, and I do not tire of them. Prints of half the works in the royal collections, even now the greatest in all Europe. In the span of forty-five years Philip IV amassed four thousand paintings. Philip. The great patron of Velázquez.

She says this sardonically, as though to take up my part in an argument, one we had last year, over my elegy for the King.

"Patron? Let me tell you—the King *killed* Velázquez. Went years without paying him for his work. *Four years once*—while they gave Rubens *palaces*."

I stand looking over her shoulder at the prints. She does not look up. I know better than to argue when she is like this. She is like this often now.

"A servant who painted was all he was. He was not treated as I treat you. At bullfights Philip made him sit with the servants—the greatest painter in the world! I couldn't bear it."

It infuriates her that Philip had paid one of the dwarves—who was it? El Primo, perhaps—a daily ration of nine *reales*.

"Velázquez, *mi amor*, was poorer than most of the misfits he painted."

The drapes are open. She sends me to the windows to pull back the cambric lining. Rain falls in the *zócalo*. A soft grey light falls across the vast walnut table, strewn with papers now like leaves on a pond: prints of the great painter's hunting tableaus, homely scenes in bodegas and kitchens, portraits of the King and of Quevedo. Her fingers stray over a fanciful rendering of Aesop, sketches of gods in the streets of Madrid— Vulcan holding court in a blacksmith's shop. A pale Bacchus, the toast of sunburnt campesinos . . .

She shows me again the work of his last years. The masterpieces.
Las Meninas.

"Look at little Margarita here. It is no surprise that the Princess comes out so well. He was very fond of her. But *las meninas*† themselves . . .

† maids of honour, handmaidens

I knew each of them intimately, and I swear to you he has seen into their souls.

"Not so very long after it was finished a painter arrived from Italy. He had come expressly to see it and left the same day, went straight back to Italy. 'I have just now seen the theology of painting,' he said, and would look at nothing else.[20] *The theology of painting*, Juana."

But the King did love him, I say, hoping to deflect her.

"Yes, he loved him. The man ruined everything he touched. He loved Mariana, too. She cheered him, she bore him children. He thanked God for the consolations she brought. And still his infidelities would not stop. Losing Felipe Próspero broke her heart. How beautiful that child was. Here—here was how Velázquez saw him as a toddler. Was this not a beautiful child? And then for her to lose him, only to give birth to that monster. . . .

"By then Mariana and Philip had been spending most of their evenings with the *sabandijas*. This was the class of diversion they sought. There was an amusing one with flippers they particularly liked. If he'd sent that one home to America with us I would have pitched it overboard myself."

How many times will she tell this? Leonor claims her physician calls it melancholy, but she does this to herself.

Leonor . . . come to the window.

"Philip *should* have felt at home with them—with his incontinence, his haemorrhoids, his nephritis. But her, even the most hardened felt sorry for her. And yet when that baby was born . . . scrofulous, hunched, rickety . . . the joke was, the real father must have been one of the dwarves. Once the jokes started, there was no stopping it.

"And now we have a monstrosity as King."

Leonor, come see the square . . . the rain has stopped.

I have loved her for her love of literature and laughter, for her loyalty to Velázquez, but I cannot help wondering now if the courtiers did not hate Philip, and then Mariana, for preferring *las sabandijas* to them.

She comes to the windows.

Is it not lovely? I ask. Below us a cat laps at a gleaming puddle. All across the vast plaza wraiths and revenants simmer up from the paving. Vendors uncover their stalls again. There is hardly a square to match it anywhere in Spain. Has she not told me so herself? She looks into my eyes, with her palm cups my cheek. "*Mi alma*, once we get back to Madrid," she assures me, "once you have seen *Las Meninas* for yourself, you will feel as I do."

About what, I ask myself—a dead king?

She tells me she needs me, just as the Queen needed her, as the King needed his great painter, needs me more than ever, with everything she loves so far away. She has only me, and this new confessor who is helping her. I should go to him, too.

I do not like the look of him.

"No, he is humble and pious and brilliant."

Perhaps. . . .

"Helping you?"

Leonor speaks of a difficulty between her and the Viceroy.

"A good and capable man," I say.

Too old and fat now to be a husband to her. . . .

I try to change the subject. It is dangerous to be put between them. He too is my patron, a friend.

"Why don't we walk through the square—just for a minute?" Now she is annoyed.

Could we sit in the patio, at least, under the trees? Or next to the library . . . ? No.

It costs her too much effort now to dress and go down before nightfall. She does not want me running off, either. Tell the pages what authors I want and they will bring them up. In the evenings she is more herself but the later the hour, the more reckless she becomes. It is the days that she dreads. Once the night starts she will not let it end. The masquerades, the Academy, the dances and the plays. My plays.

Maybe she thinks I haven't seen her watching him. Does she imagine her husband will never notice? It's dangerous for all *las meninas* but especially for me; the Viceroy sees me as her favourite, but if he could stay awake beyond eight o'clock he would see it is Imelda and Teresa who attend her once I have turned in—when else am I to read, to write these verses and sketches that so divert her? How often has she slipped in at dawn, thinking not to wake me, and found me working? She feigns surprise, each time, that I would lose sleep over her. But in her eyes the tenderness is real, and so I cannot bring myself to ask, to go back to sleeping in the dovecotes with the others.

Whole days we spend in her apartments.

A small private chapel stands between her bedchamber and the Viceroy's. It is the only point of connection between her apartments and his. Adjoining her dining room, the main salon divides into alcoves by the deployment of tall *biombos*† constructed in the Japanese style but elaborately painted with scenes from Mexico's history and streets. Late mornings before the sun is too strong, we sit on the latticed balcony, the *zócalo* before us, a wide plaza filled with life. We watch the secretaries and functionaries in black with their high starched collars. Priests leaving the cathedral, next to us. Grandees and their bejewelled trains of slaves coming back from El Parian across the square. Lay women in nun's habits selling blessed talismans and love potions to halfwits. . . .

Is this all? The question we ask ourselves. At first we do not notice it, then we try not to. The homesickness, the furies of tedium, the tedious furies. She was not always this way. Every day the same. The same conversations, over and over. And what she fears most is the melancholy, the melancholy is the worst. This could break anyone, she says, this could break a queen. Truly, I do not doubt it.

Once there were at least four maids and ladies in constant attendance. Now I am everything to her. Carver, cupbearer, dresser. . . . Her household is running half wild with nothing asked of them until nightfall. I am the only one she can be with, she says, I am the only one who can lift her spirits.

Is this all?

Yet is this not precisely how I am to serve? Do I think of abandoning her as soon as things become difficult? Velázquez stayed until the end. He watched and he saw, he consoled and he recorded, and it was not easy.

But *how* will this end?

This morning after a masquerade, we wake late, to an unholy clamour in the plaza. We are in time to watch a man hanged in the *zócalo* for breaking into a convent and attempting to assault a nun. The Indian ladies selling fruit in the shade of the gallows do not so much as flinch when the trapdoor opens. I do not like the look in her eyes. This too is entertainment.

Barefoot, naked under a muslin chemise, she languishes on the balcony and now in the salon until mid-afternoon. I have been dressing her each day for weeks, but in her bedchamber. Her near-nakedness in these semi-public rooms shocks and unsettles me; into her beauty a distracted quality has crept, the thinnest edge of madness. She is chilled, yet her forehead is hot and dry. She pulls back the carpet, draws up her chemise and lies full length on the cold stone floor. Extends her arms fully toward the unlit hearth, as if to lengthen the cold, as if a doll teaching itself to swim. After a moment she turns over onto her back, blinks, as if she has forgotten where she left me, calls me to her. She has come to a decision. There is something she needs very desperately to talk about. Something for us to . . . It is dangerous. I must only do this if I wish it. Yes? I sit close over her. The aroma of almonds rises from her, all the creams I have palmed into her skin. Do my own hands still smell of almonds? Yes. My hair spills jet across the ivory of her belly. Such a sweet confusion . . . She smiles into my eyes. Almost the same, no? Yes . . .

The new ambassador.

What . . . ?

Until now there has been no one.

Leonor, I don't . . . know how.

A hint of this would mean ruin. The Ambassador . . . do I—

Of course I know which one. *Does she think I am blind?*

Father Núñez says—what, you've *told* him? Oh yes, everything. *Everything.* Says what—no, I don't care what he says. Tell me . . .

I want you to take a message to him. Learn it word for word. I need them to be my words. *To Silvio* . . . Tonight, after the play.

Not every day is the same.

Ambassadors—the one foreign power Madrid ever permitted to post an ambassador here was from the Shogunate, before the Great Persecution. Informally the Philippines, Perú and Naples support *enviados,* but the more legitimately they conduct their offices once here, the more suspiciously they are viewed by the Crown. And yet the presence of ambassadors at a court that lacks for nothing else agreeably glorifies the majesty of the Vice-King's person, not to mention New Spain's pretensions to be a kingdom on a footing with Aragón—to the point where every man of honour is a *don* and every *hidalgo* is all but a count, and every foreigner here an ambassador of something or other. Military adventurers, fencing masters, gamblers, idle travellers, collectors of rare objects, arrangers of rare events. Any sort at all. These we call not the Special Envoy of His Serene Highness the Grand Duke of Tuscany but, limply, the Ambassador of Florence. Of things vaguely Florentine. Ambassador of florins.

Yet am I so different? Court poet—what have I let my life become? Was this not the title I once so prized?

How could I not have rebelled at the sight of the other writers and artists here? The worst reduced to the station of jesters, grown parasitic and fat at the King's table—the best, to the role of scold, and still just as much a part of the show. I thought I was above it all, inviolable behind the shield of my learning, invisible behind my masks, invincible on the battlements of my accomplishments. At eighteen the poet of choice for all occasions of state, whenever there is a visiting functionary to praise, a lavish gift to be commemorated. And now, by the time Europe's new ambassadors reach the palace gates, all have heard of me.

New Spain's Vice-Queen needs diversion—it is an urgent matter of state—so I am become her mistress of illusions, her magus, her hunting hawk. She yearns for daring, I write things Lope wouldn't risk. She is my Sovereign: I will be her warrior poet, her armoured suitor, her Giantess, her friend.

I write her sonnets. I carry her messages. Have I come so far not to create a *Las Meninas* but only be one?

Juanita, write us a comedy for Easter, another comedy for the empire. Somewhere in the Spanish dominions, they say, there is a comedy being finished every day. In a good week Lope could finish two himself, in a great month, ten. By the close of this century there will be ten thousand, with the ones I have written for her. Leonor sighs over reminiscences of Madrid, the parties in Vienna, the genius of Lotti's theatrical sets at the country palace—so I design marvels and have them built for her. Once, I build a camera obscura with my own hands, after designs by Leonardo. For two whole days it fascinates her.

I have sat in the audience among these friends of mine and watched my own plays performed. I have basked in the ebb and flow of their cultivated flattery, and believed it, no, *devoured* it. Seeing my work well received, did I so badly need to think them connoisseurs of art? The empty heads, the empty hearts ... Here we're all actors, with me the most abject of all, trapped in the plots of my own plays, lost in mazes of my own design.

All in the name of *entertainment*.

One by one, each of my lying masks has fallen away. Coquette, raconteuse, innocent. And what then remains of *me*, as finally the legend overwhelms even the charm and only the last mask is left. Freak of nature, monster of learning—*la Monstrua*. For women an object of both envy and disgust, for men, certain men, a trophy.

Carlos, I am not so different from them as you thought. Dear Carlos.

The last of the honest suitors. Even were I not now dishonoured, the only ones to pursue me still would be the giant-killers, the dragon-slayers—out to take a unicorn for their mantle. The letters that arrive now almost daily from the coast only make me feel more keenly my solitude. Poor Carlos, condemned to chase after me, just as I am condemned to love one who does not see me, even as I flee one who truly loves me. Poor dear Carlos—a scholar's mind, a mystic's soul . . . with the heart of a mathematician and the face of a clerk.

Carlos, what has happened to love?

I thought him desperate, but wasn't I the desperate one? To have remained so long deaf to the flatulent hiss of their clever fakery, to the gnashing and clashing of beaks, the endless disputing over mangled concepts, to the clatter of the finest ideas of the age spilling over the parquet like pearls from their glossy, swinish lips. How long was I to overlook their raucous, wrenching vulgarity?—gorging themselves like vultures on their gossip and murderous jealousies, on their coarse lusts and treacherous intrigues.

The decadence of Mexico imitating Madrid mimicking Paris aping the final degeneracy of the Medicis . . .

I carry their messages.

She watched me stuffing myself at a banquet of honeyed compliments and acid retorts—bitter chocolate sipped hot in the sweet night air. Cigarettes heaped on argent trays, gold braziers to light them. Intoxicating coach rides beneath wheeling stars, daring baths on the lake . . . until the worm was firmly embedded in my soul. How I hate these games of theirs now, yet I wriggle caught up in them like a minnow in a net. This puerile rage for cards. Cards, cards at all hours, while the lifeblood of a continent ebbs away through its open veins. I learned too quickly and not *well* enough, won too easily and stayed too long.

Here everything's a game, yes, but not the one I thought I was playing. She spoke so sweetly of my vulnerability, smiled reassurance down at me from the commanding heights of her unattainability. Why did she never explain to me the real rules, the true motives of the game? To keep one married gentleman out of the bed of another's wife. To lead idle nobles, unprotesting, by their privates in the service of their king—with us, the unattached maids-in-waiting, to do the leading. Games to keep a rich girl single just long enough to arrange a marriage, a marriage to someone not yet senior enough to have seen his future wife cavorting like a whore.

What has happened to love?

All around us the cloying scent of too-sweet fruit hangs in the air, as we whirl, beautiful as moths, blinded in this bright storm. Then one is plucked from the vine—for one, the dance stops, the game for her ends in marriage. Among the rest there must be casualties—disease, pregnancy, abortive loves—while for the poorest among us the games never end, except in mad spinsterhood or prostitution. At best, a few years cloistered as a concubine. Then it all begins again, but by then the player's lost her best assets, the adolescent plumpness, the limpidity of her unlined eyes, the undistracted quality of her attention.

Tonight I think of Teresa. What's to happen to her now?

Learned fool I tried to see these *galanteos*—these vile palace games—as some ancient tragic rite, as the dance of male and female satellites around a dying planetary king.[21] Like the seasons, the rules for each dance change: one night the ladies draw by lot their partners for the ball; another night the men compete not for a lady's favour but for the prize of her scorn.

This evening's little diversion called for the gallants to start off the ball in the arms of their second choice. Leaving us all to guess at their first.

But first, Juanita, give us a comedy.

She said I would have her protection. I laughed. I had not meant to wound her. . . . At nineteen, I was not a frightened child. I was not like them but I was not a prude. Was I not born on a farm in a pagan countryside? Have I not seen animals in the fields?—and I have seen things here. In three years at this palace I have seen too much. In a few hours, Silvio will look me full in the face and, with those glittering viper's eyes studying my least reaction, say it was all for a bet, that he and 'a friend' had gone double-or-nothing on whether he could have me in the space of one single night.

Tonight I would trade anything for the peace and silence of my girlhood in Panoayan, for the stillness of a village and a farm asleep on the dark shoulder of a volcano. I would give anything to see this bright whirlwind *snuffed*. I feel that mountain inside me now as smoke and solitude and stone.

Tonight I would give up even these things to see it erupt just once in a white cone of *fire*.

Ahh . . .

But instead of getting to play out my small part in a great cosmic agony I watch the next act of my life reduced to low farce—for this audience finds comedy in everything. In death, in the pathetic antics of cripples and lepers, in corruption and betrayal and loss. Anything to mask this fresh wound in their chests.

After the play she came to tell me he was waiting for me in the bowers by the Hall of Comedies. He never deigned to come to the Academy, so she led me to him like a sacrificial lamb. She even picked the place. Knowing of his interest in me, did she come to hate me because the rumours of her relations with Silvio were true, or because they never could be? Decorated soldier, veteran of a dozen duels with married men, Silvio was different, special, *más varonil, más válido. Tell me. . . .*

I am my own executioner.

Leonor Carreto—the most beautiful creature I have ever met. How could I guess that one so beautiful could be so base? The Marquise de Mancera, for all her beauty and attainments, is bored with everything but power. And knowing this at last I feel, looking back, the malice of power in her every moment with me. With a lover's cruelty she insisted I play, learn my part word for word. Make her words my own, as I had offered mine to her. But this, why this? Surely nothing so banal as my purity. Surely something more than a break in the tedium, the voyeur's thrill at seeing an uncommon spirit pawed over, the gambler's at seeing a ruinous wager lost. Learned fool, calculate the probabilities. Was it to convince herself—no, *convince him*—that I would come to be no different than she one day, after a lifetime of petty stratagems and intrigues? Or was it instead to prove one thing? To me above all.

The cut that wounds the mortal, the genius does not feel.

I went like Eve towards the serpent, Ariadne after Theseus, betraying her sex, her blood, her soul . . . only so he could then betray her. I found him at the bottom of the garden, a darker shadow among shadows—tall and powerful through the chest. I had watched him, many times. Disdaining the fashions of the French, he wore his own hair short, shoulder length, drawn at the nape with a simple clip. The beard trimmed close, streaked grey at the cheeks. Over a grey silk doublet he wore a velvet jerkin, black, lightly corsetted, so the adoring eye might contrast the breadth of the chest with the slimness of the hip, roam from the white stockings and hose full along the lithe muscular legs—to the jaunty parting of the jerkin at the jut of the codpiece. The beautiful blue hells of his eyes, impudent . . . the arrogant male, even with her. Did he imagine I might simply succumb without a word?

He stepped towards me into the moonlight, and even as I should have been thinking how deftly staged the moment was, my celebrated self-possession had already begun abandoning me. I heard myself asking how he'd found the play.

"Interesting."

"Surely the representative of Milan," I said, trying to get my footing, "has a more *interesting* response? Do you not find it something more than *interesting* that the play's hero challenges God and defies His order, but then invites punishment for his transgressions?"

"Only as a point of chivalry. But, yes, the old *and* the new. And for once, a noble man's sinfulness is not blamed on some outside force."

"I wouldn't have thought you such a staunch champion of responsibility."

"I believe it weak to blame new evils on old devils. Don't you agree?"

At last I felt myself beginning to relax. "With other causes so proximate, yes."

"Our hero took his fight directly to God, I respect that—and welcomed the return blow as an act of *nobleza*. He has committed a misconduct in his host's house, after all. But I see this subject has begun to bore."

"No, no it's just—this isn't the face you show in there."

"'This painted semblance you so admire / sets up false syllogisms of colour . . .'" he quoted, bowing slightly.

"You know it?"

"I know all your work, Juana."

"I never see you at my plays . . ."

"Good of you to notice."

When had I become such a blunderer?

"You mustn't take it personally, child, I'm just not one for sharing. Anything. But let's not waste your time on the trivial. As the whole world now knows, you're no mere poetess but a formidable philosopher. Perhaps you would help me? With a little syllogism."

"If I can."

"Excellent. Let's see . . . if it is true that to delight in evil creates a horror of solitude . . ." He glanced down at me. "Are you with me?"

"Oh yes."

"And if to flee solitude is to pursue the complete and perfect joining that is *love* . . . then this would mean that to flee solitude is both to love and to delight in evil."[22]

For an instant I hesitated. And then, instead of remarking that his syllogism consisted of verb phrases rather than common nouns, instead of subjecting him to a lecture on syllogistic figures, moods and distributions, instead of reducing the ramparts of his premises to wet straw and his propositions to so much hot air, I stood like a witless quail before the gamekeeper and found myself admiring the meagre kernels he was tossing to the ground. Already I should have guessed the whole thing was rehearsed, every word, under Leonor's direction. But I had let myself find something fatally compelling in an idea, as she knew I would. So instead of running—or standing to *fight*, I stuck my empty head through his little loop of string. . . .

"And therefore, *signor,* to delight in evil . . . is to love."

"Good girl, I knew you'd see."

"Oh I see more. I see how this makes a certain breed of man a kind of victim—at least in his own eyes—*forced* to commit evil in the pursuit of love."

"And don't forget," Silvio nodded appreciatively, "this breed of man is at the same time forced to love even in the pursuit of evil . . . especially in the pursuit of evil. Meanwhile—"

"Meanwhile the Ambassador of Milan was about to say that I must then surely see how committing evil, even as it deepens his horror of solitude, also deepens his capacity for love. Therefore," I went on, so eager to play the game, so keen to feel the braid around my throat tightening, "to love replenishes the well from which evil springs."

"*Brava, ragazza!* An observation altogether worthy of the hero of our play—"

"Yet you've also no doubt considered, *signor,* that to desire solitude sufficiently—*heroically* let's say—is to make love, for that man, both unnecessary and impossible, while removing all limits to his delight in evil."

"Delightful! Utterly delightful. You, *joven,*[†] are everything they said you were and more."   [†] young one, little one

"And you, *Señor Embajador,* are nothing they said you were."

Who was he really?

"Come child. We've begun so well. You don't want to join all these other clerks of love—insisting I find a fixed address."

I stood there in the moonlight listening to him hammering away at love. At retrograde, reactionary love that shuts the door on change, at baseless, insubstantial love—a pious vow like peace on earth or universal brotherhood. How love imposes closure, a passivity—not to choose but to be *chosen*. Love as an end to creativity, to questing, to living . . .

And though there was not a single premise I could not have dismantled, there was something in the whole, in the relentless energy of the assault, an echo of something faceless yet familiar, that I had glimpsed before.

"Still, if we must have hypocrisy," he said, his delight evident by now, "I much prefer the hypocrisy of women to that of men, don't you? I mean that for a woman, just as for a man, to delight in evil and to love both act upon the greater horror of solitude as cause and effect. But a woman . . . a woman transforms this horror into a positive, an *active* quality. She nurtures it, and it, her. Even while she is loving and sinning, this horror—the fear of loss and emptiness, this fear of becoming an empty vessel—is never far from her soul. And so, with the new anti-Christ of tonight's play, women share a special *genius* for evil, do you not think so? And a special sensitivity to the solitude it implies. Thus do they love and sin more intensely than a man, and it is this that nurtures him in his pursuit of them—even as he himself indeed becomes more . . . womanly."

So we played on under a watchful sky. The smile, the candour calculated to disarm. Into every woman's life walks at least one like him, the consummate player who knows all the steps of the dance, the feints, the pretended disinterest. How to make a show of hating hypocrisy, how to make himself an ally of the worm in her soul. And then, for all his mastery and virtuosity, to win completely, absolutely, he has to break the rules. The same rules that have served him so well.

Silvio broke the rules, but only after he had ground me down, outplayed me at a game I played with all my heart but only half my mind, a game I'd never seriously imagined losing. I never imagined how.

Hot with wine, the tumult of the evening—with years of *games*—my blood ignited. I had had enough of moonlight. I put my fingers to his lips, the lips of Leonor's lover. I had had enough of talk. I put my fingers to his heart, show me where it hurts, show me how. I placed his fingertips beneath my breast. Say it here, yes, and here, yes, and yes and here. God, my Lord God, how I wanted this, with a want and a craving that

crept and called in me like madness. At that moment I would have permitted him anything, had he only asked and not taken. At that moment
I would have gone with *joy* . . . He could have swept me up and brought
me to his bed through the whole crowded ballroom.

He could have told me I was his second choice.

JUANA INÉS
DE LA CRUZ

Alan Trueblood, trans.

Silvio that I could err and place my love
in one as vile as you has made me see
how heavy a weight sin's evil is to bear,
how harsh desire's vehemence can be.

Sometimes I think my memory deceives:
how could it be that I in truth did care
for one embodying traits I most despise,
whose every word of love conceals a snare?

Dearly I wish whenever my eyes behold you
that I could deny a love so badly flawed;
yet, with a moment's thought, I realize

there is no cure save bruiting it abroad.
For crimes of love admit no expiation
save to confess and face humiliation.

7th day of August, Anno Domini 1668[†]

TODAY I, FATHER ANTONIO NÚÑEZ DE MIRANDA, take my share of satisfaction in a great good: to have preserved our New Spain and the Viceroy's household from the mortal peril of a great temptation. Today I convinced Juana Inés Ramírez de Santillana to take the veil. Divine Providence ordained that I be in attendance at the cathedral wherein, an hour after Prime, I found her in a state of great agitation, which in turn exerted a powerful effect on me, for here was a girl of extraordinary beauty and distinction whom I had met (though not often: she confessed also to having avoided me), and of whom I had of course heard much discussion, at the Viceregal Palace.

At first I stood outside the chapel, unsure of how to proceed as she, thinking herself alone, collapsed before the altar and gave vent to a storm of wracking sobs. Her skin, already pale, was ashen, the more so in contrast to her black hair. Her large eyes, black in the dim candlelight, were wide, filled with tears and what seemed, from where I stood, like horror. At last I entered. As I drew close she looked up and at length recognized me as the confessor of her patrons. The girl and I began to speak. Though the details of our conversation remain in confidence, I can record that she expressed herself with astonishing precision for one in her state of unconcealed disarray, and with a remarkable maturity in one so young. I had the overwhelming sense that here was one whom God had marked for a special destiny, and resolved thereat, though I am not by nature impulsive, to offer her my protection, in this way to serve as His instrument.

The child spoke of an evil that followed her everywhere, saw visions of a black beast that stalked her, dogging her every step. Though she retained a rigid control of her faculties she was also clearly in anguish. She declared she would leave this world sooner than face it again. Finally I overcame her reticence to make a confession. As I listened with unrest to the distressing tale that ensued, I knew that she must be persuaded to enter a convent, a sanctuary from the temptations and predations of the world. The Carmelite convent of San José is known for its austerity and, moved by the ease with which she acceded, I have agreed to her own suggestion that her penance there be especially harsh. . . .

TAKING THE VEIL

In a chapel of the cathedral, the Viceroy's confessor has recognized one of the Vice-Queen's handmaidens, the celebrated Juana Ramírez, weeping. Later, alone in his cell, he finds cause for both jubilation and mortification.

[†]photostat copy, likely source: archives of the Seminary of the Archdiocese, Zacatecas, Mexico

The errors you have made with this girl. Read them again for yourself. Unforgivable mistakes for a man of your experience. After all you are not a young Theology professor anymore, fresh from the provinces—no, not fresh at all—yet on the eve of her profession, of her seclusion, you arranged all the candles on the altar yourself with the trembling hands of a young groom. . . .

She is far more beautiful than any nun should be, and her physical beauty pales before her qualities of spirit—such clarity of mind, breadth of learning, the incomparable wealth of her talent. With such jewels as these does one stud the mitre of St. Peter. But did you really think, Fool, that it would be so easy, that the Dark One would not fight you for her every step of the way? How pleased you were with yourself, thinking to have brought her soul safely into harbour. And now you will both have to pay.

If you are to be this child's spiritual guide, you will have to begin again. Start with what you have in common. Recommence with the awareness of your own emptiness, of your essential worthlessness except in the service of a higher power. Make common cause in your war against the flesh, the enemy you and she now share. And, books . . . you must begin all over again with her—make them *your* ally not hers. You have both lived your lives in libraries, but where you find heretics, she finds friends, comfort, bread. Her shield of learning?—*vanity,* futility is what it is, a paper army interposed between her and God. You know her, *you know her soul.*

So how then could you have been so wrong? How could you have so misjudged the fantastic power of her concentration, her mind? You thought, separating her from her books, to put her soul on the path of Virtue. Instead you have sent it careering, spiralling down to this, to vice. Did she not warn you?—of how, deprived once of her books a few short days by doctor's order, she had quickly felt the terrible energies of her mind breaking free of their ballast. But you were so anxious to dismiss this as silly self-indulgence, excess of poetic temperament.

How can you recognize her as exceptional one minute then in the next treat her as you have all the rest? She *begged* you to impose any penance but that one—solitude without books—one voice, her own, its echo turning round and round in ever-tightening spirals. . . . Thinking, thus, to humour her like some child, you permitted her one—but just one. Kircher's *Oedipus Aegyptiacus.*[23] You suggested others, but sinking a little deeper into your fatherly good humour you allowed your child to prevail. What harm could it cause.

She is not *your* child—you *deserve* to lose her. Seeking to dilute the power of her books, instead you concentrate all into one. You should have *seen* the signs, you must have. These dreams, first this black beast of hers and then the Sacred Heart. You told yourself nuns have these dreams all the time. Christ comes to the sleeping woman's bed, extracts her heart from her wide-open chest—excruciating pain then overwhelming joy. Three days later He returns and holding His own large, still-beating heart in His hands—those beautiful hands covered with His precious blood—he inserts the Sacred Heart. It fills her entire corpus with pulsating warmth as she weeps with the ecstasy of total communion, the absolute joining of body and soul. At last wedded to him, a true Bride of Christ.

In the morning they come and beg you to tell them it was not Lucifer.

Lucifer masquerading as Christ. You warn them against allowing their passion for Him to become too . . . literal, too material. You give them a special penance, the renunciation for a few days of any sustenance. They leave gratefully, smiling.

But she is not like them—is that so hard for you to remember?

You did nothing. You heard the reports. The endless hand-washing, the fasting, mortifications increasingly severe. But *you*, you persuaded yourself they were only in just proportion to the enormity of her sins and her gifts. But her soul is not yours. Her soul is not a mathematical equation. For her, you must master new subtleties: not every battle is a frontal assault. You will not have her become an *extática*, not while her soul is in your custody. All this is your fault. And now this letter. What an unmitigated disaster.

> *Padre Antonio Núñez de Miranda,*
> *Collegio de San Pedro y Pablo,*
> Pax Xpti,[†]   [†]Peace in Christ
>
> Father, it is with extreme regret that I must write you about a novice whom I know you have taken it upon yourself to protect and counsel, Juana Inés Ramírez de Asbaje. After careful consideration and much prayer and consultation, I have decided that for the girl's own welfare it is necessary that we ask her to leave the convent of San José.
>
> As Your Reverence well knows, ours is an austere order, in keeping with the vision of our founder, Saint Teresa; and the girl's harsh penitence was not at first out of keeping with it. Hours of fervent prayer, days

of fasting with only lemon water as sustenance are not uncommon with us. Neither is a certain amount of self-discipline. However, the ardour with which she has surrendered herself to these mortifications has become alarming. I must confess that to witness one so lovely become in so short a time unkempt, her hairshirt caked with the blood of scourgings . . . the icy baths, the hours spent praying on split knees, her gauntness . . . These are painful evidence of a disordered zeal. Nuns in cells adjoining hers claim she has not slept in a month. Sounds of weeping are heard issuing from her cell in the dead of night.

When these same sisters came to me about the chanting and the invocations, I felt compelled to investigate. For some weeks we clung to the hope that her fervour was for the Blessed Virgin. But the girl admits to spending entire nights poring over a tome by, I believe, a learned member of your own most esteemed and revered order. Reminded that <u>ours</u> does not tolerate the reading of books of any kind in private, she claims perhaps falsely that you, Your Reverence, allowed her to bring it in with her. It is this <u>pagan</u>—it pains me to use the word—Egyptomania that was the final straw in our decision.

By day she carries herself haughtily as though she were still at the palace, but her nights are haunted (though of this, she still admits nothing). And although she freely confesses to having broken our rules by reading, she refuses to concede that her conduct has in itself been in any way impious, or even wrong. As you must already know, it is useless to engage her in debate: no matter the extremity of her suffering and disorder, her mind burns bright and clear as the Pole star. If it were not for this, I could perhaps accept—many of the nuns here are often confused. She is not. And were it not for my deep respect and admiration for you, Father Núñez, and for all you have accomplished with the sisters of Mexico, I could not have stayed my hand this long.

She warned us that if we took this book from her she might very well go mad, and it is as if she has. I could cite other examples, but suffice it to say that the rigours of our Order have plainly unseated her too-sensitive nature. Her pain is patent, her need is real. But, however great her need, it is unacceptable that this girl, extraordinary though she is, raves of 'Naustic unions' and <u>venerates an Egyptian goddess within the walls of our cloister</u>!

I must ask that you prepare to receive her at your earliest possible opportunity. Once again, please allow me to express my deepest regret

that she has not been able to find here with us the rest and solace she so
badly needs.

Your obedient servant,
Madre Felipa de Navas
Convent of San José of the Discalced Carmelites

No, the Reverend Mother will have none of her novices cooking up
Naustical unions in their cells. She would not know a Gnostic union from
a nauseous onion. And, yes, the woman is ignorant, but *you* are the fool.
Your tactics are hardly less crude than hers, and far less subtle than the
Enemy's. You could bully the woman into acknowledging Kircher's orthodoxy in the eyes of the Holy Office and that Isis is a blessed prefiguration
of the Virgin. But you would only be compounding your own errors, the
errors of which these journals must be the unflinching testament.

The austerity you imposed on this girl is really the one you covet for
yourself. Grown fat on so many easy successes are you now to meet with
your greatest failure *just when it matters most?* To lose the greatest mind on
the continent to pagan madness?—a woman hand-delivered to you by
Providence?

No. A thousand times, no . . .

Perhaps as a spiritual director you *have* no true vocation. But you have
a *will.* To bring the great ship of her soul into port may have become your
career's crucial campaign, its greatest challenge and danger, its turning
point. You must put this right. You *will* right this ship . . .

But more gently, more patiently. A soul like crystal, lucent and brittle,
must be polished. Polished, not broken. Ground down like a lens.

Let her return to the palace. Her life there is more untenable than
ever. When she comes to you again, as she must—who else is there for
her now?—sooner or later you two will talk of San Jerónimo, a convent
known for its loose discipline and worldly pursuits. . . . And if marriage
is truly reprehensible to her, or indeed no longer practicable, then a convent is the last respectable option. Bring her to see it as the only path
from the palace that does not lead to perdition, to the ignominy of a
beaterío,[†] or the infamy of a *recogimiento,*[††] a place of reclusion so complete that the windows themselves are to be mortared in.

Arrange a visit, if necessary. If our young poet thinks the convent of
San José severe, give her a glimpse of life without sunlight.

[†]shelter for indigent
widows, reformed
prostitutes and
retired actresses

[††]women's prison
for delinquents,
thieves, murderesses,
adulteresses, street
prostitutes . . .

JUANA INÉS
DE LA CRUZ,

THE SCEPTRE OF
SAINT JOSEPH

B. Limosneros, trans.

(Enter INTELLIGENCE, SCIENCE, ENVY, CONJECTURE, LUCERO.)

LUCERO:
Beauteous Intelligence, my bride
who, from the first joyous instant
I knew myself in that most blest of Realms,
have been to me, not less than Envy, companion
through good fortune and ill, so constant
so fine, so loyal, so loving
as not once to have strayed from my side
through that most terrible of times
when, deserted by Grace and by Beauty—
they unto the Almighty Seat cravenly cleaving—
only you, in your constancy, me never leaving,
into the Abyss in my company descended;
perhaps that within me should rage such a torment
as to blaze hotter yet by the light of your eyes . . .

CONJECTURE:
Let that be for Conjecture to decide,
since your daughter am I, and your Science's;
through me alone shall you divine the consequences.

ENVY:
And through me, those of feeling, since I am Envy,
your daughter too, asp that writhes
through the embers of your breast
and from the ravel of your bowels unwinds;
for, once your Science perverse
conceived on her its monstrous stillbirth,
your favourite I became, of all the vices,
that you deploy by so many exercises,
panting ceaselessly after
war unrelenting waged on Heaven. . . .

19th day of October, 1667
Monasterio de Nuestra Señora de Dolores

Juana Inés,

Another letter from you on the heels of the last, and after so much silence. Your words come to relieve me in my torment. Each night I sit down to write you and fill the page with such trash. It seems I have nothing to write that I can bear to have you read. Then your letter arrives and my head teems with things to say.

Truly am I honoured by this sonnet on Guadalupe. You said you would write it for me one day and you have. These lines I love:

> La compuesta de flores Maravilla,
> divina Protectora Americana,
> que a ser se pasa Rosa Mexicana,
> aparaciendo Rosa de Castilla;
> la que en vez del dragón—de quien humilla
> cerviz rebelde en Patmos—huella ufana,
> hasta aquí Inteligencia soberana,
> de su pura grandeza pura silla . . . [†]

But do not think you have thrown me off the trail: I know how easily this kind of elegance comes to you.

You ask if I am truly interested in the Indians' salvation, if I am not perhaps more concerned with my 'Americanist project,' as you refer to it. The world's myths, as you say, are treasures of the imagination, not to be plundered for worldly advantage. Is this what you suspect we are doing? But even if it were true, could one not answer that the gains go far beyond politics, to the healing of the American soul? Then, you ask if the Franciscans are not more devoted to taming Eve than to venerating Guadalupe. Point taken.

And you are right of course—to 'have powers over the serpent' does not necessarily mean she must use them to destroy it.

But proceed more carefully now. You intimate that the Church has modelled the Blessed Virgin on the Egyptian Isis even while stripping her of her godhood. Then you argue persuasively—and dangerously—

[†] Marvel wrought of flowers, America's divine Protectoress, who becomes the Rose of Mexico in summoning Roses from Castile; she who brings down from on high not the dragon— whose neck she bowed in Patmos— but sovereign Intelligence, and glorious sign of its greatness and purest Majesty . . .

that the Church has struggled as much to prevent her regaining the divine plane as it has Lucifer.

As a friend I repeat the question: Are you not afraid of them making you our Queen of Wisdom? I do not think the fear an idle one.

It is becoming imperative that we develop a code so as to express these thoughts more safely. Indeed like a dragon in its death throes, the Inquisition is these days at its most dangerous, flailing out in all directions . . . at perversions, heresies and false gods. At women falsely claimed to be saints, and at female poets who make Mary into Sophia, a seductress of Christ, but cloak her in the costume of a Greek wood nymph. . . . Be very careful, Juanita, with this rash plan of yours to finish your *Divine Narcissus* after all. Be more careful still to whom you show it.

un abrazo, Carlos

 12th day of November, 1667
Monasterio de Nuestra Señora de Dolores

Juana,

I wish you the happiest of birthdays. To think that I have known you almost four full years. To think you were barely fifteen. . . . And is it really possible I shall soon be twenty-three? My senescence may even now be revealing itself to you in the gaps in my reasoning and the infirmity of my hand.

Still not one word of the palace. Each day you become more mysterious. I cannot shake this stubborn hope of mine that you have left that den of fops. But no, as you have said, where would you go? I readily admit that for one with neither means nor connections, life in Mexico is quite difficult enough, even for a man. You could of course come here, without prejudice or conditions. A woman's reputation is not a thing to be surrendered lightly—not even as the price of her independence—but can yours truly survive their palace so much longer than my jungle? I take you at your word: you have written how much you envy me the collegial atmosphere and the freedom of this place, the soberness of this work—my mind flashes to you on your way here and my heart races for an instant. But no, enough. We have each chosen our place, and this one, for all its satisfactions, is not palatial.

If you will say nothing of your present life, let me tell you of mine. The monastery has been astir with a discovery that lends credence to the rumours that brought Fray Cuadros here in the first place. In the jungle a full day southwest of here we've discovered a village, Pital, at the edge of a ruined city. Although their ways and manner of dress are unfamiliar to Brother Cuadros, the villagers do speak a dialect of the Mexican language and have moreover made themselves the custodians of a large codex, an ancient Mexican book that they venerate in one of the old temples.

We are expecting a native interpreter to arrive any day from the Indian College in Tlatelolco, but the difficulty here, as Brother Cuadros explains it, is not strictly one of language. These painted-books, which we misleadingly call histories, are only the pictorial notation, not unlike a musical score, for a performance. It is not enough to read the glyphs; they are just the cues. The performers once carried within them the script, and when they needed to, redrafted it. I am learning that history was for the ancient Mexicans a dramatic art. Nor do they seem to insist there be one sole version: it falls to each people to continually create and *recreate* its own. (To us, the Creoles, who find ourselves orphaned by history, how could this fail to bring inspiration?) While for the European, the age of myth ends and history begins with the birth of Christ, for the Mexican, the frontier between myth and history is fluid and the influence reciprocal. Time is both linear and cyclical, and so history is also prophecy and pattern, but nevertheless admitting of a series of variations on central themes.

You have perhaps learned all this at your wet nurse's knee; but for me it remains most difficult to grasp that the Mexicans not only use the past to interpret the present, as we do, but the present to reinterpret the past. Am I right, then, in concluding that they see Time's effects flowing not just forward but also backward? How strange to contemplate, as if to reverse the river of causes, make it flow uphill, see the sun setting in the east.

They keep their codex in the temple of their war god, at the western edge of this ruined city. The book rests on a stone altar the length of a man. Cut into the altar is a series of channels draining to a stone basin embellished with a relief of skulls and flowers. In the shadows, overgrown with moss, is a statue with a woman's face, one side fleshed, the other side peeled back to reveal a death's head. As for the codex, it is well cared for, and the villagers are protective of it. We now believe their ancestors were not just left with the book but also with the story.

Someone in this village still carries that story within him . . . Though we have been allowed only cursory readings, Fray Cuadros is sure it comes from Cholula and deals at least peripherally with the Conquest. Most intriguingly, images of Cortés's interpreter Malintzin appear on almost every page.

Sleep well,
Carlos

 8th day of December, 1667
Pital

Juana,

I am sorry to take so long to reply. Your letter took longer to reach me here.

Today Pital is just a fishing village on a lake, one of many linked in a network of canals and streams. The beaches are black, laced by the runnels of freshwater springs—some steaming, others deliciously cool. The shore lies shrouded in jungle and studded with curious hillocks; but on closer inspection one sees these arranged along straight broad avenues starting out from the shore. Only those building mounds immediately surrounding the village have been kept clear of the encroaching jungle.

Your letter might have taken longer still, had not Brother Cuadros's interpreter brought it in from the monastery on his way down from the capital. We thought he had come too late, but it turns out he is just in time. Just as we were preparing to return to the monastery last week, a village youth came to offer his help with the codex.

Although Fray Cuadros seems perfectly fluent to me, this new science, as practised by the Franciscans, requires that the Indian testimonies be recorded with rigorous precision. Which means, in this case, two interpreters—one whose mother tongue is Castilian, the other a native speaker of Nahuatl. The two must constantly check each other's assumptions and understandings, which are in turn tested against the testimonies of others.

This former student of his is most impressive. Brother Cuadros tells me Juan de Alva Ixtlilxochitl has become their foremost translator of the Bible into the Mexican language. Their secret project is to prepare together a version of the Song of Songs for the day when the Church deems it safe to translate. Incredibly enough, Juan's direct ancestor was

Nezahualcoyotl himself, the legendary poet-emperor. I indulge in the hope that this might finally be incitement enough to bring you here—this *is* your grandfather's work we are at. As for myself, I feel at last that my life might be close to acquiring a more weighty purpose. Surely at twenty-three it cannot be too late for me? I am like a man from the mountains first finding the sea.

And yet for all the combined skill and vast knowledge of our interpreters, the work proceeds haltingly. We suspect the boy either knows more than he lets on, or has not been completely initiated. "Did someone send you?" we ask but get no reply. At least we now have full access to the codex.

Juan de Alva and Fray Cuadros now concur: The book travelled here with a party of Mexican priests fleeing after the sack of their capital. Our codex begins where, after the kidnapping and subsequent death of Moctezuma, Cortés's army—routed and driven from the capital—returns battered and bloody to Cholula, a city swirling with rumours. Everyone, including the Spaniards, is desperate to understand what has just happened. Then, as now, so much depends on the translation. The conquest of our New Eden hanging in the balance . . .

The picture script shows us the wife of a Cholulan general, who goes to meet Cortés's beautiful interpreter in the market—the Spaniards have not eaten for three days. Each woman angles for information. The interpreter Malintzin apparently wins the contest, since at some point her new friend, thoroughly captivated, first warns then begs her not to go back to the compound where the Spaniards are housed. An ambush is planned. Malintzin is able to spin out their talk for long enough to piece together all the details of the attack. She then returns to the compound on the pretext of salvaging her personal affairs and forewarns the Spaniards.

This codex, then, contains the gossip she left with the general's wife, an account of Moctezuma's last days as a captive in the very heart of his own empire.

As I sit here among the ruins and conjure up the scene of these two women gossiping amiably in a marketplace, yet with such deadly implications, I think of Scheherazade. And of you, the palace's most enchanting songbird singing for her life.

ever yours, Carlos

2nd day of January, 1668
Pital

Dear Juana Inés,

I wish you a prosperous new year. I truly hope you celebrated it surrounded by friends, as I have.

Cuadros is kind and learned and generous, and our Juan de Alva looks every bit the Indian prince in face and bearing yet conducts himself in all humility. He is without a doubt the most handsome man I have seen. A *mestizo*, and therefore more an exile in America than even we are, he works ceaselessly, speaking with the natives, learning details of their dialect, patiently listening, gaining their trust. He and Cuadros are teaching me some of the Mexican language. So you and I shall be able to converse a little in the language of your childhood when I get back to Mexico. . . .

For my part I have been unwell, too feverish to concentrate long. At the fever's highest pitch, their healer came to sit with me. He examined me closely for evidence of bites, then, presumably to join me in my delirium, ingested quantities of a dried toadstool in order to complete his diagnosis. I give Brother Cuadros great credit for permitting his visit. It appears my condition was precarious and Cuadros had seen native healers work wonders with fevers similarly severe. My recovery has been equally wondrous. I am being treated for a loss of soul.

Cuadros smiles and tells me the diagnosis is only natural, since the native Americans have three souls to the Christians' one.

With the worst over now, I divide my time between short, shaky walks around the village and visits to the healer, where I strip naked to be swept clean of noxious spirits by egret's wings. I then drink a bitter broth and, perspiring rivers, sleep a peaceful siesta beneath leaves the size of parasols.

My walks have been fascinating. More than once have I heard the Indians' capacity for work praised in the same measure as their short lifespan is lamented. But then, I had never seen an Indian settlement not in service to the Crown. While I do see great industry, I see also many old white heads. . . .

What strikes me most forcibly is what I can only call a genius for fashioning fine tools and materials from this wild place. Cylindrical fish traps of woven reeds, three-pronged spears tipped with horn and bone. All manner of baskets and platters and ladles. Polished and painted gourds. Spinning drills for piercing jewellery, and a sort of *tarabilla:* by pulling at handles mounted on a drum one drives an axle that in turn twists fibres of hennequen and agave into ropes fabulously strong. The principle of the wheel, Juana, they seem to have mastered quite nicely on their own.

On the twentieth, we helped the people of Pital mark the winter solstice. Even in the ruins, they preserve the ancient knowledge of the heavens. How this gladdens my astronomer's heart! Four days later we celebrated Christmas Mass. I should not have been surprised that these villagers have at least a rudimentary knowledge of the sacraments. Christians have after all passed through here from time to time. But Juanita, to see a native American so willingly taking the host into his mouth . . .

I know you are not a little disdainful of this theory of ours bringing Saint Thomas to the New World. Much more troubling to me is your observation that our theory risks making the spiritual glories of the Americas mere mimicry, and the Indians incapable of getting the details straight. But consider for a moment the Mexican conception of the Eucharist. For the centrepiece of their most holy festival, their priests grind seeds and grains into maize flour, then, stirring in quantities of blood, make out of this dough a man-sized figure. After which, at the close of a month of processions an arrow is shot through the figure's chest by an archer whom they equate with the Feathered Serpent, Quetzalcoatl. Each member of the community then receives with great awe and weeping a portion of the body and, having swallowed its flesh, cries out—*Teocualo!* God is eaten.

God is eaten, is this the savage hunger of a cannibal or the hunger of the human spirit for communion with its god? They even possess an equivalent to our Holy Wafer, in the form of little idols of dough, which they call 'food of our soul.' Who could help but recall the Gospel of John?

Whosoever eateth my flesh, and drinketh my blood, hath eternal life. . . .

The great glory of the Mexican spirit is to have perceived as well as any Christian theologian the deepest intent of Christ's ultimate sacrifice. We ourselves might well have worshipped exactly as they did, had Christ not revealed to us He wished otherwise. Indeed, the Mexicans understood this alternative perfectly, for it was from the Feathered Serpent that they had chosen to turn away, their god-prince who forbade the sacrifice of men and yet sacrificed himself.

You knew, perhaps, that the Mexicans baptized their infants as we do, and that they practised confession leading to absolution. That their earthly paradise was lost when a woman ate of a forbidden fruit. Heresy, the Inquisition will call it, but how can it be heresy when we have so miserably failed to communicate a deeper understanding of our Faith? Monasteries and convents, the symbol of the Cross, and a young man-god who willingly sacrifices himself while promising to return—so much our peoples already shared! So much in fact that the Dominicans have convinced themselves Satan, no less, must have visited America to propagate a perversion of the Gospels. Who, indeed, could blame them?—to cross an ocean and find a faith in many ways more similar to ours than that of the Jews or the Moors.[24]

No, Juana, it is undeniable. An overwhelming series of correspondences exists between the Old World and the New—if, as you have often argued, Egypt shaped our beliefs as much as did Greece, perhaps we should really be looking much further back than Saint Thomas. Lucian writes of grain ships of two thousand tons' displacement leaving your beloved Alexandria. If the Egyptians could sail around Africa, and the Phoenicians dispatch fifty ships to colonize its west coast, then why not here?

Such similarities in weaving, pottery and metal work. Both architectures developing spiral staircases, sculptured doorways and lintels—pyramids and hieroglyphs. The same insignia of kingship—sceptres, canopies, palanquins, the conch shell as royal trumpet . . .

I walk through the ruins of this city that encompasses the village and see glimpses of these things. A long colonnade . . . pillars weeping lichen and lime. Fragments of fresco under moss, itself bright as paint—a face in profile, a bundle of reeds, daubs of hectic red, cobalt. Pale lintels carved with stone flowers and leaves. Sprouting from the midst of these, living rose-pink polyps, sprays of orchids and other leaves green and alive.

I have come to see this city laid out around me as a text, a living palimpsest slowly being rewritten by older scribes of Time and Vegetation—and deciphered at hazard now as I turn, wander, glancing this way and that, as if to follow the waver of a finger down a page. . . .

So now I turn your question back to you: If not through the visit of an Old World apostle how to explain such bewildering similarities in the New? We have been talking here about little else lately. Fray Cuadros can go on relentlessly reciting the lists he's compiled. Still more wondrous to me than these twinned inventions of the world are those of the spirit. In both the Mexican and Egyptian skies, a hero is birthed from the waters of darkness, beset by dragons, forges a hazardous passage through the heavens, is devoured at dusk in the Western lands of death . . . *then is resurrected.*

For the villagers here, as for the ancient Mexicans, the world has already been created and annihilated four times. And the Fifth Sun, which passes over us today, will also die, and will be the last. At the end of every fifty-two-year cycle, their universe hovers between a final, eternal destruction and a temporary renewal.

When Hernán Cortés first stepped ashore in America on Good Friday, four vast myth systems came into collision. Like four great ships rafted grindingly together in a turbulent sea, with mankind in the water, struggling not to be crushed, not to be drowned, fighting to clamber aboard any one of them and gain the shores of a new world. Good Friday, 1519, marking the death of the Son of God, was also the first day of One Reed, the year of Quetzalcoatl's death, and also the year of his promised return. Good Friday that year fell on the first day of the Mexican new century.

In Cortés the first Mexicans saw Quetzalcoatl. In this Feathered Serpent, who forbade human sacrifice and yet sacrificed himself, the first Spaniards saw a parody of Christ, and Cuadros now sees Saint Thomas. Your Athanasius Kircher finds, in Christ, Osiris resurrected. *You* have seen Narcissus. In Quetzalcoatl, the god led unwittingly to incest and his own destruction, who would fail to see Oedipus?

While in you . . . in you, Mexico sees the Phoenix.

29th day of January, 1668
Pital

Juana,

There is so much more to this settlement than we realized. Last week I think I mentioned that a string of islands reaches almost to the shore. During a walk through the village I thought to take a certain route to meet them at the beach, drawn as I was by a curious configuration of rock there. At the edge of a clearing behind the village stand two thin jagged spires and between them a gap of perhaps three armspans. The spires are not more than two storeys high, and glisten with minerals deposited by countless small springs leaking from the rock. The formation itself is not man-made, but the hollowed-out trunk that spans that gap undoubtedly is, for through a string of perforations in the wood trickles a fine mist of spring water. When I made inquiries as to its purpose I was told at first that the mist kept the clearing cool, which indeed it does. And in reason of this coolness, I thought, many women and children work there at the water's edge, on the fresh green grass, at looms and *metates*.

But what we have at last been shown is how this archipelago once was linked by bridges. Whatever its present purpose, I think this veil of mist was originally intended to conceal that first bridge from the casual onlooker. The islands constitute what I believe to have been a string of fine craters, high-sided along the periphery yet flat and open through the centres, which apparently still house many fine buildings. Even when fully populated, this city on a string of jagged emeralds would have been not just invisible from most angles of approach but virtually impregnable. And yet there is every evidence that already by the time of the Conquest, the city was abandoned save for a coterie of priests. . . .

Juan de Alva has persuaded our hosts to take us by canoe tomorrow to the islands. It turns out that the women and children of the village live there, in comparative safety, while the men defend the approaches. But then why, I bade Juan ask, do we see women and children in the clearing on the shore? *There are no villages without women,* the answer.

From the beginning this place has been an illusion maintained for our benefit. And at last we are being allowed to peer through the mist. Tomorrow night I will write with a full report.

Carlos

 24th day of February, 1668
Pital

Juana,

Thank you for writing after all this time. I will take your anger as a sign our work has at last piqued your interest.

Yes, there was darkness in the Mexican past. But Fray Cuadros and I have seen on these islands the warmth and light and joy that were its counterpoint. Juan de Alva is seeing it too—perhaps, like us, for the first time. Last night he spoke to us with enormous passion of the work of reform that his kinsman the poet-emperor Nezahualcoyotl began.[25] The poet's son continued it, as did Juan de Alva's grandfather, until his work and his life were ended by the Inquisition. It is hard, even here, not to speak of this in whispers. Talk of reformation is as dangerous for Catholics and Creoles now as it ever was for the Mexicans.

Our work of transcription is nearly done. You are right of course— our theories may, in the end, accomplish no more than making the Indians imitators of not the Christians but the Egyptians. But then so are we, it seems. Which would make our similarities to the native Americans almost inevitable, I suppose, as those between more or less faithful copies of one original. But there is so much more at stake here than originality, as the followers of Sepulveda tirelessly press the argument that these Indians no more have souls than do apes, and may therefore be uprooted and enslaved without conscience or compunction.

And yes I deserve to be reminded that it was sometimes the blood of slaughtered children the Mexicans used to bind their sacred dough. Tell me, is this why you seem so determined to turn your back on these stories of your childhood?

And no I had not stopped to consider that in one obvious respect the Mexican rite is the opposite of ours: for us, the wafer and the wine become the flesh and blood of God. For them, human flesh and blood become the divine ambrosia and soma.[26] They are more literal-minded in this than even we. But was it not the unfinished work of Nezahualcoyotl to sing of an unseen god whose hungers were less material?

These Indians are not, I know, the same people as the Mexica of the past. During these peaceful weeks here, perhaps I *have* been too willing to overlook the daily hardships and horrors of that past. Cuadros has reluctantly recited for me the gruesome calendar of passion plays—tearing the still beating heart from a victim's chest . . . decapitation . . . searing off the living victim's skin in a brazier of coals . . . riddling the victim with volleys of arrows . . . flaying and wearing his or her skin over one's own . . .

But is it not always to the stupefying scale of the carnage that the discussion inevitably turns, as it now has with even you and me? The thousands of victims scaling steep temple steps to be stretched out over the spine of a sacrificial stone. The endless, mind-dulling repetition, the stones grown slick under foot, the gut-lifting stench . . . With all the emotion of a peasant husking corn, a priest plucks a palpitating heart from a man's chest and sends the still conscious carcass flopping down the pyramid steps.

This picture you paint is not false. And Juan de Alva admits that where once the sacred flesh was to be eaten only sparingly by the reverent few, the capital's markets soon fairly bulged with meat for sale to any merchant hoping at the banquet table to impress a client with that most prized of dishes, the Precious Eagle Fruit. No one denies that by 1519 the Mexican empire had become a terrible engine of death. But Brother Cuadros insists the numbers we learn as schoolchildren are grossly exaggerated. One hundred and thirty thousand skulls found in one heap—who could have counted them? Where were they supposed to have been found, where are they now? What's more, this wild story of eighty-five thousand victims sacrificed on one temple top in the span of a single day—no fewer than sixty per minute? It is all but physically impossible.

And I ask you this: How do we weigh their hunger for mass sacrifice against our thirst for massacre?[27]

Our sky, like theirs, is dominated by eternity, but the eternities these two skies conceal are mirrored opposites—ours a brief death and an eternal life, theirs a brief life and an eternal death. For these strange and wondrous people of our America, the world, the cosmos entire, is a flowery temple dedicated to death, with the sacrificial stone its central altar and the temple itself poised at the edge of an abyss. Four suns, all destroyed. The close of every cycle a time of terror and omen and reproach—when a tenuous New Fire must somehow be struck in the open chest of Night.

I wonder, did you already know they call this wrenching-free of the heart 'husking the corn'? That to give birth is to 'take a prisoner,' and to die in childbirth is to be made a sacrifice?

Juana, if you can just permit yourself to suspend for a moment your admirable sympathy for the sacrificed, you will admit that to offer up to your god the thing you hold dearest—your life, your very heart—is at least a faint echo of Christ's sacrifice to the world. True, the victims are made to drink the 'obsidian wine' to calm their fear, but most go on to die without resisting.[28] After questioning Juan de Alva and Fray Cuadros closely I believe for the Mexican the greatest privilege was this, the warrior's death, precisely because of the sublime opportunity it represents: to choose his fate, and so take upon his own flesh the impress of the World's death. It was the hearts of men that sped the Sun, it was the Precious Eagle Fruit that fed even Time, and none fed as well or as long as the warrior's heart, of the captive who chose to die well for his captor.

I confess it leaves me sick at heart to contemplate the bloody strangeness of this history, the awful poetry of our Eden. Yet how extraordinary it must have felt, to be desperately needed by one's gods.

And I have been giving thought to what you seem to be suggesting: Christ, Osiris, Quetzalcoatl, Oedipus, Narcissus—all tricked or betrayed and brought low by love. All loved by goddesses, nymphs, priestesses. Woman as deceiver, as nemesis and whore—or the woman of sorrows, who has failed to protect. . . .

Indeed the Mexican war god BlueHummingbird of the South triggers his first war by arranging for the daughter of a neighbouring king to be married to a Mexican. The father arrives at the wedding ceremony to see a Mexican priest standing in the bride's place wearing her flayed skin. At the end of another fifty-two-year cycle, the BlueHummingbird beheads his own sister to spur the Mexicans to wage war for the promised land. Another woman of discord, another century of violence. After the office of Emperor, the second highest in the Mexican hierarchy is that of the Snake Woman, so called after the goddess Cihuacoatl, who leaves a sacrificial blade in the cradle of every newborn. It is to the man who occupies her office that the greatest number of blood sacrifices is made.

More Snake Women—Coatlicue, Serpent Skirt, wearing an obsidian blade swaddled like a child on her back, and a necklace of skulls. Chicomecoatl, Seven Snake, crying out in the road at night, some say for a lost child, others, for human hearts and blood.

The Mexicans did everything possible to exaggerate her monstrosity and, killing her, unleashed their wars.

Here in Pital, in the broken temple of their war god, the blood trail is still fresh, the pug marks still distinct. Is that it, is this the book you would have us resist opening? That in these signs—not so ancient, not quite buried—lies the contour of the Apocalypse, the key to its violence, its symbolic notation, its codex. . . .

2nd day of March, 1668
Pital

Juana Inés,

Until your last letter I had been thinking about going on to Yucatan. Fray Cuadros is leaving soon for Veracruz. From there, he and a few others will launch their peaceful conquest of the Maya, among whom there have been heard legends of a bearded god called Votan and of an underground treasure of books guarded by his priestess. I believe in Cuadros at least and wish them Godspeed.

Today Juan de Alva has asked me if I thought I could stay and live here. But for all the peace and beauty we have found, so unexpectedly, I cannot reconcile myself. Cuadros has the gift for living among an alien people; I do not. I have for too long felt an alien in my own land. For his own reasons, Juan cannot stay either, and bound together in our separate exiles, the Creole and the half-caste, we have I think become true friends.

Now that we have finished the translation and finished asking all our foolish questions, the elders of the village have come forward and offered, as a parting gift, to perform the codex for us tonight. Is it truly a parting gift, I wonder, or as a seal on our promise to leave? Brother Cuadros is worried we will be called on to share this food of visions they call *peyotl*.

I sit here alone at the top of a ruined temple in the midst of a jungle calling out to itself. The monkeys are roaring like lions. In the forest it is already night. It speaks to me, day and night, this hot forest, but in tongues I do not know. Birds that croak like goats, the buzz and clatter of insects shaped to inconceivable ends. The soughing of branches in the wind off the lake, and back in the trees a rich belling, like bottles half full of water dropped into a pool. . . .

Over the lake a half-moon rises pocked and golden. A buttery light sits on the skin like a second skin. Young girls go about the clearing lighting torches. Musicians arrive with their instruments. Slit drums, little gourds on sticks, flutes of clay and reed, notched thigh bones. A man brings a kind of *vihuela* or guitar with a pumpkin belly. A few dancers gather, bringing animal masks, shell tunics, colour whisks of iridescent feathers.

From the black forest at my back, moths the colour of vellum float past towards the clearing, eyes glinting ruby. . . . I sit brooding on the implications of the drama about to play itself out below me.

So accustomed are we to seeing Cortés as protagonist that this new codex cannot help but startle; for revealed therein as neither god nor apostle, he drives the plot merely through his insatiable appetite for the abstractions of power and gold. Meanwhile, Moctezuma, captive in his own palace, brooding on his fate, retreats to the seclusion of the fabled Black Room, its stinking walls smeared in blood. Is he the blood-spattered devil rumoured by the Mexicans themselves to gorge daily on his favourite dish, the tender flesh of newborns? Is he a monster of vicious passions with four hundred concubines, among them his insatiable sister? Or is he the chaste and mystic philosopher-king described by the Spaniards who knew him, and who after all would have had every motive to vilify?

Moctezuma knows that choosing the warrior's death at the hands of his captor means submitting unflinchingly to its ironies and humiliations. Their chief instrument is Cortés's ignorant and slow-witted country chaplain, Father Olmedo, more mercenary than priest, who has the effrontery to lecture, to try to *convert Moctezuma II*—the most learned man in the New World, its equivalent of Saint Augustine. The emperor whose title is the Speaker. Yet now, who else is there to talk to, who else will enter the Black Room, who else can help sort through the haunting intersections of their hopes and faiths?

The Mexicans are a chosen people, with a duty to convert by force the peoples of this earth—force them to worship and to nourish the Sun, keep it moving through the heavens, serve the god of war who takes and holds all other gods prisoner. Moctezuma is not merely responsible for his people, his empire. No, he has custody of the very universe, the frail Fifth Sun. Has any mortal known such a crushing destiny? In his place what man, Christian or pagan, would not have succumbed to doubt, to guilt? For by now the brief rise of the Mexica must seem, to the prisoner Moctezuma, more and more like a time of cataclysm, famine and death, perpetual war. And sin—the Mexicans understand sin, know the stench of rotting roots, of a sacred tree overwatered. . . . Fifty thousand sacrifices a year, ten to purchase each hour of sun.

You and I, Juana, have spoken often of destiny. Mine, I thought, was a simple one, until I met you. Their destiny has led them here, and his, to this: to suffer until his death the insolence of a dullard and the mocking eyes of this woman who sees everything but whose own outline is constantly shifting. If he is elusive, she is multi-form. One name could never suffice. She is forever sloughing skins, mistress of tongues, master of language, oracle. La Malinche interprets for him, who speaks for the people. But, a prisoner now, without her he cannot speak *to* the people. And so for a brief time one person—a woman—occupies the two highest offices of Tlatoani and Cihuacoatl, Snake Woman and Speaker. Small wonder the Indians revere the woman they claim to revile.

This woman controls the information. Without her he cannot act. But she serves Cortés, and her words have the power to humiliate and deceive. She knows just how to goad him, to accent the ironies, to underscore the chaplain's plodding insolence, just as once she knew how to temper and smooth the rash words Cortés first spoke to him. But the emperor knows that, more even than words, she interprets actions. This is why he needs her now, and she understands. La Malinche understands how to exploit the confusions that surround her. She knows too how to exploit the growing confusion in Moctezuma's mind.

She is everywhere, the great mother whore in the arms of all his adversaries. She tempts him with her beauty, offers to become his lover as she has with Cuauhtemoc, FallingEagle, the commander designated to replace him. But she also knows at times Moctezuma still thinks of Cortés, his captor, as his father and so must not lie with her. Mother of mercy, she holds the power to comfort and forgive. She holds the key to his redemption and to the encrypted destiny of the world. Woman of discord, she grows to fill his mind.

I cannot help reading our transcription of the codex with a sense of what might have been if not for her. And for me, had I not met you. . . .

In a marketplace, two women sit gossiping, suspended in time, on the eve of one battle and the morrow of another, reducing all battles and all outcomes to this one moment. One woman tells the other of an emperor she has known, how just before his death she held up to him his own fallen image, how she became his eyes, his ears, his voice. His nemesis.

Leaning back against a warm stone in the midst of a nervous, bustling market, this woman who is all women and none complacently pats her belly that ripens with Cortés's son, with the fruit of a new and hybrid race on a continent that she, the new Eve, has given a new destiny.

This jungle all about me lies littered with the shattered symbols of our New World, yet I think of nothing but you. And I am not alone. The Viceroy's cousins offered me a parting gift also. It is one I had thought to keep to myself but now share with you: that secretly they have begun calling you the Pythoness of Delphi.

Whenever I have asked you to join me, you have always said no, but in this last letter you say you cannot, you say it is too late. What has happened? Something is wrong, I know it. I will be in Mexico in two weeks. Please, hold on. Too late for what?

Carlos

Sappho BOOK THREE

CONTENTS

... And now,
know ye that my late-night
inquiries into Nature have cast light
on the most arcane secrets
of Natural magic,
and that through my sciences might I
feign even the moon
in the perspectives of a mirror,
or in the condensations
of terrestrial vapours;
or project spectral bodies,
by dazzling the eyes.
And failing this,
trick the mind to switch
allegorical creatures
into visible objects. ...

JUANA INÉS
DE LA CRUZ,

MARTYR OF THE
SACRAMENT

B. Limosneros, trans.

PLUS ULTRA![1]

 nd yet you have made an application to purchase your cell. How is it I am only just learning of this?"

"Perhaps, Father Núñez, you might ask the Mother Prioress, since she's held my application for two years."

"She may have wanted you to reflect upon the kind of cell you are buying yourself."

"Meaning?"

"Is it a convent cell you want, Sor Juana—or the prison cells you so exalt in verse?"

"Whatever is the matter now?"

"The life in here corrupts you with its ease."

"*Ease?* Am I softened by the barbs of envy and intolerance and vicious gossip that beset me within these walls? The Prioress now schemes to correct even my handwriting—'too masculine,' she calls it."

"Mother Andrea claims you called her a *silly woman,* to her face."

"Your superior dealt with this, Father."

"How he spoiled and pampered you. A little more each year."

"You say this now that don Payo's gone."

"*Don Payo, don Payo.* A country nun on a first-name basis with a Prince of the Church. And yes, Juana, he *is.* Gone to meet his cousin, our new Viceroy. To tell him all about you, I have no doubt. How fashionable it has become for every rake in Madrid to have a nun confidante. What am I saying?— for one's personal mystic."†

"I think I can forego the raptures of discussing mysticism with viceroys, if that's your concern."

"Once here in Mexico, don Payo's cousin can be offered the most famous nun in Christendom to comfort him during his trials among us here in the wilderness. He will not fail to find her irresistible. She will prove a marvel of comprehension who knows, as if by miracle, our new viceroy's every intellectual interest and spiritual need, can quote at length from all his favourite poets."

"I suspect don Payo has done much the same for you."

"And with your future here secured, don Payo sails for the Alcázar— *that nest of nuns*—with a trunk full of your plays and poems and treatises. Souvenirs of his travels, is that it?"

"He asked for a few trifles, yes."

"Verses for a few friends."

"Not forgetting his family, Your Reverence. After seven years in the New World, who would want to go back to one's family empty-handed?"

"Ah, you mean his *other* cousin."

"Yes, Father, the King's Prime Minister."

"And do you really believe he can protect you from there?"

"Protect me?"

"Did you think your don Payo would not show it to me before he left?"

"Show you wh—ah, I see you'll be telling me."

"That abomination! *Martyr of the Sacrament.*"

"How could I think he'd dare not to? He was only our Archbishop and Viceroy after all. But I assume your abomination of my play does not quite extend to Saint Hermenegild himself?"

"So now we have martyred you here—"

"Father, you persist in reducing everything I write to self-portraiture."

"Because it is—or no, you do not make portraits anymore, your plays contain whole embassies. The Greeks, the Visigoths, Saint Hermenegild, civil war, faith, magic, apostasy, Isabela of Castile, Columbus—"

"All that, Father. In one play? You're certain."

"You think we are in one of your little comedies?"

"Just once, before you save my soul for all eternity, how I would love to see you laugh."

"You may not enjoy the moment as much as you imagine."

"In truth I cannot imagine it at all."

"You think yourself back at the palace, perhaps. But as I remember it, you were not always laughing then."

"Just once, to see you come here without a grievance."

"Could your intent *be* more manifest? You salute not just the Queen and Queen Mother but the entire administration—you have a character addressing them from within the play itself!"

"So you've come to correct my art."

"Is there to be no end to your worldly intriguing? You are a nun, a bride of Christ, buried alive, dead to the world—"

"This, from an officer of the Company of Jesus."

"But such a clever nun—a jesting, writing nun. A nun magician. How you dazzle us with your theatrical sorcery—or do you call it science that so holds us in its thrall? Soldiers, souls and spectators all suspended between New Spain and Old, you take us back a thousand years to the Spain of the Visigoths—and not content with this, back *another* thousand to the ancient Spain of Geryon! Two continents, two centuries, three or four millennia all on one rather crowded stage. Why, Sor Juana, you are a veritable *sorceress* of space and time."

"The doctors of the Church, as you know perfectly well, Father, have defined magic as nothing more than the power to uncover natural marvels. That's all the magic I care to know about. The magic of Columbus was merely that of human genius."

"Of which you have an abundance, should Madrid still be needing any—"

"Human genius, even in abundance, is but a pale reflection of the mind of God."

"And since the natural marvel of the New World always existed, its discovery was the triumph of that genius over our own pious ignorance. You remind a bankrupt Queen of how much Spain has owed to the bold spirit of discovery, a spirit just such as yours. Not enough for you merely to play the magician, the alchemist, no, you are all the silver of the Indies, all the wonders of America rolled into one.[2] Let us all bow down now to this prodigy of piety—the writing nun who makes rhymes on the rebel martyr Hermenegild. *You try to drive a wedge between Church and Crown.*"

"And who was it, just now, lamenting the influence of nuns at the palace in Madrid?"

"At the Pillars of Hercules, the gateway of the Atlantic, the unknown sea, you have Columbus's marines shout *Ne Plus Ultra, Ne Plus Ultra,* Here ends the Universe! only to hear their echoes rebounding from the unseen shore—but no, *from the future.* Where we sit and smile down at them from the new certainties of this very clever future. How you use Time to mock at us, the ignorance of our simple faith."

"I find nothing simple about your faith, Father."

"So limited, so straitening, so narrow for one so bold—"

"Nor was I the one who made Hermenegild a saint."

"No, Juana, Pope Urban did. And thus you cunningly remind us of his unfortunate protégé Galileo Galilei—another sainted rebel in a prison cell. You would have us confuse this Galilei's impudence with the daring that once so enriched Spain and expanded its dominions! You think your hieroglyphs cannot be deciphered. You think to send don Payo with the key. To supply him with the pretext for an audience with the Queen."

"As always, Father, your learning is a wonder."

"As always, Sor Juana, you offer up a false surrender. It might shock you to know how much help I have had. There are many of us watching, more closely every year. How slyly you allude to a navigational technique you could only have read in Columbus's journals—also on the Index, as it happens. As Censor for the Holy Office, I might ask who has brought them to you. I could insist, we could make inquiries. . . . And yet you do not stop even at this. You simply cannot resist, even when you cannot hope to benefit—is all this rebellion truly in the name of liberty? Or is your own ambition even more vainglorious than the Florentine's?"

"And who, Father, cannot resist?—banning a navigator's journals when there can be no imaginable harm in reading them. Banning even the letters of Cortés to his King—under Royal Seal, but only here in America. Who, if not you, requested the seal here? And who spends his days extirpating books I could read freely as a child?"

"And look where they have led you. You might as well have written *eppur si muove.*† And so you mock at the science of the Jesuits, just as Galileo did, our Columbus of the skies! Is that your ambition, Sor Juana—to be the Columbus of a new Heaven?"

"You seem to think I have imagined a Spain—*at the time of Herakles*—teeming with Jesuit scientists."

"I think there is no end to where your imagination may lead you."

"It does *not* lead me to confuse the earth's flatness with its centrality or its motility. Even before Galileo's death—"

"Of course, of course, the Church permits discussion of the earth's motion. As a *hypothesis.*"

"To want more was unnecessary. Signor Galilei's mistake was—"

"No, do not bother. Save your rebuttal for the proper time. But take this as a token from a father who has been too lenient for far too long. You think to split us from the Church by meddling in a question upon which the whole Church is divided. Yet it is not the Jesuits, but quite another target you are striking at. And Galilei's example contains many lessons, Juana. One such is this: not even a Pope can save us from ourselves. The vain and insubordinate—"

"Revolve around themselves . . . ?"

"I see, everything amuses you now. All is fit material for your laughter. In the figure of Columbus's marines you make clowns of the faithful and the fearful. This art of yours makes fear so comical. And makes

†'nevertheless it moves'—words attributed to Galileo at the close of his trial

you bolder every year. But then, I see you are right after all. I did come to correct your art. Indeed consider this, while there is still time. That today a single work of Galileo Galilei remains on the Index. It is not a work of science but of *art*—a play, Sor Juana, a dialogue. Three good Christians—and how strange that you should use the same device—debating planetary motion. Your fellow playwright makes one of them a simpleton of faith. For comic effect. And into whose mouth Galilei puts an idea cherished by a pontiff who has spoiled and coddled our vain and insubordinate natural magician, and now is mocked for his pains. What is the simpleton made to say? That a God who has the power to create the universe—"

"Would also have the power to make its laws and regulations, its causes and effects, appear to us quite other than they truly are."

"I *knew* it."

"An idea more promising perhaps than Galileo realized."

"You just could not help showing me you have read even this most infamous of tracts. Or keep from showing us how clever you are—more clever even than the Florentine. You have seen all his errors. You will play the same game but play it rather better, you too will write a play but conceal your game from all of us, even as you announce it to be an allegory and so defy us to divine it. And see how this *promising* new idea turns God himself into a great magician, revealer of natural marvels—and you, into a goddess in her theatre, a veritable fountainhead of inspiration!"

"Truly Father it is you and your collaborators who are inspired—to fit an ocean's worth of inspirations into the shallow basin of one woman's mind, a lowly country nun, as you say. No wonder they all flock to work with you."

"When they should flock to you? It is worse with you than even *I* could have believed. It is as bad as they say. So anxious to show off your cleverness at any risk. How much better to have pretended never to have read it—instead you *quote* from it. *To me*—an officer of the Inquisition. And even here you direct the conversation to exactly where it should not go."

"And that would be?"

"Towards water, Sor Juana. Water. Your new theology, your new sacrament. Which, yes, may very well martyr you. . . ."

"Truly, Father, you find too much in it—"

"A new sacrament, a new Host—one far finer, as surely the common people will see. Because it is free. Better than bread, which we have taken as a symbol of scarcity."

"Even I thirst to hear it now."

"But you know already."

"Please."

"Water, Sor Juana. The humblest thing, the purest, everywhere free. In tears and springs and seas. Such poetry you make for us simpletons, with the simplest of things. And it has been with us *since the beginning.* God's love everywhere embedded within the beauty of creation.

"All nature as our temple—forest springs, rivers, rain. But no, not quite a temple, more like a . . . bath. A pagan bath. And all the naiads and nymphs and dryads restored to cavort again. And free, all free.

"And so you return the world to us, return us whence we had been cast out, to the garden. You have us stand at the Pillars of Hercules and make the world into an Eden of floods. Water everywhere, all is holiness—nature, existence itself is the sacrament now. What need has one for bread in Eden? What need have we for priests at sea? No—not priests but navigators, scientists—natural magicians. And they must be bold, boldness itself, to make daring from humility, from a simple washing of the feet. If we are truly to know God, we must entrust ourselves to the sea, to go beyond the humble limits of our ignorance.

"And who shall make the new theology, whom shall we make priestess of this new Queen of the Waters? Who shall interpret for us the mysteries of this new Sophia rising from the Galilean sea, this goddess in nature everywhere, who presents herself as beauty to all our senses. Queen of the Baths—in this pagan *orgy* of sensation, where to know god is to swim in god and all her sensations. *Was this your experience at the palace . . . ?*"

Was I wrong, was it madness, to think I could do without him? Was I to live in fear of him like everyone else here—my whole life? How could I work, with him coming every week to rob me of my strength, harvest it?—to milk me, his rubber tree, his adder.

Better to make of him an enemy than to let such a one near me as a friend—and arm him myself.

"You think this one of your little comedies," Father Núñez said.

Jokes, I made in answer. For the jester and only he—not statesman, knight or prince—may sometimes mock the Emperor. Núñez is impressive, I thought, and yes, there were many other clever ones working on my case but however much they might insist, they were not infallible. For in his exhaustive catalogue of my play's pernicious contents and sins of rebellion, Núñez had all but missed the obvious. Hercules himself. Ten years ago I listened to my Atlas sitting across from me, piling the weight of the world and heaven on my back, because I was not free to answer him.³ And so as not to be quite suffocated, not altogether crushed, I found myself composing, to myself, another little comedy, while he talked, while he talked. . . .

Something like this.

How the world pins poor Hercules, stoops the braided shoulders, bows that thewy nape, bends the water bearer beneath his earthen urn— ay, what persecutions of gravity! *Herakles, pobre de tí*—made passive pillar, pole and axis—mortal champion reduced to Muse. While at your antipodes, lesser men sail in fitful affray west, eyes straining ever west to the world's abysmal end. Yea, would that it had an end for one who knows it round, *knows it moves*—and still, and yet, who is forced to stand, fixed point on which all the watery world spins.

Ay Herakles, pobre de ti, I thought, sitting across from him. To be sentenced to the bond service of a lesser king.⁴ For one act of madness. But what greater madness than to choose to bend to this man's yoke? To toil twelve years, and watch my Atlas perform the labours of Hercules.

In those twelve years since finding me weeping in the cathedral, since he began to hone his sermons and circulars on me, his grindstone and paragon—what successes his service to high Heaven has brought him here on earth. Rector of the Jesuit College of St. Peter and St. Paul, he shapes not only the New World's young Jesuits, but Jesuit policy throughout the Spanish possessions. Prefect of the Brotherhood of Mary, he dispenses his ethical and practical guidance to a dozen of the most senior officers of both Church and State. Among these Brothers of Mary have been four vice-kings, all of whom Núñez has served also as confessor. And Father Núñez confesses others—the archbishops of Mexico.

Bridle the head and the body will follow.

For twelve years bridled but not blinkered I had watched him while he preached submission and humility, while he quoted Augustine to me, that with great gifts comes a greater responsibility—to endure, to be exemplary, to be strong. To suffer to lead from the rear.

While the work of Titans goes on in Europe.

Until, ten years ago, I told myself no more Hercules. No more pillars, no more *ne plus ultra*. Be their legend no longer, serve instead the daughters of the sea. Let them think me their theological Muse but quietly I will be my own—my own fountain, oracle and deeps.

¡Sí, plus ultra hay!

Or so I hear myself whispering as I sat across from him that day and said nothing.

Instead I plotted to reveal myself in increments, divert them in obliques, advance the sturdy fishing fleet by infinitesimal degrees until they found themselves far far beyond the pillars of Hercules. If Núñez is suddenly so interested in the geography of the oceans, I thought, let him read the welcome I will write for our new Viceroy and Vicereine: their Excellencies the Marquis of the Lake and the Countess of Walls. . . .

Déjame ver . . . how shall I title it? Something, like . . . Allegorical Neptune.

Sí, plus ultra, mas ultrajes, hay. More comedies.

It was another November. Not long after my birthday. 1680.

JUANA INÉS
DE LA CRUZ,

"Allegorical
Neptune"

B. Limosneros, trans.

... This other canvas paints in bellicose
hues the Triton[5] goddess,[†]
once-engendered, twice-conceived,
never-born inventor
of arms and sciences;
but here in lucid rivalry
with the deity[††] who adores the tireless
Ocean—the Sun's foaming tomb—
whose greenblack lips' myriad kiss
spurs the dawn to greater glories,
and who, with spray and sea-spume,
Minerva's regent salt-limned foot

[†]Minerva / Athena

shods in silver buskins;
yet Minerva outrivals even Ocean,[6]

[††]Neptune

and even the Great Mother, unscathed withal,
though girt in strands of seas that seethe,
no less pacific for all their teeming
than she who decks the branches of the olive tree
with signs of peace and the fruit which—if but lightly pressed—
yields the precious oil the bookworm worships
as the Apollo of night;
and yet if too hard pressed, hotly she burns to meet
with Athenian aegis and brutal armada
the watery warships
of the Trident . . .

November 1680. The new Vice-King and his wife made their entry through two triumphal arches,[7] theatre sets of plaster columns and effigies, painted canvases and inscriptions, all explicated in a quote-studded companion booklet running to perhaps sixty pages of verse and prose. The arch for the cathedral was designed by Sor Juana, the other arch, in the Plaza de Santo Domingo, by don Carlos Sigüenza. He eschewed the usual mythological treatment for that of historical fact. He contrasted the peaceful governance of pre-Conquest America with the bloodiness of European power. Indeed arches should not be called triumphal since " . . . never was an arch erected for anyone who had not robbed five thousand enemies of their lives . . ." His arch was not a success. Sor Juana's, meanwhile, depicted the Viceregal couple as a beauteously proportioned Neptune[8] and Amphitrite, naked on sea shells à la Botticelli, and elsewhere as Neptune and Minerva contending in wisdom for the guardianship of Athens. . . .

onight, at last, he comes. February 24th, 1681. The anniversary of my profession. Of course he would come tonight.

Always the theatre of his disappearances, home to Zacatecas, to keep me waiting on the indulgence of a visit so that I may know the Reverend Father Núñez is displeased. Every Thursday night since November my locutory has lain in darkness, as a sign of deference. The other three chime with music and laughter, while the one reserved for my exclusive use—the most notorious parlour in Christendom, as he is so fond of calling it—lies dark. But Father Núñez is not a man to be placated.

New Spain's most relentless mind—bright like a blade. *Tragalibros*,[†] they call him for his learning. Living Memory of the Company they christen him for his complete recall of all he reads and hears. There is another title that chills me. The Jesuits' Living Library.

Living Library? I have one more exact—*Living Tomb of Tomes*. He makes hecatombs on the books I read as a girl and loved. For now comes the honour he has coveted more than all the others: the Holy Office has made this humble son of a silver miner Chief Censor. At the Inquisition there is only Dorantes to rival him.

Scratch the surface just a little, Núñez says, to read the vein of heresy in me—and how he rasps and scours, *mi escofina escolastica*,[†] to mine that vein before the others reach it. He has built his reputation on me, plundered for his oratory the spiritual journals he has ordered me to keep. But why, why does he still come? He has no more need of me. He is done playing the Father to me. Except in his absences.

Everyone fears him now—even our Viceroy admits to his own fear openly. At the Jesuit college the novices are reduced to whispers as their rector approaches—Sssh, *el Tragalibros*, hide your books and pamphlets. Sssh, Sor Juana's confessor . . .

In those three words, I have my answer. For my fame, still am I mined; my gilt adds lustre to his hoard. But how theatrically he defuses the charge, going about in that ridiculous cassock of his, torn and thread-bare, teeming with vermin. Bleeding himself like some ecclesiastical bar-ber—his scalpel, the flail. No, *mi escofina*, humble you are not.

Why may I not be proud, why should this be a sin? To feel pride in the exercise of God-granted gifts. Am I born in a field, was I raised among weeds? Was I cradled on a crag, am I some wild beast? Or am I a woman descended directly from Adam, with the rational soul that ennobles us all, that reflects as in the mirror in the lighthouse—the panopticon of Pharos—the greatest glory of God. . . .

Mind.

Why should it have been impossible to explain this to him *of all people*, to explain myself? Why have I tried and tried? Out of gratitude—because he was a father to me once, because he has loved my soul. But that was such a very long time ago. Can my simple arithmetic be so faulty, truly can it be that in the dozen years since that first day in the cathedral, he has come to me here *five hundred times?* Half a thousand times to scour my heart. Until I can no more.

And so I have sent for him. Tonight he will know I have had enough.

He comes at dusk when he comes at all, afternoons no longer. I have begun to suspect the sight is failing in those eyes the grey of cooling lead. All the long years, all the late nights of reading and banning by the mortal light of one candle. . . . Or is it that the bonfires have been so very bright?

Tonight we will sit in the locutory without so much as a single lamp. He will not surrender the slightest advantage to me. He will not give me the satisfaction of seeing it: *the book censor will one day be blind.* At dusk he comes like an owl, like Nyctimene, to steal the oil from my lamps.[9] And so it is in this dusk that I sit and brace myself, to face that face, to meet the exorbitant eyes, to see the rage under lids heavy with humility, the dry tongue, the lipless lips . . .

Courage do not fail me now.

 "You asked for me."

"It's good you've come."

"We shall see."

"Very well, Father, we shall. I am hearing from every quarter that you are unhappy. Is it something I've written?"

"You are writing so much these days. It must be hard for you to guess."

"What are you getting at?"

"The proposals you and Carlos sent over created a great stir in Madrid."

"You know even this."

"Very bold, very inventive. Refinements to the pendulum. A musical clock—admirable. Your idea, I understand. Other notions for marine chronometers—such stunning breakthroughs for navigation, strategic advantages to the Crown . . . if they could be made to work, if the proper studies could be funded, tests of your designs. A pity to have destroyed them."

"*What?*"

"Your Queen buys bread on credit, Juana. Perhaps you think the Crown's bankruptcy a figure of speech. There is no money for studies. Yet if those designs were to end up with the Portuguese, or the English, or worse yet the Netherlanders . . . So you see, you divide not just the Jesuit scientists, Juana—you and now Carlos—but the Queen's scientific soothsayers also. About half were in favour of saving them, no doubt with thoughts of brokering a quiet sale. Yes, I am surprised your don Payo did not think to tell you. As are you, I see. But Carlos must have made copies, yes?"

"Even from Madrid, don Payo reports to you."

"To *us*, Sor Juana, he writes to us. Always this exaggeration of my influence. In some quarters, I think, your imagination hinders you. You imagine you know him, but do you know His Grace left Mexico in such a hurry so as not to miss the *auto* in Madrid? No, I thought not. By all accounts—and I have read several—it put those of our poor Mexico to shame. Thirty-four burned in effigy, nineteen more in the flesh, twelve burned alive. *Twelve.* And two women, this time. . . . You *do* know he sat with the Queen Mother. No, not even that? In the royal box, with that dwarf of hers your Leonor prated on so about. What was her name? It was so long ago."

"Had I told you a century ago, you'd still know."

"Yes. 'Lucillo.' I imagine them that day discussing your *Martyr of the Sacrament* together, at breaks. Now. You have called me here, you have come this far. Am I expected to offer my help?"

"Help, Your Reverence?"

"You stall but do not refuse it outright. Well then. How shall I oblige you—by asking how you and our new Vice-Queen are getting on? Something of a poet, this one, though I am a poor judge. And she is a Manrique! Countess of Paredes, no less. How perfect for you both."

"The knighthood of the Manriques was not always such an amusement, Father. Your saintly Loyola did not jeer at the Order of Santiago, nor did he refuse it. At least I don't recall your ever saying so. Need I remind you?—when the Marquis and the Countess first announced their intention to visit me here, did I not plead for *two days* to be allowed to remain secluded in my cell?"

"But the Mother Prioress denied you—"

"At your insistence—why *was* that?"

"And how assiduously you have been attending them, Sor Juana, to have missed confession so often lately—and how many of our Thursdays together?"

"Two, Father. Only two."

"Countess of Walls! Marquis of the Lake! How Fate makes Life convenient to your poetry—how your poetry bends you towards your fate. Allegorical Neptune! *Water*, again."

"The arch was a cathedral commission, the Chapter approved it— unanimously, as you well know."

"And do you call her María Luisa yet? Have you explained to this new one about your *past*? How it was with the other one? *Queen of the Baths.*"

"Always these imaginings of *yours*, Reverence, about the baths at El Pénon."

"Have you explained to her your new aqueous theology?"

"Is it impious on my part that duty has blossomed into loving friendship for her, whereas Your Reverence guides the immortal soul of her husband, though you harbour no feelings for him whatever? And once again you confess Viceroy and Vicereine both."

"It is not a question of feelings."

"This too has changed with you, Father. It was not always so."

"I suppose you profess some admirable depth of feeling for the Archbishop-*elect*."

"Why do you say it like that?"

"Only to say your manoeuvring with the Bishop of Puebla carries risks. But no, forget I mentioned it. He is after all another protégé of don Fray Payo."

"Is there a problem with the Bishop's election? What do the *Jesuits* know of it?"

"As for whom I confess, it will be the new Archbishop's privilege to confess the Vice-Queen, if he wishes it. But as you say, the Viceroy will likely remain with me. Or do you call him Neptune now?"

"How unlike you, Father, to misspeak. *Do the Jesuits have another candidate?*"

"Was it the comet, Sor Juana?"

"Was what the comet—the comet is gone."

"Yes, precisely. Two days ago. And here we are. Like sorcery."

"No magic I possess tells me on which nights Your Reverence will deign to appear. And on that subject might we not try the everyday magic of a lantern, Father? It is getting rather dark."

"But you *have* been busy reassuring the Vice-Queen."

"She spoke to you of this."

"We have conversations, much as you and I—"

"Told you in *confession*."

"Conversations."

"Intended to terrify her—'God's Wrath.'"

"And how did you reassure her, Juana? With Galilei's rubbish about comets hiding behind the moon? Did you show it to her in your telescope, show her the moon's face—*poxed like a whore's*? Did that reassure? Nothing divine about it, nothing heavenly in the heavens!"

"That, Father, you will *never* hear me say."

"Tell me—I never understood it, why they hide behind the moon. . . . Great elliptical orbits, was it not, out among the heavenly spheres? How helpful the Chair of Mathematics and Astrology could have been in comforting your new friend. A shame you and Carlos are not getting along."

"We will sort it out. As we always do."

"I am glad to hear it. Because the spectacle of New Spain's two brightest children squabbling is less than inspiring. You of course are entitled, you are only thirty-two, but Carlos is old enough to know better. *How like you to turn on an old friend.*"

"But such venom, Your Reverence. Is it really over me? Or still over your slip about the election? The Archbishop-*elect* will be intrigued."

"Your poor Carlos, how confused he must be. Privately, you share his view that the comet is a natural event, yet write a sonnet glorifying his adversary's position. A position Carlos has risked much to denounce as superstition, and is being attacked for it even now. These natural philosophical debates are filled with such—"

"Vitriol, Father?—spleen? Yes, how ill-humoured these natural magicians, and in comparison how benign the gentle quibbles of theology must seem."

"I have noticed how amusing you can be precisely—"

"So Your Reverence may catch his breath."

"No, Sor Juana. Precisely when you are in moral difficulties. You seem to be distancing yourself from don Carlos lately, who is, unlike you, hopeless at diplomacy. His *arco* caused the Viceroy precisely as much annoyance as yours gave delight."

"He was lucky not to be arrested."

"Perhaps this makes Carlos a hindrance to you now, or perhaps you feel justified after he insulted you. What was it he called you afterwards? *Una limosnera de leyendas!*"

"*Mendiga de fabulas.*"

"Fable beggar, yes, thank you. A sharp quill, your friend has. It might have been better to keep him as a friend."

"Why do the Jesuits not reinstate him?"

"You seek to ease your conscience, Juana, by taking up his cause. But I will tell you. We prefer to have don Carlos looking in. He does more to restrain himself this way. The Company would be too small for one such as he, whereas you, for all your attempts at caution and secrecy, your deepest impulses are—"

"After all the petitions he has made, it is pure cruelty."

"You want us to solve your problems for you. How many petitions of marriage has he made to you? Have you no loyalty? *Are you proud of what you have done to your friend*—by siding with his adversary?"

"I . . . no."

"Was it *wrong*?"

"I said I was not proud of it."

"Yet your conscience does not trouble you. It has been weeks and I have heard not one word of this in confession."

"You have often been away. Zacatecas, I imagine."

"That is why this convent has a chaplain. For the times when your spiritual director must be absent. But you have not confessed this to him, either."

"You sound certain."

"False confession, Sor Juana, is a most serious matter. I know also why you have sent for me."

"Do you."

"You have been planning this for weeks."

"And if you know—*how* do you?"

"For weeks and yet you have delayed, and delay even now. I will help you one last time. *Tell me what you are writing.*"

"If you think you know, Father, why do *you* delay—why not just be forthright?"

"That a nun, *a woman in my charge*, is now called Tenth Muse from Cadiz to Lima to Manila is already utterly repugnant to me! Had I known you would waste your convent life on verses I would have married you off!"

"You think me a dog or a slave to dispose of."

"But with this latest, you make it impossible for me to defend you, Juana."

"Defend me! You think I do not hear of them—the reproaches you make against me to anyone who'll listen? You call my conduct a scandal, you make the substance of my confessions a public matter. Defend me—there's not a man in New Spain to stand up to you. Even the Marquis himself—Regent of half the world—*fears* you. The last viceroy still writes from Spain to ask your guidance. Now I ask you, Your Reverence, to tell me what I have done to so infuriate you this time."

"In which role have you conspired to make me look the greater fool, as your confessor or New Spain's Censor?—in the plays or in the verses? *Tenth Muse.* Can you not grasp how obscene that epithet is for any Catholic, let alone one of *my* nuns?"

"Even the Holy Virgin has been called the Tenth Muse lately—would you censor her too?"

"Do not push me too far."

"But this still isn't it, is it Father? They have been calling me Muse for some time. This is not quite what makes you so . . . *passionate*."

"A bride of Christ under my direction composing love poetry—"

"Yes?"

"On *Sappho*."

"At last."

"What could possibly *be* more of a—"

"Humiliation?"

"A disgrace! *I am your spiritual director*, charged with the safe conduct of a nun's soul to her Husband's embrace. I should know every single detail of your life, every thought, every dream. The contents of your soul should be spread wide for me to inspect. And now—yet again!—you've defiled the sacrament of confession by your lies of omission."

"*I* defile it, Father? And what of the sacramental seal? And if my privacy means nothing to you, how long am I to conceal from María Luisa the contempt in which you hold hers?"

"'María Luisa.' Only your Countess could make you think to get away with this. *Sappho*. Who could even have *imagined* this outrage—poetry to a Lesbian *puta!*"

"You forget yourself, Father, you forget where you are, you forget who is the true Master of this house—and make it abundantly clear you have no idea what you are talking about."

"But I *will* know. You will bring these . . . *things* to me and we will read them together, then burn—together—each and every one, down to the last scrap, the last strip of paper!"

"No, Father, *we* will not."

"Now you defile your vow of *obedience* and revel in it!"

"No, Father, I do *not*. But saintliness is not a thing you command. No being of free will—I, last of all—can be brought to God by coercion. If it could be commanded, my soul would have already ascended to Heaven a hundred times. Tell me, does my correction fall to Your Reverence by reason of obligation or charity? I too have my obligations. If it be charity then proceed gently. I am not of so servile a nature as to bend to such mercies, as you well know—"

"I see we reach the part you have been rehearsing."

"Any sacrifices I make are undertaken to mortify my spirit and not to avoid censure, no matter how public. From you—such has always been my love and veneration—I could bear anything, any amount of injustice, *in private*. But these public humiliations, these extravagant . . . exaggerations unjustly tar this convent's good name."

"What little remains of it."

"Everyone in the capital listens to your words and trembles at their stern import as though you were a prophet of old, as though they were dictated by the Holy Ghost—"

"Go carefully."

"How many times have I found *your* words and your commandments *exceedingly* repugnant yet held my peace? But after so many years my breast overflows with the injustice. *I have done nothing wrong*—nothing criminal, nothing sinful. If sin there be it is only pride—our shared affliction, Father. I am *not* humbled as might be other daughters on whom your instruction would be so much better lavished. Your opinions in these minor matters are just that, and unwelcome. *They are not Holy Writ*. If you cannot find it in your heart to favour me, and to counsel me calmly or even harshly, but in in the privacy of confession—a sacrament *you* defile whenever it suits you—then I beg you think of me no more.

Release me from your hand and grant me no more favours, for I am doomed to disappoint you."

"Think, now, what you ask."

"God has fashioned many keys to Heaven—which contains as many rooms as there are different natures. Do you not think my salvation might be effected through the guidance of another? Is the dispensation of God's mercy limited to just one man, no matter how wise or righteous?"

"And just whom did you have in mind?"

"Father Arellano."

"That ecstatic?"

"Your disciple."

"Your *worst* possible choice! Someone who will indulge you, who will let you make him a fool."

"You claim that's exactly what I've made of you. Choice, Father. Choice is what you are always exhorting me to. Arellano understands passion, he understands faith, and penance best of all."

"You have said nothing of reason."

"Reason, *I* understand."

"Too well. Or, just possibly, not quite well enough. . . . Reason carefully then, child. You have called me here for this. Your Countess has given you the nerve. But calculate well. This thing is not easily undone. . . ."

"That much I know. After so many years."

"Do you wish a short time to reconsider?"

"Father I ask only that you commend me to God, which I know in your charity you will do with all fervour."

"So be it then. I commend you. To your God."

JUANA INÉS
DE LA CRUZ

Alan Trueblood, trans.

*Year: 1688. The
Viceroy and his
wife, the Countess
of Paredes, have
remained in
Mexico two years
beyond their second
term of service. At
last María Luisa
can postpone their
departure no longer.*

Kept from saying farewell
sweet love, my only life,
by unremitting tears,
by unrelenting time,
 these strokes must speak for me,
amidst my echoing sighs,
sad penstrokes never yet
more justly coloured black.
 Their speech perforce is blurred
by tears that well and drop,
for water quickly drowns
words conceived in flame.
 Eyes forestall the voice,
foreseeing, as they do,
each word I plan to speak
and saying it themselves.
 Heed the eloquent silence
of sorrow's speech and catch
words that breathe through sighs,
conceits that shine through tears . . .

28th day of August, 1688,
Mexico City

la excma. señora doña María Luisa Manrique de Lara y Gonzaga
Condesa de Paredes, Marquesa de la Laguna,
Madrid

Queridísima María Luisa,

thought to fast from news of you.[10] Yet it is not a fast if the hunger is not chosen. Better said, then, when you set out for Madrid, I had thought to starve. I confess this Lenten faithlessness now, as one so deliriously fed since your letter arrived. You vowed you would not forget; yet so weak is my capacity for faith, at times I could not quite believe. And even summoning belief, still I could not *hope*—so very much lies beyond our control.

The year has been a bitter one. Your leaving, and then within a month my mother's death. (But could it be you have not received my last two letters . . . ?) I did not even know of her illness.

Carlos went, thinking I suppose to represent me, though even had I wanted to, I could not have kept him here. Panoayan, it seemed, was always on the way to anywhere Carlos was going. It is hard for me to see them as friends, and yet he had known her twenty years. For nearly as long as I had not seen her.

This time he found Bishop Santa Cruz there, who had come all the way from Puebla and had stayed to celebrate her Mass—for me, but especially for my nephew, Fray Miguel now, who is devoted to him. Greatly do I doubt the honour would have meant much to her—she had little use for churchmen, or for her grandson Miguel, I gather—but it meant a great deal to me, and I was happy for the town. I doubt the church in Amecameca had seen a bishop in quite some time.

How coldly this all rings in the air as I say it aloud. As you know, Isabel and I were not reconciled.

In his visits here since, Bishop Santa Cruz has skirted the issue with great delicacy, as is his way. He has been such a friend, and with you gone

I am more than ever in his care. Still, I was stunned to learn he had been there at the end, been the one to administer her rites. Something in the scene unsettles me. Strain enough to imagine that she had confessed—yet what?

But how can I answer your first letter with such chill gloom?

You have *written*, you are safely returned, your son thrives, and your dear Tomás's prospects for advancement look more shining all the time. You even mention you have looked a little into publishing our collection, and from the way you write of it I will follow your lead and not let my hopes rise too high. As you say, securing the support of the Church there when I do not have it here will be difficult. But since you ask me for a title, perhaps I may still hope a little?

A very few small things have changed for the better since you left. With my own funds I have finally completed the refurbishment of our locutory, a project that would have Father Nunez turning in his grave—could we but get him into one. Seven years since he was last here, and now I can perhaps at last forget he ever was. The grate that divided the room, I have had torn out. In the late afternoons Father Nunez had an unfortunate way of placing himself between me and the light—hitching a shoulder or swaying at the grate—to let the dying sun strike my eyes. So now, a light grille bisects the room from the eastern wall to the middle window, and thus runs not north-south but more or less parallel with the afternoon light. The exact angle varying slightly with the seasons. The new arrangement gives me one window, my visitors another, and the third we share, sitting together at the grille.

The room seems less grim in other ways too. From the ceiling depends a silver chandelier on the visitor's side; behind an arras on the convent side is the pantry and staging area from which our guests' crystal glasses and silver cups and platters may be replenished; down the west wall runs a row of wide, cushioned benches. Two clavichords—for duets. Armchairs of ox-hide stretched over oak, carpets to cover the cold stone floors. . . Flemish tapestries and a selection of maps and paintings now relieve the impassive thickness of the walls. Polished cases and cabinets lining the south wall, on both sides of the grille. Books, of course, but also the many curiosities and conversation pieces brought by visitors over the years.

The new grille is carved in rosewood, beautifully, to resemble an arbour of wide-spread boughs, full-leafed and bent with pear and grape and apple. In places the enlacement of the boughs offers the suggestion of a private garden of warm redwood and rose. . . slants of light play in the turns of brights and darks, and as the space behind each recedes into glades of shadow and cool, we might almost forget where we are. And who.

Just once more—how I wish that it might be you, for one more hour.

To this small bright thought I venture to add others, and kindle myself a small new fire here in the hearth. I share its little glow now with you: the Bishop, you see, has brought not just support but help and company. A secretary, who should be taking this down even now. *No 'Tonia, that's what a fair copy is for. Take down everything. We decide what to cross out afterwards—and you, we do not cross out—*

Would I, the Bishop asks, have any use for a young woman, with little fortune but with a good orthography, a decent Latin he himself has seen to, a passable style in Castilian, a rough familiarity with Italian and Portuguese—and who, if that were not enough, plays the clavichord beautifully? I have since learned she has a fair and improving knowledge of Nahuatl, too, and she is in return teaching me phrases of an Angolan dialect taught her by her mother. What's more, in the privacy of our cell Antonia has been sharpening my fluency in curses, which she spouts with more flair—should she dislodge a book or drop a plate—than a seafaring apostate.

She is also lovely, with a brambly thrum and tangle of tresses such as I have never seen.

My Most Excellent Lady Countess, I take great pleasure in presenting Antonia Mora, ~~my godsend and salvation~~—*did you just cross that out?*—until recently resident in Puebla and now an oblate here in San Jerónimo. Officially her dowry was paid by me, though Bishop Santa Cruz arranged for everything. She lodges here and half her time may be spent working at this table. Henceforth, you shall never have cause to complain of the brevity of my letters. In fact I promise amply to repay (if not in quality then in lines) each line you find the time to write.

The Mother Prioress raised few objections to the Bishop's arrangements. Four thousand pesos is not an inconsiderable sum for a dowry, even were Antonia a nun. The Bishop shifts the credit to me, arguing that I bring the convent treasury many times that amount in donations and commissions. But I have been doing that for years. No, if Mother Andrea is more tractable now, it is for the same reason that she acquiesces in the Bishop's wishes: that nothing short of seeing every nun in

Mexico barefoot will placate Archbishop Aguiar.[II] In the past few years the Prioress has discovered that in the Archbishop's eyes whatever good we do is little, whatever ill incalculable. I cannot help but laugh remembering that first day he came from the backcountry after his surprise election, the hasty plans you and I laid to win him over with an evening at the palace. Not knowing of his hatred of theatre you made him our comedy's guest of honour; not knowing of his hatred of worldliness in nuns, I dared to write it. Win the Archbishop over— what a fiasco.

Strange to think that I have never once laid eyes on him, on whom so much now depends.

The Bishop of Puebla, meanwhile, has proved in almost every respect the Archbishop's opposite. And while the Archbishop of Mexico has never been to San Jerónimo or any other convent in his city, the Bishop of Puebla rarely misses a chance to call. He comes to the capital so often lately it's said Mexico has two archbishops. Though there is little he may do to soften the Archbishop's anger, there is much he may do behind the scenes, as he does now. And so at long last it seems there is help for me.

As an oblate Antonia is bound to the rule of our convent by every vow but that of enclosure. In the way of the Indian cooks and the servants of the wealthiest sisters here, Antonia, our sole oblate, is freer than we sisters are, if only in this one regard. So trivial it must seem to them, this liberty, and yet so enormous to me. She insists on doing everything within her power, from the cooking here in our rooms down to the most repellent of chores. She persuaded me finally to divest myself of my one servant, who had become pregnant—which started up all the speculations again about just what sort of errands Sor Juana sends one on. She swore the conception was immaculate, and while I did not doubt that it seemed so to her, I sent her nevertheless to my sister Josefa, who will treat her kindly.

A secretary is of course a source of vanity, mortifying in a nun—and in employing five secretaries simultaneously, truly the Learned Aquinas must have been an Angelic Doctor not to succumb; so it would be ungracious of me to reproach my friend the Bishop for not having arranged something like this years ago. In his own defence he might simply answer that there are not five Antonias in all the New World. In addition to taking dictation and writing out fair copies, Antonia arranges for their delivery, wears a penitential groove into the flagstones between my bookshelves and the convent library, treads out still other channels from the porter's gate to the city's printers and booksellers.

And yet she persists in vexing me with complaints that she would prefer to stay here, when a walk in the streets is for me a dream slow to fade. She might not go out at all, could I not bribe her with a few classes in poetry. In exchange for which she pretends to enjoy helping me with two new duties I have been given. Nominally similar, one I dislike as much as the other I enjoy. Leading religious instruction in Nahuatl for the servants is the first, but the second is preparing classes purely of my own devising for a dozen of our more promising novices. With respect to the former, I well know how their thoughts bend our Faith to flow in courses more natural to them, and who am I of all people to say they should not bend? It makes me feel like a Jesuit. But as for our academy, bending our thoughts is precisely the object of our academic devotions, even as one bends both in penance and in pleasure.

Once again it is the Bishop's intercession I have to thank—and Mother Andrea's newly tractable mood, but even here Santa Cruz presents her with an argument worthy, in its cunning, of a certain Florentine counsellor to princes.[12] 'My dear Mother Andrea, while so many of our leading citizens come to consult the myriad wise and learned nuns throughout the capital, and come to be edified by still other sisters skilled in music and poetry, San Jerónimo—in competing for patrons— depends more than do all the city's other convents on so very few of its gifted sisters. . . .'

Sly enough on the face of it. It also quietly reminds her we must work doubly hard to repay his favours here, with the new convent of Santa Monica taking up so much of his time in Puebla. And lying beneath this reminder is one not so gentle. For while Father Núñez is vain about his humility, Bishop Santa Cruz is supremely serene in his considerable vanity—unless the compliment of his favour is returned with too little gratitude.

In evidence I give you a recent sample of the gossip that the sisters bring by my cell in any unoccupied instant. If there is one treat of which we are insatiate it is news of our sister convents, and this particular story even I cannot resist, since it concerns not only ours and the new convent of Santa Monica, but a young woman from near Tepeaca, about a half day's travel from Puebla. (Antonia's eyes have gone wide—she is from near Tepeaca herself, a town with which I have associations of my own.)

The young woman of our story, having one sister already professed at the convent of San Jerónimo in Puebla, had been trying for twelve years to take the veil. Living in an outbuilding on the family hacienda, mortifying her flesh, praying in her solitude, fasting and having visions. The people of the town had taken to calling her the Hermit—with scorn by some, no doubt.[13] But among the *campesinos* of the haciendas were those who revered her as a *beata.*† A vocation that the Holy Office has been making more than perilous. So this and a terrible loneliness, I suspect, gave her excellent reason to seek the protection of the veil. Bishop Santa Cruz had initially found sufficient cause to take her. She was of a good family that after the death of the father fell into straitened circumstances. Despite her emaciation she must have been pretty, for it is common knowledge that Santa Cruz favours pretty nuns. For obvious reasons, I have never quite found a way to ask him if this is true, or why it should be so. Does he imagine a plain woman needs no protection, or is there no pleasure in a secret possession unless others, knowing, would covet it? In any event he was disposed to take all seven remaining sisters into the college that was about to become the convent of Santa Monica.

†a holy woman not under vows to the Church

What, then, could possibly have happened that even months later she had still not been granted entry? She was further away from it in fact—as far away as could be imagined. The scene I'm about to present is still almost unimaginable to me . . . Santa Cruz has just celebrated Mass. A half-starved girl throws herself at his feet, begging admission to his newest convent, as she has done every day for weeks. And indeed, though she has done nothing differently today, he loses his temper, shouts at her to stop harassing him, and thrusts her angrily away. The cathedral of our second greatest city was filled that day with worshippers. He still wears the chasuble, the dalmatic, the stole. Stunned, anguished, in a weakened state, as the girl makes her way from the cathedral she stumbles and falls heavily down the steps.

Having ears to hear, Mother Andrea needs no help to grasp that the only thing worse than the Archbishop's enmity is compounding it with the Bishop's. Thus, in the matter of our new classes for novices, it now pleases Andrea no less than it does me that in our refectory once a week I am training a whole *generation* of my own replacements.

And as for our collection of verses, I promise to think about a name suitable to an introductory volume. All year I have felt myself slowly sinking beneath the weight of a thousand unasked tasks and cares; as a consequence, the titles that have come to mind are quite ghastly. My ideas run to such as the Danaïdes: the fifty granddaughters of Poseidon and the Nile condemned unfairly by the judges of the dead to haul water in sieves for having murdered (but in self-defence!) the fifty sons of Aegyptus. From which tender reflections spring such inspiring titles as *Hypermnestra's Sieve, Lernaean Lake* . . . I had almost settled on *Amymone's Spring,* as it is a source that never runs dry even during the cruellest droughts on the driest of plains. But since the water springs from holes in the stone where the trident's tines went in, just before Amymone's ravishment by Poseidon . . . Well, you will see the problem instantly.

If a nun absolutely must be pagan, she should at least be chaste.

All my love, and to your two men my warmest embraces.

día 28 de agosto, Anno Domini 1688
del convento de San Jerónimo,
de la Ciudad Imperial de México,
Nueva España

Castalia [11th day of September 1688]

la excma. señora María Luisa Manrique de Lara y Gonzaga
Condesa de Paredes, Marquesa de la Laguna,
Madrid, España

Lysis,

second letter—so quickly. (I have your letters of the 1st and now the 13th of July.) As Antonia placed the envelope in my hands I knew it couldn't be the answer to my last to you, which will be weeks reaching you—crossing uncounted mountain passes, one Atlantic and all the vicissitudes of storm and tide and fog and faulty charts that this implies. And then besides, two sets of censors, one on each side—as if from Veracruz to Cadiz they faced across a functionary's desk, to make the sea of faith for censors but a pond.

And yet even knowing all of this, when I saw how slender your letter I could not help feeling some careless phrase of mine had angered you. In this frame of mind (askew) I read and read once more the opening line.

Send me a title, Juanita. Our daughter needs a name.

How have you managed it so quickly? Licences from the Holy Office, thirty letters of support from theologians. Thirty!—have you so much as unpacked your travelling cases?

You say the printers have *started*? A title then, a title . . . to do with the Muses? but no, one hears far too much talk of Muses over here. Wait.

There is a spring on Mount Parnassus, sacred once to Ares. It lies a little north and east of Delphi. But that was Ares's day, and then there was a nymph and then it was Apollo's time to shine. Castalia. (Pagan, *and* chaste, Castalia.) To escape Apollo's attentions she plunged from a cliff to a spring far below, a small spring at the bottom of a deep rock basin. Here in the tale, the spring transforms into a source of inspiration, to both Apollo and the Muses, who were for this reason called (if rarely) the Castalides. All this is quite fine, and the idea of our Castalia as the Muses' muse quite gratifying, but what amuses me not a little is a glimpse of Apollo's 'inspiration' as his quarry launches herself from the heights and dissolves into a shower of silver.

So, yes, 'Castalia,' but what? *Fuente de Castalia? Manantial Castálida? Salto de las Castálides?*—*Chubasco, Aguacero, Chaparrón, Diluvio*—*Haz Castálida?* I am at a loss. May I surrender the decision to your most exquisite discretion? *Hazme este favorzote?*

Of a sudden, nervousness consumes me. Nymph. What *sort* of nymph—naiad, dryad, nereid, hamadryad—which? This is not some backwater we are publishing in, this is *Madrid*. You have hinted that the printers, who are holding the first signature till you hear from me, would have room in it to print my *Letras a Safo*.[†] How it thrills me to know you have not forgotten them. If I say 'not yet,' will I break your heart?

[†]*Lyrics on Sappho*

I lack the courage still. I am afraid to break this truce. Núñez has kept to his word, and for these last seven years I have not heard a word of his against me. You will lose patience with me for being cowardly. And yet in these quiet if not peaceful years I have been able to work, much bad, some good—but some of that work we are publishing now. If honesty forces me to concede it is not yet my great work, modesty does not stop me thinking that in *First Dream*, at least, I have given something of my measure. There is not a poem quite like it in our language.[14] (You have said precisely that of *Las letras a Safo*, I know.)

But if the Inquisition here can ban Montalbán's albeit terrible play (seen throughout Spain without pleasure perhaps, but also without censure) for the blasphemy of having a character *pray God hasten the course of the sun*, then the holy officers would not hesitate to ban our Castalia for a dalliance with Sappho. And even in the unlikely event that their decision be overturned someday by the Holy Office in Madrid, it could take years. I do not know whom it would bring more pleasure to see our collection seized and held till then—Father Núñez or Fray Dorantes. Both consulted on the Montalbán case. For Núñez, any brief pleasure he took would surely have been in banning a play by the author of *The Nun-Ensign*—an old favourite of mine. Dorantes was, meanwhile, the more vociferous in his ruling and would take pleasure now in seeing Núñez chastened for his past association with me or for any lack of zeal in condemning our collection as soon as it appears.

Already, then, it takes all the courage I can summon to have you publish, along with so many love poems, *Martyr of the Sacrament* and *The Divine Narcissus,* knowing as I do how angrily Núñez views these. Sappho's hour for the stage is not yet nigh. Infinitely worse than the frustration of holding back this one suite a little while longer is the pain of imagining the whole collection seized.

Can you forgive me, then, if I send you another rarity in its place?— to fill the signature, and if you approve it and accept it as a portrait, might you let it open the collection . . . ?

The other night well past Matins, after reading your letter for the dozenth time, the verses I enclose came all in the most marvellous flood. I pray you read them as token of my love and gratitude, a tribute in seventeen quatrains. Sálazar has written something using this structure of dactyls, but I have strengthened it and even bettered it, I think, after a practice poem or two. Even after these, if someone had offered as a wager that a poem of sixty-eight lines each beginning in a dactyl† could come out any better than the beating of a beggar's drum to the thin jingling of his purse, I would not have taken it—would fain have taken the purse.

† one stressed syllable followed by two unstressed: rárity, líberty, álgebra, cínnamon

> *Tránsito a los jardines de Venus,*
> *órgano es de marfil, en canora*
> *música, tu garganta, que en dulces*
> *éxtasis aun al viento aprisiona.*
>   *Pámpanos de cristal y de nieve,*
> *cándidos tus dos brazos, provocan*
> *Tántalos, los deseos ayunos:*
> *míseros, sienten frutas y ondas . . .*[15]

Though I had tried to give it something of the tabor and pipe, yet does one hear in this tribute to you the fife and drum . . . there is a stirring on the plains of Troy, for it seems a fighter of great moment has joined the fight; only it is not Achilles but Helen who moves among us. Or one as beautiful.

You are a Manrique. It is your way to face the field and if there must be a fight to force it, choose the day, the place, the arms. Only wait a little longer, wait a little more. They are strong and many, and you are so very far.

And farther still with the hurricane season descending full upon us.
The wait for your answer will be an agony.
With all my thanks, with all my heart.

día 11 de septiembre, Anno Domini 1688
del convento de San Jerónimo,
de la Ciudad Imperial de México,
Nueva España

SANTA CRUZ

here is a house from whose top floor, and looking south, one may see the last of the arches of the aqueduct where it spills into the basin of the Salto de Agua. The house is large, one of only two on that block, and without adornments of tilework or cornices or coats of arms to call attention to itself. The two gates leading to its courtyard are backed with heavy canvasses, to deny the passerby so much as a glance of the interior. Carriages come and go frequently, but at night.

The servants' entrance is deeply recessed, down a passageway tunnelled with an ivy oddly untamed for a house so well kept. A tall, strongly built woman in her mid-twenties, dressed in the plain brown *sayuela* of a convent or hospital domestic, has walked swiftly yet indirectly to the house: east, past the convent of San José of the Discalced Carmelites, then several blocks south, weaving gradually west among the corrals and outbuildings of the city stockyards and stables. Once, she briefly halts and reaches between the rails of a corral to feed two crab-apples to a colt that comes to the fence at first sight of her. She hurries on along the canal of the Merced, crossing west over a bridge three blocks south of San Jerónimo, wending north and now west again to enter this passageway. A door opens at the first knock. She is taller by half a head than the elderly porter, and seems taller still by reason of a wild mane of waist-length hair tamed at the nape with several turns of orange ribbon.

She is shown upstairs. He is standing a step back from the window, the drapes drawn back just sufficiently to see the pure water of the aqueduct fall in a long clear muscle, a fold of silk. In contrast the room is dark. Turning, he beckons her to the plain wooden chair and seats himself comfortably upon the purple velvet divan facing it. The plush is of a shade very close to the piping and cincture of his Lenten cassock. She sits without moving, looking slightly past his face, as unhurriedly he studies her. His hair is a pale brown, the forehead high and broad, the crown of the head slightly flattened. His features are fine, the long slender brows slightly knit, as with a hint of temper. The eyes are large and dark. The nose is strong, the cheekbones wide. The jaws taper to a frail point of chin beneath a small-lipped mouth. Above it, a charcoal line of moustache. The pinkish icing of a burn scar shows just above the high collar. Only after several moments does he speak.

The voice is a sweet tenor.

"Convent life seems to agree with you. Who would have thought? In other ways too, I feel you coming along nicely. Your handwriting is more like hers all the time. And your style—she has been working with you to improve it, hasn't she. . . ?"

She does not respond.

"Let's not begin awkwardly. Has she or has she not?"

"Yes."

"It is only right that someone with so many correspondents, and of such calibre, should have a secretary. Someone discreet for her messages, someone for delicate purchases, books. . . . What was the purpose of your outing today?"

"To come here."

"No, what did you *tell* her? Come. Tell me."

"Something I needed to do for my family."

"Not untrue. Clever. And she asked you no more about it. . . ."

"No."

"Excellent. Trust and consideration. I would say she has begun to like you. Would you say she has begun to like you?"

"*Don't.*"

"Does she *trust* you?"

"I don't know."

"Of course she does. May I see the list of books she has had you purchase this month? It was not in your last letter."

"I forgot."

"But you have it now."

"I haven't made it up yet."

"Now you see? This is the problem. The handwriting is good, the style is more literate all the time, but the reports themselves have become . . . disappointing. They lack detail. They are not concrete. Detail is exactly what I ask of you."

"I can't do this."

"But you can. You have more than proved yourself capable with many others."

"That isn't—"

"You can't do this *anymore.*"

"No."

"You can't do this to her. Is that it?"

"Yes."

"To her *anymore*. . . . Answer me."

"Yes."

"Those things which you have, nonetheless, done until now."

"Yes."

"You are too hard on yourself. I have no doubt that you still can. It is the only reason you are here now, in Mexico, after all. Where your duties in this regard are, overall, less onerous than in Puebla . . . ? *Are they?*"

"Yes."

"It is good that you display loyalty. To earn her trust you must have this quality. Do display it. Just not here. For me, to me, but do not display it *with* me."

"Manuel, I—"

"You do not help your cause by calling me that. We have an agreement, and that part of it is finished. We do still have an agreement? Unless your feelings for your dear sisters have changed. Have things changed?"

"How *could* they have? *¿En este mundo de la chingada, las cosas—cómo van a cambiar?*"

"I am prepared to endure a little petulance, because I value your sincerity. A useful quality. Perhaps not much frightens you, after the life you have led. Though you must admit it was more frightening before we met. But *they* do frighten. I think they *are* frightened. I have explained to them that they may not be able to stay in Puebla much longer. They are doing very well in school, though they may falter a bit now. I have brought their letters, as I agreed to. You may read everything here before you leave. I think you will find them enjoyable. Even the little one traces out her letters quite charmingly. And can sing out her whole alphabet, too. If you could see them, there is such a bloom on their innocence just now. . . . So. Our agreement stands, nothing has changed."

"Nothing."

"Details. *Not* evidence. I am not documenting a case. It is the state of her soul I would gauge, its dispositions, its readiness. You understand, these are only for me. I am not the Inquisition. They have their own sources there, and if anyone can protect her from those, it will not be you but me. You do see this."

"Yes."

"Excellency."

"Yes, Your Grace."

"No, dear child, this we reserve for the Archbishop. Excellency is quite enough. Will you say it now?"

"Excellency."

"There. In this arrangement, I too make sacrifices. And penance. You have not been easy to replace in Puebla. You see, it is not just your information I miss. Your absence has been painful to me in every respect. As painful as was your presence, come to think of it, though of course differently. But now I am convinced, once again, that we still have it, this understanding of ours, and so I am resigned to my sacrifices. In my own life I have found happiness fleeting. But you, I think, are happy there. Are you happy there? Otherwise . . . ?"

"*Otherwise?*"

"Yes?"

"Yes, Excellency, I am happy there. Otherwise."

"Then I can be happy for you. Do be happy, dear child. Be happy as long as you can. The letters are in the top left-hand drawer. Face the window if you like. You have earned a little privacy . . . there is so little where you are. *Left.* There. Go on. I will watch from over here. . . ."

JUANA INÉS
DE LA CRUZ

Alan Trueblood, trans.

Silly, you men, so very adept
at wrongly faulting womankind,
not seeing you're alone to blame
for faults you plant in woman's mind.

　After you've won by urgent plea
the right to tarnish her good name,
you still expect her to behave—
you, that coaxed her into shame.

　You batter her resistance down
and then, all righteousness, proclaim
that feminine frivolity,
not your persistence, is to blame.

　When it comes to bravely posturing,
your witlessness must take the prize:
you're the child that makes a bogeyman,
and then recoils in fear and cries.

　Presumptuous beyond belief,
you'd have the woman you pursue
be Thais when you're courting her,
Lucretia once she falls to you.

　For plain default of common sense,
could any action be so queer
as oneself to cloud the mirror,
then complain that it's not clear?

　Whether you're favoured or disdained,
nothing can leave you satisfied.
You whimper if you're turned away,
you sneer if you've been gratified . . .

[6th day of January, 1689]

CASSANDRA

la excma. doña María Luisa Manrique
Condesa de Paredes, Marquesa de la Laguna,
Madrid, España

Dearest María Luisa,

weet friend, beautiful Thetis of the Seas, you seek to fashion me a peerless armour at the glowing forge of your cares. How I love that you would protect me still. First, to let you know we are alone. Antonia has gone out on an errand. Please know that we will always have these moments, these letters written in my hand. But the simple fact of being alone does not leave me free to speak. And things we said here in this cell, just we two, I am not free to write, when the mails may be opened at any time by the Holy Office or the Crown. I know you know this—I want you to hear me say it. Still other things may be written to be read obliquely, as one reads fables written by a friend who has read and loved the same stories, as have you and I. And then there are lines that may only be spoken in the theatre you and I make here, that no longer resonate in the world outside, as with an instrument whose sounding board is split. If together we could not create such a place where the instrument could be heard again, what use would writing be, what use theatre?

Last, let there also be things I may say in these letters that I could never say with you here with me, sitting so near. We must always make a place for these, as I will before I stop tonight.

But if I am to keep my promise to write often, I will need help. To burden you with tedious plaints in the too brief hours we had alone together in this cell would have been too graceless even for me. Even now I hesitate, but hope you will give me leave. . . .

You write to warn me that these seven years of quiet I celebrate as a truce are in truth a siege. So I tell you now that Father Núñez has indeed caught wind of our plans and has begun to rail against our Castalia before she even reaches here. It is as if he believed Sappho's lyrics were in it—but how can that be, if the source of his information is the Holy Office there? Surely he knows they would have mentioned any verses on Sappho had they been there. And if he has some other source so early—who?

And yet, sweet Lysis, even with these fresh worries, what I most suffer from has little to do with Núñez or Archbishop Aguiar. Not a siege but a blockade—and I am that grain ship, that silver galleon straining at its hawsers to run the line, anxious, chafing to put to sea before I sink beneath the worthy new duties they heap on me almost daily. These will keep me from any work I might call mine more surely than any Church injunction can.

The daily Masses, the Friday chapter of faults, the public acts of contrition that bring the envious among my sisters so much satisfaction . . . yes, these weary me a little more. But there is yet much more than these. The prayers of the Divine Office I barely mention—these you yourself have grumbled about often enough in my stead. The very thought of being woken mid-night for the prayers of Matins (with those of Compline still on our lips), you find hideous; but I sleep little anyway. Often as not I am reading or writing when the chimes call us, and these at least I do not mind. Have we not always found them among the loveliest bells of the capital?

I have been elected convent accountant for the third straight term. Few convents in the city have ever earned six percent per annum. Of course we must first have money to invest, so by far the task most prodigal of my time lies in hosting the convent's many patrons. To do this effectively, though, means rehearsing our *niñas* and novices in skits and our choir in musical entertainments. Then there is the writing of these—if something better suited really cannot be found. And because I have not been clever enough to conceal my familiarity with Nahuatl, I am become a sort of Solomon of disputes among the three hundred servants here, though far from all *speak* Nahuatl. Worse, because one set of apartments or another is always being renovated to accommodate still more servants, I very often find myself Superintendent of Works:[16] most of the workers are also native Mexicans, whose overseers are seemingly selected for their inability to let them work in peace.

Other charges I take in turn with three or four other sisters. Besides the classes I wrote you of, four of us see to courses in reading, music, dance and arithmetic for thirty young girls. Then there come occasional turns in the infirmary, the cellars, the archives, the library—this last, as you can imagine, I do not resent so much.

Having now quite exhausted myself (and surely you) I pass over a few other, minor tasks, to close with the sermons and arguments I am consulted on by various monks, priests, bishops and inquisitors, never forgetting the carols, lyrics and plays I am asked to write for the churches and cathedrals—these I do on my own time, though the commissions go chiefly to the convent coffers.

Perhaps you will understand after all this complaint why I can almost not bear the thought of doing without Antonia now that I have found her. I was thoughtless not to explain all this to you first in a letter in my own hand. (Even as sensing your hurt has made me see, if belatedly, how the similarity of her hand to mine only made things worse, and troubles you still.)

You have always been anxious about my friends. But I depend on so many people for so many things; I would be consumed with anxiety if I felt I could trust only the friends I did not need. This would be no way to inspire alliances anyway, but this you know better than I. A spirit of mistrust entrains its own surprises.

The Inquisitor Gutiérrez I admit to needing as much as liking, though I liked him instantly . . . he of the bland looks and feigned bemusement that clothe a sharp mind in an almost childlike frankness. Scarce a fortnight over from Spain, he first ambled into my locutory to register his disappointment that so many otherwise serious individuals in this city were making fools of themselves with ridiculously exaggerated praise of a certain nun in a certain convent. He stayed three hours.

On his next visit we worked through some of the briefs he was preparing; I took a no doubt wicked pleasure in suggesting corrections he might make to a certain priest's newest manual of devotion for nuns. Later, when one detailed argument in particular was singled out for commendation, Gutiérrez openly acknowledged my help—at the *Holy Office*, before a roomful of his colleagues! Everyone was talking about it. Can one even imagine it, the impertinence of the thing? The Jesuits and the Dominicans disliked him about equally for it, with the result that—we laugh about this—he's now seen as something of an honest broker. One wry Augustinian to keep the Dominicans and the Jesuits from each other's throats.

My prickly friend Carlos, for his part, made a terrible start with you— *con ese asunto del arco.*[†] Certainly you of all people owe him nothing, not

[†]'that business of the arch'—the triumphal arch of 1680

even the gift of your comprehension, having stayed your husband's hand and kept my slightly seditious friend out of irons. You scarcely knew me then, yet heard my petition—which said so much for your openness of mind and heart. But if Carlos had made a better beginning I know you'd have seen under all that awful pride and irritability a beautiful mind and such a generous spirit. Yes I do take his employment with the Archbishop as a betrayal, but of our principles, not of me. In the matter of serving His Grace, Carlos has little choice. The University's stipend is a mean provocation—among his relations he has a dozen mouths to feed—and you've seen for yourself how profitlessly he conducts himself at the palace. Almost any extra income he gets is at the Archbishop's sufferance: his chaplaincy at the hospital, his commission to write the history of the convent of the Immaculate Conception (and you cannot begin to know how galling his newfound 'expertise' in convent life can be), and now this post of Almoner.

It is only fitting that your questions turn to Antonia's origins, for the defence of our good name is our best guarantee, however imperfect, of honourable conduct. What's more, it is entirely in keeping with your own nobility of spirit that you have been able to forget the towering elevations separating your origins from mine.

I was born a natural daughter of the Church. My father was an adventurer barely of the hidalgo class whose name I do not even have the right to take. Antonia's origins are not much different from mine, and if she has been so very much less fortunate, it serves to show me, as nothing ever has, how things might have gone with me. She too was born in the countryside. East of Puebla, not far from San Lorenzo de los Negros. Her father was a military physician who retired to the country to sire a score of daughters on the mulattas and negresses in his employment there. His less common passion, though, was educating them, and thereby proving to his satisfaction a theory of his that women, even of mixed race, may become *gente de razón*,[†] if thoughtfully trained. I cannot decide if this lets me like him a little more, or a very great deal less. And yet I profit by his results.

[†]creatures of reason

Dearest Lysis, I know you will not let yourself be repelled when I tell you she was once forced to sell her body as a courtesan. In the better houses the men would ask for the educated one, the tall one—for White Chocolate, as though to order a hot beverage from a palace steward. But it is clear that in the beginning she was not in such fine houses.

There is the frailest line of scar—by glass, or sharpest steel—that runs from the corner of her left eye all down her pale cheek to the corner of her smile. Yet it has neither disfigured her face, nor maimed her spirit. She has been willing to tell me much more, but I do not want to know—while unspeakable, it is not quite beyond my capacity to imagine it. I have seen them in the streets. For years I heard their screams at night. We hear them even here.

Knowing that the situation of those dearest to her is precarious, I have begged Bishop Santa Cruz, who has done this much, to do whatever else he can. She has become a friend to me. You cannot know my loneliness when you left, my thoughts during this cold year. Until I met you I was content to stay in here, within the walls of this cell, with these friends who are my books my only company. But since you left how I hunger to see the streets again, to walk in them *just one hour.* . . .

I have forfeited that liberty, but at least I have Antonia—a warm salt breeze, salt in speech, strong as the sea. She is tireless in my service, sleeps almost as little as I, though rather better, and though she is not yet twenty-two to my forty, fusses over me like an anxious mother hollow-eyed with worry and nights of care. (And as you are always chiding me for not making copies of the verses I give away as gifts, here is someone now for that work, too.) Know that in her you have the strongest ally, for she is always trying to warn me against one prideful folly or other. She has been my Penthesileia—no, like the Angolan warrior princesses of her grandmother's ancestors, such strength, to see her in the orchards and the gardens they say . . . the quiet rage in her that must find its release somewhere.

If I have never seen her there, it is because I do not go. . . . For you see, dear friend, the flowers in the orchards, the smell of the earth, the hard rain that lays bright bracelets of coin on each blade of grass, all these things bring too near the absence of another time. And of a kind of poetry now lost to me.

As the years go rushing, rushing by, in things absent I feel a presence as of stone—your absence as of a stone in my breast; your distance the darkness behind it, and all that holds it in are these letters from you: the presence of your absence. Absence—yours, others'—is become a presence ever before me, an ever constant pressure, the mass of a stone I am afraid to roll back. Always for me lately, this absence, this dance. This too is a kind of siege.

I have been afraid to speak to you of all this, *amada dueña de mi alma*, for fear I will not know how to stop, or when I must.

There was the day you first came to this convent. . . .

Sweet Lysis, I too regret, bitterly, every hour together we could not have. With this letter I enclose a few verses that, hesitant yet, reach for your hand. . . .

I send you all my love and anxiously await word.

día 6 de enero del año 1689
de este convento de San Jerónimo,
de la Ciudad de México,
Nueva España

[2nd day of April 1689]   HELEN

Her Excellency, Lady María Luisa Manrique de Lara y Gonzaga
Condesa de Paredes, Marquesa de la Laguna,
Madrid

Mi querida Lysis,

ur daughter has safely arrived. Castalia has reached the New World. I have our collection under my hand now as I write, as I have written for thirty years, so many countless hours, with serried rows of books in friendly ranks, standing watch close at my back.

Something else I have never said to you, I say it now. That a man I loved more than the sun, my kinsman, loved your kinsman with all his great heart. How beautiful it would have been, and how strange, to have known so very long ago that today—under the aegis and seal of the House of Paredes—I would reach up to shelve my own first book only to discover that it fits between his two best loved authors. Between these two books I still have of his, between Homer and Manrique I stand: Juana Inés de la Cruz, Sor.

I exist.

This book. Our first. I open it. I cradle her, this child of ours, run my ticklish nose down her bumpy spine, snuffle out her newborn's scents. I hold up a world in my palm. A life entire.

I laugh a little through the springs in my eyes at the saucy title you have found. *Castalian Flood.* Run, ye mockers and sinners and poetasters, run for the arks!

Such a feeling of dangerous peace creeps over me, Juana Inés de la Cruz, Sor. Between Manrique and Homer, between peace and fight. One book—isn't one enough? Why do we have to struggle so much not to be crushed? Surely now all the fighting could stop. And yet I know it does not.

For a long time after my girlhood ended it was hard to love the *Iliad* as before. Even now I prefer the *Odyssey,* and there are parts of his *Iliad* I dislike still. For a while after leaving Panoayan I disliked it all, every chapter. As a young woman at the palace, what I saw in those chapters was the endless waste and horror of all that is most beautiful in men. The finest flowers of an age cut and trailed through gore and dust. This epic of deflowering men. And then just when it all becomes too much, a Homer transformed writes a kind of miracle for us, an interlude, as though by a different pen, as though the Homer of the *Odyssey* drops by for a turn. The working of Achilles' shield at Vulcan's forge.

On that shield, as Thetis of the silvery feet stands tiptoe at his shoulder, anxious yet marvelling, the smith Hephaistos works the heavens and beneath them two cities. In one, a civil peace: festivals and marriages, through the streets wind bridal processions by torchlight; women crowd doorways to watch the maidens pass. A marketplace wrought in silver, sober heralds and arbitrators sit in open court . . . sage elders in session on benches of stone slow-worn to gloss.

The other, a city under siege. Outside its walls not one but two contending armies ring the ramparts in glittering bronze. Beyond, Hephaistos works soft fields triple-ploughed . . . teams of oxen till in the sun, to each teamster a man brings sweet wine in gold flagons. Under a silver tree a feast is spread. Women scatter white barley for the workers to eat. Beside a fire a brass ox lies jointed and trimmed. Copper reeds sway in a silver stream, sheepflocks gleam. A player with his lyre refreshes the harvesters, as with light dance steps—for their fardels were light—they keep time. . . . And enclosing all, the deep gyres of the Ocean River running at the shield's outermost edge.

Why has Homer given us this shield, this paradox of an object of war, yet a refuge from it? Is his an act of defiance, or does he merely tease out the moment, an idyll before the bloody climax? Whatever his purpose, it is an interlude of all that is beautiful and fine, all that is worth living, striving for, all that made that war terrible and cursed. All this was lost, the Poet suggests, over Helen. We should despise her, even when the Trojans themselves cannot. This daughter of Zeus and Leda, Delusion and Nemesis, hatched from an egg to a beauty unbearable to men. But which Helen? For there were two. . . .

The poet Stesichoros was struck blind and his sight restored only once he had admitted that Helen was never in Troy, that she had instead been spirited to Egypt by Hermes and replaced with an illusion fashioned by Hera from a swath of cloud. It is an illusion so real as to trigger a war, a myth so real to us now it may as well have happened. A myth wrapped in an illusion cradled in the hull of a dream.

Among those who have been to Ithaca and know its coast are some who believe that Odysseus never made it home. That the coast described at his landing was not Ithaca at all, but Leucas, Isle of Whiteness, Isle of Dreams. And that his return, therefore—or the *Odyssey* entire—was a journey in a dream, real as a city on a shield.

Two cities on a shield, two Helens, each looking out to sea. One over the plains before Troy, one over the shores of Egypt. Helen of Sparta, Helen of Troy. One the illusion of a possession, one the dream of a release, both of an impossible beauty.

Since my childhood I've known, as one knows an old dream, how the fires and floods and storms conspire with the illusions of the years to keep us from Ithaca.

Sweet Lysis, let our daughter be the siege raised, let this book be our shield, let these pages be our dream of release from all cares of consequence, all delusions of possession, all the torments of absence. Let us make of this book—this shield, this dream we have shared—the place where we come from so far to meet, I from the west and you from the east. To our island of dreams, our dream of an impossible beauty, and in it, together, we walk the white shore.

Juana. . . .

*día 2 de abril del año 1689
de este convento de San Jerónimo,
de la Ciudad Imperial de México*

CHRISTINA   *[29th day of June, 1689]*

María Luisa Manrique de Lara y Gonzaga
Condesa de Paredes, Marquesa de la Laguna,
Madrid, España

Lysis . . .

o the incomparable Christina of Sweden is gone. As your letter arrived, the first rumours had only just begun. It is true, then; she was interred at Saint Peter's Basilica. The Pope forgave her every excess after all. In abdication, poverty, obloquy, even in death, she commanded a queen's respects.

For another moment after finishing your letter I could not quite believe—in the sense that one could hardly ever believe she really was alive, so very alive was her legend. Here at the convent, as it had been at the palace, the talk was often of Christina, just as she was fascinated by convent life. (For Christina, it was the married woman who was truly a slave; nuns were only prisoners, and even the queen was not free. . . .) They are probably talking of her now in half a dozen cells around this patio. All the rumours that she would come, was coming, was in Seville, then in Cadiz itself, waiting for a proper embarkation. For an entire fleet, more likely. From my earliest days here—and perhaps it never quite stopped—I had the notion she would come to stay a while with us at San Jerónimo, with her menagerie of parrots and apes, with her equipage of fourteen thousand books, and we might sit together and while away the days. I would tell her of our academy, of Antonia and Tomasina, María and Belilla, and she would tell me of hers, of Bernini and Corelli and Scarlatti. And we would talk of Descartes and astronomy, of languages and the fighting spirit of queens, of horsemanship and marksmanship, of a life of the mind and men's breeches.

When they asked her about this—her loves and her pistols and her breeches—do you know how she answered them? *The soul has no sex.*

You write me gently of her death, but it is I who should be consoling you. You had much higher hopes than I that we might one day win her patronage for a nun in the wilds of America. How could our Castalia fail, you wrote that day in such high spirits, how could *Sappho's* lyrics fail to enchant Christina of Sweden? By the time I read those words, she was two months dead, and only now the news is confirmed. How cruelly time and distance work at the edges of irony: one edge they blunt, its opposite whet.

Her influence was enormous, you write trailing off. . . . Between the lines I read what you do not quite say: if Sappho's lyrics had *been* in *Castalian Flood*, Christina might already have read it and taken up our cause.

The collection has gone through two print runs in two months. You write that we should be thinking about another collection—surely there is something to be done about Núñez. What is it, *really*, that fuels this grievance of ours, you ask, that it blazes up from embers banked long ago? Can he not somehow be persuaded to tolerate *Las letras a Safo* in our next collection, when that bright day comes? By which I take you to be asking if there is anything you can say to overcome my fears. In answering the first, perhaps each of us will find our answers to the second.

While you were here, your protection sufficed, but the House of Paredes is back in Spain now. My relations with the Viceroy are cordial but not warm. The Count is decent enough, but it does not help to know he is part of the faction that has brought such grief to your husband's brother. As for the Countess de Galve, if it did not so inflame the Archbishop to hear of her visits here, she would not come at all any longer.

Do you know what she has just done? She put on *Amor es más laberinto*, knowing full well from what happened to us that he would not come to any play, least of all this one. All this may bring her a childish satisfaction, but I do not see what good it can do her or me, and though I cling to my love of comedy more grimly each year, it is not exactly why I stayed up from Matins to Lauds for two months writing it.[17]

The Archbishop persists in his refusal to serve as her spiritual director, even as he did with you. Unlike you, she takes it personally, though he would gladly do as little for any woman. Since His Grace will not minister to her, the Viceroy stays with Núñez as well. Father Núñez is happy to oblige. You kept him as your director because in your life you had found so few with the nerve to challenge you—better the adversary one sees, you said, as befits a Manrique. But it was you who convinced me to find another director precisely because I did have much to fear. Now you wonder if I have not become 'more timid in my rebellion than I was in my submission.'

The question is a fair one. As I say, in the answer to your first, perhaps we'll find our answers to the second and now this third.

Twenty-one years ago the Reverend Father Antonio Núñez led me to see the service of Christ as Loyola himself first had, as a mission of chivalry. The verses of Juan de la Cruz speak of the soul's longing to be ravished by Him, a prospect Núñez can just countenance. But that in the verses of Juana *Inés* de la Cruz a nun should speak to Christ as to a courtly lover . . . no, this Núñez cannot bear.

For all that, things had not acquired the bitterness you have yourself witnessed between Núñez and me until near the end of what was already a dark time. In 1674, the Holy Office sentenced a Franciscan—Carlos's dear friend—to burn at the stake for his activities among the Maya in Yucatan. Father Núñez had not yet reached his position of eminence at the Holy Office and has always claimed he was not intimately involved. Until the end. For he was one of two Jesuits assigned to bring the condemned to contrition. The harshness in my relations with Father Núñez dates from that day.

Much of the rest you know, but for a detail or two. Almost immediately after Bishop Santa Cruz's election was overturned (almost certainly with the connivance of the Jesuits), Santa Cruz took an interest in a text by an Irish Jesuit whom I had known in my locutory. Father Godinez had been highly critical of the Jesuits here as spiritual directors, the gist of his criticism being that they too often clipped the wings of their penitents for fear that our mystical flights might soar too perilously high, commending us to penitence rather than love, to obedience rather than communion.[18] The Society of Jesus refused to publish it.

Núñez is himself a veritable apostle of self-mortification, I know that he believes such extremes and rigours are not for women, for we fall easily prey to the ultimate wickedness of ecstasy.

But to compensate for the relative moderation of our physical trials, Núñez would substitute a cruelty of the heart. I give you your former spiritual director, and a sampling from his latest circular to us. . . .

I very much desire, for the *alivio* and *decoro* of your convent and the estimation of your persons, that you avail yourselves of all good tokens and qualities, from the infinitesimal firsts to the supreme and ultimate . . . and, finally, that you gather unto yourselves all the good works and talents that you can.

And why, you might ask? To use them for ostentation and proofs of your efforts? Not in the least: that you might keep them protected and ready to hand, and only take them out and use them when and as the convent may have need of them. . . . That you raise and fatten and spoil the plump flesh of your talents and commitments, but in order to slit their throats and bleed them with the knife of Mortification, on the altars of Charity, in the temple of Obedience. This is sacrificing to God your thanks; the other, is offering your talents to the idol of Vanity.[19]

You will perhaps recall the sentiments.

And so it frequently amuses me to note how many of the churchmen under his direction have become just such *extáticos*. His Paternity don Pedro de Arellano, now my nominal director, was a Núñez disciple. During his time with Father Núñez, don Pedro acquired a most holy fear of sin, most notably his own—as he found himself stabbing the patron of an inn after a twenty-four-hour gambling binge. And we have the Archbishop himself, who now takes to his bed in murderous rages a few days each month. Even though Núñez is the only one who can so far control him, he controls a depreciating asset, for everyone here watches with malign anticipation for the day when the most unpopular Archbishop in living memory reaches that apoplexy of wrath from which there can be no recovery.

But now, in the span of a few months, Father Núñez has dedicated to Bishop Santa Cruz first a rehash of a text he wrote years ago on the reforms of the Council of Trent, and then recently some new text—I am still trying to get the details, but I hear it is another tome on penitence.[20] So Núñez has begun courting my most powerful ally within the Church. It seems he was only waiting for you to leave.

Finally I have admitted it, you will say. What more evidence do I need that this is no truce? But at least he does not defame me, and his courtship does not succeed. I will not let it. (One cannot walk two blocks in Mexico without tripping over a theologian. Bishop Santa Cruz has only one of me—indeed is the only one in the Church who can now claim to *have* me in his collection. He has known me for fifteen years, and yet however often I tell him the *via mística* is simply not in my temperament, Santa Cruz has never given up hope that he will one day find the mystic in me. The risks of (my) ecstasy he is prepared to run, for the nun's transports are the oil that lights the altars of the Church, the blood of renewal, the blood of Christ himself. So you see, Núñez detests the very thing the Bishop has never given up hope of finding in me. But finding it, what then? I suspect that Santa Cruz has this idea that he will one day shape my holy ravings, or play John to my Teresa. Or perhaps it is the reverse. . . .)

It occurs to me tonight that since the first rumours of Christina's death, I've been half dreading Núñez would come to bring me the news himself. The Nun-Empress, he used to call her, with that sarcasm, that Philistine tone and that memory he wields like a scalpel, with which I know he has made you suffer, too. 'Beware of her, Juana. Christina of Sweden did more to silence Descartes than we ever could.'[21]

Silence Descartes? If Núñez ever does come to gloat I will offer him this—from among those letters of hers she had published, here is her note to a Descartes who had recently expounded his ideas on the infinite amplitude of the Universe.

Monsieur . . .
Were we to imagine the world in the vast extension your theory assigns it, Man would find it impossible therein to preserve the place of honour he assigns himself. On the contrary, he will in all probability judge that these stars also have inhabitants, or even that the planets surrounding them are populated with denizens more intelligent and, on the whole, better favoured than he; doubtless, then, will he lose the conviction that this limitless world is a sacred gift placed at his service.

Who can doubt that Christina, who had negotiated the Peace of Westphalia and knew the hearts of men and the tides of politics no doubt better than he, imposed upon Descartes a quiet moment or two of reflection then?

There it is. Now you know the circumstances that fuel the fires of our old grievance. Núñez has taken up too much of our time this night. It is late, soon it will be day. Antonia is asleep.

I want to tell you a secret. As you know I am widely envied the location of my cell, for its sunny mornings, its views of the mountains. You are among the few from the outside world to have seen those views. But there is quite another reason I would not trade this cell. Behind a tapestry, there is a small door opening into a stairway. A century ago many of our cells had such doors, as one may see from the architect's designs (to be Superintendent of Works has its compensations). But not long after the convent was finished, the stairways were ordered walled over, for the nuns had begun to congregate on the roofs at the slightest pretext, at street festivals, religious processions—there is no end of things to watch in the streets once one begins to take an interest.

A convent has many secrets, and this is among our best kept. I am not the only one to have restored my cell to the original design. There are three of us, as far as I can tell. We know who we are. We do not go up by day for fear of being seen, even though the Archbishop who ordered the stairwells sealed has been dead half a century.

But very late at night, when I cannot sleep, or a scream in the street or in a cell has woken me, such things in a telescope I have seen. . . . Some nights it is only the stars that bring relief. The stars were always distant, the stars do not change. Looking up at the night sky— unchanged since in the childhood of our race we first traced their constellations—have you ever felt your spirit mounting to those heights up through your eyes?

The Twins, the Fire-Bow, the Great and the Little Bear, Cassiopeia . . . And is it not with a child's eyes that we trace again in letters of wonder this starry alphabet, and through those eyes feel our own childhood reaching back down to us?

When it is very clear and the magic lantern of the night glows brightly, when the horizons stand traced in stars like figures cut from black and laid on lantern glass, I swear to you, even when it is cold, I smell fresh-picked corn baking in the sun as I once did in Nepantla. That, for me, is what these moments on the roof have come to mean.

Eight years I have waited for the Archbishop's permission to buy this cell and I wait anxiously still. For in these rooms, so long as they are not mine, even this secret doorway can be taken from me.

And now, as I say good-night, I promise you before this ink is dry to slip up to the roof and think upon the infinite expanses of the universe,

the limits on the hearts of men, the closeness I feel to you despite the
distances that separate us . . . and to look into the east to you, for you.
Love . . .

día 29 de junio, Anno Domini 1689
del convento de San Jerónimo,
de la Ciudad Imperial de México,
Nueva España

Post Scriptum. Mid-morning: remembering last night's stars, I have yet one
more favour to ask. I should tell you right out, it is less for me than for
Carlos. All his studies and observations, his proofs and calculations—it
breaks my heart a little these past few years to see him so freely sharing all
this with visiting scholars (while rounding on the local ones like a wounded stag). He has understood that he can never publish most of his work,
and so tries to advance the work of those who perhaps one day can. For
six months now he has been attempting to obtain a copy of *Philosophiae
Naturalis Principia Mathematica*, a new work of natural philosophy.
Technically speaking it is not banned, but since this Newton is a
Lutheran and apparently goes further than Copernicus, Galileo and
Descartes combined—indeed pulls together and builds upon their
studies—most booksellers here sensibly assume his text will soon be on
the next Index and want nothing to do with it. Apparently the holy officers at the port in Veracruz are of the same view and have confiscated at
least one copy that we know of. If, however, as happened earlier this year,
a nobleman from Madrid happened to be travelling to the Indies with a
parcel under seal of the House of Paredes, it would not likely be opened.
I hasten to repeat that he would be committing no infraction. Technically.

he locutory stands in readiness. By a bookshelf I sit radiating an admirable, a mighty calm. Gutiérrez has just left. I need not remind myself that in the past he has brought reliable information from the Holy Office: rumours of cases, advance word of rulings, gossip of the Inquisition's inner tensions and debates—monthly casualty reports from the war between the Jesuits and the Dominicans. Today, as one of two consultants on the case, Gutiérrez brought news of a licensing application—routinely approved, yet whose implications for me cannot be routine.

Father Antonio Núñez de Miranda is to be granted licence to publish *The Penitent Communicant*. It is written, Gutiérrez assured me, in a prose as rigorous and subtle as it is dead. Following Thomist doctrine, Father Núñez holds that the act of transmuting His flesh and blood into the wafer and wine is Christ's most sublime expression of love for Man. Not a half-dozen theologians in all the Catholic commonwealth can match Núñez's learning on the Eucharist. And it is his secret conceit, as a good Creole, that to further deepen our apprehension of this supreme mystery, no one is better placed than the (sufficiently disciplined) theologian raised among the ruins of cannibal Mexico. According to Gutiérrez, who has dubbed it *The Shriven Communicant*, the work's underlying message is that anyone who finds grounds for an ecstatic communion, in so holy a mystery, had better think again.

But while I was speaking of this with Gutiérrez, my mind could not be deflected from a detail I found sobering enough to meditate upon. *The Penitent Communicant* is dedicated to don Manuel Fernández de Santa Cruz, Bishop of Puebla. The Bishop is my friend, the Bishop is not here yet, the Bishop was to be here an hour ago. Suddenly it is not beyond imagining that the Bishop has come all the way from Puebla to look over Núñez's manuscript, not to see me.

Antonia sits fidgeting at the desk, having filled the inkwells and twice restocked the paper and quills. At the middle window, the little table is set for two, one to each side of the grille. While I radiate calm, the afternoon sun streams brightly through crystal wine glasses, blithely over bowls for whipped chocolate, blindingly across the matching sideplates—pleasant peasant patterns of pheasants and ferns on the blue-on-white ceramics of Puebla. No, *calm*. On the visitors' side rests a platter of the *dulces encubiertos* for which San Jerónimo is extolled by our sweet-toothed patrons. Candied figs and limes from the orchard, candied squash and peppers from the garden. Behind the arras in the back, the giggling has stopped, which almost certainly means that today's *escuchas,*[†] Ana and Tomasina, have abandoned their listening posts to search the street for signs of our eminent guest. It has been some time since the Bishop's last visit from Puebla. The times are anxious— Antonia, ever incapable of hiding her feelings, looks more worried than I would admit to feeling.

Carlos has been home from his latest expedition for several days now, but chooses this precise moment to pay a visit. Thinking it is the Bishop in the passageway I rise to stand fetchingly by the grille. As Carlos comes through the doorway I would like to be angry—and try to look it, but in truth it is good to see him. He has been away through most of the winter and all of spring.

A bachelor dressing without a woman's touch, Carlos has today achieved somehow a shadow of mournful elegance in a black cape too heavy for April, a small, reasonably white collar and a high black tunic laced firmly at the neck.

"Have you run out of people to see, Carlos?"

"This is lavish even for you," he says, glancing over our preparations. "Are you so pleased to have me back?

"I am, exceedingly."

He takes the Bishop's seat. I stand a moment longer trying not to look exceedingly pleased, staring down at the broad pale forehead, the hairline seeming a little higher than six months ago, *con mas canas*. He is almost handsome, the cheekbones finely formed, over cheeks a little too hollow just now.

"So this isn't all for me."

"You don't eat sweets, or still didn't the last time you graced us with a visit."

"I've been a little unwell."

"The malaria . . . ? 'Tonia, will you bring our friend a cordial?"

"Probably."

"Lime, beet, tamarind?"

"Lime . . ."

Antonia, who is fond of him, hurries over with a glass. *"Gusto en verlo, don Carlos."*

"Hola, Antonia. Gracias."

"Something more substantial, Carlitos—a soup, a stew?"

"I'd be glad to make you something, don Carlos."

"The cordial is fine, 'Tonia. I'm fine. And yes, it is nice to see you too. But *you*—I leave for a few months and come back to this. What deviltry have you played on Núñez now, after so many years? *?En qué avíspero te has metido ya?*†"

†'What hornet's nest have you stirred up now?'

"Aside from publishing without seeking his approval?"

"You couldn't have sent one copy to Núñez?" He shrugs, a maddening little hitch of one shoulder. "Not even as a courtesy?"

"You mean, Carlos, as an invitation to meddle. But you're right—had I realized there'd be advance copies turning up everywhere . . ."

"He's the one turning up everywhere. The university, the *Audiencia*, the Brotherhood. Criticizing your spiritual director—"

"Before Dorantes can blame it on him instead."

"Was that Gutiérrez I just saw leaving? Tell me the Inquisition isn't involved."

"He had been hoping to see Bishop Santa Cruz."

"Ah, a war council."

"What have you heard?"

"Something about a sermon. Given by Núñez, I take it."

"He preached an old sermon by Antonio Vieyra, so he could— with suitable humility—knock it down again in private at the rectory afterwards."

"So, for a few select churchmen," says Carlos, "you knocked his straw man down, what—more *elegantly* than he?"

"Something along those lines, yes."

"Have things been so dull?"

"If he's so bent on talking about me, let him have a sturdier quintain to tilt at."

"I thought you'd cured it, this mania of yours for taunting him."

"Unlike you, I do not have the option of running off for months at a time. And if you know so much about my affairs before even showing your face here, it just goes to show how little privacy I *have*. Nor do I have the option of being ignored."

"Thank you."

"You know that is not what I meant."

"And now the Bishop is coming all the way from Puebla. . . . I should tell you, then. I've invited an interesting young Frenchman for you to meet."

"When?"

"In a minute or two."

"*Estás en tu casa.*"

"Don't be annoyed. Most of these types are rather less than they seem to be, but I'm convinced this one is rather more. He's spent half his young life at Versailles. He has brought me a letter from the King, in fact."

"Not theirs."

"Louis XIV."

"You're serious."

"Perfectly."

"We could be at war again with France any day now—how has he been allowed to come?"

"Well for one, he appears to be a near relation of every monarch in Europe. I haven't really the head for this sort of thing, but he seems to be the grandson of Henri IV and Catherine de Medici—"

"Marie. Catherine was her mother."

"He is also the nephew of Isabel de Francia—and therefore first cousin to María Teresa by his aunt Isabel, making Philip IV—"

"His uncle by marriage. But this would also make Louis XIII his blood uncle, which in turn makes Louis XIV his first cousin . . ."

"By blood *and* by marriage. Yes, Juana. Moreover, on his father's side are Stuarts. So I may be about to introduce you to the future King of England. Or France, or—"

"Spain. Permission to come, then . . ."

"Would not have presented an insurmountable difficulty. What I have not worked out yet, is *why* he's come."

"Other than to deliver your letter."

"He says he is in America to round out his education, is quite wide-eyed at the prospect."

"What better education than Mexico for a future King of Spain?"

"He claims to have no interest in politics."

"Then what does he claim claims his interest?"

"Generally speaking, literature . . ."

"And specifically?"

"You."

"Me."

"He wants to translate you. To France. All of France, I gather."

"So now you want *me* to help you find out what he's really up to."

"They have a way of revealing themselves to you."

"Because naturally he couldn't have come so far for a thing so trivial as his stated purpose."

"That's not—"

"Juana, don Carlos—*disculpen* but there's a French gentleman here. Tomasina swears he's as beautiful as an angel."

"Yes, that will be him." Carlos smiles.

Antonia used the word beautiful. And so he is, with the beauty of sculpture—features pale yet warm like finest Carrara marble, lips full with just the faintest hint of rose, ice-blue eyes shading to lilac . . . older than the face, more knowing. His hands are pale, blue-veined, with long, finely-wrought fingers, broad palms. An angel's hands, and clasped with no apparent effort in one is the strap of an impressively heavy-looking satchel.

"Sor Juana Inés de la Cruz, *je te présente René Henri de Borbón. Vicomte d'Anjou.*" Adds Carlos, in accents vaguely Italianate, "special envoy of King Louis XIV *de Francia*. The Viscount has just arrived from Paris after a few weeks in Seville. We spent a marvellous afternoon yesterday discussing the latest astronomical discoveries—a wonderfully educated young man."

"I apologize for the intrusion, Sor Juana," begins the young nobleman, "but it's really out of clemency to your learned friend don Carlos, whom I've been hounding for five days straight to be given the opportunity of at last meeting you. An honour all Europe may now envy me." He adds, with a little flourish and a low bow, "My compliments."

"And my compliments on your Castilian." I indulge myself in another moment of looking him over. There is nothing quite like French men's fashions on Frenchmen. The hair is beyond doubt his, but his habiliments are those of the latest fashion doll. It seems the ostrich-plumed hat is no longer. The petticoat breeches are of course an incalculable loss. The collarless, fitted coat is almost knee-length now, this one in lilac-coloured silk, and embroidered at the cuffs and buttonholes, with violet sash and waistband. I sense Carlos following my appraisal and avoid his look. With Carlos drab is good, drab is wise—it is in the flourish that disaster lurks.

"You are kind, my lady. The languages of France and Spain were spoken in our household in almost equal measure, but I confess that the Castilian tongue always gave greater joy. . . ."

"Carlos tells me you were able to take great pleasure, too, in walking about Seville."

"A good deal, yes. It holds up much better than does Madrid these days." Brightening, he adds, "But even in Madrid—everywhere I've looked, in fact—the booksellers are out of your *Inundación Castálida*. Three Spanish editions sold out in five months—and here the first shipment gone, I'm told, in three days!"

"Carlos and I were just talking about my local channels of distribution. Have you been able to get a copy yet, *Vicomte?*"

"Don Carlos was good enough to give me his."

"How kind of him."

"I *had* read them, Juanita, or most, in manuscript. . . ."

"How I envy you that privilege, *señor*."

"Or the unenviable duty. Our Carlos has so many."

"I'll get another copy eventually, Juana."

"Now it is his patience that we are to envy—"

"*Pardonnez-moi*, Sor Juana, but was not Castalia the Sibyl granted eternal life by Apollo in exchange for her favours?"

"That was Deiphobe."

"You must think me entirely lacking in culture."

"But not at all. You were exactly right about the connection with Apollo."

"If I might exculpate myself a little. My thoughts have been with the Sibyls since yesterday. At the house of don Carlos, we were speaking with a Brother . . . ?"

"Bellmont," Carlos says gloomily.

"Bellmont, yes—where I heard him refer to you as the Sum of the Ten Sibyls."

"Come, *Vicomte*, we have so many more interesting topics before us. Tell us about your King."

"But you must call me René Henri—please do me the courtesy of informality, my lady. Now where to begin? Aunt Ana taught Louis a passable Castilian, which, after his marriage to my cousin, *la Infanta*, he spoke often with her. Even after her death he takes a great interest in Spanish affairs—"

"An interest some find worrisome." Carlos is about to continue when Tomasina and Ana burst shoulder to shoulder into the locutory—barely suppressing giggles—each bearing a freshly heaped tray, but with eyes only for our beautiful guest.

"I've heard rumours he has remarried."

There seems an excellent chance that Tomasina will step on Ana's robe and one or the other of my *escuchas*—or both and the trays—will crash through the grille into the Viscount's pretty lap.

"We have heard those same rumours, Sor Juana," continues the young noble, plainly accustomed to such attentions from novices. "The happy date is not something he disposes to announce. She is well beneath his station. His lover of many years, even before the death of her husband, the poet Scanlon. Not that this has, for me, the least importance. What matters rather more is—"

"That the King and his new wife have a shared love of poetry?"

Carlos is being particularly obstructive today, given that the guest is his. The Viscount seems not to have noticed. Perhaps the wit at Versailles was too quick for our young émigré.

"Tell us what matters, René Henri."

"Gladly my lady. Louis' great interest in the lessons taught us by Spain have led him to emulate her in proclaiming our own golden age. And what better model for a palace life than that of our uncle Philip's *Palacio del Buen Retiro?* A great patron of learning, Louis has empowered me to offer don Carlos a singular commission. *Royal Cosmographer!*"

"A gallant offer."

"He's serious, I assure you, sir. Your income would be handsome. Your skills as an astronomer are well known to him. And you, Sor Juana, if my king had the faintest hope you might be persuaded—"

"*Nonsense!* She can no more leave than I. We're Mexicans, our place is here."

"Yes of course." the Viscount looks slightly bewildered. "I intended—"

"No offence given, René Henri, it's an old debate," I say soothingly. "After all, you will have noticed with what equanimity Carlos ponders his own departure, if not yet mine. Tell me, is it true they've taken to calling your cousin the Sun King?"

"Perhaps because he throws about so much gold," Carlos mutters.

"Spoken like a true astronomer, Carlos."

"Indeed they have, my lady. It is a title which doesn't displease him."

"Might the title fit so well, *Vicomte*, because his new home is a palace of light?"

"*Ah le Palais de Versailles! Mais c'est une merveille!* Which is not to say Mexico—Mexico City outgleams even Paris. But Versailles! Apollo's palace of the dawn *a du luire ainsi a l'aube du temps!*"

"I hear he's lavished almost as much on the palace," says Carlos, "as on the artists he stables there."

"Louis does seem at times to love his artists more than their art. He's spoiled Boileau beyond redemption and *Racine—mais* what a *pauvre type* I am! Sor Juana, I've brought for you from France—" says our young visitor, reaching into the leather pouch at his feet "—Don Carlos wrote . . . that no gift could be more precious to you than books. You've read Molière I'm sure. And Corneille? Yes? I must be making a terrible impression—blathering away like an idiot."

"Not at all, René Henri. The candid is one of my favourite modes. You wear it well."

"I had only wanted to say that to gaze on Racine today, once the brightest light of all, is to make one fear our brief golden age is already in its sunset years. When as a boy I first met him, you should have seen the man. But, already at thirty-eight—"

"Not quite your age, Juana."

"Carlos's sympathies remain with Deiphobe."

"But no! Were it not for your air of gravity and—"

"Ah, my *gravity*," I say, unable to resist, "another little reminder of time's swift transits and steep descents. Carlos will be grateful to you."

"Forgive me, my lady—" he stammers. I feel myself blushing now at the pleasure of seeing him blush, as he struggles gamely on. "I express myself poorly. It's just that if you could see Racine now—hero of my youth—a genius, now grown docile enough to accept the King's commission to write nothing but the Royal Historiography."

"I suddenly see my existence there as Royal Cosmographer."

"Have you forgotten, Carlos? You've already refused our guest's offer. Or does it suit you to do so twice in the same hour?"

"Don Carlos may be right, Sor Juana. When I see you both here working at the height of your powers . . . He might well find the spectre too haunting."

"If you'll permit me, René Henri, perhaps I might restore some small part of the regard you once held for your Racine. For although it doubtless helps to have served perhaps all Europe's last great king, it will not have escaped an artist of Racine's stature that the burden of service grows heavier these days to the precise extent that the king himself loses the gravity of substance. Though they command realms and empires larger by far than any of the old principalities, how our kings today envy the humblest Asiatic princes the strut of their unthinking despotism, their thoughtless hold on power. How much less need have these little satraps for painters and plays and soaring panegyrics, whereas even the Sun King grows desperate for any art magnifying the faint lustre of his divine right . . . rather than simply reflecting it as the Moon cannot help reflecting the Sun."

The Viscount, flushed, struggles in the grip of some beautiful emotion. He seems about to stand. "Clearly, my disappointment has made me ungenerous, my lady. I *am* grateful to you—I think you've come very close to the mark. For it has always seemed to me his collapse began with the failure of his *Phèdre*. By far Racine's greatest work, and not one that much glorifies kings. I've summoned up the nerve to bring you a translation I've made into Castilian, for Mexico's author of *Love is a Greater Labyrinth*. What a masterpiece," he says, passing the book through the grille. "They had it in for him. The most famous, the most gifted, the most brilliant—he was too . . ."

"Superlative?"

"Antonia, will you get Carlos a refresher of the cordial? Perhaps not the lime . . . something sweeter. And another for the Viscount."

"But yes, exactly, don Carlos. Superlative. Just half a glass. Thank you, Alexandra. Is it futile to hope my proposed translations of your Iberian classics might help" —he asks this as though it could be anything but futile— "bring a fresh blush of dawn to our French letters? Beginning, as Carlos and I discussed yesterday, with a few of the lesser known poems of his own illustrious progenitor, the great Góngora. And, if this does not come as both premature and presumptuous, some of your own, Sor Juana?"

"Certainly of the obscure variety," I say pleasantly, "you'll find many more of mine to choose from than among Góngora's."

"What an oaf you must think me!" Again the beautiful blush. "*Justement*, the whole point I was about to make is that the one luminous quadrant in the French literary firmament is the irrepressible vitality of our women of letters, clearly one thing we share with New Spain. I've brought you a sampling of my favourites. How often have I pictured you, America's Phoenix, in her nest spiced and feathered with books. . . ."

"Candied *jalapeños, señor?*"

"Why yes, thank you, I have been wondering what these were. Candied, are they. Your servant here—"

"Antonia's an oblate here at San Jerónimo and a friend."

"*Je vous prie pardon, chère demoiselle. . . .*"

"Oh, I'm sure she's already forgotten it, René Henri. You'll no doubt find women's memories as short here as they are in France."

"I was about to say she probably saved me from another indiscretion, but perhaps that would have been too much to hope for. It's just that meeting you in person, it's just so . . ."

"Fabulous?"

"Antonia . . . save a pepper or two for Carlos."

"Peppers, you say?" the Viscount asks, having just bitten into one. "Let me—oh, oh yes, so they are. Perhaps some of that cordial, Alexandra?"

"Antonia."

"Eh?"

"Antonia.

"Of course. *Antonia.*"

"The lime, *señor?*"

"Yes, yes, Antonia, any kind at all."

"You were telling us," Carlos puts in before he can take a drink, "about France's women of letters."

"Yes—Louise Labé, *bien entendu,* but we have more than just *femmes poètes.* There is also Christina of Sweden—who was of course not one of us but wrote French like a Frenchwoman. There are those among our women of letters who have been in mourning for months—but perhaps I should be extending my condolences. The world's two most learned women—you two must have corresponded."

"No."

"Truly what a pity, for you both. She maintained quite a lively correspondence with France. But among our contemporaries is one still more notorious. Madeleine de Scudéry is making a new kind of literature, very novel—offering the delicate folds of their inner landscape as an intimate response to the swell and thrust of the great massed forces of History as written since Herodotus—"

"The Viscount," Carlos observes, "fairly peppers his speech with vivid metaphor." Although the tone is still dry Carlos seems somewhat anxious about the turn in the conversation.

"So wide is her renown," the Viscount presses on as though he hasn't heard, "so broad her popularity and so great the respect for her erudition, all France has begun calling her Sappho—as I believe you yourself, Sor Juana, are called the Tenth Muse here . . . how curious! She's very subversive."

"Sappho?" asks Antonia sweetly.

"Subversive in what sense, René Henri?"

"She makes Sappho the daughter—the offspring *plutôt*, of Scamandrogine, an androgynous entity. To her discerning readers it's very clear that all creators—all humanity really, not just artists—*sont au fond bisexués.*"

"*Monsieur*," Carlos sputters, "*estamos en un convento!*"

"You're entirely correct, *señor*—as a nun, such ideas must be repugnant to Sor Juana. But surely," adds the young aristocrat, eyeing me appraisingly, "to the scholar and the poet, they cannot be so entirely offensive."

Such an amusing child. Does he expect with such a pallid challenge to get me to raise my colours for him?

"Carlos has spent enough time at convents to know they are less an island of virtue than an isthmus. The heart, *Monsieur*, is the same, no matter how tightly bound the breast. No word or idea is in itself offensive to me. It's a question of intent."

"If I have expressed my intent poorly . . ."

"If you have, you must feel free to express it more precisely. Please, go on." And how my strange young visitor does go on. I had been willing to help Carlos discover what the Viscount was up to, and whether the offer from Versailles should be considered sincere. For if it is, Carlos is in no position to be dismissing it so lightly. But I have begun to sense where this is leading—let him at least get there quickly.

"De Scudéry's Sappho inverts the conventional picture. De Scudéry has Phaon propose marriage—Phaon is—but of course you know. Sappho accepts his suit but not his proposal. She will not submit to what she charmingly calls the *long slavery of marriage. . . .*"

"Now there, *Vicomte,* is a subject fit to discourse upon at length. Carlos will bring you another day, perhaps . . . ?"

"I do hope we may, for I know you will not fail to be fascinated by what Mlle de Scudéry is attempting. The signs are all there for those willing to probe a little—Louis would never stand for open talk of *l'amour lesbien*—"

"*Señor!*" barks Carlos.

"Sor Juana, do you not think this might be the singular gift of women's art? To ennoble yearning, and imbue with a kind of grace the grotesque impulses of our inner life . . . ?"

"You seem to insist, Viscount, on the grotesque and the debased," says Carlos heatedly. He can at such moments be very dear. "Clearly this is neither the province of women's art nor the special province of art itself."

"Yet is Sor Juana herself not at this very moment making a poetical study of Sappho . . . ?"

Carlos goes pale, Antonia positively flinches.

"Does everyone on both sides of the Atlantic," I ask looking at each in turn, "think they know what I am now working on?"

"Juanita, I'm sorry. It just slipped out—in the spirit of yesterday's free exchange of ideas."

"Such a rarity, Carlos, the free and equal exchange. Your generosity gets the better of you at times. And *Vicomte,* you should bear in mind that as a confidant Carlos is something of an amphora—straight necked, wondrous capacity, but susceptible to gushing forth suddenly on all sides."

"Please don't blame don Carlos. I know I shouldn't have been the one—but might we not speak of this? I was so hoping to bring us around to it. It is precisely this work I hope most to translate."

"You do, *Vicomte,* seem rather to insist. An insistence that leaves your intent looking decidedly unnatural. And were I ever to devote a work to Sappho, I would avoid the grotesque and the debased altogether. Of this you may be sure. If you insist so on the names of de Scudéry and Labé, Sappho and Christina—is it to intimate that one might find in France, or is it Versailles itself, *toda una comunidad Sáfica?* Am I then to take this Sapphic community to be a refuge, or just one more exotic birdhouse for the palace grounds? And is there some point to this? Does one hope to incite me to some brazen action or blushing declaration?"

It is as I thought. The mask of shyness, the blundering and blushing are gone. The Vicomte d'Anjou sits smiling through the grille, world-wearily amused. Is there more, I wonder? What lies beneath this next mask?

"Perhaps, *Monsieur*, a man of your beauty believes he may speak with no particular purpose at all. Just what sort of translation is it you hope to make to France—of my poetry, my person, or do you merely hope to make a diverting report of me? Or perhaps you serve your King not as his procurer but as his proxy, making your mission the inversion of what you say it is: to translate France rather to *me*, by way of the salacious flirtations of a bored king who has proclaimed himself nothing less than the state itself. This is the Sun King's notion of a golden age?—to interrogate a bride of Christ on her sensual inclinations? Or is this what passes for wit at Versailles . . . ?"

Were it not for the anger that a jaded smile from one so beautiful and so young strikes up in me, I would be the weary one. Once I thought I would suffocate without the diversions of this locutory. Now I am suffocated by them. Was Carlos right after all? Have things really been too quiet?

Tomasina rushes into the room, "—excuse me, Sor Juana—the Bishop's carriage. It's *here*."

JUANA INÉS
DE LA CRUZ,

"Carols for Saint
Bernard: the
House of Bread"

B. Limosneros, trans.

chorus

To the new Temple
come all and find
how its stones are made Bread
and its Bread made of Stone.
Ay, ay, ay, ay!

verses

If there in the Desert
He refused to transform
stones into bread for
His sustenance,
    Here, for our own,
He saw fit to conceal
the foundation, which is Christ,
in the Bread of His Substance.
    Now on this, His new altar,
to us He reveals,
that He is of His Temple
the cornerstone,
    and since he would sustain
us with a delicacy,
the sweetness he feeds us
is a Honey of Stone.

[22nd day of June, 1690]

Lysis,

 t is a giddy time. One notices we have been cele-
brating the king's wedding to the new queen for
over a year now, though we hadn't quite intended it.
A sort of accident. With the first queen's sudden
passing and the haste to secure another upon which
to sire an heir, the dates we've been getting to celebrate were all long past; and since we have never known when the next
occasion was coming, except to hear we've missed out, we have never
really taken the banners down.

And so it almost seems we find ourselves transported back to the
Mexico City of my early years, for through the streets and late into the
night flood upwards of seven thousand coaches drawn by silver-shod
horses—coachmen in gold lace, their hatbands struck with pearls—
wedding bells and serenades, bullfights and bawdy festivals, wild
rumours of fertility rites held at the outskirts of the capital . . . but then
we at San Jerónimo are at the outskirts here and have seen little of this
for all our vigilance.

A giddy time and a desperate one, for it is not only the Viceroy and
the Creoles who would make their mark. The Church initially joined in
with special Masses and midnight orisons, but lately the theme from the
pulpits is more often the hoary one of Sodom and Gomorrah. Perhaps
it is only the lost dowries that has them vexed, but I believe our year may
be ending—

On your side of the Atlantic everyone, you say, is clamouring for a second collection. Five Spanish editions now of our Castalia's flood—your
printer weeps Castalian cataracts of gratitude each time he hears your
name or mine, or talk of a second collection. Your friends in Mantua are
ready to translate our Castalia to Italy, your friends in Vienna, to
Germany, and a fresh new friend of mine asks nothing more than to
bring her to Versailles.

I glean from your teasing that you've had nearly enough of my timidity. Since *Las letras a Safo* are an open secret and since Núñez rails against

them anyway, why not publish and at least silence the speculation? What is it that so exercises Núñez, you ask, in *not* finding Sappho's verses in our collection? Does he read in their omission not respect for him but weakness? Cowardice . . . though you are too kind to say this. I know how it must look to a Manrique. Please, María Luisa, please do not give up on me. I need to believe too that Sappho's time may come soon, even as Castalia's has.

Yes, these verses are an open secret, more open than you perhaps realize, given that Núñez now roves from pillar to pillory pronouncing darkly against this new and unprecedented wickedness. Here in Mexico—where so much may be spoken, and spoken almost freely if not open sedition or undisguised heresy—to publish is quite another proposition. In this respect we are not like Spain, and so it has been difficult to make this difference clear. What is written is not just better evidence for the Inquisition, the written is Writ: it occupies another realm of existence entirely.[22] Picture Cortés reading his *Requerimiento* in Latin over the heads of the Indians he is about to attack. There, you have it. Things since then are not so much changed.

But I also need to help you to see that in another respect things are already not as they were when you were here. I ask you to read me now obliquely, in the way we have spoken of before. Think of Aeschylus and the art of lyric tragedy, in which an entire story may be told though almost none of it happens onstage. So . . .

The Inquisition has asked Carlos to furnish a complete list of the reading materials in his possession. In Spain I know this is rarely done any longer but the Holy Office here is its own beast and master. Carlos blames me. Which is only fair, since any blame I can remotely connect him to, I do. He has decided the demand for a book inventory is linked somehow to Núñez's campaign against me and what he, Núñez, insists on calling *The Sapphic Hymns*. Very sanguine is dear Carlos about my publishing difficulties, as he reminds me of how many of his own manuscripts go unprinted. So while he understands my frustration, and yours, as no one else does (he will tell you he understands most things as no one else does), every risk I take makes his caution seem, well . . . cautious. Caution beseems the woman, and as a complement to her modesty can never be excessive; whereas in a man it is, in anything but the quantities required for his barest survival, a disgrace.

So yes, you are right to ask. I have withheld my favours for eight years now, and what has it brought me? What I offer these Churchmen I am now scarcely in a position to withhold. Núñez has me almost completely encircled. I can no longer sit by and watch him undermining me.

I *know* you are right. And so since April I have been pressing a number of counterattacks, but obliquely—as Aristophanes resorted to comedy so as to beard the tyrant Cleon. How else are we to answer the tyrants, how else to raise their siege? Here is how the campaign stands.

Picture, María Luisa, a stage set by Aristophanes, from *The Wasps* or *Lysistrata*. A whole little Troy town on a mountaintop—Mount Eryx, or the Hill of Ares, or better yet the sanctuary of the Erectheum on the Acropolis. Yes, the very thing. A great hive then, with dozens of locutories, open in profile to the auditorium. A play of comic comings and strange goings on. Let us set it during a siege, but in a castle with honeycomb walls and the soldiers of both sides—paper wasps in red, honey drones in gold and lilac—all slipping in and slipping out for the honey of the harlots of the hive . . . all the while the harried queen crouches off to one side laying eggs in moments of privacy as fantastic as brief. Her cell too is open to the gallery.

Enter in stunning array the thirty theologians of Castalia's preface to a fanfare of ram's horn trumpets, a stately pavane across the boards and then another blast to rival Jericho as once again they exeunt by thirty different exits.

Enter two platoons of holy officers carrying torches, Jesuits and Dominicans jostling. Our defenders of the ramparts against the Saracens, Jews and Lutherans, and yet for these keepers of the wall, no glorious fanfare of shofars.[†] The Theological Thirty have made them look quaint—keepers of a mighty fortress over a mere mill race. So far, these stalwarts will not quit the stage, though they stand near the exits and get in the way.

[†]Hebrew war trumpets of ram's horn

Enter Núñez declaiming, as he moves from cell to cell to cell, three lines of Castalia's poetry, over and over, the three having remotely to do with Sappho.

Enter Dorantes reminding the audience that Sor Juana was trained in theology by none other than Núñez.

Enter Bishop Santa Cruz, bent on rescuing all pretty nuns from perfidy.

Enter the Creole delegation paddling out of rhythm, a longboat at their waists, its figurehead a carven effigy of Guadalupe. And yet who is it they ask to intervene with the Vice-King to stay their charges of sedition? Not Guadalupe, certainly.

Enter Carlos carrying the Archbishop's magical hat—the mathematician and natural philosopher as archepiscopal mendicant bartering alms for miracle cures. And this one once called *me* a fable beggar.

Enter an officer wearing the coat of arms of which Archbishop Aguiar never stops boasting, of a family so ancient they trace their name back to the Centurions. The venerably outfitted officer tows a trundle of books to the booksellers. See him wheedle and threaten until they surrender all their comedies, which he exchanges for his copies of *Consolations for the Poor*.

[†]cockpits and bullrings

Enter other officers fanning out to close down the *palenques* and *cosos*.[†]

Enter the Vicomte d'Anjou who may be the next King of England or Spain, or even of France, or he may be here to translate me, or he may be here to spy on us.

Close Act I with the Archbishop walled in by stacks of comedies by Quevedo and groping myopically for an exit. . . .

How I weary of these silly wars and the siege they lay upon our thoughts.²³ Even as Lysistrata and the lusty women's assembly so wearied of it all they were willing to withhold their favours (O supreme sacrifice!) until their husbands made peace. A sacrifice, Aristophanes tells us, made all the more stark by a war scarcity of Milesian comforters to help them bide their loneliest hours.²⁴ So you see, these comic women of Aristophanes were serious. As are we.

Tonight my thoughts turn to the end of war, to the weddings and the banquets that seal the peace—and to the difference between the false peace and the true, the siege and the truce. Thoughts that form the basis of *este entracto* and the parabasis for Act II. Picture next, dear Lysis, a stage set for a series of banquet scenes. As for some other antic comedy by Aristophanes, but to be read remembering the art of Aeschylus. Prudence calls for us to practise this art of lyric comedy for the next letter or two. . . .

The first banquet scene here was three months past, after the Maundy Thursday sermon at the Metropolitan Cathedral, to mark the feast in the olive grove of Gethsemane. Taking its inspiration from Christ's washing of the disciples' feet, the sermon's theme is humility. Naturally, then, Núñez would see himself as the obvious one to give it.

My locutory soon filled with Churchmen who came to hear what I might make of it. What's more, one of the late arrivals had come directly from the college rectory where Núñez rebutted in private the very oration he had just given in public. Caught up in the mixed emotions of the moment—their outrage and perplexity, my merriment—I upstaged his rebuttal with a full demolition. Since then, I have had misgivings I cannot dispel. Not for fear of reprisals so much as over my own motives. The Last Supper. Of all the beautiful banquets in the stories of all the world, surely this is the loveliest, the most terrible. Two courses: a *plato fuerte* of the bread and the wine; and a *postre* of a delicate, an ineffable sweetness . . . Christ's humble washing of the feet. Then, as a final toast of Grace, there comes the Mandate to His companions: *A new commandment I give unto you, That ye love one another; as I have loved you. . . .* And on the morrow of the Passion and on all the morrows ever after He leaves us to ask and ask and ask: but *how* has He loved us? That night He showed us, so beautifully, how we may be made humble by love.

Act II, Scene Two. A few days after the sermon, the sisters of Saint Bernard sent to ask that I write a cycle of lyrics for the dedication of their new temple just two blocks up our street. For weeks I cast about for a fitting subject. Here was a fit challenge, for me especially, something simple for Bernard, advocate of a holy ignorance. Hearing that Núñez was to celebrate the penultimate Mass and with my blood still up, I chose my topic and wove into the lyrics an entire sermon to rival the one I could predict Núñez would give. On the Eucharist. There is no mystery more sublime than this; none finds my heart more surely than the mystery of this sacrifice. If Father Núñez so detests water, I thought, then he shall have his sacrament of bread. And though the reasons for my choice had been so vile, it was conceived as is a life, and from that passionate mire grew a small simple miracle for the simple people of the neighbourhood who would come to fill their new temple. This temple of Christ as the womb of Mary, this flesh of her Son as the Host rising in her womb, this temple of Christ as a house of bread.

Here is a mystery to feed the hungry, here, in three voices, a mystery the simple people need no theologian to understand.

> 1.–You who hunger,
> come and find
> Corn grains and Wheat Spikes, Flour for Bread.

2.–All you who thirst,
Love has provided
Green Grapes and Ruddy, Must for Wine.
3.–They will not find them!
2.–They will!
3.–Not these shall they find—
but Flesh and Blood!—
not Bread and Wine . . .

The house of bread is the temple, the temple is Word and world. The bread of Christ springs from her nature, the wine is her harvest, the love of Nature springs from her beauty, as beauty itself springs from love, and love from the greatest Beauty of all.

This cycle too was to have been a banquet. The dedications in the temple begin next week. Núñez has read my lyrics and in them found what I had woven there. A sermon by a woman, expressly forbidden now by the Council of Trent. The issue is clear. To press matters too far here would be foolhardy. It is almost certain that my lyrics will not be sung.

Act II, Scene Three. With all this, the prospect of peace seems more beautiful than ever to me. And more like a dream. We turn to *Lysistrata* for comic relief. As is fitting for a comedy, it ends with a picnic, but spread in the solemn sanctuary of the Acropolis; for as a dream of peace, *Lysistrata* is a serious comedy. After drenching the men's chorus with pitchers of water, reversing thus the unfair judgement against the Danaïdes, the women's chorus sits down to eat with the men. A picnic of peace that serves as preamble to a wedding feast.

Act II, Scene Four. Two camps and their aides are sitting down to dine, out in the open air—next to our academy, let us say, at the refectory. The long table is laid in the passageway beneath the boughs of our pomegranate trees, as was laid for us and the ladies of your court half a dozen times here in the convent courtyard—where our talks and our dreams ran to topics thought impious by many. You will remember the ones I am thinking of. Plato's *Symposium* was another such night, another such dream. Under lamps bright with finest oil, the two sides face one another, raise toasts and make gentle, generous jokes, and pass the vegetables and gravy boats. The guests Plato has assembled are to make speeches in praise of love. As the others discourse, Aristophanes sits silent until Socrates enjoins him to speak—a matter of duty for one who has devoted his life to Dionysus and Aphrodite. To this challenge and this banquet we owe a lovely legend of the sexes. You see, at first there were three: male, female and hermaphrodite. And here, as I recall, the story takes a turn, for it is from this third sex that we are descended, says Aristophanes, as can be plainly seen in our lurching about half our lives in search of our lost half.

No one could doubt, after such a wistful rendering, that the great comedian liked to be taken seriously. One might almost pardon Aristophanes his role, not long after, in the trial and conviction of Socrates. How strange that Socrates' great disciple Plato, so mistrustful of the theatre as it was, should befriend Aristophanes. Perhaps it was some secret shared love of contradictions, for such a bundle of them was this Aristophanes! Mocking the gods yet not denying their existence, mocking old-fashioned Aeschylus yet accepting his greatness. Mocking the art of lyric tragedy that died with him, even as the comedy of Dionysus would die with Aristophanes.

The old theatres had been of wood. Pericles, in his wealth and his love of glory, remade them of stone, to outlast the age. Yet stone is for Apollo; the art of Dionysus is not made to last. In his art lies something Pericles has not grasped: that in its decay, the temple and the theatre, the city itself, possess a greatness that the original could not capture. For now in the mossy lineaments of each ruined façade, in the tumbled furniture of rotted dados and cleft pediments, scrawl the worm-scripts of chance and circumstance, whispering of a different plan. The ruin invites us to reimagine it, reseed it, it needs *us* to complete it, as the perfect original never does. The art of Dionysus does not outlast its age. It laughs it off the stage.

Act II, Scene Five. Lysis, there are things we may no longer write to be spoken aloud, for it would mean we must first rebuild the theatres, which Apollo would never permit. Even so long ago, Aeschylus knew his art was dying. I believe he must have, for in this art the chorus writes the artist. The lyric tragedy is a drama not so much of *héroes y heroïdes* but of the great race that bore them. Homer may begin in the tenth year of the siege, aware that the audience knows the first nine fully as well as he. Centuries later, Aeschylus begins the greatest play cycle ever written and laces the *Agamemnon* with the briefest of reminders.

But Athens is changing quickly and by the time the trilogy is complete, the lyric tragedy of Aeschylus is dead. Dead without an epitaph. In the end it is the guile of the judge Athena, her wiles of Reason and Persuasion, that win the Furies' parting blessing on Athens and its harvests.

> Let there blow no wind that wrecks the trees.
> I pronounce words of grace. . .
> Flocks fatten. earth be kind
> to them, with double fold of fruit
> in time appointed to its yielding. Secret child
> of earth, her hidden wealth, bestow
> blessing and surprise of gods . . .

The audience for the *Eumenides* no longer truly knows and feels who the Furies were—or rather of what they were born, these daughters of Night. The new Athens has lost its fear of the dark. The play opens before the temple of the Pythoness at Delphi and closes before the Erechtheum in the sanctuary of the Acropolis. The comedy *Lysistrata* ends in the same sanctuary, with all kneeling before the shrine of Victory.

> Athena, hail, thou Zeus-born Maid!
> Who war and death in Greece hast stayed:
> Hail, fount from whom all blessings fall;
> All hail, all hail, Protectress of us all!

The greatness of the comedian Aristophanes is to see his art as that epitaph, to know that the death of an order, even one day Apollo's, must be sung drunkenly, by an old reveller of Dionysus. And for all that, Aristophanes could not bear to see the new move beyond the old. The greatness of Aeschylus was to see that a new order just might, if it is built upon the old, but he could not bring himself to write its epitaph as a ruin. In the *Oresteia* he has given us the greatest play cycle made. In the ancient Furies' blessing on a young Athens, he has shown the way. But he could not take that path himself, he could not end the *Eumenides* in comedy. He was too great to ruin it.

Who am I, with one book, to stand in judgement of Aristophanes, much less of Aeschylus who wrote seventy tragedies, with the seven to come down to us each greater than our greatest? What work is left to us who follow giants such as he? Perhaps a few small steps are left. What indeed would be the last great work of a golden age but both the proof and chronicle of its dying? A lyric end to the cycle, a tragedy written by a comedian, to be played in a burning theatre. Now the paradox: that its end be written by one not great, whose worst fear is not ruining the work but no longer knowing what greatness is.

For our next collection, María Luisa, here would be a purpose and a dedication, no? And yet once written we could not publish—it would not be heard, its place does not exist, except we rebuild the old theatres of wood. No, we live in an age of stone that calls for guile and persuasion, and it is not the righteous Furies we must cajole but Apollo, choleric now in his middle years.

Act II, Scene Six. And here is the final scene of our lyric comedy tonight. I ask that you read this one, too, obliquely, and by its conclusion I may have convinced you it is not yet time for Sappho to take the stage. There is another banquet I am thinking of. It was in 1611 or '12, at any rate not long after Galileo Galilei was made a member of the Lyncean Academy. The banquet was in Florence, at the palace of the Grand-Duke of Tuscany. Galileo Galilei was there, as was a Florentine cardinal. After the meal, before the dessert, a debate was staged, much as in the *Symposium*. That night the contest was between Galileo and a professor of the Natural Philosophy of Aristotle. The question addressed floating bodies: why some float in water, like ice itself, and why others sink. Galileo took up the question eagerly against the Aristotelian. The contest was not close. Those companions not among the judges were invited to take sides to make the affair more interesting. Taking what was clearly the winning side, Lord Cardinal Barberini expressed eloquent support of Galileo. Galileo had skill and knowledge, the Cardinal had skill and subtlety; both debated with passion. The two easily carried the evening. Afterwards His Grace the Most Reverend Lord Cardinal, one day to be elected Pope Urban VIII, was reported to have prayed God preserve Galileo and grant him a long life, for such minds were for the enduring benefit of Man.

The book I asked if you would get for us a few months back, that you say you now have and are only waiting on a messenger to bring it across . . . you know the one, on the floating and sinking of all sorts of bodies. It might be best not to send it for a while. The climate, just now, is not good for ice.

I cannot tell when we will be able to write in the old way again, or pub-lish Sappho's lines, but for the next letter or two let us make little songs of prayer for fair weather, and sing blessings over the land.

Love,

día 22 de junio, Anno Domini 1690
de este convento de San Jerónimo,
de la Ciudad de México,
Nueva España

Late spring, 1690. Writing daring theatre and poetry is far from the most dangerous of Sor Juana's occupations as she finds herself increasingly embroiled in theological questions, disputed by the Princes of the Church with quiet savagery. The mind of Sor Juana Inés de la Cruz, even half-engaged, is a prodigious resource. Her letters and arguments are coveted and examined by bishops, confessors and inquisitors alike.

JUANA INÉS
DE LA CRUZ

AN
ATHENAGORICAL
LETTER, 'WORTHY
OF ATHENA'

. . . His Excellency may well have thought, seeing me draw towards a conclusion, that I had forgotten the very point on which I have been commanded to write: what is, in my view, the greatest expression, the greatest *fineza*, of Divine Love. . . .

As Christ our Redeemer preached his miraculous doctrine, and having performed so many miracles and marvels in so many places, he reached at last his native country, in which he should have been owed greater affections, and yet directly he arrived, instead of singing his praises, his neighbours and compatriots began to censure him and list his supposed faults. . . . With the result that Christ, who had wanted to work miracles for his native land, and to award them all manner of benefices, saw then in their bad faith and dark mutterings how they would receive Christ's favours, and so He withheld them: so as not to give them occasion to do ill. . . .

And regarding Judas, upon whom He showered many particular favours not given to the others, in the hour of his betrayal Christ lamented not that Judas had hanged himself, but rather the damage such favours had done him. . . . By which He seemed to regret having favoured Judas with the benefice of creation, saying that it were better he had never been born. . . . And from which we may conclude that the greatest expression of his Love would be to withhold His favours. Ah me, my Lord and God, how blindly and clumsily we lurch about not seeing the negative favours You give us! . . .

ABYSS

aturally enough my thoughts keep returning to this one afternoon, and each fresh return yields some small new detail. What I do not ever recall is the slightest premonition. Just before the Bishop of Puebla arrives I am forced to spend another hour in the locutory when every free moment has become so precious—only to discover that Carlos's latest guest has come for a flirtation. Once I might have been amused, or flattered that he had been sent to me across an ocean by Louis XIV, in the sort of gesture the French King so likes the world to expect from him. But those times are past; I am no longer a girl at the palace.

I see the beautiful young face of the King's emissary, recall deciding to bring points of colour to those smooth, pale cheeks. . . . I ask if a man of his beauty believes he may blunder along with no particular purpose at all. If the rest of the distaff world stands before the blunderbuss and counts itself disarmed. I suggest that my young friend press on, as earnestness may yet win the day. But why not raise his aim—and set his sights not on mere flirtation, but on a conquest less abstracted—

Always at this point Tomasina returns from her watch at the archive windows and rushes into the room.

"The Bishop's carriage, it's *here*—parked beside the canal," she adds, as if this in some way added to the drama. Then there comes that moment after an arrival is announced when conversation falters. Carlos gets up grudgingly from the Bishop's chair and pulls another to the grille from the far side of the room. Antonia hastens over with the chess table. As she places it within easy reach behind me she bends to my ear and asks to be excused. She does not look particularly well.

"Ah, chess," says the Viscount, "I'll wager you play like Greco himself."

"Stay, *Toñita*—just till he's settled in?"

"Did the great Greco not die near here?"

"Not at my hands, *Vicomte. Gracias, 'Tonia.* As a child, *Monsieur*, I'd always intended to learn. And then I ran out of time. But the Bishop sometimes consents to a lesson when he has business here."

"One of the better players in New Spain, I understand."

"What a curious thing for you to know."

"I've been hoping to meet him."

"Have you? Of course you have . . ."

As Bishop Santa Cruz enters, the change in the Viscount is quite complete. It is clear that he has some business to transact. I find myself half-admiring the young man's duplicity even as I am resenting being used as a stalking horse. Bishop Santa Cruz is also, for an instant, quite transformed. At first I think it is recognition, or surprise, but it is not quite either. He is our most handsome churchman. Indeed many of the sisters here, and I can only imagine how many in Puebla, confess at our weekly chapter of faults that when Satan visits at night, he is as likely to take the guise of Bishop Santa Cruz as to masquerade as Our Husband. Santa Cruz's features are boyish, which in a man of fifty can be appealing. Fine brows carrying the suggestion of a frown in perpetual warning to triflers, the chin slightly too delicate for the width of his jaw. The teeth are good and big, indeed better fitted to a slightly wider mouth. . . . More than pleasing enough, but the Enemy appears to me rather differently. A little taller, a little younger, more . . . statuesque.

The Viscount on the other hand—though he is now beyond any doubt a viper—is angelically beautiful, with his gold locks and lilac eyes and hands of marble. The features and the hands, though, are not a cherub's but the warrior Michael's. Square chin, wide mouth, pale, full lips, a nose prominent yet fine at the bridge. For an instant they face each other: a younger man, beautifully masculine, an older man, boyishly handsome. And in that instant, the Bishop's face is almost unrecognizable. It is the clearest moment in what remains of the afternoon. What appears, what seems almost to rise up—as the Viscount's beauty strikes it like the slap of a glove—is the figure of an enormous vanity. And though Bishop Santa Cruz and I are old friends, I shudder to think of that poor girl in Puebla looking into his face as she begged to be permitted to enter Santa Monica.

For a moment I fear some real violence must pass between them, but it is only the usual cut and thrust. An insult here about the Bishop's lineage, another there about the Viscount's immoral king and country, vague hints of war and excommunication . . .

"Obviously a spy," says the Bishop, as the Viscount's footsteps die out.

Santa Cruz fixes his dark eyes on Carlos.

"Don Carlos, you spend so little time in Puebla anymore. You must still have many friends there."

"A few. Who tell me your work on Genesis is nearly complete."

"That's so, yes."

"Two thousand pages, Lord Bishop. Monumental."

"A book like any other, don Carlos. To be read a page at a time. But you, *señor*, almost daily I hear of you winning some new distinction for the Chair of Mathematics and—is it Astronomy or Astrology? I never remember."

"Astrology."

"We are told you are predicting an eclipse of the sun for next August."

"The margin of error is still considerable."

"Yes, isn't it," he says, holding Carlos's eyes an extra heartbeat. The Bishop's gaze shifts to Antonia. "I bring good report of your sisters at the convent school. The youngest takes after you, I think. Very clever with her languages. What was her name . . . ? *Antonia?*"

"Francisca."

"Will you play something for us, Antonia? I haven't heard you at the clavichord for—how long has it been?"

I ask Santa Cruz if she could play something brief, she is not altogether well. To which, after listening a moment, he answers that brief will be best if she finishes the way she has begun. Antonia plays well, and yet her playing just now is not quite soothing. She is unhappy, no doubt, that I have kept her.

"I notice you have something of a Puebla reunion on your hands, Juana."

"So I have."

"The time may not be far off for those carols we have been scheming about."

"For Saint Catherine?—you're in earnest?"

He has not quite promised but the commission is clearly mine now to lose.

"It would be good to hear Puebla talk of Puebla again. There was a time when our little Puebla de los Angeles stood up very nicely against the brilliance of the capital. We have our splendid volcano, though Mexico does have two. . . . While Mexico has its cathedral, we have ours, lovelier and almost as large. We have the Jesuit Seminary, Mexico has the great Colegio de San Pedro y San Pablo. But while we have a children's choir, Mexico has Sálazar. And since don Carlos left us, Mexico now has the two of you."

It is the second allusion to Carlos's unhappy departure from the seminary more than twenty years ago.

Santa Cruz shakes his head ruefully. "And now during Holy Week to have the great college's rector Antonio Núñez, giving a sermon by none other than the immortal Vieyra. Your four-time winner of the Seal of the Holy Crusade delivers a homily from the Prince of the Catholic Orators!"

After the false modesty regarding Puebla, the mock heroic tone of the tout nicely inserts the skewer: a delirious prestige attaches locally to the Seal, our highest prize for eloquent sermonizing, but even in Núñez's case, it is quite eclipsed by the informal title of Prince of Orators, which was devised for Vieyra alone and by which he is known throughout the Catholic dominions.

"Don Carlos, I suppose you were here for Sor Juana's analysis after the sermon?"

"Regrettably, his Lordship the Viceroy wanted some prominences surveyed on the coast, for gun emplacements."

"Your holy crusader and our Catholic prince both out-manned, outgunned by a simple nun—they should have seen the emplacements ranged against them and put out to sea. A pity, don Carlos, that you were not there. You at least could have given me a competent summary. So I've come to sort it out for myself. Our Mistress of the poetic *fineza* corrects—"

"Questions, don Manuel, merely questions."

"Of course. *Questions* New Spain's most original thinker on the Eucharist."

Carlos glances at me, a look of warning that finds me torn between cheer and dread. He knows what the Bishop's patronage means to me, now especially. He knows how long I have wanted this commission. But Santa Cruz has been provoking him since—well, since he stopped provoking the Viscount. Is it something Carlos has done, something he has said—everyone here hears everything, or thinks they do—is it to do with his services to the Archbishop?

Carlos is not one to hold his fire for long. I fill my return glance with the fervid hope that Carlos follow the Viscount out.

"I should be going," Carlos says, getting arthritically to his feet. "*Su Ilustrísima* the Lord Bishop has important matters to discuss. And I have some records to check at the Archbishop's palace. From the time of

Bishop *Zumárraga.*" His eyes glitter as he looks my way. It has come out with a strange emphasis but now he is bending to add, conspiratorially, his smile including Santa Cruz, "You can tell Antonia it's not the music."

As the slight, stooped form disappears through the doorway, I sketch ambitious plans for his next visit, to shower him with proofs of my gratitude. The remark about Zumárraga, Mexico's first bishop, is not so very odd, I tell myself. Carlos is always nosing about in some archive or other for the chronicles he is asked to write. And the jest about Antonia's playing defused the whole situation wonderfully.

All in all he has handled the Bishop with unwonted forbearance and grace. Yet what I distinctly recall feeling as he leaves is annoyance. Annoyed that so many of the people upon whom I most depend seem to dislike each other. Annoyed, as always, at Carlos for half a dozen things. Annoyed, too, at my own weariness, the sense of wasted time, that I will be up until dawn now finishing the convent accounts. And at Antonia for the mournful music she has chosen, when she knows so many pleasant lays; at her ingratitude towards the Bishop who has brought her here, and just perhaps towards me. Annoyed at the Bishop—for his shabby treatment of Carlos. And at myself again, for giving voice to my great pique with such a little peep.

"You were cruel to him."

"I thought his temper might get the better of him."

"And what would his temper tell us that it hasn't already?"

"It may only be prudence, given his friendship with the Franciscan they burned. But it bothers me that he always manages to be away when something happens. Like this sermon. And his silence on the Eucharist. Fifteen years ago he talked of nothing else, and has abandoned the field to Núñez ever since."

"But you've said it yourself. Prudence."

"It is not *why* he goes that I wonder about, but *how* he always knows far enough in advance to arrange things so tidily. It is not *why* he has been silent for fifteen years, but *how* Núñez from that time became so knowledgeable on the old cults. Are we all to retreat from theological questions the moment Antonio Núñez shows an interest—are you to hand over all the beautiful verses you have written on the *finezas?*"

The compliment is sincere. If I persist, this will become unpleasant.

With Carlos gone I am determined to be done with this quickly. It is as he has said—the Bishop does have matters to discuss.

"You do know, don Manuel, that Father Núñez has dedicated this new work to you."

"A sobering look at Communion."

"Are you here for the manuscript?"

"I have it." His hand starts towards the tray. He checks the impulse, then takes up a candied fig with a kind of languor. "But I don't have to come from Puebla for that. I am more interested in his motives than in his book, more still in his motives for the sermon."

"A straw man. Vieyra has written—what is it, thirteen orations on the Eucharist, many of them sublime. Núñez attacks perhaps the weakest. Why not strength on strength? There would have been a contest to watch."

Santa Cruz asks my opinion on the local edition of Vieyra's work on Heraclitus. "I admire it. Though I haven't read their translation—but some sense of the grace of his style could not fail to come through. No one in our tongue is writing a prose to match his."

The Bishop smiles before biting delicately into a walnut square. "Certainly not the plodder your Royal University found for the translation. But I am told the editions in Madrid—the '76 and '78—were awful translations also."

"I haven't read them."

"But you've seen them."

Not having seen either, I answer instead that any speaker of Castilian should really read Vieyra in the Portuguese, the quality being so high, the languages so close. I promise to send Santa Cruz home with my copy. He promises to bring me the Castilian editions next time.

He pauses to dust sugar from the purple cassock. "Now to Núñez. You had begun to say why that sermon suited his purposes. Our discussions in Puebla have run along those same lines, though going somewhat further. . . ."

By 'our' discussions I take him to mean the Dominicans, whose stronghold is Puebla and whose warlord is the Lord Bishop Santa Cruz. They still find something not quite clear about Father Núñez's motives. It is a game with them to analyze the adversary's positions endlessly. I brace myself. Núñez, the rector of our Jesuit college, invites to his chambers not just Jesuits but Dominicans, a Franciscan and three officers of the Inquisition. And yet he does this to attack a fellow Jesuit. Why? Yes, Vieyra is influential, but he uses that influence not for the Company but to persuade King John to suppress the Inquisition throughout Portugal.

The Jesuit Vieyra has become the greatest living threat to the Inquisition just as the Jesuits are infiltrating it; the Holy Office, through its rigour and universal reach, stands as the main obstacle to Jesuit designs on global power. In America but also in the Orient, the soldiers of Christ have only to adapt certain points of Catholic doctrine slightly to make it palatable to local rulers, certain other *minor* points in the Philippines to counter the incursions of the Moor.

The Jesuits, unchecked, will destroy the Church.

Santa Cruz makes no effort now to conceal his passion. I rarely see him so unguarded. The heavily bejewelled fingers delicately prowl the platter. Walnut, date, fig. *Suspiros* and *aleluyas*. A bite from each. The platter's losses mount up on the Bishop's side plate of Puebla porcelain. I try very hard to share his passion.

Were I a writer of romances, were I a general or a prince, were I half so brave as the nun-ensign, I would surely fly to the fight. I would not fail to seek my place in the universal theological struggle. But I am pledged never again to set foot beyond these walls, a nun who may not freely walk across this room.

With Father Núñez, my chief interest in speaking on theology was that he did not want me to, whereas Santa Cruz has always tried to draw me into these questions more deeply. It would be an insult to our friendship to show a lack of interest now, especially with him in this humour, so pleased that I have let myself become—*fool*—involved. And in his unwonted candour I have a measure of his frustration. Santa Cruz, a bishop at thirty-five, is still a bishop and has been for seventeen years.

Antonia is playing more brightly now, a sonata that sounds like Scarlatti, but even if it isn't, I am almost sure the Bishop once mentioned a dislike for Scarlatti. Tomasina and Ana watch attentively, so sober and discreet.

Suddenly Santa Cruz has my full attention.

" . . . one of just several signals that Father Núñez is distancing himself from Archbishop Aguiar." What has he just said? "Quietly the Inquisition commits all its resources to overturning Vieyra's exemption to its jurisdiction, and he is losing ground. The Jesuits do not like working in the open, yet Vieyra does precisely this. Just as the Archbishop does now in his defence. As a show of support for Vieyra, the Archbishop asks Núñez to deliver this sermon."

"So although Núñez will not refuse a direct order," I murmur, "his refutation of the sermon afterwards serves notice that if the Company of Jesus must choose between Vieyra and the Inquisition, Vieyra loses."

To which the Bishop responds, fully including me now, that we have it on unimpeachable authority that Archbishop Aguiar and the Portuguese Vieyra have never so much as *met*.

"And yes," the Bishop continues, "if Núñez is forced to choose between influencing real events in Mexico and accommodating an archbishop's fantasies of eminence, His Grace the Lord Archbishop also loses. . . ."

It is vital that I make sense of this day if I am to find the source of the misunderstanding with Santa Cruz. And yet each time I think this hour through, so much remains unclear. Clarity is a thing to prize, clarity of mind I prize most highly. And yet at about the time of Carlos's departure things become considerably less clear. I am clear about my annoyance, I am clear about the sensation of unreality. And now I am clear about one other thing: this annoyance I know. I know it exactly. It is that which precedes waking at three in the morning at one's work table as one is being shaken by the shoulder and called to choir. The dream need not be particularly good, but is preferable to opening one's eyes.

As Santa Cruz asks me to reprise my arguments in this crisis over a sermon, the sensation is of being asked to explain a complicated joke, which, moreover, was never amusing.

Forty years ago, with great flights of oratory already behind him, and decades more ahead, Antonio Vieyra wrote a flawed sermon that, worse, boasted even as it was exposing its own flaws. He is blind now, ill. Eighty-two. He has left Portugal to return to the country he has loved for half a century. Brazil. Sworn enemy of an Inquisition that has real reason to fear him—five defiant years in its prisons and under attack again for the past decade, and also now by the landowners who hate him; outspoken defender of the Jews and New Christians; tireless protector of the enslaved Africans and the Indians; master of twenty languages and American dialects.

Antonio Vieyra is a flawed man, and a great one. The New World has not had such a holy instrument of Christ's true conscience since Bartolomé de Las Casas. And the writing is the least of his greatness. It is one thing for me to be impulsively foolish, quite another to be rehearsed in it. How have I come to this place? How do I find myself on the wrong side, with the buzzards circling a great, embattled, eighty-year-old man? I too am flawed, I too am not humble. And I have not fought all my life for others as he has, accepted prison and torture. For others. Yes, I have made other choices.

And now I remember something I should have remembered then, from a time that is gone. . . . My grandfather speaking of Sahagún and Las Casas, with that fierce pride of his that was itself like firelight. These two, he said, and Vieyra, were the proudest sons of the Iberian Peninsula. For all the horrors perpetrated by us since Ferdinand and Isabela, not another race in Europe would have produced three such men. He spoke to me of this at the firepit, the last night we spoke of anything.

Bishop Santa Cruz assumes an expression of absorption. And as I prepare to begin, I would be anywhere but here, saying anything but this, thinking any thoughts but these. Weakly I ask why he even needs my arguments.

"Whatever Núñez is up to, Juana, if he plays the jack again, as Jesuits do, quietly behind the scenes, we answer with a queen."

Amused, he asks Antonia to bring the chess set over. I could easily reach it myself but I suppose he wants her to stop playing so we may concentrate. She looks like she might have been crying. It's so selfish of me to have forgotten she is ill. As we are shifting the candy tray to make room for the little chess table, I touch Antonia lightly on the shoulder and tell her she should go. Santa Cruz has the idea she should take notes for me to help with the dictation later. Instead of asking why write any of this down, though the answer is obvious, I am saying she is not well and agreeing to write it out for him myself. And there I have promised it, with not so much as a demur. There is no turning back. But instead of letting her go he asks her to stay anyway. Antonia has a temper and coldly now insists that no, she really would like to stay, as though he's instead given her permission to leave. The scar in her cheek stands out pale against her colouring.

"Excellent, Antonia. If you are quite up to it." Indulgently, the Bishop includes her in the conversation. "A few details, so that you may be useful later. In the service of your mistress, what counts are the details. *Fineza*, Antonia, in its theological sense refers to the subtleties of love at work throughout Creation. Such is the love of Christ, masked, reserved, discreet, and above all, Antonia, *watchful*. . . ."

Conceding the advantage, Santa Cruz accepts Black. White takes his pawn, Black takes mine. And then I am beginning in this language

I am not far from despising, the language of canonical lawyers playing at theology, "First, don Manuel, the Jesuit Vieyra boasts that he will contest the findings of not just Augustine, but Aquinas and Chrysostom, too, then improve upon their positions, finding a *fineza* no one can match. Augustine holds that Christ's greatest sacrifice for Man was to give His life for us. Vieyra responds that since Christ loved Man more than life itself, the greater sacrifice was to absent himself from Man. But to this, we must answer that Christ is not absent at all but is present in the wafer and the wine."

Bishop Santa Cruz nods in satisfaction. He has been over this point carefully with me, has corrected me quite gently, as a friend. But I am not at all satisfied. It is not just the language—for the sake of this argument I go against everything I most intimately feel. "Present not only in the Eucharist but also in His Word."

I take another pawn, Santa Cruz takes mine. "Next, the Reverend Vieyra treats the Host as a remedy—a substitute for His presence rather than *being* that living presence. A confusion as fundamental as between metaphor and analogy. . . ."

"¡*Vale!*" approves Santa Cruz. "Augustine vindicated."

In his enthusiasm he reaches out to sample a sweetmeat, falters, then gives in, but this time with deliberation. "I know you are loyal Augustinians here at San Jerónimo, but will you only intercede," he wonders, "for one saint and not the other two?"

Black takes my pawn with a knight. I take Black's knight with mine. "In claiming to refute Saint Thomas," I say, "Vieyra illogically argues from genus to species; in attacking Chrysostom, he confuses cause with the expression of its effect. . . ."

I carry on in this fashion until I feel I have refuted myself, and Antonio Vieyra only incidentally. Santa Cruz takes my knight. "But surely," the Bishop suggests, "complete victory lacks one final step. Proposing a *fineza* greater than Vieyra's."

I answer that what makes this whole matter vain is that among so many sublime demonstrations of love we insist on deciding which one is best. We are like children picking blackberries. With our jars filled to overflowing with a harvest of such sweetness, we set to squabbling over who has picked the most. For Chrysostom it lies in the washing of the feet, even the feet of Judas. For Aquinas in the wafer and the wine, for Augustine in the Passion. We should give thanks to all who have discovered such richness in the Mysteries, then find what sweetness we can in our own little jar of blackberries.

"What Vieyra has found," I add, "is undoubtedly rich and lovely. So if I seem now to repeat Vieyra's mistake it is only to say he should not speak of besting the *finezas* of three maximal Doctors of the Church when a simple nun might find one, if not better then at least not worse than his. . . ."

White queen, with a glance of triumph, takes his rook. Black pawn, with a glance of amusement, takes my queen.

"Look at it this way, Juana," he says, queen in hand. "Vieyra's faring no better here today."

"And here," I continue, more cautiously, "I direct my attack not at Vieyra's logic but instead at his imagination. But since in all matters theological, errors of the imagination are infinitely more dangerous than errors of logic, you must promise, don Manuel, to correct instantly the slightest unorthodoxy in my position—anything that, by sheer inadvertence or feebleness of mind, might exercise the Inquisition. Errors in art, after all, are rightly answered by mockery and contempt"—he must have known my reluctance was not feigned—"but errors in theology must be answered before the Holy Office, and for all eternity."

"Of course, of course." His frown is one of impatience.

Clinging to the slim purchase of that promise—*his promise*—I press on. Black queen takes my castle.

"Christ's greatest finesse, Vieyra claims, was that He loved humanity without wishing that we return His love. Unless it be for the good that loving Him does *us*."

I wonder if it is really possible that Santa Cruz has not seen his own queen in danger. In taking mine he has left his unprotected. The sense of unreality only deepens. I have never beaten him. I feel my annoyance and self-disgust dissolve to a slow-rising elation. White knight takes black queen.

For just a few hours it's as though I am waking not from but to a dream, to find myself a citizen of Plato's submerged Atlantis . . . speaking the language of Atlantis, flooded by Atlantean cares and intrigues in a parlour at the bottom of the sea. Antonia's pallor, the Bishop's languor— the slight displacement between his gestures and his words—all seemingly the natural consequence of our submersion . . . occasional echoes of speech rising to the surface of my recollection in tremulous bubbles.

"Surely if Our Father's house has so many rooms," I am proposing now, "it is because there are so many ways to love and as many dispositions. What shall we call loving for the good that being in love will do you? Let's call this *amor egoista*. Loving for the good your love will do your beloved? Call it *amor magnánima*. For the benefits accruing to you from the return—the requital of your love? Call that love mercantile. Loving for loving's sake, with no *desire* that it be returned? Vieyra's *amor fino*—selfless love. And truly, this *is* beautiful, but in this he only follows Saint Bernard. Loving without desire is perhaps a feat the greatest among us may manage. Whereas loving for loving's sake, but without any *need* that it be returned—this we may truly call a divine or sovereign love, for such a love lies beyond us. . . . God alone is not completed by His love's return. His love is already complete. Divine Love is for Him alone."

White rook mates black king. The Bishop has lost his first game to me, gracefully. His face is curiously open, with a nakedness that in a simpleton we take for Good.

"The queen sacrifice was particularly nice."

"You taught it to me once." I no longer feel particularly triumphant. Against a more experienced opponent he would have seen it for what it was.

"I thought your mind elsewhere. . . . But as Vieyra and Father Núñez before me have discovered, humility is a most democratic virtue whose benefits apply equally to all. The mortification you bestow upon me in my defeat is a favour."

With my loctutory crowded after the sermon a fortnight earlier, this was as far as I had gone. These were the arguments Santa Cruz had come to hear for himself. But now he has said, with the most disarming simplicity, this curious thing: '*my defeat is a favour*.' What I say in reply is spontaneous precisely where my other foolishness has been rehearsed, for here is an idea that touches a genuine chord in me. If I could just say one true thing today, one thing I *feel*. . . .

"But in Christ, don Manuel . . . in Christ we feel this mortifying Love drawn and tempered to a fine and lacerating edge. Of such a gift we have already a thousand times proven ourselves unworthy. So to chasten us for our unworthiness of His *finezas* is also a fine thing, for He chastens whom he loves. But God's greatest *fineza* is a still more negative favour—to release us from his hand, to spare us his *finezas*, to grant us no favour at all."

The Bishop—startled from his languor—asks for an explanation.

Of errors in judgement and character I was already a hundred times guilty, but my single sin that day was speaking aloud thoughts that should have remained silent. For if the Word made flesh is God's greatest gift, then returning that gift to God—in the soul's gift of silence—is our most sacred offering, the highest of which we are capable.

And yet I do not keep silent.

"As I have said, don Manuel, God is not completed by our requital of His love. But by making us incomplete, he gives us the chance to choose completion. By leaving us free, he makes it the highest expression of our free will to *choose love*. How beautiful this is. But when He asks that we respond to the boundless favour of His love by loving as He loves us, the most faithfully we are able to reciprocate is by loving Him especially for the favours He does *not* bestow upon us. His greatest gifts we shall surely crucify. Withholding them, God spares us the opportunity to commit the most diabolical evils. So you see God's greatest benefaction, his subtlest finesse, contains in its belly another: the gift of not having to revoke our freedom.

"And what is its highest expression? Loving *without hope*. This we may call loving heroically. This, even the worst of us at the best of times can do. . . . To love without the slightest hope of being worthy of our love's Object, or of His love's return. And to exercise our free will as if with hope, as if we were in fact capable of good, of love, of being loved, in the terrifying absence of His Grace. . . ."

I sit here in Atlantis replaying that dreamlike hour in a mind filled with a silent roaring. Is this deafness—a roaring we can no longer distinguish from sound? Swelling to drown out all other sounds and then receding, the mind no longer able to hold to the featureless din. Caught up in the moment, I go further in ten minutes with my friend the Lord Bishop Santa Cruz than in twenty years of confession.

n the island of Mexico, from the old barrio of Nacatitlan, a street goes north through the new streets intersecting it, running west and east straight down to the lake. North of the barrio of Nacatitlan, the street is called Calle de las Rejas where it approaches the porter's gate of the convent of San Jerónimo, and from there past the slaughterhouses and butcher shops to the monastery of San Agustín, the richest in all Mexico. Here, in the days after the first Sunday of Advent and leading up to the festival of Our Lady of Guadalupe and in the fortnight beyond this to the Nativity, the beggars gather in great numbers at the monastery gates. It is the hour approaching sunset in this season of festivals and the end of rains. As though upon a living coat of arms, the central plaza of the Imperial City of Mexico lies embossed and embroidered and criss-crossed and braided with tens of thousands of people, afoot, on muleback and horseback, and in litters and carriages.

Over at the Cathedral and unconstrained by the solemnity within, celebrants have hemmed its walls about with exuberant bouquets the violet of Advent—irises, jacarandas, violets, hyacinths.

Three blocks farther north, the street reaches a smaller plaza at whose southeast corner agents stream in and out of the Customs House, its west windows reflecting a sky orange with the approaching sunset. Hemmed too in violet bouquets stands the small rose-coloured temple of Santo Domingo, on the north edge of the plaza itself. Across Calle Puente de la Aduana to the east stands the edifice of an austere authority: two tall storeys, a stone coat of arms, a cloth banner above the tall front gates at the southwest corner. There the sky blazes red-orange in the glass; farther along, the light slanting over the plaza leaves some windows in shadow on the upper floor. In one of these, six north of the gates, a lamp burns.

A second is lit as the first arrivals enter. Their carriages come in not through the front but by the rear gates, backed in black canvas to discourage petitioners and relatives and to frustrate the few inevitable daredevils. From the courtyard, where carriages wait in deep evening shadow an attendant leads each new arrival down a long black corridor lighted by rough torches. There are many doors; all are shut. Among the cracked and battered doors one is new: torchlight gleams dully in its heavy bosses and rivets.

Second-last to arrive is one who walks this corridor for the first time. He is young. He carries in one hand an Italian tricorne hat. His hair is blond; he wears it fashionably long, in ringlets. The tall robed attendant walks swiftly ahead. The young man tries not to fall behind, while trying not to try to keep up either. Tall himself, long-limbed, he is nevertheless hampered by the high-heeled shoes, canary yellow to match his long velvet *justaucorps* and yellow satin suit. He curses himself for a fool, first for accepting a last-minute invitation to leave the comforts of the palace, no matter from whom, then for getting into a carriage without knowing its destination. He knows it now. The shudder he has so far managed to suppress gathers at the base of his spine and skull. He reminds himself that he comes to give what amounts to a literary assessment, which he intends to render concisely and then just as quickly leave.

Led now through a small patio behind the front gates, he sends a last wistful glance out and climbs a tall staircase, its railing wrought of flat iron, unturned, unadorned. At the second door on the left, the attendant leading him knocks and returns swiftly the way he came. The most important guest is yet to arrive.

The door opens. Inside are five men. Straight ahead, behind a desktop as deep as it is broad, its clutter of dossiers pushed to one side, sits a burly man of about fifty in a white tunic and scapular. His beard is full and heavy, thick, starting high on his cheekbones, almost at his eyes. The heaviness of the beard and brows make the alert eyes, deep in their well of wrinkles, seem small. The heavy black curtains to his left are closed. Before them a secretary sits attentively at an *escribanía*. Another Dominican sits on a plain chair midway between a divan and the door. Over his scapular he wears a black mantle, the hood drawn back. He glances up briefly from a dossier on his lap as the man in yellow makes his entrance. A red-bearded friar sits at the edge of the divan. His habit is black, the hood especially large, of a soft material. The Augustinian's smile seems friendly.

To the right of the desk the drapes are parted a little, letting in the day's last light. Through the smoke in the air over the city, high thin clouds trail plumes of crimson. Just beyond this armspan of sky is an unoccupied chair, thickly upholstered, walnut arms inlaid with ivory and nacre. Beside this a low table, and upon it a small platter of sweetmeats. Across the room a Spanish gentleman paces to pass off his unease for impatience. He gives a familiar nod as the young man enters, crossing over to him. Without rising from behind the desk, the Master Examiner beckons to the empty chair next to the Spanish gentleman's. For several moments no one speaks. Sounds are heard in the hallway. All come to their feet, the young man reluctantly, as a man comes in, removing his travelling cloak on his way to the chair by the window. The servant hurries from the door to take the cloak and broad-brimmed hat.

In this season, the cassock the man wears is black, its piping, like its cincture, purple. The hair is a light brown, his eyes large and dark. The other men sit once he is seated. The young aristocrat is briefly chagrined that he has not been shown the same courtesy.

"Refreshments, Excellency?" the Master Examiner asks. "Water? Nothing at all . . . ?" The secretary leaves the room. The servant follows. "We'll begin, then. Your time in the capital is short—at least for now. Our foreign visitor, you know. And don Francisco here, as the Viceroy's representative, comes as a neutral observer."

The Spanish gentleman sits with his elbows on the armrests, fingertips resting lightly on the gloves in his lap. He inclines his head towards the man by the window. The Master Examiner continues, "In the unfortunate event that His Grace the Archbishop were no longer able to carry out his functions, the Viceroy would share our need to have as much warning as possible—"

The Viceroy's man raises a hand in a gesture of caution. "But I am also here to prevent any unpleasantness attaching to the Viceroy—that is, if his spiritual director *or* the Viceregal Cosmographer were ever indicted. Our particular interest would be any evidence connecting don Carlos with the Creole seditionists, which is of course a secular matter. Your cooperation will be noted. And of course, appreciated."

The Master Examiner turns back to the Bishop. "Our new *Calificador*, you have met."

The red-bearded man shifts in his seat. "Lord Bishop."

"And Prosecutor Ulloa here is with us so as to be familiar with these proceedings from the outset. Ulloa?"

"Even in complicated cases, Excellency, some of our best evidence is gathered through simple tactics," says the Prosecutor. "The simplest have stood the test of time. Apply pressure, watch for cracks. How and where depends upon the case, with which I am just now acquainting myself. . . ."

Master Examiner Dorantes glances at the red-bearded man.

The Calificador smiles affably. "Perhaps, Prosecutor Ulloa, I might begin. Having learned of the so-called *Athenagoric Letter* from an old associate in Puebla, I felt it my duty to obtain a copy of the printer's proof and show it to His Grace the Archbishop. To whose quarters I was accompanied by Master Examiner Dorantes, two weeks ago today. November 22nd. Understandably His Grace, who had taken to his bed, takes this attack on the Jesuit Vieyra as one upon himself. He has been nothing if not loyal—"

"To a man vehemently suspected of heresy," puts in the Prosecutor, "whom our Office in Portugal has once condemned and now has under examination again."

"I next expressed to His Grace," the Calificador continues mildly, "my bitter regret at not having heard of the nun's letter of attack earlier, given his recently announced intention to deliver a more recent sermon by this same Jesuit Vieyra. I did point out how things might have been much worse."

"And did His Grace the Archbishop wonder how they might?"

"He did, Lord Bishop." The Calificador smiles. "To which I answered, first, that the attack was published, taking it out of the realm of vague rumour and into one where we may prosecute. Second, that the *Letter* was signed, saving us valuable time. And third, that if the Archbishop would care to consider the matter philosophically, the prologue by this Sor Philothea—who has thus done our Office a great favour in arranging for publication—significantly rebukes its author for her worldly pride and vanity, thereby mitigating what would otherwise be a most grievous insult to the veneration in which His Grace is everywhere held."

Not quite pleased with the tone, Master Examiner Dorantes takes over the recitation himself. "The purpose of the visit was to put the full weight of this Office at His Grace's disposal. Unfortunately Father Núñez has allowed himself to be absent during this moment of distress."

"If you'll permit me, Fray Dorantes? At this point we were able to confirm that His Grace had been unaware of Father Núñez's own criticisms of the Jesuit Vieyra directly after the sermon. The Archbishop was so incredulous that it was fortunate I had witnessed Núñez's refutation myself in his chambers, and could confirm it personally."

During the interruption the Master Examiner sits quietly contemplating a point near the centre of his desktop, a scratch in the varnish, an ink spot. He lets another moment pass before concluding his report to the Bishop.

"Our discussion turned to certain speculations, lent substance by the timing of his absence, about Antonio Núñez's possible duplicity in this *Athenagoric Letter.* That it seemed close to using Núñez's own arguments from the rectory that day. This did little to quiet the Archbishop's unrest. The idea of cancelling his own participation in Gaudete Sunday and the Nativity was entirely the Archbishop's idea. I did caution that his absence on two such holy occasions would only draw further public attention to the affair and fuel the most unhealthy speculations. At this point, speaking more to himself than to us, he raised the possibility of going 'home' to Michoacan for the entire season."

In the chair beside the window the Bishop sits unmoving, his expression neutral, the large, dark eyes extraordinarily alive.

"There we have the Archbishop's reaction. Meanwhile the affairs of this Office do not rest, in any season. We have a disinterested party ready to make a formal denunciation of the text as heretical, when the moment to increase the pressure arrives. A series of anonymous leaflets has already been written, taking the denunciation further. Our printers are standing by. As to the *Letter*'s author, the Viscount here has been good enough to accept our invitation."

"Anything to oblige the Holy Office."

"The Lord Bishop mentioned to us your business here, and that you are so recently arrived. What you may speak to are her current resources in Europe. We have our own assessments. But we will add yours to the file."

"Yes, do feel entirely free. In return I shall be grateful for any intelligence you may be able to provide, and especially for material assistance with travel permits. As you may know," he turns to the Bishop, who seems to be looking not quite at him, "I am charged by my King with the mission of bringing one or, ideally, both of them—a matched pair, as it were—back to Versailles. If forced to choose, his preference is for her but he understands that her vows make this is a matter of some delicacy. So I must ask you one last time, Lord Bishop, is there no way of securing the necessary permission to have her taken?"

Raising his left hand to the curtain, the Bishop inspects something farther up Puente de la Aduana street. To the beating of drums and coronet fanfares, students of the Jesuit College of San Pedro y San Pablo are advancing on the Plaza of Santo Domingo; it is the *procesión burlesco* that by custom marks the six-week break in instruction. During his boyhood in Spain, the Bishop himself participated in several, though perhaps not quite matching the notorious Mexican exuberance. As in Spain, such displays offer useful glimpses of issues of concern to a diocese. In the street now the theme is a common one, the world upside down. Men costumed as women, women as males, others as fanciful animals, feet waving in the air and heads dragging along the ground. Still others as infants holding up placards marked *Senility*, or dressed as prostitutes waving *Chastity*. . . . But what has caught the Bishop's interest is at the head of the procession. A giant on stilts garbed in a purple chasuble, over it, a prisoner's *sambenito*, and on this Archbishop Aguiar's coat of arms. A horn sprouts on each side of the mitre. Costumed bulls and fighting cocks caper just out of reach as the Archbishop whirls and staggers and lays all about him with his wood sabre. . . .

The Bishop continues to gaze out the window. In the plaza the lamps of the workshops burn bright. Apothecary, printer and engraver, candlemaker, carpenter, farrier . . . the last straggle of communicants after Vespers.

Imperturbably watching the young aristocrat's colour mount, the Master Examiner eventually answers. "The nun, Viscount, is a problem of our own creation. We do not need France to solve it for us."

"It is of course as you wish," the Viscount says with elaborate casualness, "but if I may not have her and therefore may not have both, I must absolutely have him. His Majesty is remarkably uninterested in failure, even mine."

"Your King should thank us."

"He may thank you, but he will not thank me. He had his hopes set on her."

"It would be irresponsible of us to turn such a pox loose within his borders."

"A pox against which even an ocean, I notice, has not so far imposed a perfect quarantine."

"Do not trouble yourself unduly. The reach of our Office is long. As for the other one, you do understand that should he be called before the Tribunal, we can reach him even in Versailles."

"My mission is to get him there, not guarantee his piety."

"I remind the Master Examiner," interjects the Viceroy's representative, "that we have as yet heard no evidence of misconduct—ecclesiastic or civil. We are speaking of a distinguished natural philosopher—"

"Not an occupation that this Office inclines to take as an endorsement."

"The most distinguished in all the Spanish dominions."

"That he finds so few colleagues *in* the Spanish dominions we take as cause for rejoicing."

"Rather take it as a reminder, Doctor Dorantes—that I am here because his maps and studies have rendered valuable service to the Viceroy and to our King."

"Reminding me," says the Viscount, "of my services to mine. So, gentlemen, if I might continue, I should be going soon." The Viscount rises as though to announce a considerable grandiloquence. "As I was leaving Spain it was vividly impressed upon me that the support of the Countess of Paredes is unshakeable. On the other hand her husband's family's fortunes are, as you know, at the moment somewhat vulnerable. Her husband's brother, the Duke de Medinaceli, is more likely to be recalled to Madrid on charges of treason than to be reinstated as the King's Prime Minister.

"As to the first collection—this *Inundación Castálida*—it has proved wildly popular among ladies of the finer sort. That said, neither the collection nor her name is as yet well known to the other courts of Europe. Were the ties that bind the thrones of Spain and France not so very close, she would not yet be known in Versailles either. But I can also assure you, and I travel as widely as I read, there are not three poets in all of Europe today writing at this level. In ten years or even five, your nun may not need a Christina to be heard in Rome. There, Master Examiner, you have my assessment."

"One that gives no further cause to expect interference from Europe, which fits with our own assessment. Thank you, Viscount. So we have, in the matter of the *Letter*, the means to apply pressure to a number of points at once, as Prosecutor Ulloa has put it. Our anvil, let us say. Similarly, there are a number of potential hammers, one being a line of inquiry we have maintained for many years. . . . I apologize, Ulloa, for waiting until this morning to turn this other file over to you. But you will have read enough by now to understand why."

Glancing over at the two outsiders, the Master Examiner continues, his tone neutral. "Whenever a widely respected servant of Holy Mother

Church has used her auspices to win widespread trust and high esteem, there are repercussions when that individual is condemned to the stake. Upsets are to be expected, divisions within the Church itself, even within our Office. The trial of the Franciscan Fray Manuel de Cuadros fifteen years ago is an incident that I am sure the Lord Bishop well remembers. The charges were of a varied character. Some minor, most not. Eventually Brother Cuadros was persuaded to make a full confession and, as often happens, confessed to particulars unknown till then to us. Particulars to be found, Prosecutor Ulloa, in the dossier you now hold. I was at the time only an assistant to one of the examiners on the case, and so had little direct contact with the man. Antonio Núñez, on the other hand, whose task it was to secure his full repentance, spent a great deal of time with him. We were able to secure a number of manuscripts— translations and the like—enough of them to make his sentence inescapable. But certain other papers vanished. Heretical monographs on Indian practices. Blasphemous comparisons of their demonic rites to our most holy sacraments, or rather of these to . . . cannibalism. The examining magistrates were confident of seizing them in a raid that was to be carried out the next day. But by then they had disappeared. Fray Cuadros, a stubborn man, could not be induced to give testimony confirming our suspicions, but all the signs at the time pointed towards Carlos Sigüenza, who was prudently absent during the trial. We had drawn up plans to move against him, but after the Franciscan was burned, feelings in the Church and within this Office were, as I say, divided. The Archbishop of the time, being also our Viceroy, urged us to wait until we had more conclusive information. To date, it has not surfaced.

"The difficulty is that no one has seen these manuscripts for fifteen years. Were they destroyed? And if they still exist, where are they? Sigüenza is not stupid. It is doubtful that he would try to conceal them either at his house or the university—"

"Doctor Dorantes," says the Viceroy's emissary, chin lifted, cheeks faintly colouring, "what strikes me as *doubtful* is a line of inquiry that by your own admission has turned up nothing in fifteen years. Until credible evidence is produced, the palace shall suppose that both don Carlos and the Reverend Father Núñez continue to give faithful service. The Viceroy's administration will not be undermined, as the Archbishop's clearly has, by baseless suspicions."

"Of course, don Francisco, of course. We are aware Sigüenza is a friend of yours"—the Master Examiner raises a weary hand—"*and* that this can of course have no bearing on your deliberations. But your concerns are temporal. We take a longer view. Fifteen years is but a heartbeat."

"Unfortunately, *messieurs*, like don Francisco here, I do not have an eternity either. And if you have been hearing the same reports I have about an unfortunate and ill-considered alliance between great Spain and a certain insignificant enemy of France, time is scarce indeed. I would really rather not have to make arrangements to smuggle a subject of the Spanish Crown out of Spanish territory in time of war. Unless you have further need of me this evening, I will leave you to get on with things. For my part, I leave reassured that you do not have enough to be arresting him any time soon."

The Viceroy's representative rises to follow the Viscount out. "In the morning I make my report to the Viceroy. Keep us apprised."

When the two have left, the Calificador runs his fingers through the red tangle at his throat. "Did he say keep us surprised?" he asks, of no one in particular.

"Coming late to this case," Prosecutor Ulloa frowns over the open folder, "I do not yet see why the foreigner has been brought here tonight. How do we know this *Francés*," Ulloa says with distaste, "will not run and tell Sigüenza everything he has just heard?"

"If only he would."

The Prosecutor considers this.

"You see, Prosecutor Ulloa, the good don Francisco and the Viscount," explains the Calificador, "are part of the pressure."

Dorantes looks up from pondering the scratch on his desk. "Were the foreigner to do just as you suggest, Ulloa, although it is almost too much to hope for, Sigüenza might, in a panic to destroy the evidence, lead those watching him directly to the documents. What we can be sure of is that he will not leave New Spain until they are destroyed, since he cannot doubt that we may reach him even in France. So as long as he is here, there is still a chance. All the better if he has both reason and opportunity to leave. But where are those manuscripts? The most likely thing is that they are not in the city."

"Still," says the Calificador, glancing about him, "what if these papers *were* here? A question interesting to contemplate, no? One place would be a convent. Almost impossible to enter without giving warning. Too many corridors, too many escape routes, too much time. San Jerónimo, for example, is just such a warren."

"But has the publication of this letter," Ulloa asks, "not put her on her guard?"

"It's hard to say with her. She has so very many interests—her poetry and her little fables, her locutory and her library. It is touching. And the few things that do not intimately concern her . . . hardly exist at all. His Excellency knows her better than I, but I would say she knows nothing of the world—has she ever lived in it, I wonder?"

The Bishop looks at him, his eyes glowing darkly.

"What the Calificador is taking so very long to say, Lord Bishop, is that she has no reason to connect the letter's publication to our interest in the missing manuscripts."

"Forgive me, Master Examiner," says Ulloa, "but we do have sources at San Jerónimo. Before taking the risk of alerting her, would it not have been wise to at least try to reassure ourselves she does not have the manuscripts right now? Could a way not have been found?"

"A way has been found," says Dorantes.

"I have been wondering—this time the red-bearded magistrate does not look at the Bishop, who has turned his attention back to the plaza, but addresses himself to Master Examiner Dorantes—just how reliable we consider this 'way' to be."

With a scowl at his confrere Dorantes says soothingly to the Bishop, "With a little more experience, the new Calificador may come to understand that even when the end result is assured, there are no certainties in the moment. The nun or the Frenchman may lead us to the manuscripts. The manuscripts will give us Sigüenza or even give us Núñez. Núñez will give us what we need against her—he can hardly hide behind the sacramental Seal now. Or in the matter of this letter, the Archbishop— that is, should he be well enough to continue—moves against her on his own. Or, finally, we press this question of heretical quietism in her *finezas negativas* and clean up at least one mess the Jesuits have made.[25] *Dejada, alumbrada, gnóstica* . . . she has given us options."

"Excuse me," the Calificador offers, "but have we not missed a step? How are these manuscripts to give us Núñez? Is he not more likely to be taken in the event that he has failed to burn her journals?"

"There are other proceedings, Calificador. Many others, which you have no present need to know about." Dorantes runs the heel of a small pale hand wearily across one brow. He leans forward, weight on his elbows, and places his interlaced palms on the desk. "You may go now, Calificador."

When he has left, Ulloa asks, "As to the sequence, does the Lord Bishop have a preference?"

"Who falls first?" The Bishop turns from the plaza. "No. I do not much care."

"We take our exemplum in patience, then, from His Excellency. Anything before we adjourn?"

"Master Examiner, Lord Bishop . . ."

"Yes, Ulloa."

"While I, for one, am satisfied that the case holds promise, one final worry occurs to me. Bringing don Francisco here was prudent—he now knows himself to be the prime suspect if don Carlos is warned. But are we prepared to have the foreigner go to her with what he has heard?"

"It is as you yourself have said, Ulloa. Pressure at as many points as possible. He would be doing us a favour. But he has not the slightest chance of getting her out if we do not wish it."

"And we do not wish it?"

"We do not wish it."

The Bishop seems about to rise. The others tense to rise with him. For the past half hour he has seemed unaware of the tray of sweetmeats on the table beside him. His hand sways idly now over them, stops, settles on a choice. A slice of candied squash. Raising it to his lips, he stops. The heavy rings glow in the lantern light. It is full dark outside.

"Not knowing quite what he expects to get," the Bishop says softly, "the Viscount may indeed go to her, as he has once already. At first he will find himself enjoying again this power he has over her, which lies precisely in her not knowing that he has it, and this knowledge that she does not really see him. But since he cannot get in, and since he cannot get her out, he will see that this is all there is for him.

"I do not think he will go again."

Something has been troubling me, a care
so subtle, so fleeting, it appears,
that for all that I know of the feeling
I scarcely know how to feel it for me.
  It is love, but a love
that, failing to be blind,
only has eyes to inflict
a more vivid punishment.
  For it is not the terminus a quo
that afflicts these eyes:
but their terminus being the Good,
so much pain in the distance lies.
  If this feeling that I harbour
is not wrong—but what love is owed,
why do they chastise one
who pays on love's account?
  Ah, such *finezas*, so rare, so subtle are
the caresses I have known.
For the love we hold for God
is one without a counterpart.
  Neither can such a love,
ever meet with oblivion,
since contraries are not
to be conceived upon pure Good.
  But too well do I recall
having loved in a time now past
with a quality beyond madness,
exceeding the worst extreme;
  yet since this love was a bastard,
of oppositions wed,
swiftly was it undone,
by the flaws with which it was cast.
  But now, ah me, so
purely is this new love enkindled,
that reason and virtue
are further fires to feed it.
  Anyone hearing this will ask,
why then do I suffer?
Here an anxious heart responds:
for this very cause, and no other.

What human frailty is this,
when the most chaste and naked spirit
may not be embraced
except in mortal dress?
  So great is the longing
we have to feel loved,
that however hopeless it becomes
we are helpless to resist.
  Though it adds nothing to my love
that it be requited,
though I try to deny it—
O how I crave this.
  If it is a crime, I avow it,
if a sin, now it is confessed,
but however desperate my attempts,
I cannot bring myself to repent.
  Who sees into my secret heart
will bear witness
that the thorns I now endure
are my own harvest.
  And that I am the executioner
of my own desires, fallen
among my longings,
entombed in my own breast.
  I die—who will believe this?—at the hands
of what I most adore,
and the motive of my death is
a love I cannot bear.
  Thus, nourishing my life
on this sad bane, I find
the death on which I live
is the life I am dying for.
  But courage, heart,
however exquisite the torments
through whatever fortunes heaven sends,
this love, I swear never to recant.

JUANA INÉS
DE LA CRUZ

"Divine Love"

B. Limosneros, trans.

DEIPHOBE

[*27th day of November, 1690*]

la excma. María Luisa Manrique de Lara y Gonzaga
Condesa de Paredes, Marquesa de la Laguna,
Madrid, España

Queridísima María Luisa,

 or weeks I have no news of you. And now your letter opens saying you will not be able to write for some time. Were this not agony enough—there is the why. I beg you, write even two lines the first instant you can, just to say your Tomás is recovering. How galling for you to hear his physicians changing their diagnosis like so many weathercocks. And how very selfish I have been to burden you—can I have forgotten you might have cares of your own?

I continue to believe Tomás's recent difficulties with our new Queen are temporary. It saddens me to be so far away and so ignorant of matters there that I can now offer such thin comfort and no advice at all except, believe all will be well even as you act all the more resolutely to make it so.

Let me at least try to allay fears I myself have raised so unkindly, with regard to the recent activities of the Inquisition here. The time for reading obliquely, as one reads Aeschylus, has passed. As soon as Carlos duly supplied them with a book inventory, the whole business faded away. The Inquisitor Dorantes was only sending a message to our distinguished Chair of Mathematics and Astrology. No, not just a message, a reminder. For it is ten years ago now that Dorantes censored a set of observations Carlos had published on the phases of the moon. (Twenty years ago Dorantes even censored Núñez—for 'an excess of enthusiasm over the immaculacy of the Virgin Mother's conception.' Truly, one hesitates to imagine what this could have meant . . .)

I am sorry to have alarmed you unnecessarily. You once said you thought my fear of the Inquisition exaggerated. These days, anyone in the capital will tell you that the Holy Office's power is on the decline. That if you are circumspect and curry favour with the authorities, do not rise too fast among your neighbours or speak out too frankly among strangers, do not think the wrong thoughts or read the wrong books, that if you miss no opportunity to express your enthusiasm for the Faith, you have nothing to fear from the Inquisition.

At any rate, if the Holy Office had launched a proceeding against Carlos I would have heard—first the whispers of the well-informed, then a great murmuring among the ignorant. And soon after that he would be a guest of the Tribunal.

There has been nothing of this. So I hope to have laid your doubts (and most of all your loving fears) to rest, if by this somewhat gloomy avenue.

Things have been otherwise calm. Right now, all the talk at the cathedral is of the Archbishop's sermon for the Vigil of our Lord's Nativity, or perhaps it was for Gaudete Sunday, I'm not sure which. The point being that he seems to have decided not to give it. I will send Antonia out this morning to find out what she can. The affair has occasioned as much mirth as curiosity among the clerics here, since it has become an open secret that the Archbishop, who never misses an opportunity to trade on his intellectual connections in Europe, has become all but incapable of delivering much less writing a sermon, such is his near-constant state of upset.

As I wrote you recently, the Bishop of Puebla has followed through on his promise to secure for me the one commission from the Church that I have truly coveted in recent years. A suite of carols on Saint Catherine of Alexandria, to be sung in the cathedral in Puebla. In a few more weeks I hope to have finished, but I may say with a small shudder of poet's superstition that they are on their way to being my best work since *First Dream*.

I am not quite over my bitterness. I have written you about my lyrics for Saint Bernard, that Núñez had his way in the end and that they were not sung. This has brought more hurt than anything in the years since you left. And yet because in all these months you have not mentioned it, I cannot help suspecting you've not received that letter either. No matter, it's over now. I brought much of it upon myself. Such squabbles over theology are no place to speak one's heart. I do not much care for loose talk of God.

You asked last year about my grievance with Father Núñez. I gave you what it is built on, the circumstances, but what lies at its heart, what lies on its altar is simple beauty itself. Though Núñez might fulminate against this or that formulation of mine, and insists on seeing attacks against him any time I encroach upon his holy exclusivities and prerogatives, in the end it is about this. His positions on the Holy Mysteries lack for neither learning nor subtlety. What they lack is beauty. He sees it, and it enrages him that this should enter into it at all. But from the simplest peasant to the most exalted sovereign of the world, we are swayed by beauty, we turn in its orbit. Womanish thoughts! Paganist poetry! he fumes, yet sees the evidence all around him. Even he. For it is said that at the Jesuit college Father Núñez has built with his own hands an altar to the Virgin that only he is permitted to tend. They say that the altar of Rector Núñez is very beautiful, that its beauty is of an Asiatic extravagance. When I remember this altar, my thoughts wander to a day in the distant past when things grew so bitter between us that I asked he be replaced as my director. It was your husband's uncle, don Payo, who tried to mend things between us. In refusing my request, he let slip a small detail I would never have guessed at, but without which I would find the altar incomprehensible. That as a novice, the boy Antonio Núñez wrote beautifully, of a beauty reminiscent of Saint Jerome's. As a result his noviciate with the Jesuits was made especially hard; his punishments were of a cruelty almost fantastic, until he had stripped the least marks of grace from his thoughts and writings. Is it for this, I wonder, that I could never quite bring myself to hate him? Oneness, Goodness, Truth. The transcendental attributes of God. But there is a fourth. It is in Her; it is in Her Son. Our souls sway to a fourth transcendental.[26] Beauty. The poets overrunning theology! he cries, but I am only following Saint Jerome, the Ciceronian. And Núñez, better than anyone, knows this.

Obedience, forbearance, humility, resistance to suffering. This is what he answers with. In Núñez's Church of the Holy Infantry, to have a gift is indeed a great burden—the burden of annihilating it. To be an ordinary infantryman is more than burden enough.

I understand our sacraments as well as he, if differently, and while I find them of a majesty and depth that goes beyond our comprehension, they do not console me. I am not fed, I am not filled, by this bread.

He has made himself our authority on the Eucharist, but if others could only read the monographs Carlos will never publish on the ancient Mexican sacraments. The Reverend Father has made himself our authority on communion, and takes the *finezas* of Christ to be his exclusive province. He treats the *fineza* like a demonstration, a proof, an axiom of love. Yet the *finesses* are an expression from which we *infer* love. They derive from our gift for inference. Love is not a truth that insists. We infer, Christ does not insist. And so Núñez's positions are never beautiful—they insist, they prove and reprove. And against the love of beauty and the beauty of love he knows he cannot win.

A love of Christ that is passionate, yet pure and disembodied—we both claim to believe in it. I believe that to develop the capacity for such a love here on earth, here in the flesh, would only make our love for Christ all the deeper and truer. Núñez cannot believe that any such love may exist among us, and reviles my need to feel it. I believe in this Love with every fibre of my being, yet from Him I do not feel it and so can find no way to return it.

What I feel is His absence. It is why I once sought for him in the beauty of the world. This at least I can feel. My mind infers it, but so does my heart. This is an absence at least bearable to me—and in the hours when it is not, I look to the mountains in the east, I look to the stars, and feel my love returning, flooding me. . . . I know you will understand but I add this in the event this letter is intercepted: if I could be less than utterly convinced of His existence, how much more bearable would my Lover's absence be.

Núñez hates this. Every tone and syllable. Father Núñez has extinguished his gift. Only to find it reborn in me, rising to oppose him.

I am the books, I am the beauty, I am the gift.

And so my thoughts return often to that day with the Bishop when I went too far and yet, even sick with self-disgust, I continued to abuse the gift of speech from the heart in my lyrics for the humble Saint Bernard. I have heard Bishop Santa Cruz was in a rage when he learned they were cancelled, for it is precisely this heart speaking its secrets to God that for fifteen years Santa Cruz has pressed me to reveal to him. In banning them, Father Núñez has dashed any hopes of an alliance with the Bishop. So one less worry, a boon it is hard to feel I deserve.

Santa Cruz calls this failure to feel the presence of Christ entirely normal. Spiritual aridity is the term, and it is a step on the *via mística*. What he mildly disapproves are the traces of worldliness still clinging to my sacred verses. Worldliness, the Bishop does not want either; what he wants is rapture.

My, but how melancholy this letter has become. If this was to be my attempt to set your mind at rest, it is hard to pronounce it a success. I pause for now and will start tomorrow afresh. My thoughts are with you, the thoughts and prayers of the entire convent are with Tomás. Sweet Lysis, I pray that a note from you of happy news is but a league or two off from here, and that I shall be able to start again on a note of joy and thanksgiving. And if that note has not yet been written by the time you receive this one, give not another moment's thought to writing until Tomás is well. Unless, dearest María Luisa, you should just need to talk. . . .

There. I hear Antonia on the stairs. She has news. And more energy at times than either of us knows what to do with. It is like trying to curb wild horses. More soon.

Love,

día 27 de noviembre del año 1690
del convento de San Jerónimo,
de la Ciudad Imperial de México,
Nueva España

Extract from Sister Philothea of the Cross (I)

My Lady,

I have seen the letter in which you challenge the *finezas* of Christ predicated by the Reverend Father Antonio Vieyra in his Maundy Thursday sermon. So subtle is his reasoning that the most erudite have seen in it his singular talent outsoaring itself like a second Eagle of the Apocalypse, following the path laid out earlier by the Most Illustrious César Meneses. . . . In my view, though, whoever reads your treatment cannot deny that your quill was cut to a finer point than both men's, so that they might rejoice to find themselves outdone by a woman who does her sex honour.

I, at least, have admired the liveliness of concept, deftness of proof and energetic clarity that you have brought so convincingly to bear, this last being wisdom's inseparable companion. For this reason the first utterance of the Divine Wisdom was *light*, since without illumination comes no word of wisdom. Even the words of Christ when he spoke of the highest mysteries, but under the veil of parable, did not evoke much wonder; and only when he chose to speak with clarity was his universal knowledge acclaimed. Such clarity is one of the many favours my lady owes to God; for clarity is to be had neither by effort nor persistence: it is a gift instilled in the soul.

So that you might see yourself in letters more clearly traced, I have had your letter printed; and also that you might take better stock of the treasures God has invested in your soul, and be made thereafter more appreciative, more aware: for gratitude and understanding are twins born of the same childbed. And if as your letter claims, the more one receives from God the more one owes in return, few creatures find their accounts more in arrears than yours, for few have been bequeathed such talents, or have incurred thereby such a debt to Him. So if you have made good use of them thus far (which I must believe of anyone who professes religion), hereinafter may you use them better.

My judgement is not so harsh a censor as to condemn verses—by virtue of which you have seen yourself so widely celebrated—a skill Saint Teresa, Saint Gregory of Nazianzus and other saints have sanctified with examples of sacred verse; but I would wish that you follow them not just in metre but also in the selection of your subjects.

Nor do I subscribe to the vulgar prohibition of those who assail the practice of letters in women, since so many have devoted themselves to literary study, not a few even winning praise from Saint Jerome. . . .

Letters that engender arrogance, God does not want in a woman; but the Apostle does not condemn those that do not lead woman from a state of submission. It has been widely noted that study and knowledge have made of you a willing subject, and have served to hone your skills in the finer points of obedience; indeed, while other female religious sacrifice their free will to obedience, you make a captive of your intelligence, the most arduous and pleasing holocaust that may be offered up for slaughter on the altars of Religion. . . .

see her pale face in the doorway. This news, I do not think I shall like.

But her news is not of the Archbishop at all, and for just an instant I mistake the two booklets she holds for the most recent issue of our city's *Chronicle of Notable Events*. She is trying to explain, so breathlessly as to have likely run the whole way. . . .

"I was at the Hindu's, the one with the turban—"

"Hindus—"

"'Two copies for you and your mistress,' he says. 'My compliments.' They all have them—*all the booksellers*, dozens of copies—next to *Inundación Castálida*. People are already buying them as if they were *yours*—"

"One *is* mine, I gather. Come, I'll take the one you haven't quite crushed yet. . . ."

"Juana, who is Philothea? *E igua puta*—how did she get your letter?"

THE ATHENAGORIC LETTER
by the Reverend Mother
JUANA INÉS DE LA CRUZ
a nun professed to the veil and choir
of the very religious
Convent of San Jerónimo of the City of Mexico, capital of New Spain.
Printed and dedicated to her by
SISTER PHILOTHEA DE LA CRUZ
her most studious and devoted follower
of the Convent of the Holy Trinity of Puebla de los Angeles.
Licensed in the City of Angels, Diego Fernández de Leon, Printer. In the year 1690.
Available in Puebla at the libreria Diego Fernández de Leon,
under the Portal de las Flores

This is not possible. Printed by Sor Philothea, costs assumed by Philothea. Using the Bishop's regular printer. Licence signed by Santa Cruz, dedication by Philothea. The preface addressed to *me*:

Sor Philothea is the Lord Bishop Manuel Fernández de Santa Cruz y Sahagún. If Antonia wants a harder question it's this: what is

the use of a disguise that lasts not five seconds? What is he doing—
what has he *done?*

I have seen the letter?—seen it, of course you have! I sent it, you *asked.*
Why not 'received' it?

But no, it was not Philothea who asked. Santa Cruz asked.

"The Bishop did this? But Juana, it was *private.* He said—you said . . ."
she adds helplessly.

He said, I said. He said little, I on the other hand said rather a lot. No,
but *this,* this is beyond belief. *Like a second Eagle of the Apocalypse . . . her
quill cut finer . . . Deftness of proof, energetic clarity . . . Even Christ when he spoke
of the highest mysteries, but under the veil of parable, did not provoke so much
wonder. . . .* He cannot think this is helping anyone—to be compared to
Christ. *Favourably?* He cannot think this helps *me.*

"Who is the Eagle of the Apocalypse, Juana?—*¡caray!*"

"Tonia, if you're angry now, look at the third paragraph, where he
complains about your handwriting."

*So that you might see yourself in letters more clearly traced, I have had your
letter printed . . .*

"What? Oh." She almost manages a smile. "And now *ese hijo de la
mierda* expects you to be grateful?—what he wants is everyone to see
how clever he is!"

Pacing in and out of the room reeling off questions and curses, reading out loud, whirling about at each turn, tresses swinging out like rope
ends, Antonia is becoming quite magnificent in her fury. I would not like
Santa Cruz's chances if he were here. It is almost as if she truly hated
him. But whatever her past grievances with Santa Cruz I have my own
to nurse just now. And yes, talk of the Apocalypse I also could have done
without.

"Toñita, would you give me some time to think this through? Then
we'll get to work, *mi amor. ¿De acuerdo?*"

She goes into the study, greenish eyes glowing, rattles purposefully
about at the workbench, getting ready to take dictation. I have no idea
what 'work' means, but it felt good to say.

This beggars belief. How can he be so stupid—can he not see what
he's done? We've done this together a dozen times. A private letter has
every advantage, advantages a published one lacks. Power: in possession.
Control: in choosing who gets access. Elusiveness: the letter is a ghost.
The target hears snippets, conflicting versions, is never sure to have

heard it all, to have seen the whole shape of the plot. Fighting it, Núñez feels himself flailing about, sees the hapless spectacle of ridicule he makes. But all the advantages are as dust: it's the *liabilities* that count. The letter in private circulation is a rumour—published, it is evidence. And here the target is the Chief Censor of the Holy Inquisition! Publication plays right into his hands.

We have made him a gift of his revenge, and made taking it his duty.

But Santa Cruz has never been stupid. He knows the game better than anyone. He taught it to me. This is not a blunder. Is this to be some sort of lesson in the finer points of obedience? Then there has been some misunderstanding, I have given him no *cause*. He talks of gratitude—but how have I been ungrateful? *And if as your letter claims, the more one receives from God the more one owes in return, few creatures find their accounts more in arrears than yours, for few have been bequeathed such talents.* . . . He paraphrases Saint Augustine. . . . *Indeed let the rich galleon of your genius sail freely, but on the high seas of the divine perfections* . . . This is my examination by the scholars at the palace! But twenty years ago? I have never spoken to Santa Cruz about this. He was still in Spain—or is this about my Columbus and the *Martyr of the Sacrament*? He mocks me through my works. Mentions the mastery of Saint Joseph to tar another of my plays—or my carols, sung in Santa Cruz's own cathedral this year—then deliberately confuses Joseph with Moses as a pretext for maligning the learning of Egypt. Calls it barbarous, and slyly denigrates my passion for Alexandria. . . . *movements of the stars and heavens* . . . *disorder of the passions* . . . Can this be about my carols on Saint Catherine? Yet if he was unhappy, why give me the commission?

No, this is not a lesson, this is a *provocation*. Catherine, Athena—he mocks me through my past, my work, my sex—*our* sex. Sor Philothea. *Athenagoric, worthy of Athena,* she titles it. Such wisdom, such energetic clarity. Such honours to our sex.

But these are just provocations, dear Philothea, these are not so far from threats. *Nor do I subscribe to the vulgar prohibition of those who assail the practice of letters in women.* . . . *Letters that engender arrogance, God does not want in a woman.* . . . *lead a woman from a state of submission.* . . .

A friend would not do this.

It is night. Pleading illness I have asked to be excused from the prayers of Compline. Everyone knows why. I insist Antonia go.

Publishing the letter, Santa Cruz deliberately exposes me. He publishes it in full. Even where I close stressing once again that this is for his eyes only. In a private letter, such a closing is what it seems to be. Published, it makes me look like an intriguer. The transparency of the pseudonym is now an asset—plainly Santa Cruz was making no effort at subterfuge. Philothea was merely to keep any worldly indignity from fastening upon the princes of the Church.

And so the full weight of their opprobrium attaches . . . to me.

By the time Antonia returns I am in a fury.

Santa Cruz and I have been friends for seventeen years. I simply cannot believe he came that day intending to do this. Then what has happened since? Something in the letter itself. He is obviously angry about the negative *finezas*. He cannot think I meant him—that the greatest *fineza* is receiving no favour at all. Does he think I am asking to be free of his favour, my obligations to him? Free of him? Could he not see that for once I was speaking my heart? Is he so unaccustomed to my sincerity in questions of theology that he could mistake it, think I was playing him for a fool? When I write of those who are 'blind and envious' in my letter—does Santa Cruz not see in the humble Núñez, almost blind, a more likely target than himself? It is incredible. Can Santa Cruz be that dim, that proud, feel that unsure of my sentiments for him?

But then maybe this can yet be undone! A misunderstanding after all?

No. Yes. Quite incredible. No, not believable at all.

Morning. Through the east and south windows a brilliant morning light streams past me and over the floor on either side of the writing desk here in the corner. It is as if I am hiding from it now, this energetic clarity. For almost a full day I have explained nothing, and for the past twelve hours have refused to see the obvious. The obvious is quite terrible.

Our target was never Núñez. The target was Francisco Aguiar y Seijas. Archbishop of New Spain.

 I have been answering the wrong questions. Yes, yes, it's clear why the pseudonym, even such a transparent one—but why a woman, why a *nun*? I had thought the irony directed at me. It is not. Archbishop Aguiar will see himself fairly surrounded now by nun theologians, Sor Juana and her followers. An attack of the Amazons, led by Athena herself. And everyone will see that he must see this. And he will know himself mocked for his hatred and his fear of us.

Sor Philothea is a fiction, a figment, a demon. Sor Juana is real. Mine is the only name that is real.

In my own letter so worthy of Athena I name neither Núñez nor Antonio Vieyra, nor even Santa Cruz. It is a letter, requested by a superior, on a certain sermon delivered by a certain predicator. I sign it only because anonymous documents send a dangerous signal to the Inquisition. But Sor Philothea in her preface—to *me*—names not just Vieyra but Vieyra's own teacher, his mentor: Meneses. Just to say my quill is cut finer than even his. Why?

Or might it just possibly be that Menenses is to Vieyra as Vieyra is to the Archbishop?

Philothea, seeing no one named, sees her opportunity: she makes it seem as if my letter strikes at the Archbishop himself. The last vestige of an unstated connection to Father Núñez is quite forgotten. There is only the Archbishop now. How is the reader to think otherwise? I would believe it myself. Then, admonishing me, Philothea sidesteps his wrath.

Sor Philothea is the matador, Sor Juana is the cape.

Seventeen years. Santa Cruz has been a *friend*—to me, my nephew, my family. He gave my mother her *last rites,* took her confession, celebrated her funeral Mass. Have I been such a terrible friend?

This makes no sense. He sounds more and more like Núñez. He writes of the haughty elations of our sex, exhorts me to obedience, to sacrifice my will, to hold my mind captive.

I have done this thing out of obedience, put my mind at his service, done everything he asked. Then he turns on me that old shibboleth of Saint Paul, that a woman should not teach—yet even Saint Bernard admitted women might profit from study. I should really write more theology, Philothea says, even as she admonishes me in the preface to the theology I have just written. My lyrics to Saint Bernard *were a sermon*—and though such a thing is forbidden by the Council of Trent, Santa Cruz was furious when Núñez forbade the singing of them on those grounds.

I have not answered it: what has happened since then?

I should read occasionally in the book of the Lord Jesus Christ? How cruel, how cruel is my sister Philothea. I should write more on sacred subjects, she chides, when I have written how many religious plays and sacred *loas*—even as I was writing for Santa Cruz a suite on Saint Catherine.

Now I am turning in circles. For even if Santa Cruz's target was always the Archbishop—why *publish?* The question is the same. A private letter directed at the Archbishop has almost every advantage. Unless the Archbishop is so close to madness—does Santa Cruz imagine His Grace might collapse before he takes action against me? Does Santa Cruz even care?

I see the face of my friend. Yet knowing what he has done I do not trust my memory of his face that day. . . . The eyes shine. A face like an adolescent's but slightly bloated by the intervening years. The boyish smile that stretches the sparse moustache across a row of teeth perfectly formed yet overlarge for the narrow mouth. The thin lips, the impish chin, the muscular jaws, all this might have rendered the face squirrel-like, were it not for the incongruous languor of the Bishop's voice and gestures. No. I would have it be incongruous but it is not. I have seen it many times before—his hand hovering over the confections of our convent, and it always seemed dear and comical, the way he attempts to resist his sweet tooth. Fairly torments himself before giving in. He thinks it is not noticeable. We think our notice is not noticeable. . . .

There is a moment, something from that afternoon . . . But am I recalling it or planting it now, in the light of what has happened? The Bishop has just entered, the Viscount rises to greet him. Something comes into the Bishop's face. Even as it strikes me that the Viscount's beauty, for all his youth, is masculine, it crosses my mind that with the stickle of moustache shaved, and with it the little ridgeback of bristles that runs to the chin, Bishop Santa Cruz in a cowl could quite easily pass for one of us. Sor Philothea . . .

No, this memory I do not trust at all. But neither am I quite certain that somehow I did not see too much that day, as well as too little, and showed too much of what I saw. . . .

No, no and no. I do not accept this. All this for some *thought* of mine he might have guessed at? Ridiculous. This is just not good enough. Whatever happens next, I want to *know* why a friend has done this to me. And I want to know why *now.* That was *Easter.* It is almost Christmas. Why wait seven months? Easter, Christmas . . .

The Archbishop's cancelled sermon, his trip to Michoacan. It can't be about this.

"Antonia! Get Gutiérrez for me, please. Quickly? If you hurry you can be back by Vespers."

I will not be going down for Vespers either. Let them think I am afraid. Let them think I am scheming. Let them think what they will.

Why *now*?

If Gutiérrez had not been an officer of the Inquisition the turnkeeper would have challenged him, arriving after Vespers unannounced. Antonia shows him into the locutory. She lights a lamp over on his side of the grate and hurries down the corridor, through the porter's gate and back in, fusses with the lamp on ours. . . .

One does not expect cheer from a visit by an Inquisitor but in the three years I have known him, this is often exactly what I have been given. A funny gnomish face, the sparse little beard, as though the entire scraggle were attached to his lower lip. I have liked him from the first, having from the first an intimation of our secret bond. He has precisely as great a vocation to be an Inquisitor as I to be a nun. He has his ideas on faith and Faith and how to serve them, but that he should find himself in his present profession still seems wildly improbable to him.

He has come quickly. Everyone has seen the letter by now. A sheen glistens on his freckled forehead. With just two lamps lit I am reminded of Núñez's visits.

Has Gutiérrez heard anything?

"His Grace is 'home' in Michoacan. He hadn't made a formal announcement but the topic of the sermon he was to have given was no great secret either."

"You're not telling me, Gutiérrez. Is it bad—is it as I thought?"

"Another sermon by Antonio Vieyra, yes. He must have decided to deliver this one himself, Núñez's having gone over so well."

"He had no idea what Núñez did at the college rectory after. . . ."

"I think we can suppose not. But His Grace of course has many . . . distractions."

"Is he really so unstable? Could Santa Cruz believe this might unhinge him?"

"Who is to say it hasn't? They might be able to tell us in Michoacan tonight."

"Can you find out?"

"We'll know soon enough, I suspect. But yes, I might find something out. This letter, Sor Juana. Very neatly done. It was also an enormous risk."

"You do understand, this was to be about Núñez. It is Philothea's letter that makes it seem otherwise."

"Yes, now that you have pointed it out. Publishing it is incomprehensible, as you say. In fact, I can see him finding the phantom letter, as you put it, even more maddening. But Antonio Vieyra . . . His Grace has been nothing if not loyal."

"If one were to exempt everyone in Europe the Archbishop imagines he knows, one could not discuss anyone *but* phantoms. And you do see that not having heard about Núñez will have skewed his perception from the outset—"

"Clearly, clearly. And His Grace has been nothing if not a bit embarrassing. To hear him trading on his contacts—"

"He seems never to have grasped the basic point that one already expects an archbishop to have them. Like someone who cannot stop auditioning—"

"For the job he already has, yes. But I hardly think Vieyra qualifies as one of His Grace's many phantoms."

"How so?"

The watery blue eyes blink owlishly. He seems almost to be about to tell a joke, then frowns, lightly clears his throat. "Juana. I assume you have your own copy of Vieyra's sermons." I do. He asks to see them. Summoning the patience to indulge him his bit of theatre, I turn to send Antonia up, and find her already at the doorway. . . .

She comes back with a single volume. Gutiérrez asks if I don't have both. I explain that as far as I know the Portuguese edition collects the complete sermons in a single volume. My heart is sinking. There is something unpleasantly familiar in this turn of conversation.

"I'm sorry. I was referring to the Spanish editions. Could you have her bring them down?"

"I don't have them."

He thinks about this for a moment. "But surely you've seen them."

"Any reader of Castilian should really make the effort and read Vieyra in the Portuguese." *As I was saying to someone else a few months ago.* "What is it, Gutiérrez?"

His eyes are of a childlike roundness. "I'll let you see for yourself." He gets up to go. "I'm sorry to drag this out but there are a few things I want to look into before it gets too late. I'll be back first thing tomorrow."

Antonia sleeps downstairs tonight. She has been quiet since Gutiérrez's visit, as have I. After clearing away the dishes of a light *cena*, she stokes the fire and goes downstairs. Though it is dark, I find myself as often as not looking out one window or other. One to the south, from the library, another east from the bedroom, two looking east from the *sala*. I am awake when the chimes call us to Matins. It is not fully light. When Antonia does not meet me at the bottom of the stairs I go into her room, thinking she has slept through but she has gone on ahead.

In the past I have not spent much time dwelling on Archbishop Aguiar. There are unseen prospects and faces that it is as well not to contemplate too often, lest they begin to set themselves like hooks in the imagination. As has happened, apparently, in the mind of the Archbishop himself.

But now the stories of his near madness run endlessly through my mind. His famous bed of vermin . . . the bedding he has not allowed to be changed since his installation at his palace. His fear of poisoning. His refusal to eat food cooked by a woman's hand or to eat the meat of any female animal. His furious hatred of a woman's traces—our bodies, our perfumes, our voices, our singing. His loathing for cats. There was the time he had the flagstones of his palace replaced on the rumour a woman had walked across them while he was away at the Cathedral. The story of how his mother gave him up as an infant to be raised by the Church at the death of his father. The countless, laughable pretexts to boast of the antiquity of his family. And, of course, there is his vast acquaintance.

But now it seems I am the one who may have let her mind be overrun with fictions. It seems he has become *my* phantom, and with this letter I am now made his. A figment, a demon, and yet unlike the others, this demon is real, has a name, has a place, has taken a woman's voice and form. And now this Sor Juana incites others to follow her example, such as Sor Philothea.

But this is idle brooding. I have a more active brooding to do. These past few years the Archbishop has acted as if I did not exist, for reasons not unlike mine no doubt: for the horrible aspect the fact of my existence presents. God, O God, after the insult of this letter, after the discovery of this intrigue of an attack on Vieyra, and on top of this, the mockery these direct toward him . . . he will loathe and detest and abominate my very name.

The night has not been a pleasant one. Gutiérrez returns, but not first thing. It is mid-morning, windy. The sky is white, the light carries tints of faintest orange.

"Fires," shrugs Gutiérrez. "An infestation of some kind in the crops. *Mira*. Nothing yet about the Archbishop's state of mind. I do know Núñez has left for Zacatecas and will not be back before the new year. The Spanish editions," he says, handing them through the grille. "The '76 and the '78. See for yourself."

"Yes?"

"The first page," he says, watching me intently.

The first page. 1676 . . .

"Go on, now the other."

1678 . . . Both Spanish editions of the sermons of Antonio Vieyra . . . *'are dedicated by the author with respect and affection to don Francisco de Aguiar y Seijas . . .* Then, Bishop of Michoacan, now His Illustrious Grace the Lord Archbishop of New Spain.

Gutiérrez and I sit in silence for a while. I hold the books, closed, on my lap.

The connection is real. But it is not a connection, it is a *friendship*, and the friendship is deep. Once one contemplates the thing seriously, they do not altogether lack for things in common. The younger Jesuit who seeks a bishopric in New Spain writes to the greatest Jesuit in the New World. Now the one is Jesuit Inspector General for Brazil, the other Archbishop of Mexico. Both hated by the local authorities, though for very different reasons. But because a man is widely disliked it does not mean he has no friends. It may even be that His Grace is loved. By one man, a great man. Of an age to be his father. . . .

"I am informed," says Gutiérrez, "that they have been close correspondents for almost twenty years." He scratches the red tuft under his chin but for once the effect is not comical. "His Grace's secretary is in deep shock, and will be spending the Christmas season in Michoacan condoling with the Archbishop. Sor Juana, I cannot for the life of me tell you why, but the how is clear enough. Bishop Santa Cruz saw you did not know."

"The whole afternoon remains gallingly unclear but I do remember we had a nice long digression. What did I think of the Spanish translation? I said one should really read him in the Portuguese. And then he used almost your exact words. 'But the Spanish editions, you *have* seen them.'"

"To make absolutely certain."

"And then he tested me. To see if I'd correct him, if I knew of their correspondence. Santa Cruz let it slip that the Archbishop had never so much as met Vieyra. It must have been then. The haziness could really, I think, make me scream. He claimed he had just learned of it. . . . He had it on unimpeachable authority," I add, my face beginning to flush. It sounds like an excuse.

"It might even be true," Gutiérrez says graciously.

"I'm sure it is."

"I reread it last night. My copy." He shakes his head. "Unpublished it could have been so effective. But this, this is about something else entirely. I've been thinking about it all night. I'm at a loss. I'll keep checking around. But I don't want to stay too long."

"It was good of you to come. Don't make that face. Truly, I'm in your debt."

Gutiérrez gets up to go, checks himself, turns back. His freckled hands come to rest on the back of the chair.

"Just a thought . . . This business of haziness, vagueness. It would be better if you did not talk about this too much."

"What do you mean?"

"You're familiar with the guidelines for assessing mystical visions. Well, the principle is the same. The main criterion of distinction between a God-gifted vision and an intervention by the Enemy is exactly this. Clarity. Heaven forbid, but you may eventually be called to give testimony about this day. No shadows, no diabolical vagueness, only clear recollections. . . . Whatever you say, say it with your usual clarity."

I shouldn't keep him but suddenly do not want to see him leave.

"Gutiérrez . . . which sermon was the Archbishop to give?"

"*Heraclitus Defended*," he says, a smile swimming into the watery blue of his eyes. "The printers at Santo Domingo have a thousand copies they are not so sure they will be paid for. I can get you as many as you like. The price, I'm sure, will be reasonable."

Philothea's letter is neither a mistake nor a misunderstanding, neither lesson nor pique. These are not just provocations and threats, this is a betrayal—not even in the heat of anger but deliberate, premeditated for years, or months, or at least weeks. If the Archbishop's connection to Vieyra is a deep and abiding friendship, then without question Núñez would have known. And even he, even acting under Jesuit orders, would not have exposed himself and his career to Archbishop Aguiar's rage without seeking assurances. The rebuttal of a Jesuit by a Jesuit, a gesture made moreover in a Jesuit college rectory, marked the boundaries of their support for Vieyra and for the Archbishop himself. Of what Santa Cruz had led me to see, that much had been true. But the gesture sent *two* signals. The audience for the first one being the Holy Office itself and the Dominicans within it—but the second embedded within the first had a separate audience. The message was personal, from Antonio Núñez to Santa Cruz. Far more than offering his services as he had in the past, Núñez was indicating his readiness to switch allegiances from the present Archbishop to his clear successor—perhaps even to work, as Aguiar's confessor, to hasten the man's collapse. Responding to the signal or to the risk taken in sending it, Santa Cruz had come to Mexico to hear Núñez's proposition.

Arduous and pleasing holocaust for slaughter on the altars of Religion. This may as well be from Núñez's latest circular. Philothea speaks like Núñez far too often for it to be hazard. There can be no more escaping it. She is speaking *for* him, from him, of him. The Apostle Paul on women's learning . . . Augustine on gifts and responsibility, the whipping of Saint Jerome—beauty, obedience, the *galleon* . . .

It has happened. The thing I have worked so many years to prevent. Núñez has won Santa Cruz over. As Philothea has in so many ways been telling me. And if it happens to be true that Vieyra and the Archbishop have never met, Núñez will have known of this too. Santa Cruz's unimpeachable authority in my locutory that day was Núñez himself.

Núñez and Santa Cruz have found a common enemy.

 I will be clear, I must. Núñez and Santa Cruz. I should be flattered they have laid down arms, lain down together, the ox and the dog. The beast has two heads now. I will stop being such a fool. I will stop asking and asking why.

Why?

Why ask me for theology—why are sacred verses no longer enough? Why praise sacred verses, *if they are not enough? . . . not so harsh a censor as to condemn verses . . . a skill Saint Teresa and Saint Gregory of Nazianzus have sanctified. . . .* As examples of skill in verse, why use these? Why Teresa— whose skill as a poet was secondary—and not John of the Cross whose mastery was sublime? And if it is because she is a woman, why mention

Nazianzus at all? A vulgar poetaster, a dog in the manger who gave the order to burn . . .

It cannot be. All of this cannot be about the *Letras a Safo*—just because I did not leap at the chance to have Santa Cruz read my lyrics? For this, I was ungrateful?—and all this is just a bout of pique? But his face showed none of this. I see him getting up to leave that day. . . . He asks if I do not have something for him to read during the long carriage ride back to Puebla. "Something other than our Father Núñez's *Shriven Communicant*." I offer to send Antonia for the Vieyra sermons in Portuguese. He smiles, asking if he might not read instead some of these lyrics for Sappho he has been hearing about. Antonia pales, as I remember Carlos had earlier with the Viscount. I say the verses are not quite ready yet to be read. He accepts readily enough, saying something about the perfectionism of poets, and that he looks forward to reading the transcription of my negative *finezas* very soon.

He didn't even try. Who could be that petty? No. Not even Santa Cruz could be so vain. He had what he came for, the promise of my written arguments. Or was it that he resented having to hear of her lyrics from someone else? Someone more vulgar, someone who does censor verse, who does speak of them to everyone. Someone like Núñez. . . . Are *Las letras a Safo* Núñez's price? His prize. No. No. It can't be this.

The night is cold. Tired of pacing from window to window to desk to bed, I move into the sitting room. Antonia comes out of the library, where one has more room for pacing, and lights a fire in the hearth. She goes out and leaves me to my thoughts.

Gutiérrez is right. The haziness is not amusing, and 'dreamlike' is not comical. It is dangerous, for many reasons.

This is certainly a betrayal, but there is something else here, something more. I can't help thinking the preface that introduces it is only secondarily about my letter, or how Santa Cruz feels about it, or me, or even about telling the Inquisition why he publishes a tract so dubious. No, here too is a gesture. To show the world what he has done, and tell me what he may yet do.

In one stroke Sor Philothea publishes the nun who bests both the Archbishop's idol and Núñez, his captain. Pronouncing herself a follower of this nun, Philothea shows His Grace how his horror of Woman is become an object of general merriment even as Philothea slays the dragon herself. In binding all this up in the skullduggery after the sermon, Philothea flushes Núñez from cover, who has been working at cross-purposes behind the scenes. In this she drives a wedge between Núñez and the Archbishop, or rather burns Núñez's bridges and his ships, for in now speaking for Núñez she signals to all a switch in his allegiances without having to name the beneficiary. Any criticisms Philothea makes of the traits that the nun displays in her letters—want of humility, excess of worldliness, ingratitude, insubordination—apply equally to Núñez's conduct towards the Archbishop. Indeed should that final apoplectic crisis come now, let it be on the heads of Núñez and the nun.

The next move is of course mine. Which the Holy Office, now called publicly to attention, will be watching. Philothea does not even fear to raise the head of Cerberus.

One move. The breathtaking beauty of it. All question of causes and effects aside—and speaking only of the beauty of the game, for beauty's sake—how often can even a consummate player, even one such as Santa Cruz, expect to be offered such a move?

 When?

But can I not let this go? Surely it doesn't matter now, to know when my friend of seventeen years decided to do this. Or whether he came from Puebla to Mexico with at least some of this in mind. Perhaps he had sensed his opening in Núñez's latest overtures, a chance to humble me and capture Núñez in one move. Or maybe it was only in my locutory that he began to contemplate the possibilities. Coming to collect my letter and Núñez's manuscript as one does minor pieces; then Núñez's proposition, a slightly more important piece. Discovering next that a fiction planted by Santa Cruz himself had taken root in my mind: that I was unaware that the Archbishop's friendship with Vieyra was neither pretence nor another delusion. Sensing, in this, the most tempting hint of an ironic symmetry: my scorn of Núñez's manuscript dedication to a knowing bishop, my ignorance of Vieyra's to the Archbishop, a man he'd never met.

And now Santa Cruz has Núñez, too. It seems to be what Núñez wanted. Well then, they have each other. But Santa Cruz's fury over Saint Bernard would not have been feigned—he was afraid Núñez and I, in our resumption of hostilities, would spoil things before it was time and rearrange the pieces on the board. What ecstasies of anticipation Santa Cruz must have suffered!

Now I have at least an answer. All the answer I will likely ever have. And it is a mercy to see something clearly, if even just this one instant, during our chess lesson that day, something suggested to him by the game itself. . . . This is the moment. The most spectacular gambit of all.

Bishop Santa Cruz has sacrificed his queen.

The gambit he himself taught me, an extension of our lessons, brought now into the world for all to see. We are not to take this as a betrayal but as a sacrifice. It is one thing to do it on a board. How many can execute it in the flesh?

I see the hour. The late afternoon light angles through the window bars, strikes a painting on the north wall, filters through the boughs and leaves of the rosewood grille. Tomasina and Ana moving back and forth, refilling bowls of chocolate, replacing half-empty trays of sweets and fruit. The light falling across the board, the chess pieces clustered in one corner. Black has just retired, its king mated. I have never beaten him. Santa Cruz is being gracious, but clearly had I been a more experienced player he would not have mistaken my queen sacrifice for inattention.

"I thought your mind was elsewhere," he said simply. "But . . . humility is a most democratic virtue, whose benefits apply equally to all. The mortification in my defeat I take as a favour."

It is the sort of thing I expect him to say with irony. But his dark eyes are liquid and full. Neither anger nor hurt, not mortification. Almost . . . gratitude. But for what? Of course—I have released him from the scrupling of his conscience, whatever that might be. But no, it is not that. His boyishness has never been more manifest than in that instant. He is leaning back . . . crumbs of sugary crust lie in the purple folds of his cassock, sugar crystals in his small moustache. I had never thought of him as anything but relaxed, but all the tensions in his face I see now are gone.

In his eyes, all the affection and goodness of a child after the most severe punishment, and yet deserved. A guilt not purged but absolved.

And then the moment passes without my quite seeing it. Seizing upon this idea of defeat as a favour, to ease his embarrassment at being beaten by a novice, I launch into my own earnest effusions on the negative expressions of God's love, the withholding of his favours, which we shall surely abuse and for which we show the foulest ingratitude. And permitting Santa Cruz to glimpse it—just the possibility of answering my insufficient gratitude for his many favours with a salutary correction, a negative *fineza* so sublime . . .

Is it possible that the affair turns on the fortunes of a moment? A stroke of hazard: the conjunction of a game and a chance remark. Is it possible that one without the other might not have been enough?

Six months later the opening presents itself. The Archbishop lets it quietly be known that he will follow the Maundy Thursday with a Vieyra sermon of his own. In this, Santa Cruz must indeed have seen the hand of Providence, a blessing, a sign of *favour* for his strategy, the negative *fineza* of his sacrifice. For the great players, there are days when one plays with such a brilliance. It is as if the game is guided by another hand. . . .

Then the game is up. It was just a game: the consummate player lives to play his queen again. For I am more in need of his favours than ever. Now he will teach me a deeper gratitude. Favours I will not take so lightly. Favours I shall crave desperately. My very life is in his hands. My teacher teaching me still the ways of the game.

 A lifetime of shoring up defences. A bishop blocks a priest, a vice-queen holds an archbishop in check. Then she leaves, the bishop wants promotion, it all collapses. No one expects an accounting, no one demands to hear your excuses. Just a game you lose, then disappear.

But it is not a situation that lacks for humour. One has only to work at it a bit. One may of course win a battle and lose the war. I find myself entering a new stage, exploring a more extreme hypothesis. That I, Juana Inés de la Cruz, Sor, can win every battle and still lose everything.

For the game is not up at all. And he is a fool if he thinks he can control the Holy Office. He only thinks he knows where this may lead, and my redeemer may soon have to look to himself. No one controls them once they begin. It is why even kings do everything they can to give them no reason to start. Even the Sun King. Insubordination to popes is one thing, but Bishop Bossuet keeps him from offending against the Sacred Canons.

On Friday, the first leaflet appears. It is the Feast Day of the Immaculate Conception, the eighth of December, 1690. Yes, Gutiérrez, let us be clear. The moment is chosen to heighten the outrage. The leaflet rants, the leaflet raves. It is signed 'the Soldier.' Not long after, a second leaflet by the Soldier. It refers to a certain nun's *Sapphic Hymns*. Núñez. The phrase was first his, a deliberate distortion of the title, but he has been speaking against them for years. These things take on a life of their own. Their life now is blasphemy.

The leaflet inveighs against the only verse I recall having published that refers, alludes to or in any way hints of Sappho. *Sáfico,* I shall tell them, is a dactyl.

Elación, arrogance in a woman, disobedience, ingratitude.

Now the hay cart starts to run downhill. Next come the sermons of attack. My friends scrambling to plan a defence. Better, I say, to give no answer at all. Let it lie, let it rest. So far there have just been threats. By the Feast of the Epiphany, the furore may have died down; the people will have had Christmas. It is the people the Holy Office will not see troubled. But I fear there is no stopping it.

It is the work of convents to pray for the well-being of the community that supports us. For the surrounding neighbourhoods, to take their sin and suffering upon ourselves. But now Mother Andrea calls for special prayers to be said for the convent of San Jerónimo itself, for deliverance from the threat that hangs over us, the shadow that has fallen across our good name. My fellow sisters file past the door of my cell with looks askance. They seem to find me somewhat unlucky these days. But what do they *want* from me?—to waste my life gossiping mindlessly at the convent grate? Is this so becoming of a nun? The whole convent savours seeing me stumble—*ah maybe her life is not charmed, after all, her intelligence not quite divine. Seems like she was over-reaching . . . perhaps she would have seen this coming if she'd lifted her head out of her books for once. So it took the Bishop of Puebla to put her in her place. At last! She wouldn't dare defy him now. She needs his protection more than ever. . . .*

I've done everything they ask! Entertain the Viceroy?—I do it weakly, meekly, weekly. *She's too worldly.* I remain in seclusion. *She's too good for us, standoffish, selfish*—I hold classes, direct plays, direct the convent's finances —*she's trying to take over. Just like the Spaniards—she prefers them, you know. Like Malinche did, Cortés's whore*—so I write Mexica *tocotines,* reams of popular verses in dialect. Now I'm pandering to the rabble. *Her mother's half-Indian they say.*

Yes, write verses, says Philothea. But write on theology. And here is a taste of how it is for women theologians, how it is when the Muse takes up the quill. Can Santa Cruz not see what Núñez has known all along?—if I take up theology they'll have me a heretic by the end of the week.

Theology was the last thing Núñez wanted. It is why he burned my journals fifteen years ago. It is how I finally escaped his command that I write for him. If Santa Cruz speaks for Núñez now, how can he ask this of me? How can they even want the same thing? What is it? *What do they want from me?*

They implicate me in order to attack each other. They reconcile in order to see me punished.

Without a doubt the Archbishop wants me destroyed. The Holy Office is now at least curious, and Santa Cruz cannot be sure he can stop it. Núñez, on the other hand, has given me fair warning. He said I would destroy myself. Is this is what they want?—to see me destroy myself?

How? What would permit them to orchestrate it? What little manoeuvres and adjustments? Something I will write, something rash, ill-conceived? Something I'm writing now. Is the Saint Catherine commission a trap? Or is it something I have already written? What would hurt the most, humiliate best, give the most satisfaction, what would be their most negative finesse? Something I might refuse to give up, too intimate, too painful to let them paw over. And in refusing to hand it over, to repudiate it—and in the writing itself—all will see how the arrogant nun has brought this upon herself.

To prove their correction is just, what might I be asked to surrender? . . . as the ships of the alliance fill the horizon. An armada of men schooled in the affairs of the world, who send a message, who bring a lesson. To teach us our abecedario, to bring us our primers. Egypt taught us our first letters, but Athens is our first school. Lesson number one. No one stands apart. There is no neutral ground. Lesson number two. Give way to the greater force, that takes itself for a force of nature—the volcano, the quake, the flood. Lesson number three. Loyalty and justice are only questions among equals. The rest must choose. Slavery and criminal cowardice on the left. Or annihilation on the right.

Left. Or right. Decide. But we are children who know not our left from our right. Where is Athena, wise Athena now? Does she hover still over Athens, as the Dove broods upon the abyss? They come to set the dice upon us, and the dogs. Whom shall I call to defend us? Perhaps Antonio Vieyra, who saw the needs of others as no impediment to his pursuit of greatness. . . . Is this the irony they want me to see at the end?

Extract from Sister Philothea of the Cross (II)

Trusting to this analysis, I do not intend that you curb your genius by renouncing books; only that you elevate it by reading from time to time in the book of Jesus Christ. . . .

Was there ever a more learned people than Egypt's? With them began the first letters of the world and the marvels of their hieroglyphs. Such was the wisdom of Joseph that the Holy Scriptures call him a past master of Egyptian learning. Nonetheless, the Holy Ghost plainly states the Egyptian people are barbarians: for at best their learning penetrated to the movements of the stars and heavens, but did nothing to rein in the disorder of the passions. Their science aimed to perfect Man's political life without enlightening his journey toward the eternal. . . .

Study not ultimately consecrated to the Crucified Christ and Redeemer is wicked folly, sheer vanity. Human letters are mere slaves that may occasionally be used to serve the Divine. . . .

Angels scourged Saint Jerome for reading Cicero and for having preferred, as if a bondslave and not someone free, the seductiveness of eloquence to the solidity of Holy Scripture; yet this Saintly Doctor of the Church did at last come to make exemplary use of secular learning and letters. . . .

What a pity that so great a mind as yours has stooped to a base acquaintance with the world without desiring to know what goes on in Heaven; but sullying itself on the earth, let it not descend yet further, to discover what goes on in Hell. And, if that mind should ever crave for sweet and tender demonstrations of love, let it direct its apprehension to the hill of Calvary, where, observing the *finezas* of the Redeemer and the ungratefulness of the redeemed, your intellect should find a limitless scope to examine the excesses of infinite love and to derive, not without tears, fine formulas of atonement at the very summits of ingratitude. Or, at other times, indeed let the rich galleon of your genius sail freely, but on the high seas of the divine perfections. I do not doubt that it would go with you as it did with Apelles who found, while painting the portrait of Campaspe, that for every brushstroke he applied to the canvas, love sent an arrow into his heart, thus leaving, in the end, a portrait painted to perfection and a painter's heart mortally wounded with the love of his subject. . . .

I am quite certain that if, with your great powers of understanding, you formed and depicted a concept of the divine perfections (to the limits permitted within the shadows of faith), you would find your soul illustrated with such brilliance, your will in an embrace of fire, your heart sweetly wounded by the love of its God, so that this Lord, who in the sphere of nature has so abundantly showered you with positive favours, does not feel obliged to rain purely negative ones down upon you in the supernatural. . . .

This is desired for my lady by one who, since kissing her hand so many years ago, lives still enamoured of her soul, a love which neither time nor distance has any power to cool, for a spiritual love admits not of change, nor grows save in purity. . . .

From the Convent of the Holy Trinity of Puebla de los Angeles, on this the 25th day of November, 1690.

Your devoted servant kisses your hands.

Philothea de la Cruz

Phoenix BOOK FOUR

CONTENTS

What kind of sorcerer's brew
did the Indians confect—
the herb-doctors of my country—
to make my scrawls cast this spell?

JUANA INÉS
DE LA CRUZ,

"Herb-Doctors"

B. Limosneros, trans.

NE PLUS
ULTRA

wo long months had I been given to consider my situation. Sor Philothea's preface to the letter so worthy of Athena was dated November 25, 1690. The first leaflet denouncing it appeared on December 8th, the Feast of the Immaculate Conception. The leaflet was signed simply *the Soldier*, who fairly wrung his spleen dry. And though he used phrases I was sure he had heard from Núñez, truly was the good soldier all but deranged—raving, emotional, unable to follow a train of argument, and I could not help wondering if the author was not His Grace the Archbishop himself.

On the third Sunday of Advent, a new series of leaflets appeared, all signed *the Soldier*. Polished, learned, theological. Sane. Now there were two soldiers. This one's denunciations branched out, amplifying on the hints Sor Philothea had obligingly given the Holy Office. The negative *finezas* were clearly and foully heretical. As for Sor Juana, the list of her heresies was long, and would grow. *Illuminist. Gnostic. Arian.*

The inventory was unnerving enough. Surely we had to do something, my many friends urged—write a response, mount a defence. But so far the Inquisition's involvement was unofficial. It would be undignified for them to display the least sign of haste, in moving against a mere woman especially. The people themselves must be seen to clamour for protection, yet the *vulgo* had thus far been quiet—no, not quiet but Decembers offered much else to talk of.

January was a quieter month. Though the days were lengthening, the nights were longer.

The day after Epiphany another run of leaflets flared up, these ones signed. Manuel Serrano, Franciso Ildefonso—two non-entities from Puebla, along with five other complete obscurities. *My seven slanderers, my impugners, my persecutors.*

On the second Sunday in January the sermons of attack began all over the city. There was no stopping it now, and no stopping my friends, who had taken to meeting without me, since I would do nothing to help myself. They had to have Father Xavier Palavicino. Palavicino was ambitious, brave, eloquent, and a great admirer of the much slandered nun. Here in the temple, before the month was out, my attackers would have our answer.

Most Sundays, the only threats to the calm of a solemn Mass are the neighbourhood delinquents who have made a sort of ball court of the plaza. The double doors giving onto the ball court, while thick, are in such poor repair as to let bright brawling day sift in through the rifts and splits in the thick oak panelling. On a crisp Sunday morning in January there may be two dozen children outside, and it can sound as if there are twice that number. As Xavier Palavicino waded ever more perilously into his discourse, I found myself praying for another hundred young scufflers to drop by for a game outside.

Father Palavicino chose his moment carefully if not his words. The date being the feast day of the learned widow Santa Paula. Our convent chapel had received distinguished visitors before, but rarely in such numbers. Front row, centre, kneeling on cushions, were the Viceroy and Vicereine, the Count and Countess de la Granja. On her right the Archbishop's Vicar-General. On the Viceroy's left a nobleman from the highest ranks of the Spanish aristocracy, exiled to Manila and sufficiently forgiven since then to make his way back as far as Mexico. Beside him the fallen angel of Versailles, le Vicomte d'Anjou. Three rows back is a Creole suspected of sedition on whose behalf I had once interceded with María Luisa, to secure his early release from prison. Though he perhaps meant well, his presence was not a comfort.

Standing as it does on the compound's north side, our chapel is notable for its cool, and can be quite icy on winter mornings. Notable also for its tranquillity—when not a ball court—a place where I have spent many quiet hours. This January morning our chapel offered neither calm nor quiet. Never, I would wager, had the Holy Office been so well represented here. Consultors and familiars, assessors and censors, prosecutors and examiners, one by one they filtered in, in all the sulphurous pomp of their offices. Even the Holy Tribunal's accountant put in an appearance, who rarely partakes of anything more carnal than the inventories of iron tools and personal effects. Even our Reverend Father Antonio Núñez de Miranda himself was there. Slowly, from where we sat behind the chancel lattice, the whispers among the sisters of St. Jerome rose in fits and gasps—at the entrance of each new official—to a pitch of strangled panic; until finally the Prioress was forced to rise, and striding before us at the grillwork—quenching light as she advanced, shedding it in spokes—furiously gestured for silence as our guest began to speak.

And as he commenced, the quills of half a dozen secretaries seated at little writing desks in the aisles scratched like dogs at a kitchen door.

To the nave of our chapel now I saw drawn every rift and resentment, Dominicans to port, Jesuits to starboard—patterned like filings scattered on a parchment—no, arraigned along the axis of a needle pointing to a nun hidden in the upper choir. Who diverts herself with conceits such as these.

It would be saying too much to claim that Father Palavicino's discourse was in my defence, as indeed he did, say too much. He began by predicating a more conservative position than mine on Christ's *fineza major,* His greatest expression of love for Man. But even though taking a position somewhat distanced from my own, Palavicino did not contest the propriety of a woman, a nun, *taking* a position, and this would have been all the defence I could have asked. For then he did a brave thing, given his auditors, whose attendance he may not have predicted but by now was well aware of. Xavier Palavicino looked the Chief Inquisitors squarely in the eye, and opened with a quote from Jonah: *'Now the Lord had prepared a great fish to swallow up Jonah.' And now this bride of Christ, our Minerva of America, has been summoned as a great fish to bear us up her prophecies, and to cause many a holy doctor to shake the dust from his books and sharpen his wits.*

With Father Núñez, half-blind, somewhere below us in the chapel, Palavicino defended me against the blind depredations of the Soldier, this Soldier of Castile. Palavicino praised my intelligence, the deep learning implicit in my position, my grace in stating it. He was only echoing, in this, the published judgement of a bishop-nun but if I was not mistaken, much dust would indeed be shaken, many quills sharpened. What kind of black mirth would the fishers of souls make on this one day? Why did he not come to me first? Still am I treated like a child in theological matters, *un menor de edad*—speak when consulted, theologian's muse. They do not need a woman to tell them how to act—to think, perhaps—but action requires courage. Yes, gentlemen, but thinking requires *thought.*

Still, who was I to criticize anyone for this?

Minerva, pagan goddess . . . Letter Worthy of Athena, her prophecies . . . a great fish—this last he said knowing I was writing carols for the cathedral on Saint Peter, fisherman. The allusion no doubt struck him as clever.

Oh yes, and glaring down at the Inquisition's saintly officers, Father Palavicino likened my persecution to the persecutions of Christ.

My defender qualified me as an innocent lamb, spoke of a *wound in my side* from the Soldier's cruel lance. What on earth or in heaven's name had made him think to say this?—another helpful friend comparing me with *Christ*. Was he completely mad?

With defenders such as these . . .

Worse, it was not even me they defended—woman, prophetess, leviathan—nor any living creature at all. It was a principle they made of me. Some new category. They were like men born to the desert: rain they had seen, small springs, salt lakes, storm-born freshets foaming into sand—yet coming over the last dune at the world's end, what they saw was mere water no longer but the *gates of Atlantis.*

Irony or iron consequence? For I had been the one to play this category game for them, lead the merry chase through monster, muse, paragon, virgin—the female in me being thus incompleted uncoupled unachieved, the dam of our perfidy not yet burst in me—they presumed to praise me as all but a man in *validez y valor.*

In my locutory afterwards the mood was somewhat glum. Each of my visitors had been at the sermon, but as the parlours were not opened Sundays until three, all made the trip back by their own separate paths, presumably to see how I was bearing up. Ribera was sitting in an ox-hide chair at the grille nearest the clavichord. Dean de la Sierra had not taken a seat at all, but stood rummaging in the bookshelf against the east wall. Carlos sat next to Ribera but not quite at the grille, as if he too were less than keen for a good frank talk. First to arrive, our convent chaplain sat quietly on a bench by the window closest to the door while I tried to cheer things up. I was becoming not a little resentful, not only of my lack of success but that it should fall to me, in the circumstances, to do such a lot of cheering.

Palavicino arrived last, and had a choice of the bench beside the chaplain or the armchair next to Gutiérrez, who had not been here for weeks yet appeared now. Slumping down beside the chaplain, Palavicino told of being accosted outside the chapel by a raving madman who had denounced the sermon in my defence as heretical. As Palavicino pronounced the word it took every mite of self-possesion not to glance at the Inquisitor Gutiérrez, who was staring at the chandelier.

Just then, a small new personage dropped by on his way to the palace to present his credentials. Baron Anthonio Crisafi gave the general

impression of being the Sicilian envoy of the Spanish viceregal administration of southern Italy. I had not known we needed one of these. There
was something funny and flighty about his eyes, which seemed never
quite to meet mine. Although in better days I would have found his presence in every way comical he quickly proved much better informed than
could be expected of a recent arrival, and moreover was taking pains to
make clear that his information extended to me. He had arrived knowing that on my locutory wall was a copy of Velázquez's portrait of a
geographer—more improbably still, he knew that the painter's model
was a lunatic at the court of Philip IV.

Glancing about him, the Baron took the empty armchair and as he
sat, pulled it closer to the grille. He was all but telling me he came from
Spain with a message from María Luisa. And yet I did not trust him. I
had been having some trouble lately telling my friends from my
adversaries.

Trying to marshal my wits I launched into a little peroration on the
portrait's true subject: Democritus, the laughing philosopher—a man so
ruled by candour, the people of his own village thought him insane. I had
the distinct impression the Sicilian knew this, too, perfectly well. *Who has
sent him? If it is María Luisa, why has she sent him knowing this?* Lest the frantic workings of my mind show in my face, I rose and made my way to the
back of the room to pace back and forth, I hoped theatrically—the nun
beneath the globe beneath the lunatic on the wall—as I cobbled together
a few ideas from bits of Justinian,[†] and from Mondragón's treatise on the
virtues of insanity and the holy truths of the mad.

[†]Byzantine emperor
and lawgiver

"Indeed, *mis señores*, we the sane, who never cease to thirst for conquest—to rule, found cities and cultivate our own holdings—can only
look with envy on the estate of the one we call mad. *El loco* pays neither
tax nor tribute, suffers neither vassalage nor servitude. Small wonder
kings seek his candid councils, and the slyest of the sane feign holy
madness. . . ."

This won a few wistful nods from the *cuerdos*[†] among my interlocutors.

[†]the sane

"In the ears of the king, gentlemen, such sooths are bittersweet, but
in the eyes of Democritus are so filled with gall he puts them out to
maintain his philosophy of cheer. . . ."

The Sicilian may have known all about the gravity of my situation
and all about the painting—nevertheless he looked slightly dazed by the
shift in tone. Foreigners—even the Spaniards themselves—were never

quite prepared for the intensity of this game the way we play it, we the children of Spain and Mexico. The blood in the lace, the sword in the cape, the red in the tooth as we smile. I was thinking to draw the 'Ambassador' out, but in truth there was something I could no longer quite trust in such jests. It was a loss of dexterity I found unsettling.

"What say you, Baron—does not the lunatic's smile as he contemplates the world make elegant comment on the philosophy of cheer?"

"*La Casa del Nuncio*," the Baron blurted, "in *Toledo*, Sor Juana, is not to be missed."

What was this? What was he trying to tell me? "Has the Ambassador visited many of Spain's *casas de locos* during his travels?" I asked. "They are a great favourite, I understand, of foreign visitors."

"Yes, Sor Juana, that is true."

"And do foreign noblemen come expressly to such houses, as in Lope's day, to shop for a suitable fool to return home with?"

"They do."

"And you've seen them at palaces other than Madrid's?"

"In fact, yes."

I left off pacing, making my way somewhat absent-mindedly to my seat by the grille. Of course the House of the Messenger was a madhouse famous throughout Europe, fools and gold being Spain's last remaining exports. But it was the way he stressed its location. . . . I racked my brain for the rather-too-much I knew of Toledo—eighteen Church councils, capital of the Visigoths, of Saint Hermenegild and the Arian heresy—the royal seat of Alfonso, Emperor of the Two Faiths . . . of El Cid, El Greco, La Mancha and Quixote, the ancestral castle of the falconer López de Ayala . . .

Seeing me at a complete loss the Baron bent to extract a small packet from his satchel. "I had planned to present this once we knew each other better. But I think this is the moment after all." He took the book from a soft wrap of oiled leather. "I have heard that you read Italian."

"From whom, Baron, may I ask?"

"Perhaps the most original and most daring poetry written in this century. On *our* peninsula, at least."

The Scelta. Campanella's *Scelta* was written in an Inquisition prison cell after a plot to expel the Spanish from Calabria.

Thanking him, I rose quickly and placed the book on the shelf farthest from the grille. Would there be a message tucked in its pages? From

María Luisa, perhaps? But no, this was the worst sort of book to conceal a message in. The message had to be the book itself—but what?

There was so much to consider, I was relieved to see him rising to go. When he had taken leave of us, the chaplain took the opportunity to see him to the street.

"Someone has sent him from Madrid," offered Ribera.

"Or even Sicily," added Carlos dryly.

"Or else Rome," said Gutiérrez. He had not asked about the book. The tone was casual.

In the silence after 'Rome' was let fall, Palavicino sat stewing. De la Sierra had been standing by the bookcase nearest the exit for half an hour, and I had begun to wonder if he would be back. As Dean of the Cathedral and the Archbishop's Vicar-General, his presence here before today had already been barely tenable. Father Xavier Palavicino was the next to find an excuse to leave, a plea for forgiveness in his eyes, a man with much on his mind. Well, no matter, it was good of him to come.

Who were these men in my locutory? Which were foes, which friends? And which had the capacity to do me greater harm—maleficence, accident or foolish acts in my defence? It was dawning on me that a fate might be decided by questions such as these, and by such men, as much as by my own actions. I could not quite decide whether to feel fury first or make straight for terror.

I had had enough of company. It was time to clear the room.

Reverting to my disquisition on lunacy and cheer, I reminded them it was always like this. Each time a new Viceroy arrived. You make too much of it, dear friends. Remember? The threats, the manoeuvres, the betrayals . . . it goes on for years. You've just forgotten. Things looked so much darker ten years ago, and yet for these ten years, have I not seen my freedoms multiply? I am not free to travel, but yet the world freely comes to me. Half the gentry of Europe files through this locutory; half the books we here are not free to buy, they bring over as gifts. The thoughts I am still not free to write openly, I have only to ply in parables and allegories; while whatever I am too cautious to publish gets published for me. Even the learned Inquisitors bring their proofs and arguments now for my candid opinions, too freely given.

Gutiérrez, slightly flushed, edged for the door.

Come again, Gutiérrez, come again soon.

The Dean chose that moment to give me the news that my commission for the Feast of Saint Peter had been cancelled. And this with barely an apology, though I knew the final decision on this was at least technically his. What Dean de la Sierra wished to impress upon me instead was that the Archbishop did not even bother to consult him before announcing it.

I answered that, as the Dean himself had admitted, *while approving my lyrics,* the common people needed a voice for their hardships and grievances, which were proving especially painful this year. Returning his book to the shelf, he was good enough to concede this again, before slipping out. Once he had, Ribera told me Agustín Dorantes had dropped by yesterday with an offer to help him rewrite my lyrics on Saint Peter. Dorantes was a passable rhymer and before my time had been the man most often favoured with such commissions.

Agustín Dorantes was also Master Examiner of the Inquisition. The man most likely to preside over a process against Palavicino's sermon.

Many came to the chapel that day, but Dorantes was not among them. Many explanations were possible but the most likely was this: he was already involved. It would not do for the Chief Magistrate to be present where and while evidence was being gathered. There could be little doubt the Holy Office's involvement was now official. But the case could not yet have been Palavicino's—

No. Though there might be a file opened against him soon, the Holy Office did not move so quickly. The case was not Palavicino's, the case was mine.

But Núñez, Father Núñez *had* come. Could that mean he was not involved? How very curious the sensation, seeing him in the chapel. He had not changed so much these past ten years, not so much as I might have thought. It was clear the young monk walking with him was less assistant than guide, but other than in the decline of his sight, he seemed no more ancient than he always had. Ten years earlier, almost to the day, we had spoken of Hermenegild in prison—Núñez had never been so threatening.

Choose, he said, a convent or a prison cell. I answered then with Herakles. How should I answer now?

Why neither, Father. There are as many thralls among the free as there are follies among the sane. Just so many mad slaves to honour, romance, lust, necessity. But not you nor any other shall ever make a prison of my mind. Irons are not all iron, yet they hobble. Bars are not all wrought, yet ring and girdle. Stays are not all of whalebone, but detain us only if we let them.

How like empty bravado this sounded, ten years on.

"You think this one of your little comedies, Sor Juana, but this sacrament of water may well matryr you," Father Núñez had said, exactly ten years ago. "Just how far are you willing to go, Juana? As far as Galileo?—or *plus ultra,* as far as Bruno."

It was late in the locutory. All but two of my guests had left. The *escuchas* were washing up behind the arras, speaking in whispers. Ribera had been working at something quietly on the clavichord. He rose to leave, promising to return soon. He had an idea for a new musical project for us but had to go straightaway to consult someone. Only Carlos remained, leaning quietly against the wall, over by the window. He had secured a commission to write a chronicle of our Viceroy's great naval victory in Santo Domingo. We were sure the actual news of it must arrive any day. Carlos was trying to persuade me to write a dedicatory poem to open the chronicle. A show of loyalty to the Crown should be a welcome opportunity, for both of us. Things had never been easy between the new viceroyals and me, with her especially. They arrived with the presumption that I would serve them as enthusiastically as I had served past viceroys and vicereines, and rather more blindly.

"What can it hurt now?" Carlos asked, coming to sit across from me.

I had been thinking there was at least one other message in the *Scelta:* the perils of a person of the cloth meddling in worldly matters. But after today's events I had begun to wonder if doing nothing was a luxury I had.

"So tell me please about his great naval triumph. Is it fair to say the French in Santo Domingo—and *where* else?—would have been rather heavily outnumbered?"

"Tortuga. And yes, heavily."

"You have a title?"

"*Trophy of Spanish Justice in the Punishment of French Perfidy.*"

"Stirring. We might actually win."

"Yes."

"I can't bear her."

"The Vice-Queen."

"I assume her husband did little more than relay Madrid's orders to the fleet?"

"Correct."

Another commission. The very thought. . . . Such a lassitude I felt. Even the carols to Saint Catherine, which I had wanted so badly, I was barely a week from finishing and yet could not. I could only dread what use Bishop Santa Cruz might yet put them to.

Antonia had made her way finally through the *portería* and along the corridor to join Carlos on the visitors' side. Quietly, listening to every word, she went about the room collecting dishes and depositing them where we on our side could reach them. I envied her the freedom in this humble task, a freedom she would say meant nothing to her, who wanted only to be on the other side, with me.

"Was I so very arrogant, Carlos, or too weak? Should I have forced the issue ten years ago, while don Payo was still Archbishop? Would I be better off now?"

"Or incomparably worse."

"Truly, things did look so much darker then. Don Payo gone, then news of the *auto* in Madrid, then the comet. . . ."

"A nice test of your scientific principles."

"Listening to the Sicilian today, as we talked about *nuncios* and madhouses—and then that remark about Toledo, I was thinking that for some games one may know too much."

"Too much . . ."

"Too much to solve it, to bear not finding the answer, or finding one. Too many answers to bear."

"Such as?"

"Things, facts . . . That the onset of the Thirty Years War was remembered for the three comets of that year. That while all Europe watched them through his telescope Galileo was too ill to get up and look at them. That his troubles with the Jesuits began with the one event he did not see, with the facts he did not observe."

"Yours sound like facts in search of a hypothesis."

"That at the death of Caesar, who had declared himself emperor, a comet hung over Rome for six months—and who is to say the Archbishop does not owe some facet of his election to the effect of a comet?"

"I ask you again, are you so sure it would be better if Bishop Santa Cruz were Archbishop now?"

He was right, of course. Such a curious instrument was this chronoscope that is memory. One had only to look through it a second time to see the whole world inverted. And yet a third glance did not right things.

Núñez, who was surely my enemy now—could it be that day he had still been acting as a friend? Ten years ago it looked like madness to stay with him. Was I to think now it had been madness to dismiss him? Better or worse, then, to have refused every commission . . . and watched every special privilege I have won in here evaporate. Watched the thousand leaden chores and communal tasks here close over my head like the sea . . . accountant, peacemaker, Superintendant of Works and Masonry, paymaster, catechist. Explaining the sermons, chiding the novices, leading the choir.

And now I sat here envying Antonia's freedom to pick up dishes.

Curious inversions these.

Next to the window, Antonia's gatherings accumulated on the little table that spanned the grille. Glasses and decanters, flasks and cups, a city of glass in the setting sun—smudged glass towers and crystal minarets, inverted cones and earthen domes . . . a city of the sun on its own plateau, rising up against a plain of roses crossed in shadows.

Answer the question, decide.

I got up to help Antonia with the dishes. Carlos bade us good-night.

As we finished, the last light fell across the rose bushes outside the window. The little courtyard lay in shadow. The Prioress came to stand at her balcony, looked down a moment at the locutory, then faded into her apartments to light the lamps. I set the Ambassador's gift on a chair by the doorway. I would send Antonia to him tomorrow, ask that he return at his earliest convenience. It had come to me, what I had been trying to remember since the Sicilian left.

After the rebellion in Calabria, Campanella feigned madness to save his life.

For an hour, sad thought,
let us pretend
I am happy
though I know I am not:
  since they say what afflicts us
has its conceiving in the mind,
to imagine ourselves blest
is to be a bit less wretched.
  Oh that my mind this once,
should serve to bring me peace,
that it not always run
counter to my ease.
  The whole world holds convictions
of such divergent kinds
that what one deems black,
another proves white.
  What entrances some
enrages others;
and what this one finds irksome
adds to that one's comfort.
  He who is sorrowing says
the happy man is heartless;
and he who is joyful smiles,
to see the sufferer in his toils.
  Those two thinkers of Greece[†]
long pondered the matter:
for what brought the first to laugh,
to the second brought grief.
 Famous has their opposition
been these twenty centuries,
yet without a resolution
that can so much as be divined;
  to their two banners even now,
the world entire is drawn,
with the colours that we follow
determined by our disposition.
  Democritus claiming that our one
worthy answer to the world is laughter;
Heraclitus that the world's misfortunes
are cause for lamentation . . .

JUANA INÉS
DE LA CRUZ

B. Limosneros, trans.

[†]Democritus,
Heraclitus

unday, January 28th. The bells of three o'clock, two hours more to Lauds.

On the Friday night after Xavier Palavicino's sermon, I did finally sleep. Antonia woke me at daybreak or I would have slept through prayers. During these, the coldest nights of winter, when we woke to frost on the flagstones and ice on the *tinacos*, she would often sleep on a cot by the fire in the library. At midnight I sent her in to sleep in my bed, preferring to read the Sicilian's gift with my back against the chimney. I doubted she would sleep much either, but she liked it there.

It had not been easy to be with her these past two months. She took the letter, the pamphlets, the sermon, hard—raged at him—quite refused to see that Santa Cruz had done anything at all for her sisters, and she was very close to rage with me for doing too little to defend myself. It was true, I'd done little but brood. Yes, brooding I was doing rather a lot of.

In the hours since the sermon I had been going over the entire day, the Sicilian's visit, the gift . . .

After writing his *City of the Sun,* after the uprising in Calabria, Campanella lived twenty-seven years in the Inquisition's prisons, feigning madness to stay the proceedings against him. But reading his *Scelta* I wondered what kind of madness this could have been, and what kind of prison, that he could write such poetry there. How did his madshows seem? Were they ever the same, or different each time: did he laugh, did he cry, did he tear his hair, bring himself to grief? I wondered if he ever, for an instant, lost his mind, I wondered if he ever, for a moment, forgot his lines. I wondered, if I were to feign madness, what kind I might try. There were so many kinds.

There was the lunacy of the court buffoon; there were the rages and fears of His Grace the Archbishop, his hatred of us, of all things that give pleasure; there was the sad and yet laughable madness in his choice of Heraclitus for the Gaudete Sunday sermon. Gaudete, 'rejoicing.' Heraclitus, 'the weeping philosopher.' Which is to say, if one may not laugh on this of all days, then one must weep ever. Or brood.

In June they had cancelled my lyrics for the sisters of Saint Bernard, in December my lyrics on the Nativity. Now those for Saint Peter, fisherman. How was the poet to feel about this, what was she to say? It was not so very far from madness—but whose? That of Democritus who finds comedy where there is confusion, and puts out his eyes to preserve his vision? That of the geographer, the dizzy simpleton bestowing his simple blessings on the globe as it spins by too fast?—or perhaps it is his head that spins too fast.

It felt like illness, it tasted like bile. Was the geographer seasick, did he need to rest awhile? Perhaps the geographer was only lost. No, it felt like falling. It truly did. A sickness not of floating bodies but of falling ones. Which only made sense, after all. The sane objection to the world as globe was always that at bottom one must fall off. And yet even the mad geographer couldn't have it both ways, he had to decide: round or flat, floating or falling, convent cell or prison cell—

Or madhouse. For the sensation now was very much like falling—up. This madness of mine, this madness of the mind that spins too fast, that finds comedy where there is none, yes, but also threads of mystery everywhere and signs, always signs and holy messages. Where there were none. As here, in the coincidence of Democritus and Heraclitus, about whom I myself have written . . . in my first volume for María Luisa. Two holy messengers—I found myself swinging from one to the other now like a kind of pendulum for marking time: the philosopher who laughs, the one who cries. Two holy authors: Vieyra and Campanella. Two thought mad but not: Campanella and Democritus. Two gifts: a painting and a book. Two Vieyra sermons.

Too many twos, one too many coincidences . . . but wait. Madness is not the message, for the messenger is *not* mad.

The messenger is not mad. . . .

"Antonia!"

Just as I'd thought—she was in the doorway almost at once, pausing there, hollow-eyed, to slip her nightshirt on. "Bring me Vieyra's sermons, please? Down at the end. I *know* you know where. Red leather. Next shelf up—left. There."

She padded back, greenish eyes curious, my pale Angolan warrior princess in a torn nightshirt.

"Put something on your feet—here, take my slippers—how can you walk around like that? As soon as it is light, I want you to go to the palace and try to find the Sicilian. First thing on a Sunday morning it should not be too hard, if he is in fact staying there. Ask him to come at his earliest convenience—but bring him back with you if you can."

"I could wake the turnkeeper right now."

"No, we may need the favour later. Go down and get dressed—it's cold enough for *snow*. By the time you're ready I'll have a note for you to take to him. . . ."

I laid my hand on the cover of soft red leather. . . . Vieyra's sermon was a famous one. Less for its content than for its origins: Christina of Sweden's drawing room in Rome. Vieyra had just arrived from Portugal to seek the Pope's protection from the Inquisition. He'd had the general idea for his oratory already, but during a visit to her apartments improvised the exposition with such stunning success Christina asked that very day that he become her spiritual director. Which he declined. Vieyra served one man alone, the King of Portugal.

Here it was . . . 'The Tears of Heraclitus Defended in Rome against the Laughter of Democritus.'

> Democritus laughed, because the affairs of Man seemed to spring from ignorance; whereas Heraclitus wept, because these same affairs seemed miseries. Heraclitus therefore had greater reason to weep than did Democritus to laugh, for in this world there exists such a host of miseries that owe nothing to ignorance, and yet no ignorance that is not a misery . . .

What ignorance was a misery, an ignorance of *mine?* These emblems were not threads fallen together at random. These were the makings of a message—*and I knew what it was.* The message Baron Crisafi had brought me in the gift of Campanella's *Scelta:* the Archbishop was not mad.

 In the two hours Antonia was away at the palace I had the idea of launching a counterattack.

None of the libels in the other pamphlets mattered, but those penned by the second Soldier, those we had to answer. For in them the Holy Office was sounding out its own arguments. But even more urgent now was to repair the horrible, gaping breach Palavicino had opened in my defences. This nightmare of the Soldier's cruel lance in my side, as in the side of an innocent lamb, as in the side of Christ. . . .

Just then, seeing Antonia come swiftly up the steps, cheeks flushed, a strident scarlet ribbon in her hair, it came to me how we might do it. The wound in the side, there was no wiping away the image—but if we changed the soldier, the wound, the side . . . the lance. The shepherdess Camilla. Virgil's own Amazon, I had her right in front of me. It could not be more perfect. It must be Camilla's lance, through another side altogether. . . .

The Tyrrenian giant Ornithus advances through a wood. He is a colossus dwarfing his little war pony and bearing savage arms never before seen. Espying Camilla in a clearing he turns and bears down on the one he has been searching out. Ornithus springs from his war pony—three swift strides swallow up the meadow. Smoothly, quietly, swift as Achilles, she runs him through the chest with her lance. . . .

And then the insult as he falls.

'The day has arrived for your vaunting to find its reply in a woman's arms. To the afterworld, hie!—and when you get there tell the shades of your fathers that the one who sent you, and how swiftly, was a woman!'

I looked into her greenish eyes. She read mine. "Work . . ." Antonia said, her smile engagingly grim.

Yes, *work*. Something for us both to do. We would answer Sor Philothea with a letter of our own, published in this case under a pseudonym—Sor Seraphina de Cristo. Christ's finest angel. And even as it poked a little angelical fun at our devoted follower and friend, and this for missing the point of a certain recent letter of ours, missing even whom it was meant to address, we would make it clear that dim Philothea had been involved in it all from the start, indeed had commanded that the sword be made, only to grasp it from the wrong end.

Then we would see what the world thought of clever Philothea. In this affair there was mud enough to cast about.

For our purposes today, Antonia, think of irony as having not two surfaces but three, its blade a triangle in cross-section—inserted, the wound it inflicts takes a good deal longer to heal.[1]

Baron Anthonio Crisafi arrived by three, having cancelled one appointment and rescheduled another for that evening. He cut a dignified figure, in a fitted velvet doublet of an almond brown, a high collar, and across his chest a heavy emerald-studded chain.

"The Countess of Paredes sends expressions of her love and concern. . . . They are in Seville, at the home of her brother-in-law. The

Medinaceli Palace has every imaginable comfort. As you may know, her husband, the Marquis . . ."

The Sicilian could tell me no more than that Tomás was still unwell.

"The Countess asks me to tell you that your second volume is ready for the printer in Seville. All that lacks are the endorsements and licences. She is holding the text you asked for, in hopes of 'a climate more favourable for ice.' Did I get that correctly?"

"Yes, thank you, Baron."

"She also emphatically agrees with the idea of publishing in Spain your letter on the Vieyra affair—of having it approved there before it can be formally condemned here in Mexico. She already has letters of enthusiastic support from nine poets, but the theological endorsements are not coming so quickly. She wishes you to know that in every free moment she is working to that end—and I can assure you she is working with great passion and energy. So far she has three. . . ."

"She had thirty for *Castalian Flood*."

"So she said, yes. Vieyra is an enormous figure in Seville—not much less revered than he is in Portugal. But during King John's suppression of the Holy Office in Portugal, many Inquisitors took refuge in Seville. What the Countess wanted you to know was this: while soliciting approvals she has learned that certain distinguished officers of the Church in Seville *already know something* about the Vieyra controversy here in Mexico."

My guess had been correct. The Archbishop's correspondent had hinted, the merest hint of a hint, that His Grace was perhaps not quite so unstable as was thought here. "Baron Crisafi, I do not know how to thank you. Perhaps one day I may be in a position to render you some small service."

"I am afraid, Sor Juana, there is more. This was the Countess's message *before* your package arrived. What I am about to tell you now, she had not wanted to worry you with, at first. You see, it appears the Archbishop's correspondent in Seville has also read a good deal about *you*." The Baron leaned forward, lowering his voice. He did his best to meet my eyes. The emerald chain about his neck swung free, sparkling in the light, sending splinters of green across the chocolate doublet.

"The Archbishop has never given the slightest sign he knows I *exist*."

"But Sor Juana, that is exactly right, that is precisely how the correspondent put it. On bad days, His Grace the Lord Archbishop pretends you live in someone else's archdiocese."

"Does he indeed, sir? Why, this happens also to me. But then I take it His Grace has his good days as well. Truly does one wonder what such days might be like."

"I will tell you. On a good day, apparently, he almost manages to forget you are alive."

Baron Crisafi looked genuinely pained to have said something so unpleasant. "And I am afraid that's all I know, Sor Juana. I should be getting back," he said, straightening in his seat. "This is not a day to be away from the palace—especially for foreigners."

"I'm sorry, I don't see what you mean."

"My quarters are just down the hall from the French Viscount's. He mentioned you have met. Yes? Well it appears the Viscount d'Anjou has made an unannounced departure."

"The stewards have checked the silverware by now, I hope."

"In a manner of speaking, yes, Sor Juana. You see, a treasury official was found murdered last night. His wife says he left home late yesterday afternoon in great excitement to be meeting a very distinguished foreign visitor, but could not say more."

"You are going to tell me this official is privy to information about the silver fleets."

"It appears a shipment left for the coast recently."

"The Viceroy will be happy to see you are still among us."

"I am hoping he has not sent out a search party. It might be hard to convince his men I was on my way back to the palace."

After thanking him, urging him to come again and expressing the very keen regret that he had not arrived in Mexico much sooner—last year, just for instance—I rose to let him go.

Two entire days the Baron had spent with María Luisa—*just weeks ago*. I wanted to ask him about each minute, I wanted to ask him how she was, how she moved, if she smiled.

I could keep Baron Crisafi no longer.

I hoped he might come back, and gave a little wave as I stood at the grille, which was as close as I might come to seeing him out.

Gutiérrez did not come until Thursday morning. From Sunday to Thursday it snowed. I could not remember five consecutive days of snow down in the valley. As he entered the locutory the enormous capuchon of the Augustinian habit was drawn up, obscuring his face. It was the cold, I knew, but I could not help thinking he did not want to be seen entering. The hem of his habit was sugared in snow, even the long black cincture that hung at ankle-height was white-tipped, like a tail. He shrugged back the hood. His face was ruddy with the chill. I remembered that his mother was Flemish and, as I recalled, a Lutheran.

He was sorry to have been so long. It was a busy time at the Holy Office. He said this as only Gutiérrez could, the tone light. I apologized for my pique in the locutory last week. He answered that I was holding up better than most.

Today the novices were hopeless, dropping things in the back, hands trembling as they set down cups of hot spiced chocolate for us. Again I told myself it was the cold. And again there were no platters of convent delicacies for our guest. The kitchen says no, Tomasina whispered, wide-eyed. They won't say why.

I asked Gutiérrez if he thought Xavier Palavicino was doing someone else's bidding. My defender was of course a learned fool, bent on showing us how much he knew. But did he not perhaps know too much? How many people knew of the carols for Saint Catherine—was it not conceivable that Palavicino was acting in concert with Bishop Santa Cruz?

"Well if he is," Gutiérrez ventured, "he should look to himself." He looked down gratefully at the cup of chocolate warming his hands, bent his head to sip.

"But then," I added, though not quite believing it, "perhaps everyone's forgotten the sermon already—with the vanished Viscount and the murdered treasury agent to gossip about."

He looked up at me sharply. "Hardly. Since one of the last places either was seen was here in the chapel on Friday."

"The treasury man was *here?*"

"As was a convicted seditionist called Samuel, also a foreigner, I believe. And who, like the Viscount, has also disappeared. It *would* have been a convenient place to exchange messages."

"But were they seen together?"

"People have seen all manner of things—including horns on the Frenchman and a halo on the poor fellow from the treasury." Gutiérrez scratched speculatively at the scruff of his beard. "Such rumours are sometimes of some use to us, but I would not want to be the secular authorities trying to find out what actually happened."

It had been two months, and I had never congratulated him on his promotion. Examining Magistrate. Something of a change from correcting and censoring texts. Was it more awkward for him to come here? No, not so far. Lowering my voice I asked if he had ever heard of any arrangements to intercept my mail. He looked startled that I would ask such a thing of him so baldly. Before answering he glanced over at Antonia and the novices.

"No, but I'll look into it," he said quietly. "You know I can't tell you what I learn. . . ."

"Of course not."

"But you would feel better if I knew."

"Much."

"You've been careful."

"About doctrine, yes, careful enough. About certain personages, I'm not so sure. If Núñez, for example, has intercepted certain letters and shown them to Santa Cruz . . ."

"I see. As I said, I can't tell you what I learn. But I can let you know *when* I know—if and when."

"*Gracias*, Gutiérrez. Don't take too many risks. San Jerónimo can hardly be considered neutral ground at the Holy Office these days."

"No, Sor Juana," he said, "but then it never was."

He set down his empty cup, and added after a moment that if I could think of anything to do to help myself, I should do it. It came out a little coldly, but he was anxious to be going. There was some checking he needed to do. For me but also for himself, I saw. He did not credit the poisoning story. The Archbishop had been crying poison for ten years. But to the possibility that I had raised—that the Archbishop's madness might be a device of some kind—this, Gutiérrez was giving some sober thought. It was not often I saw that insouciance falter. I could only imagine how many of his own actions he was re-examining in this light. And he confessed now that one thing had been bothering him for weeks: the rift one might have expected between Núñez and the Archbishop over the Vieyra affair . . . there was as yet no sign that it had opened.

He promised to return soon. The last time he promised this he was gone six weeks.

If I could think of anything to do to help myself . . .

Yes, and if Bishop Santa Cruz was still thinking of swooping in as my Redeemer, he should swoop very soon.

Antonia, who had doubtless heard every word Gutiérrez said, insisted we finish our Seraphina letter and send it to Santa Cruz. I did not have the heart to tell her the letter was ridiculous.

Satirical verses are like wolves: once loosed they close straight on the weakest, fattest offering. Whoever the second soldier proved to be, the first still stood every chance of having been His Grace. If in my letter on the Vieyra sermon I had struck the Archbishop a glancing blow, the Seraphina letter was making straight for His Grace's throat. . . .

Worse, I was no longer at all sure who the second Soldier was. It had startled me to hear Palavicino protesting that he was not the Soldier. Not once had it occurred to me that people could suppose it was anyone but Núñez. The thing was so obvious—Sapphic hymns—the phrase was his; the charges of heresy, especially that of Arian, were precisely those Nunez had threatened me with. It had to be him. Or someone wishing to sound like him. . . .

But who could have managed this? Master Examiner Dorantes could.

Dorantes did not come to Palavicino's sermon, did not want to seem to be involved, though this had not stopped him offering to help Cantor de Ribera—what, rewrite, *repair?*—my lyrics on Saint Peter.

Why had no rift appeared between Núñez and the Archbishop? Could the second Soldier have been Dorantes, doing Santa Cruz's bidding? But then what if Núñez had never been involved? Just listen to me—such contortions to believe Núñez was not the one. Why could I not bring myself to think the worst of him? Why after all these years, after everything that had come between us, had I not rid myself of my affection for him? *Father Antonio Núñez de Miranda was not my father.*

 I had been walking in the snow.

When Gutiérrez left, I set out for the kitchen to see Sor Vanessa and Concepción, who were among my few friends within these walls. That there were no platters of *delicias* today for my guests was a painful turn, and yet I found myself stopped outside, standing in the lightly falling snow. I looked back.

I'd come out along the high temple wall, the cool stone slots we confess through partly snowed in. Parting from the wall, tracks wound through the orchard and ended with me, here in the midst of the winter growing season. After a moment I added to them, wending through the branchless lances of papaya trees, green growths in massy cluster at the tips—a line of maces groaning beneath the extra weight of moistened snow. I ducked in among the pomegranates and apples, ruddy-cheeked amidst the little hods and barrows of snowy leaves . . . in through branches broken where not bowed or bent to their stays like Bedouin tents. A finch startled ahead of me and, catapulting into the air, freed the softly nodding bough—such glory for that tiny weight, such masses to dislodge . . . launched not up but down.

There was such a stillness out here now, and for a moment, I was not sure how long . . . it had come inside. A cool, a quiet in my mind. Thoughts falling to rest, not memories quite, but everywhere falling, the presence of what was past piling up in drifts. . . . The quiet in the orchards after snow in Panoayan.

As I came in through the refectory it seemed I had quite forgotten my grievances. I did not come to visit the mistresses of the kitchens often enough. Vanessa, descended from the aristocracy of Navarre, small-boned, elegant. Concepción, an Indian servant old enough to be her mother, round and bent. And yet they were very much a couple, a partnership in here. It was like another country, indeed one in which Spanish was rarely used, since it would have returned to Sor Vanessa the very advantage she had chosen to surrender. What speaking they needed to do, Vanessa did in the Nahuatl she had learned, and Concepción in her few set phrases and words for food in Basque.

I had once had the idea of learning Basque, which Vanessa warned me from the outset I would not have time to learn. And so the joke among us was that I would tease Vanessa about her Nahuatl, which was good now, while Vanessa sadly warned how far Concepción was ahead of me in Basque. And then I would ask when she was going to take the time to teach me. Now they were mortified to see me come in through the kitchen doorway. I saw it was not their doing—that the Prioress had ordered that there be no more special courtesies for my guests—and so my coming could have been a painful moment that just now I would have given anything to avoid. It was too late to turn back. My wet feet saved us.

Concepción scolded me in Nahuatl, dragged me over by the fire and pulled my shoes and stockings off as though they were a child's. She had hardly towelled my feet dry before Vanessa thrust into my hands an aromatic cup of chocolate spiked with some kind of *aguardiente*. They would not let me leave until my stockings had dried, and in truth they dried too quickly. As I sat before the fire Concepción came by to stir the pot from time to time, and Vanessa brought morsels of this or that on which I was asked a grave opinion. Concepción told her to make me try everything. I was too thin, too thin. I listened to them softly chaffering over sauces and spices. I stared into the fire . . . along the walls . . . at the clusters of clay *ollas* and copper pots, strings of peppers and of garlic, baskets of red and white onion, all strung from the rafters. More than once my eyes had sought out the open doorway to the pantry at the back. . . .

As I was leaving I asked Vanessa when she was going to take the time to teach me Basque.

"You do not have the time to learn," she said.

If it came out a little awkwardly, it was only that her face had fallen, to hear what she had said. I smiled and shook my head.

On my way out through the refectory I glanced at the rostrum. It was a shame to let drop all Antonia's work on Camilla. She had done a fine translation of Virgil, another of Catullus. I would ask her to give us a class on Camilla at our academy on Monday.

 At first I was afraid it was the typhoid again. Even before the symptoms, the sense of something gone wrong. Then hot and cold, fever and chills, bouts of drowsiness between the headaches, a vise about my skull, forehead and back.

I was a fortnight in bed. In that time Antonia had gone down to meet little delegations of well-wishers, a bookseller, a theatre-manager come with an actor or two, and tears and flowers. And gossip. A day or two later, a few impresarios from the bullrings and cockpits, with bottles of good wine and still better gossip. *There* was a visit I was sorry to have missed. Write one sonnet on a bullfighter, make fast friends for life. We shared a bond, I realized. The Archbishop's hatred. Next the Creole seditionists would be bringing me chocolate.

The Viscount and Samuel and the treasury man had all come to our chapel—perhaps had even chosen it as a meeting point. What drew them *here*? Rebellion was in the air, and our convent was fast becoming a symbol, if not of insurrection then I did not know what. It was not just my locutory now—all the parlours were brewing rumours and gossip. The French were coming, the Viscount was leading them through our defences! It was not completely implausible. Eight years earlier the pirates had held Veracruz for six weeks, then sailed off with fifteen hundred Spaniards to be made slaves. Still, one might doubt that all were virgin girls. . . .

Then Antonia brought up from the locutory a story I made her repeat twice. That Father Xavier Palavicino had been in Veracruz at the time, having boasted of going among the dead and the dying, giving last rites even before the French had returned to their longboats. I teased Antonia for wondering if Palavicino were somehow in league with the Viscount. Xavier Palavicino, pirate curate. But if not, what did this mean?—nothing at all, except to the simple people of Mexico, which was not nothing. It did not matter if it was true, it could seem true enough to them.

Comedy where there is none. Palavicino among the pirates—it was absurd yet somehow chilling that events so incongruous should so conspire. What *had* brought them all to the chapel that day? *There was no connection.*

The connections are in the weave of the net. The fish in it are not cause but <u>*consequence*</u> *of the weave. The fish do not weave it, nor are the fish woven into it. The fish are only caught up in it. Change the weave, change the fish. A different weave catches different fish. The word is* coincidencia.

I am not the fish, I am the net.

February 12th. There were to be no more classes at the academy, and the other teachers would take up my classes of music and dance. The Prioress had chosen this moment to announce it, while I was in bed. She thought me weak. We would see. Rebellion was in the air.

I got up and dressed, still tottery. Mother Andrea was expecting me. Yes, she had told the kitchen no more special favours. These had been for friends of the convent. She was no longer sure that I knew any. She was unusually sure of herself—as I recalled it, Palavicino had been her idea, not mine. She could not hold my eyes.

I told her I did not care about the food, but the classes, these would continue.

Yes, the classes, she said. They had not been her idea in the first place; as *she* recalled, they were the idea of Bishop Santa Cruz—who was also, it appeared, not such a friend of this convent. And cancelling them had not been her idea, either. They were suspended by order . . . she held up the letter by a corner. I might read it myself, if I wished. And if I wished, I could take it up with him, His Grace, the Lord Archbishop of Mexico.

That afternoon I sent for Gutiérrez, where had he been? It had been two weeks already. *I am stronger, I am not weak.* A little dewy at the temples, a little clammy under the tunic—but far from the only one, in this place. I was better, much, or would be if the headaches would ease.

February 15, 1691. Gutiérrez came. I went down alone to meet him. No news on the letters, but he had been wondering, what if Núñez had not burned all my spiritual journals? Just a thought, but what if the journals—not the letters—had been what he used to so change Bishop Santa Cruz's stance toward me? How did Gutiérrez know about these? But I had told him, had I forgotten? In making his inquiries this week he had discovered there were men at the Holy Office who had not forgotten Núñez's talk of my journals so many years ago. *Who*—Dorantes? It was no sooner said than regretted. Gutiérrez risked enough by coming here. I apologized. I had not been well.

Yes, he could see that for himself. He insulted me wryly enough and the moment of awkwardness passed. He had other news.

Palavicino still persisted in his mad intention to publish the sermon. He had found a printer, and most of the necessary signatures. One was the Viceroy's. Gutiérrez was surprised, but I explained that the Viceroy had been grateful for my poem on his great naval victory in Tortuga. He was only too happy to license the excellent sermon written in my defence. He had been trying to do me a favour.

 February 24, 1691. The twenty-second anniversary of my profession. The day I entered here I was not quite twenty. . . .

The second time I left the palace I went out the main gates—not by the servant's quarters, the way of shame—straight into the main square, with Perico alone to see me off. He led me out through the Hall of Mirrors, as if to remind me I had nothing to be ashamed of. Of course not, Perico. On the way to the door I saw her passing through mirror after mirror: a young woman fighting for her composure, at her hip gliding just above the mirror frames the tousled head of a dwarf.

Mostly it had been a relief, not having to face her after that day. Her nakedness in too many mirrors, too many rooms, the nakedness in her face. I had not had to look into a mirror for twenty-two years.

I caught glimpses of course. Drawing water from a well . . . a face in the lamplight on the baths we drew. And there were nights I missed her, that passion, that pride and rage. Was she still here, had she gone away?

And I missed Antonia, the way she had been when she first came. For though we looked nothing alike, she had been about that age, had something of those traits, that pride, that rage.

A breeze from the sea . . .

Look at her today. It seemed the cloister did this to all of us. This anxiousness, this anger. This frustration and bitterness. She was not happy here any longer. I should have let her go. Where, where would my Antonia go?

We were at the table in the sitting room. Beyond her left shoulder a fire burned low in the corner. We had not spoken much all day. She'd prepared a beautiful meal for the anniversary of my profession. Vanessa and Concepción had sent up a lovely stew, chicken and *chayote*, peppers and squash. There was no hope of finishing all this food. Antonia was eating quietly, not looking up. Her hair was draped back over her broad shoulders in long black coils and streamers. Sometimes on festive occasions when it was just we two, we wore dresses. But tonight she still wore the rough brown *sayuela*, and I a damp white tunic of cotton . . . too thin, too thin.

Losing our classes was a bitter thing. Explaining it to the novices more bitter still. These past few days I had so wanted to bring the other Antonia back to stay. I wanted to tell her we would get them back, our classes. I wanted to say, I know you are not happy, Antonia. Let us pretend, a little while, make believe for a week or two, that we are. . . .

"I have been thinking, 'Tonia, that you and I should write a play together." The window over the table was closed against the cold. Her form moved through the warps in the crystal panes as she cleared the dishes from the table. She did not yet look at me, but paused—about to lift a bowl of grated jícama and beet. "We have all the elements we need for a marvellous comedy—like *los empeños* that the Archbishop would so have hated, if he'd given himself half a chance." Her eyes, hazel in the light, met mine. She straightened. She was allowing herself to hope I might be serious. "I am serious. You and I. A play of mistaken identities—like

Amor es más laberinto, which you know as well as I, having copied out all those drafts for me." I could see her excitement now—to be *doing* something.

"But how can I . . ." she asked. She shifted the bowl in her right hand to rest on the plates in her left, and nervously tucked a strand of hair behind her ear.

"Don't worry—we'll take another play as a model. There's one by Tirso that might be just perfect. With a maid named Serafina, I recall, and a secretary named Antonio. Tirso has all the tricks. You'll get the hang of it." I saw the light going out of her eyes. She thought I was making fun of her. Could she think me so cruel after what had happened with our classes—with Camilla? I pressed harder. Truly—I actually wanted us to write it. A play of masquerades, cloaked figures, assignations in the shadows of a garden. Couples reflecting other couples reflecting each other. Servants mistaken for their masters, and vice versa. Two hooded soldiers, each passing for the other. Archbishops feigning madness, bishops veiled as nuns. A Sicilian count we take for an enemy but who represents a friend. A French viscount introduced by a friend but whom we discover to be a seducer on a king's behalf—but who then reveals himself to be a pirate king bent on treasure and conquest. Seizing the moment in the capture of the silver fleet, the Creole seditionists rise up, proclaim the pirate viscount king! and thereby achieve their dream of making the viceroyalty a kingdom. We have all the elements—we could write it together in a week or two. . . .

And yet with every word it had gotten worse. Dishes still cradled against her side, she stood, head bowed, hair veiling her face. Her shoulders heaved—she set down the dishes violently. The bowl of salad tipped onto its side. "You wouldn't defend yourself from him!" Her hands shot up—the long blunt fingers splayed, tendons standing out in the strong wrists. "Someone had to."

The gesture was of imprecation or pleading, but it was only when I said his name that she would look up at me.

"Who—*Santa Cruz* . . . ? 'Tonia, what is it? Why are you crying?" I got up and rounded the table to her side. I took her hands, folded the angry fingers up against her palms. "Toñita, look at me. Tell me . . ." I smoothed back her hair, with a fingertip touched the fine scar at her cheek, the damp tip of her nose, raised her chin. Her eyes brimmed.

"I sent it."

"Sent what? What did you send?" But already I knew . . . I was remembering her in the locutory—turning from the clavichord the day of his last visit as the thought had flickered through my mind that she'd been crying.

"The Seraphina letter, to Santa Cruz."

Our letter—did she have any idea what she'd done? There was much more she tried to tell me. No, Antonia, not now. I had never asked to know about her and the Bishop. I already knew where she had come from. Of course there was more, Antonia, there was always more. I did not need to hear it. I had chosen to trust her—*chosen*. I would not live my life racked with suspicions. Their gossip, their stories, their envies, I did not hear them. I did not listen. No, Antonia, I am too angry to hear it tonight—it was cruel but I would not give her the relief of confessing it. I do not care right now to hear what he has done to you—do you have any idea what you've done to *me*? If you hate him so, if he has done so little for you that you should find yourself trapped in here with me, then write your own letters—don't send him *ours*—or go to Puebla yourself and tell him how you feel, for you are not nearly so trapped in here as I.

No, Antonia. I will ask you when I am ready. Not before. Just now, I do not have time to help you with your conscience.

Now there really was work to do. Now let Santa Cruz have my answer. And in it let the Inquisition know I would not go without a struggle. Let them take their time, make their preparations, polish their arguments, for they would have such a fight.

And tell the shades of your fathers the one who sent you was a woman.

JUANA INÉS DE LA CRUZ, 1 MARCH 1691

abridged and adapted from the translation of Margaret Sayers Peden[2]

[†]published only posthumously, five years after Sor Juana's death

REPLY TO SISTER PHILOTHEA[†]

My most illustrious señora, dear lady:

It has not been my will, my poor health, or my justifiable apprehension that for so many days delayed my response. How could I write, considering that at my very first step my clumsy pen encountered two obstructions in its path? The first (and, for me, the most uncompromising) is to know how to reply to your most learned, most prudent, most holy, and most loving letter. . . . The second obstruction is to know how to express my appreciation for a favour as unexpected as extreme, for having my scribblings printed, a gift so immeasurable as to surpass my most ambitious aspiration, my most fervent desire, which even as a person of reason never entered my thoughts. . . .

This is not pretended modesty, lady, but the simplest truth issuing from the depths of my heart, that when the letter which with propriety you called *Atenagórica* reached my hands, in print, I burst into tears of confusion (withal, that tears do not come easily to me). . . .

I cast about for some manner by which I might flee the difficulty of a reply, and was sorely tempted to take refuge in silence. But as silence is a negative thing, though it explains a great deal through the very stress of not explaining, we must assign some meaning to it that we may understand what the silence is intended to say, for if not, silence will say nothing. . . .

And thus, based on the suppostion that I speak under the safe-conduct of your favour, and with the assurance of your benignity and with the knowledge that like a second Ahasuerus you have offered to me to kiss the top of the golden sceptre of your affection as a sign conceding to me your benevolent licence to speak and offer judgements in your most exalted presence, I say to you that I have taken to heart your most holy admonition that I apply myself to the study of the Sacred Books . . . I confess that many times this fear has plucked my pen from my hand . . . which obstacle did not impinge upon profane matters, for a heresy against art is not punished by the Holy Office but by the judicious with derision, and by critics with censure. . . . I wish no quarrel with the Holy Office, for I am ignorant, and I tremble that I may

express some proposition that will cause offense or twist the true meaning of some scripture. . . .

I have prayed that He dim the light of my reason, leaving only that
which is needed to keep His Law, for there are those who would say that
all else is unwanted in a woman . . . I deemed convent life the least
unsuitable and the most honourable I could elect if I were to ensure my
salvation. I believed I was fleeing from myself, but—wretch that I
am!—I brought with me my worst enemy, my inclination, which I do
not know whether to consider a gift or a punishment from Heaven. . . .
it seeming necessary to me, in order to scale those heights, to climb the
steps of the human sciences and arts for how could one undertake the
study of the Queen of the Sciences if first one had not come to know her
servants? How without Geometry, could one measure the Holy Arc of
the Covenant and the Holy City of Jerusalem, whose mysterious measures are foursquare in all their dimensions, as well as the miraculous proportions of all their parts? . . . And without being an expert in Music, how
could one understand the exquisite precision of the musical proportions
that grace so many Scriptures.

In this practice one may recognize the strength of my inclination. . . .
What have I not gone through to hold out against this? Strange sort of
martyrdom, in which I was both the martyr and my own executioner.

I confess that I am far removed from wisdom's confines and that I have
wished to pursue it, though *a longe*. But the sole result has been to draw
me closer to the flames of persecution, the crucible of torture, and this has
even gone so far as a formal request that study be forbidden me . . . 3

[And yet] I see many illustrious women; some blessed with the gift of
prophecy, like Abigail; others of persuasion, like Esther; others with pity,
like Rahab . . .

If I again turn to the Gentiles, the first I encounter are the Sibyls,
those women chosen by God to prophesy the principal mysteries of our
Faith, and with learned and elegant verses that surpass admiration . . . I
see the daughter of the divine Tiresias, more learned than her father. An
Hypatia, who taught astrology, and read many years in Alexandria . . . I
find the Egyptian Catherine, studying and influencing the wisdom of all
the wise men of Egypt . . .

Then if I turn my eyes to the oft-chastized faculty of making verses —which is in me so natural that I must discipline myself that even this letter not be written in that form—I see verse acclaimed in the mouths of the Sibyls, sanctified in the pens of the Prophets, especially King David. . . . The greater part of the Holy Books are in metre, as in the Book of Moses; and those of Job . . . are in heroic verse. Solomon wrote the Canticle of Canticles in verse; and Jeremiah his *Lamentations*. . . .

And if the evil is attributed to the fact that a woman employs them . . . what then is the evil in my being a woman? I confess openly my own baseness and meanness, but I judge that no couplet of mine has been deemed indecent. Furthermore, I have never written of my own will, but under the pleas and injunctions of others . . .

That letter, lady, which you so greatly honoured . . . I believe that had I foreseen the blessed destiny to which it was fated—for like a second Moses I had set it adrift, naked, on the waters of the Nile of silence, where you, a princess, found and cherished it—I believe, I reiterate, that had I known, the very hands of which it was born would have drowned it . . . for as fate cast it before your doors, so exposed, so orphaned, that it fell to you even to give it a name, I must lament that among other deformities it also bears the blemish of haste . . . If I ever write again, I shall as ever direct my scribblings towards the haven of your most holy feet and the certainty of your most holy correction, for I have no other jewel with which to pay you . . .

y spring, the fears of winter had faded, yet the atmosphere had scarcely changed—the winds might change from excitement to anxiety to giddy folly, but unrest and shifting alliances had become our constants. It felt as if we might wake any day to a new state where stones would rise up and floating bodies fall. One had only to glance away for the kettle to come to a boil.[4]

She should not have sent our Seraphina letter, but it had taken Antonia to rouse me if even a little from my latest bout of melancholic humours. In fanning sparks Antonia had struck, I found the flame flickered up and fed itself a while—the letter ran to over fifty pages, which I had only just sent off when Carlos at last published his panegyric on the Spanish naval victory over French perfidy and piracy—a testament writ on water to Spanish valour and overwhelming numerical superiority.

The rain had not stopped since the naval battle, nor indeed at any time during the dry season. It been raining for ten months. The flooding in the outlying neighbourhoods was grave enough that Carlos had agreed to lend a hand designing new diversion schemes. This year was already the worst since '29, and the wet season had scarcely started.

Then a new danger. During the dredging operations, the men working under Carlos had discovered in the foul ooze at the bottom of the canals thousands upon thousands of small clay dolls in European dress, men and women in various postures of torment—pierced by lances, cleft at throat and chest. Though there was no saying how or when these effigies had found their way into the canals, Carlos had promptly warned the Viceroy that an Indian uprising might be imminent, thus dredging up the oldest fears of our colony.

I had never stopped writing carols for the humble—on the Nativity and the love of a child, on fishermen and the miracles of abundance, on temples of bread. But for a year, almost none of these had been sung or published. All that had been heard from me were praises of a childless king's potency and the beauty of an unseen queen.

Not long after the Viceroy's last visit to San Jerónimo, the Cantor de Ribera brought two pieces of news from the Cathedral. The surprising: that he'd persuaded the cathedral dean to allow my carols on

Saint Peter to be sung after all, to the music Ribera and I had written. The theme of Peter the fisherman had proved irresistible this year. I managed not to ask Ribera if Master Examiner Dorantes, who had volunteered to rewrite my carols, had lost the knack. The second piece of news was a simple delight. We'd often spoken of a manuscript I had started during my years at the palace and subsequently lost. *Caracol.* Now he'd finally convinced the dean that in these anxious days the cathedral needed something rare and unusual, an eight-day cycle devoted to sacred music. I would set down my ideas for *Caracol* again and together Ribera and I would develop the companion lyrics and musical illustrations. I had written so many verses on music that it might simply be a matter of adapting the existing ones. There would not be much money but enough for three. Three? Yes, he had persuaded Sálazar, no less, to join us.

Certain to be Ribera's successor, Sálazar was already the finest composer in the empire and in his better moments the only one able to approach the great Italians, Monteverdi and Scarlatti. Where Ribera was at his best with a simple melody, Sálazar was a master of the polyphonic. My friend was the first to admit that by Sálazar he was quite outstripped.

As Ribera sat across from me I remembered that when he and I had first met some fifteen years earlier, I'd composed in his honour a sonnet painting him as a swan, sacred bird of Apollo and Orpheus. In truth he did resemble a bird, which had almost made the sonnet come off, but the bird one thought of with Ribera was another. He was lanky and tall, grey-headed for as long as I had known him and beardless, though never quite clean shaven. His neck was thin; and as with long thin necks, his Adam's apple protruded and bobbed, but more like a peach pit than an apple on a bough. Though the nose was too short to be thought beaked, and was from that point of view disappointing, his heronness lay—and bounced and dipped—in the long black brows, glossy and sweeping. Still, while one might compose all manner of sonnets on the singing of swans, herons were a stiffer challenge.

His eyes searched mine, his brows signalling antically. Did I share in his excitement?

If his idea had been to cheer me, it was a magnificent success. I felt a rush of warmth and was happy not to have to worry for once about seeming ungrateful.

June 29th. The children have a game here in the capital, one I arrived too late to play myself but of which I had often made good use in class. In this game the city itself was the music and each church and temple, each cloister and monastery, was a saintly instrument on a musical map, each ringing at a certain pitch. The lowest of these was the bell of San José— *Ut,* our C. San Bernardo, three blocks north, got *Re. Mi, Mi, Mi,* was for our most elegant, Jesús María, whose bell was said to be of pure gold. The cracked brass bell of Santo Domingo got the semitone, *Fa. Sol* went to the convent of Santa Teresa. And the highest of these was our own, *La.* The low note on the overlapping hexachord gave us an *Ut* in F, and so on. Depending on whose bell first struck the hour, the map gave a different melody of pitches and chords—time running through the city as Re, Mi, Sol, Fa—or Ut, Fa, Sol, La, Mi, etcetera, children leaping up when their note was struck, a good deal of laughter . . .

At first I heard the ringing, then Ribera's music from the cathedral. As the bells died out I could almost hear the words. The rain had nearly stopped, the sky almost cleared. I leaned far out the window over Calle de las Rejas, startling my neighbours across the way. Saint Peter Fisherman . . . did I hear my verses, or only imagine them?

> . . . *Pescador de ganado,*
> *o ya Pastor de peces,*
> *la red maneja a veces*
> *y a veces el cayado,*
> *cuyo silbo obedece lo crïado . . .* [5]

After the music had faded away, I stayed by the window, my eyes roaming the bases of the hills beneath the low cloud. I had been hesitating to do *Caracol.* If anything, recognizing how badly I wanted to do it made me more hesitant. What I resolved to do instead was write a second birthday poem for the Vice-Queen. The one written on her birthday, when she'd come unannounced with her entire retinue, I had composed not merely in haste but in anger. Not with her for once but with one of the handmaidens, who had begun gossiping about the affairs in the palace dovecotes with the express purpose of making a slighting allusion to stories of my own nights on the upper floors.

It was during my timé in the dovecotes that I had lost the manuscript of *Caracol.* Speculative harmonics. The beauty of the world as a music cascading from the mind of God. I had not been that far along. I could have started again, and yet I let the idea go, something so beautiful. For the first time in all these years I wondered if I had perhaps believed that I'd tarnished it in the puffery and the vaunting of my examination at the palace. Or that in the dovecotes I had perhaps tarnished myself.

Why, Señorita, if you are beautiful, is there so little harmony in you?
And why, Soul, dost thou know so little peace?

I saw what taking up *Caracol* again could be for me, and wondered how much of this Ribera had seen. Not a commission, but a second chance. A chance to say good-bye to the girl who had been seen out through the Hall of Mirrors.

 To set the proper tone for *Caracol,* our eight-day cycle required an opening note of cheer. I well remembered how dark and cold the cathedral felt when it rained. Something striking, new astonishments, fresh hopes. For it seemed to me that what we found most dispiriting just now was this sense that everything was being stripped from us, by Spanish incompetence, by French predation, by blights of pirates and weevils, by the waters themselves that gnawed away at our island.

And yet there was so much here that we might yet accomplish. What Ribera and I would offer them was the example of a musical clock, another project I had left unfinished years ago.

Ladies and gentlemen, *compañeros, compatriotas . . .*

It is often said these days that the age of discovery has ended. And yet Europe has never seemed farther away. But the age of discovery never truly ends, for it is always starting somewhere else: and it is time for us here to make discoveries for ourselves.

No empire has had more to gain or lose than ours in the question of longitude, for on this depends Spain's claim to all the lands lying beyond a certain meridian line imaginatively traced north-south on the sea in 1493. The trouble being that in the two centuries since, we have still found no method for tracing such a line out of sight of land. So while we have long been fond subjects of the Spanish kings, we here in Mexico may yet wake up one morning to find ourselves Portuguese. . . .

No country in Europe began with a greater advantage than did our Spain of the Two Faiths, for our learned Moors once had access to the writings of the mighty Persians—the astronomers of Baghdad, venerable Al-Tusi and Abu'l-Wafa, and the geometers of Kabul, Mansur and Al-Biruni.[6] How circuitous are the tracts of history: it seems one has only to digest the problem, in 1493, to discover one has just expelled the solution, in 1492.

Perhaps this is why it was our Spanish kings Philip II and III who first envisioned a great prize to the solver of the problem—six thousand ducats outright, and two thousand a year for life! And still, we in Mexico await the solution as anxiously as ever. What city suffers more grievously than our own the losses in mercantile shipping on the world's two greatest oceans? Or the pillage of our silver in the Caribbean? Or depends more upon a healthy Spanish treasury to fund its own defence?

The *Académie Royale des Sciences* of our great Bourbon adversary has lately made some little progress—if it can be called that, for the most recent calculations have reduced the map of France in the west by a full degree of longitude; such that the mighty Sun King complains of losing more land to his geographers than to his enemies. And so, inspired by these great pirates of land, the geographers, it is indeed the piratical nations of England and France that are pursuing the solution to longitude at sea most doggedly—to catch our laggard age up with the Persian tenth century, and catch up with our silver fleets.

If anything has saved us thus far, it is that the pirates do not know where they are. . . .

You will say we do not know where they are either, but surely our best hope lies in finding out where *we* are before they do. Waking up Portuguese is not the worst to be imagined: we might find ourselves, not far hence, the westernmost city of France. Which could be even worse than it sounds. For if we do not know where we are, or in whose empire, or even whose language we should be speaking, *it is because we do not know what time it is.*

To which problem we humbly propose a solution: the Mexican musical clock.

The sailors tell us that could they but tell the time with accuracy, they could greatly increase the precision of their navigations. We begin, then, with the science of the publican, who raps on his casks to check their volumes. And as we have just heard with our own ears, different volumes of water can be calculated to make the vessels they fill sound out the hexachord. As the curtain rises here in the atrium, the musical clock we see before us is composed of six water vessels shaped like funnels, each of increasing volume, each designed to tip into the next larger as the water level rises to a given height. And so unto the largest. To the height of the water corresponds a volume, and to the volume a tone when the vessel is struck lightly with a baton.

Aboard the ship, the water is made to flow at a constant rate from a reservoir filled each day by sailors at a water pump. Every six seconds Vessel I tips into II—and if struck at any instant it sounds with one of six notes. As the water level rises the note drops. Vessel II is a basin whose tone every ten seconds drops by a note and tips itself once a minute into Vessel III. The sum of the first two vessels gives the timekeeper his seconds. Vessel III drops by a whole note each minute and spills itself every six minutes into vessel IV, whose tone changes by a note every ten. The sum of III and IV gives the timekeeper his minutes. Vessel V changes by a whole note each hour and tips every six. Vessel VI varies by a whole note every six hours. The sum of V and VI gives the time-keeper his hours.

The timekeeper does not need to check the time continuously. Rather, when the navigator calls *Time!* he takes up his baton and lightly taps each vessel, smallest to largest, yielding the precise time by way of a sequence of six notes. When the navigator is seated at his table, the timekeeper sings them out or pipes them back to him. Ut—Sol—Mi—Re—Fa—La!

Converting these back to the corresponding values (6—2—4—5—3—1), the navigator proceeds to multiply each by the appropriate unit: 6 units of 1 second, plus 2 units of 10 seconds (equalling 26 seconds); 4 units of 1 minute, plus 5 units of 10 minutes (equalling 54 minutes); 3 units of 1 hour, plus 1 unit of four hours (equalling 7 hours). Time: 7 hours 54 minutes 26 seconds.

Which translates, depending on one's habits, to the hour of breakfast, between Prime and Terce.

In theory, then, we have the musical clock, and the practical demonstration that music is our most perfect and pragmatic idea of Time....

 It was evening, after Vespers. The storm outside was worsening. At dinner, beneath closed shutters, the candle flames dipped and quivered to each big gust of wind. After the meal we moved into the library. Antonia was taking dictation for *Caracol* as I paced about the room to various tempos, here and there a pause to pick up instruments and curios, pull musical texts down from shelves. Over five months since she sent our letter to Bishop Santa Cruz, and in that time I'd refused to let her unburden herself to me. She had tried—had gotten as far as saying our Seraphina letter was to blame for everything. Ah, the vainglory of writers. But that night during the wildness of the storm, there was no stopping her. The weather explained everything now if we wished. Perhaps I could blame my cruelty too on this.

I had already guessed at half of it, or not quite the half. I understood that it had to do with her sisters, but her hatred of him had less to do with the ones he had not helped than the ones he had, the little ones in the convent school of Santa Monica. She and Santa Cruz as lovers would have seemed common—but he had never touched her, she had only watched him disciplining himself, and afterwards tended his back. Here, too, there was more, but I deflected her by asking where she had gone to meet him. A house near the Salto de Agua, at the end of the aqueduct. It was a relief to her to describe it, though I had not asked as a kindness. And since that night, the room has come into my mind many times—always clear but with slight variations. Santa Cruz wearing the black cassock of Lent, or a violet mozetta. On a desk by the window there are cigarettes or flowers, chocolate or wine. Oddly the one constant is a detail she did not give. The view from the window of the Salto de Agua, where the water of the aqueduct falls in folds, like clear silk. . . .

But when I asked Antonia if he had read out my letters there, I saw how close I had come to breaking her heart. She had never shown him a single letter—nor ever discussed a single one. The truth was he never asked, and if he had she didn't know what she would have done. *What then?* Reports—but I had to please believe that not a word she told him had been true. Reports . . . She had to tell him something, but lied about everything. He said all he cared about was the state of my soul. This sounded like Santa Cruz. He asked if I still kept a spiritual journal for myself, he asked once if I had any manuscripts not my own. He said he didn't care about doctrine or secret books. He said it wasn't for the Inquisition, that they had someone else watching—someone in here— and that only he could protect me from them. Unless she thought she could. So if I was reading X she told him Y, if I was writing one thing she told the son of a wayward bitch another. But most often what he asked for had been details, personal things. Where I brushed my hair at night, brush or comb, left hand or right, if she had ever seen me disciplining myself . . . and so she lied, had been lying for three years and the bastard knew—she was sure of it. This was part of the game, that he made her lie—once he asked which she thought might place me in greater danger, a lie or the truth. And she was terrified—she didn't know, it was true, how could she know that? And then he came that day for my arguments, the day I beat him at chess. My pages for him were the one letter she almost didn't post—but if she hadn't, what then? She didn't know how to protect me. He was the only one who could. I had to see, I had to believe her. . . .

The truth was that I did, and yet I was not sure she would ever let herself believe *me*. So I told her things, about myself, my past. I spoke to her simply and quietly, as though she were a child, for she was quite childlike by then. About my own years in Mexico as a young girl, about how frightened I had been. I spoke to her of how happy I had been to know her, and have her here with me. That it had been too long since I had seen her laughing, the mischief in her. Yes, I'd known there was more, flashes of darkness and trouble. But she had been like a secret book I had never wanted to leaf through, a sort of miracle that she had made such a difficult journey to me intact. Well, not quite intact. She smiled then. And I told her that I had always known there was more between her and Santa Cruz, that it had been a point of pride that if I treated her with love and friendship I needed never worry about any of that, and I had been right after all. That even friends have secrets, that friends could risk hurting each other.

And so we lay on my bed and I stroked her cheek and kissed her hair, as the sky paled in the windows in the east. We missed the prayers of Lauds and again at Prime, even knowing not a few of my sisters would be saying that it was for sins such as these that it did not stop raining anymore.

She told me how frightened she had been for me. She had never seen me as I was after the letter from Philothea. Not writing—not even to María Luisa, hardly reading, melancholy, sarcastic—who? not me . . . yes, you. How she hated him, how she had wanted to die when she came into my room and saw the fragments of the *Letras a Safo* in the ashes on my desk.

I had thought of Seraphina as our first work together, but she had felt those verses had been ours. She and María Luisa were the only ones ever to have read them. Though it had been six months, it was still painful to talk of them so I asked what she thought—what we might do for her sisters.

There was no place safer for her sisters than where they were, in the convent of Santa Monica, nowhere he could not reach them if he chose to. And nowhere he could not reach her. He had threatened once to take her away from me and put her back where he had found her. But she thought Santa Cruz was finished with her now. She had not been summoned to the house by the Salto de Agua for over a year.

But has he finished with you, Juana? she said, after a little while. Is it love? she asked. Could it be he is in love with you?

I asked her if she knew what the Mexicans say about someone who takes a gift back, for she has been a gift to me. What do they say of persons such as these?

Oppa icuitl quiqua.

They eat their excrement twice.

Caracol . . .
> *Dulce deidad del viento, armoniosa*
> *suspensión del sentido deseada,*
> *donde gustosamente aprisionada*
> *se mira al atención más bulliciosa.*
> *Y luego:*
> *pues a más que ciencia el arte has reducido,*
> *haciendo suspensión de toda un alma*
> *el que sólo era objeto de un sentido . . . 7*

We take up again the case of the spiral shell, cut now with a very fine saw not cross-wise but at a parabolic angle. The section yields not the orbit of a circle but an ellipse. And if, as we have just argued, the celestial harmony were conceived not as Pythagoras did, as a circle of fifths, but as a spiral, a winding stair, ever widening in its compass, then we should soon see each turn on the stair offering a mutation on the scale with respect to the position just beneath it. As a symbol then we may say the winding stair is Grace and detect, in the very properties of the spiral, its structure and agency. For as we have seen in the properties of the speaking trumpet and caracol, the spirals of the ellipsoids propagate sound, lending it strength and amplitude.

On this voyage, Mind is the guide, Grace is the strength we are given to rise.

Music is the Mind of God brought into Time, spiralling down through the Creation. The spiral shell is the voice from the depths of the sea, that silence from which the echo springs, the instrument through which we speak to the sky. Here in Mexico the Lord of the Wind wore a conical hat and here in this city his temples were round, with no sharp angles to stand against the wind. He was called Ehecatl. Here, the wind was the breath of heaven; the storm, the music of the sky—the thunder his drum, the wind his strings, the rain and the snow and hail on the ground were his water sticks. And the caracol was his wind-jewel . . .

And so we find in the caracol the hidden emblem of our soul, the secret shape of Grace, the echo of a celestial correspondence; even as we hear in ourselves, if we listen, a distant echo of God.

 July 5th. The composer Sálazar came, alone. Would Cantor De Ribera be joining us later? First one musician was missing, then the other. The world of course revolved around musicians, but if we were serious about setting the *Caracol* to music we really should meet all together, very soon.

Ribera was ill. Truly?—please say it was not serious. No, a cold was all. The cantor was only a little hoarse. Sálazar was smiling now and I found myself glad he had come, even though we could get little work done. Cantor De Ribera was always hoarse, the irony being that a musician whose title derived from chant and song should have such a raucous voice. This was his speaking voice; his singing was a truly pitiful thing to hear. But with perfect pitch. He was particularly hoarse when excited— which, when speaking on musical subjects, was often. He was good, Ribera, and a good musician, and knew Sálazar to be a great one.

There had always been something stiff in Sálazar's demeanour toward me—perhaps it was only the younger artist thoroughly sick of hearing about the older one. He was making a special effort to be cordial today. To both of us the Heron Ribera was especially dear. And yet I had the distinct impression Sálazar was considering a withdrawal from our *Caracol.* Though we had talked but a few times, he and I had known each other much longer than he realized. Almost thirty years ago he had come to the palace as a boy of six to play the violin for the court. He had spent a horrible day waiting to be called upon, had sat for hours with his violin in an adjoining room. Finally a page was sent for him, only to return saying the child seemed too frightened to play. As the youngest member of the court I was dispatched, one child to another, to coax him out. I found him sitting on the floor in a corner, lonely and over-awed, and angrily hurt now that someone had finally condescended to talk to him—though what could there be for *us* to discuss? And so we had a talk about being a prodigy.

Today I considered asking him if he had any memory of this, but did not want to spoil it with worries, mine or his, that I was trying to influence him to stay with our project.

Sálazar had just been saying, with some delicacy, that the cathedral had never seemed a promising venue for *Caracol*, but neither he nor Ribera had expected the Palace's patronage to be in doubt. Until yesterday. The Viceroy began by expressing his untiring admiration for Sor Juana . . . but the year had been difficult. Sálazar was explaining this to me as though perhaps I had just arrived from Perú. Very difficult for the Viceroy. Yes, I saw that. Hastening to reaffirm his favour for me and friendly feelings, the Count de Galve joked that the past year of our association had been dogged by ill-luck. The tone at first was rueful, then mock-dreadful and dire, as when one eggs on the teller of a ghost encounter. Blight, flooding, pirates, rumours of insurrection, the Viscount's disappearance, the French, the French, the threat to the silver fleets, the dolls in the canals. . . . Before long the Count de Galve, his thin face already anxious and careworn, was visibly frightened. It had been clear from the first he was not a strong man, but he had once wanted to be.

It was don Carlos who'd partly succeeded in changing the subject. Carlos? Partly . . . He pointed out that recent days were *not* the worst in memory. The year 1611 had still to be given the edge. Many of course had heard about the earthquake, the most devastating in over a century. A few had heard of the eclipse. The hall grew quiet. The empire's greatest scholar since Juan de Mariana was in his element. When Carlos had finished his relation of the events of that fateful year, no one noticed for several minutes that even the musicians had stopped playing and were raptly listening.

I tried to put a brave face on this for Sálazar. 1521, 1611, 1691 . . . note the pattern of declinations in the intervals of calamity, I said. Sálazar put in something about mutations and musical intervals, I answered in downward spirals and rates of fall.

In the art of Aeschylus there are stories in which what happens to the individuals tells the fate of a people. But though the calamities of 1611 had involved many others, and though many died and suffered throughout the valley, our Viceroy took all this to be about one person, himself. It was not hard to picture him, his darkling thoughts returning to the year of ostentation in honour of the king's wedding, the exaltation of his offices as the King's representative, the balls and debauches, the Church's dire warnings.

And if Carlos had told his tale to such stunning effect at the palace, I thought it only a matter of time till the recital reached the Archbishop. Twenty or thirty courtiers, as many servants—in a week the news would be spreading from every church and brothel in the capital. Like the Viceroy, His Grace would find lessons to draw from it.

 They came a few days later. Two lackeys in the Archbishop's livery. Safety in numbers, it would seem. By the Archbishop's dispensation they entered into the cloister, entered this cell without knocking. But so swiftly does word fly through the alleys and corridors that we were already waiting for them. This is a women's place—no man enters here without this warning.

Wordlessly one of the lackeys handed me the order, under the Archbishop's seal. Silently, mercifully, they turned and left. After a moment to compose myself I followed them to the door to make sure they'd gone. My sisters in the cells across the way stood gaping in their doorways.

> . . . the petition dated January 4th, 1679, received by the Secretary of the Archdiocese on November 20th, 1681, for the purchase of one cell. Pursuant, a complete inventory of its contents is required, for the purposes of determining if said cell in its dimensions and appointments is adequate and appropriate to the purchaser's requirements.
>
> By order and disposition of His Illustrious Grace,
> Lord Archbishop don Francisco Aguiar y Seijas,
> signed this, the sixth day of July, 1691

The game was obvious enough, if subtle for a man of the Archbishop's temperament. The inventory would reveal the cell to be too full and therefore inadequate to its purpose . . . until an as yet undetermined number of items had been auctioned to raise funds for the Archbishop's ferocious campaigns of charity. The people's need was insatiable in these trying times. Who would deny it, who would refuse? Even if she could.

I wondered if he would next send Carlos, his Chief Almoner, who knew the contents of these rooms as well as any man. Almost thirteen years I had been waiting to buy this cell. All these years without a response, and yet the request had been neither forgotten nor lost. Was the Archbishop's secretary so very competent, or were they aided by a memory in which nothing is forgotten or lost?

I had begun to wonder if there had ever been a rift between Núñez and His Grace.

But the cell, Your Grace, is it too full or instead too small . . . ? For I have so far found no room for a botanical garden, or pleasaunces such as those of Versailles. A full astronomical observatory would be a splendid addition, and a bestiary, too. If not so large as that kept by the great Khans, then something more modest, such as Moctezuma's own. . . .

The soul of Teresa of Avila is a palace, one of the most beautiful that has ever been. That we may understand a little, she presents it as a palace of passageways reaching inward, an enchaining of seven chambers or abodes. In the innermost, on a priceless rock-crystal throne, waits her Beloved.

My soul waits at the top of ten steps, behind a lacquered folding screen in the Japanese style, in a long narrow room that houses my *studiolo* and library. Here is where the Inspector will wish to begin his list; it is this room that contains the most priceless of marvels; in this chamber my Beloved rests.

But before entering, the gentlemen may wish to get their bearings, to fix this particular arrangement in their minds. At the top of the stairs, there, to the left, is one of three doors connecting this room to the other two. Just inside the doorway is a second folding screen, also in the Japanese style but decorated with scenes from Mexico's past and streets.

Nine *varas* in width by ten in length, the upper storey is six *varas* high. Three rooms: on the east side, a sitting room with dining table, a bedroom with a desk; the third room runs the full length of the west side and occupies a third of the total width. The geometry will not be difficult, though the accounting may so prove. While there are writing desks in every room, here by the window is the largest. The window has been altered, is large and low; as the Inspector sees for himself, the view across the rooftops is to the south. Note the step-ladders, the shelves built to line the walls from floor to ceiling—the workmanship is excellent. Note carefully the openings cut to the exact contour of the window, the fireplace and doorways; see the hooks set in the dim top shelves from which to hang a lantern while one searches. The four transverse display cases stand at two-*vara* intervals, each successive case from the south window a little wider than the last to catch the light. Take note that all must be dismantled if they are to leave this room. Yes, the cot and the reading chair by the fireplace, these come out easily.

That space beside the stairs, there behind the low shelf? No, not a hidden stairwell, I assure you, just a chimney shaft.

If we think of the library as a window looking out from an enchanted palace, then the prince's *studiolo* is the world brought in to stock the cave of the magician, the workshop of the alchemist.

Its elements are to be deployed with care, in sections and harmonious intervals. The *studiolo* is a theatre of the soul, the mind is its orchestra; its sweetest solos are played on its finest instrument, *admiratio*. We may imagine this instrument of wonder as a slender violinist seated, a little nervously, among the reeds and flutes and clarions. In the ideal arrangement featured here, in which the library and *studiolo* flow one into the other, the two chief sections—perhaps think of these as the strings and the winds—consist of instruments of spirit and sense, the upper and lower choirs. And yet this business of upper and lower is really a convenience, for the instruments are free to move about, and really owe it to themselves to do this. So it happens that we so often find *logica* down in the kitchens, where the knives come out.

But you will want to get under way. First, the musical and audible instruments, since this is a sort of auditorium. No, I do not play them all unfortunately, but quite a few. Clay flute, clavichord, *vihuela*, violin . . . There you see an echo chest, here two automatons that dance and sing. Try them if you like, they are very lifelike. One pendulum, which, courtesy of Signor Galilei, we can use to regulate the tempo by lengthening and shortening the string. One musarithmetic box such as in the famed *studiolo* of the Reverend Kircher at the Jesuit College in Rome. Oh yes, the Jesuits have these too. Bigger. One music box, one speaking trumpet, one conch shell trumpet, yes, a *caracol*. I was just coming to that.

If you don't mind, I really must sit down, I really must stop a moment. You would not consider coming back another day? Surely the Inspector must see this will take a little while. What you are asking is the inventory of my soul.

 Friday afternoon, a cold grey rain. It was the turn of those of us who confess with Father Arellano. The Mother Prioress preferred that the most senior of the black-veiled nuns not go to our own chaplain, who had influence enough here among us. I had been called and could not delay long—our patio being the closest to the chapel. Reluctantly I made my way along the arcades to stay out of the weather, down the short passageway, past the chapel entrance and out into the rain. The orchards were ahead, a drab of yellowing leaves, the gardens to my left, mostly mud and a sprig or two of green. Sister María Bernardina was kneeling on a stone slab, soaked to the skin, confessing through a small slot in the thick chapel wall. She finished as I drew near, blinked water out of her eyes. More drops tumbled from her brows. She almost smiled. The *craticula* is the width of the mouth, such that on neither side of the wall may we see each other with both eyes, leaving one feeling not unlike the Cyclops confiding in Odysseus. I was not even sure I knew any longer what Father Arellano looked like, to those with sight in both eyes. For ten years he had been my nominal director, entitled to meet with me more comfortably in the locutory whenever he wished. He never wished. I am too beautiful, he had once explained. Nice that he still thought so, for a Cyclopean attaining a certain age—though were it intended as a gallantry, and it was not, it would have meant somewhat more were he indeed able to see me.

It was cold, it was raining, there was pain in my knees, I was prepared to be brief and Arellano rarely spoke beyond prescribing a light penance. But today he did speak; through the patter of the rain and a channel in the masonry the depth of a forearm, I only heard him with difficulty.

. . . failing you . . . I cannot much longer . . . protect you. When had I ever asked such a thing of him? He meant to protect himself . . . The rain, the stone was cold now. *A time to study the writings of John of the Cross . . .* But I *knew* his work—he was the poet I most revered. *Another spiritual director. Father Núñez . . .* Father Núñez what?—he could not mean . . . protect *me*? This could have been amusing, from someone else, in another circumstance, in sunlight. But from Arellano it was not. For Arellano found nothing amusing in the monstrous face of sin—at least since he had looked down fifteen years ago to find his dagger separating a fellow gambler's ribs.

I had wanted to listen to the pain in my knees, but changed my mind when Father Arellano admitted he'd approached Núñez without my leave. . . .

Father Arellano, you must not worry yourself overly about failing me. My previous spiritual director did so utterly, was quite unable to answer questions such as these, or not satisfactorily—can you hear me all right, can you hear me clearly? It is awkward to speak to one's spiritual director in this way rather than in the comfort of the locutory, but at least His Paternity don Arellano is dry? For while I treasure John's poetry, in his commentaries there are concerns. . . .

John writes of even the adepts in spiritual matters as being like children in their knowledge and feelings, in their speech and dealings with Him. In the first night of the soul, ours is the love of a child, for this is the easiest love, our love of the infant Christ and our sadness for his destiny. In answer to that love, He sends the sweetest milk flowing through our prayers and meditations. But through this night He will wean us toward a more adult love, so that in the last watch of the first night, the soul is more like a young lover slipping out of a darkened house, the house of the senses, to be with her Beloved. *Beloved of my life, I run to you.* Delectable moments, stolen, brief, promises of a still greater richness and fullness to come.

As in the Canticles.

Yet as the first night draws to a close the love has become difficult and painful: we are to be deprived again, but of joys now of the spirit, weaned again. And the first trial of the second night is this frustration, for one is a lover and not a child anymore. But why must it always be thus? If in His house there are many rooms, why must love abide in each indifferently? And the love He returns, is it the same for everyone, or is it a love of each of us? Surely he would not love as if we were other than we are, surely he loves us knowing *who* we are. Does this love take no colouring from its vessel—is it ever and forever the same?—while the face of the ocean, the wide eyes of a lake change with every tick of the sun, every shred of mist, every lake-bottom and sea-floor lift, every alteration of the deep—silt, sand, rock, mud—every angle of its run and pitch?

What is more constant and yet more various? What is more constant in its variations than water? If not love?

Silence from beyond the wall.

I should have known by now. I was not, in fact, a child. I did not need his advice, I did not need direction. And so I started out, as so often happens with me, clever . . . as a child hoping if she were only clever enough she might keep him. . . . And then I end up kneeling in the rain, pouring out my heart to a slot in the wall—scent of stone and must, rain in my mouth, taste of salt—to a man who once found me beautiful and cannot bear to see me now, who probably cannot hear me, who has perhaps already gone.

The books, I could see, were different. The books might be dangerous. But these other things of mine, would they take all this from me? What harm have they done anyone when only I may see them?

Please do not take these away. These are only instruments of beauty and wonder, these are only innocent things.

1 astrolabe, 1 helioscope, 1 telescope, 1 set of compasses
1 microscope built to designs by Reverend Athanasius Kircher; an assortment of fine steel scalpels, 1 of obsidian, suitable for the most delicate dissections and slide preparation
1 magic lantern, 1 camera lucida built to designs by Leonardo
1 magic square (& alchemical equipment & materials)
1 collection of glass paperweights, 1 of seashells collected from the seven seas
7 magnifying glasses of different strengths and sizes
1 toadstone; 1 fish skeleton embedded in limestone; 8 gallstones of divers and disputed origin; 4 *perlas barruecas*; 1 horn of an Atlantic unicorn . . .
1 chronoscope . . .

No more brooding on how little I had accomplished these past ten years, or the past twenty-two—a few verses to take pride in, the glimmerings of an idea or two. I would not ask how much time I had. I would not lament that it was not enough. I lamented now only wasted time. Work harder, work faster now.

I finished the last remaining lyrics on Saint Catherine in a day and sent them to Puebla, city of Angels, to Santa Cruz. If he had any intention yet to play my Redeemer . . . Let that be up to him. It could not hurt now.

One morning a little before noon a young nun came to say a man had come for me. The way she had said this put a small spur to my fears. Her expression was kindly and solemn, almost pained.

"From the Inquisition?"

"No, no, Sor Juana, a composer."

One composer. Which one was it now? One or the other, they could wait if they would not come together for me just once. I finished the page I was reading at the window, and an extra three, slowly, for good measure, then went down. Sálazar. Looking angry and wounded in his pride. My gaze went out to the little courtyard, past the rose bushes to the long yellow grass, less like lawn than sedge. The rain was making the ground frail, everywhere returning the island to the marshland it was. Gardening had branched into masonry: the gardener's every step these past months laying tiles of sky in the earth.

Sálazar stood waiting some way from the clavichord and well back from the grille, hands down at his sides. He was tall, a man fully grown, but it was the expression of the six-year-old he wore—a proud artist kept waiting like a page. As I studied his face what softened my anger was that his own seemed quite dwarfed by his hurt. I almost apologized, for I was just then remembering him as he was the second time we spoke together. A tall boy of seven, Antonio de Sálazar was by then known by all to be a prodigy. He had come to the Palace again, to play the clavichord this time, not the violin—and to play no one's music but his own. He had not been made to wait. He recognized me among the many who came afterwards to congratulate him. Later we had a moment to talk. He led me to the same vestibule and thanked me for my kindness on his previous visit. I had been like a princess to him—he flushed then. "But how stupid, perhaps you are one."

"No, Antonio, I am from here, just like you. And do you remember the advice I gave you?"

"I do, and won't forget it."

"And will you tell me?"

"Take time from my music, to make friends and keep them. Save a little of myself, for myself."

"Anything else?"

"A genius can be hurt like anyone else."

Now I was forty-three, he was still ten years younger, and the one who had given him the advice was now the one who had wounded his pride. He had forgotten the princess in the palace, or did not see her in a middle-aged nun. Or rather a middle-aged nun in her. That was understandable. But I wanted to ask if he remembered what she had said, so many years ago. Her advice. And if it had been of any use to him.

Instead I thanked him for coming, made no excuses for the delay, and was the cantor perhaps coming later?

Fury stood in his eyes then—no, Sor Juana, he was not coming later, and he, Sálazar, did not like to be kept waiting. He had a lot of work to do—many new commissions—now more than ever. This *Caracol* had never been his idea but the Cantor de Ribera's, and another thing he did not appreciate was being asked by the Vice-Queen to look through my poetry to her for musical insults. At last night's ball the Countess had drawn him aside to tell him at length of her conviction that she had been slighted during her last visit to this locutory. She'd had the distinct impression that in my verses on that day I had called her hand-maidens whores. Which made a musical composition I had penned on the occasion of her birthday at the very least suspicious, and who better than Antonio de Sálazar to ferret out the insults most certainly buried there? And precisely what, he wondered, was he to do?—pretend he could find none the least bit suspicious, only to have someone else do it for him and make him look either a fool, or very much like the man who has played the Countess for one? Half his commissions *came* from her, and if I was determined to throw away what was left of my career—which I seemed to be, however little *that* might be—he had no such intentions for his. He would not lie to her, for Ribera maybe, but not for me. And so as he was saying, he had more work than he had ever wanted and a burden of responsibility he wasn't even sure he could cope with, so this was not at all the right time for a collaboration.

I was glad I had not asked him about that day we first met, for though he stood as a man speaking of a great career to one who had not quite had one—he looked so terribly hurt. He was that boy, about to cry, and I was no longer sure what was happening.

Well, Maestro Sálazar should do as he saw fit. Who knew indeed what the future would bring? For the present, Cantor de Ribera and I would be fine. We could finish what we started.

Sálazar's eyes went cold, the boy quite gone, but he had already shown me his hurt. I had not been the one to inflict it after all, but he was nothing averse to passing it along.

"No, Sor Juana. I am afraid that will not be possible. That is what I have been kept waiting so long to tell you. Cantor de Ribera died this morning. Two hours ago."

The rain had stopped. Sálazar had gone. I sat at the clavichord working out some notions Ribera had once had for *Caracol.* From the courtyard, quiet now, I heard water running in the gutters, droplets falling into puddles from the rose bushes, without blossom in this season. Those leaves that remained had gone yellow.

Did you ever wonder where the princess went, Antonio? Don't you ever won-der where they go?

I think Sálazar had remembered after all. The advice. I was happy he had taken the time to know Ribera, to love and keep him. Ribera was proud of that love, of the younger man's gift, not at all like a rival.

Suspende, cantor Cisne, el dulce acento:
mira, por ti, al Señor que Delfos mira,
en zampoña trocar la dulce lira . . . [8]

I had had a thought for Cantor de Ribera that morning, two hours before. To have been there. Though in a convent one grows used to friends dying elsewhere. I could not quite picture him then, or quite hear. On other days, yes. The hoarseness in his voice, as he announced he had secured for us this last commission. The long neck, the big Adam's apple, the long black brows darting up, dipping down. I wished I had tried that sonnet on a heron, so many years ago. My problem had not been entirely poetic. In praise of a cantor, a song heralding his voice as a heron's could not help but be suspected of irony.

It could not be good to be a heron and called a swan. In truth if the swan was the emblem of Apollo and Orpheus, it was as likely for the graceful curve of its neck. For Apollo and Orpheus were lyrists, first of all. An injustice to herons . . . the swan's neck was graceful, the heron's just long. And yet I wondered if the heron's song was any more raucous than the swan's . . . save its last.

Who could live a life anticipating how every act, every step, every gesture, good or bad, might be remembered one day? Every line said or written in earnest or anger or jest. Who could live this way?

After our father Saint Jerome, maximal Doctor of Holy Mother Catholic Church, we may see Beauty in terms of the three transcendental attributes of God: Oneness, Goodness, Truth. Beauty is the transcendental perfection of God in time. Beauty is God's plenitude, an overflowing—vast yet in nothing superfluous—pouring down in a cascade of music through the orders of Creation, through the stars and heavens, through the whole sublunary world—human, animal, vegetal, mineral—down to the smallest of atoms. Since the Fall, so is it also with our human senses: each being an instrument crafted to resonate differently. In full possession of our senses we are like unto a prism breaking beauty into its spectra and gamuts and separate registers—red, blue, gold—mi, fa, sol—sight, hearing, touch—that scatter in tints and tones and hints and hues, in flocks, in flights, in schools, through water, into air, over ground.

But to return us whence we have fallen is a long climb and arduous. And in assembling our provisions for this ascent, it is not enough to lay the evidence of the senses side by side. These instruments of mind must be fused, in the sense that Lope tells us the painting of Rubens is a poetry for the eye. Imagine poetry, then, as painting for the ear. It is the mind that slowly teaches us to weave together these separate elements into a score, and in this sense we rightly call Theology the Queen of the Sciences, for it is she who enters the final chamber, the abode of the Beloved.

Even as to the lover every aspect of the Beloved is beauty . . . the turns and pauses of His mind, the fragrance of His skin, the warmth of His breath as if the radiance of a perfect fire . . . but here one must not go on too far. In recollecting these, the Queen in her actions is like a lover straining to learn every small and separate thing of her Beloved. These are the notes, and she strives to show us how to compose them in their very fullest arrangement, to fuse them in perfect union, making full use of each and every instrument.

Mind is the shepherd, Mind is the falconer, Mind is the net that recalls and collects, Mind is the guide that shall one day bring them all home to rest. Our mind is an instrument of collection, and a collection of instruments. *Logica, inventio, divinatio,* and the finest of all is *admiratio,* for it is this gift of marvelling at the world that brings us most closely on its own to our condition before the Fall.

But it is the soul in Grace that plays them. The soul is in the grace of the orchestra, the Soul is the orchestra of Grace. And its Music is Love.

Entreme donde no supe
y quedeme no sabiendo
toda ciencia trascendiendo . . . [†]

 nnumbered times had the capital been warned, a dark day was to come. Make ready. It would be for all to see, a terrible majesty written in the sky.

It was Carlos's plan to prepare everyone this time. With the mood in the city now, could one even imagine it, the pandemonium?—to which I wondered why the authorities feared our panic so much more than our fury.

With the Archbishop's blessing, Carlos had spent the past weeks going to the churches to explain what was to come. Forecasts of doom and darkness from the pulpit were hardly a departure. The predicators were agreeable, pleased at last to have a date and that date so near. And even an approximate hour. Sermons were polished and studded with quotations from the books of Revelations and Amos, dark references to the breaking of the seals, and to Nineveh. The forecasts propagated from the churches and spiralled out through the plazas, amplified by doomsayers in the streets and echoed in the marketplaces. The people were frightened, the people were prepared. They had no sense that the source of this foreknowledge was in any way different from prophecy. All had the date now and the hour was drawing nigh. August 23rd, 1691.

There were small flaws in the plan, but chief among them: no one is ever quite prepared for a total eclipse of the sun.

Carlos had only just purchased a new telescope and with a generosity typical of him gave the old one to Antonia. He explained to her, and again with diagrams, how the parabolic mirror had greatly enhanced the quality of the sightings since Galileo's day. He came to San Jerónimo several times to instruct us in its features, and the day before the eclipse spent all afternoon with me reviewing patiently, despite his growing agitation, the geometric formulas I would be using in *Caracol*. Before leaving that evening he fitted several layers of dark brown glass over the telescopic eyepiece and stressed that they must not be removed until the sun's eclipse had reached its totality. The plan was that Antonia

[†]I entered I knew not
    where
and thus and there
    remained:
all sciences
transcended . . .
—John of the Cross

should set up the telescope in the very centre of the patio, for there were numerous events to watch for in every quadrant of the sky. I did not think the chances particularly good. It had been raining for a year.

 Thursday dawned cloudless. On this of all mornings, a clear blue sky was itself an uncanny sign, but particularly for those who still doubted. The sun shone over the city on the lake and the lake within the city, scintillating in ten thousand places, in the sloughs of the streets and in garden puddles and cattle troughs. Just before nine o'clock in the morning, two before the hour fixed by the prediction, the street dogs disappeared from the alleys of the barrios. Not long after, five thousand Indians along the canals stepped from their traces—to be restrained by neither shouts of threat nor curses, by whip nor iron goad—and according to the witness of their overseers, melted away like wraiths. At nine o'clock on August 23rd the sun died.

The imperial capital of Mexico, city of the centre of the earth, was cast onto an otherworldly plane of night as the Sixth Seal was opened, and the *Sun became black as sackcloth of hair and the Moon became as blood.* Swiftly, with the bellringers standing by, the bells of the city began their tolling from fifty belfries and campaniles. Many who had lived through the comet of 1680 said this was far worse, the fear, the wretchedness, the loneliness in the violent milling darkness, as the streets filled and the light failed. To four hundred thousand people came the moments of greatest terror they had known.

Moving as though blind, stumbling, falling through the dark, the people of the city made for the sound of the bells. Beneath the belfries lay shelter. In the movement of the bells lay life and hope of Life. The churches were lit by thousands of candles, the churches were Light. The plazas before the churches were thronged with the bereft, crying out for succour, calling out for comfort.

Before the sermons ended—indeed before they had quite begun— the light was already returning to the world, though the people did not seem directly to notice it.

By noon, processions of ascetics groaned their way through the streets, like carts heavy burdened, from the churches and temples past the convents and monasteries, and echoed within the walls by smaller processions moving round the patios like larger wheels of penance and within them cogs.

It was to have been a moment of triumph for human learning and science. We had been prepared, to prevent panic. There were small flaws in the plan. Yet the Grand Plan had emerged triumphant.

When he came to San Jerónimo afterwards, shortly past noon, Carlos and I quarrelled bitterly, but it would never have occurred to me I might not see him again. This is not to say I had no sense of approaching danger. It was never far if we were not careful, and I at least was not—how pleased he was that the plan had proven useful. The Church had not been caught off guard.

There is a peasant science of prediction that has not yet been fathomed, one that links eclipses to earthquakes. When the first quake came three days later we half expected it—the half who did not dread it. The quake itself was not violent. Anyone raised here had experienced worse. More unusual were the aftershocks, their intensity, undiminished from first to last over the course of a week, but most of all their number: I had not thought to count, but it came to be said there were forty, forty exactly.

It seemed that a people in distress was versed in an older learning, its holy texts in the scripts of stillbirths and deformities, in the flights of birds, in the spill of fresh vitals in the dust. . . . Known to this ancient wisdom is that eclipses exert malignant influences—stillbirths and live births of disharmonious proportions, deformities of ominous shape and configuration—infants with limbs shaped like stars, the heads of animals.

It was not long before there appeared an anonymous leaflet plastered to walls in the plazas and public markets, near the prayer niches and places of worship—and all around San Jerónimo. Were women *monstra*, the text began, were they too without souls—like the stillborn and malformed they brought into the world? The author had assuredly read Paracelsus. The leaflet might simply be the latest in the series of attacks on me, a warning or some kind of crude slur. But it might be something else, for in just this manner did the Inquisition sow its seeds to determine what fears might find congenial soil. In Spain the fear of witchcraft had never taken, whereas in France that horror and its harvest seemed inexhaustible.

September, 1691. Gutiérrez paid a visit unannounced. I had seen little of him since late spring, when he had been unable to discover if the

Inquisition was monitoring my mail. As for the authenticity of the Archbishop's madness, it was an open question at the Holy Office, with adherents on both sides even today. Gutiérrez no longer had an opinion. He did not know anything about the leaflet and knew little about Paracelsus. The truth was, Gutiérrez seemed to know less all the time.

As if reading my thoughts he excused himself for not having come sooner but there had been little to report, till now: on June 4th of this year, Doctor Alonso Alberto de Velasco, priest of the Tabernacle, member of the Brotherhood of Mary, advisor to the Holy Office of the Inquisition, had made a formal denunciation of the sermon of one Xavier Palavicino, pronounced in the convent of San Jerónimo at the feast of Santa Paula. In response, Prosecutor Ulloa had written to the Tribunal, attesting that he had received the denunciation of the sermon and naming two Inquisitors to examine its propositions for pernicious error. The Inquisitors were said to be Mier and Armesto, thorough, capable men.

I did not want to seem ungrateful, but June 4th, this was almost *three months past.* Gutiérrez shrugged. He had only found out about it a week ago. Or two. The thing to note was that the prosecutor made his decision to launch an investigation less than a week after receiving the denunciation. By the standards of the Holy Office, this was particularly fast; this seemed very much like haste. Antonia looked at me strangely after he left. How could I take this so calmly?

But in October Gutiérrez brought better news. A printer's proof had been submitted in an application for a publishing licence from the Holy Office in Puebla. It was the same printer that had published the Letter Worthy of Athena and Sor Philothea's preface last year. Diego Fernández de Leon. A pause for effect. Bishop Santa Cruz's own printer. Yes, go on. The licensing application was for the printing of my carols on Saint Catherine of Alexandria.

It appeared Santa Cruz was to let them be sung after all. After Gutiérrez had gone, I turned to see Antonia's face younger by years.

Is it love? Antonia had asked that night. Surely if Santa Cruz is in love with you, she said, there is a chance. But how much better my chances seemed today if he didn't, if none of this was personal at all. And now this, after everything else. *Was* it love? How was one to know with such a man—who was to say what certain men were like in the secrecy of their rooms? The things he had asked of her. This was lovemaking for him—with a young woman so beautiful, so carnal—only that she watch during his mortifications?

But perhaps this was precisely the point, that he had always resisted such sublime temptations. Asking nothing more than to have Antonia making reports to no worldly purpose—not even caring if they were true, perhaps even knowing they weren't. How I brushed my hair? Did I use a mirror? No, for him the game had been to picture it, *to watch her watching me, and suffering for it.* Watching me just as she had watched him. Lord God, did I discipline myself? harshly, strictly?—did he imagine he and I were alike?

Is this love?

At San Jerónimo the stories that held the greatest sway over the mind of the convent were those of the *beatas,* not witches but false saints and holy women held in the Inquisition's secret prisons, soon to be secretly tried and burned at certain convents across the city. The rumours were repeated in the work rooms, the gardens and orchards, at the water basins and in the refectory. Rumours became near certainty, confirmed in letters from sisters and cousins and friends in other convents, in other cities. The number of letters multiplied. Eighteen convents in the capital alone, three thousand nuns—all writing and reading letters, all circulating the same stories in endless permutations. The letters flew like flights of startled doves.

There came an item of news from this time that I could not help believing. It had come in a letter from our sister convent in Puebla. Bishop Santa Cruz had asked *la mística,* Sor María de San José, to put to paper for him an account of her spiritual journey. It was a singular sign of favour for a countrywoman from Tepeaca he had once all but kicked headlong down the cathedral steps.

Eleven months had passed since the publication of my Letter Worthy of Athena, eight months since my reply to Sor Philothea, three since I had sent Santa Cruz the *villancicos* he had commissioned on Saint Catherine. Four weeks remained until they were to be sung on her feast day at the cathedral in Puebla. I had begun to let myself believe that he had no further wish to bring out the *mística* in me, had found his Teresa. Perhaps, as Antonia had hoped, he was truly finished with me.

If music can be seen as our most perfect idea of Time, then perhaps History too is a musical science. The mutation to a higher key felt inevitable when it came: soon the talk in our letters and the locutories was of not just one *beata* but several, then not just *beatas* any longer but nuns, adulterous nuns. But . . . had not the people been saying that the cause of these calamities was instead the eclipse? This was only asking to be told that fornication had brought on the eclipse.

Carlos and I had not spoken in the three months since, though he still came to the locutory for Antonia, for their classes of mathematics and science, and history. She left sheepishly to go to him, while I tried to let her know I did not mind, without ever quite saying why. I did not want her to misunderstand, lest I hurt her too. Her friendship with Carlos was real, and growing, the gallant preoccupation of the older gentleman with a beautiful young woman at a delicate age. For her part . . . no, those thoughts were for the privacy of her heart.

And yet for all this, when he came for her, I knew he came for me; what had come between us that day had never really been about the eclipse. In all the turmoil of the day's events, the last thing either of us was thinking about was a quarrel. Antonia and I did not even know when we would see Carlos next or in what state we might find him, but he came that afternoon. He found us in the locutory with Gárate, the convent chaplain. Chaplain also of the Metropolitan Cathedral, Gárate had been there at the appointed hour, and had just been telling us of the Archbishop's immense satisfaction with the turn of events—had an archdiocese ever served more effectively in an hour of sudden calamity? There had been a great cleansing in the capital. Many a lax Christian saw his faith forever renewed, many a secret Jew saw his faith in the law of Moses shattered and forever forsaken. And then there was the rate at which alms had been pouring in all day, to the cathedral, to our own temple, no doubt to every church and cloister in the city. Gárate had heard about the Archbishop's requisition of an inventory of my cell, and wondered now if His Grace might feel less need to resort to auctions to raise funds for his charities. I was determined not to entertain false hopes, but found my mind racing, nonetheless, to the other consequences that the Church's great success might have, for me particularly.

Gárate rose to salute the man of the hour with a ceremonious bow. Carlos shook his head. "I only thank God for having put me in the way of a conjunction of events so rare and about which so few observations are dispassionately recorded." Never had I seen Carlos look happier. I held my tongue. This was the fulfilment of a dream, his no less than Galileo's—of science in the service of the Church.

Carlos was too excited to sit, but rather stepped stiffly about the locutory closely inspecting things on the walls he'd seen many times before and today was clearly not seeing at all—almost a bust of himself, stiff-necked, stiff-jointed all over, heaped in glory. There was something in the long face, in the long, broad-bridged nose and the huge dark eyes, that reminded one of a terrifyingly intelligent fawn, grown ancient—bending arthritically now to examine a map as the chaplain continued to sing his praises, marvelling at the precision of his art.

"*Science*, sir," Carlos corrected, still facing away from us, hands clasped at his back. "Merely the rigorous application of a method." Half turning toward the chaplain, he added, "And we still missed the prediction by two hours."

Here he remembered his old telescope and asked Antonia if the moment had been worth all the preparation. In no time they were leaning close to the grille, Antonia by half a head the taller, conferring volubly and leaving me with Gárate sitting at the window, listening more to them than to our chaplain discussing the weather, which, yes, was holding. It was the first fair afternoon in months. The sun was all benevolence, the sky a radiant blue. Across the room, Antonia was asking Carlos how it could be that the moon had fit so perfectly over the sun.

"Do you hear, Juana? Such a natural philosopher we have here in our Antonia!" At this angle, few gaps showed in the grille. His face ducked into view as I sat back to see him more clearly. He turned back to her. "And yet what you so accurately observed, Antonia, is merely a stupendous coincidence."

Again I bit back a reply. If the phrase 'stupendous coincidence' had any meaning whatever, it was surely an invitation to probe more deeply, instead of an irrelevance—which I knew Carlos had not meant—for, with so many bodies in such a busy heaven continually swinging in front of one another from some perspective or other, an eclipse did not exist without a point of view. And what was a perspective separate from our experience of it?

Just then Gárate ventured how helpful it might be if, after such a universal display of penitence, the rains were now to cease and the city were given a reprieve. I could hold my peace no longer. "Tell me, Carlos, how does glossing over the stupendous improbability that produces a total eclipse allow us to properly account for its most significant effect—the power it exercises upon our minds and upon our times? Were there ever odds more properly called *astronomical,* that the angular distance for the sun and moon—their apparent diameters—should prove identical, two bodies so vastly unequal in size and in their distance from us? Doubtless you can fill in the trigonometry for yourself, but pull the little moon in closer by a few thousand leagues and suddenly the eclipses that have for dozens of centuries moved admirals and histories and kings fade to a pallid glow in the darkness; nudge the little moon out another twenty thousand and in a flash—no totality at all, but rather a small dark smudge against the glare, a bit of soot on lantern glass. Instead, what we are given—in this coronet of ice in the heavens—is the overwhelming impression of *Design* and *Intent.* But whose design and what intent?"

At the gap in the grille the smile faded, succeeded by the bemusement of someone who has bent to inspect the contents of a cage and found something unexpected. But if the chaplain had not taken it upon himself to defend him, our quarrel still might have ended there.

Carlos said nothing. How convenient to let others answer for him, how delicious to have the Church itself uphold the righteousness of one's scientific principles and not have to speak to how they are used.

"Is this also your view, Carlos? Your vision of the new science? To terrify people in churches even as the Jesuit Kircher used to do with his magic lantern—projecting devils into the air! And what of the science of history to which don Carlos has dedicated his many monographs? Are the fatal events of this day too insignificant to merit the historian's notice?"

"Juana, don Carlos, I . . ." Antonia began, bewildered.

"It's all right, Antonia." Carlos came to stand where he could speak to me without raising his voice. "An eclipse is many things, Juana. But surely it is also a rare opportunity to test hyphotheses of the sun's composition, to refine estimates of its mass and, yes, distance, and to theorize on the properties of light." His tone was grave, dignified, as he then asked if I might care to discuss my own observations of the event. I could still have stopped. I had only to be evasive.

Instead I told him the truth, that I had not looked through his telescope at all.

At this, Carlos turned his enormous sad eyes on Antonia. "You see, it is just as we feared, Antonia. No, it is worse. Not only does the artist challenge our empirical observations with poetic cavils—she makes this poetry on what she has not even bothered to *see*. It is forever this way with Sor Juana. As with mathematics in the past, as with virtually everything else, she has lost all interest in science now . . ."

What happens between even true friends, why do we not take more care—indeed insist on being careless with our most dear? Are we hoping to prove our friendship indestructible? That morning as if by a miracle the sky had cleared long enough for him to take detailed sightings with a fine new telescope, one of the finest in the world. And I begrudged him this. For weeks Carlos had toiled long hours selflessly and all but pointlessly over the infernal dredging projects at the canals; the disappointments in his life were not few. Then, one day of glory, a day when for once the deepest of his passions had no need to be hidden, from me or from the Church, when his faith could be served by the depth of his learning and his love for astronomy openly declared. How could I have let this happen—how many times have I turned it over in my mind? We could have stopped there, avoided the worst, had I not let myself be goaded—and shamed, on a day of such appalling events—into feeling a petty stab of jealousy, of Antonia.

I asked Chaplain Gárate to leave, and then Antonia.

How dared he say I had lost interest in science—in everything!—in front of them? Did he have any idea how many people Gárate might tell, to what uses they might put such information?

Carlos's face was pale as always, but the eyes behind the spectacles were enormous and angry: this was a formidable fawn. How dared *I* impugn his feelings for this city, this country—and truly, he wondered, was my first concern the people's plight or my own? And was this compassionate concern of mine quite historical—or was it for how a day of triumph for the Church might diminish my precious liberty? And was the heart of my interest truly Mexico, or only in those parts of it that affected *me*? As always, with me—everywhere a conspiracy.

Conspiracy. How interesting to hear don Carlos sound more like a Jesuit with each passing year. On the subject of conspiracies, what could he tell me about the Archbishop's demand for an inventory of my cell? Ah, so don Carlos was truly claiming to have no knowledge of this—perhaps one does not see everything in a telescope after all. But such concern in his face now, and would that be for me or the fate of his own manuscripts? Equally curious that *in* some of these manuscripts were recorded the

Mexica testimonies of comets and eclipses, yet among us here and now such things were only superstitions entirely devoid of interest.

Indeed yes, *superstition*—this childish notion of a destiny inscribed in the sky between a comet and an eclipse. Sor Juana's distresses had all the seriousness of astrology, a weak excuse for persistent melancholy—

A thirty-year-old quarrel is itself a natural wonder. This was the only man in the New World who could ask when I had last done work the equal of my talent, and chide me now for my loss of interest in the passions we had once shared. But for years it had been clear to me if not to him that we could never practise here a true and free natural philosophy. Most of Carlos's colleagues in Spain had forsworn the practice of science altogether. But he had persisted for the love of it, though we could only follow distant developments, confirm conclusions made in freer places, and in places not so much freer. He and I had quarrelled more than once over Galileo, whose fate, Carlos insisted, owed to an excess of pride, chief among his many character flaws. Over Descartes we argued less harshly, over the change in him—unflinching in the *Discourse,* conciliatory two decades later in the *Meditations.* For Carlos this softening was a sign of maturity, a judgement that he pronounced with all the dignity of someone whose best work would always be unpublished.

In a quarrel of decades, each thing said echoes with the hundred said before. So when he said 'melancholy' I heard his laments that in me the masculine virtues—intelligence, analysis, curiosity, independence, scepticism—were forever undermined by the feminine vices—moodiness, willfulness, faithlessness, inconstancy, duplicity. Particularly the last three, which for him were the true reasons I had not married him. But hearing these in turn cut me so deeply not because he was saying 'marriage' but because I was hearing 'betrayal.' Of a friend, of an ideal, of a love, of a gift. These past years the few moments of sweetness Carlos and I had found were when discussing our various ideas for inventions. Musical clocks and maps, wind harps and steam clocks. When I thought of all these whimsical creations, it seemed we had begun to find a poetry together for what could not be done here, could never be published, for the great synthesis that would always float just beyond our grasp. And so perhaps the heaviest blow to our friendship had come only recently, in a book by a Lutheran with a good biblical name, but then, they loved their Bibles. Isaac. We still had not read it, but had read formulas and arguments copied into letters from Carlos's correspondents in Europe. From what I could see, this Newton had accomplished it—fused the Archimedean infinitesimals with the Cartesian translation of geometry into algebra, next integrating these into the Galilean equations on falling bodies, all to solve the riddle of Hermes Trismegistus: universal attraction at a distance, expressed now in the language of mathematics. Just such an enterprise had been my great dream as a child. Carlos and I had been outstripped. We would never catch up, and now to follow even the rest of Europe meant to be left ever further behind. This was something I had never been able to endure. To hear him say I had lost interest in mathematics was to hear him say I had betrayed a gift. What he could never understand was that I had not betrayed it but had failed that gift terribly, and so, abandoned it.

And then just the day before the eclipse, had I not swallowed my pride and finally asked him to verify the formulas I'd used in *Caracol?* He had been generous as usual, and gentle. No simple business, this, he said, frowning over my calculations for cross-sections cut by various spirals winding through cones of differing amplitude. It was a good afternoon in the locutory, a good journey without moving, with the rain falling in the courtyard past the window bars. I noticed his threadbare clothes, the skinny legs and patched hose, the little chest and shoulders under the great faded cloak. The conversation had turned from the conic sections to the Cartesian vortices, to Christina of Sweden and back to her famous tutor. There had been much gentle talk and laughter. How grey his hair was becoming. How thin I was, like a girl again. How pleased he was that we had at last built a model of my musical clock. And so for once I gave no utterance to my faithlessness, my doubts that the essential Catholic doctrines, which Carlos so tranquilly expected to confirm through his new telescope, could ever be construed as having foreseen not just a sun-centred heaven, but a cosmos of infinite extension crowded with an infinitude of suns like ours, and spiralling through these, the turbulent music of the starry vortices. Infinite worlds, infinite presents and pasts and futures, coincident—all things number, the number infinite.

It was one thing to know this about our Faith, another to make him admit this. But having hurt Carlos on his happiest day and so grandly placed History on the winding staircase reaching up to God, was I not then bound by conscience to turn the instruments of that science upon myself? As opposed to viewing an eclipse through a tube, the challenge of a historical science lies not in the rarity of observations but in not being engulfed by them.

And it was true my faith was not so great, my science not quite like his. But I was not so inconstant, Carlos. I had not lost interest in everything, had not betrayed the loves of years, or not so completely. I watched the eclipse, it came to our convent too. . . .

 We had made our preparations at San Jerónimo. While there could be no contesting that this was a Sign from God, Mother Andrea did permit it to be said at our weekly chapter of faults that eclipses did not always portend disaster. As far as I could establish, the chief danger was blindness, and while prayer at such moments was only right and natural, I asked the sisters to please pray in the manner usually pleasing to God— eyes closed. For there was every reason to believe staring at the sun would be as harmful then as on any other day. I had spent some days rereading the old accounts of eclipses. It was hard to winnow the truth from the exaggerations: there was the suddenness, the total darkness; there were descriptions of birds falling from the sky. I arranged for lamps to be primed in the convent patios and in the infirmary in case of need. Our preparations seemed sensible.

There were small flaws in the plan.

The sisters around our little patio had been standing just inside their doorways, casting dark looks at Antonia and the telescope, and over at me, who had surely put her up to it. I was standing just inside, like the others, waiting for a sign. At the first indication I intended to light the lantern from the breakfast fire we had left lit in the kitchen.

I knew what an eclipse was, yet I felt the nervousness, too. There was nothing wrong with the sky. So calm, so blue, the sun sovereign, unassailable. The darkness came upon us. I was prepared for the suddenness—it had to be like a thundercloud drifting across the sun. I knew the cause yet the temptation to look up was all but impossible to resist. It was for this that blindness was such a danger in the old accounts. But the darkness itself, I was not prepared for at all. The moon's edge was at first invisible against the sun's glare, fast diminishing. There *was* no cause, no moon, no cloud—and through this no-cloud passed no light at all. Something unseen was wrong with the sun—then a scythe moved against the fields of light.

The sisters came through their doorways and fell to their knees as one, and from them as one a groan of prayer went up. The onset was so sudden, the reactions as if rehearsed—the sisters of our patio streaming into the open—half-moon faces turned toward heaven—a practised play set swiftly into motion. I had forgotten to light the lamp. I too found myself in the courtyard, calling out that they should please close their eyes. Though I could scarcely see by then, I felt they must be looking up, even as I was. At the sound of my voice Antonia bent to the eyepiece. A chill fell upon us with the darkness, as if we had stepped into an icy room, the room that was the world. The screaming started with the chill—I could not distinctly hear the screaming in our own courtyard though it was all around, but felt I heard it in the *gran patio* and blankly started forward, to be away from where I was. Howling dogs in the streets and plazas—if they had run off, it was toward us.

Full dark came upon me as I was crossing toward the orchard thinking, not-thinking, to take the quicker path. I had a rueful thought for the lantern, then another to think of the little good it would do unlit. My steps faltered, a dizziness coming over me, as I had sometimes felt in an earthquake. It was not so much to see the stars at that hour, or even their breathless number, but seeing them *coming out* before my very eyes. An eclipse does not need a telescope, Carlos. The eclipse within a tube is one thing, and the eclipse without, another. The spectacle above is only the stage: the drama is below and spreading through the theatre. Rapidly.

The chill was of draft, of premonition, of the devil and death. The warmth still lay on my left shoulder as if I had turned away from a fire, as if the sun had just gone out. I stopped just at the trees. It was too dark to go forward. The sensation was of blindness, the impression of total dark, yet it was not—no, the eye saw and what it *saw* was darkness. Then a stirring, darkly, in the branches. Hundreds upon hundreds of grackles were roosting in the trees. At dusk the clatter they raise is ungodly. But here was utter silence, and in that instant I felt it, sheerest terror—the still panic of a groundling hunted from the sky. I had the thought that they were blind, countless chattering birds silent now, helpless, too frightened to cry out in their blindness.

Design. Intent. Terrible flaws in the Plan.

I looked into the branches, stood staring but did not understand it, like a child, all science transcended.

With time, the senses seeped back through their prism. Venus and Jupiter glowing red as blood. The howling of the dogs, subsiding. The braying of a donkey. Crickets nearby, it seemed all around. The crow of tentative cocks in the *gran patio*—was it dawn, midnight, dusk? Nine o'clock in the morning—midnight dark, but for the frail pink of a sunset in every quadrant of the sky. Chaplets of rose, shimmering coral rings in the puddles in the mud. Then a pearl light on the walls of a convent I had come to understand I hated and in equal measures loved. Nuns crying, whispering, though I saw none about. My eyes clearing. Vanessa and Concepción standing outside the kitchen, a flicker from the fire behind them, Concepción's arm over Vanessa's shoulders.

Bells tolling in the churches, a summons, a sounding, a song. San Jerónimo, San José, Santo Domingo, Jesús María—Sol-Fa-Fa-Re-Fa-Sol-La—Sol-Sol-Sol-Fa-Sol-Fa-Re-La—Sol-Mi-Sol-Mi-Sol-Re-La—a babble like baby talk, more and more bells joining now throughout the capital, its map crumpled and convulsed. Dancing across the city now, not Time but the echoes of its stop.

As if a dreamer has forgotten to breathe and woken up.

> . . . *De paz y de piedad*
> *era la ciencia perfecta,*
> *en profunda soledad*
> *entendida vía recta*
> *era cosa tan secreta*
> *que me quedé balbuciendo*
> *toda ciencia trascendiendo* . . . 9

I too had written verses on the night, the finest I had ever made, had thought her a friend, had found the glory of the day sky blinding. I thought in that moment of John of the Cross, our great poet of the night, of his love for her beauty, of the verses that had inspired mine.

Yet first was there Night, then Terror, only then did Science and Beauty and Holiness come.

The Jesuits who stop over in Mexico, coming home from Cathay, tell us that in the Middle Kingdom eclipses are suns seized in the jaws of vast dragons. In the tenth century, Al-Biruni and Abu'l-Wafa used the happy event of an eclipse to chart the slight difference in longitude between the cities of Baghdad and Kath. Fifteen centuries earlier, the Medes and the Lydians listened to the wisdom in their hearts—that there are few wars we are not better off without, and any war we can stop we must—and a peace was sealed in that place with a double wedding.

And yet the courses of wisdom are less easy than eclipses to predict. Only fifty years later, when calm Thucydides tells us eclipses and earthquakes were more frequently reported, the most cautious of the Athenian admirals neglected his own counsel after an eclipse of the moon. Nicias had been against the fated expedition to Sicily all along, had quickly called for reinforcements, had now decided on a withdrawal from Syracuse. But the sailors were fearful of putting out to sea, and the soothsayers were foretelling calamity for any sailing within the four weeks of the eclipse. The fate of Athens hung on this delay. The result was the annihilation of the world's greatest navy—those who made it to shore numbered forty thousand, hunted from Syracuse, herded like deer by the tens of thousands and brought down.

. . . of all the Hellenic actions which are on record, this was the greatest—the most glorious to the victors, the most ruinous to the vanquished; for they were utterly and at all points defeated, and their sufferings were prodigious. Fleet and army perished from the face of the earth; nothing was saved, and of the many who went forth few returned. Thus ended the Sicilian expedition.

The heart of Thucydides just this once moved with his pen.

Este saber no sabiendo
es de tan alto poder
que los sabios arguyendo
jamás le pueden vencer
que no llega su saber
a no entender entendiendo
toda ciencia trascendiendo.[10]

Dearest friend, I should have listened, I did not mean to hurt you. It is you I should have written to. You built the first telescope I looked through; my stories of the land first coaxed you to leave the highways between the cities. This land that has become your life, that you love as I once did. Our love is a difficult one. But if we love each other, is it not because we love the same stars, the same land? Please let us be friends, let us stay friends forever, let us not always fight. This was what I should have said.

The account of an eclipse, without us, is like a play without actors, a story half told. I did not betray the loves of years or our principles today but only failed them a little. I will try not to be ashamed of losing my head, of standing as a child who did not know the night; and you must not be shamed by astrology, whose proper study and wisdom should be, perhaps, coincidence itself—to see that we look through the telescope from both ends, taking note that the views do not quite match, and taking wisdom where we find it, where they overlap. The courses of the planets, bird flights, stars—if we read these for clues to our destinies, is it not because first they are written in the heart?

This was all I had wanted to say to my friend, as Christina had once written to hers about the hearts of men, and wars and ending them. One does not remake the world from first principles, but neither do we truly see it by observing each thing separately, as if from nowhere. We are not nowhere, we are in Mexico. We are not separate, we are here together for an hour. And though each eclipse might be tracked through infinite pasts and into infinite futures, this one hour will only happen this way once. In everything we feel and see and know lies this more ancient wisdom. The dying of the Sun, in all its terrible beauty and glory, comes only once, for us.

How doth the city sit solitary, that was full of people! how is she become as a widow! she that was great among the nations, and princess among the provinces, how is she become tributary . . .

THE
LAMENTATIONS

n the weeks after the eclipse the rains returned to the city, hard, unrelenting, while against the mountains broke thunder and black storms it was said one could not breathe through, save with a hand cupped against the face—rain plunging not in drops but unbroken sheets as from upended cauldrons, and much hail that laid waste the fields, flattened grain and the tall corn, stripped orchards and the long plots of beans, scattered flocks, killing many lambs outright and even calves in the upper pastures. Flash floods such as had never been seen rolled down the bare mountainsides, and from the volcanoes as down the sides of a field tent, gathering mud and rock over slopes stripped of trees, sweeping the soil itself now from whole fields, flooding the watercourses with high walls of water. Behind these, slurries of mud, tree trunks and boulders rasped out the arroyos. Bridges, roads, whole farms were carried off, churches and monasteries broken apart and sloughed into the pleasant draws they had overlooked. How fragile a building of stone, once the foundations are made to shift. So it was that in the next weeks and months, the provisions that might have come from the surrounding hills to the valley flooded and blighted and infested with weevils did not come, or came so meagrely as to nourish old grievances and ever kindle the rumours of hoarding, through autumn and into the first months of 1692.

Increasingly did the valley of Anahuac depend on cities farther afield. Pack trains and heavy wagons heaved and plodded over muddy tracks and mountain passes from Puebla and Oaxaca, Queretaro and Guadalajara. Many mules and burros and draft horses died. Beasts of burden grew scarce, with ever more needed to haul ever smaller cargoes over roads steadily nearing disintegration. Even within sight of the city the wagonmasters and muleteers were unsure of delivering their cargoes. The roads approaching the causeways now were fields of mud where thousands of Indians toiled. In heavy rain the men deepened the ditches, dug drainage channels in the sloughs that were once fields, sectioned small tree trunks and laid these cross-wise in the roadstead, and over this laid gallet and gravel from the lakeshore.

Sections of the new causeways built in the last century subsided, weakened by the constant rain. Covered ever more deeply in mud, they clogged with the slower traffic even as the shipments dwindled in size. As the pack trains and wagons queued to cross, cargoes of vegetables mouldered in the damp. Ripe fruit rotted. Disputes arose. The shippers and wagoners demanded compensation. Fewer were willing to risk the journey. Contracts were rewritten to make the delivery point the lakeshore not the city. Whence the cargoes had to be transhipped, onto beasts of burden supplied by the city administration. Food, coal and fire-wood were reloaded in smaller bundles into lighter carriages, into enor-mous corn baskets to be ferried across the causeways by Indians on foot and into any available canoes.

The Indians were no longer needed to dredge the city's canals. Now they laboured from first light to dark building dikes. The lakeshore encroached; the canals overflowed their channels and spilled through the streets, a few passable now by canoe. The Merced canal along the west wall of San Jerónimo had overflowed, and could be distinguished from the streets on each bank by deeper tones of red and black. Black with the usual filth and sewage, red with the mud of foundered adobe houses and blood from the slaughterhouses where the livestock sickened from the damp and hunger and rotting feed. At the first sign of infirmity they were slaughtered, eventually in the corrals themselves.

Then the bakers and *tortilleros* began to close—one day no wheat, the next no corn, on other days grain but no fuel.

By March there was hardship enough for all. The greatest markets in the world were humbled. The grain was wet in the garners. The lack of bread was hard for everyone, but the want of corn—for tortillas, gorditas, tamales, *pozole*—was especially cruel for the poorest, for the mothers, for those of an age to be warriors, for those old enough to remember. This had once been a people of the corn. The new corn was a child in its crib, the young corn a warrior, the hard corn a blade of sacrifice, and this sacrifice the shucking of a heart.

The mud dikes, while not easy to maintain, were at least not as hard to build as they might have been, for as the houses of the poorest foundered, the adobe slumped into the streets. The rivers in the road beds and alleys ran with little sticks of poor furniture, bits of cloth and rag, baskets.

Many died.

By April, what was once the best growing season was drawing to an end. It had been raining for almost two years. In the convents the cellars lay under water to the ceilings, the kitchens ankle-deep, the provisions piled now on the floors of sitting rooms and in bedrooms on the upper storey. We subsisted nervously, guiltily, on stores of rich conserves, jams and sweets, on the rare piece of fruit coaxed from the orchards. The young children in the convent school no longer chose blue for the sky but shades of grey, blue-black, purple and brown. Books on the shelves mouldered and mildewed, the pages warped and swelled, the boards bent, the bindings split, packing the volumes more tightly, making them harder now to take down, often not to be returned to the same shelf.

Books, letters . . . were we never to attempt poetry on human afflic-tion, how much space would be left vacant on our shelves. The Old Testament reduced to a few spare passages read in the pleasant gleanings of an hour, Sophocles and Aeschylus to be dispensed with entirely. Thucydides and Herodotus thinned to a recitation of places and dates. Much of Hesiod—and all that was fine in *Works and Days*.

On the sufferings of animals we make no literature; except we give it a purpose, their agony bears within it nothing of the redemptive. It is not tragic, it is obscene. But on a human suffering, neither may we make free to spout just any sort of poetry. It is one matter to take from Music a per-fected idea of Time, and to make thereby of History a musical science, but it would be better to say why this should be so—though we cried out for answers, we might still find consolation in detecting some machinery of redemption, the mechanism of a purpose, though these remain ever fugitive, ever mysterious.

This. That a people, to the extent that it is a people or becomes one through just measures of joy and pain, might be considered possessed of a soul. A simple soul, instilled with an ancient learning, instructed in a Music old and simple and terrible, in the beauties of eclipses and the earth itself rending, in the detonations of lightning and of mountains that erupt.

And so perhaps needing to find some purpose, we might speak of a nation entering a night of trial. Of this dark night we are told by its poet that if the child-soul of a people is to be instructed it must first be weaned of the pleasures of the senses and all delectable things. Though the soul is being fed manna, the tongue does not taste it. For the flavour is delicate after the flesh-pots. In their hunger and their want the people of our valley dreamed of different things, some of meat, some of oranges, pomegranates, some of good fresh bread.

In a person or likewise in a city, one cannot properly speak of constant panic—panic either subsides or else ends in destruction, self-destruction or madness. To see a beggar on a street corner or in a market, a starveling in rags muttering in singsong and telling stories to himself, it is lunacy we first think of. During those days, in the ceaseless repetition and mutation of our rumours we had become in this sense one lunatic; they were as if the rumours and singsong of one mind. There was anguish and hunger, moments of panic, and the rumours were our delirium.

The blight worsened. The *chahuixtle* spread like locusts, though people from the city were not sure how these creatures moved—if they crawled or flew. It was said that a farmer would look over a fine field at sunset and wake to its devastation, that the infestation travelled now as a swift horse galloping. A deeper fear was disease, that the sicknesses that had attended upon the Conquest, and so greatly abetted it, would be returned now as our harvest. Cholera, and typhus, and the most feared, for its hideousness, was the small pox. Disease did come—not from the country but from the barrios nearest the slaughterhouses to the north of San Jerónimo, and the feedlots to the south. The cattle especially were frail, and their handlers and slaughterers seemed most afflicted by these new fevers and died quickly. Many prayers at our convent were said for the dead.

And still the rains. Even in our prosperity, we could not get dry in the cells and workrooms of the convent. Leaks in ceilings, along window ledges, water standing on the ground, mildew high on the walls. Even in the shelter of the colonnades clothing never dried on the lines. If it were raining during confession, one might be wet from one Friday to the next.

The waters rose until long spans of the causeway decks went under. It had been hard to imagine, was hard still to believe. The causeways were a mighty thing, the city's pride, leagues long, and straight and high. So wide as to let six carriages pass abreast. The water was wider. Those few who imagined they might find a haven on the sea of mud that had been the mainland waded out over the long causeways with what belongings they could shoulder. Then the raised borders went under and the water on the decks stood waist deep, and no one sure of the way. It was said that among the last waders were some who had stepped off the edge. Heavy-laden they sank without time to call out.

Strange the sensation to see the city cut off—the causeways vanished were a fearful sight, and maddening to the eyes, as of a figure hastily painted over on a canvas—there, yet not. Though in a convent one could not see this. To see nothing for oneself, this was also maddening to the eyes.

The city was made an island once more. Four hundred thousand souls sustained now by a few hundred canoes, their passage from shore to shore growing longer, slower, by the day. A few barges had been completed but the work had begun too late. For weeks now the water had depth enough for deep draft ships, yet these had only plied our lake once, caravels built by the marines of Cortés to lay siege against the capital. As in that time, the hunger grew terrible. The poorest ate insects and grass, fodder and rotting hay. The street dogs disappeared once more—into cooking pots, when there was fuel for the cooking. And now the soul of the people took instruction in irony, for it was noted that the residents of this city had always eaten insects and dogs. Other people noted differences: there were caravels then, and only canoes now; the mission of the Spanish, who were not loved here, had been to starve the city, whereas the work of the Indian boatmen now was to keep starvation from us.

From the want and the deprivation, the breasts of the negresses and Indian wet nurses dried up. And among the mothers better fed, yet who had let their own milk go, there was sorrow as the infants were weaned on sops of bread. Sorrow, too, among the wet nurses who had no sops for their own.

In a city all but inundated, there was some thirst and more fear of thirst. Many wells were already fouled by the water standing on the ground. And each time the earth shifted with even minor tremors, a clay water main broke in one barrio or another, and could not be repaired or even dug down to through the water on the surface. To drink that red-black water, poisoned with blood and mire and the offal of diseased cattle, was as yet unthinkable, even if there were enough dry fuel to boil it. But there was still the aqueduct, which brought good water from the springs of Chapultepec. For some, indeed for ever more people, the walk to the Salto de Agua was long, the wait longer, the return a long torment. Our anxiety in the convent grew, for should our water main break, our vows did not give us leave to go out to fetch the water ourselves.

And so when there came a quake not violent yet not so mild, and reports arrived of cracks in the arches of the aqueduct, there was terror. And the murmurs that the water would no longer come were difficult to quell. But there was still rainwater where there were barrels to catch it, and there were many cooking pots free for this, since there was little to cook. Our small patio sprouted a garden of such pots—of enamel, clay and iron—and though we could not hear it, one could imagine a music of water drops as they fell throughout the valley at different pitches into divers vessels filled to various levels. Such distractions were welcome and brought relief but not much, for the hours between prayers seemed ever longer. And all our prayers were special prayers, for the Salto de Agua, for a family, a barrio, a house. Many hundreds died.

The question arose, how much can a people bear? In the mouldering books many stirring answers offered themselves but the simplest was that it depended on the people itself. Some seemed outwardly strong but soon lost the strength of their purpose, the heart of their convictions. The fortitude of the *conquistadores* could not be contested, and even now the Spanish *tercios* were feared throughout Europe, yet the French had begun to say of our empire that while its limbs were immensely strong, its heart and head were infinitely weak.

Other nations were born for trials. Israel was one. Such were Israel's sufferings that John draws upon the prophets Jonah, Job and Jeremiah, and David, royal poet of the *Psalms,* to speak to us of the night of the soul. The people of this valley of Anahuac were another born to trials, for this was a land of plenty in which the heart of the earth trembled, flash floods struck from a cloudless sky, mountains groaned and burst into flame. The last of the valley's peoples was the Mexica of the Triple Alliance. They too thought of themselves as chosen for a special destiny. And even to such a people come times when it is asked to endure more. The days of sea and fire ending in the year of the caravels on the lake was one such time; also the year 1611; and now. Our valley was filled with a babbling, of waters, of fables, of demons, of the confusions of the soul in darkness.

For a time it had seemed that in our suffering we had become one, that the fates of the peoples of the valley were not separate. But how much can one people take before it breaks apart and its soul falls into discord, before it bursts, and its heart.

On April 7th of the year 1692 the sermon at Easter Mass was given by Father Antonio Escaray. Two years had passed since a pleasant day in a locutory when those assembled had discussed the Maundy Thursday sermon. Father Escaray had been among us. It might have been two centuries.

With the Viceroy, Vicereine, and all the magistrates of the Royal *Audiencia* in attendance, Father Escaray decried the scandal of the scarcities. He hinted openly, baldly, at the rumours of hoarding and price speculation among the Viceroy's favourites. Rumours as true as they were persistent, and in their persistence lay their proof. *Vox populi, vox Dei.* Father Escaray's too was sacrilegious abuse of the solemnity of the pulpit for profane ends; yet he was applauded—roundly, deafeningly, in the Metropolitan Cathedral during the most solemn of Masses.

In the days following, people talked openly of uprisings in the provinces, and revolts on the plantations led by the runaway slaves based in San Lorenzo de los Negros. And yet such stories, if they were not invented here, would have had to come to us by canoe. The boatmen, who fed us and nourished us and had little time for gossip, themselves came to be feared and resented, for upon them we were as dependent as children. And had anyone forgotten the dolls in the canals, and the pagan rites still practised in the mountains? Whispers came now against the Indians of the countryside who were surely hoarding their crops, which was a cruel injustice since any crops they tended were not theirs.

The Indians did not lack for grievances. Remembered from the days when there was food were the wealthy Spaniards and Creoles who had helped themselves to whatever tempted them in the markets without a thought to paying for it. Now there were the fourteen-hour days of hard labour without rest; now the half-*real* of pay that bought almost nothing when prices were low, not even tortilla to replenish a man's strength; now the cold and sickness, the infections and fouled water, the drownings and foundered houses; now the breasts that would not draw, and much death among the new corn.

But we did not know what was said in those houses and in the streets unless the people there came to tell us. In the convent there was helplessness, that we could do so little, see or know so little for ourselves, and frustration that even so recently as Teresa's time, the sisters might go among the people and be of some use. The Franciscans were busy in these days among the Indians who had been brought in from the villages in work gangs. But the people of the nearest barrios did come, to the chapel, and to all the locutories; this was work all of us could do for the people who could not read, and for the women who came after the worst of all losses. Some came for answers, answers I no longer had; some came to know how others had suffered, that others had lived through such trials. There were books and verses for this. Most of all the work was to sit with them . . . Filipinos and Africans, Creoles and Spaniards. But for the Indians who turned to us, the poorest of the poor, I felt I could do a little more, listen to their stories of how they had come to live in the city, remember little songs to sing with them. The same scriptures brought comfort, though never enough. Perhaps the Indians appreciated especially the Lamentations. In Nahuatl, the voice of Jeremiah could seem familiar, not unlike verses they had heard as children.

. . . because the children and the sucklings swoon in the streets of the city.
They say to their mothers, Where is the corn and the wine?

In our valley, the burial songs had been not so very different from the songs for births. I was surprised to remember so many of the words. But I did not know enough of them, and there were few elders. Our capital was made up of many peoples, yet none quite whole any longer. And though many of the instruments lacked, and the music in its movements was perhaps no longer vast, many simpler melodies remained, beautiful in their own right. For only when the last of a people is gone, in its language, its way in joy and suffering, can the music be properly said to have gone out. Then may we take up a fragment, a bit of pottery or a shell and hold it to our ear.

It became hard to remember the purpose; then, to hear the music; soon, to imagine these could exist.

Though Father Escaray was a Franciscan, the Viceroy and Vicereine had begun frequenting the Franciscan monastery, a place of refuge in a time of need perhaps not far off. From their choice it was clear they feared the poor more even than the wealthy Creoles, for it was the Franciscans who were closest to the people, and could best protect them from the people. Six men were said to have died in knife fights in the *pulquerías* in just the first week of June. On Friday, June 6th, an uproar broke out at the public granaries on the rumour that they now stood completely empty. A restless mass surged about the granary doors, thrusting a pregnant Indian woman up against the nervous troops. They clubbed her to the ground. She miscarried there on the stones. A way was cleared;

a delegation of fifty Indian women and twenty men bore her up to the Archbishop's palace where the women were turned back, were always turned back. And again from the gates of the Viceroy's palace they were turned away. There were several hundred by now in the square—men and women. At nightfall they dispersed in knots and clusters of twenty or more, toward the taverns and *pulquerías*. Shouting and fights were heard through the night.

On Saturday nothing happened, though the *pulquerías* were said to be thronged with insurrectionists, with people drinking and hatching plots outside in the streets. Here at San Jerónimo, Concepción came with a dozen of the older servants, most of whom I had given religious instruction in Nahuatl. They were wounded by the stories: yes, there had been many drunk at the granary yesterday—but not half were of the people— and none from among the women who had attempted to get justice for the brutality of the guards. The drunkenness was a slander, for as I surely knew, *pulque* was once a sacred drink. Not the actions of drunkards—but of women, and had it not always been thus in the face of injustice? Had not Our Mother one day challenged the war god to nourish the people on milk not blood? And maybe Madre Juana had heard of the time . . .

The title they used for me was one of respect but it felt uncomfortably formal now, for they were very much at ease, visibly proud of what the women had done. I suspected that some of the convent's servants, Concepción in particular, had been among them. I thought of telling them a nickname I had once had as a girl. But to persuade them to use it would have required a long story, and they had so many of their own and some of these were new to me. How the women of this valley, in their defiance, had always given the people their new destiny.[II] There was Coyolxauqui, the war god's sister, who opposed him, and whom he slew to inaugurate war. Even Malinalli, who had translated for Cortés, was only avenging upon her own people the injustice of being sold by them into slavery—was that not true? And so we passed the afternoon quietly in my sitting room, nodding as each began a story the others knew, Antonia trying to make them comfortable with cold tea, these women unused to being served.

On the morning of Sunday, June 8th, a large assembly of women had waited for the Viceroy after Mass and had insulted him openly in Santo Domingo square. A mob was milling in the central plaza. It was said they were a drunken rabble and Indians. It was also said that the Viceroy had come to the balcony to speak to the people and been felled by a paving stone. But though we did not know it, the Viceroy had already slipped away to the Franciscan monastery, disguising himself in the robes of a monk. In the late afternoon, as a mob numbering in the tens of thousands pushed toward the palace gates, another woman, an Indian, was bludgeoned to the ground. The crowd was chanting *México para los Méxicanos,* and for one more hour, it seemed, we were a people in our suffering.

The woman, near death or now dead, was taken up by the crowd— many women—and brought down the street to the Archbishop's palace, as had happened before, where they were again turned back without a chance to be heard. At dusk a paving stone was thrown up at the Vice-Queen's balcony, then another. Abandoned by the Viceroy, an outmanned palace guard assembled before the gates to face the mob, which turned briefly to looting the stylish shops of El Parian. The guards charged the looters. The mob charged back with stones. As the guards retreated a few opened fire, taking a hail of paving stones in answer. Two soldiers were knocked down—the mob fell upon them.

Others tore apart the market stalls for torches. The *ayuntamiento* was first. Then the palace. Through the barred gates, fire was set to the doors, then to the window shutters; then firebrands were thrown up at the balconies. The latticework of the Vice-Queen's balcony caught.

With flames already raging through the administration offices, Carlos led a party of students inside to retrieve the city's collection of Indian documents and histories.

Then, at the height of the revolt, the cathedral doors swung open. A priest flanked by a guard of altar boys emerged bearing the tabernacle of the Holy Sacrament. Seeing it raised on high, the crowd—blood-lust in their eyes, paving stones still clutched in split-nailed hands—fell to their knees while the procession traced the slow perimeter of the square. The young priest spoke for a few moments to the crowd in Nahuatl and Castilian. There the uprising ended for the day. When the rioters had left, many dead lay untended in the square.

Distressing to me in a way I could not grasp was the idea of the balcony itself, burning. True, I had spent many hours there, but few happy. Was it the image of the paving stones breaking through the lattice, or the rosewood in flames—what was this, grief?

That night we stood in the courtyards, near the locutories, took turns there, exchanged word. The rumour came at dawn that Puebla had been destroyed, that Malinche itself had opened and engulfed Puebla in fire—Iztaccihuatl too had woken, a thing that had not happened in all the histories of the valley. It was not credible, and yet hard to disbelieve. In the half-light, a fine grey ash was falling, the hills obscured by cloud.

All day, the story persisted. Surely the ash was from the Smoking Mountain and the fires in the plaza. And even if Puebla had been destroyed—how would we have heard so quickly? But our role seemed simply to echo the others, as throughout that day the people of the barrio stopped to tell what they had heard and to hear what others had said before rushing out again. By nightfall the effect of the rumours reaching in through the walls had become uncanny, as when by candlelight one first hears a hidden choir in a darkened church, voices sourceless in the air, hidden behind a wall or a curtain or a lattice. . . .

And yet we were that choir, we were that chorus, a chorus that was blind.

In the night, Monday, the arrests began. It was a night for the settling of grievances, parties of armed men in the streets. This, one could see from any window. There was no cause to believe the Inquisition would choose this night to make its arrests, for the Inquisition was accountable to no one and needed no pretexts. And yet it was hard to disbelieve, hard not to look for faces in each clot of men coming down the street. Hard not to run to the window at each shot fired, each flicker against the ceiling, each shout. I could not stay in my cell any longer.

Don't let them come for me, don't let them find me in here, behind so many walls. Let them take me in the open, not from my bed, let them take me from among the others.

Chaplain de Gárate sent word he would lead special prayers in the chapel, deserted except for us in the upper choir. Not a Mass, no vestments, a few candles on the altar. I did not know what he should read— he sent for me, he could not think. I could not either, I could not let myself. What should he read? *The Lamentations of Jeremiah*, I thought. But these would bring neither calm nor comfort.

Is this the city that men call the perfection of beauty, the joy of the whole earth . . . ? Thy prophets have seen vain and foolish things for thee . . . false burdens and causes of banishment . . .

It was while we were filing out of the upper choir afterwards, crowding at the top to take the winding stair. A sister just going down turned back to another, above her, and said something. It was in her tone, or rather that there was no tone at all. "Unless we are already dead . . ."

It was perhaps this, as much as anything.

I joined in all the prayers that night. No longer could I hold myself as one apart. I moved in all the processions, out in the open—women on their knees, ash falling, blackening us, our foreheads and faces, the makeup of actors, court clowns. Steam from a torch, mud and cloth, sharp stone, a knee gashed. Frightened novices, a young nun. Nothing separate, none of us separate now—all the fragments collected, one.

At the end of the night, with the sky gone grey, we went in to the prayers of Lauds. When we emerged at first light I thought to look one last time, truly look, to see for myself. To lay to rest the stories, the destruction of Puebla, the old volcanoes burning. La Malinche, Iztaccihuatl. To know, perhaps, that none of this night had been true, that we had been in no danger at all. I moved the shelf from the wall and lifted back the tapestry, reached in and felt for the latch. Stiff with disuse the hinges shrieked—I stopped, listened for Antonia, who might only be pretending to sleep. On the rooftop in the early light of morning I looked into the east, out over the grey lake to the volcanoes, the sky behind them blue-black. If I could just see, with my polished eyes. Iztaccihuatl lay dormant, as always, as she had since my earliest memory. A pale grey plume rose from the cone of El Popo. And yet for all the violence in that cauldron I saw such a majesty—how little touched by events, how still.

If I could but see to the camber of its hills, to the roots of its ravines, to the boughs of smoke holding up the sky. With polished eyes. Yet how changed the world below that horizon, the grey flooded fields, the vales of mud, the flood wrack floating all about the city as the *chinampas* had once done. Oh my city, white city of the sun, the lake in among your buildings now, the long mooring cables of your causeways gone. City of Empires, Venice of America.

White Sunflower. How solitary now.

I looked down over the dikes in the streets, the beggars crowding as ever at the gates of San Agustín. Beyond that, up Calle de las Rejas, to the charred timbers and scorched stones of the municipal building tumbled into the square. To the palace blackened to the parapets, the corner closest to the cathedral gone, carrion birds above the plaza. And to the sun, a sickly slug of tin.

There were verses I knew of consolation, that had given and brought it. And there were lamentations, and I sought them out, this time for myself.

Woe to the bloody city! and from the eyes of Ezechiel fled desire. . . .
And the Lord came as an enemy, and devoured her palaces. . . .
And David stretched out his hands in his affliction, and cried. . . .
And the flesh and the skin of Jeremiah were made old, and his bones broken,
  and his liver was poured upon the earth. . . .

But it seemed then the prophets of old spoke for their own people, and not to me. I thought of the heron Ribera, and many things besides. But the closest I could come to giving voice to that anguish was this. It was as if Music itself had died.

THE FURIES

On Tuesday came the first executions. It began slowly; for we had learned that during the rioting someone had put a torch to the public gallows. Four Indians given death for insurrection. Three lived to be executed; the fourth killed himself. At each corner of the central plaza a pair of hands was stuck on pikes. On Wednesday, the Viceroy moved into the residence of the Marquis of the Valley, the title and the palace Cortés had been awarded. Six more Indians executed, one *mestizo*. It did not rain. On Thursday, a man from Madrid. No one had expected this. Insurrection from a Creole perhaps, but not from a Spaniard.

If even ten thousand had risen up in the plaza on Sunday, there was work to last a thousand days. It was hard to find a limit to what to believe, hard not to be drawn into imagining what was to come. Without the anchor of the Church, it did not seem impossible that the Viceroyalty might be swept away and all trace of Europe with it. What was to become of us—were we a people?

Work began on a new gallows. By Friday came the news that the Viceroy had ordered the hanging of twenty-nine negroes in the *zócalo*. The men had not been involved in the riot, but on Tuesday had lost control of a herd of pigs they were driving from one of the barrios to the slaughter-houses. The pigs had stampeded just beneath the Viceroy's barred and shuttered window at the palace of Cortés. The Viceroy ordered his troops into the streets, his nerve being insufficient to bring him to the windows. It was said he was hanging the herders now to silence the jeers and restore the dignity of his office. The charge was to be sedition.

I did not believe the rumour, but the stampede and the hangings had happened—after the unnatural events leading to the sudden vacancy of the posts of Archbishop and Viceroy. In 1611. Such confusions were not surprising. We had acquired a hunger for strange events, portents of end-time and what must come next. Only the previous week there had been the story of the Viceroy coming to his balcony and being struck down by a paving stone. This too had happened, but to Moctezuma, in 1521.

In truth these were echoes of older stories. The fear of sedition, the war on the enemy within, these were as old as the valley itself, as the stories of the dragon twins. I thought I heard in their resurgence now a kind of rhyming.

The people of our valley were once a people of poetry. Their leader was the Speaker. Those who had not learned the people's tongue were mutes, and so the enemies to be feared came from within, for how could the Mexica be overthrown by a people lacking even speech? When the translator Malinche found her way to Cortés, the enemy was no longer mute.

In the week of the riot in our plaza there had been an uprising also in Tlaxcala. Here, it was remembered, uneasily, that for many years prior to the Conquest the Mexica had permitted Tlaxcala its freedom so as to keep a ready supply of war captives within the frontiers of the empire. When the moment came, the Tlaxcalans had fought beside Cortés. The enemy within.

These stories had not been easy to keep from my mind; within them I heard still other echoes of an older tongue. The volcanoes WhiteLady and La Malinche had not come to life, but the women of the valley had. And though Puebla had not been destroyed as we had heard, there had been a kind of rebellion, and there too the enemy within had spoken. For when the Viceroy sent men to commandeer Puebla's grain stores, it was the Bishop of Puebla who barred the way. In Puebla, Santa Cruz was the supreme authority and for weeks before the crisis had been buying grain at high prices and selling at a loss, precisely to pre-empt all talk of hoarding and speculation. Facing down the Viceroy's troops he vowed, before an anxious crowd at the granaries, that the grain of Puebla would not be taken before his vestments were soaked to the last drop of his own blood. I did not doubt his readiness. To sacrifice his martyr's blood before a multitude would have been such an ecstasy. A few days after the riot, the Viceroy addressed to the Bishop of Puebla a public letter of apology.

How it must have haunted the king's representative, that moment in the rioting, here in the zocalo, when ten thousand Mexicans of every race and class fell to their knees as if with one mind at the sight of the Sacrament. A moment the Count de Galve did not see, having slipped away in the dress of a monk. One cannot know what goes through a mind at such times. Perhaps he had most feared being dragged to a balcony and stoned.

In the week after the uprising, a crude sketch was affixed to the gates of the deserted palace and beneath the drawing a caption. *For Rent: Coop for Local Cocks and Spanish Hens.* This piece of sedition was authored neither by Indians nor by rabble but by the Creoles—even here their wounded pride showed, for at the palace in fact there were never many local cocks but not a few local hens. I knew this, for I had been one. Everywhere throughout the capital, the Count de Galve was the butt of jokes portraying him as a dandy, a coward, a cuckold. Without the Archbishop he could not govern. His Grace moved vigorously to guarantee public order by threatening hoarders and speculators with anathemas and excommunication, but in truth there had been little to hoard. Within a month and in the Church's hands, the worst of our fears passed, just as they had after the eclipse. If recently the incidence of irregular births had truly risen throughout the parishes, the obvious cause was the months of privation endured by pregnant women, not the work of the Enemy within the womb. But the Church was quick to respond to our hunger for strange events. Neither was the insurgency of the women in the plaza forgotten. From the pulpits came warnings against insubordination, exhortations to obedience, of daughters to their fathers, women to their husbands, sisters to their older brothers, servants to their masters.

For a time, the star of Dean de la Sierra burned brightly. It had been his inspiration to send the young priest and altar boys into the midst of the rioting. Now he sent word through Chaplain de Gárate to ask that I write the carols again this year for the Feast of Saint Peter. He was sorry it was no longer prudent to come himself. I might have tried writing a cycle to placate the Furies, to pronounce words of grace. But this was not what was wanted. I wrote them quickly, hymns to Saint Peter. Father of light, man of the sea, master of the air. New Caesar, great lover of Christ.

Much was said in this time, much was false. Little was said of the Inquisition. I had no reason to expect them. And yet there were days I could not quite face the idea of being in the locutory if they came. I preferred to be where I was happiest, among my books and collections, and my thoughts. Perhaps I still imagined these to be a form of rebellion. I looked through the shelves, shaking my head at the deterioration there, taking inventory of the damage. The Italians were in a bad state, above them in the ceiling a hairline crack we had not seen. Many volumes waterlogged, the *Commedia* falling to pieces. *Purgatorio*, the journey up that mountain, unreadable. Sitting by the window, I thought of Dante, his part in the fratricidal fighting of his youth. Civil war . . . his betrayal by the Neri, his banishment from Florence on pain of death by fire. It was not long before I remembered that Galileo had once given two mathematical lectures to the Academy of Florence on the configuration of Dante's Inferno. I was not certain, but I thought the figure had been a spiral. That evening in the library I came to see the Inferno, too, as a sort of instrument. Devised for the amplification of suffering.

In August a letter. This handwriting I knew so well. A letter from a friend on a day when it was needed. I felt my spirits rise as I turned it in my hands. If we were already dead, it was at least a place where letters were delivered . . . if slowly, for as I opened it I could see the date: April 22nd. There was no saying whether it came directly from the mails, or from some other source. No one had seen the deliverer.

22nd day of April, 1692
Seville

My dearest Juanita,

I shall permit myself to forego the histrionics with you. You were a friend, he was a friend to you. Tomás is dead.

The first great benefit of widowhood is asperity, the second, that it allows me to retire from court life. Even after all we have endured these past two years I cannot quite say it killed him, but Tomás never fully recovered from his early difficulties with the new Queen. Yet I pity her—the King cannot conceive a child. She has said she knows she is intact but is no longer sure she is quite a virgin. These things are never a secret at court. The watch on his efforts has been like watching a three-legged calf lurching about in a barn. He can scarcely walk or hold his head up. You can imagine the jokes this has tended to, but it is too sad now even for the courtiers. The mirth is quite wrung out of them. And so it is in sober tones that the latest makes the rounds, that the King has begun to consult certain nuns in Oviedo known to be possessed by demons. One has informed him that his impotence was induced when he was fifteen by a potion of dead men's privates mixed into a cup of chocolate by Queen Mariana. One could weep. Because the King and Queen Mother are involved, the Holy Office pretends to consider a distinction offered by the King's confessor: that is, between Satanic divination of the future and now these of the past.[12] In the end someone will likely burn for this, the King's confessor, or a nun.

We have had news of troubles in Mexico and of floods. If I do not quite bring myself to hope all is well with you, I may at least send my hopes that you are safe. The Council of the Indies has received complaints against the Viceroy and chances are he shall be recalled. If he has not been thus far, it is only that there are few men left here to send into a bad situation, and bad news arrives from all over the Empire. And now to have the French sniffing at its carcass, after all the battles my family has fought. I should let myself off too easily to say 'had I only been a man.' I have seen good men fail here, men like Tomás, and men more capable. Tomás was also a little unlucky, prone to gaffes; some of my advice he listened to, but it was not uniformly good. You have made much of my family's greatness but it is unclear to me what we have accomplished since the Manriques took the field to fight for Isabela. We have had two great centuries, but what does the Order of Santiago stand for now?

Yet even as our hopes have failed all around us, there has at least been the glory of our art. This century has been of a brilliance only France even dreams of matching. They have the playwrights but not the poets, Italy more sculptors but fewer painters—it would take all Europe, or as you have shown me, it would take the court of the old Medicis. Yet for all this time we have been failing. As a girl I saw Velázquez knighted, but by then his heart was already broken. I do not understand it. I wish I could have you here, to help make sense of it for me.

And now I must tell you I am withdrawing too from my efforts at publishing. I retire with unfinished business. *Las letras a Safo.* They meant so much to us. You said the time was not right then and it is not right here now, but there was a moment, I thought, when all seemed possible. Yet with Tomás ill these past two years, I could not have managed more. Your *Second Volume* I will have shipped in three separate sailings and, God willing, at least one shipment shall soon be reaching you. Although this is a stronger collection even than the first, the endorsements did not come easily. There were moments I feared we would not get the Holy Office's licence at all. I must warn you there were only eight theologians willing to lend their names to this, even though your letter on the Vieyra sermon is well thought of privately. Someone has even written from Majorca or somewhere for permission to publish it separately. But officially I am told the Spanish Inquisition stands with Mexico's, even though its judgements often seem unnecessarily harsh to us in Spain. If the Holy Office here is quiet just now, it is not resolve that lacks but prey. In these times no one is eager to offend, still less for a sermon written over fifty years ago. The great Antonio Vieyra has left many scars in his battles.

So, there are not many endorsements, but the quality of the people is high, as is their praise. It is a considered opinion among the leading figures here that you have, in this one volume, matched the greatest poem of our century's greatest poet, the prose of our peninsula's greatest stylist, and the theology of the greatest predicator of the age. I know you, and I know you will take this praise hard, and the encomium as irony. Phoenix of America, Pythoness of Delphi, Sum of the Ten Sibyls. I ask that you take it simply for what it is, and perhaps also for the truth.

You have said that little lasts, but we Manriques believe in the few things that might. So I prefer to think of my own efforts as having had a small hand in that rare thing. It is as close as I have come.

You will think I have abandoned you, but if money can be of any help to you now, know you have it, or a word or a letter.

I prefer to do my grieving here alone. But in the fullness of time I expect to enter a convent. Then you and I shall be sisters together.

There are things I shall miss. I shall miss my Tomás. I shall miss your letters of times past, of weddings and great banquets, and War's end. You.

With love,
María Luisa.

MALINCHE

There came the illusion that after the flooding and the revolt the world outside might be again as it had been. The lake returned the city to us, street by street, though as lake bottom. It would be for us to make them streets again. The dikes came down. Some were used to rebuild houses, though this work went slowly—for so long as there had been such habitations of adobe, they had been built by work parties, but many neighbours were lost or had walked back into the country when the causeways rose up. Trading houses went under and did not rise up. Shippers, feedlots, shops. This time there could be no help from Europe. The Viceroy could be replaced, but it seemed certain the empire and the illusions it rested upon were never to be restored. He himself may have sensed this, for the killings stopped. Ten thousand executions would not have been enough. The Church alone was stronger than before. Never had the Church here seemed so powerful, the world of princes so weak.

There was much praise for Archbishop Aguiar. He had been decisive, though his decision to turn the women from his gates, twice, did much to spur the riot. The Archbishop was strong, because he had been the voice of Wrath all along, because he had not fallen. The Archbishop was strong because the Viceroy was weak, strong because we needed him to be, strong because from that day forward he would be unopposed. Everywhere the Church's power, incarnate in the person of Archbishop Aguiar y Seijas, was in the ascendent. His coffers were full. His men had much success in the bookstores exchanging *Consolations of the Poor* for the texts of comedies. But I have misjudged many things, among them the Archbishop's magical hat, which in those days was said to be working great wonders for the sick. This was not superstition. Again I had been too hard on Carlos. The object of the hat was not to cure, the object was to bring consolation to the suffering. And in this, it had been more successful than all my learning.

History I had always sensed as a wind that moved just beyond these walls, to be brought inside only through the portal of books. But repeatedly these past two years, History had come to me and I had not known how to answer. History was all around us, trying the gates, rattling the bars, tapping at the shutters. And when the world did finally enter here—the responsibility, yes, I felt, but I found no use in my great gift. In the face of so much suffering, I had lost the purpose. My city had been tearing itself apart. How had I answered? *Caracol* unfinished, a few carols. With the Empire collapsing all about him and the Vandals at Hippo's gates, Augustine *had* written—kept writing, to restore the faith of the world in the world. *City of God*, the *Confessions*. John's *Canticles* written between sessions of torture . . . Campanella in prison, feigning madness to write the *Scelta*.

On the worst night, I had thought only of myself, feared only for myself, yet could not think for myself. No purpose, I had had no vision. A vision of nothing at all. In our valley we were once a people of poetry, and to its Speaker there had come a judgement more to be feared than the enemy, a presence more troubling than the poetry within: its end. The revelation of an emptiness, the end of a music.

September brought its own questions and judgements. There arrived the first of three shipments of the *Second Volume* of the collected works of Juana Inés de la Cruz, a nun professed under vows at the convent of San Jerónimo. Whatever its reception in Europe, the reappearance here of the letter on the Vieyra sermon was as gall, the theologians' endorsements bright *banderillas* to goad the bull. A bull that loathed bullfights. The letter had been retitled. "Crisis of a Sermon." More impudence. The dangerous proposition of God's negative *finezas* had not been withdrawn, and the criticisms of Vieyra's positions on Christ's greatest expressions of love for Man had not been softened by so much as a word.

Towards the end of September, a visit from the Holy Office. A requisition, signed by Master Examiner Dorantes, for an inventory of all books, monographs and manuscripts in my possession. To the Inquisition familiar who had brought the requisition I answered that the Archbishop already had such a list. But I was forgetting myself, for they knew that.

Not long after we had submitted our new inventory, the Holy Office requested another, and warned that omissions from both lists could only be considered deliberate, if an unlisted book were subsequently traced back to me. This we had anticipated. Antonia had kept duplicates of all our lists. Then came another missive: certain manuscripts already known to be in my possession were missing from both lists. Yes? If Master Examiner Dorantes would describe them in detail—titles, author, contents—we would be sure to conduct a thorough search. There were two small victories in this, and against the Inquisition this was no small thing: the first, to have it even partly confirmed that not so very much was known about these manuscripts; the second, that the Holy Office did not immediately pursue the matter, meaning Dorantes was far from sure I in fact had them. So if I thought the victories small, it was in knowing the much that he could yet do to reassure himself.

My *Second Volume* had arrived in time to be added to the inventory. There had been three thousand four hundred twenty-seven books. Then, twenty-eight. It had been childish to count them, for it was only the list that was required, not the count, but it had been the ambition of my girlhood to have four thousand. At this rate I would have them collected in five more years. This, though the titles were not always easy to obtain, or to hold on to. I had arrived in Mexico thirty years ago with two hundred favourite volumes and fifty pesos, and it was then, in my uncle's house, when I let slip something of my ambitions, that I had first been told of the book collector Pérez de Soto.

Now, as the days and weeks passed, I felt myself coming to a better understanding of his case. Born in Cholula, son of a mason. Cathedral architect, astrologer. A practical man, a man of numbers and plans, but with imagination, as I have, and with many friends at the cathedral, as I had. A man knowing himself largely innocent, holding out reasonable hopes for his release. The collection of Pérez de Soto totalled sixteen hundred sixty-eight books, all but eighteen returned to his widow, from which it was plain that the evidence against him had been slight. He had gone before the Tribunal, given a full and frank accounting of his activities, stoutly declared himself innocent. Though of charges unknown to him. And then, without even bothering to question him, the Tribunal sent him back to his cell: that he might make a full and complete recollection of his trespasses. A bad shock to a man who had braced for an interrogation. He was given time to recollect. He was given weeks. He was given months.

He was killed trying to murder the mulatto cellmate they had just that day given him for company. It happened in total darkness, when the lanterns in the hall were put out after the supper. I have been told there are no windows there.

Toward the end of November a possibility came to mind, stayed for some time: Pérez de Soto was already mad. Because, long before he was arrested, the rumours had half broken him. And then, as arrest became imminent, every conversation ended as he entered a room, a tavern, a workshop. The other half was broken when the rumours stopped.

There were always other possibilities . . . the solitude of his confinement, the Tribunal's indifference to his testimony, the impossibility of a full recollection, his confessions to an escalating series of false crimes— if only so he might be lightly convicted of charges he could at least know the basis of. All were possible, any of them sufficient if Time in the Inquisition's prisons was as I imagined it.

This was how it might have happened with him, but Pérez de Soto's was a different life. He did not live in an echo chest; neither was he called to worship eight times a day, there to face his neighbours. For my part, I did not go to taverns, though I had once, in disguise, during my time at the palace. One did not go far disguised as a nun. Our cases were not the same. I thought it best nonetheless not to walk into so many rooms without knowing who was in them. This would have been a harder thing for Pérez de Soto to manage. Few friends came for me now, so another difference. Gutiérrez and Santa Cruz, to name two, but since I was not sure they had ever been friends I did not think their staying away counted. Carlos I no longer saw, though this I could blame on myself. He still occasionally came to give a class for Antonia, and once when he learned of the book inventory. Since he had not asked specifically to see me, I told her to go back down and tell him not to worry, his manuscripts were safe for now. Scientific treatises, tables of celestial observations, studies of the old Mexican calendars . . . Antonia and I had worked long hours, late nights, had recopied them, hidden the originals in the convent archives, disguised as account books and registries, sent copies in separate packets under assumed names to distant friends. The next time, I told myself, he could go to his friend the Archbishop's office for secretarial services.

I came down for prayers, less often for walks. In the orchards, one or two trees had to be cut down, their roots pulled up, the gardens restarted. It was work Antonia was keen to do. Vanessa and Concepción worked long hours beside her.

Briefly there was the illusion that the world outside was returning to normal. It was painful, but now is gone. Inside we had fewer illusions. It is the work of convents to take on the sufferings and prayers of the neighbourhoods, but we had been marked by this, had taken many sufferings and written them into our backs and onto our knees and the convent was a darker place for it. By December there were nightly processions around *el gran patio*. Mother Andrea had tried to maintain rules against excesses of mortification but the rules had given way. The factions now were against their reinstatement—had the floods not abated, the riots and executions ceased? The flails had always been of braided hemp, to be knotted at the ends if a sister wished, but never to be pierced with tacks. Ever more of the sisters came to the refectory and choir wearing barbed crosses, iron gags and branks. The younger sisters had had no experience of this. Many were frightened, a smaller number were lit from within. I had seen it before. It is a sort of enthusiasm. And unless we are fortunate, it is the start of what no earthly force can stop, once it has begun.

When it might still have made a difference I had undermined Andrea in a dozen ways. I had so resented the slightest infringements on my liberty. How easily I had given up even the duties I had loved, the academy, the music classes for the youngest children.

If a convent could be said to be possessed of a soul, San Jerónimo's had changed. Could we have withstood together the tide of events outside? I did not help them try. This had been a good place, precisely what I thought it would be. I had not been deceived. But it was a convent. Instead of blaming it for my own failings, I should have been grateful for the excuse.

In the refectory, at our Friday chapter of faults, I went to the rostrum before a hundred and fifty of my sisters and pledged what I had always refused, never again to miss our communal prayers, for the rest of my life.

1693. Early in January a novice came to say don Carlos de Sigüenza y Góngora was waiting in the locutory. *Please,* will you come? Antonia asked. But he and I had reached a place where there was too much to say. I had no wish to see him—for it was seeing him that always softened me. I had heard the story of his quarrel with the Archbishop, had at first thought it exaggerated, but though it had happened weeks ago, Antonia assured me the marks were still hideous and pitiful. During a discussion, Carlos, never one to tolerate another's inattention, had asked if His Grace could please make an effort to concentrate, since he was being spoken to. The Archbishop rose in a rage, walked across the room and struck Carlos full in the face with his cane, smashing his glasses, cutting him deeply. The cheekbone, crushed, had set badly. The scar healed jagged, livid, the full width of his eye, an eye he must have come very near to losing. Of course an astronomer has two.

I had generally found it difficult to hate anyone I had never seen, but though I had felt many things for the Archbishop—pity, fear, disgust, contempt—hatred I managed the day Antonia described the injury.

This in no way lessened Carlos's capacity for infuriating me. At the end of his last visit, he had managed to give Antonia a few parting words of advice to pass along. That though the Archbishop's ways were strange, Carlos was sure there was still a way forward—if I could just let a few months pass without some fresh provocation. A way *forward?* Only he could say something like this with his face disfigured by that man. I had no wish to repeat the experience of the day of the eclipse. We had counted on each other for so much. How we had wearied ourselves, our friendship, with these quarrels. The best it seemed we could manage was not to speak them.

In a few moments Antonia was back.

"He's asked for you."

"Has he."

"He is leaving today—*para la Florida.*"

"Another dramatic exit."

"He wants to say good-bye, he says it might be a *year* this time. Please go to him. You know it's you he comes for."

The regrets would start before he had even left the room. Today it would be his scarred face, the sight of him in his travelling clothes again. The ancient buff coat, the spyglass tucked into a baldric, the belt with pouches dangling—a notebook, magnifying lens, powder horn. A small military adventurer. *Don't go again. Don't leave me behind.* Then I would remember the times I had said good-bye to him like this before, once at the palace . . . the many injustices I had done him over the years. I had punished him in so many silent ways for becoming a traveller, but not like my father; for becoming a scholar of our past, but not like my grandfather—and especially for never letting heartbreak stop him. Yet he was sufficiently like them that I resented him each time he left. And how I'd resented his friendship with my mother, that he had insinuated himself into my past.

No, I would not go down to him.

Anger served Antonia best—better certainly than melancholy and regret served me. She was only mildly angry when I first refused to go down to him, somewhat less mildly when I refused a second time even knowing he had come to say good-bye. But her anger was as much with Carlos as with me by the time she returned with his manuscripts.

"How can he leave these things with you?"

Still at the top of the stairs, she stood as though unwilling to enter without a satisfactory answer. She held the bundle hanging at her side as one would hold a brick. But I did not know which manuscripts she held. And when I did know, I knew also that for once I had made the right decision, not to see him. This time the argument would have been inescapable—bitter, and still more bitterly regretted—the damage irreparable, for I would have voiced then what I had never said: that though he cherished the memory of Fray Cuadros and the memories of their times together in the jungle, he would abandon even these and suffer a thousand deaths himself before he would blame the fate of Manuel de Cuadros—or mine—*on a single defect of Our Faith.*

Antonia spread the papers out on the table beneath the library window. Precisely the sort of documents Examiner Gutiérrez had once been fishing for, the very ones perhaps: a translation of the Song of Solomon into Nahuatl, which had been expressly forbidden; land titles Carlos had rushed into a burning building to retrieve, belonging to his friend the translator Ixtlilxochitl; my letters to Carlos in Veracruz, several verging on heresy; three letters of his, unsent, to me. And at the bottom of the pile, the most dangerous. The recitation of a painted book they had discovered there: Moctezuma's last days as Cortés's captive, and the outlines of a theological discussion between the Speaker and Cortés's ignorant chaplain. But I suspected Manuel de Cuadros was the author of this text. It was the sort of work he had gone to the stake to protect.

My greatest fear in that time had been that Carlos might be implicated. His friend Cuadros I scarcely knew, had met just the once, a few months before the trial. And by then, Carlos said, he was not himself. Perhaps Fray Cuadros, too, I understood better now than I once had. Thirty-four years he had spent among the Indians, first as a student then a teacher of their languages, then as an instructor at the Indian College of Santa Cruz, then finally as the leader of an ill-fated mission to the Mayan highlands. Carlos said Cuadros was never the same after the Church ordered burned a lost cache of ancient Mayan books and artefacts he'd been instrumental in unearthing. A year later there came the Franciscan's turn. At first light, they stripped the balding heretic naked, smeared him with honey and daubed his body with feathers. All day in the punishing sun he perched—a heaving mass of wasps and flies and stinging ants—wavering barefoot on the thorny palm of a *nopal*. The pyre was lit at sunset.

And now Carlos had made me responsible for the fate of his friend's manuscripts. Was this to be punishment for all my injustices, to suggest that I too had had even a small role in what had happened to Cuadros—in that my stories of the countryside had set Carlos on his path? But the question was not how or even quite why, but why now?—when it was these very legends that had been so much on my mind. But in the end Antonia had the better question.

What are we to *do?*

Lysis,

I cannot simply send this without a word, so if circumstances dictate that I answer your letter only now, months late, I am sorry.

I am sorry.

I had thought not to write again, to let your last letter be our final one, to have answered it only with the verses I wrote the night it arrived. There was nothing then to add—it was so wrong of me to think I could guess at the feelings of one who has lost a husband, and yet for those few hours while I was writing for you, I thought . . .

I am sorry also about the pseudonym, and that you will have received this package that you will not want, signed with a stranger's name and delivered by a stranger's hand. It is only that I do not know whom else to entrust it to. I have bound these manuscripts under a separate seal for your protection, though you must please feel entirely free to open them, or to destroy them, seal unbroken—the choice and the responsibility will be as unwelcome to you as they have been to me.

For my part, I will not do the holy officers' work for them, or Time's. What I fear most is not their power to silence us, but to erase. Here, they have the power to erase whole centuries; before long they will have erased ours, as already they have blotted the boldest pens of Spain.

The climate here is not favourable to ice, and will not be for a very long time.

But though there are troubles here and fears, at least are we spared the sadness at court in Madrid, spared what you have seen, the sight of our king—spared the news that arrives from the other corners of the Empire.

Yet here in Mexico too, the French circle nearby, as though we were already dead.

Or, perhaps we are, perhaps we have long been—and this, our golden century, was merely the soul of an age making ready to depart. Who can say that this is not all that a golden age ever was? . . . a sort of afterlife, a golden shade hovering above the carcass of empire. We are left here, we are left behind, to watch a greatness that has dimmed. Had the heart of the Velázquez you knew as a girl been smaller or harder than it was, he would not have been the one for that work. Athens and Alexandria, Florence and Madrid. Mexico. Versailles. When finally the French breach our fortifications here to tell us we are dead, we will explain it to them—that what they scent on the air is not their glory, but the fresher vigour of their own decomposition.

Lysis, I will never see Athens. But we have many ruins here, built into living monuments of shops and churches, city gates and bridges. Our stones here are used again, as was the custom once in Alexandria. So it is also with our stories. Those of our valley are ever with me now, their murmurings in the night are little serpent's tongues licking at my ears.

Lately the convent's servants have reminded me of a lesson I had once learned and since forgotten. Here, there are not so many Helens. The women of our valley are more like Iphigenia, when they are not like Clytaemnestra, the other hatchling, the other city on the shield.

One last tale, then, though it ends with no wedding, though it brings little peace.

Malinche. Tell me about her, Antonia asks, to draw me out, as we sit copying together at a table, like two children over spelling lessons. Her bell-clear voice, my reluctant, mumbled answers, the scrabbling of quills, their clattering in the inkpot. Conversation of the ordinary sort has become almost unbearable to me. I feel my jaws, the string beneath my tongue, grow each day more stiff and strained, like curing meat. Another day, another turn on the vise, another turn on the cleat. Antonia says I've become cruel so as to have no one weeping over me. Perhaps it will be for my cruelty, in the end, that I am remembered here.

For the woman called so many names in life, history has reserved just one. Malinche. All call her that now. Born a princess near Veracruz, named after the sister BlueHummingbird slew to propel the Mexica toward their destiny, sold at the death of her father into slavery to the Maya. Malinalli, Malintzin, Marina. . . . Her beauty spares her the numbing drudgery of the fields; her gift for languages lifts her from the foetid anonymity of the brothels. Precisely these gifts of hers make her the perfect gift for the foreigner, Cortés, when he arrives. More than just a consort, she speaks for him, tempers FeatherSerpent's vengeance, interprets his actions. Do the Mayas have an idea of what they have just loosed against the Mexica?

On the night Moctezuma is felled by a paving stone, Cortés and his men are attacked and driven from the capital. They flee to Cholula. There in the marketplace, Malinalli meets the wife of a commander. Each seeks information, each attempts to beguile the other. Malinalli tells a story of the Emperor. In turn the commander's wife says there will be an attack on the foreigners—Malinalli should save herself. The Mexica reinforcements are due at any moment.

Two women sit in a marketplace on the eve of a battle, two others over their orthography at a kitchen table recopying the story, two more over one letter a thousand leagues and a thousand years apart, and in it, a fable. Malinalli's mastery of tongues brings to life the strangest friendship in all the world, and the shortest. She conjures two interlocutors—without her, they would not even have known how to find each other interesting. Only she knows what Moctezuma and Cortés are really saying to each other.

Love or hate? Antonia asks. What . . . ? You haven't been listening, she so gently chides. She wants to know why Malinalli returns to the Black Room even after the chaplain begins to stay away. Perhaps she is troubled that her lover has abandoned Moctezuma just as he begins to fascinate. Cruelty or kindness, love or hate. Is she drunk on love? Seduced by power? Bent on revenge—has she gone to gloat? She is there for what they share. He'd thought himself untouchable, she'd thought herself loved. She cradles Moctezuma's head to her breast, comforts an emperor who's mistaken himself for a god, been seduced by an imposter and cast aside. Both now feel the burden of their choices. He, the Fifth Sun's divine priest, she, the woman of discord, come to lead the Mexica to their destiny. How Moctezuma aches to submit to it, to what is ordained . . . if only she will help him determine what it is. This she consents to try, for in Moctezuma's fate she has a foretaste of her own. He, the scapegoat for a god, she, the stand-in for a bride.

Loving and hating now are as immaterial as words. Oracle, she has just seen how quickly interest wanes once the other is possessed, sees this in the straining instant she conceives the son who will be called Martín Cortés. The tyrannies of a woman's flesh—forced to love the sons of men we've grown to hate. Traitor to the powerful, liberator to the weak, she who speaks and speaks has been by her own tongue betrayed. Speak oracle, speak. What speech can redeem the Sibyl now but silence? Now that the conquest has been made.

Dear Lysis, dear friend, I sense in these legends a script so configured as to be read by me . . . or completed. And yet it is as if a cloud had settled over my mind, my eyes. If I could but *see, know* if it is already written, or whether I might yet change it.

I pray that a tender God keep you close to his breast, until the day we are made sisters again.

Your loving servant,
don Juan Sáenz del Cauri[13]

had not paid sufficient attention. My mind had not been clear. There were messages in the days, months. Years. It was in the dates. The visits, the rulings. The judgements. One could see the orchestration, the patience, the planning. I had missed so much, been careless. Days of sun, days of cloud—I must pay more attention now. Every minute of every hour.

January 26th, 1693. Word came that Examiner Gutiérrez of the Holy Office was waiting in the locutory. He was leaving for Manila. His work was finished here. A bright clear day, warm for January. During his last few visits, not suspecting him had become impossible. And now his work here was finished?—I had *been* his work. I had forbidden him ever to come again—leaving, he'd vowed that should he ever return, the visit would be official. I had not seen him for fourteen months.

Was it official now?

In September of 1691 he had brought word of the denunciation of Palavicino's sermon and the names of two Inquisitors assigned to investigate. That October he came with the news the carols on Saint Catherine were to be licensed and published—but *when* in September, *when* in October? November 12, 1691, he arrived with the identities of two of the three examining magistrates appointed to try the case. November 12th, my birthday. I apologized that the convent had so little to offer visitors now. A few sliced apples, a green papaya Antonia diced and sprinkled with chillies. Gutiérrez thought us lucky to have our own food supply in these trying times. The magistrates were Master Examiner Agustín Dorantes and Examiner Nicolás Macías, two Dominicans. To maintain the appearance of objectivity, there were to be no Jesuits, Gutiérrez said. In this case the proprieties were paramount. I had misunderstood. Why should the Jesuits be thought partial to Palavicino?

"Not partial, Sor Juana, *hostile*." He paused to finish the unripe fruit before turning with satisfaction to what remained of the apple, soft and withered and worm-eaten. He did not seem to mind a little calamity. "And this seems no longer about Palavicino."

He glanced down to produce his latest piece of intelligence from the folds of his black robe.

. . . I, the undersigned, Prosecutor of the Holy Office of the Inquisition, do therefore reiterate that said sermon merits harsh punishment, and so do ask and plead that an edict be drawn up for the recall of all extant copies and that its condemnation be published in the convent of San Jerónimo, with an additional order that any and all desist from all discourses praising the fame or person of the nun in question . . . [14]

Strange that a script so crabbed, so hard to read or even in that instant to see, should prove so hard to clear from the mind.

"But this reads like a sentencing. . . ."

"Unusual, no?—for Prosecutor Ulloa to have already written it out . . . since the judges have not yet made their rulings."

"But, Gutiérrez, something here is not right. Why would a prosecutor— even if he's written it—*file* his sentencing request, if there is such concern for the proprieties?"

In times of old, the smile might have seemed less forced, the answer less hasty. These were not times of old. "It appears the Prosecutor is overly eager."

What had Gutiérrez let slip?—either they did not care so much about appearances as he had suggested, or the sentence had not been forwarded to the eventual judges at all, and if it had not been, then it was not part of the official record. Which meant Gutiérrez had not retrieved it from the files but had been shown it by the Prosecutor, who either trusted Gutiérrez or was feeding him information. It was Gutiérrez now who seemed overly eager.

"Do you remember, Gutiérrez, the first time you asked about the spiritual journals I had once written for Núñez, so long ago? I see that you do. I asked how you knew. The Holy Office was aware of them, you said. A reasonable answer. But it was not your first. Tell me the first answer that came to you."

"I said you must have told me about them once yourself."

"But I never did that, did I?"

What came into his pale blue eyes then I would not have expected, not anger, or triumph, or guilt or even shame. Relief, it was relief. That came as a comfort to me.

I would not have been surprised if my dear friend had simply never returned, but it had turned out otherwise. The date of his last visit was not difficult to remember. It was two weeks later, the Feast of Saint Catherine. November 25th, 1691.

Rain fell each day that month—the waters gaining on the streets, puddles joining to form ponds. Painful for as many years as I was willing to recall, Novembers reached their lowest ebb at my birthday on November 12th, their high point near the end. November 25th. It seemed heartless in a time of such hardship and distress to wish for even an hour of happiness. But once one gave in, gave oneself over to it, the thing might prove irresistible. Not for a day, just for an hour. This was all I hoped for the celebrants that day in a city thirty leagues to the east. After I had long since given up hope, it seemed my carols were to be sung after all.

I had never seen Puebla but knew its cathedral was thought beautiful, up a short flight of steep steps from a shady central plaza much smaller and more intimate than our own. The cathedral choir was considered excellent; I had met the choirmaster. And so I could not help myself—the joy I felt to close my eyes and imagine the people filing in, to hear the music Ribera and I had written rising through the vault, the voices in the choir . . . to see the girls from the schools coming to hear verses on the learning of a girl, reading them afterwards in the libretto on the way home, reciting her story in the convent schools all across Puebla.

Three centuries after the Crucifixion, when the *Acts of Pilate* were drawn up to promote hatred of Christians, a girl of eighteen went before a Roman emperor, to denounce him, and to refute his paganism with arguments. In Catherine of Alexandria there was much to love, and to fascinate. Her courage, her audacity—a Christian, a young girl, going before Maximinus, persecutor and mutilator of Christians; then, her victory over the forty pagan sages the emperor sent to refute her. . . . Or some said fifty. With a saint so well loved the story ever ramifies—finally to a second emperor whose cruelties were instead attempts to seduce her and force a marriage. Since then she had been reverenced for her patience, her fortitude, and above all for the restraint of her passions. Many believed she had achieved as her reward a mystical marriage with Christ, some said first consummated on Mount Sinai.

Burnings and marytrdom, a serpent and a sacred ring, a bladed wheel, a beheading, a headless trunk flowing milk . . . Catherine had proved irresistible. Among the girls of the valley of Anahuac, the first saint we love is most often Teresa, for her strength and humour, for the palace of her soul, for her writings in a language and from a time so close to our own. Teresa was my second love. Among all the saints my first was Catherine . . .

We went in to church from Panoayan scarcely six times a year, and one extra time at Pentecost when Father was there. Each of us had a favourite occasion. In the spring came the feast of the Annunciation— this, for Grandfather, Good Friday for our mother, and Easter for my sisters. And in November, the Feast of Saint Catherine, for me. First the slow torture of the ride in to Amecameca, then taking a turn around the *manzana* before Mass . . . the special gaiety of the girls that day, and in the church itself, for Catherine was the patroness of cloisters for maidens and female scholars, and of young women at risk in the world.

In the Church afterward, we were given time to spend at her altar, a little statue of white marble not much bigger than a doll, quite overhung by the bushels of roses hemming her in—roses of Alexandria, or so they were for me. During the cart ride home it was not Catherine's martyrdom I worried over, but the fate of those she had persuaded by her learned arguments. Those scholars who had admitted their defeat to the emperor had been burned, but it was even worse somehow with the empress and the general Porphyry, who had gone to her terrible dungeon to convince her to renounce her faith and save herself by embracing the worship of idols. And by Catherine's great learning, the empress and Porphyry had been saved from idolatry, to live as Christians for barely an hour, before they too were martyred by the idolators.

In those years it had been difficult to keep separate in my mind the idols of Egypt from the little statue in Amecameca and the dolls of Panoayan. For many years afterwards I thought the path of learning the more dangerous, the path of mysticism the more burdensome. Until the years came when I wondered if it might not be the other way around. It was Teresa who reminded us—through her acts, her books and her trials—that the paths were not separate at all, nor were these incompatible with friendship. But by then I was in a convent. San José of the Discalced Carmelites, the order Teresa had suffered so much to found. What had happened, what had gone wrong? Where had the spirit of her humour gone?—of a woman who spoke to God in loving friendship, who, complaining of her trials, heard Him answer, 'But Teresa, this is how I treat my friends.'

'Yes, my dear Lord, and it is why you have so few.'

The great gift of the saints is not sanctity but to take from us even the humblest instruments of our everyday humanity—a bowl, a scrap of cloth, a gesture, a doll—and return it to us immensely enriched. Teresa was one who could immeasurably enrich even the most precious of gifts. Illumination, friendship, laughter. The paths did not separate unless we let them. I had tried to make this a matter of faith since then.

All these odds and ends I remembered the day I learned the carols were not sung.

That afternoon, a man in the Archbishop's livery was waiting in the locutory. It appeared I still had a place in the Archbishop's calendar. It had been almost five months since two of his men came, requisitioning the inventory. Unlike the others, this one met my eyes. Good news, he said kindly. The inventory had been reviewed and the cell purchase approved. No, Sor Juana needn't get up, he would set the papers right here. For me to look at when I was ready. I had only to file a full statement of savings and assets, to be used for purposes of collateral in case of default. His Grace's secretary would expect a response by the 31st of December or the application would be voided.

Gutiérrez came that same afternoon. The omen did not seem a good one at the time, but not everything was a sign. The sky was lightly overcast, the air very cold. Though it had not rained yet, there was still time. He was sitting by the window, the enormous black hood pulled back from his face. He no longer felt the need to come hooded to see me. No more games of *capa y espada,* no further pretense of having smuggled copies out in the black folds of his habit. His face was serious, composed, the pale blue eyes mirthless. Resting on his knees was a small scrip of Inquisition documents.

"You know you cannot come here anymore," I said before he could speak.

"Yes."

"Good. You may begin now."

"I am the third examiner, Sor Juana. Dorantes, Macías and I. I am to judge Palavicino, and will be forced to follow this through. I am here to tell you now that my verdict will be the same as that of Dorantes. We can both see where this is going now, and no, I cannot come here any longer. If I have to come again, it will be because I will have been given no choice. I can go now if you like. But because this visit is still *ex-officio,* I have come . . . let us not say as a friend, but prepared to tell you everything I know or can anticipate, knowing what I know, hearing what I hear. And in return, if you have anything for me, any information, a manuscript, any statement to offer, I believe this will be your last chance to choose your ground. Once it becomes official, you can only choose how to respond. The offer I am about to make expires at the end of this year."

Before continuing, Gutiérrez retrieved two folio pages from his scrip and passed them through the grille. He sat back, giving me time to read.

Dated that day, November 25th, 1691.

At the instigation of his Lordship the General Inquisitor, I, Agustín Dorantes, Master Examiner of the Holy Office of the Inquisition, having studied with particular attention the attached sermon, find the author to have been making a vain show of theology . . . making plausible dangerous subtleties and futile novelties . . . *such as making even speculative provision of a three-dimensional wafer the length and volume of a man in order to restore to Christ the use of His senses in the host.* . . .

The sermon's author then makes an allusion to Our Lord Jesus Christ on the cross, whom the author claims was already transformed into a lamb, and whom a soldier then wounded in the side with a lance, an allusion being made to a Sor Juana Inés de la Cruz . . . by way of using the Latin name Agnes ('Inés' deriving, as all know, from Agnes and meaning 'lamb') . . . with the more fundamental intention being clearly to praise said nun, thereby abrogating in spirit the reforms of the Holy Council of Trent, and thus contravening Regulation 16 of the Expurgatorio of the Holy Tribunal of the Inquisition.

In respect of which I declare to the Lord General Inquisitor that it appears on this point intolerable, despicable and deeply troubling that, to indulge and gratify the ingenuity of a *woman meddling in theology (this so-called scripturist)* and applauding her subtleties, the author should make of the pulpit an arena for a settling of profane accounts, using for satire a mystery of our faith as grave as the Eucharist, and publicly citing a woman he refers to as 'Maestra,' moreover referring to her later as 'Minerva' in citing a passage of hers that contains a certain form of indecency, if not in her lack of authority, at least in materially traducing the seriousness of the pulpit and of the Holy Scriptures; and that he should cite her among a list of saints and fathers and doctors of the Church such as Augustine, Chrysostom and the Angelic Doctor, all having distinguished themselves in treating of the question of Christ's greatest *fineza* of love. . . .

Gutiérrez waited until I had looked up from the page. "Henceforth, Sor Juana, anything concrete I say will be regarding Palavicino's case, whereas anything regarding a hypothetical case against you will be precisely this, hypothetical. I have persuaded Dorantes to let me bring you an offer. I would like you to consider it seriously. A statement from you, ideally an expression of contrition and conformity, but in fact discussing anything you like—any manuscripts that might still come to light, or your negative *finezas*, or responses to the leaflets attacking you—even a denunciation of Bishop Santa Cruz, though I would recommend against this. Technically, the statement would be entered into the proceeding against Palavicino, which is ongoing—we have begun to look into his other activities. Your statement, however, may be on any matters likely to come to our notice, *before* they do . . . in the event, for instance, that damning pages of your spiritual *Vida* should be found in the possession of anyone who had failed to report them. As you write your statement of contrition, you might construe such earlier writings as indiscretions of youthful pride, since regretted—an excuse not available to your spiritual director. Any deposition freely given before a notary of the Holy Office will be scrupulously accurate—you can count on this—every word you say, every pause, every expression of your face, every gesture of your hands. There are one or two precedents for this, and advantages. Conversely, an interrogation would leave you considerably less latitude in your replies, less still in the choice of topic. And in your gestures, no choice at all."

"When you speak of an interest in my *Vida*, you are speaking hypothetically. . . ."

"It is the only way I may speak—and even this is the most dangerous thing I shall do today. The penalties for discussing an actual proceeding with its subject are extreme."

"But we have had many such conversations."

"If you will examine your memory, Sor Juana, you will note any mention I have ever made of your theological views made no reference to the Holy Office. I could not hope to match your memory or the mind that contains it, but if, hypothetically, we are ever asked to compare our accounts, I will be consulting not my memory but the field notes signed, dated, and filed with my superiors after each of our meetings over the years. It is not personal, Sor Juana. Most of us do it, even when we are not encouraged to. It is the path of success at the Holy Office. Generally we fear each other more than we do outsiders. Please do not reject out of hand this olive branch. I went to some trouble to convince Dorantes. It will be offered to you only once. . . ."

No. I could not give a statement—it would not be the end but a way to begin. The Inquisition needed no help with the end. I could not afford to trust him.

"How clumsy of you, Gutiérrez. This should have been left to someone else. This can't have been your idea. Are they trying to humiliate you? You've been the third examiner for some time now—the time to tell me was when you first knew."

This won me a change of tactics, all pretense abandoned now. And it came as a relief, it came as a consolation. Was it too late to tell Sor Juana that her mulatta had been meeting for almost four years with Bishop Santa Cruz? That she had come to me as his spy? Yes, Gutiérrez, you should have told me that last *year*. Did I really believe she had stopped? *Liar.* And was it too late now for him to tell me she had been delivering my letters to the Holy Office for inspection before posting them? *Liar!* And was it too late to mention that once a month for the past four years the Holy Office had held meetings on the circle of those closest to me?

Then, though I had not asked and would rather not have had it enter my mind, he described many of these evenings in the Master Examiner's office across from the rose-coloured church. Who had attended? Santa Cruz many times. The French Viscount twice. And so Gutiérrez took pleasure next in anticipating for my benefit the conduct of a plenary session of the Holy Office, nine days hence, when the Dorantes verdict would be read, along with the other examiners' rulings. Yes, including his own. Prosecutor Ulloa would then be allowed to read the sentence he had already written a month before the verdicts were handed down, not being able to help himself. To which, on December 4th, he intended to add a further request: that Palavicino be excommunicated, banned from receiving the sacraments anywhere in the archdiocese, defrocked and banished from New Spain. He might be permitted to go to Quito or Manila—but never again to Spain. Palavicino's sermon would be recalled—the entire print run to be accounted for and burned in the plaza before the chapel doors of San Jerónimo. This was the best that Xavier Palavicino could hope for.

On the other hand, the matter lay largely in his hands, for the way ahead was straightforward, if narrowing. Should he refuse to abjure, all available methods of persuasion would be brought to bear. In any event, before he departed he would be forced to give information on his other associates and activities, after which, the path of his salvation was clear: the appellant should state his guilt with expressions of sincere humiliation, declare himself convicted, beg in all earnestness for pardon in appealing to the judges for special leniency, express his sincere and vehement desire to purge his sin and offence, beseech the saints to intercede in his behalf. . . .

Gutiérrez asked next if it was also too late to tell me my carols would not be sung in Puebla that day, in the cathedral, or anywhere near it, or on any other day.

Whatever Santa Cruz's true purpose in publishing my carols, the result of not allowing them to be sung was foreseeable also, that those verses touching upon Catherine's audacity, her defiance of imperial authority, her pride and learning—all published in my name—could not but further madden all those shocked by my Letter Worthy of Athena. Even the printer was the same, if anyone needed reminding. Catherine, Athena. Alexandria, Athens. The names might change and the places, but not Sor Juana's impudence, her willful pride and disobedience. And this time there was no preface of kind admonishment from a loving friend. Here *was* a difference, not in my attitude before God but in the Bishop's toward me. A shift Santa Cruz could not have signalled more clearly than by barring my carols from his cathedral.

"Sor Juana is pensive. She will want time to think. The Holy Office's time is limitless, but its charity is not. The offer, as I say, expires on December 31st."

Two visits on November 25th, two deadlines of year's end—not everything was a sign, but neither was everything a coincidence. For if it were I would have to call coincidence the next piece of information Gutiérrez brought: the date of the judgement filed by Master Examiner Dorantes, and which I had just read. November 25th, 1691. Yes, Gutiérrez, today, the Feast of Saint Catherine. I was quite aware. No, he was afraid it was not quite that, or not just—but rather one year to the day from the publication of the Letter Worthy of Athena by Bishop Santa Cruz in Puebla. *This I had not seen.*

Santa Cruz had been planning to forbid the singing of my carols for a year, had awarded the commission purely to cancel it, and Dorantes by dating his ruling on that anniversary was telling all, telling me, the Holy Office had been part of this all along. The Palavicino case at the Inquisition and the publication of my letter had one sole object. The interests of the Master Examiner of the Holy Office and the Bishop of Puebla had one sole object. The same hypothetical object, one point of convergence: one Juana Inés de la Cruz. One hypothetical nun. Not everything was a coincidence. These were signs. And the visit from the Archbishop's man on the same day was another—but of what? Santa Cruz wanted my annihilation and my adoration, Núñez my subordination, Archbishop Aguiar my public humiliation, preferring this even to my private destruction. And their wishes were not the only ones in play. Núñez was accountable to the Archbishop, but also to the Jesuit Provincial, his Inspector General. Dorantes to the Dominican Provincial, perhaps to Santa Cruz, and both Núñez and Dorantes to the General Inquisitor. Yet now I was to believe that they had laid down arms and were working together—fist in glove—in a miraculous convergence of hostile and competing interests. All joined now in a sort of fraternity, along with a dozen scurrilous and anonymous pamphleteers, and Velasco of the Brotherhood of Mary, the denouncer of the sermon. And at least one Augustinian. Most of them detested each other—what could possibly bring all of them together? I did not believe it. I would not. Why would they want me to believe this? I could not bear to.

"Tell me, Gutiérrez, if the Inquisition has so much time at its disposal, why do you look like someone with so little?

"You look more and more the desperate rat, my good friend. Do you face penalties at the Holy Office for your insufficiencies?"

The convent had seen a lot of rats as the waters rose. I'd been thinking of their morality, but I could not help seeing how Gutiérrez might take the remark as a reference to his appearance—how near both the sublime and the tragic cleave to the childish. From the first, Gutiérrez had been funny to look at even when he didn't intend it—scratching under his chin, accentuating his chinlessness, as he had just been doing. The next few minutes were quite out of character. He became vulgar, spoke of heresy as an illness, one that did not end with death—just as banishing Palavicino unbroken would not so much be to expel an ordure but pass along an infection. And as for the Inquisition's use of time, I might profitably study its employment now with Palavicino. The Holy Office was disinclined to move against him until its inquiries were completed, and would only do so if Sor Juana attempted to warn him, though she should feel free. As the only person outside the Holy Office who knew, let her choose—let her give him the truth or leave him with the illusion. So I would feel the blow twice, twice watch him fall, be in no doubt where the responsibility lay. Twice.

But if Sor Juana wanted to know why she should expect the Inquisition's patience in *her* case—did she want to hear? Then he would tell her.

There was always a certain anxiety with heresiarchs.

Since by definition they were adjudged to have the power to corrupt princes, the cases had to be handled delicately. Such investigations were likely to cost a prince or two along the way. Executions of that kind poisoned relations at court for decades. The case of the Florentine was taken up early enough, yet so leniently as to merely aggravate the problem. There had loomed a real danger of having to open proceedings against not only a Medici Grand Duke but the Archbishop of Siena.

Further, the corruption of the heresiarch did not necessarily end at death. One heresiarch, it seemed, begat another and then who knew how many others over time? At least in her case the potential for a problem was caught early—

Meaning. Hypothetically speaking? Yes, Gutiérrez, yes. The Holy Office had been receiving reports on a certain case for . . . years. From whom—how *many* years? If he would not give me a name—a year then, *when*, 1675, 1670? Oh, earlier. At the *palace*? Oh, no, before.

Before.

Consider the year 1663. But perhaps he had already gone beyond his brief. To sum up, then. Time, the Inquisition had a great deal of, a very powerful advantage. With the heresiarch, not an advantage to be surrendered too easily. Care should be exercised. This one had quite ruined one priest, with two more likely to follow, had corrupted royalty—just how many viceroys now, and vicereines?—had seduced one prince of the Church and set two more at each other's throats. It had come to poisonings. Spying with France.

To take on such a case without a measure of reluctance was a thing only the very ambitious or the foolhardy would do. Master Examiner Dorantes did not seem to be one of the latter. He was determined that the Holy Office in Mexico make its own mistakes and not repeat those of the Inquisition in Lisbon or Rome. But no one was so sure of his

theology as to oppose her in print. Everyone had seen what she had done
to the Prince of Catholic Orators. Proceed slowly, indirectly for as long
as possible, and only with force as a last resort. Until her mind was broken. Hypothetically. It would not happen straight away. It would take
time. It was the safest path. She shouldn't take it personally. He was sorry
to have upset her, but she had asked. Still, she was entitled to her doubts.
He admitted he had often lied to her, and was perhaps no longer credible.
She would want to draw her own conclusions.

Sor Juana should study, next, the Inquisition's way of proceeding
against the *beatas,* which there was every chance now she would be able
to do at close range. The rumours long abroad were correct, a trial was
pending, and a sentencing: a woman had been in the Inquisition's prisons
for some years now. The campaign against false sanctity was to receive
more resources. There had been two secret trials in just the past few years.
When? February of 1688. March of last year. I had heard nothing of
this—why were we hearing about these now?

A glint of amusement. This was why they were called secret trials.

But this next one was to be different, special. There were other locations, yet San Jerónimo was felt to be promising . . . spacious, the orchards,
the *gran patio,* the home of Sor Juana. No, a date had not been set, and
would not be before the Archbishop's new *beaterio* was completed. A place
for unattached women of fervent faith to have their visions under a
watchful eye, under lock and key. Speaking of which, did Sor Juana perhaps remember Sor María de San José, Bishop Santa Cruz's hermitess?
Certain irregularities had emerged in the relation of her *Vida.* Years of
visitations from the Enemy, who came to her in the form of a naked
mulatto—came still, apparently. Quite prodigious. It was not at all clear
to the Lord Bishop Santa Cruz that she hadn't sought these visions
actively. Clearly the quality of recruits was everyone's problem.

 Not everything was a sign, not every sign was of a conspiracy, not every
conjunction was in the stars, not every influence heavenly, not every irony
was a coincidence, not every coincidence a sign.

That poor girl—struggling to be allowed to live as a holy woman in a
cave, prepared to sacrifice everything to be with her Beloved, dreaming
of nothing more than admission to a cloister, denied it—again and again,
while for twenty years I had dreamt of escape. Had they decided to connect our fates in some way, to make examples of us? But examples of

what?—we were so unalike. One of us saw the Enemy as a naked mulatto and rebelled against his touch, the other had first seen him as Lucero, shining, Prince of Scholars, divided against the light within himself. And as his demon assistants read him the verses I dreamt of one day writing on the Nativity, he saw prefigured there the story of his fall.

But who in the depths of the night had not heard his mockery? Would she and I have heard him so differently? Truly, how different were we? One who dreamed of nothing but knowing the touch of His graces, the other to touch the grace of His mind. A hermit's cave, hers, a magician's, mine. Both born in the countryside on a hacienda, both families fallen, indebted, impoverished. For her the danger was a charge of false sanctity, for me, heresy. *Via mística, via intelectual.* Write freely, write a *Vida,* as had been commanded of Teresa. For how many months had even Teresa's *Interior Castle* been torn apart line by line by her enemies at the Holy Office? The paths were separate only if we let them be. It was Teresa who had shown us this. We walk the same path, María de San José. I must warn her. Could I write?—no, send word to her through her sister at San Jerónimo in Puebla. But I could only guess what terrors she was enduring now. I might only terrify her more—in a time like this, in this frame of mind—in hers, in mine—I might only make her see in me another demon trying to deflect her from the path. Had I not heard what Gutiérrez said about warning Palavicino? They would move against her if I tried, *because* I had tried. This was the trap—the special trap for me. Two fates in my hands, and yet neither, for one was already condemned, the other I could do nothing but harm. *Stay away from her.*

The rains had continued through November of 1691 and into the following month. Before December ended I had furnished the Archbishop's secretary with the inventory and a statement of means. The other deadline, the other statement, I had allowed to pass. I would not be taking any commissions from the Inquisition that year. The first days of the new year went by anxiously. But as January wore on, I saw I had been foolish to fear the Inquisition would come for me so soon, for Gutiérrez had promised it would not be like this—that there would be time, a great deal of time.

On February 1st the Archbishop's contractors completed his new *beaterio,* on time despite the weather. This was fact. The *beaterio* was built and consecrated. This could not be denied. People had seen it, entered there for the inauguration. The date was February 24th . . . the anniversary of my profession. The timing was a reminder from the enemy that everything was orchestrated; every thought had been given to my discomfort.

Not all was true, not all was false. But these had become facts and observations in another science, conceived not to lessen uncertainty but to increase it, not to remake a world from first principles but to tear one down, in time. Its instruments of spirit were not *admiratio, inventio, divinatio, contemplatio,* but doubt and isolation, bitterness and suspicion, dread. Its instruments of sense were not astrolabe, compass, vacuum flask or pendulum, its instruments—that is, the work of the senses in this science—but no, these did not bear thinking about, these should be avoided by the imagination. But if I had let him, Gutiérrez would have agreed to describe them for me, in time. And with instruments such as these, with this new science, somewhere they were building a new cell for me.

This was the game of the Enemy. These were the paces through which Gutiérrez had been instructed to lead me all these years. One part truth, one part lie, the third made up of what was missing—not seen, not said, not imagined or expected, not properly read. A kind of triangle, and this third side, this edge of the blade, was by far the most terrible. Events conspired—events were now arranged—to make each day, each hour rich in possibilities, abundant with hypotheses, each single moment inexhaustible. And now it was very important to have missed nothing, if I was to face him again—not to give him hope, a sign. For the date of his coming again, this was no accident, no more than the last time had been, and not a coincidence. January 26th, 1693, the Feast of Santa Paula, the second anniversary of the sermon—so either the visit was official now, or his departure was a lie. Before going down I sat fidgeting at the studio window, the sun bright, looking across at the farrier's, the cartwright's, trying not to notice Antonia watching me collect myself.

I had been careless. There were messages. And now Gutiérrez was in the locutory. Why had he come—was it official? What had I missed? I could not get Palavicino out of my mind. January 26th, 1693 . . . Palavicino was fine, still unaware his sentence had been written. Time yet for one more dream, another plan, for a life to which he had already died, a life he would still be in love with. I told myself it was not bad to imagine him in love with his life, that this one thing was not a lie, and that they would not move against him until they felt close to having what they wanted from me, or until they had it already. One difficulty had been in keeping a firm grasp on what this was, if there was any limit to this, if it would ever end. How. Another difficulty in all these months was in keeping myself from wondering without let or cease, if I was already dead to mine. But I should not think so much about this—if I was not to give them a sign of weakness, submission, collapse. Palavicino, María de San José, the *beata* in chains, Catherine of Alexandria—reminders all, all together, not coincidence but signs, of what I had refused for as long as I could bear to recall. The charge and care of another's life, of any life save mine. A convent was the safest place, a place with walls, safer for both sides, and yet I could not protect them all, or myself, not even from inside.

And now I would go down to him. He was leaving for Manila. New Spain was finished. His work was finished. On the 27th day of January of this year, Antonio Gutiérrez, still with the Inquisition or not, left for the Philippines, or did not. They came the next morning. The sun was shining.

KILLING
FLOOR

. . . viviendo en tanto pavor,
y esperando como espero,
muérome porque no muero . . . [15]

ll one day and then a second, the cell was stripped. Eight men, three in the Archbishop's livery. I wondered what the other five did when not doing this, I wondered where they lived. Not stripped. Some furniture was left, many pots and plates. Two beds. Upstairs a table. The glass cases, especially, had to be taken down, the bookshelves broken out. I begged them to leave the folding screens. Instructions left no room for doubt.

The table under the window, then . . . the tapestry at the top of the stairs.

This also they took down, but showed no interest in the door behind it. Instructions did not extend beyond these rooms, to the locutory downstairs, or views from the roof. I expected Antonia to be hurt, but she gave no sign of having seen it there. I had not known anyone could be so discreet.

The sisters of our small patio were considerate, standing pale in their doorways. Though we take a vow of poverty, we are each attached to our cells. We come to think of this place as our home, of each thing as our own. Our belonging. The cell itself is mine now: the men brought a bill of sale.

One of the men in livery I knew, the one with the kind eyes. He had come before, to bring news that the sale had been approved. I had wondered then, how a kind man could succeed in the Archbishop's service. But I had made this mistake before. When he came into my cell now with the others, he did not look up from his work. I watched him carrying out boxes and bundles, delicate instruments rolled into rugs. And watching, I was given to wonder whose eyes had been averted these many years. The Archbishop's coat of arms . . . I had seen it frequently. A family among Spain's most ancient. An ancestor had been a knight attached to the court of Julius Caesar, had met the Apostle James on the Spanish shore. A story if true, incomplete. Hearing it, I had once asked how an apostle of Jesus might feel, to be met by a Roman officer after Judea.

On a maroon ground, within a silver border, the Archbishop's shield encloses five seashells set against a cross.

The smallest things, at times. Of these do they build a new cell for me.

Antonia took their coming so bitterly, imagining this to have been some fault of hers. As well to say she brought the floods. Shhh, Antonia. Emptiness has many positive qualities. A caracol makes no sound at all, until it has been emptied out. And then you can hear the sea. Shhhh. There, can you hear? The difficulty can be in persuading the animal who lives inside to leave.

'Tonia, hush . . . John of the Cross was asked, repeatedly, severely, Since God is Light, how can the approaches to God be dark? Even in a soul purged of its attachments and impurities.

The poet's answer was ingenious. Listen.

Imagine a room with nothing in it. Two windows, facing each other, the Light of God streaming through, one window to the other. One never sees the light, only what it strikes. As a hand lifted between the windows is lit, or as motes of dust whirl as if sparks in a wind. Do you see? It is why a cell must be stripped.

We obstruct the light.

In all these months, in the refectory, the workrooms, the choir, the *sala de devociones,* the one rumour that had not ceased was of the *beata,* the trial. It was a prospect some of us dreaded, but not all. I knew when the sisters were telling it by the way they looked over at me. There was little doubt why our convent had been chosen.

I had been supplied with details the others did not have. That she was half-Indian, that she had been a midwife, arrested years ago. Gutiérrez claimed never to have seen her, but said that he had walked many times past her cell; that its door had been more recently replaced, its newer braces and rivets glowing softly in the torchlight of the halls; that the trial was to take place at night. He did not say why, but the possibilities were obvious. It made for better theatre. Gutiérrez was a liar.

I had been weak then. I had asked him if he truly did not know who she was, if she existed at all—or if the *beata* . . . if I were she.

Then in a letter from our sister convent in Puebla, word of Sor María de San José, that Bishop Santa Cruz had read her *Vida,* the spiritual journal he had commanded her to write, and turned it over to the Inquisition. But this I already knew, and here also had I been given knowledge the others did not have. She was to be examined by the General Inquisitor himself.

Were the visions frequent, were they actively sought or passively received? Did they follow the path of previous mystics? Did the visions uphold or break with doctrine? Were they frenetic or calm? Were the recollections hazy or clear . . . did they bring a sense of peace? Did they lead to God or toward the Enemy?

This was how *beatas* were to be examined. Now Sor María would have to find her own way to answer. I had asked myself what Santa Cruz had ever wanted from her, wanted from us. I wondered if it was merely to raise her up and make me fall. Or to make the writer a mystic, the mystic a writer. To reverse our fortunes. But it was clear now, what Santa Cruz wanted. He simply wanted what we do not. He had never wanted Núñez to join him, but by turns favoured and thwarted him to divide him from the Archbishop. He had not cared if the Archbishop were mad, only to drive him mad with the possibility that everything he touched was poisoned. And then to teach this to me.

They say Sor María is half-Indian, but that is what they always say if one learns Nahuatl. I could write to her, too late, but now at least there was little danger. Send a message in Nahuatl through a servant. María de San José, our paths are not separate. Here is a man who takes back what he has given, who eats his excrement twice. Here is a man who does not care about the outcome, only that there should be conflict. Here is a man for whom the game does not matter, only that he should set two sides upon one another—that in playing him they play against themselves, that to everyone he brings pain and trials. You know this, as I do. You have entrusted to him your secrets too. But the traitor is a gossip—*in necoc yaotl, ca chiquimoli*.[16] This expression we have in your valley and mine. We have known him here, we have known him all along.

Necoc yaotl. Enemy of Both Sides.

Once I had been afraid of the dark.

First as a child, then as a girl, in Mexico. Now though the nights of trial were filled with doubt, my fear of the dark returning, I ceased trying to sleep except during the day, between the hours of prayer. I wanted to be awake, on my feet, when the Enemy came. I ceased going down to the workrooms, the refectory—though I did try to eat. They wanted me weak. But there is something else I have feared. I have feared it all my life.

This void . . . this lightness, without books or ballast, without work or measures for my mind, this mind turning round, emptily, hungrily, upon itself. Now in darkness. It was clearly explained, why they would not leave a lamp or a lantern. If the Church requires something of Sor Juana for which she has need of light, then she will be brought a candle.

For one who does not sleep, the nights are long. Longer yet in darkness. But the cell is not always empty now. The emptiness comes and goes. When it comes, it is, but when it has gone, I am sometimes grateful for the company. The demons come in many forms. To some they come as a naked mulatto. This is to be preferred. Sometimes they come as revenants of the dead.

I had a visitor, in the locutory—I did not take visitors. She said she was my cousin. Magda. Magda was dead. But then what harm in seeing her? This was cunning. Had Magda said that?

The locutory was dusty. Mould and rust at the base of the window bars. Mildew had crept down from the ceilings, the finish on the grille scored with it and dull. The clavichords, the things on the walls, in the shelves, they should have been taken with the things in the cell. I would no longer be attached to these. These were not to die for. They could come for them when they liked.

A sour smell, as of fermentation, hung above the stench of the canals.

The woman was not Magda, but she had Magda's eyes. An onyx cross. Cunning. A long white dress, silks and silver. She dressed like Aunt María had, if without the veil. Ravaged face, blossoms about her nose and cheeks from drink. Almost hairless. Dead, Magda might come to look like this. And if she were not dead, a veil would have been wise. But the eyes, these were alive, not terribly so for eyes but for inanimate objects. Like Magda. Small, hard, polished. Like beans, lychee pips. They were alive with their hatred of me.

"Hello, Juana."

Magda died not long after her mother had, Uncle Juan many years before that. María had sold off all his enterprises but one. She kept the *pulque* concession, the most profitable. At her death, Magda inherited. She married soon after, and followed her husband into the north. Zacatecas . . . ? No, it was Queretaro. When he left her, she died there by her own hand.

Magda had been exhumed by the Inquisition, and sent to me.

"The Archbishop has asked me to come."

"A recent one?"

"I'd heard you were like this."

"And I you."

She did not quite understand but never could, and hated me now a little more for it. A spiritual hatred, it seems, is not unchanging, but grows beyond the grave. Like hair they say. I looked over her sparse pate. She was not long dead, maybe.

"Why send you?"

"I asked to come."

"To see for yourself."

"More or less."

"To bring a message."

"More than one."

"How does he look? Describe him."

"You know His Grace does not consent to see us."

"You spoke to a secretary."

"I bring an offer, a last chance."

"To save myself."

"Not you, Juana. She will be condemned. The sentence will be death. She will burn here."

"Will you come?"

"Are you prepared to have a woman *die* for your pride?"

"Who?"

"Don't pretend. It's weak."

"Tell me her name."

"They did not give me leave to speak of that."

"Just a last chance."

"Her last chance."

"To have her die not here."

"Or not at all. Perpetual imprisonment. The trial and the sentence to be carried out elsewhere."

"She cannot hold out much longer. The difference is small."

"You don't believe that."

"You know not the first thing about it—"

"Yes, how small of me."

"And now I am to believe they would modify her sentence. Or is this merely to spare myself the trial?"

"Think of your convent, at least."

"The conditions."

"No contact with the court. Here or in Madrid. No letters to or from. No visits, except as directed by the Church."

"There is more."

"A general confession of your sins, a renewal of your vows, a return to the state of novice."

"A stay of all proceedings against me."

"The Secretary did not mention that."

"Was there anything else?"

"Two things. A reminder, and also a message. If you want it. I have it here."

"From?"

"From you, Juana. From you. . . ."

The seal had been broken.

"Did you know, Cousin, your father took care of delicate business for my father?"

"Why are you telling me this?"

"No harm can come of it now."

"You mean, no good."

"Yes, I mean no good."

"Then why, Magda, listen to you?"

"Because you want to know—always, everything, or to think you do. You agreed to see me today, didn't you?" Into her eyes came a look of triumph. The letter would come at a price. Knowing the contents, she already believed I would pay it. "But first you shall hear everything else I have always known. About you, Juana. And for this, there is no charge. Did you know that our grandfather—*our* grandfather—introduced my father to yours? Or that my father was engaged to your mother when *your* father met her? He had heard so much about the beautiful daughter. Uncle Pedro wanted to see for himself. So you got her looks, and I got the other's."

"You have them still."

"Tell me, Juana, when was the last time you saw your*self*? But no, let's not quarrel yet, not when there's so much left to tell. . . . Did it never once enter your head you were named after my father? There, you see? It was only when Aunt Isabel had *you* that he gave up. I was almost four when he married my mother."

"You owe your legitimacy to me, then—take it as payment for the dresses."

"And always so clever about your fifty pesos. Such a bargain hunter. My father paid *thousands*, ran around to wherever you'd been, paying off your debts like a *secretary*. But I am forgetting the reminder now . . . from Bishop Santa Cruz: when he went to give your mother her last rites, they had a long talk about you, about their many hopes for you."

"I suppose you'll be taking the canal back."

"He said you would see. . . ."

"Swimming again, I imagine—you should have insisted on a boat."

"Did she never tell you about the other fifty pesos?"

"When you get back, do give my regards to Sáenz de Mañozca."

"Did Isabel ever tell you it was the name that broke her heart—?"

"And my respects to Torquemada—tell them the one who sent you was a bastard, too."

"Amanda—the cook's daughter. You remember her—"

"Get *out*."

"But you don't know why yet, Juana, *why* it broke her heart. You will want to know this, Cousin. . . ."

 Gutiérrez had promised me I would be brought to remember things, bear witness against others, as others would against me. Gutiérrez was a liar, Gutiérrez was a Judas, Gutiérrez was my friend—surely it was shame that had made him leave the Inquisition, book passage for Manila.

Magda did not leave the locutory for some time. And if I did not either, it was because there were things I needed so badly to know. She was right about this, right about me, and would not leave until I had heard them. She had made no move yet to hand me the letter. I added a condition, before giving her what she wanted, a single piece of information. Hearing it, she nodded in satisfaction, as though it had only confirmed something she had already known.

If I felt shame, then, I told myself it was because of the condition. I told Magda I wanted to know the *beata's* name if I co-operated. More childishness. They could give me any name they liked. Magda did not answer directly, though I could see she wanted me to believe she knew who the woman was. But I knew they would bend to my will. I would have a name, eventually, for the holy officers who had sent Magda knew it would be worse once I had one. It was only afterwards that it seemed like haggling over the *beata's* name to get what I wanted.

As the hours passed, my mind returned to what I had told Magda—because I could not bear to see that letter in her hand, and the seal broken. I told myself they had already known about Carlos, about his last visit, about the manuscripts, of course they had. I had suspected him for days, since he last came. No, I had suspected him for months—Gutiérrez had said there were testimonies and reports on me dating back thirty years, even before I moved from my uncle's house to the Palace. Why tell me this unless the identity of my betrayer would be a devastation? *Carlos.* Magda was dead. Even if I had thought of her, even if it were true my own cousin had informed against me, this would come as no great surprise, at best would make me furious yet not hurt me. I could not possibly think less of Magda. And Magda was dead. What would be the object?

After Carlos had left for Florida, of course I began to wonder why he had truly come. To say good-bye, or was it to test my defences, my readiness to express contrition? But I was forgetting: he had come to show me a way forward with the Archbishop. Yes, His Grace and I had so much in common, much common ground. Our interest in the philosophies of Heraclitus, our regard for Antonio Vieyra—like a father to one who has never known one. And, of course, our friendship with Carlos. What did I know about friendship—who had my friends been? The seed of doubt sown by Bishop Santa Cruz had long since put forth its flowers. Carlos always knew when to leave, always managed to be away when unpleasant things befell his friends. Had he so much as tried to warn me the day of the chess game? He had merely left, excused himself. He was going to the archives to study the papers of Bishop Zumárraga.

Zumárraga—why even mention him if not to make reference to stories I had heard from my grandfather the night he died? Stories I had told only Isabel after, because I could not help myself. Mentioning Zumárraga the day of the chess game only reminded me Carlos had gone behind my back to be her friend, who in turn had betrayed to him my confidences. Isabel I knew I could never count on, or turn to—but Carlos was only telling me that everyone here informs on everyone. A little earlier would have helped, dear friend, but I had it, now. Thank you, Carlos.

Carlos was exactly the one to have been sent to strip my cell—he was the Archbishop's almoner, after all—yet Carlos was always leaving, just as he had been away when Fray de Cuadros went to the burning ground.

And now the Holy Office knew without a doubt that I had his manuscripts. It was clear that Carlos had brought them to incriminate me and save himself.

Magda too had come to show me a way forward with the Archbishop. And surely here was the meaning in the message she had brought from Santa Cruz, that he had taken my mother's last confession, had taken from her my confidences and my secrets—everyone betrays everyone, everyone informs on everyone. This was a lesson Santa Cruz had been giving for some time, the same lesson someone had been preparing for me since 1663. It was not too late to believe it could have been Magda: it was too late to believe it could not have been Carlos.

They have turned me against a friend.

Who is the Enemy of Both Sides, if not I. . . .

 Emptiness. It is the sound of such a vastness.

It brings other sounds with it, other voices. Sometimes, hearing them, one would leave, go anywhere, distant times, places. The holy officers can arrange this, change verdicts and sentences, book passage to Manila, send fools into exile, spare the *beata*. They can bring Magda back from Purgatory, where mortal sins are purged not with the Light of Love but by dark fire. They can bring me to fail another friend, to fail the living or the dead. Magda came many times. I did not like her visits. I did not know why I always saw her. I was not to have visitors. The Enemy comes in many forms now, living and dead. They come as payment for too many questions and doubts, for the petitions for special knowledge, for this hunger so displeasing to God.

Does the vision bring peace, is it actively sought or passively received, does it lead toward God or the Enemy . . . ?

Sometimes they come in visions, but sometimes take no form at all. As when Antonia comes to sit in the dark with me. Remember our lessons, Antonia, remember irony? Close your eyes. A blade with three sides, in profile, diminishing to a point in an infinite regression of triangles—inserted, the wound it inflicts takes an eternity to heal.

Philothea, Bishop of Puebla. Theophilus, Bishop of Alexandria.

Philothea, Loving God. Theophilus, Beloved of God.

This is the knowledge the Enemy offers me.

Theophilus, Christian tyrant. Hypatia of Alexandria, pagan maiden.

Maximinus, pagan tyrant. Catherine of Alexandria, Christian maiden.

And note, Antonia, how a fine-drawn wire wound round the blade forms a spiral. With a wire fine enough, one may turn around the three-sided blade endlessly. Like this . . . the minions of Theophilus pull Hypatia down from a chariot, scrape the flesh from her bones with oyster shells. The henchmen of Maxentius behead Catherine spun upon a wheel. The followers of Hypatia turn upon themselves. . . .

But I knew now why Magda came. She had given me the hint I needed. To desire vision, to hunger for knowledge excessively, this was to admit the Enemy. This was why Magda had been sent to me, with messages and reminders. *For the Enemy has no power over the soul except through the operations of its faculties, and especially through the medium of knowledge that lodges in the memory. If, then, the memory annihilates itself with respect to the faculties, the Enemy is powerless.*

They had sent Magda to keep me from annihilating my memory.

Turtle shells . . .

I did not want to remember. Not here, not now, not like this.

We had gone out through the tall corn behind the hacienda, a herd of deer going over the fence ahead of us. . . . She had a surprise for me, hanging from the branch of a cedar, something in a bucket leaking water. She wanted me to take the bucket down. Her eyes glowed with excitement. Wide, almond eyes. I also had a surprise. The night before, there had been an incident at dinner, an old story I had led Diego into telling, about a bridegroom impaled on a wedding tree, and something about a wolf. . . . In the telling, it had become clear that he had been using his dog to track us into the woods. After, my mother had said nothing to him in our defence but had spirited me out of the room instead. I would be going to live with my aunt.

Reaching up for the leaky bucket that morning I said we were going away to Mexico. Her face stiffened—she asked if she was to go as my maid. She ran away from me then, too fast for me to follow. In the bucket that morning were two turtles . . . we had had such turtles at a special place of ours, high on the mountain. I walked back alone to the hacienda, water trickling onto the dust beside me and across my feet. I came through the passageway leading from the portals and saw Diego in his dress uniform in the middle of the courtyard. Before him, he had lined up the *campesinos* as though for inspection. But it was my mother, rocking calmly, he looked at as he drew his sword. Impassive, she watched him pacing up and down the file, screaming questions in pidgin Spanish at the bewildered men— *Who did who did it, point him point him, save you, not save him, I won't kill . . .* I could not tell what he was asking. They could not have understood. He questioned the next man, holding the sabre beneath his chin. Wild with frustration he turned to the man next in line and waved the sword-point back and forth close beneath the *campesino's* eyes. He twisted the flashing blade a hair's breadth above the bare chest of a third, as though to drill a hole. They were too terrified to answer. Wilder yet, he stepped to the next. As he raised his sword in both hands, something relaxed in him.

Isabel's voice was not loud, yet rang clearly over the ranting man's, rang through the run of blood in my ears.

"Diego, *enough.*"

She had not moved, had not so much as sat forward, but the rocking had stopped. The baby let the nipple slip from between his lips to look up at the source of that voice.

"You do know innocence, don't you, Diego? You do *see* . . ."

Or perhaps she truly did mean innocents.

The tone, calm, agreeable, lent the words an edge of menace and contempt. Slowly Diego lowered the sword.

"Back to work," she said, without taking her eyes from his. The workers vanished. Eventually he looked away, as I knew he must. Beaten, he turned and went out, the sword arm hanging loosely at his side. In a moment or two we heard his horse gallop by.

I set the bucket down and went, legs wooden, to Xochitl, to discover what had been happening. While we had been out, a man had rushed in from the fields to spread the news. Out in the maguey field a *campesino* had found Diego's mastiff at the killing floor, suspended by its hind legs from a cross-beam supporting the roof thatch. A heavy bludgeon lay by its head. It had been clubbed to death. Gutted. Skinned and dressed. The hide was staked out, to be made into saddle bags one day, a scabbard, a woman's boots.

 I had been three months in the convent of San José when I sent for my uncle. It was mid-winter, then as now, 1669. At San José, visits were rarely permitted, except in cases of greatest urgency. I had written out a message, a letter I could trust no one else to deliver. And I knew without a doubt that it was that letter Madga now held in her lap. I had written it to my mother, a call for help. Only Juan could deliver it, because he would have to read it to her, because above all Diego could not be the one for this. Would she please come for me, would she let me come home? I had nowhere left to go. San José was a house of anguish and agony, a place of blood and instruments of torment, a place without light, without books, or laughter or wonder. She had been right all along, she had been right about me.

And now I saw my cousin's eyes shining with the knowledge of those lines, with her knowledge of me and the memories of her hatred. How many years had Magda known—the years since Aunt María's death, or for all the years since Juan's? All the years I had been in here, at San Jerónimo, waiting for my mother's answer.

I had guessed the essentials. Magda gave the details as she handed my letter back after twenty-four years. And for this also there would be no charge. But by then she had my information, and I had from her the real reason she had brought the Bishop's message with the letter. A simpler reason. To remind me that I had once refused his dispensation to leave the cloister, to be with my mother as she was dying.

"So, Cousin, you have your letter back. I would have returned it anyway, even without your information. I loved him. He loved her. And now you know why my father would have been such a willing messenger. Do you want to know the rest? Are you ready to hear? Don't just nod— tell me you are."

"Yes."

"Aunt Isabel told my mother she had already guessed about your father and the Indian. But what broke your mother's heart was a name. Did you realize she had been planning to call you just Inés? But hearing that other name, she named you after my father instead. This part he told me when you were leaving for the palace. And for the past many years I have known the rest. *Amanda*. Would an Indian choose such a name on her own? No, Amanda was your father's choice. Amanda, loving, conceived in love. So then, Cousin, whose choice were you—and what were you conceived in? I know your mother wondered.

"You and the cook's daughter were sisters, Juana. And your father was a Jew. And you are welcome. For the dresses. . . ."

The night of trials contains a good deal of pain, we cling so to things. Our illusions of sense, our instruments of mind, our memories, we would cling to these even when they hurt us. We forget we are another's instrument. Our grasp must be prised open, our fingers parted. All affections and attachments and faculties must be burned away, like a log in a fire, like grime and rust encrusted to base metal. And the soul is to be its crucible.

It is said the sensations are as of one lying beyond the walls of a familiar city—one's own, perhaps, forbidden to enter, forced to keep watch, tracing lovingly from afar the shadows of the parapets, the chapels and towers. Or the longing is as of a lioness who goes forth in the night to seek her cubs, who have been taken from her. It is said she cannot long endure this state, and must soon recover what she has lost or die. On other nights it is like being released by a hunter to be hunted again.

And again.

Again.

Again.

And in the deepest dark in the last watch of that night, there is a crossroads.

Fate, was my crime of such enormity

that, to chastise me or torment me more,

beyond that torture which the mind foresees,

you whisper you have yet more harm in store?

  Pursuing me with such severity,

you make your heartlessness only too plain:

when you bestowed this gift of mind on me,

you only sought to aggravate my pain.

  Bringing me applause, you stirred up envy's ire.

Raising me up, you knew how hard I'd fall.

No doubt it was your treachery saddled me

  with troubles far beyond misfortune's call,

that, seeing the store you gave me of your blessings,

no one would guess the cost of each and all.

JUANA INÉS
DE LA CRUZ

Alan Trueblood, trans.

FEEDING
THE SUN

Carlos,

 ne letter, the most difficult, the last. Then I can get on with what there is left to do. I send this through your friends at the monastery in Veracruz, and hope they will find some way to make this reach you—I must risk it. If it's intercepted by my holy censors here we are lost, but if I do not try to warn you, Carlos, and you are taken, I am the one lost.

I have told them, about the manuscripts—not all, and the papers are safe yet—but that you brought them here, that we had quarrelled months ago, that I turned you away. How fortunate my coldness to you just this once has proven. I told them I did not know what the packet held, but that I thought they were scientific treatises.

So upon your return you must not be manoeuvred into thinking they know more than they do—and while you are away you must contrive an accident, with witnesses, so you may say the manuscripts were destroyed or lost. I have thought and thought and thought through everything I have told them, and this is the one thing that poses great danger.

You are asking yourself how I could have done this. Or it may be that from me it comes as no surprise. They came so soon after you left. . . .

The almoners brought a bill of sale—as if to say I had purchased these things from myself, only to donate them again. It was as if they were *taking them from me twice.*

Only now as it all sloughs away like scalded skin do I realize how deeply, bitterly angry I've been, and how unjustly. Not coming to you when you came to say good-bye now leaves me sick with remorse. I know you didn't betray me. Life is not so simple, so symmetrical. The friends of my enemies are not my enemies, any more than your friendship with me makes the Archbishop my friend. Might it be that day he broke your cheekbone with his cane, you were defending me? But what I have also come recently to learn is that neither does being the enemy of my enemy make that someone my friend.

And now, what I have come so late to see is that if you've left your most precious possessions with me it's because from this fool's errand to Florida you never expected to return. What made you think you would be the first to die? Too proud to refuse the commission which may end your life, too sentimental to accept the one which might have saved it. Who is to say you might not have made a life at Versailles? You just can't leave her, can you, this New Eden of yours? After all these years, this is how you still see her. The ever faithful suitor you see her as she was, not as she's aged. Faithful generous suitor, you share whatever you've learned of her with every passing scholar—a lifetime of discoveries reduced to footnotes in the books of lesser writers.

I have recopied carefully each of these letters of yours from Veracruz invested with so much tenderness, and blush at how much less was returned in mine to you. So critical was I of your Americanist project— why invest your life, risk a career on a pursuit so unpromising? To find political virtues in the Mexicas' tyranny, to make FeatherSerpent out to be the twin of Christ—doubting Thomas, the most sceptical of all the saints. Christ had a brother, Carlos, but his name was Satanael.

Yet you were unworried by consequences, and unwilling to believe me indifferent. How could I be? you asked. These were the stories of my own childhood. Do you have any idea how it felt for me to watch you take possession of those stories, one by one, when I'd let them go?

And now I hold the last remaining account of Moctezuma's last days even as my own conqueror approaches. All my strength it takes now to look forward without blinking. Carlos, I have sent a plea that Father Núñez return as my confessor. I will not even try to explain. Through Arellano, he has demanded a sign that I at last see the enormity of my transgressions. A sign. I see nothing but signs. I have written for him the one he seeks. Mine, I do not seek.

You think you'll be the first to die. You may be right. For see how death eludes one who desires it—even death, when in demand, will rise in price. The Archbishop's auction raised a good part of the ransom, but not all, for they knew I had something left to sell. . . .

How can I ever make you see how I could have thought—for half the span of an hour—that you had brought these things to implicate me? *Who has sent him? Does even Carlos know? Who has brought us here, to this pass? How can he do this—after all that has happened, to Fray de Cuadros, to us?* I could not understand it—to remind us of what might have been? Of what cannot be brought back, what we failed to prevent?

You who knew me—surely you could see how dangerous their stories were. The Mexica. The most rigorous and unsparing, unblinking, glaring straight into the sun . . . people devouring their idols, a people swallowed by the sun. And now Fray de Cuadros is dead. Carlos, I am not indifferent. Carlos, I have not forgotten. Stark, the invitation: who will feed the sun. How dangerous all the little love stories we tell ourselves of god. The conqueror approaches, see his footprints in the rock . . . ? After each slow step a dust of dreams trails up. The Emperor of Dreams awaits his destiny, awake. He tries to flee, to hide himself within a cave, but the earth will not harbour him. He returns in shame. Desperately he consults the sorcerers, the oracles, the ancient texts—the ones not burned by his own father's order. Through dream-plagued days and sleepless nights, prodigies, portents, ill omens drift like smoke through the capital. All who dream of the end of the world, all must come before him. The capital is made to pay a tribute of dreams. The *Massacre of the Dreamers* is what one day they will call it. So many dreams . . . Moctezuma sifts them, immersed in one vast dreaming.

Tell me your story.

"I saw a strange bird with feathers like ashes. Its head was a mirror. I looked into it and saw the sky full of stars at midday. I looked again upon a plain full of armed men surging forward on the backs of deer. . . ."

Tell me your story.

"Last night I saw a smoking star dripping fire, like an ear of corn bleeding fire. The night sky was filled with blood and smoke. . . ."

Tell me your story.

"The temple on the great pyramid burst into flames. Lightning struck it from a clear blue sky. Even now it's burning. We keep throwing water on it, great quantities of water, we cannot put it out. We cannot put it out. . . ."

Tell me your story.

"Everyone in our precinct heard her again last night. Weeping for her lost children. Weeping for the city. . . ."

Tell me your story.

"On the lake I saw a waterspout as high as a mountain and through it saw the gods descending. . . ."

Tell me your story.

"Last night the streets were filled with two-headed dwarves and hunchbacks asking for the king. . . ."

Tell me your dreams—who will feed the sun?

Destiny approaches him who knows the histories. The histories he knows himself condemned to repeat, for this history is prophecy.

Tell me your dreams.

The jails are full of sorcerers. But all those brave enough to tell their dreams, the Emperor of Revery has had put to death. The flood of dreams that left the prisons awash in dreamers now runs dry, and more terrible to him than all the dreams is the moment of their ceasing.

"This Christ of yours," he'll one day soon now ask the startled chaplain, "he died to save his father? He gave his heart to feed the sun?" The beautiful interpreter smiles and shakes her head.

Tell me your story. Tell me your story of the end.

Dreamers given death, sorcerers grown still, seers lost from sight, jailed prophets, shrouded, silent . . . slowly silence falls.

Drums booming, flutes piping . . . the last sounds from the outside world to reach his ears. Soon even the dreams of the Emperor, the last to dream in all the world, fall silent.

Soon enough, soon with great relief he elects the warrior's death. Death at his captor's hands. The nobility of the captor vouchsafes the nobility of his dying.

Who will feed the sun? the captive asks, but gets no answer.

I am sorry, Carlos. Can you ever find it in your heart to understand.

Your friend,

Juana Inés Ramírez de Asbaje, *la peor de todas* . . . [17]

MESSENGER

. . . y abatime tanto, tanto,
que fui tan alto, tan alto,
que le di a la casa alcance . . . [18]

n the evening, I went to find Xochitl, still hoping to convince her to let Amanda come to Mexico. In the kitchen the door to the fields stood ajar. Moths whirled at the lantern glass, throwing shadows over the packed dirt of the yard. I remember that it was a clear night, the moonlight a burnish on the blades of corn. We sat at the small table, the evening's unwashed dishes piled behind us on the blue-tiled counter. Xochitl had said no for the second time, and for the second time I had asked why. Instead of answering she began to tell me of her youth, as a girl respected by her people, a fish of gold. But I had heard this. Though young, she had been a healer, was soon to be a midwife, as Amanda would be one day. I had grown impatient, for this was precisely what she had never wanted to teach me. Xochitl talked then of first meeting my grandfather, when he came to her village on the far slope of the volcano. Soon after, something had slid, and she was no longer honoured. *Tla alaui, tlapetzcaui in tlalticpac.* Fish of gold, what happened to you?

She had been returning late to the village. It was after dusk. She was pregnant. The horse, going fast, had stepped into a *toza* burrow. I saw so clearly then how my grandfather would have blamed himself for the accident, though it was something that might befall even the finest horsemen. It was only afterwards that she came to Nepantla to nurse me. Xochitl had been trying to tell me the one story I had always dreamt true, yet I was hardly listening at all, and afraid, just perhaps, to hear that she and my grandfather had done something improper. I had always thought of her as his age, her hair had been white even before his.

Something had slid, but she did not mean her fall from the horse. Something had broken but she did not mean her hip. This something had broken months before. Two Spaniards, not one. Pedro Manuel de Asbaje, Pedro Ramírez de Santillana. Two don Pedros, a father and a grandfather. Two superb horsemen, two horses . . . The horse was not my grandfather's. The horse Xochitl had fallen from was my father's. Pedro Manuel de Asbaje. *Aca icuitlaxcoltzin quitlatalmachica.* Who arranged his intestines artistically.

I had heard this as a child, on a cart ride from Nepantla to Panoayan, and had vowed to resolve it for myself one day. And so I had. And now another from that time—I believed Magda: Xochitl had been trying to tell me Amanda was my father's daughter.

Even as Magda said it, smiling through the grille, I knew it to be true. Because she knew how it would hurt me to know this, now. Amanda was my sister.

Four years after I had left for Mexico I made the long return journey by ox cart only to discover Amanda and Xochitl had been sent to another hacienda. They never arrived. It was from Diego's lips I had had to hear this, and that he had sent men searching for them everywhere.

Isabel had only been waiting for me to leave. She had sent them away without so much as sending me word. I had been thinking precisely this when I saw her, riding fast along the maguey field, past the killing floor, slowing towards the house. In a moment or two, from where I sat among the trees, I saw her go in. She would have been waiting for me to come back to the house; but as the wagon staggered on, I ran to catch it, vowing never again to look back to Panoayan.

I broke that promise to myself. I looked back once, from the convent of San José, my new home among the Carmelites. And when my mother did not answer my call for help, I believed she was paying me in kind for having returned to Panoayan only to leave without speaking to her. I had never forgiven Isabel for never replying, for not coming for me. We never spoke again. Not a word ever again passed between us, not a message; never had I a kind thought for her, never did I permit myself a fond memory.

And I also believed Magda about Uncle Juan. He had promised to deliver it himself, the next day. He always kept his word. Some weeks later he was called to Acapulco on business. In the wide bay before the city, his body was found by a fisherman. Juan had not gone to Panoayan, had hesitated. He was still in love with her.

My mother never received the letter.

February 6th near dawn a light rain stopped. Father Arellano came not long after Prime. One by one the other black veils around our small patio went down to confess at the slots. Terce had come and gone. All that morning I waited for my turn to be called. María Bernadina was the last to come back from the *craticulas*. His Paternity would see me in the locutory. I wondered if he had conquered his fear of beauty, or had been told there was less to fear. He had not agreed to see me there for years. As I entered he turned his chair to face the window bars, his shoulder to the grille.

We sat shoulder to shoulder looking into the garden, out over the rose bushes. It might have been pleasant, a visit from among the living. We might have talked about the passing of the years. I looked more closely at him. His body had run to fat, his jaw to jowls. His hair was still black at the crown, had greyed at the temples, whitened around the ears. I had forgotten that it was not just the thickness of the walls—Father Arellano, when in the presence of sin, mumbled.

"*Este* . . . as of today, Sor Juana, you must no longer consider me your director."

He was very sorry, but it went hard for the confessors of heretics. He said this glancing sidelong, his voice high for one of his bulk. He did not think he could face it. This I could believe, if he could not even face me; just as I could believe him a man who had just recently made his first visit to the offices of the Inquisition.

Was it true Sor Juana sought the protection of the Prefect of the Brotherhood of Mary? Yes? Then His Reverence had sent him, Father Arellano, to say that she would have to agree instantly, that day, to meet his conditions, meet them all, meet them fully, lest she soon come in for a more rounded discipline.

By what token was I to believe he came from Núñez?

Prefect Núñez had expected this. His terms were these, which Father Arellano would now try to present verbatim, that there be no misunderstanding. Having heard them Sor Juana could judge of their source for herself.

First, Sor Juana was to cease all visits to the convent archives, all study of any kind. She was herewith forbidden to read even among the saints and learned doctors of the Church. The time for Augustine was past. For the moment, as a kindness, she was to be permitted one text. Father Arellano placed it on the table that spanned the grille. If she cared to, let Sor Juana read her John of the Cross as often as she could bear. Not the verses. These she was never to read again. But *The Ascent of Mount Carmel*. This was the only mountain left for Sor Juana Inés de la Cruz to climb. All else was vanity. One candle per week would be permitted for this purpose, if she was prepared to meet the other conditions.

Which . . . ?

Sor Juana was to cease all writing, except at the express command of her director. And this next point the Prefect had enjoined Father Arellano to make with some clarity: Sor Juana was never again to write poetry.

Not in any form, no devotional verses, no carols for the Church. This condition was not negotiable, and was never to be rescinded under any circumstances, for the rest of her days. God did not need her poetry here, and in Heaven are enough who sing.

Sor Juana would first draft a preliminary statement of guilt, in preparation for a full examination of her conscience, of all the unnumbered crimes and vilest sins of her worldly life, from the beginning. . . . Father Arellano was sorry. These had been the Prefect's exact words. Nothing had been forgotten. Nothing is ever forgotten under the eyes of God. Gaps, omissions were no longer to be tolerated. With even this simple condition the Prefect doubted very much she could comply, after so many years of evasions, for *the thing that hath been is that which shall be . . . and there is no new thing under the sun.* It was the Prefect's view that she could not change, would not. And even if Sor Juana might delude herself for a while, he was not given to delusions. Too much of the Prefect's time had been wasted on her already—his time, and that of so many others working on her case. So much waste and vanity and vexation of the spirit.

No doubt Sor Juana would want some time to make her calculations.

Vexation of the spirit. . . .

It was with Magda I had first seen the Palaces of the Inquisition, the banner above the front gates, two girls flirting with the sentries . . . the rose-coloured church on the plaza, the workshops, the forges. It was with Magda and María that I had first learned of the great *auto* of 1649, retraced the route to the burning ground, heard described the uncanny likenesses of the effigies. It was in Magda's voice I heard whispered the names of the Grand Inquisitor and his nephew Sáenz de Mañozca, and those of the family Carvajal, Ana and her brother Luís. Magda had even learned the brother's poetry. *And from myself, without You, who would deliver me, And to You, without You, my Lord, who would carry me? . . .* Magda, too, was a scholar. A chronicler of family and the familiar. And it was on that day that I had first heard of the book collector Pérez de Soto, who had also too little respected the Holy Office. She talked then of a smaller *auto*, more suitable to the edification of children, the *auto* of 1656 . . . the year Pérez de Soto was arrested.

Magda had made it clear from the first that she was prepared to bear witness against her own father's parents. Nor was I sure it was untrue that they had been secret Jews. If they were convicted of Judaizing, their remains would be exhumed and burned, *sambenitos* hung in their parish church, in Mexico, and in their birthplace in Spain. I did not know if even Magda could give evidence against a father she had loved, though he was beyond hurting now; but she would not hesitate against mine. Others would believe. Was this truly why he had left us, as Magda said, to escape the *auto* of 1656?

No, I would not let myself believe it, because she would know how I wanted to—which from Magda would make it false. What else did the scholar Magda know, what had she told, to whom? What lies could I refute? What truths . . . ?

1663. This was the year, according to Gutiérrez, of the first testimony against me. For Magda, her first visit here would have been a kind of anniversary. Thirty years . . . perhaps to the day. *There are many working on your case, Juana. You would be surprised to know just how many.* . . . Núñez had said this to me a dozen years ago. Núñez too would have known about those first files—had he been warning me even then about Magda?

But though she might be an asset to Dorantes and to Santa Cruz, as her files had been to Gutiérrez, Núñez had never needed Magda. Father Núñez had other assets. And so in the night after the first candle burned down I saw Núñez come to stand vaunting over me, brandishing his war tools, felt the rasp of his mockeries, heard him boasting of his advantages, of the perfection of his memory. It would be as with the second inventory of Dorantes—I would need to remember all I had told him, every confidence in a dozen years of confession—even *how* I had told him, and everything I had not, beginning twenty-five years ago. I could face the Inquisition or else Núñez; I could face the Dominicans or my own conscience. This was the challenge in the message, which he had always believed me too cowardly to accept. At least before the Holy Office I could protest my innocence. *Vexation . . . no new thing under the sun . . . remember thy Creator in the days of thy youth.* Three times Núñez had recalled Ecclesiastes, and in doing so, warned me of where we might make a beginning. . . .

On the day of the service, the old men of the town had come out. The priest from Chimalhuacan read gently from the Gospel of John; then Brother Anton from Texcoco came forward and recited beautifully from Ecclesiastes. My grandfather would have liked it. It made me think of Hesiod. Uncle Juan had not come. I had not met him yet, and had not imagined they had been friends. Across the hole in the ground stood Magda, behind her my aunts and other cousins, my sisters beside my mother. I had been furious to have been asked to choose the place, had refused to—*choose?* I choose that he still be here with us. Amanda cried quietly beside me, her arm about my shoulders. Xochitl sighed once, and stroked my hair. There came my turn to read, from an old book with a broken spine. Kneeling in the fresh-turned earth I read the first four stanzas without crying or so much as pausing, it seemed, to breathe. But when I did pause, I did not go on.

By that evening the last of the guests had left. My aunts were not guests, as my mother pointed out, but had grown up in this house. They were to have my sisters' room, which had once been their own. Josefa and María were to be in my room with me. It was just for one night.

Late that night I was still in the library, asleep in the corner armchair where he had used to sleep. I thought it a dream, at first. I saw my mother standing before me. The lantern guttered, its oil run down. Her veil was drawn back. I thought it strange she had not changed, though the dress was beautiful. She had bent slightly, then seeing me awake, seemed to hesitate.

"I wanted to be sure it wasn't him." She smiled faintly, embarrassed. It might have occurred to me, she had bent to pick me up.

"I thought you never came in here."

She straightened, the swelling of her belly formidable, pronounced.

"Who do you think put him to bed all these years?"

It was the kind of hidden knowledge that I had always known lay all about me, and had always sensed about to rush in at me from some unexpected quarter. "Your eyes are clear, Inés, for seeing far. But up close you're as blind as the rest of us."

I looked away, to the floor, the cold hearth, the desk in the shadows behind her, unshelved books in a jumble on the near side. On the other, stacked neatly, the four books he had been reading, on them a thick envelope. *A mi hijita Isabel.* My eyes had lit dully upon it that morning, but it had lain there for the week since. Embarrassed, I slipped past her and went quickly to the desk.

"This was for you."

It did not occur to me to offer to read it for her. She started down the aisle toward me, casting shadows over the ceiling ahead of her. I could not see her face against the flicker of lamplight. She would be angry that I had forgotten. It would seem typical of me. "I don't know when Abuelo put it there. It wasn't there . . . that night."

She came to stand very near, very tall, waiting perhaps on a better explanation. Her fingers touched the envelope but did not quite grasp it. I did not know what she was feeling, but craning up with her so near I saw it was not anger.

"Did you really paint those angels for him . . . ?"

Startled, she looked up into the shadows of the cross-beams, which divided the composition into three, the figures crudely painted but finely drawn. Cherubs, seraphim—the thrones and principalities, the seven choirs . . .

She stood a long moment, remembering. "Your grandfather loved angels, like a child. I was a child myself. I thought it was . . . nice."

Unable to stop, I asked why she had given up drawing. Her eyes left the ceiling, glanced over the desk covered in books, at the map above it of the southern oceans. She looked at me finally, in their hollows her eyes large in the unsteady light. She drew in a long breath. "Inés . . . no matter how clever you are, no matter how—"

"A library is no place for a woman—you've told me."

"That's not what I was going to say."

It was only partly because of what she said then, that I told her about the last night with him . . . to give her something more of him than a letter. And so we sat up late, and I told her the stories he had told, how animated he had been, how his eyes had seemed like emeralds once again. How I had woken up as he put me to bed. I told her because of the angels, and because he loved her. I told her because I needed to tell her, more than anyone. When I had said that the library was no place for a woman, she had started to replace her veil, but then gently placed her hands on my shoulders.

"No matter how clever you are, *hija*, no matter how hard you work or you try, you can never bring them back."

Núñez would not care why my father had left. Núñez would not ask me about the *auto* of 1656. He would demand to know why I had left her—left refusing to speak to her, twice. He would ask why things were not better between us, even after this night. He would ask how in a rage, just three months later, I could accuse her of driving my father away and ask if she had ever loved anyone.

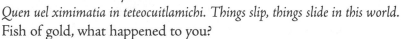

Quen uel ximimatia in teteocuitlamichi. Things slip, things slide in this world. Fish of gold, what happened to you?

I sent for Arellano on February 23rd when Núñez had still not come. I had given a statement of my guilt, agreed to the terms, and I had requested—no, I had been hoping that he might come for the 24th of February, for the twenty-fourth anniversary of my profession, that we might begin my noviciate together, my year of trial. Why had he not come?

Father Arellano was sorry, but he did not decide for Prefect Núñez, nor did Sor Juana. He would come when it was time, when there were signs that she had truly understood what she had been given to read, had truly *heard* this time. I reminded Arellano that he and I had spoken of Juan de la Cruz in confession not so very long ago. His Paternity might remember the rain. Did he have some new direction for me now?

"Sor Juana, that is the day I was referring to, when I communicated to you a final warning from Prefect Núñez . . . that while there was yet time, you should study the writings of John of the Cross for a path to God that still included a little poetry." Even so recently as then, the Prefect had indicated he was prepared to confront the Archbishop and defend Sor Juana's practice of poetry on purely devotional topics. "But the Prefect's warning went unheeded, and that time is now past."

Unheeded? No, Father, I had not heard. Would it have made any difference, you ask? How, Father, could either of us know that? And *why* had I not heard?—because His Paternity had been unable to bring himself to meet with me in the locutory. So why, I wondered, did he come now? Was it not true he had been forced to, as a punishment? And how could Father Arellano make accurate report of me, if he could not look at me, if he did not examine me? Why would anyone send a messenger to give messages I could not hear, or who warns me that I might next come in for a discipline 'more rounded' when Father Núñez had in fact said *circular*? Was that not true—yes? Why, then, should anyone rely on such a messenger?

As he rose, he glanced at me without wishing to, his eyes round and dark. They looked as mine might. He had not slept, looked more frightened than I, or I hoped he did. It was as I had guessed, that he was being sent for his negligence. And if they so chose, his penalty could be the same as mine. And it could be death. He had confessed a heretic for almost a dozen years without raising the alarm. To defend himself he would have had to admit what I had guessed all along. That he had been unable to bring himself to *listen,* had been too frightened to.

I sat for a time when Arellano had gone, and looked out into the garden. What could it *mean*—that I had tried on my own to take the very course of action Núñez had urged upon me through Arellano that day, two years ago? What was it they thought I had not heard, had not yet grasped? I understood that the poet I had loved, whose echoes in my own poetry Núñez had most despised, whose voice was never far from my mind, was to be turned against me. For the one book I was to be permitted, now, was of the night of trials, not the poems. I understood also that this was to be done to demonstrate that everything could be turned against me, to make an enemy of a friend, to remind me of how much Juan de la Cruz had endured not for his poetry but for his faith.

Núñez would say that God had guided his hand in this choice of book, but then why had I not heard his messenger—had I been guided not to hear the warning? If He has guided the hand of Núñez to triumph, has mine been guided to fail? Was I to be returned to the beginning only to be shown that the night of trials never ends, but only opens into deeper trial? I had looked down that path, into a darkness that Juan had made beautiful. I had drawn from the springs of his sources to bring comfort to others, to bring some sense to their suffering, but I could not make that path my own.

If only Núñez had come, we could have talked together. With him I would have spoken my heart, I would have tried again, in a manner more sincere than with Arellano. Father, why have you offered this path now, you who warned me from it, the path of the ecstatic, you who said it would lead me to destroy myself? Why send Arellano to me, when for twelve years he and I have been as strangers? It would be better to have left me to myself, to turn on myself, than to send such as these to me, who are afraid even to look upon rose bushes without startling.

But Núñez had not come. And to this last question at least I knew the answer. We had been sent to punish each other, Arellano to me, for his concupiscence and fear of sin, and I to Arellano, to mortify my pride.

The next day, for my twenty-fourth anniversary, I put on again the rough *sayuela* of the novice, much as Antonia wore, and cropped my hair. I chose the evening, after Compline, so as to have some hours before being seen. My vanity cost me much of the week's candle.

I was afraid Antonia would try to stop me. She was stronger, angry. I explained that it had been shorn thus twice before—surely harder on those who would have to look upon it than it was for me. I could not stop her cutting her own in turn. I was not strong enough. I had loved her hair.

We helped each other, in the end. The places farthest back were hardest to reach.

I sent Antonia with an apology to Father Arellano. He did not come for weeks. It amused Núñez to send him on April 13th, the Feast of Saint Hermenegild.

I could see Arellano dreaded coming now. I had won that much from them.

Would Father Núñez be coming soon?

If and when Sor Juana had given positive signs of her will and disposition, the Prefect would come to examine them himself.

But had I given no indication considered positive?

The cutting of the hair was positive.

What other sign had I failed to give? Arellano was sorry, but as Sor Juana herself had said, he was only a messenger. No, Sor Juana's apology was unnecessary. Her criticism had been correct. The Prefect had indeed said 'circular,' and said now that there was perhaps time yet to choose between a cell and a closet, to follow a circular path or one still more tortuous—neither should she imagine such pleasant quarters as had held John or Hermenegild. *Ne Plus Ultra.* Here the Prefect had instructed Father Arellano to ask Sor Juana if she understood. Yes. To repeat it. Yes, I had understood. No, to say it.

Ne Plus Ultra.

Perhaps this talk of signs had been misleading. Sor Juana, as a natural philosopher, a master of navigation and circular paths, would prefer to think in terms of treatises, observations. Evidence. In the absence of which, the Prefect continued to believe that a path without poetry and philosophy would be far too narrow for one such as she. Now if the message had been communicated adequately, the messenger should be going.

Circular paths . . . closet or cell. In the last century Teresa had written to Philip II about Juan's abduction to Toledo and his imprisonment by the unreformed Carmelites, his former Order. She said she would have preferred to see him fallen into the hands of the Moors, who had more pity. Had he not effected a daring escape in the night, he would almost certainly have died there.

He was kept in a cupboard. It was not high enough for him to stand upright in. Juan was not tall. In the refectory he was made to eat sardine scraps from the floor. There where he knelt, the monks went round him flaying his bared shoulder blades with leather thongs. The circular discipline.

In purgatory God purges the soul with fire. In this life, with love. The same love with which he purges the angels of ignorance. The monks of Carmel crippled Juan's shoulders for life.

The ignorance went in roughly where the wings would have been.

Some paths were narrow. How straitened a path could I be made to follow, how narrow were the straits I could be made to pass? Núñez was taunting me. He mocks my work, he mocks me through my works. How silent the machinery that turns the tides. How now at the antipodes? Great Herakles, now that we have you here, explain it to us. Now that you have decided. We have time. How did one such as you come to take up *Ne Plus Ultra* for your banner? You who stole the milk from Hera's own breast, milked a goddess like a cow, who dammed the Nile, freed Prometheus, raised the pillars of Calpe and Abyla.

Even of such gifts your shining Bridegroom, rich beyond imagining, has no need it seems. Look around this cell, Sor Juana. Tell us what you see. For twenty-four years you have worn the habit of a clown, the King's fool in the ermine, with sceptre and crown. The Queen's handmaiden posing in her gowns. Or would you rebel even now—pull pillars, sky and pedestal all crashing to the ground?

Look once through the chronoscopic lens: Hera's Glory, Theologian's Muse.

Now Herakles, look again, two dozen years along: Hera's lunatic, God's clown.

How differently the poetry of prison rings now. And these echoes from the future, in these cells, how unlike themselves they sound. But that should not surprise us, after all, for so it is with echoes that what one mostly hears is the end.

Twice more that month I sent to ask when he would come. Always Arellano instead. The second time the memorized message carried a suggestion. If Sor Juana was in a hurry, if Sor Juana insisted on knowing when, she should practise her sciences of prophecy, by which the nuns in Madrid had so ably served the Crown. Thus did he summon to my mind Sor María de la Agreda, spiritual advisor to Philip IV, and the book of her prophecies banned across Christendom, recalled and burned. Thus did he recall to my mind the Inquisition's power to erase, which I feared more even than their power to silence me.

How it must have amused him on the Feast of Saint Hermenegild to remind me of my *Martyr of the Sacrament,* and its verses on natural magic. For by now I must have seen: that it was the holy officers who mastered the arts of illusion and the sciences of uncertainty.

The more that is stripped away, the less that remains to be taken.

I began to use the stairway again, late at night, while Antonia pretended to sleep. One did not need a telescope for stars in such multitudes.

The weeks passed quietly. Father Núñez was a subtle man. Four months since Magda's visit, four months since I had first sent for him. Time and quiet in which to brood on each message, to solve the riddles each concealed—to wonder if they had ever been there, if Núñez had taught this game to Santa Cruz or learned it from him. Time and quiet in which to ponder the completeness of my acquiescence, the emptiness of my rebellion, the contents of his messages, the terms of my defeat, to let these grow to cover me like a second skin, to all but heal and then be torn again from me. Four months without poetry, four months with one book. Four months in which to wait for the most terrible riddle to be answered, of the *beata's* identity, the secret dread that Magda's visit had awoken.

What did he still want from me? Evidence of what—that I had found the path on my own? But the path is another's, this path is not my own. I lacked the faith to follow wheresoever it led, I lacked faith in the administrators of the circular discipline.

Late one night, the light of the candle almost spent, I thought I found in the pages of the one book permitted me an answer. *When the understanding lay in darkness, the will in dryness, the memory in emptiness, the affections in bitterness, and the feelings and the faculties lay stripped. When, all senses consumed, the soul lay as helpless as a prisoner bound hand and foot, able neither to move nor to see nor to receive any consolation from earth or from Heaven.*

And had been thus bound for years.

Then, and then only, would Father Núñez come to examine what he had wrought.

On May 18th the Archbishop published an edict against the insufferable disorder of women's friendships in the convents, in particular among women of different quality, between nuns and servants, between the sisters and their favourites. Penalties for those who persisted could vary, banishment, lashes, excommunication. In some quarters the edict would be met with satisfaction, in others taken up to revive the rumours of sodomy. Unless I preferred not to heed it, I could take it as a warning, that Antonia would be the next to suffer for my sins.

The more that is stripped away, the less we may offer in surrender. What was left to offer them that was not Antonia? I was not sure how much I had still left. But if I could do nothing else—I could perhaps force the moment.

Arellano came quickly, as one who had been readied for the call.

So it was true. How long had Sor Juana's eyes been banded like this?

Father Arellano would please convey any messages, before he became distracted. Of course, yes, it was no longer his business to inquire. The Prefect had asked—would Father Arellano please raise his voice?—*The Prefect asked* if in these twelve years in which Sor Juana had had her perfect freedom, she had accomplished what she had set out to do. Her poet had his *Canticles,* her Velázquez his great canvasses. Had it been worthwhile, that so many others, the lowly, should have suffered so and might suffer yet more? Had she worked enough magic, had she had enough of fame?—for who knew what new triumphs her countess would bring her to, what bold lyrics she would next publish. Truly, having achieved so much or so little, could Sor Juana be content now to give service as an ordinary nun?

Had Father Arellano brought no other word? No, that was all. Then to His Paternity's own question: First, he should notice that my secretary had served to guide me here, and note that if anything were to happen to her, I would lose my way entirely and never find the path. Second, the question was not how long but how much longer, for the next time Father Arellano came, he would find my writing hand splinted and bound, not just my eyes. And if on that occasion he could still not announce Father

Núñez's arrival, then he would return to find them put out, as evidence of my sincerity. Father Núñez would of course want evidence. Now if His Paternity would try very hard to remember the gist . . . ? That there were orbits within circles, and circles without orbits, and if I was to walk a circular path, perhaps I was also to take this as a sign that in the circular manner of things, Father Núñez sought in me a Christian Herakles. I had shorn my hair, I would bind my hands, as I had my eyes. And next I would offer up to the Prefect of the Brotherhood of Mary the final *evidence* that he and Mexico lacked—so that we might together take sightings of these fresh new orbits by the light of our mutual darkness.

There is a false peace, when for a time it seems the Enemy sleeps while we wake, wakes while we sleep. One day this peace must be cast out, back into the darkness whence it springs, and as it leaves there comes a spirit of dizziness in its wake.

Solve the riddle. How he had tormented me with his knowledge—my childhood love of riddles—to set my mind riddles whose answers were in the book, so that I would be forced to read it only as he wished me to. The circular discipline. *When the mouth was pierced with sorrows, the vitals were consumed with hopelessness, the heart lay gasping, like a fish on hot coals, and the eyes blinded as those of an owl in the sun of noon*—and when I had read the poet I had loved, read him not with my eyes but through those of Núñez—then would he have me believe he was to come.

But I would not be deceived. No, what would more surely bring him was the threat to put them out, his eyes. The poetic solution.

Little fool.

Antonia tried to help. Cook, talk, draw a bath. Yes, she could draw me a basin of cold water to wash in, leave it on the table, go to bed herself, leave me in peace, not come up again until she was called. I said again, perhaps she should not live with me. Her only answer was to bring me a vase of flowers. Iris, marigold, rose. She set them on the window ledge. If I did not want them, shove them off. Her anger was better for both of us.

He had not come. Núñez was not a poet.

For two days now, Antonia had respected my wishes, left me to myself, the upper floor to me. Two days to contemplate where pride had brought me, the prideful threat by which I had trapped myself, the narrow road out. Two nights to turn about from room to room, up to the roof and back to this.

Perhaps Sor Juana would prefer a closet.

Bed. Table. One fresh candle. Materials for writing—what? Another plea that would not be believed—one upon which he might look favourably? Table, vase, basin, light silvering on the surface, breaking through my fingers. Whose hair was this, whose black eyes, who was this novice? Núñez had heard the hollowness in the threat, the weakness within it, and had not bothered to answer. At the table I picked up a pen, dipped it, idly trailed a thread of black across a page. How was I to do this, with a quill tip?

Once I had used the years to mark his absences, and exulted. Since February I had marked the months, then the weeks. Now the days. Soon I would be counting off the hours. They could wait decades.

Late in the night I rose, moved into the next room, simply to listen to my steps moving through the empty studio, then soft on each stair to the roof. I went cautiously to the ledge to sit above Calle de las Rejas, looked down past the windows of my cell to the *portería* grate, a single lantern flickering. Warm night. Stars. Lean into the light to see down, lean out to see up.

The chapel bell tolled once, quietly. In the distance others sounded. A noise from below—*una india* arriving to set up her stall beneath the lantern at the grate, an infant sleeping in the sling of her *rebozo*. Fresh *tamales* and *atole* for the worshippers at Lauds.

What more could I be instructed in dispensing with? I did not need their books, if there could be only one—I did not need this book, which Núñez had poisoned now. In my mind I had the verses. Juan's and many others, many hundreds. But what of the rest?

How many stars did one require? I thought over how many I might remember, more or less, over how I should recall them, as they had been on some other night or as they were tonight? If I could fix them in my mind, tonight, hold them fast, glowing still in the simple sketches they traced in the sky, as if a finger a thousand years ago had traced them behind my eyes. Perhaps it was the constellations one remembered, not the stars. After all these years I still could not connect them, knew so few of the names by which they had been called by other peoples in other places and times. Fire-Bow, *Los Astillejos*, Orion. Taurus, Gemini. How many constellations would suffice? I wondered how I would remember Night itself. Like this, or as I had once feared it as a child? And this new night, as final and complete as the living may see, there was no way to know if it was more to be feared.

Poetic nonsense.

And having taken out his eyes, could I at last be free of his voice in my mind?

I had thought to force the moment—but had left myself no way out. They who could wait decades had only to wait now a little while, a week, a month, to see if I would follow through. If I could, nothing in their files had changed—I was only where I had been—but if I could not, they would have the measure of my weakness, would know that I am beaten. Would know that I know it.

I wondered what it was that led me to this. Was it only pride, or weakness? No, there was something more.

It was in his messages, his taunts . . . *prediction, natural magic, divination.* He had something more in store, something better, someone else, after Magda—*I had to know.* What—charges they could bring against Antonia? But she had done *nothing.* Or the trial, it was to be any day now, was it the *beata*—was that it, that the charge against her was to be divination? But I could not see how that was to make for a more devastating discovery. What had I missed? Were these to be the charges against *me*? Divination, sorcery? There was the hex on Sister Paula, the *sorcerer who passed* through the classroom in Nepantla, but it was only an expression—this was childishness. What else would Magda testify to? Or had they found someone *else* . . . ?

Another possibility had slipped into my mind, into the quiet, with a dread unlike anything I had ever felt. The one final truth the holy officers were only waiting for the moment to reveal. One last discovery. That in the Inquisition's secret prisons, in a cell whose occupant had been held for years, only to be used one day as an instrument against me, as Magda had been . . . a holy woman from the country, a healer, half-Indian, a midwife . . . that the secret within the secret trial, was that the *beata* was Amanda.

And within this vertiginous spirit there dwell such intolerable blasphemies that even in desolation it were better not to pray. Far better to kiss the dust with one's mouth . . . for the remembrance of past evils, the ignobility of past actions, reveals such vileness as to make the soul believe God its Enemy, and itself the enemy of God. . . .

How long they have instructed me in uncertainty, how long I have been fed on doubt. When was the first lie told that brought me here, now? Days, months, weeks, thirty years, three thousand. I cannot wait longer. It must be tonight, while I have the strength to pray for strength.

I thought the answer hidden in those pages—that to know what would bring him, I had only to read with care, closely, deeply enough. But I have not solved it, because the answers were never *in* the book. The solution is the book itself. This is not about evidence or messages or instructions. It is not a question of my willingness to change or submit. It is not that he disbelieves I could be made to follow the path, but that he is afraid I could, for a time. For if it goes so hard on the confessors of heretics, how much harder on the director of the heresiarch. There is a safer path. It is as Gutiérrez said. A convergence of interests. The paths are not separate. Núñez will come when I have destroyed myself in search of answers to the false questions he has planted. This too is a kind of divination, circular discipline, a natural magic. The book serves as both method and sentence. It is his instrument. This book is killing me.

And when the work is done, the magic course is run, together will they come to pick over what is left, strip off whatever yet has worth, put away the rest. In a cupboard, or a closet.

I do not know what else to do, what else to pray for. I have lost faith that he will come at all. He may leave this work to others. How am I to pray for answers when I know no question I can trust?

No, there is one. One question . . . for all the answers I will never get. Who is the *beata?* One name I would give anything to know, one face I would give everything to see.

To know, to see. Can I give my eyes to see?

No one sees more clearly than blind Núñez how much I fear this place he has led me to. My mind. An empty room, a night with nothing in it. How much strength need I pray for, to lift a feather? Twice. To let the madness out.

Christian Herakles, set me free.

I will not rise from this table until I have chosen, will not leave this room until it is decided, till I have done it, or discovered I cannot and know that I am beaten.

Table. Basin. Vase.

How small has the world become. Brown. Turquoise. Red. How plain the palette. For twenty-four years I have sat at these windows overlooking the spectacle of other lives passing by. The neighbours across the way whose routines I know so well—I have never heard their voices. Never spoken with the old widow lodging in the lower rooms, helped her with her packages, exchanged greetings with the wheelwright. And I will never see more of their lives than I have seen until tonight. The chapel bell chimes the hour. Two past midnight, three to dawn. How brief, how few the hours ahead . . . how long, how many, those behind.

Convent, palace, prison. The worlds in these. Firepit, pantry, library. Prolix memory. Cornfield, river, killing floor. Prolix memory, what did she want from me, for me? Her lamb. *Your eyes are good, Inés, for seeing far. But up close, you are as blind as the rest of us.* Isabel. How must it have felt for you to hear me call you that? To watch me—driven by this hunger—turning away from you, turning to Xochitl for the things she could teach? And to be deserted by my father, only to see your own father turn to me for the one thing you could not offer him?

Window, night, cloud. Three, the chapel bell. Ink, paper, quills. Take one up. Feel free. Remember . . . ? Delicate scratch of quill over parchment. The quill's cool, lacquered shaft . . . unvarnished tabletop, worn to the roughness of petals. Again, more softly with ink, its pitch on the page a little lower. From the canals an ever fainter croaking. Stench of black water. Scent of flowers faded in a vase. Faint, sharp sizzling of candlewick . . . bare footsoles on stone slab, rough wool on skin. I sit here unmoving, a ghost haunting its body, and yet how far these senses are from extinction, keen to every fading sound and texture. Taste. Smell. Sight. Study the quill tip, its bead of ink. Not yet?

Horses. A coach crashes blindly through the streets toward some unspoken assignation.

Once I thought I had a gift, a special gift, a greatness within me. *Why.* Why give me a mind that devours my heart, enslaves me to my pride? Words—why this curse of easy eloquence? I choke on it. It has choked this cell on its wages. Books, instruments, curiosities—loyalty for trinkets. I have lent my voice to every passing cause until it no longer recognizes me. When did I agree to barter greatness for fame? Show me the contract—where have I signed it? Show me my name.

Show me my name.

Is it for this that my work has not served? Why must so many others suffer for me, so pointlessly? How do you see me—do you see me? Will you not lift, Bright Lover, your shining face to me? Beloved of my life, so happy and so new, I run to you—lover of my life, in the darkness of the night, so high and so wide . . . I do not find you. Where have you run? Why is there so much pain in this love you offer us? Why must we be broken to love, and crushed—why may we not love as lovers—with a love that is our own, even one willful and rich and turbulent? Surely there is One with a heart to answer such a love. What woman ever brought a lover to love—or having lost him won it back, by waiting on her knees? Why can I not suffer this, to lie with my face in the dirt of the yard?

Four. See, you have me counting now the hours. Below, hear the *tamalera*, palms slapping flatly at the *masa*. Inspect the tip, closely, bead of ink, small globe of night. How little left to surrender. How much.

Five. For the third night running I hear the piping. Is it a festival? A day of feast on the calendar of some unfamiliar subject tribe? For three *madrugadas* running he pipes against the dawn. Three notes rising and falling, shrill—shattering insanely against the empty stones. He must be in the street just below. I lean to see. The turquoise basin slips from the table edge. I leave the shards where they lie. There is not much time. You gave me a sky to conquer—a night I now cower beneath. Why give me these gifts, then not allow me to use them? Why shower them upon me only to let me forsake them, turn them against me, upon me, abandon me to my self, my Enemy? Court freak, *mujer de placer, menina*. You bring me to the brink of this black prospect only to turn your face from me—didn't I sacrifice, didn't I try, who is the sower of discord, who is the enemy of both sides if not I?

Or am I not . . . me?

If I must be another, then let me be another's—if I may not be mine, make me yours, not theirs. Manipulate me magnificently, make me round and roll me in your palm, dance me and sing me divinely, let me make you laugh.

Let me make you laugh.

Hera's lunatic, God's clown. Christian Herakles, who cannot lift a feather to let the madness out.

You mock my eyes. To make them see what I have not been—and yet see nothing of what you have in store for me. He mocks these eyes. Take up the quill. Prepare to sign for him with Night. Two beads, each a small globe. Shoulder them, now, whole worlds. Take them up. Feel how light, the lightness one feather brings. What shall I write . . . how. Guide my hand. A sign.

Silence. The piping has stopped. Still no word. Still I must wait. As I thought . . . you remain hidden. More silence.

False dawn . . . dawn. Rest . . . false peace. The first light coppers the cathedral spire. Hear the map of bells.

Lauds.

Where does the piper sleep?

So I had lost, and soon enough he would know. This path, this ecstasy
was not mine. I could not make myself one even to defy him. The *ecstatics*
have an answer, and I only questions. No face in the darkness, no sudden illumination. I do not know who the *beata* is, or even if she exists.
But whatever comes I have found an answer of sorts, a kind of negative
answer lit as by a small ray of darkness. The *beata* is not Amanda.

My faith in this is unshakeable, because I choose to make it so. It is a
kind of certainty.

Whatever else I may be brought to doubt or fear it will not be this.
Whatever else they still wanted from me, whatever the action, whatever
the surrender, if they had Amanda, and knew whom they held, they had
only to show me her face and I would have done anything they asked.
Until the moment she is brought before my eyes, with this love shall I be
purged of this fear of the face hidden from me.

It is perhaps with such a love that the angels are purged of ignorance.

Núñez will never come.

PLEA

*Plea, in forensic
form, entered before
the Divine
Tribunal, in
entreaty for forgive-
ness of her sins.*[19]

I, Juana Inés de la Cruz, the most worthless and ungrateful of all the creatures fashioned by your Omnipotence, and the most obscure of those
created by your Love, appear before your divine and sacred Majesty, in
the sole manner and form permitted by right of your Mercy and infinite
Clemency; and prostrate with all the reverence of my soul before the
most august Trinity, I do hereby affirm:

That in the proceeding before the Tribunal of your Justice, against my
grave, enormous and unequalled sins, of which I acknowledge myself
convicted by all the witnesses of Heaven and Earth and by all that is
alleged by the Criminal Prosecutor of my own conscience, which sentences me to eternal death, and even this will be treating of me with
leniency—that I were not sentenced to infinite Hells for my unnumbered crimes and sins; and whereas of all this do I find myself convicted,
and recognize that I merit neither pardon nor so much as to be heard, in
spite of all, knowing your infinite Love and immense Mercy, and while I
am still alive to this life and before they have closed off from me all
avenues of appeal . . . I beseech you to admit this plea in the name of that
intense and incomprehensible act of love by which you suffered so terrible a death . . .

. . . You well know that for many years now I have lived in religion
without Religion, even as a pagan would; as a first step in the purgation
of these faults, in faint proportion to my derelictions and yet in token of
my desire to assume again those very obligations that I have so poorly
met, it is my wish to take up once again the Habit and submit myself to
the postulant's year of trial under the examination of your Minister and
the father of my soul, acting as your Prosecutor and testing the will and
liberty by which I am disposed to these trials; and as concerns my dowry,
I offer the alms I have begged of the Community of the Blessed; and if
there should be any shortfall, I count on the intercession of my Mother
and yours, the most holy Virgin, and of her husband and my father, the
glorious Saint Joseph, who will (as I commend myself to their pity)
undertake to pay said dowry, candles and gratuity.

Wherefore, I implore Your Sacramental Majesty to grant all the
Saints and Angels your permission, licence and leave to readmit me to
the good graces of the Celestial Community; and this being granted—as

I might hope of their pity—that I might be given again the sacred habit of our father Saint Jerome, upon whom I count as my advocate and intercessor, not merely that I be received into his saintly Order, but also that in the company of my mother Saint Paula he entreat you to grant me the perseverance and increased virtue that I have always asked of you . . . All of which I shall receive by the good and charity of your infinite *misericordia,* provided in the appropriate degree. And for all these do I beg mercy, &c.

SOVEREIGN

What is destined for Zeus but endless rule?
Ask not, neither set thy heart on knowing.[20]

fter Vespers, Father Arellano brought a message. The Prefect was coming. Coming? Tomorrow. *At dusk.* Possibly, yes, Sor Juana.

Arellano was sweating still from the streets, though it was cool inside. Was there more? His lips had begun to move before the words tumbled out— his relief to be finished this penance, evident.

"Prefect Núñez will determine for himself the sincerity of Sor Juana's dispositions, whether, having been given the tip of his golden sceptre to kiss, she could truly settle now for such humble burdens—to lead the choir, instruct the servants, keep the books. *Superintendent of Works.* Or whether she still seeks to serve her prince by a more wandering path, farther afield. Blind poet, prophetess, seer . . ."

But why now? Sor Juana could ask the Prefect herself, tomorrow. And now he, Arellano, would leave her to her doubts.

What sign had I given, what sign had he read—none. But after some hours I saw. That for four months I had misunderstood completely all the taunts—it was not these I was to draw his lessons from. All the messages were *one,* made of the events of my life, of what I have known, one message that explains everything. Explains *everything*—why, all this time, he had even *pretended* to want to shield me. For I am not the one he comes to keep from the rack. I had not seen. . . .

Why come after so many months? Because I am exhausted. But why tomorrow, why not two more days' wait, three more days' exhaustion? He could come without warning—why the annunciation?—and if he *is* coming, why the message, why a message so much like the last? Because I have missed something. Try again, Juana Inés, try harder.

Superintendent of Works. He is telling me he has intercepted my letters to María Luisa. But something more. *Blind poet.* How this amuses him, the wandering . . . farther afield. *Service. A prince in the field*—the poet

Homer. This is about my grandfather—something I am to be made to remember. This. He saves the most painful for last.

"Even in America, Angelina, even here we serve the Sovereign of the Two Worlds. . . ." It was the last night we were together.

Even now the fund of Núñez's derision is not spent. This blind man who hails my new career as blind poet, mocks my threat, applauds my decision—there being so few poets who know how to write for our kind—who afflicts me now with the one confidence I would give so much not to have disclosed to him. But oh how I do grow weary of reading my past through this man's eyes, seeing only what and whom and how he wishes.

It is in the darkness after the last prayers, Father, that the visions come most clearly. I see you now in the only way you may now see me. I close my eyes, I open them. And you are the same. Antonio Núñez de Miranda, Master of the Collections, the Sources—now the Visits. My Turnkey. And was it not you who arranged my uncle's permission to visit the convent of San José? This I had forgotten. And were you not the one who'd guided me there? Antonio Núñez de Miranda, Controller of the Book. How studiously you read—and *I was the book* whose pages you would cancel and correct. Antonio Núñez, Master of the Recollections, keeper of the keys to the palace of my memory. Who maps the rooms, the halls, registers their contents perfectly, then slides the bolt and bricks the windows shut.

Who is this Jesuit, who does not live among us but is never far, who speaks to me through silence and absences, who still asks *whom* I would serve—and where and how? Head or heart, heart or soul, soul or flesh. What vast wrongs have I done, that Fate has sent him to me—*and what has this man done* that he should appoint himself my judge? I who have raised arches of triumph to the failing, worked hollow magic with theatre sets, drafted scripts to make gods of the king's representatives and make kings of God's.

Yet not everything do I repent. I have composed things for people I have loved, for the hurt made carols, and for the hungry. Even as he once suggested. And I have never been ashamed of my elegy for the king, though they laughed even then. Planet King. And since those days I have wished the son of the Planet King a happy birthday many times. Invalid, incoherent, impotent—Carlos the Bewitched, descended from Juana the Mad. He is thirty-two now. Sovereign of the Two Worlds. It has been hard for him, and I am sorry for that, but I am glad the Monster survived.

So there are certain things it were better not to deride, certain friends it were better not to attack. It is unnecessary, when he has won; it misjudges its effects.

Or might Antonio Núñez de Miranda be nostalgic? Does there perhaps remain one piece of information he had always wanted to have—to see his inventory of windows and doors completed before the palace is pulled down? No. A man with such a memory does not feel nostalgia.

He does not know he has *won*.

Tomorrow he brings one final brutal revelation to finish me, warns me to expect it, transmits the subject to amplify his effects—ever my magnifying lens.

I am come to make war on you, Juana Inés, against the Evil in you, against the Enemy, for the dominion of your soul. And because you are a house divided in all that you do, I am confident of defeating you.

He comes to tear the palace down himself.

But it seems even the Prefect errs. He had only to wait. The time to come here is when the admission of my cowardice is before us both. Then, how much more easily do the palace walls crumble. Misjudgement, tactical error . . . what is this that I am feeling? Is this hope? There is time yet to find some advantage—what *is* it about that last night with Abuelo, what has Núñez discovered since, that he would threaten me with it now? How much did I tell him then, *in what words,* about this night I have not mentioned since, scarce returned to in my mind for a quarter of a century? He would remember as if it were yesterday. What is it, Father Núñez, that you would have me remember, what fresh horror do you bring—or is it hope?

 Princes, golden sceptres, blind poets, wanderers . . .

I think I remember . . . fireflies. The night was cold. We had stayed up late by the fire, leaning close, pausing now and again to poke at the coals. He had rarely spoken about the war, this war half again as long as the siege of Troy. *No wonder the Poet had gone blind, he said, straining to see the end.* My grandfather's war had begun in a year marked by three comets, hanging over the horizon even as the Soul of Caesar once had over Rome. Summers of fire, autumns of plague, winters of hunger. A war to announce the coming of the end. He had always dreamt of travelling; he travelled then. Westphalia, Prague, White Mountain. He left in '24, happy to have missed Magdeburg. And yet he was proud to have fought for the young king.

The stars were fading to the last constellations. . . . I was leaning toward the fire, my elbows resting on a book in my lap that I had hurried into the library to retrieve. Abuelo had been speaking of the chivalry of Spinola at the raising of the siege at Breda, and regretted never having served any such prince in the field. *Iliad*. . . . I had found it quickly, on his desk, to read for him the speech of Zeus's mortal son to Glaucus. It was to be years before I could read the *Iliad* again.

> . . . He leads his people. As ye see a mountain lion fare,
> Long kept from prey, in forcing which his high mind makes him dare
> Assault upon the whole full fold, though guarded never so
> With well-arm'd men and eager dogs—away he will not go
> But venture on and either snatch a prey or be a prey . . .

Alone and hurt my grandfather walked home from the front, through half-empty villages to his own on the bank of the Guadalquivir, but everyone was gone. His family, the friends he had known. He followed the river to where it ran into the sea, then kept walking, to land's end, to the pillars of Calpe and Abyla. And as he talked over his plans for explorations here, in America, his eyes glowed green as emeralds, as they had not in many years. And so it was that he began to speak of the end of the Mexica and the last sorcerer, Ocelotl.

"As I have followed his trail, Angelina, it has sometimes seemed to me that there went the last honest man. . . ."

Kings and princes . . . service and counsels . . . honest men . . . Ocelotl, Vieyra . . . Vieyra defending the Jews . . . condemnation, to wander to the end of the world. The Wandering Jew—

Magda. Magda will testify Abuelo was a secret Jew.

No—Núñez does not need to do this—why? To show me the full measure of my cowardice? Would you tear the palace down, Father, or rally its defences? He cannot think even me such a coward, to recall this of all nights to my mind and then expect me not to fight. If I know you, Father, your motives are not these. If these are your motives, I do not know you.

Could it be he has concealed a *code* within Arellano's messages, woven from all that Núñez knows of me? He does not ask me outright so as not to give me the opportunity to lie; rather I can only break his code if I have the very information he needs to know if I possess. He has trapped *himself*—four months of getting no answer from me, four months without the reassurance he seeks. It is not merely a question of what Núñez knows, thinks he knows or pretends to, but of what he *doesn't* know, thinks I *may* know, *fears* I do. There is more here, more than a threat, there is weakness, and not merely mine. Wandering, world's end, prince, sceptre . . .

In the legend, an old Jew taunts Christ at the foot of Golgotha. Why does the mighty King of the Jews drag a humble cross up so slowly? *I go on*, Christ answers, *and long shall ye wait for my return*. For his jeer the old Jew is condemned to wander without rest until the day of Judgement. And yet the story mentions no war—no golden sceptre.

Núñez has sent messages through Arellano *because it is dangerous to come himself*. For if there is danger, the messages Arellano carries must not appear to be in code but instead seem what they have seemed even to me—mortifications of my soul. What sort of code is this—with a clue that seems to be about my letter but is not? His is a code with a missing key—it must be, for if any message or even all of them together were to carry all the necessary elements, Núñez could never be sure it would not be decoded by someone else, someone other than . . . me—I alone hold the key. No, I am the lock. Núñez has inserted his code into my memory.

There is another children's story Núñez would recall. One that contains every element of Arellano's messages. *Wandering, war, world's end, prophecy, divination, service, a chosen race, a king's favour. Escape. Resistance. The time of sea and fire.*

The Conquest. One night holds the key.

 The moon was rising, late, high above the mountains. . . . He had asked for my help, to look out for Amanda and Xochitl. Yes, we would watch over them together.

"You remember I once told you that Ocelotl had a twin. And that together, from here in these mountains, they launched an uprising against us—do you know it started right around here? Maybe from a campfire exactly here, on a night just such as this. . . ."

Though the fire had burned down to red embers, the night was no longer dark. The snowfields glowed faintly violet.

"Ocelotl's second summons to the capital had gone quite as disastrously as the other—first with Lord Moctezuma, now with the Lord Bishop Inquisitor Zumárraga. So it goes for one who would serve the Sovereigns of Two Worlds, eh, Angelina? At least this time things had begun better. This new lord had offered him his friendship and protection. But then after a few months came the request that should have sent Ocelotl running. Before long he was arrested on the charge of divination. He found himself in prison again, this one too the nightmare of a race. . . ."

Tracking the sorcerer Martín Ocelotl through a countryside Grandfather had travelled so far to call his own, this was the last great passion of his life. Ocelotl might have been the one man to have escaped both from Moctezuma's prisons and from those of the Inquisition—twice, and Abuelo's fascination with those escapes was perhaps more personal than I had ever realized. In the months before the Conquest, Ocelotl had gone to the archives of the Triple Alliance, in the city of Texcoco, for it was a time of strange events such as had been related in the old histories. Ocelotl was next summoned to Tenochtitlan to give advice to the Speaker, and was imprisoned there with the other seers and sages. Abuelo was never able to determine how Ocelotl escaped, but some said he had been released by none other than Cortés. The sorcerer returned for a time to Texcoco and worked with the Franciscans there who were recording the things of the past while there remained time. The archives had been put to the torch shortly after the fall of the city on the lake, and FastingCoyote's temple to the Unknown God razed. The memory of an entire race survived now only in the minds of a few elders.

Ocelotl's reputation among the Franciscan brothers led to his invitation to meet Bishop Zumárraga, which led in turn to their friendship and to his second imprisonment. It was the patterns of likeness and contrast that had fascinated my grandfather, on that night and other nights. Texcoco of the Unknown God, Tenochtitlan of two thousand gods. The warnings from Texcoco to Tenochtitlan, of one emperor to another, father to father, then son to son. FastingCoyote to Moctezuma I, FastingPrince to Moctezuma II—then the three warnings and the three escapes of Ocelotl. Twins, doubles . . .

"The same and yet not the same." Abuelo shrugged. "Almost the reverse, *verdad?* It reminds me of a company of knights I once watched riding along the banks of the Guadalquivir. So many ensigns and banners, differently patterned, and yet all part of a deeper emblem of—what would you say, Angel? Honour . . . ?"

"*Sí Abuelito,* and truth—and *valour.*"

"*Eso.* Honour, truth and valour. But in the histories here, though I have tried I can never quite name the deeper emblem. Do you know they stopped for the night in our village, those knights? Of course, even in my boyhood they no longer wore much armour. It was only a hunting party, and yet how proudly and how high the pages had borne the old standards and ensigns—but I have never told you of the great knight companies of the Mexica! Truly, have I? The Eagle Knights and—"

"The *Jaguars.*"

"Ah, so I have. Companies as great as our Order of Santiago, reduced now to two men. And they had one last battle to fight, those two, under the old banners."

The uprising began not long after Ocelotl had quit the capital, having escaped his fate a second time. "The jailers claimed he had help, but it was what their kind always said." Ocelotl and his twin Mixcoatl—even knowing it to be hopeless, with so few men of fighting age left—invoked the ancient prophecies and launched a series of attacks leading toward the capital.

"The Indians Martín Jaguar and his brother Andrés CloudSerpent were arrested and convicted by the Holy Office of falsely claiming to be gods, or the doubles of false gods. The Inquisition could not even decide on the charges! As in the ancient prophecies, CloudSerpent went to the burning ground but, that morning, Martín Jaguar's cell had been found empty—ha, for a third time. Ocelotl had vanished in the night."

 Why has Núñez used one children's tale to refer to another—why not refer to the second directly? What is the deeper pattern he would have me read? So long as his code is not broken, even if I myself were, I could give no other answer even under torture, and he would be in no more danger than before. But with each fresh message, each new hint, he brings me closer to guessing what he would have me reveal unwittingly, and the danger to him increases.

It is a code that points to one thing to point to a second to a third to what the messages never quite say . . . from Persia to the courts of Europe, to the Jews of Africa and Asia, to Golgotha and Mount Carmel, the hills of the Holy Land . . . but the land that he never directly mentions is this one, these hills, this continent, these old palaces, this New Eden.

Scrolls . . . the burning of the painted books, Sahagún, the Franciscans, an honest man.

Not nostalgia, not cruelty—there is one last window in the palace of my memory Father Núñez needs to look through, into a room whose contents he very much needs to inventory. Though I do not yet know what it is, the basis of Núñez's code and the source of his fear are the manuscripts Carlos has left with me. And if he comes now, it is because after four months he is becoming desperate—and if he is desperate he cannot afford to come to me empty-handed. There *is* hope here, but I cannot delude myself. Even he does not have the power to offer me my freedom. He cannot raise the siege himself—at best he offers a trade, an exchange of prisoners. The manuscript and my silence for . . . and now I see. In the darkness after the last prayers one sees most clearly, as on a blinding page.

Somewhere on the south bank of the Guadalquivir is a village, and in it the parish has its church. Within that church, the sacred canons stipulate that a yellow <u>sambenito</u> be hoisted into the vault, such that the light that filters past it through the high windows and over the parishioners casts shame in hues of sulphur. And thereafter shall begin proceedings against all those related to the family Ramírez de Santillana by blood or association, who, if convicted of following the law of Moses, shall be condemned, and if dead, burned in effigy. . . .

He trades with this. But I do not yet see how—no one controls the Inquisition—and if his offer is to suppress the evidence, how, if Magda began giving testimony in 1663? I did not even know Núñez until . . . 1666. Three years. Who gathered that testimony? Dorantes is my age. He would have been a boy. Gutiérrez was in Spain, also a boy. Santa Cruz, also in Spain.

It could have been anyone, it could have been Núñez.

But he does not control the *files.* Gutiérrez has seen them—but seen exactly what? And yet even if Núñez has somehow held back parts of Magda's testimony, and comes here to offer them in trade, there is still Magda now. . . .

She did not come from the Archbishop. That was a transparent lie. Even she did not pretend he'd agreed to see her. Magda does not care about Faith. Magda's love is the Inquisition. Núñez does not control the files, he does not control the Inquisition, Núñez controls Magda. Magda the scholar. A father to a fatherless child. He is good at that, a man of books. There is a chance. . . .

No, there *was* a chance, there *would* have been hope, had I the manuscript he needs. But I have recopied them. There is nothing there that Núñez should particularly fear, nothing with which I could trade. But *think*—he cannot not know this either—because of course there are other manuscripts. It only makes sense that Carlos would not bring them all to me.

It is not yet dawn—I have a few hours at least. What is in the manuscript that Núñez fears enough to come now with the danger to him greater than ever? Even to guess the general contents might be enough to convince him I have what he seeks, to induce him to speak of it more openly. . . .

Prisons, ~~gallows,~~ pyres. Archives, libraries, burnings. Books: *The Ascent*, the *Confessions*, Ecclesiastes, Esther, the Scrolls. ~~Kings: Ahasuerus, Hermenegild, Moctezuma II, Philip II, Carlos II~~. Poets, scribes, chroniclers: ~~Homer, Augustine, FastingCoyote, Manrique, John of the Cross,~~ Manuel de Cuadros. Noble servants: ~~Mordecai, Sarpedon, Glaucus, Spinola, Velázquez, Ocelotl,~~ Manuel de Cuadros.

~~Doubles, descendants of gods: Sarpedon, Jesus, Moctezuma, Ocelotl, Mixcoatl.~~ Presumed heretics: ~~Hermenegild, Bruno, Galileo,~~ Manuel de Cuadros. Sentenced, imprisoned: ~~Mordecai, Jesus, John of the Cross, Moctezuma, Ocelotl,~~ Manuel de Cuadros. ~~Escaped: Mordecai, John of the Cross, Ocelotl.~~

Did not escape: ~~Hermenegild, Mixcoatl, Moctezuma~~ . . . Manuel de Cuadros.

Judges, Inquisitors: ~~the Vizier Haman, the Bishop Inquisitor Zumárraga,~~ Father Antonio Núñez, Jesuit. . . .

It is only a theory, the slimmest of possibilities. What if the missing manuscripts were not an assortment but a collection, with a theme, the raw materials for a book . . . a book of conversations, say, between prisoners and their captors: Ocelotl with Moctezuma, Moctezuma with Cortés, Ocelotl with his Inquisitors . . .

Fray Manuel de Cuadros with Father Antonio Núñez.

 On the day Cuadros died, Núñez came here well after Vespers. The day had been clear. Then a fine rain had begun to fall. The pyre was slow to catch fire. He arrived well past his appointed hour. He came in like a basilisk—stooped, heavy lidded, the small head, the jutting chin—ordered everyone to leave, spoke as a superior even to the Dean of the Cathedral. Always so grimly deliberate, so controlled . . . that day the sight of him—exalted, enervated, the light of Truth burning in his eyes. I could smell the *leña*, and something else. He told me he'd just come from the Plaza de San Diego. I would never again smell smoke without thinking of Padre Antonio Núñez de Miranda on this day, or see him without smelling smoke. I recall the rasp of deep feeling in Núñez's voice. At the last possible instant, Cuadros gave some sign. They took his confession. They gave him absolution. His confessors embraced him. Such a great shedding of tears up there on the scaffold. In the emotion of the moment even the executioner embraced him and apologized for some slight—then strangled him, quickly, leaving the Adversary no time to snatch the lamb back from the fold. A great shout from the crowd . . . the *leña* was lit.

I rose to leave the locutory—where was I going? He had told me now—what more was there to be said? I asked if he had come to confess with me, I asked if he had been the one to give the executioner the signal. It came out before I could stop myself. Yet had I stayed—to hear what, I did not know—how he *felt?*—he would hate me today, I am sure of it, with an all-consuming hatred.

But now I wonder what he might have come to say.

How often before that day had Núñez gone to see Cuadros in his cell?—how many subtle attempts had he made to bring his charge to contrition? Might Fray de Cuadros have made a record of some kind and had it smuggled out? He would have needed help but had many friends in the Church. His trial was a bitter controversy for years, even after he was taken to the stake. It was why his contrition was such cause for relief. It would be this record that Dorantes has been after for so long—he would like to add a chapter, or two, possibly, to the collection: the conversations of Master Examiner Dorantes with Antonio Núñez, certainly. And, if the hunting was very good, with me.

An hour to Lauds. So frail a shield it seems to protect Abuelo now, and so many ways—even if I have guessed correctly—in which this becomes more dangerous. For if I convince Núñez I have what he seeks, or know its location, and he falls first into their hands, they will have it out of him, with all the conviction of a man under torture, and then will come for me.

Abuelo, I would repay your gift of fifty pesos now, and Uncle Juan's. I have been mistaken about so many things; I could be wrong about this.

But of one small thing I am certain now. There were fireflies. Or no, only one. . . . I was almost asleep. It had been circling lazily about us. Abuelo noticed it after a while. Lifting the tip of his traveller's staff from the flames, with a smile he traced its green track with an ember. . . .

Why these stories, why that night? Why did I find the *Iliad* so quickly, on his desk, and the Manrique poem beneath it the next morning, among the few books he was reading at the time? Why two books he had read so often, why the two he had perhaps most loved? And on top of these, in the morning, though not that night, an envelope. *A mi hijita Isabel.* Did you hear death coming, Abuelo, while I slept? Through the courtyard . . . did you know her step?

And I am certain he had started to tell me these stories for a reason that night. But then the last of his stories had ended—of Bishop Zumárraga and the sorcerer—and he had not told me. Perhaps he had raised details in the telling that he had not fully considered beforehand. One twin escaping his fate while the other did not. Or if it had not been about Amanda, I cannot help but wonder if that night at the fire he had been trying—knowing I was soon to leave for Mexico—to warn me of the dangers ahead, in my appetite for secret knowledge, in my childish passion for visions and natural magic, and to speak to me of a threat he had felt hanging over our family for his entire life, and which, just perhaps, he sensed hovering also over my uncle's house.

Or else, as I listened to the rumble of his voice, and watched his big hands grappling with the traveller's staff as he poked at the night's last embers, I had only fallen asleep. Perhaps he told me as I slept.

Dawn. The bells of Lauds. I may have hours, or only minutes. It could be anything: a record of their conversations, a list of certain monographs Núñez might have failed to report to the Inquisition—or Cuadros's monographs themselves if they have somehow since gone missing. The most dangerous would be something on the Eucharist that Dorantes might link to a sermon or paper Núñez has delivered. The best I can do is lead him to think that I may know but, also, may not, and in this way he will be hampered in his questioning lest he reveal more to me than he learns.

Yet if it is divination Núñez would have me practise, then what I divine is a weakness in his position, an uncertainty in his design. It rings hollow, like a boast. The strong do not boast or threaten, or prepare the ground with books or messages, and if it is the science of uncertainty Núñez would still practise upon me, perhaps the alchemist has too long handled the mercury, and quicksilver poisons the messenger.

This natural science as they practise it begins to seem inexact, its illusions not yet perfected, for in Núñez, they have given me an adversary of flesh and blood, however formidable. It were better to leave me to myself, turning in upon myself, my worst enemy. They think to deprive me of my collection, but return to me my memory. Now Núñez comes too soon—yet already they have left me too long in the darkness. In the hour after the last prayer, in the last watch of the night, there is a crossroads. And at that crossroads something waits. It is a jaguar.

I fear it, but if Núñez in his blindness thinks I fear it more than he does, I am no longer convinced of this.

Threats, weakness, boasts . . . to their science of uncertainty, I answer with a faith built on disbelief. All interests do not converge in me, not everyone betrays everything, not all the sources can be controlled or collected, time exists—if not for the Holy Office then for its officers. Gutiérrez is a liar: Gutiérrez ran out of time. Neither will I believe Carlos knew of Bishop Zumárraga by way of a betrayed confidence, but instead came to his own knowledge of the story, and thinking I might know it, used it to warn me. And whatever Santa Cruz may have learned of my early life, he did not hear it at my mother's side. She did not like churchmen, she would not have liked that one. She would have told him nothing, even at the last. And as for fear, it is human to fear the worst, but our strongest reason for expecting the worst imaginable is fear itself. I will fear the worst but without proof I will not *believe*—howsoever Núñez might imply that the other prisoner in the code is the less fortunate twin. Of this unbelief I make a fortress until it be proved otherwise.

Divination of the past leads in unintended directions. It were better not to deride certain things, stir certain memories. Even Magda I am indebted to, as one held long under water is grateful to find the bottom of the swamp. *Thus far and no farther—Ne Plus Ultra.*

Whatever may come, whatever stratagems and half-truths may yet be revealed, our position is better than it was three days ago. I cannot know what to expect today, cannot divine all the possible alliances.

But if the game be to pursue the secret Jew, then I invoke the great King Alfonso!—and stand with the Emperor of the Two Faiths.[21]

And if the game be to teach me more of chess, I invoke the great tacticians Ruy López and López de Ayala—and together we shall serve the Lord Instructor of the World. For though there are stronger players, even the Inca Atahualpa honed his game in prison—and let them remember who once inspired Santa Cruz in the sacrifice of queens.

And if it be a hunt of those who would wander in the open without cringing or cover, then I invoke the great falconers, Frederick II and again López de Ayala and an unnamed Moor on the banks of the Guadalquivir —and together we shall fly the colours of the Lord of the Two Horizons. For who does not fear threat from above?

And if it be simply to give honest service, I invoke the last sorcerer, Ocelotl, and don Pedro Ramírez de Santillana, my grandfather. And together shall we serve the Sovereign of the Two Worlds. This is whom I would have served, and would still. Heart *and* head, soul *and* heart, body and soul. On the banks of the river Guadalquivir we ride under the banners of the Eagle and the Jaguar, under the Ensign of the Trout and on our shields the Salamander. On the south bank there is a village where we shall stop the night, and a little parish church where a yellow *sambenito* shall *not* be hoisted into the light. For there are colours we will never consent to put on, and a chapter in our family chronicle I will not live to read.

If Núñez comes here to threaten this, or to lie, with no credible assurances that he can return that spite to her jar, then he will discover for himself that it is not the all-powerful who grips the helm of Necessity, but the unforgetting Furies. My memory is my own, hereinafter. He will not take this palace again. And not all the windows are bricked shut. I remember those grey eyes—colour of cooling lead, yet not quite cool, the horror and the elation in them. I remember his strange speech, curious un-Christian admissions, the smell of his cassock. I smell it still, and I have begun to wonder if Núñez does not also. I remember other things, on other days, and still other rumours that I have heard, and can attest to. And I too will be believed. There is a weakness in his position. It smells of smoke. And he should hope that I find it before long.

For if he miscalculates again and Magda gets her chapter, then so too does Dorantes—at least one to add to the collection of Manuel de Cuadros. Even if it means giving him two. And they will have their rebellion and their fight, though against the Holy Office we cannot win . . .

. . . . O friend, if keeping back
Would keep back age from us, and death, and that we might not
    wrack
In this life's humane sea at all, but that deferring now
We shund death ever—nor would I half this vain valour show,
Nor glorify a folly so, to wish thee to advance:
But . . . there are infinite fates of other sort in death. . . .
Which (neither to be fled nor scap't) a man must sink beneath—
Come, try we if this sort be ours and either render thus
Glory to others or make them resign the like to us.

SECOND
COMING

 prayed that you might come."

"Your prayers did not bring me. I was sent."

"You're looking well."

"I am not looking well—I am told neither are you."

"Might we not light a candle before it is quite dark?"

"No more of your evasions."

"Surely a little light—"

"Even with your life in the balance you cannot help yourself. Insolent wretch—I see perfectly well like this. I see *you* better—throne room of the Nun-Empress. I could not bear the sight of this place then—this auction house, these *toys*. Candlelight will not improve it now."

"Does nothing remain of your feelings for me?"

"As much as remains of my youth."

"And has age so hardened you?"

"Age does a lot of things. As you are now discovering. And in you I discover my worst mistakes. I should have left you with the Carmelites."

"I would be dead today."

"At San José you would be buried, but not lost—dead, but not for all Eternity. Yet what is even this, next to Sor Juana's boundless knowledge, immortal Fame? I do not hear you. Perhaps you would like me to believe you have changed. That you now believe worse things exist than death."

"This I believe."

"Than obscurity."

"Yes."

"Than *ignorance?*"

"I only sought to make of my mind a vessel worthy—"

"This is why you begged that I come?—to sing me this old song, to justify yourself? None of this matters now, Sor Juana. None of it, not to anyone. Not your poetry, not your experiments, not your precious studies. Except as each and all attest to your total indifference to the life of a bride of Christ."

"Indifferent?—never."

"Your conduct betrays you. You have reproduced within these walls the earthly world you vowed to forsake, surrounded yourself with—"

"Gifts. Most from friends of the Church—I've given them away."

"No, you let him take them. Hardly the same. But things can be reacquired. As you say, they cost you nothing."

"No, Father. I only said they were gifts."

"They assured me your suffering was genuine, but they do not know your theatrical talents as I do. You feign illness, distraction—"

"What do you know of this?"

"Do you think you are not watched in here, Sor Juana, do you think you are not *seen*? And now you feign contrition. Anything to persist in your defiance—"

"Father Núñez, could it be you have not heard my statement read?"

"So vast the sins, so meagre the details. Yes. The statement, *the plea*. Nothing has changed."

"No, Your Reverence, you're wrong. This winter . . ."

"This winter."

"The 24th of February . . ."

"A *Jubilee?*—you dare mention that to *me*. A general confession? The fasting, the trials, the meditations—it was too much once, why go through this with you again? All the sins of your life?—twenty-five years of *new* abominations. It would take *weeks*."

"I am ready."

"You think you are but I am not. Neither of us is young anymore. I have not been well. No. Find someone else."

"There is no one else. You must see that. Who knows me as you do? I need your clarity—"

"Seduction—more flattery. It's always the same game with you. But even you, Sor Juana, cannot seduce them all. If you could, I would not be here. The Vice-Queen despises you. The Viceroy has let himself be convinced your sympathies lie with the seditionists, if you are not yourself one of them. Those Creoles who do not hate you for your service to him are made anxious by the spectacle of your rebellion before the Church. Even your don Carlos is away a lot these days, I notice."

"He too was sent. He too performs services for a higher power. Another mission to map bad-weather harbours. A prudent undertaking, in such uncertain weather. He has always travelled among the people, Father, as have you . . . wandered quite far afield."

"I am told you would not say good-bye to this dear friend you are somewhat late in defending. Have you ever said good-bye *to anyone?* So quiet now. No clever reply?"

"Truly, Father, why have you come? Have I given no sign that those who have sent you seek—no proof, no *evidence?* You once said there were many working on my case, to interpret my hieroglyphs. Is there not some writing of mine that might now satisfy them? Please, Father? A letter, a *manuscript* I might surrender?"

"Your cell has been voided."

"Some ill-considered offence against the sacraments—my House of Bread, my writings on the sacrament of water?"

"Your cell has been voided."

"Yes."

"No. You are playing for time. If only the weather would improve, the earthquakes would stop, if only, if if if. So many hypotheses. But in a time of so much strangeness, Sor Juana Inés de la Cruz is one prodigy too many. I once heard you boast this city was yours. It is not yours now—you are detested by the pious no less than by *los nepantlas.* And it has scarcely started. The things the rabble already says: Malinche, Malinchista—how painful, given where you are from. Yes, the sacrament of water, the house of bread—soon it will be the humble people of the barrios who denounce you, those for whom you have written such heart-felt carols. If only you could convince them that the time of calamity is truly over, it was all happenstance—hazard and not God's wrath, but that is impossible. They are not natural philosophers, they do not reason as you do."

"I have read their histories. Some have survived, some we may still interpret, Father. Do you not think it possible that some new wonder might surface to surprise us all?"

"What do you *mean*—would you win my confidence with this double-talk? The only tales of wonder the people of your city have an appetite for now, Sor Juana, are told by my condisciple, Martínez—and that appetite is insatiable, and these are people of every class. On a Thursday afternoon he could fill the cathedral itself. Six editions of his sermons, stories largely about the Devil. *There* is a publishing success for you. How is it that you, Juana, who are so quick to make poetry on our theology, have written so little of Satan? I have always wondered. On this point you were always so evasive, even for you. Do you ever give him a moment's thought? Is he still a scholar, your Lucero—yes, there is a clever character, sly. You might make him comical now. Such comical stories Martínez tells of Satan thanking false priests, bishops with concubines, the mighty making false confessions. You have seen how quickly they turned even on the mother prioress whose case has become so notorious these past days. Condemned to eternal perdition for a single omission of a carnal sin during her girlhood. How the people applaud this, Martínez tells me. And how they would turn on you, if they knew the depths of viciousness your false confessions conceal. *Queen of the Baths.* That balcony where you and your Marquise spent so many jaded afternoons, Juana Inés, it is gone. It is ashes. The people of *your* city have burned her wing to the ground."

"Have you come to hear me beg? This time will be different. My word must still be worth something. If I promised those who sent you my discretion . . . ? My submission."

"You used me, you use me now."

"I needed you."

"My influence. You used it to abuse the generosity of a Church that gave you a home when you had nowhere else to go. *Take your word*—do you even know what the truth is anymore?"

"I need you. It is the truth."

"But you do not say why—"

"But I have tried."

"Why *else.* Tell me. The plain truth, from one whose word I am to take. Tell me why I am the one, why Arellano will not do—why *else.*"

"Your influence . . . with the Holy Office."

"Yes, better. So let us speak calmly and plainly, one last time. As we used to. Father to daughter. Your friend Palavicino has destroyed himself defending you. He thought to make his mark. He has made it. The man has no idea. And now he has made an application to enter the Holy Office as an *examiner,* when he is about to be examined *before* it. Ulloa has already written out his sentence. Lashes, banishment . . . In a few days the Tribunal will issue a proclamation, naming him in the sentence and you among the charges, to be posted and read in every church in the New World. And throughout Spain I take it. You may take this as a compliment. Any proceedings against you here, I have not been made privy to. But then, that is the procedure. And Dorantes will miss no opportunity to use procedure to embarrass me. As for any remaining influence I might have with the Holy Office, I have it very much in spite of you. How long did you think it would be before I had the preface of your latest volume read out to me? 'Phoenix of America . . . Glory of the New Eden, Glory of her Sex.' Did you think that if every poet and scholar in Spain wrote a letter in praise of you that it could protect you for *five minutes* here? Do you think that your countess, the King, Queen, Pope—all eight Urbans—all the civilized world banded together could stay the Archbishop's hand on the day he decides to move against you *here*? This is the New World, Juana Inés. Our New World. *Do you?*"

"No . . ."

"That day is not far distant, I assure you. You are a nun of the convent of Saint Jerome of the Imperial City of Mexico. Our authority over you is absolute, inescapable, implacable, eternal. Or is it truly possible you still fail to understand this? Do you imagine the Archbishop needs the Inquisition to deal with a miserable country nun, be he so moved? The Inquisition, Sor Juana—you would be begging for it within a week. Do you doubt it?—*do you doubt it.*"

"*No.* No, I do not doubt it."

"So this time will be different."

"Yes."

"And what of this 'destiny' of yours—have you now abandoned it? *You thought you had a calling.* So now, yet another change of heart? I do not hear you, Juana Inés."

"I thought . . ."

"A calling to what? Do you even know—did you ever? If you are to have me believe you have abandoned it, should we not know what it was? To *greatness*, perhaps? But, no, that was my error. If you thought that . . . And another of my mistakes to tell you my hopes. I was wrong. There is none in you. And now you want me back."

"All my life—"

"If those are tears I hear, I want none of them. The time for us to cry together is long past."

"Father, since I was a girl, you have asked a choice of me. Palace or convent, convent cell or prison cell. All my life I have fought you. I *choose* this now."

"Choice? I asked you to *serve.* Choice was always your idea. I have never cared how."

"But Saint Ignatius . . ."

"I asked you to search your conscience, I asked you to reflect upon the sins and crimes of your past, even as you now beg me to do with you, just as you refused me then. I only mentioned Loyola when I could not rid you of that antiquated nonsense. *To serve a prince in the field,* wasn't that the phrase—that was *your* design. Not mine. I have never much cared how you served. Was that not your *calling,* or have you forgotten it? To serve one who asks more of himself than he commands . . . ?"

"Father—"

"I—Sor Juana, I am not the one!—this is not *poetry,* now. He has been with you all along. Your Prince has stood so nearby and watched you. *With such pain.* You say nothing. Could it really be you had not seen it? If you will not answer plainly even now, there is no point. . . ."

"Father, don't leave. Please. Not yet."

"It is too late for this. I am old."

"Can it be too late if He wishes it?"

"My faith in you . . . in us, is spent."

"I would do anything to restore it."

"Nothing you could ever say. Actions, Sor Juana. Actions."

"Anything I can give. . . ."

"No, give it to your Husband, not to me. For me no one thing can be enough. I am rather smaller of spirit, rather lacking in Charity. Somewhere within myself I would have to find at least a faint ember to rekindle, a spark of faith. And even then I would come only if my Provincial ordered it. Nevertheless . . . there is a certain pagan manuscript. If finally you see how inconsistent all such matters are with your profession, a nun's vocation, if this manuscript were to make a miraculous and silent reappearance, your secret could remain between us, and you might begin to gain my trust."

"But—"

"Do you try now to back out?—it is you who have been hinting at this."

"Your Reverence . . ."

"What I *will* take your word for, is that by then you will have destroyed all the outstanding copies. Then, were I to hold that manuscript in my hands, it might be possible for us to make a beginning."

"Father—"

"That is, *if* I am ordered to come again. . . . In the meanwhile, your friend the Bishop of Puebla has told you what you must do. Take his friendly advice. Sor Juana, you are already forty-five. On insignificant trifles you have spent more than *twenty-five years*. Contemplate the mysteries of our Faith. Nothing else matters now. The cleverness, the comedies, the double-talk, the lies of omission. These go, these end here. The inventory and record of all your crimes and sins must be *complete*. No evasions."

"But Your Reverence, I don't—"

"Gaps will not be tolerated—do you *hear* me?"

"Of course, Father."

"Are you prepared to surrender that manuscript, *today?*—do not even pretend not to know which."

"Yes, Father. Father?"

"What is it."

"I *have* heard you, and there is something I have told no one else. It should not wait."

"Go ahead, Juana Inés."

"About this manuscript you have called *The Sapphic Hymns* . . ."

Verde embeleso de la vida humana,
loca Esperanza, frenesí dorado,
sueño de los despiertos intrincado,
como de sueños, de tesoros vana;
  alma del mundo, senectud lozana,
decrépito verdor imaginado;
el hoy de los dichosos esperado
y de los desdichados el mañana:
  sigan tu sombra en busca de tu día
los que, con verdes vidrios por anteojos,
todo lo ven pintado a su deseo;
  que yo, más cuerda en la fortuna mía,
tengo en entrambas manos ambos ojos
y solamente lo que toco veo.

JUANA INÉS
DE LA CRUZ

Alan Trueblood, trans.

Green allurement of our human life,
mad Hope, wild frenzy gold-encrusted,
sleep of the waking full of twists and turns
for neither dreams nor treasures to be trusted;
  soul of the world, new burgeoning of the old,
fantasy of blighted greenery,
day awaited by the happy few,
morrow which the hapless long to see:
  let those pursue your shadow's beckoning
who put green lenses in their spectacles
and see the world in colours that appeal.
  Myself, I'll act more wisely toward the world:
I'll place my eyes right at my fingertips
and only see what my two hands can feel.

LORD PROSECUTOR

The craft of the forger is weaker far than Necessity.[22]

Date unknown, year 1693 . . .

. . . charges that in clandestine distribution from America even unto Europe, and in conspiration with Lady María Luisa Manrique de Lara, Countess of Paredes, with the Creoles Carlos de Sigüenza y Góngora and Antonio Núñez de Miranda, Jesuit Prefect of the Brotherhood of Mary, and with the aid of the mulatta Antonia Mora, the nun has trafficked in heretical tracts, monographs and forbidden translations, including those of the Franciscan Manuel de Cuadros, already consigned to eternal damnation on related charges.

Ask the nun's response.

The heresiarch will state a response for the record.

A: Before the Lord Judges I freely confirm that manuscripts were copied and sent, but there was no traffic, no profit, no distribution ring. Further, the orthodoxy and character of the manuscripts are still to be determined here before this very Tribunal—but if even a single one were deemed heretical, I do not doubt, Lord Judges, that all the parties named here would willingly—

Tell the nun again to address herself only to the Lord Prosecutor.

A: I have only addressed myself to whom addresses me as an expression of respect.

Should the Tribunal require expressions of the heresiarch's respect, we will extract them.

Reverend Lord Judges, our Office begs the Tribunal's indulgence: that it abide the heresiarch's impudence a little longer. The next days' testimony will show her to be descended on both sides from a long line of false Christians; to be infected with Judaic and pagan abomination from her earliest years; to be weaned on necromancy and superstition. A sworn statement will be presented, and attested to tomorrow before the Tribunal, to the effect that her own wet nurse was a sorceress descended from an Indian insurrectionist condemned by the Holy Office long years ago.

Proceed.

Núñez was not wrong. I could not help myself. Rebellion. It was this—the falsity of my courage, the weakness in my defiance—that I wondered if he had wanted me to see on the day he came, to see this as a danger to us both.

For his part he had not been so foolish as to threaten me with Magda before knowing how badly I could hurt him in return. I had so few advantages—that he was forced to be careful of not revealing more than he learned, and his fear of being spied upon in the locutory. How much easier for him to question me in a prison cell. My one hope had lain in drawing him out, letting him lead me to where he feared to go. Instead he had only to scratch at the surface, rasp a little at the vein of defiance in me, and within five minutes we were already at manuscripts. I would not have Sappho to divert him a second time. His next such visit would be his last, and my next gesture of rebellion the thing most certain to lead us both back to those chambers.

But no longer would I permit myself to doubt he would come at least once more. It were better that he not delay too long, *but I shall tarry, Father, until you return.* Neither would I let myself wonder when, or about his motives. Even about the web of his alliances, I would try not to care. Like this, I could only destroy myself, tilting at every shadow.

Not an hour after Núñez left and already late in the evening, I was allowed to take delivery of a letter from Lord Bishop Angel Maldonado, informing me of his visit, though Father Núñez had told him he was wasting his time. But since Maldonado had not been dissuaded, and since the journey was not just long but dangerous, I wondered yet, would he come just for this, does he come as a friend, why would he have written of me to Núñez to begin with? It was painful to be reduced to this. It was Maldonado who had my carols on Saint Catherine of Alexandria sung at his cathedral when Santa Cruz had refused them.

The morning after the letter, the Archbishop's secretary came in person to explain about my new cell.

"It is on the northwest corner of the *gran patio*, where Sor—where the postulant Juana will be more comfortable with the other novices, though they are somewhat . . . younger." I forced myself to take an interest, at last to be seeing him, a sleek and officious man with a long nose, over which he was studying me for some reaction.

There would be a great deal more noise, voices, cries in the night, the nightly turbulence of the processions. The secretary might see the new arrangement as a hideous coming down in the world, but my concerns had nothing to do with either noise or privilege—I would be one step closer to the convent prison cell, a barred door opening from a cellar onto the southwest corner of that courtyard. I pointed out to him that I had a cell, for which he himself had signed the bill of sale. Ah yes. A careful review, however, of the contents since removed had shown the current cell to be too large for my future needs. They continued to play at their games of irony. And I to fly to the lure, at each slow swing, though I had had weeks to see this coming.

The new cell they had found for me proved to be half as large, and there was no stairway to the roof. *Superintendent of Works* . . . I had persuaded myself to believe Núñez had intercepted only one—but in that one letter, I had mentioned the hidden stairway.

> . . . next, the Reverend Lord Judges are asked to consider how the heresiarch has made her nest in corruption, and with corruption feathered it. Over the course of decades and in flagrant violation of her own vow of poverty, she had, by the performance and peddling of various favours, amassed a collection of curios, instruments and books lately confiscated and valued at thirty thousand pesos. Most recently she has attempted to suborn Bishop Angel Maldonado of Oaxaca for the purposes of gaining illicit foreknowledge of the present proceedings against her. Previous to this, she had induced another Prince of the Church, since stripped of his charges and titles, to publish under his licence an insolent suite of verses on the holy virgin Catherine of Alexandria, therewith subverting the veneration of a saint of the Church in order to draw the thinnest of masks over the true intent, being to praise and exalt a pagan sorceress, also of Alexandria, and a mortal enemy of our Holy Roman and Apostolic Church. In another letter to the former Bishop, the heresiarch praises this Hypatia's learning overtly and belligerently. And it is

a perversity no doubt fulfilling the heresiarch's perverse designs that even as a pagan once corrupted the Prefect Orestes, so also has this paganist of our day corrupted the Prefect of the Brotherhood of Mary, not least in the trafficking of documents. Leading to the question of how long the heresiarch's own collection might take to burn.

A: Lord Prosecutor—

Instruct the nun to wait to be addressed.

The heresiarch will wait to be addressed, or will be gagged until her responses are called for. All of the foresaid, Reverend Lord Judges, being of a piece with other writings by the heresiarch sympathetic to various heretics and schismatics from the early Church. Which returns us to the heretical proposition of the *finezas negativas* of God, this also published under the Bishop of Puebla's licence, and the charge which the heresiarch still guilefully avoids addressing. . . .

Get the nun's response.

The heresiarch will make a response.

A: Lord Prosecutor, any confusion of Catherine of Alexandria with Hypatia does not originate with me but has persisted for some centuries, and for good reason if, as seems the case, the pagans in their treatment of Catherine took inspiration from the Patriarch's work with Hypatia. As to corruption, the destruction of the synagogues across Egypt coincided with the takeover, by Christians, of the Jewish monopoly on the grain trade between Alexandria and Constantinople. Corruption comes in many forms. As to the burning of my own collection, it is a technical question, but one traditionally within the competence of this Church to answer. Certainly the destruction of the Serapiana was a test and precedent available to Caliph Omar as he made ready to burn the main library. But let us say, if indeed the Lord Prosecutor requires my response, less than six months.

Instruct the nun to answer specifically to the *finezas negativas*. . . . The Tribunal awaits its answer.

A: The Lord Prosecutor has not yet conveyed to me the Tribunal's instructions.

The heresiarch will answer to the *finezas negativas*. . . .

 The day's warmth had not yet ebbed from the column at my shoulder as I stood, unnoticed, at the door of our new home, looking down over a courtyard lively with activity. On the *gran patio* I would not have expected laughter of the sort I so craved to hear, to share, based in neither fear nor anger—not these torments of irony.

It was as the Archbishop's secretary had said. The sisters for the most part were younger, many wealthy, with one foot still planted firmly in the world, the wealthiest with their favourites, then the novices, the slaves and servants, the young girls from the convent school.

Lying as it did on the far side of the chapel and refectory, the workshops and orchards, the *gran patio* was another world though I had once imagined I knew it well enough. Like the others, I came for the torch-light processions; and after quakes I had often come to supervise the masons. While the colonnades around the first and second storeys had been preserved, to anyone acquainted with the original plans, the place was a bewilderment. Each according to her means and whimsy, various residents had made modifications, all being expansions of one sort or other—a third storey kiosk on pillars in a vaguely Turkish style, or ground-floor additions shambling a third of the way into the plaza. Flat roofs with crenellations, peaked roofs of thatch or of canvas, all more than likely propped on untreated uprights. Walls were of adobe brick or simply mud over wattle, some painted, a few limed, most left bared to the elements. Then another extension is built to abut on a wall that may or may not survive the next tremor . . . leaving more or less at hazard, blind alleys, light shafts and hidden recesses, and balconies giving onto blank walls. In appearance it was as I imagined a bazaar of Persia, or a market town at the edge of a desert. Our Santa Paula's first convents in the Holy Land might have looked thus.

Late afternoon was becoming a favourite time, for though the blood-sport of the processions was to begin again in a few hours, there was no sign of this yet. The nights were as written in sand. By the first light of each fresh morning, *el gran patio* was itself again. In the looseness of this order lay a resiliency one had to live here to notice. The fuss and fluster of chickens darting under foot, the call of songbirds from their cages . . . throughout the day, servants gossiping at the fountain, hanging laundry, fine articles of silk, others of cotton, and among them, ranged indifferently, hairshirts torn and darkened. Schoolgirls strolled in pairs, novices and lay favourites sat on the stone benches in the passageways.

Our new neighbours had grown used to us. At the outset there was bound to be resentment. Though small, it was still a corner cell with two storeys, and views to the north and west. More, my presence threatened to mean more scrutiny from the other patio and beyond. But when Antonia and I arrived, barefoot and tonsured, all our belongings in our two hands, perhaps the resentment grew a little less.

I wondered if it was not another dangerous fantasy but I let myself imagine Antonia and I might grow to like our new home . . . though so far she was having the more difficult time, to find her place. The nun's return to the noviciate for her Jubilee is provided for in the statutes; a good deal rarer is the secretary to a novice forbidden to write.

After Núñez had come and quickly gone again, there came a change. The Church began to authorize the visits of friends to the locutory once again. For the longer walk, one of several minutes, I was grateful though it was an occasion for more gossip, as I now had to walk past the entire convent.

San Jerónimo had not had a bishop's visit in over two years. His Excellency Angel Maldonado kept his promise, and I let myself believe he did indeed make the long journey from Oaxaca for me. Save for the bright blue eyes and the purple cassock, he might have been taken for a native of this country, his cheekbones high, his nose prominent, fine-bladed at the bridge. He seemed surprised that I was aware of the *beata* trials—but he knew María de San José well and though he disliked Santa Cruz, he did not believe there was any immediate threat to her. He did not mention any rumours concerning our convent as the site of the next trial, and it was a relief not to have to discuss it. What he had made the six-day journey to tell me was that the Holy Office was mere days away from publishing charges against Father Xavier Palavicino, whom I must know well, given that he had risked so much to defend my letter on God's negative *finezas*. Very gently he asked if even Sor Juana Inés de la Cruz did not have a few small sins she could freely confess for her Jubilee?

Bishop Maldonado was a decent man. It would have served nothing to point out that Oaxaca was very far away from the affairs of Mexico, that Father Núñez had been withholding his intercession for months, that I hardly knew Palavicino at all—and to tell the Bishop he was bringing me news of charges I had known of for almost two years, this would have been callous while leaving me to appear all the more intransigent. There was little he could do to help me here, but I preferred to think I might still have a good friend in Oaxaca, who before he left did his best to impress upon me the precariousness of my situation—certainly I must accept Father Núñez's offer of protection, at least from the Archbishop. The progression of events was in the bishop's view methodical, and his main concern was with what or who should logically follow now that the Palavicino affair was coming to a head. We parted on my promise to give our discussion my most urgent consideration.

> . . . that for three generations the family Ramírez de Santillana, of the province of Andalusía, has here in the New World intermarried with other families of false converts for the purposes of perpetuating secret worship of the laws of Moses. And that of this third generation, the nun calling herself Juana Inés de la Cruz has not ceased in her open defiance of our Holy Roman and Apostolic Church even while exploiting the trust owing to her position within it in order to publish various pseudo-theological tracts purporting to defend the Sacred Canons but which covertly undermine them. And that the nun has been recently so emboldened as to go beyond even this, publishing a tract (and within this, the proposition of God's *finezas negativas*) vehemently suspected of heretical Quietism and the Illuminist heresy that so persistently springs from the ranks of her cohort: new Christians, false converts, false Christians, crypto-Judaizers.

> Ask the nun's response.

> The heresiarch will make a response for the record.

> A: To the first charge: it is false, inspired by pure malice. Charges of this sort shame Holy Mother Church. To the second: if the Lord Prosecutor adduces particulars I will answer to each. To the third as to the first: false. This is not my cohort. But I remind the Lord Prosecutor that from it have

come not only saints Ignatius de Loyola and Teresa de Ávila but Juan de la Cruz—a year under torture, three times his writings denounced before the Inquisition. The torture was the shame of his century, the denunciations, of ours. The latest being so recently as 1668, even during the proceedings leading to his beatification. I repeat, those who make such denunciations before the Holy Office abuse it even as they shame our Church.

Instruct the nun that not Juan de la Cruz nor any saint or beatific person is here charged; that she has not properly answered the third charge; that she desist from presuming to make pronouncements imputing shame— to this Church above all; that it is not her place; that this is not her place.

I could not bear to ask it—to be brought by such as these to ask: was it possible that my grandfather had been a secret Jew? Could a truth and fear so vast have hovered, sensed yet unseen, over all our years together— could we have shared so much, yet not that truth, that pride, that fear? However much I searched my memory, I scarcely recalled his mentioning the Jews at all, even while he had talked so often of the other great peoples, those of Cathay and Egypt, the Persians and the Moors, the Spanish and the Mexica.

But if ever there was a fact, a truth, a pride he found painful above all others, it was that the Spain he so loved had once had a special gift, an example to all Europe. The gift was tolerance, and the Moors had given it. Under the Almohads, in their capital on the Guadalquivir, the city of Córdoba alone fathered, in the span of eight years, two universal geniuses: a Moor who would go on to write the great commentaries on the Greeks, and a Jew writing treatises on medicine and philosophy in Arabic. In Córdoba, the Jews had embraced Arabic, writing only their poetry in Hebrew, *the secret language of the heart*. The phrase had been my grandfather's. And among the early Christian kings, some had been inspired to lead by the Almohad example. But the inspiration did not last; the gift withered on the vine, and the expulsion of the Jews began, under Isabela. A great queen, Abuelo said, and a great error. Here was the true Spanish heritage that the Conquest had betrayed, the great hybrid that Christian Spain had failed to coax into flower. And yet, for all this, Maimonides was the sole Jewish writer I ever heard mentioned by name, his *Guide for the Perplexed* the only text, and this only in passing: a work of paradoxes on the unknowability of God, denounced as heretical by the Jews themselves—or rather, Abuelo added with that sad smile, by the still perplexed.

And that was all. But was it, truly?

Why did he come to America? the prosecutors would not fail ask, after their false witness had given her testimony. They would say it was to hide himself in the wilds of a demonic country, as a place conducive to the practise of his secret rites. *No.* He had served his king, he was tired of war, a commoner who loved books and Spain equally, and who dreamt now of exploring. But what first brought him to Xochitl's village? What was the source of his lifelong fascination with the escapes of the sorcerer Ocelotl, or with the verses of the poet-emperor of Texcoco who had built a temple there to the Unknown God? I had only to remember some of the books in Abuelo's collection to glimpse the paths he had travelled. I had only to think on this to see that it was a collection of just such works that I myself had greatly added to.

And I had only to consider these researches seriously for a moment to realize that Abuelo would surely have *written.* If only notes—knowing that these had to remain strictly hidden, perhaps to be destroyed at his death. And if he had truly heard Death's step in the courtyard that night, he might have been burning his life's work at the firepit as I slept. My fear took on a new guise: that his writings were not destroyed but concealed—at the hacienda, its hiding place a secret my mother had taken to the grave—or in some hidden recess behind the bookshelf at Uncle Juan's, near me all those years. And that the Prosecutor would next bring forward these papers to ask if I had seen them—claim to find it incredible that I had not, had not in fact *based my own heresies upon them*—before demanding that I repudiate them, that I watch them burned before my eyes.

How better to explain this rage like the pique of a child whenever I heard them—and I had only to close my eyes in this darkness to hear the holy doctors judging the beliefs of the country of my birth as superstition and heresy. Or whenever I felt them turning to derision the loves and passions of my childhood—the riddles and puzzles, the hidden forms and secret knowledge.

There were answers I would never have, fears and doubts I could no longer let myself entertain, but what was true beyond any doubt was that the hidden connections I had sought in stories and in the world all around me were real: the flesh and blood people in my life, the stories I was not to be told. No need even to close my eyes to see him, a man in his prime, a fine horseman riding into Xochitl's village, and now see her as she must have been then, before the accident. His daughter's age, with Amanda's grace, for that grace had first been hers. A young woman wise beyond her years, except perhaps foolish in love, even as one of his own daughters had been once. And how those two must have talked, for Xochitl had stories quite the match for his, of jaguars and walking fish, trout that were not there and the masks of god. Eventually a thing had broken that had made their friendship impossible—and yet after all the injustices of the Conquest, he must surely have seen this as but a feather in the scale. Perhaps it was precisely this, the scale of the incommensurate, that left him unable to resolve things in his mind. Like a problem with zero in algebra. Impossible, yet impossible to abandon altogether. Over the past few months it had occurred to me that she'd chosen to come to live with us as an act of contrition—to serve the daughter of her friend by nursing the daughter of her lover. But though Xochitl had lost her place in her village, she would not have agreed to come to Nepantla if she had not loved and trusted my grandfather. There was something between them she did not wish to twist—they never spoke again, and lived together until he died. Friends for life.

The untold stories, the unspoken correspondences between the legends, were real, as real as mountains, and strong. And it had become troubling to think on the ways in which their hidden influences and sympathies had not ceased. Is it possible to walk a path all our lives and not know—even refuse it, to think we have turned our back on it—even as we think we are following another, making each choice at every crossroads for reasons we do not see, and which might as well be the opposite of what we think they are? When every choice seems a turning away. And might one not end thereby in hating choice itself . . . ?

And so who was to say that one mention of Maimonides was all I had learned from him of the Jews, whose god they seek everywhere to know by his secret name. But if that god were my grandfather's, how painful that I should only hear of this from his accusers. Had he ever tried to tell me? How much of this might my mother have known, if I had known how to ask? I had wondered if he was trying to protect me, but perhaps he only hoped I might be fearless. It had worked for one of his daughters.

Without so much as rising from the rocking chair where she sat nursing the baby, my mother had stopped Diego with a word and a look, and sent him slinking off with a question. *You do know innocence?* She looked at me then, another question in those black eyes, but I had as yet no idea what had happened. And I remember Xochitl, hair glowing softly in the light, her face strangely youthful, I thought, as she watched my mother. She was standing in the courtyard, a few steps beyond the kitchen door. At her bare feet, a rag lay forgotten. Mother's eyes met Xochitl's, whose face had split into a grin of almost painful width. The two looked at each other for a long moment as though each daring the other to laugh first. Just then the baby coughed and cried, fists like tiny angry planets making small arcs in the air. My mother frowned down at the balled hands, the bald head grimacing, and with a little shush gave him her breast. Xochitl bent stiffly to pick up the rag.

Eleven years they had lived together, raised daughters together. Between those two women lay an entire world that I could scarcely begin to guess at. The moment had passed, but it had happened. I no longer doubt there had been others, though this must have been one of the last. In a few days I would be in Mexico. In a few weeks, Amanda and Xochitl would leave for a destination they would not reach. But that night Xochitl served us dinner herself, for the only time that I can recall. I was relieved, this once, that Amanda had remained in the pantry, for it had been just that morning that she'd asked if she was to go to Mexico as my maid. When I saw Xochitl coming in with our plates I jumped up to help, but she answered in Nahuatl, "No, let this be my privilege."

The main course was a *mole*, a meat dish in a sauce of chilli and chocolate. While this was now common in the recipes of Puebla, *xocolatl* had once been a sacred aliment and Xochitl had never cooked with it or, if she did, had never served it to us. Instead of making a solemn event of it though, Xochitl was relaxed and smiling as she limped about. It seemed now that around my mother she had always been conscious of her hip, standing very straight when she spoke with her, often waiting to move until she had left the room, out of pride, I'd assumed. But I wonder tonight if it wasn't, instead, consideration.

As Xochitl leaned down to clear my plate, I murmured in Nahuatl, "Delicious, Xochita, but that *was* lamb, wasn't it?" I was half-joking, but she had a way of squinting that could make me laugh even when the joke was mine.

"*Tepescuintle*," she said, then hobbled off towards the kitchen, leaving all the day's tensions draining from me in laughter—gales, *carcajadas*. At the far end of the long table, Mother had looked up from nursing Dieguito, her long brows raised. *Escuintle*, she knew. A Mexican word Abuelo had often used for a naughty child. So I explained, feeling the humour of the moment fading, that it was short for *tepescuintle*. She had only been mildly curious and I regretted starting, for not only was she unlikely to find it funny, I might end up getting Xochitl into trouble. And I felt confused, as well, for only now was I giving serious thought to who had actually killed the dog. Seeing Xochitl, smiling, hobbling around the table, I knew it had not been her after all.

Tepescuintle, I began, cringing inwardly, was a small, voiceless dog the Mexicans used to fatten . . . to eat. And even as I said this, I recalled that just the night before, when I had told the story of the bridegroom impaled on the wedding tree, my mother had not been amused in the least. She didn't laugh now. But to my surprise, the hint of a smile played over her lips.

"But you *like* animals," I said.

"There was always something not right with that one."

"Is he gone for good?"

"I would say the dog is."

"And you'd just let Diego come crawling back." From long habit I shot this back before I'd really heard her. I saw her joke too late.

The baby began to fuss again, as if needing those great black eyes as much as milk. When they met his little fox eyes, his fists eased again and loosed stubby petals fingering the air. She crooned to him a lullaby in a singing voice it shocked me to hear.

But by then I had decided to be furious that she should find this a thing to joke about after what Diego had done. How could she keep a man around that I knew she did not love? Had she loved my father, at least? Love was not everything, she said. No, not for her, obviously. I would understand when I was older. Truly I hoped not—

"*He* was older—*he* didn't understand, did he, why love was not everything. Wasn't that why he spent so much time away?"

"Maybe he knew he couldn't stay."

Was she saying he had avoided us?—why, so we could get used to it?

"I'm sorry if this hurts you—you're too young to be hearing this, but we've run out of time, you and I. . . ."

"Hearing what?"

"Yes, Inés, he avoided me, as you put it. But the one he avoided most of all was you."

It was a mother's instinct, to repeat the child's words to convey an adult thought. I knew even then she had not been trying to hurt me, but having heard her echoing the very phrase I had used to conjure the ghost—of my father avoiding me, staying away from me, who waited only long enough to get to know me to stay away completely—the words went like a knife through my chest. She tried to go on, but I'd heard much more than I'd wanted to. Before leaving the room—so I would not cry in front of her—I asked as calmly and coldly as I could manage if she even knew what love was. If she had ever loved anyone.

The night before I was to leave for Mexico, she came to find me again in the library where I was choosing books among the shelves for the dozenth time, adding just one or two more to the already-too-many, making the trunk all but immoveable. Perhaps that had been the idea after all. I had a few hours left, just time enough to finish the argument. I was sorry it had to be there. She had come to give me the fifty pesos. Her face was guarded. I saw with some satisfaction that I had hurt her.

I felt more than saw her expression soften. Perhaps it had been finding me standing in the shadows amidst the ranks of books. "This is the countryside, Inés, not Madrid or Mexico. A woman does not always get her first choice. I love his son, now."

"Why a man at all?" I wished I hadn't asked. I had her thoughts already about a woman's place in the world, and her judgement on my ambitions for Mexico.

"Your father did not care for cities. . . ." If by this she was trying to say he'd feel as she did about my plans, I did not want to hear it. In fact, I never wanted to hear her mention him again. "He was like you, Inés. He always had somewhere else to be. I had been planning to move to the city with your aunt. After your sister María was born I went back there a few times to visit. You might like it. I did, more than I expected. But your grandfather had already rented the hacienda in Nepantla for me. Most fathers would have disowned their daughter. You only saw me helping him, but first he helped me. He showed me a way to make a life for myself here, and for his granddaughters. Whether your father returned or not. And in Nepantla I would be easy to find. About what I said . . ."

If she would just let it lie, just let me leave like this, not make it any more painful than it was.

"You weren't wrong about everything. . . . So maybe it was true, he didn't want you to love him too much. But there was another reason." I told myself I wasn't even listening.

"I hadn't thought of it this way until the other night, but he might also have stayed away so he wouldn't love us quite so much."

"I should go to bed." It was too late for this, too late to see the past other than as it was.

"Yes. Tomorrow will be a long day."

When I did not move, she went ahead of me. I thought she had gone, when I heard her call to me. She stood framed in the doorway, behind her a few stars. Among them beamed a planet white and still. I could not see her face.

"As for the other . . . I was distracted with the baby. I thought you two were too young. But you could have come to me. I would never have let any of my father's granddaughters be hurt." With that, she was gone.

She did not come out the next morning to the wagon, though for once she had not gone out to work. She had stayed in her room, but had left the door open. Amanda had gone out into the fields very early, and did not come back to say good-bye. Xochitl held me briefly, but we did not speak.

My father's granddaughters. My mother had been thinking, then, of Abuelo's other bequest of fifty pesos, as much a message from Abuelo to Xochitl as a gift for Amanda. It would be four years before I learned of its existence, another twenty before I learned from Magda that Abuelo had borrowed the hundred pesos from Diego. But I had remembered my mother's words clearly, for it had been an odd way of putting things. It was the one concession I had ever heard her make to the game of twins Amanda and I had used to play. It had struck me as generous even then, and had only deepened my confusion, generosity not being a quality I had associated with her. Generous. I did not know her at all.

Friends, enemies, it seemed to make little difference now. Bishop Maldonado's gentle remonstration on the subject of confession felt not so very different from being asked by Núñez if I had ever said good-bye to anyone I had loved. It felt some days like being asked if I have ever loved at all.

Other friends came to the locutory, and after a few such visits I no longer doubted their sincerity, but neither were the choices that my friends urged upon me easily distinguishable from those of my adversaries. On the question of winning the protection of Núñez by my confession, my friends were divided by how full and how sincere it should be. They fell between two extremes—of a partial confession as a tactic of expediency, or a sincere expression of contrition.

But surely those who urged sincerity saw how this might well entangle me more deeply in questions of heresy, and could the camp of expediency not see that my confessor was attentive and experienced, not easily deceived? Even this was not the true dilemma, because it admitted of a third possibility: choosing to face the Holy Office. And in its implications that third avenue left me more dependent on Núñez than ever. For if commanded to recant the negative *finezas,* I could not choose to, even knowing the consequences. Why could I not, because I was right and they were wrong? I might be a heretic, but not in this.

Before all the Holy Community of Saints and Angels and the Celestial Tribunal I still ask—and ask again even after all that has come—what is a heretic? Giordano Bruno's case was clear. He had simply pursued the mysteries so far as to become a stranger to the world. Galileo Galilei was no stranger to the world—and attacked nothing in the world so righteously as unquestioned authority, and the Jesuits. The manner of Hypatia's death was Alexandria's penalty for sorcery, but one might as well ask if Hypatia was just as truly the heretic, not for charting the flights of ravens and the courses of Sirius as her father had taught her, but for challenging barbarism and hypocrisy.

But if she was a heretic, it is as well to call Galileo a witch—his witchcraft was his method, his heresy defiance; her heresy was her eminence, her witchcraft, memory. Again of this Holy Company I ask: is it heresy to recall an older faith? A wisdom before the Light, a fall before the Fall, a woman of more ancient tears, a sun, a son, before the Son? is it heresy in an age of iron to remember one of gold?

What, then, does the Lord Prosecutor's idea of heresy amount to but a fear of choice itself, and a superstition rooted in the fear of that which is older than itself?

On this night the Prosecutor made no attempt to interrupt. I was allowed to speak at length, for the secretaries to record. A witness was brought to challenge certain of my assertions, but I was allowed to question the witness in turn, though this was unusual. And yet each session had in its own way become more frightening than the last; and as I was shown courteously from that room and back into the darkness, I could no longer ignore that these fantasies were not harmless, though at first they had kept my fear from overwhelming me entirely. In the first days after Núñez left, little scenes such as these ran swift and incessantly behind my eyes—with Gutiérrez's depiction of those chambers all I had to go on. Unusually high, windowless, stone floors, stone columns of eight sides. With time I had flooded the chamber with light, colour, turned stone to marble, iron to brass. But imagining the room differently did not make it any less likely I would one day be taken there.

Thus was I about to send myself to the stake still upholding my negative *finezas*, in defence of free will, I who have always hated making choices. This was not the calculation of longitude at sea. There were no prizes for making discoveries such as these—or that the *ostrakis aneilon* used in Hypatia's death were likely to have been the tiles of ostracism, that doubt itself has become heretical and that the punishments of Hypatia and Galileo were less for witchcraft or heresy than for a new kind of treason. One from within. And with each passing night it was becoming harder to imagine standing my ground before the holy officers, because through Magda they might know things even about my own life that I did not. Even as I dreaded how these would be revealed to me, when, in what tones of irony and triumph, it became more urgent to anticipate what might be coming. Truly frightening was the eagerness with which my mind returned to that room, to confront the false witnesses, who were now almost always Magda, examining me. And in the midst of my rousing defence of heretics, it was Magda the scholar who had drawn the link from oyster shells to turtle shells—and I had stood revealed then as a hypocrite, as she forced me to admit it: I had always seen that Amanda had my father's eyes, that she had been his choice, and that what I had most envied of Amanda was not her secret knowledge, nor merely her grace, nor even her gift with a gesture. It was her heart. I am not a child anymore—certainly I could bear this coming from one such as Magda, but only for so long as I can cling to my faith that they will not bring Amanda before me in chains.

After I had slept a little, I saw how far things had gone. They had made of me an officer of the prosecution.

There is a curious remark Núñez has made more than once. *Gaps will not be tolerated*—and well do I know that the fear of these can be intolerable. I have already sensed it in Núñez's vaunting of the perfection of his memory. *Nothing is ever lost beneath the eyes of God*—before the eyes of God, perhaps, but beneath them, much is lost upon us. The weakness I have smelled was fear—but hardly mine and his alone. For it is precisely what the holy officers do not know and cannot see that is a torment, for them as it has been for me. I detect it in the careful reports Gutiérrez had filed of our every meeting, against some future treachery among his compeers. This same fear abides in the inventories of Dorantes, in the careful comparison of the first with the second. It lies in the method of their interrogations, scribes trained to record in teams so as to miss nothing—they have made a special lexicon for the language that goes beyond speech, a shorthand to mark the crack of bone, the sinew's snap, the long vowels without consonants or stop. And if I permit myself a memory of my tour with Magda to the workshops of Santo Domingo, I see it even in the instruments their smiths and forgers make—the branks and gags and pears—for the plugging of gaps.

These sealers of windows, these cloisterers, with their mortar and shutters and locks, they too fear all that escapes them. They cannot rest until they have seized it, known all, had this allness tallied, until they have entered into their logs all the testimonies. Until the record is complete and buried in the archives. Just as I had once made myself trace the constellations, to make a friend of Night, they are as children afraid of the dark, who cannot bear to see the sky until they have made an inventory of all the stars.

And so as if by a long ride in the desert was I returned to the dilemma of my confession and perhaps, I thought, to the beginnings of a solution. A confession not full, for there can be no such thing, but of a fullness that yet gave the enemy no comfort, no rest, no peace—for whose conscience did not trouble him in the night, whose mind did not contain an inventory of secret doubts? Who is to say what Núñez feared most, a missing manuscript or darkness, or what he dreaded—if there was a dread we shared—more than the images conjured in the scent of smoke.

Gaps will not be tolerated, yet are everywhere. It would be for me to forge a confession of these, and let the holy armourers see what I had glimpsed, through long trials in the night, that mail is lighter and just perhaps stronger than plate.

Yes, there is some knowledge of me in the punishments and torments the holy officers inflict, but how much, and how much of this is from me? What brought Galileo Galilei to his knees? It was not that they had found someone more clever—a Jacobi Topf, some anti-Galileo of the Soul—nor that Galileo was old, or ill, or almost blind. It was not even quite the pain and the fear imposed on an old man's mind, but the special shape he alone could give these. More likely, Rome and Florence supply the same crude materials as are furnished here. Time. Doubt. Fear. With these, we forge the instruments ourselves, from our own faculties, and yes, the soul is to be the crucible.

It is not that a fated few bear within them some secret flaw—neither is this to be found in a single trait or faculty. It is not that we contain the seeds of our own fall, but that the shape of that fall—forced upon us— takes its imprint from us, our whole selves. Not only our conscience but our reason, memory, heart. Our imagination. And also our defiance, freely willed and chosen. So many olive branches Galileo was offered. What is a heretic, even one who recants, and why could he not take the olive branch? Why could he not curb his strength in strength, and not wait to have it broken? And what was it that brought a book collector and astrologer to attack the mulatto with whom he shared his cell, to try to murder him with his bare hands in total darkness? What had he seen, what had been summoned for his sight, if not the most appalling vision of himself?

But, then, I could not be sure if these were fantasies at all . . . or rather prophecies a mind in that dark had driven me to fulfill.

JUANA INÉS
DE LA CRUZ

B. Limosneros, trans.

When Pedro, as a man of the sea,
finds himself denying
Freshets, Springs and Streams—
all run down to the sea,
they laughingly
and Pedro to weep.

verses

The Freshet does not forget
its beginnings in the spring,
the font of all its being;
since from the silvery rills
of its laughter springs forth
the most pleasing of confessions
to the Source:
but if Pedro denies all this
with ungrateful evasions,
Freshets, Springs and Streams—
all run down to the sea,
they laughingly
and Pedro to weep.

   The Spring laughs on
as it crashes from the summits—
in an oblivion without sorrows—
recollecting on the lowlands
the Flashing Eyes, the Lucid Matter
of its earliest existence:
but if Pedro denies all this,
though with a mortal shudder,
Freshets, Springs and Streams—
all run down to the sea,
they laughingly
and Pedro to weep.
   The mightiest stream, unswervingly,
with impetuous fire
surrenders unreservedly
to the sea, meeting there
its Final Destiny,
finding there its quietus:
but if Pedro denies even this,
turning his eyes from such glimmerings,
Freshets, Springs and Streams—
all run down to the sea,
they laughingly
and Pedro to weep.

EPIMETHEUS   The heresiarch will cease her denials and respond fully to the third charge, concerning the so-called negative *finezas* of God, and then recant them.

A: Lord Proscecutor. God is a superabundance surpassing every category, even that of divinity, flooding the three transcendental qualities of Oneness, Goodness, Truth, overflowing these as Beauty, cascading in a Music down through the Creation in Time. We have called this Mystery, we have called this Night. And well we might, for its darkness is not dark nor absence of light but the mystery of an immense plenitude overwhelming our small faculties, as the brilliance of noon floods the pupil of an owl.

So when I say that the restraint of such a superabundance may come to us as a favour and mercy, language itself is found wanting. To my persecutors I say the negative is in the eye of the beholder . . . as when we close our eyes on a scene brightly lit and find projected against our lids the brightest things dark, the darkest light. To my slanderers I say that if there is darkness, it lies not in God but in the overturning of our categories. The negative lies in the reversal, but the negation lies in us.

Is the negative bad, the positive good? This is heretical Manichaeism that the pamphleteers beneath the mask of their pieties are near to practising. Good Evil, God Devil, Light Dark. This is the very heresy that first seduced Augustine until such time as he had seen the teacher Faustus with his own eyes, heard him for the first time. A negative favour is still a favour, God's restraint is not a negation but a finesse, the finesse is not evil for being indirect, and this very hostility to the negative, the oblique, and the hidden is itself a kind of childishness, superstition abetted by language. Yes, Good; No, Bad. Even Odd, Straight Bent. The thinking of infants, who do not know night from day, their left hand from their right. Are these any less superstitious than the beliefs of the country of my childhood, whose practices are called diabolic, their sacred images idolatrous? It has been claimed by those whose offices are holy that I have held myself to be above faith as a thing no better than ignorance, paganism, superstitious visions, as beneath contempt. It is simply not true, it is not simply true—for I have felt contempt for none of these things. As a child I was taught that the face of God was unknowable, and its masks only mirrors in which the peoples of the world might find themselves.

And so to my attackers, my slanderers, my persecutors among the pamphleteers I say that even if it were my authority alone that Xavier Palavicino had cited, my authority is not mine alone, as the figure of the pupil of the owl is not mine but John's, as the ray of darkness that strikes the eye is from Saint Dionysus—these are my authorities. John, Jerome and Augustine, Dionysus and Hermes Trismegistus, FastingCoyote and Maimonides . . . poets of the flood of superabundant Mystery.

> . . . *Sé ser tan caudalosas sus corrientes,*
> *que infiernos, cielos riegan, y las gentes,*
> *aunque es de noche . . .* [23]

hether I could recant. The one question left, for me. The rest I leave for others.

Truly, who can say what secret springs and silent vectors have carried us to any given moment, and what hidden currents had brought me to speak of the negative *finezas* on a moment's impulse that for two years I had found myself unable to repent by choice, and left me unable to imagine anything I would not say—no matter the danger—to evade the judgements of the holy officers upon them? What is it now that I still cling to, through great pain and perhaps tragedy, like a child to a fable? Is it to the fable of trout, there and not there, at the bottom of a pool, or to a certain wise way Xochitl had of making me laugh? Or I wonder if it is to the gesture of two trout speared, together on a platter, or to some notion of justice written in an anagram.

Or only the weight of my grandfather's hand I've felt on mine, all these years, each time I took up a pen to write.

Recant or refuse. This choice is not false, not a fantasy, though dangerous, nor is it complicated. Once the question is put and the decision commanded, any third option—silence, indecision—is merely an illusion, to be dispelled by a torture that is not at all a figment. And then the question is put again. I who have lost so many, to come so far, for all I claimed to care for—is it all to end here in a battle that cannot be won?

Recant or refuse, a simple dilemma but the true one. I know this in my heart. What is it I cling to?

It is only a gesture.

I may never hear the exact charges I am convicted of, but heresy is not always punishable by death—the unrepentant are. A statement of error: brief, no longer than a sentence. If I cannot resolve this, compose it— now, in my mind—the choice will be made and the sentence written for me. The outcome is not in doubt. And if I am to find a way forward, I can only hope I find it in choosing to look back. For if it is to some fable of truth itself that I still cling, or to a sentence spelling ruin in a child's anagram, if I am to rewrite it, there is one journey to be made again, to a place where the paths begin and to a moment where they intersect.

 On the landing above the canal Uncle Juan said good-bye and sent his respects to my mother. I did not trust myself to answer. He apologized for María and Magda, asked when I would be returning. I did not know how long it would be. The boatman pushed off. We were soon out of the canals and out on the lake. Flotsam and deadheads bobbed at the surface. Most of the streams and rivers feeding the lake had been in flood. The sun was briefly out, and hot, thinning the mists that lay in the valleys. I had hardly slept the night before, and through drowsy lids thought I saw a seal ahead of the canoe. Then two, which could not of course be seals. Two . . . three . . . six . . . The canoe surged powerfully under me with each paddle stroke. The sun was warm. Into my mind swam the sea calves of Proteus and among them Menelaus, disguised in sealskins on the shore of Egypt. Homecomings . . . how long had he been away from Sparta, and Odysseus from Ithaca? Little shards of sun glinted on the water.

It was mid-morning of the second day as we entered the highest valley. The lower slopes were shrouded in a drab mist—shifting, softening land-marks. The young ox driver grew more animated, asked a hundred ques-tions. He had never been so close to the mountains. As we turned off the main road onto the track running up to the hacienda, I looked back, though I knew there were no other turn-offs to mistake ours for. And yet while the landscape had seemed changed, it began to seem as though the changes its tenants had made had somehow never taken. There were no workers in the orchards. Close beside the road the plots of tomato and squash had been ploughed under and no one worked there.

We rolled over the brook and past the sentry box. The black cedar shingles on the house faintly glowed with pale green moss. Around back, the cart pulled to a stop. The mist had begun to clear. The cone of Popocatepetl floated above the earth upon a plane of white billows stretching south. In the calm air a white plume of steam went up as if pouring through an inverted funnel, an upturned hourglass of cloud. Fresh snow gleamed in the sun like fields of white obsidian. I got down, stiff, hesitant. . . .

Up on those slopes is a place with a waterfall, and a rooster tail of water bursting from a dry rock face. But for all its beauty it is not Ixayac I would give the most to visit again for an hour, nor even our library, but a shady spot at the base of a giant cedar among the pines. On the banks of the river Panoya, between the cornfield and the plot of maguey. In hindsight it is not always from the highest point that one sees farthest. From here one sees the orchards and the green rows of vegetables, the house itself with its watchtower and chapel, the corrals and the mountains, the windmills, and in the mind's eye at least, the trout pool and the waterfalls of Ixayac.

And here, next to the granite cross, was a place in which to have solved some of the mysteries that had always surrounded me. And who is to say that my destiny—a butterfly pursued as by a toddler—would not have altered its course? Solving one of these at eleven I might have refused to leave my real and true half-sister in Panoayan and, like my mother, never left for Mexico in spite of all my plans. Solving it at fifteen, when I returned to find Amanda gone, I might have set out to pursue her through the wilds of the New World as the nun-ensign would surely have done.

But for clues, it is to the objects spread before me in the shade of that tree I look now, more carefully than at fifteen when in my distraction I felt more than saw them. Corncob doll. Bird's nest lined with a blue-green down. Cornflower crown, pressed between the leaves of an old book. The beginnings of my first collection. They were never mementoes, nor did that collection, so much grown, ever serve me in this way. It is closer to the truth to say that I had carried them back home from Mexico as keepsakes, or as evidence against an accusation, though I cannot say what charge I most feared—of having forsaken the past, perhaps, or of emptiness itself. I had *not* forgotten, but had carried them away precisely so I would not have to remember.

Here it is tempting to see so many lines converging and patterns laid.

A wedding tree and a turtle pail, a shady spot in which to sit with Amanda, and to read from Ecclesiastes and the poet Manrique, on the day I first met Magda at Abuelo's graveside.

Of Necessity, the imagination of the ancient Greeks fashioned a net, of Fate, a thread. Then what is Destiny?—of the many riddles I'd set myself as a child, this was one of the earliest. And to this, I did arrive at a solution of sorts. If fate is a thread, necessity a net, then a destiny must be found in the weave, in the gaps between. So it seems I have not come so very far since then. It would be better to remember this from now on. Had I done so earlier, it might have come to me why I found Gutiérrez sympathetic from the start—though the rodent chin was but the faintest hint, for in fact my grandfather's chin was quite prominent. But each had a habit when amused of scratching at the beard below it, and Abuelo's had once, very long ago, been more red than grey. And if any of what Magda has said is true, there were other things too that might have occurred to me, about my own family, the secrecy in which my uncle's parents lived, my grandfather's friendship with them; and to ask what my mother and María knew about the secret poetry of his heart, and the language it was written in.

So if anything was to prove fateful, it was my resolution, leaving Panoayan, never again to look back, at the age of fifteen.

So many fine reasons I had found for this in the works of the famous poets and philosophers. *Life is an ever-living fire kindling in measures, being extinguished in measures.* Heraclitus. Nothing lasts, says the poet Manrique, and all our lives flow to the sea that is death, such that we may wonder if the past ever was. But it was the story of the poet Orpheus that exerted the decisive influence, for it was precisely by looking back that he had lost the one thing most precious to him.

Here. If there is an answer, still some way out, it is here.

 The convent chaplain's visit this morning brings it back, my doubts, how frail my defences and all my resolutions seem. He had gone to the cathedral for me, to learn what he could about the new developments Bishop Maldonado had warned of. A warning now confirmed. It continues to be harder with friends, harder to pretend. After Vespers Antonia comes into my room and asks me to go for a walk with her. It is so hot, she says casually.

Down in the courtyard the heat radiates from every stone and column. Down here, at least, one does not smell the canals: a light breeze agitates the smoke of a dozen fires. It is too hot to eat inside. Tables of different heights and sizes have been laid under the trees around the fountain. As we cut across the patio Antonia shifts to that side as though to guard me. I am not sure she even notices. Most of the women have finished eating, the servants moving among them clearing, the young girls chasing each other about, playing at hopscotch, skipping. Strumming a *vihuela* quietly by the water is a girl I recognize. She could not have been more than five or six at the time but was soon good at her scales. Wearing the habit of a postulant now. Our path takes us quite near.

"Sor Juana."

Others glance up. Nuns, novices. Not all the looks are hostile. Some sympathetic, a smile or two.

"Sor Juana."

"Sor Juana."

"*Dando un paseo, Sor Juana. . . .*"

"*¡Qué calor de infierno! eh Sor Juana?*"

I say to Antonia they should not be calling me that. I am a novice now.

"Of course you are."

I see she is taking me to another part of the convent, through a long arched passageway that leads from the patio. At the end of it the orchards and gardens stand off to one side. A breeze blows here, gains strength as we advance. All down the passageway, along the ledges, clay vessels of water stand; from the ceiling hang water bags for cooling. Simple convection—cool orchard air rushing through to replace the hot, rising from the patio. It is as if, just ahead, someone has opened a door onto the sea.

An arch of soft light before us, more light behind, in the passageway it is all but dark. I pause a moment, to stand in the breeze, lift the rough woollen cowl from my neck. "These things are itchy in the heat. I'd forgotten."

Wordlessly Antonia turns to take the lid from a large clay jar sweating on the ledge, lifts back the cowl from my head, sprinkles cool water over my scalp. In three months the hair has come back slowly, straight, black, like bristles.

"I feel like a porcupine."

"You look like one."

"You're one to talk. Take yours off."

Swiftly she stoops to lift the hem of her shift, stops at her thighs. A few years ago, the faint light of the patio well behind us, she would not have stopped at a threat. I reach up to remove her headpiece. She inclines her head. I free her hair.

It is like a roper's workshop, little finger-length drills and twists of cord. On tiptoe now, I reach up slowly to take down a smaller water jar and in one motion pour it over her head. She gasps. I feel her strong hands at my wrists, watch coils and rills spin from her hair to fall against the light.

"Where are you taking me, 'Tonia?"

"It's a surprise."

"So was that."

"So we're even."

"I'm not very good with surprises today."

It is not too dark to see the change in her expression. "Of course—I'm sorry."

"No . . . it's just this heat."

"I'm taking you to Vanessa and Concepción for supper."

I know it is not the whole surprise, and that it has to do with the chaplain's news, but I had been afraid she was taking me to the locutories. It is not a question of trust. The dread is never far.

"Show me your herb garden while you dry off." I need a moment, and the detour I know will please her. It is where she grows the herbs and essences she puts in our baths. "If we go to those two like this, who knows what pranks we'll put them up to."

We skirt the edge of the orchard along the infirmary wall, faint grey, texture of muslin. The branches nearest us are heavy with blossoms. Something is always in bloom. Now it is the pomegranates. After the herb garden we take the long way around, drawing out the hour, before the quarrel we each know is coming starts up again. Plots of beans and squash, *jícama* and *chayote,* past the trellises. I do not know how to say good-bye. But for weeks I have been trying to persuade her to leave. I have some money put by for her and for my nieces, an attachment on the convent accounts. It is not an inconsiderable amount. I have shown her the location of the codicil in the archives, and though she did not want to listen, made her promise at least to inform my nieces of its existence, in the event I should be taken.

We turn at the water tank below the windmill on the roof, blades spinning, water knifing from a clay pipe angled just over the surface, the tank nearly filled.

She must see that it is more difficult for me that they can still threaten her here. Can I not see, she's asked in return, how cruel it is to say this when I know she is not leaving?

But we do not continue. The evening is warm, the first stars are out, and Venus and a sliver of moon. Bats flit through the branches, their cries a glimmer of sound less heard than imagined. And so I walk in the quiet with my not-quite sister, not-quite daughter, barefoot in the soft, deep earth, sandals in one hand. Left again at the chapel wall, past the refectory, toward the kitchens. Vanessa's slim form in the doorway. Concepción's round bulk appearing behind her.

It has been thirty years since my carriage ride with Magda, thirty-eight since the hex in the classroom of Sister Paula, thirty-nine since my father left us. I have resented, hated, then feared the Holy Office of the Inquisition for almost a lifetime, even, it seems, before I knew what it was, and even now I suspect I may yet find new reasons why. But it seems that there are times when to look back is to see more clearly ahead, for precisely there, where Magda and I neared the end of our first and final journey together, I see another about to begin. A cortège, duly consecrated at the rose-coloured church, sets out from the Plaza de Santo Domingo. In all, four outriders, a wagon and a carriage whose coat of arms bears a rough wooden cross that matches the banner above the iron gates through which the convoy departs. In the wagon, otherwise empty for the outward passage, are implements for digging. In one of the trunks lashed to the carriage roof is a quantity of *sambenitos*. Inside the carriage will be at least one senior official of the Inquisition. I cannot prevent myself imagining it to be Dorantes, though I have never seen him. But Magda I see clearly enough. And over the past few days and nights, her journey is like a waking dream.

The holy officers with their shovels and *sambenitos* will not be embarking from Mexico in canoes as I did. But departing from the village on the far shore, where the deadheads lie high on the strand—dry now amidst the flood wrack—the path is the same. There is only one way for carriages and carts to take. At this time of year they should have no trouble fording the river at Mexicaltzingo, to arrive in Chalco by nightfall. Even setting out well before dawn, the cortège will not enter the highest valley before mid-morning. When they turn off the main road, they will be heading east, the mountains towering high above, seeming almost to lean down over the path. Beyond the oaks along it lie orchard rows. Apples and limes, peaches, pomegranates. By mid-day the first rays of the sun reach this side of the hacienda, with its square watchtower on the north. And in the watchtower a little bronze cannon. If the day is clear, the sun strikes a stained-glass rosette set high in the chapel face, and in the rosette the image of the angel Uriel framed in gold. It was my grandfather's idea that should the little cannon fail, the hacienda should be defended by a higher, purer fire.

My grandfather's first child was born here at the hacienda, and here she was baptized, Isabel. So it is here that the first of the *sambenitos* is to be raised, up behind the glass, to take the light. And as with the firstborn, so it shall be done with my aunts, and finally a *sambenito* will be hung in the church in Chimalhuacan where I had my baptism. But there is other work to do here first, once the outriders have unloaded the digging implements.

Recant or refuse. Choose well, choose carefully. The letters are the same, but the sentence now is changed. Recant, and protect the place while betraying its spirit. Refuse, and preserve an idea of justice but see its site desecrated. It is not a dilemma to be solved by a simple defiance. I have come back for a clue, a way to relinquish a fable of truth that once lived here, or that I brought back with me at fifteen. Perhaps I am to find it in a story I ignored then, for I had not let the Poet himself have his say.

When the enchantress Circe sent Homer's Odysseus into the underworld to know his fate—if he would ever make his way back to Ithaca—she gave precise instructions. Beyond the stream of Oceanus, which forms the outermost limits of the living world, they would find a level shore. Enter Hades' house by the groves of Persephone. *To call the one you seek, the blind seer of Thebes, you must sacrifice a black ram there at the entrance and fill bowls for the bloodthirsty shades who assuredly will come.* Odysseus was to stand just within the gates, the ram's head facing into the Underworld. But as the beast's throat was slit, he was to cast his eyes back, to Oceanus. *Don't look back* is not the injunction of poets, but against one poet by the Judges of the Dead.

 After the meal under the trees outside the refectory, as Antonia and I are making ready to leave, comes the moment for the surprise I have been expecting. With a nod at Vanessa, Concepción disappears inside, to return a moment later with it held out solemnly before her: a candle easily the thickness of her wrist and the length of her forearm. To cover my emotion I ask what such a thing could be for, a sure occasion for the sort of ribaldry Concepción tries to shock us with. But the two of them are as solemn as children with a handmade gift—and this gift they have made for me themselves.

"Madre Juana is permitted a candle a week," Concepción offers. Clearly they have heard something of the chaplain's news. Knowing them to be my friends, perhaps he has told them, to make me see sense. They are trying to keep me from giving up.

Vanessa too has rehearsed an offering. "Maybe now, Juana, you'll take the time to learn Basque."

"How far is Concepción ahead of me?"

"Leagues."

"For Madre Juana we can make one bigger next week."

"No, this will be big enough. I don't think Basque so difficult."

I am eager to be away. We say our good-nights. There is no mistaking Antonia's elation. I am regretting not having pursued our quarrel in the orchard, now to have to dash her hopes. She carries the candle for me like a spear or a standard clutched in her fist, a gesture of defiance to a patio almost deserted; the women are preparing for Compline.

"You could carry that more discreetly."

She begins to ask how it would look to be caught with it underneath ... then sees that I am serious. I tell her that nothing has changed, that what I said was for Vanessa. For Vanessa, she says, but not for her.

"No, 'Tonia, you don't understand."

She detests hearing this from me. By the time we reach the cell we are each close to saying things we would regret, and are fortunate to be called by the bells to prayer. She argues now with a kind of desperation, perhaps senses that tonight will be her last chance. What can I still find to say to help her now, how will I explain? It is not so much giving her reasons to leave, but to convince her that she leaves for the right reasons. Once, I had been more persuasive.

The vigil after prayer is less bloodthirsty than it can be. It is too hot for the extremities of piety. Our argument is not long in starting up when we return—I am barely halfway up the steps. It is Antonia who has found a new tack. She agrees to leave—but only if I will. An opening that permits her to take up all the past weeks' arguments in reverse and turn my own against me. We should be at it most of the night. And so, although she has been accusing me of being cruel to drive her away, it is only tonight that I explain what Bishop Maldonado was anxious to make clear, that my hatred of the Holy Office risks blinding me to the more immediate and perhaps greater danger: an ecclesiastical tribunal, its rules of evidence and procedures entirely at the discretion of the convening bishop, or in this case, archbishop. Unlike the Holy Office, the Archbishop has little in the way of contacts or reputation to cultivate across Europe, so the Inquisitors here are pleased to allow His Grace to take the lead, and will limit themselves initially to deposing evidence. Only after what remains of my own reputation has been destroyed will the Inquisition instigate its own proceedings. It is the tribunal's composition that Archbishop Aguiar summoned Bishop Maldonado from Oaxaca to discuss. His Grace wants one judge of the *Audiencia*, to represent the Crown, and wants Church representation at the level of bishop and provincial, particularly since His Grace hopes evidence will be heard that implicates a bishop. Maldonado's cold relations with the Bishop of Puebla make him a leading candidate but as my friend hastened to add, they have also given him leeway to decline.

The tribunal will be constituted to investigate errors of doctrine, insubordination, alleged violations of the nun's vows and the holy sacraments, but also—and most worrisome to my friend Maldonado—accusations of secular and political abuses committed within the walls of a holy sanctuary. What sort of abuses? I wondered. In such times as these, he said, hints of sedition are heard with the same hostility as is the mere suggestion that the Crown has ever been susceptible to private influence. The Crown, too, will be pleased to let the Archbishop proceed. Evidence, grievances, denunciations of every possible stripe will be entertained—and what will emerge, as much as any particular crime or sin, is a portrait.

I tell Antonia, whatever my success against the other charges, breaking my vow of enclosure is the one I would find impossible to contest.

"Only if you're caught—we could just disappear."

"I can disappear in here, 'Tonia."

"No, Juana. You only think that."

I answer that the threat of an ecclesiastical trial is what Núñez holds in reserve. He too is fond of surprises. So I have become cruel, it seems.

Maldonado insists Núñez is my only chance. For while Núñez cannot claim to control the Inquisition, he holds sway over the Archbishop. It cannot be stopped once begun. A general confession is the one way to keep it from starting. Bishop Maldonado seems to know nothing about the manuscripts of Manuel de Cuadros.

Mail is lighter than plate, but stronger only if it can be made more supple. There are so many unknowns. Does Núñez control Magda, or only think he does, or pretend to, and what if Dorantes in the meanwhile finds the very manuscript I only pretend to have, or hope to? And what if I cannot manoeuvre Núñez into betraying what it contains before he detects that I do not have it? And what of Panoayan? For unless I learn to play at his game more deftly than I so far have, and unless Fortune takes a friendlier hand, the ways of the false dilemma and the true lead to the same terminus, and the shades and judges of the dead will have their bowls of blood. Down the path of confession it is Núñez who waits at the pyre to extract my contrition. Down the path of defiance it is Dorantes, with Núñez lashed beside me. The paths are not separate. For one way or the other Magda would have her chapter—and while I may succeed in destroying Núñez, it is a resolution—even should my courage not fail me—not a *solution*, not an escape. At the end, Manuel de Cuadros did not escape his fate, and far braver than I, could not even cling to his defiance, but changed his mind before the brushwood even fully caught fire. If I am to go there, at least let me have found one resolution I can keep.

For himself, Núñez *has* a solution—more dangerous than if I had collapsed, yet a path with at least one acceptable outcome. For once I have submitted myself to his power and protection, if it seems I have evidence that may be used against him, it is within the setting of an ecclesiastical trial that he can have the Archbishop negotiate immunities with an Inquisitor General pleased to let His Grace take the lead. And then Núñez will have solved, once and for all, the problem of the missing manuscripts.

I have shared no more of this than I thought strictly necessary to persuade Antonia. But it is myself I have thought to spare most of all, for it can be more disturbing to see her frightened than to face some things myself . . . she has been my Camilla. She was upset, pale, but on the whole I thought she had taken it well. On even this subject I can be persuasive after all. But well after Matins, when I think she has surely fallen asleep, she comes upstairs in her nightdress to see the new candle. I am caught, sitting at the table by the bed. The flame flutters lightly next to the window open to the west. For the breeze I have left the door open on the upstairs colonnade over the patio.

We talk quietly for a moment or two. She seems tired. There is not much fight left in those hazel eyes. But as she turns to go she looks at my hands and asks if I am starting a new collection. Her face is drawn, the faint white scar from eye to mouth more noticeable. She does not wait to hear my answer.

Good-night, Antonia.

 Through the room moves the scent of flowers from the trees by the fountain and the smell of horses from the corrals to the south. I look out over the Merced canal, low now, a solitary canoe slipping under the Monzón bridge, rippling the quarter moon. The dry season is ending. With a little rain, but not too much—one hesitates to ask—and cooler days, the smell rising from the canal will not be so bad. There is a young family on the upper floor of the old house across the street. I think they have just moved here too. I will have to ask one of the sisters on this side. The flower market below is interesting to watch. Funerals, festivals, young lovers. The time, long or short, will pass quickly enough.

With the idle hands that are a source of such anxiety here and new hope to Antonia, I have fashioned from common garden clay a puzzle much as I made once as a girl. The puzzle offers a test of dexterity. The object is to roll a small clay ball, against its natural inclination to fall, up the spiral. A simple spiral tower in miniature, modelled on a diagram of such a puzzle from the territory of Persia. I believe, somewhere in that land I shall not see, one may make a pilgrimage to climb the spiral ramps of temples following this design. Nothing is easier to build, nothing is harder to climb. I climb it now.

Such rousing contortions—such hip sways, such elbow fluxions and wrist rolls. Then as now, just such were mine, that day in the shady spot by the granite cross in Panoayan, as I gave myself over to the puzzles that cannot be solved—or if they can, not with hand and eye but heart and soul. Where I tried so hard not to choose by choosing . . . everything.

Then, failing, I had thought to put all such childish notions out of my mind. Now it seems incredible that I thought it all behind me. The riddles and puzzles, the alphabets and anagrams, the forms hidden in the land, the house divided against itself, the wars of the past. The lost ages of Man. And I would not have liked to think—no, not at all—that the destiny I had always looked forward to could be woven merely of these, of such emblems and patterns and habits of mind. Just behind me.

Refuse or recant, erasure or silence. Consider well, choose carefully.

Perhaps one begins to answer by wondering if it's been a mistake to think such puzzles only childish things and by asking if the Persians were so very different, and if their spiral temples were only for children.

Down by the river Panoya, windmill blades turn sleepily like pinwheels on a breeze. The shadow of a cedar branch nods over the arm of a granite cross. The sun's warmth lays a soft sash across my back. Over at the water troughs, the driver stirs, wakes from his nap under the ox cart. A cluster of fresh-picked wildflowers leans against the cross beside me. Beyond it, I notice a clump of weeds, freshly pulled up. The long mound of earth is pocked, subsided in places like bread left out in the rain, like an old hut covered in sod. A green rabbit satchel lies at my knees, its contents spread out among the cones and dried needles before me.

I take up an old book. With a forefinger I bend the corner of a page. It arches like a cat stretching after a nap, trembles in the slight breeze and tugs at me, a sail eager to be launched. At the outer edge of the maguey field a movement catches my eye, my mother's chestnut mare spinning out trains of dust behind her.

I no longer believe it is fate that brings us to meet here, or not fate in the way I had once understood it, but it is a moment of decision. For Amanda and me it may already have been too late: the nun-ensign did not always triumph. And in spite of everything that went wrong between us, everything we needed to know had been there all along. Amanda and I were *cuates*, *cuates* were enough.[24] Nor is it any longer so clear that the destiny I chased was so unlike the fate I did too little to help her escape.

Perhaps the two things are only the same—one we see in looking ahead, with hope, the other in looking back.

I feel a kind of peace, letting my eyes wend and stumble in the way of bees over a field of wildflowers—bumbling comets trailing pollen—who in their windings weave a fine canopy of yellow muslin against the sun. The weight in my lap is a comfort. The book, mildewed and waterlogged, opens to where it always does. And yet now I read in the shapes arrayed about me that the keepsakes were not precisely evidence, or not only that—not proof that I had not forsaken the past. Not evidence against a charge, but charms in a magic against loss itself.

And for this, for us, it is still not too late. Mother passes quite near, riding hard. Her hair and the horse's long tail run together on the wind gusts, like rain driven through a fountain. The ox cart rattles and groans along the side of the house.

What has changed is not so much the evidence but that I let myself remember it. I have heard her sing to Diego's baby. I know this voice, and that it is not only Xochitl who has sung for me in the night. *My father's granddaughters* . . . I have heard this, too, such an odd way of putting things. I have the fresh flowers at my side, the fresh-picked weeds. It was my mother who chose this spot for him because I could not bear to choose. Even angry and hurt I knew she had chosen perfectly. If there has been a piece of evidence still lacking, it is perhaps knowing a little more of how a woman can need a man, and the need to be fearless to make another proud. And now I have my letter back from Uncle Juan. The swarm of thoughts, the memories that have returned me here, even as they had once driven me down from Ixayac, ease . . . Past the sentry box the spokes falter and at the grassy stream, almost stop. The driver snaps the traces twice down hard on the oxen's backs. The Inquisition cortège waits for it to cross. The wagon staggers on, makes its laggard way over the bridge. No, for this, it is not too late. And for us, that moment is now.

I gather up my things. I get to my feet.

I go into the house . . . to discover some small part of what my mother knew of love.

Brother Francisco Manuel de Cuadros came to the locutory only once, a few months before his arrest. Carlos had given me some warning of what to expect. They had not seen each other for almost five years. He was small even next to Carlos as they came in, Carlos in black, he in his faded brown cassock, ragged with the quantity of its mendings and his poverty. Fine sandy hair, what little hair he had, scorched white at the tips, his skin mottled by the sun. The impression that has lingered was of sand— the hair, the skin, the cassock lightened by the elements. Carlos had been shocked by the change in him. I remember his quiet, the slight tremor in his hands. But perhaps Carlos meant the eyes, a colour one would have said once blue, as of an unclouded sky whitened ahead of a dust storm or fire. Or this is how I remember them now.

He and his fellow Franciscans had been two years among the Maya, earning their trust before being allowed to meet the priests of Votan. "It was an archive," he said quietly. "Thousands and thousands of manuscripts. Like those we know here, but more detailed, more intricate, as if the work of great painters, but these were painting canvasses of text. Speaking figures. . . ." It took two more years to learn the basis of reading them. "It felt like watching not just all of a literature but all of an art burn at once."

His whitened eyes in the mottled face had a staring quality even when averted. The painted books piled in the square in Valladolid had been like a small mountain, a pyramid. He had broken faith with his order and hidden a hundred, for what use was the science of reading them if there were no books to practise it upon? But choosing them had proven worse than watching them burn.

After the Franciscan's death, and when it seemed at last safe for Carlos to make his way back to the city, he and I vowed to each other that should any of those manuscripts ever come into our hands we would defend them with our lives. It was twenty years ago. We were younger. It was an emotional time.

During most of that visit Fray de Cuadros had kept his eyes just slightly down, as if something moved on the floor behind me. I am accustomed to such things in one form or other. They all perhaps learn this at seminary. But I was sure then it was neither in fear nor in distaste, as I like now to think it was not in shame. It seems to me tonight that simply because Manuel de Cuadros expressed contrition as the smoke was rising to his eyes, this does not mean, after all, that he did not keep to some secret decision or pledge. I cannot know what it was, but I like to imagine that for him too there was a place that had inspired it. A place from his youth, or somewhere in the mountains of the south, a waterfall, a village of faces, a text on the wall of a ruin.

But a resolution made in strength and not against himself.

There are two small crosses now at the base of the cedar tree. The cross of granite I have seen, the one of obsidian I have only pictured there. Even five years ago, though I had a bishop's dispensation to go, I did not see why I should, with everything I had loved there gone. The site I chose because she chose it for him. And because it is the place I would choose also for myself. It is a place where with every step you take, you walk in halls of jade.

But the stone—this I chose for her. A stone that is also a glass. It is one of an uncommon beauty, native to our region. We do not always get good-bye.

Among the last of the shades to come to the bowls was Achilles. There, Odysseus began to sing his praises, of his fame among the living and the glorious fashion of his death, but Achilles silenced him, with this: it were better to serve as slave to the poorest of the Living than rule as king among the Dead. *Recant.* And yet, as I turn this puzzle in my hands, I wonder if I have returned to relinquish a notion that I have too long held, or just perhaps, to detect the fable in theirs.

At the margins of the living world there is a secret spring, the origin of all things, and some have called it Oceanus. And Oceanus . . . the ocean river that forms the outermost rim of Achilles' shield, flows in reverse. One does not look back leaving Hell. But being there, one looks back if one ever hopes to emerge.

And among all the living, the one Achilles looked to was Odysseus, for news of his son.

Erasure or silence, defiance or submission. There are puzzles to which the hardest answers last, the earliest endure. At Xochitl's knee I had once learned that Time itself could be looked upon as a spiral. Hold it up, turn it in the hand. Time as a spiral, memory as a cutting plane: the truths it reveals follow from where and how one begins. Roll the ball up the spiral again: the sum of all possible angles is as true as a fable, but the One Truth in the sum is not for the reckoning of Man. Much is lost upon us, a few things remain. Remember these—with pleasure, remember again . . . my mother firing off an arquebus during a jaguar attack in the dead of night . . . the angels in the library. And there was a moment after a dinner, when together we almost laughed.

As it is with magic charms, so is it also with good-byes. Or with refusing even choice itself, so as not to lose the path not taken. But if I have not lost him, and not lost them, it is not because there is something I have not let the holy officers strip from me, or even because the sod remains undisturbed in a shady spot beneath a cedar tree. We do not always get good-bye, but moments such as these. And who is to say if Time itself can take these back from me.

 Heraclitus has written that one never enters the same river twice. But the greatest of rivers and the smallest streams share a destiny, however obscure it may remain, as they run to the sea. Though their currents be muddy or clear, shallow or deep, though they run swift in the shadow of their *rives*, yet do they bear up, in the trains of their passing, gold and ochre and russet leaves. To spin slowly, dreamily, on their surfaces.

And even as the Nile brings the cargo of her seasons in tribute to the sea, these, all these have come down to me through the intervening years, and down through this night . . . as afterthoughts.

It is almost light, the square of sky pales beyond the window. Beneath it on the table, my collection of two. The newest, the most ancient; the oldest, the first. One I have made with my hands. The other I have brought from the convent archives. A battered book, the husk of its bindings split. I take it into my lap one last time before returning it to its hiding place in the shelves. I close my eyes. . . .

What is a childhood but the end of all past times forgotten, beginning again? And to leave the highlands of childhood for the valleys and currents of one's own time is to lose something akin to prescience, to lose sight of the far ranges at our life's end. Now I cannot see ahead an hour and yet, looking back, how curious to remember, only now, the place where I was born at the hacienda in Nepantla: the gaps in the walls, the breezes blowing through, the stars . . . a hut of pale fieldstone that the people of our region sometimes called the cell. Remember with pleasure, remember it all again, for yourself, remember for them.

More than by the little of the world I knew, my mind has been shaped by books. So it is not so strange that I had come to think of my own life as a book, strongly bound, beautifully made. I had never doubted I would find there my legend and my destiny, and even if its end escaped me until the last page, the last day, I had never doubted it would on that day feel necessary, even familiar, the page already marked. And though I now see at last the briefest glimpses of that text, its language I know well. I learned it as a child. A broken book is still a book. To be mistaken in this is to make of it another kind of destiny, to succumb to the patterns already woven there, even of broken threads. Or, I had thought them broken, but the body offers up its own evidence. For as night ends, I feel that ache even now, so fresh . . . and in my legs, a honey-gold thread of pain.

What is the path that is no path, to an end that is a return? Each time without precedent, to an embrace that is a relinquishment.

What is the collection that cannot be taken, the text that cannot be erased? The silence that cannot be broken.

In the silence in the darkness there is a spiral stair. It leads up and out and into the night, where at a crossroads in the desert, at a secret spring, an unknown god waits, hidden even as the soul is from itself.

And offers us water.

But here I let fall the invocations of the famous poets, the herbs and the potions, the magics, the charms and enchantments, the brilliant feasts and the sable rams. And this last charm with the battered spine, which has been my life, this too do I lay aside. For there is other work, and it will soon be light.

To this alone do I commend me.
This alone do I invoke,
truly,
that in a world of living,
this world knew not
its deity.

Guided by a silent Clarion
along a path that is no path,
blundered across, stumbled upon,
in search of an end that has no end.

Jerome sat in contemplation of
the Trumpet of the Judgement,
but soon was troubled
to be hearing the very echo
of what he feared most;
and thus, pondering an event
to strike terror in the heart
of the most exalted Seraphim,
advanced a step, without moving,
guided by a silent Clarion.
    He walks toward that City
where his spirit dwells
in ardent Charity—
and though the road is unknown to him,
in truth God is the way—
and, in the manner of a pilgrim, spans
in one long peregrine flight,
the gulf from earth to Heaven
without ever losing his way,
along a path that is no path.

JUANA INÉS
DE LA CRUZ

B. Limosneros, trans.

    Leaving the track stained red—
holding his blood scant price
to have covered such terrain—
he came to be thought mad
and was subjected to brutal stonings . . .
these, the Holy Doctor answering:
—Since by an easy path
no one to heaven has ever ascended,
let none wonder it should at last have been
blundered across, stumbled upon.

    That it comes to me by happy accident
dampens not the ardent
fire that enkindles my soul:
to find the end of my love's quest
in One who has no end.
Thus, eagerly do I go
spilling all of the carmine
that these veins enclose,
till now not a drop is left
in search of an End that has no end.

Horus   BOOK FIVE

CONTENTS

chorus

Seraphim, come!

Come all and find

a Rose that is cut

and yet it lives on;

  that withers not

but revives

to a fierce new bloom,

one stemming from

her own deepest being;

  and so it proved a blessing

to have bent her to the knife.

Harvesters, come!

Come all and find

a Rose that is cut

and yet it lives on.

verses

Against a frail Rose

a thousand north winds contrive:

how hedged in by envy she is

in the brief hour Beauty is given to live!

  Because she is lovely, they envy,

and because she is learned, they ape:

how ancient now is this story

in a world that pays merit with hate.

A thousand panting breaths
give vent to a thousand whirling blades on edge—
that for each fresh distinction score and mark
a great and lonely heart.
  So many deaths
against a single life conspire;
yet none meets with success,
for having sprung from cowardice and rancour;
  so do not read too much into the ignorant,
blind, malignant fate
she suffers on the wheel of blades,
for with this God constructs the chariot of her triumph.
  Although the circling engine
is a cutting courtesan,
it is one whose machinations
serve to restore Catherine's fortunes.
  And to the Rose herself
it is not new, not in the least,
that upon her august splendours
pungent barbs should mount an honour guard
to mark her final glories.

I copy her words like a parrot incapable of grasping their meaning. And now its mindless mimicry has brought the parrot's master to her knees. Don't blame Juana, blame *me, this is my doing.*

This is to be my punishment. How perfectly it fits. Isn't this what she once wrote? Now I'm left to fill the void of her voice's silencing. Parrot's imitation of the nightingale—a mockery all the crueller for its sincerity.

I, Antonia Mora, copyist, whore, have read every word you've written these past five years, Juana Inés de la Cruz, every verse, every letter. There is not one of your sonnets I can't recite. How I have slaved to make myself indispensable to you, who raised me up out of the gutter, taught me to think, to give those thoughts form, to write, imitating your flourishes, striving to become your instrument, a projection of your voice, to have you clutch me as tightly as the quill between your fingers.

All I asked was to hear your terms dictated, to catch your thoughts in quivering flight and soar with them an instant aloft. Saint Thomas had five secretaries—I would be the only one you'd ever need!—to be for you a dozen, as you strode across the room spouting verses like a dragon—rhymed arguments yoked to flame.

I pored over your writings, how you formed your letters, each letter a gesture, tracing in their whorls your turns of mind, conforming mine to yours, becoming your forger, a hunched Vulcan to your Venus—*you, Juana, taught me these stories.* This is what you've made me. I am your creation.

At night I would read and reread each day's work aloud to make my voice more like yours, to hear it as I wrote. At night, I dreamt those soaring thoughts were mine, your grace my own.

How many of your correspondents knew—how many?—where your words ended and mine began? Soon only the most delicate of letters did you even bother to reread. How many times did I finish a phrase, a paragraph you'd started, start a letter for you to polish only to have you say: "Go ahead, 'Tonia, finish it. You write more like Sor Juana Inés de la Cruz than I do. . . . You'll be a poet one day, Antonia."

CODEX: FORGER

Sor Juana's secretary, Antonia Mora, finds herself ordered to write her own journal. But she has done this all along. For the Bishop of Puebla, she made dutiful report. Except, her reports were deliberately falsified. Like a duplicitous accountant, she has always kept two versions of her books.

No. Not even you could make it so.

It got so I could see your every thought written in your face—your arching brow for me an entire paragraph, your wry smile a sharp riposte, your pallour a defence, a heartfelt plea. I made myself your paper forgery—deceiving hundreds but the one I made a fool of was me. Listen to me!—even here I echo you. The vulgar wry-necked chatter of Echo's errant daughter.

Parrot mind in a scarecrow skull—I've ruined everything, understood nothing, not a single thought my own. . . .

Thank God Carlos is back today from Florida, just when everything seems lost, back to help me now, lead me by the hand, explain it all to me like a witless child, show me how to make it all better.

Only thinking about him now, so near, do I realize how quickly things worsened once he'd left.

 And now this new interest in me, in my scribblings, after all these months. Who is really behind it? If it's Núñez, is he testing the sincerity of her petition for him to return, or is he gathering testimony for the Inquisition? As an oblate, my one vow is holy obedience. Obey or they keep my dowry and return me to the streets.

I would never see her again.

And just what is it they want me to explain? They don't need me!—every woman in here is watching Juana's every movement. Do they think she still confides in me? If only I could make it so, but I'm the last one she should risk talking to after everything I've done.

Or is it the Bishop behind all this after all? They say he now has every nun in Puebla scouring her soul for fresh transports to record for his correction. For him to 'decipher and organize'—as though a convent were a grotto of raving oracles. He thinks after betraying her by my stupidity I can be ordered to do it again deliberately.

He knows I'm a liar! He trained me himself. Is it a forger's handbook he wants to see? It's lies he wants, knowing how I ache to tell the truth. I *have to* lie—but what lies can he use against her? Which truths condemn, which absolve her? Which lies protect and which endanger her?

So I keep two handbooks again—one true, one false. One version to deceive and one to protect. One to mislead, one to bear witness. But when the time comes will I know which one is which?

And what if she doesn't want absolution? And what if she doesn't want what's best for her? They all say they want what's best for her. *You're just like the rest, copyist.*

Don't make me speak for her . . . again.

CODEX: TEMPTATION

Carlos receives a letter from Antonia and rushes back from his mapping expedition in Florida. Sor Juana will not see him. She will take no more visitors. Needing as much as Antonia to understand, ever the scientist, Carlos, too, urges Antonia to take careful notes for them to interpret together.

I ASK CARLOS FOR HELP, what does he give me?—he reminds me of our classes, the Mexican painted books. *I don't care about books.* The books of the Red and the Black, of knowing and death. *I want her to speak to me.* The ancient codex is more than a text composed of images. It is like a shorthand notation for a performance that goes beyond speech. *Speech is quite enough for me.* Carlos tells me I mustn't be like the Franciscans—me! That I shouldn't be so hungry to change her that I don't really see. He can only help me if I will be his eyes and ears. If we're to understand a phenomenon, have a controlled effect upon it, then he and I must observe it carefully, describe it faithfully. Faithful to what, to whom? To the one I'm to spy on? To the truth, he says. And just what is that, I'm about to ask, when he waves me off: *he understands.*

Yes he understands but nothing's changed. They're all still asking me to speak for her, still asking me for signs to decipher.

Gestures, times of day, colours, scents, weather, situation . . . but Carlos, how will I know what's significant?

"When in doubt, record. Get it all. The codex must attempt a complete reckoning. Texts can be burned, contexts . . . die harder."

All right, I will. Everything. But won't she see me? Won't her knowing what I'm doing change what she lets me see?

"One thing I did learn among the Franciscans, Antonia, is that the observer is always under observation."

She returns from the garden, fingers stained as they had once been with ink. Is she still writing? Using gardening to cover the traces? Writing secretly in the middle of the night?

Carlos asks if it didn't look like ink because I wanted it to. He says this calls for a hard-eyed observer.

Juana, what kind of observer do you need? What kind of eyes. . . .

If I'm to record everything, then that includes her words.

Can it hurt to try to make her speak to me? Carlos says not, as long as I continue recording everything else faithfully. But he knows me unable to resist this temptation, this craving to hear her speak.

I've started bringing her books, ones Carlos has chosen for me. I told her I couldn't bear the empty shelves grinning at me like a mouthful of missing teeth. She knows better. What I'm doing is perverse, a test. It's one thing to stop reading when there are no books left.

Carlos is teaching me, again, I tell her. Can I store the books here? How long can Sor Juana Inés de la Cruz contain her appetite for books Carlos thinks even she has not read?

Not all unread: the first one I bring is Tirso de Molina's *El vergonzozo en palacio.* Isn't this the play with the maid called Serafina and the secretary named Antonio? Have you foreseen all this? Her warm eyes, wry smile. Is that the only answer, a smile? How do I record that? A thousand variations on a smile, a million unsaid subtleties. I CAN'T DO THIS!

I'm not up to this.

Snatches of conversation wrung like diamonds from a mop.

If not a lot, you still speak to others—cooks, masons, gardeners— why not to me? Sure, a few words, now and then. Thrilling confessions like: "Good-night, Antonia." Your eyes glitter with . . . is that amusement? You know I've started watching you while you sleep. A few nights ago, just after three, you find me slumped against the wall next to your open door, sound asleep, notebook in my lap. Some spy!

Carlos, what does red mean? I rush into the locutory overcome by the sensation of seeing her just now in the orchard, standing on a crate, the red, red juice of ripe plums running, intemperate, between her fingers, down the backs of her hands, staining her slender wrists. Juice welling from the corners of her red lips, plum-red runnels like liquid ruby along the cheeks of her laughing face, head thrown back, jubilant . . . a veiny tracery under the pink shell of her ear and down her nape. Plum-red soaking into the hairshirt's rough brown wool.

Red, Carlos! What does it *mean?*

He answers with some dry thing about Mexicans and Egyptians.

I try again. Have I helped you get here?—maybe this is where you want to be. Did you use me then—would you do it again—manipulate me to deceive your enemies?

Do you know I'm keeping two versions of these handbooks?

Do you know which I'll show to my confessor?

Can the observer change the observed? Does the observer have a right?

Carlos wonders if you wanted me to finish Sor Seraphina, wanted me to send it. To sever your last ties to the Bishop for you. If I've been sick with guilt for nothing. Am I a character in a play, Juana? Is my role to betray you? Would you let me do that to you? Do you want them to think you're some kind of saint? I think at last I will bring her to speak.

"I'm just flesh and blood and breath, Antonia. You, of all of them, should know."

"But how are *they* to?"

"I'm counting on you. . . ."

"For what?"

"To tell them."

Throwing myself against the blank wall of her silence.

Father Arellano asked to see my handbook today, Juana. What should I do?

There's your vow of obedience. . . .

You want me to show him, then.

An almost imperceptible shrug.

Is she trying to say she doesn't care? I don't believe you!

The shades, degrees, gradations of your silences. Silence of the sun spilling across a darkened doorway. Silence behind my eyes, below your belly. Behind sealed lips, what they never say.

At the base of a mountain in the depths of the sea. At the bottom of a flooded mineshaft . . . a silent, soot-spent coal-seam on a cloud-cast night.

You . . . the blaze just one unspoken word could ignite.

I AM SUPPOSED TO RECORD only where she goes, what she does. What about where she no longer goes, things she won't ever do again? Locutory, library, choir . . .

Am I to do these things in her place? Laugh, read, write, sing. Paint her movements through sacred space . . . for now a kind of space has opened up around her. The strict routine of places and times that rules the rest of us parts wide now like the Red Sea as she moves through the courtyards to the orchards, the kitchens, the workshops.

And to a degree I am allowed to move with her in that parted space. Less freely, less visibly, but still. . . .

The others scurrying along on their appointed rounds in ruler-straight flights and crossings, while, path eccentric, she wanders among us like an island of ice, the kind Carlos says number as grains of sand in the northern seas. Cool, self-possessed, immense, visible for leagues.

Even in a courtyard criss-crossed with bell-summoned sisters and novices, she is the one the eye now finds and follows.

Carlos tells me what it is that the Bishop is so avidly mining the convents of Puebla for these days: the biographies of nuns approaching death. Silver or gold, iron or lead?

And what lessons would he have this dying teach? What little treasures is it to yield?

Afternoon, heat abating. She waters plants I've installed before her open door for privacy, as our fellow inmates still stroll by so casually. Knowing this, Carlos has given me a rose of Jericho to add to the screen. This is the one she tends most carefully.

We stand together. A moment's stillness. Suddenly, pigeon wings flap like sheets snapping in the air.

Waking others now. Warbles, frail rumbles . . . a whole brood of bird calls, unfledged, tries the cooling air—its speed, its draft—fading faintly past.

How could I have ever thought to take refuge in this swamp? Juana mutters, bent frowning over the convent's architectural drawings. After each rainy season it seems the lines of pillars and beams yaw farther out of true. . . . Of all her old duties here, the one she's not relinquished, in fact refuses to, is supervising the construction and renovation works by crews of Indian masons. The Indians are preferred, as the least likely to force themselves upon a nun.

I took a vow of enclosure, I heard her say once to the Prioress, I did not promise never again to speak to a man. And so each day for two or three months each year they come to her. The men huddle, cap in hand. Then—the same thing I saw happen in the kitchens—when she begins to speak to them in their native tongue, dark faces beam, excited glances fly among the new men, bowed shoulders draw a little straighter. . . .

Today, with the season's rains abated, an old workman I've never seen before, tiny, bent, face of leather, kneels before her. The same confusion in both their faces as she hastily bids him stand. The foreman barks something out at him. She helps him to his feet.

The first time I've ever seen her uncomfortable among them. . . .

 In the kitchens just before New Year, the five of us—Juana, Vanessa, Concepción, Asunción and I—a Creole, a Spaniard, two Indians and a mulatta (I feel just now like I should be telling a salacious joke). . . . High spirits all round, general merriment. We are making one of Vanessa's desserts for a banquet the Vicereine is giving:

> fresh-baked, unleavened wafers
> sliced apple baked between
> upon one half of the plate a bed of burnt-caramel cream, chocolate sauce
>   upon the other
> stewed crabapple garnish
> wafers pierced by taffy cane, a waving, bannered flourish. . . .
> Multiply by number of settings (200), assemble twenty minutes in
>   advance and let stand until serving.

Concepción, unthinking, licks her thumb and reaches up to wipe a daub of pale flour from Juana's cheek, tanned from the orchards. Her gleaming thumb raised, flour-daub still intact, Concepción hesitates, murmuring: your skin is dark, like Our Mother, Guadalupe. Then laughs a little and wipes the flour away.

They will say that in the end your skin was like Guadalupe's.

How do I know this? I would bet my life.

Juana and I spend the afternoon with Vanessa, copying out her recipes for an edition to be bound and sold to raise money for the convent.

I weep, to be sitting here at a stained and rough-hewn table in a fragrant kitchen. To see her writing again! To be sitting next to her. As always, copying. . . .

Her handwriting is changing. The bold masculine hand everyone here claimed to find so scandalous is giving way—'masculine' because the lettering was once firm and full, and beautifully-formed; 'scandalous' because beauty of any kind in a nun is an incitation and a temptation. Handwriting.

Who to, an incitation to what poor, pathetic creature . . . ?

As I look over at what she's written her script now seems both more elaborate and more . . . hesitant. Go ahead, write it: feminine.

Isn't it here then I should also mention that, speaking so infrequently, Sor Juana Inés de la Cruz is developing the slightest stutter?

Isn't it here I try to say how this makes me feel?

Stay me with flagons, comfort me with apples: for I am sick of love.

You in the orchards, a wind through the pomegranates, figs and apples. *Ariel*—a crystal crash among the apple boughs. Pale undersides of leaves, wind-canted: the startled modesties of petticoats.

Comfort me with apples.

And am I supposed to copy out too the angry script of lash-strokes across her naked back? Record their obscene utterance? The colour is pink—soon, blue-welted like berries—a flailing alliteration: why not make merry on our way to damnation? The slender lash-lines straight though not parallel. Welted quill-strokes of different lengths and thicknesses—

The way the braided cord hisses through the quilted air.

In a convent, this too is considered manual labour.

Is this the kind of hard-eyed observation that will save her? Then, decipher this.

Cloud-burst, exploding thunder, torrent of rain. Then just as suddenly it stops, sun battering the gleaming stone again like waves against a cliff. Little tendrils of mist rising from the patio's volcanic flagstones.

Nuns in every doorway, staring out, eyes sceptical or filled with rueful wonder. Beneath a startled blue sky Juana crosses the misted yard like a lonely ghost, to see how the garden has fared. Water cascading from the roof's carved waterspouts in clattering, prismed arcs. All eyes upon her as she nears—if she's not careful!—hands balled into little fists, elbows bent, shoulders slightly hitched she walks briskly through the sheet of tumbling light—all eyes upon her—our collective gasp—and calmly disappears, soaked to the skin, through the arched passageway. . . .

Her little joke.

 The kitchen's lost Poetics:

Asunción washing up, Concepción putting water in an *olla* to heat for mint tea. Darkly beautiful, compact, determined, fiercely blushing now, expression critical, Vanessa stands off to one side of a table spread with sculpted dishes heaped with colour.

Juana's forty-sixth birthday. Our little surprise party, just the five of us. Caught off guard, trying to deflect our attention, Juana says to the room at large that Vanessa's such a genius it would take an eight-day week, *un octavo dia*, to make another like her. I feel a pricking of unworthy jealousy. . . .

Chicharrón salad—baked pork rind, fresh basil, picked by Juana's own hands, vinegar.

Plato fuerte—sauce of ripe papayas, freshly puréed, uncooked. Chicken stock, flaked chillies. Sauce served cold. Fresh-caught whitefish, amaranth seeds floating in a clear, dark sauce round a mould of bulgar wheat flecked with chilled cucumber. . . .

Dessert—the smell of baking peaches wafting through the low vaulted room—how I love this room, it seems the only place we can be happy now. . . .

Another private masterpiece that will never grace the refectory's communal tables.

 Near evening, already dusk. You have not returned from the orchards. I run a bath for you: you will be tired. Into the steaming water what scents shall I pour, what essences shall I choose for you to carry into this night's sleep? To cloak you, every mound and furrow, and still at dawn like fallen dew: cassis, angelica root, Italian bergamot, cloves? Marjoram, spearmint, olibanum, rose? Cinnamon . . . I pore over bottled roots and barks and essences like a wizard, a *curandera* over her healing incantations.

Can you be healed of this? Can I heal myself?

The water cools a little, the moment passes. A little later you come in, weary, as I expected. You see the water and smile, beginning to undress. No, wait! An eyebrow arches—your dusty face—as if to ask, What's the matter?

It's ice-cold, I lie, putting on more water to heat, making you wait, cruelly.

Gardening, cooking, embroidery . . . Carlos asks me if this sudden interest in women's work—work she would never permit herself in here—is a parody of feminine servility?

I am thinking of this as I watch her silent among the weavers, taking her place at a loom, half-listening as the others weave and spin, telling stories to pass the time. Sitting across from her as she begins to work the loom, hesitantly at first and then more surely, I see her look up at me, dark eyes shining with awe, as a lost skill returns to her forgivingly from a bygone time, as though it were only yesterday she was girl in Panoayan. . . .

Dedicated, rat-sated, battered, ears in tatters—convent cats in their leisure hours stalking wary birds. Juana watching.

The next day the *curandera* returns to her potions, a delicate case, this one, I mutter.

If what the ancient Mexicans believed is true—that a colour, a sound, a scent is as significant to a ceremony as any word—and if to change any one of these recasts the whole, couldn't this extend even to the play's outcome? Dear Lord, let this be so!

If I can't change that outcome with words, why not with scents and flavours? How am I to believe there's no such thing as magic when I have heard you speak of this so often, when I see you now under this spell?

Carlos always says the first step to understanding a thing is observing well . . . a careful description of its properties. The *bruja* unstops her bottles, passing them beneath her nose, one by one, eyes closed: the cream finish of sandalwood. Lavender's true, high notes. The rasp of pepper, deep and feral. Rose: warm and cream, but fine. *Nardo*, rich butterfat;

with jasmin—low-pitched and gritty—its perfect complement. Violet: cool and powdery. *Lirio* root: a mushroom's musk—what will it say to the hard-eyed observer to smell that on her skin? Anise mixed with berg-amot—a baby's pink fragrance, flesh of velvet creases.

Is this madness? I said I would try anything. Shall I wring my hands over what right I have, again? Am I not entitled to a little hope? Of undo-ing the hex I've helped put on you?

The cool, sweet convergence of vanilla and cassis, the eggshell whiff of *aldehidos,* the leather waft of *habatonia*. Regal essence of *Acahar*. . . .

From a dream of flowers I wake before dawn, looking to put names to the scented melodies in your bathwater: Temptation, Incantation, Jubilation . . .

Obsession.

Still in bed, arm flung across my eyes, I hear you moving through the darkened rooms.

I follow you everywhere now. You hardly seem to notice, like a wild crea-ture grown used to me. I stand by you tending flowers; I cut a shock of white narcissus blossoms for our table.

You turn to me, your shirt splashed with pollen.

Gold. Carlos has already carefully explained this. The colour of the West as the evening star sinks into the swamp of night. Where souls taken prisoner in childbirth lie in wait.

I kiss your hands. On such and such a day, someone here will soon be saying, her palms tasted of clay. . . .

Weeding, she uproots shoots of basil she planted just last week. She's started forgetting little things.

Dawn, fog. Sky the colour of time. This place is filled with ghosts! I *live* with one—no, five hundred. I look out into the time-swept streets and see still others—past or future? Streets filled with mists, miasmas, phantoms. Spectres of vanished instruments and books, and cruel instruments of iron and timber soon, now, to come.

The ghosts of young men playing a ball game against the massive convent walls. And on those grey walls others sketching bright, crude symbols with strange cylindrical brushes. A few words I recognize: *Crisis.* PAN. *México para los Mexicanos* . . .

San Jerónimo: the crumbling ghost of a ball court, an altar, an ancient book.

Tremulous blue light in the rooms across the street.

Mid-afternoon. Sun in a sky of brass. Thousand-throated roar of a bull-ring, five blocks away.

Thread of hairshirt wool stuck in the bed of rough-planed timbers where she sleeps. Strand of hair caught in the scaly bark of a potted tree. Ragged fingernail recovered from the garden soil. Peeled whorls of fingertips, wedged invisible in a pocked column of volcanic rock abrasive like a file. Flesh wedded to a flail.

With these, your textured leavings, I brew your returning's counterspell.

**CODEX:
TEMPTATION 2**

WHAT MORE CAN I FIND TO SAY TO SOMEONE who doesn't want to go on speaking? *Find something!*

What can I bring to bring her back to me? Dreams, memories, news of the world—echoes from the streets.

Check the cellars. Make a list.

A scrap of paper on the floor by a shelf—whatever it says, it's in Nahuatl. . . . Carlos has suggested I ask her to read it for me. Another of our pathetic temptations.

So, a scrap of verses in her handwriting. When was it written, hours ago or months?

Her stained fingers. There are a hundred and eighty-nine books and manuscripts hidden in the archives. I wonder for the thousandth time, is she writing again—or still? And in the language of her girlhood? Is there ink concealed beneath the dirt? Is she working in the gardens to conceal it? Again no answers.

Eyes enormous now, luminous, whites stark in their sockets. Glossy ridge of cheekbone, drawn thin, like her clavicles, her sickle-boned hips—skin stretched tight like a canvas before the brush's first shy kiss. Keyed in ivory and bone like a clavichord too delicate to play.

Cheekbone ridge drawing down to tanned hollows. Her jaws' muscular swell. Curved, cracked lips. Hairshirt fustian like a tamarind pod. She looks each day more like an Indian, a gaunt field hand.

Strong still, I thought. Only an occasional unsteadiness after climbing stairs.

I told myself.

This morning she has trouble getting out of bed.

Asunción is bringing the poultices. I will spread them out like grape leaves across her cicatrices.

Hunger scrimshaws your ivory form. Some long-dead navigator's graven altar—a map, some enchanted isle, its rough topography in bone.[1]

Today much better. Everything back to normal, if that's what this can be called. Only the slightest unsteadiness in her hands.

Núñez is coming! *Next Sunday*—the report reverberates through the convent cells like a shot. As though it's been confirmed—it hasn't been confirmed?! My growing desperation. He will be here *next week,* ten days . . . then it'll be too late, it will have started.

To bring Juana news of the world I need to leave this place! . . . just an hour or two each day. Nothing has ever prevented me. Permission of course I need. The Prioress has already awarded me a lot of liberty, but this?

Enter the womanly conspiracies of kitchens: Vanessa calls on me to join Asunción for the shopping when old Concepción pulls up lame. A recurrence of gout is blamed. . . .

As we approach the market, Asunción turns to me and asks, well what are you waiting for?—just be back in two hours.

Free!—that's how it feels, though I know it really isn't. The eyes of men all over me, the oldest game still awaiting me like a dog lolling at the door.

That first day I just walk and walk, hardly seeing, just feeling the wind all over me.

Carlos says I must make your America sing to you like a siren. Just as you've made it sing for me. But what does someone like me have to offer you? What clumsy lyrics can I lay at the feet of someone who has brought the world so much beauty?

I offer you every sunny morning since the day we met. . . .

Every rain-laved dawning these past five years. Each high-waisted noon, each stooping dusk. Five years of full moons high-risen. Five years of brief-locked eyes and stolen glances quickly broken. Of breathless grazings, staged accidents and soft collidings. Of slow-drawn baths, petals swanning across a tile-bound tub. The plump pad and whisper of languid towellings.

Antonia Mora, you will make a poet one day. No, Juana. Not even you can make it so.

At the market I buy a little bracelet for her wrist. Will she accept, will she refuse to wear it? A string of little silver bells and the shells of tiny snails, a talisman to chime and charm and faintly mutter, to fill the silence as she works.

The bracelet was my second choice. I knew she would never wear the brooches I saw the Mayans selling: live scarab beetles, pierced and tethered to a pin by a thin, golden chain. . . .

According to Carlos, in the rituals of the ancient Mexicans the brush of certain words across the vocal chords can be more important than their meaning, and the soft shush of shell anklets more significant than a word—gesture translated into sound, word into thing. Meanings that change, subject to the occasion.

Núñez's approach, murmurs massing like clouds. Ten days, now five. Five years of our lives telescoped down through these five remaining days. I refuse to let her out of my sight for one instant. And even as I feel her drawing away from me, I touch her at every opportunity.

For the first time in two years I sleep in her bed, sleep there each night, holding her. She strokes my hair.

Tell me another, Carlos . . . another engine of torture. The cap they call the Cat's Claws. Carlos submits to describe it.

Another morning. Another day gone. A rising tide of panic. And fury— what is left to say? What's left that she'll still listen to from me?

And so the game begins. A game she seems to find touching in a way I can't quite grasp. Each day back from my staged outings to the marketplace, I tell her a series of lies—fables, say, with at least one containing a grain of truth.

The game: guess what I saw today. Heard, said, did, touched, smelled, tasted. Guess which life I lived, bore witness to.

(For you, I mean.) This part goes unsaid.

Close your eyes. . . .

. . . *The wobble of a newborn colt* . . .

A single thread of tobacco smoke rising fine, then fanning into a plume that bulges and checks and eddies as my finger passes through . . .

The starched whisk of a black-pinioned bird past the window, fan tips across stone . . .

Cold stone floor against my back, *pulquería* air a fermented stew, raucous songs, taste of *pulque* wrapped viscous right round the tongue, like a burnt milk's clotted skin. . . .

Holding out my closed hand as if to drop a little coin into hers, I ask, guess, Juana, which of these things I've brought back for you.

Three days. I can't think, can't see properly, a kind of film before my eyes. I can't help her, can't help anyone like this! We're running out of time—hundreds of possibilities to try. Find the word that breaks the spell. Makes her look up and see. . . .

Carlos, help me! His face haggard, drained of colour. The last few days of waiting are harder on him. At least I get to *see* her. All he can do is come to me, every day now, and wait.

Maybe the problem, Antonia, is that you're looking for a single truth. Juana said something to me once—this should be interesting to you, who play the clavichord so beautifully. Look at the clavichord's harmonics. We approach the truth not head-on but in tangents, he says.

What's that supposed to mean?

Press the keys. The metal tangents strut across the fretted strings, producing not a single note but a chord. The same set of strings, depending on where the tangents strike them, can be made to play several different chords at once. . . .

Tangential truths. Harmonics keyed to chord and discord. Gradually comprehensible to the patient ear. . . .

No. I am running out of time.

Guess, Juana. Guess what happened on the way to the marketplace. What took place, fell beneath time's relentless sway.

The gravel rasp of scissors slicing through a plait of hair.

All the colours called green.

The sensations called pain.

Shark-skin roughness of a young guard's emery cheek, there at the top where a woman's thighs first swell to meet.

Sound of a fist opening, frisk of fingernails across a callused palm.

Smell of poverty and darkness, low-ceilings. A public executioner sitting, leaning over his mother's bed, alcatraz lilies crushed in a pale, muscled fist, rust-red loam beneath his broken nails. The soft plat of white petals striking the stone floor.

Against a hill in the middle distance, a torch flickering forgotten under the noon-day sun.

Guess.

 How can you bear to have Father Núñez be your confessor again? *To have the same confessor as the Archbishop?*

A ghost of a smile crosses your lips—you think it's ironic, don't you? Well, I call it sickening! I'm shouting now: so when Núñez arrives from confessing you, will the Archbishop smell you on him, over the odours of their own so-piously-unwashed bodies?—stench of sulphur and cheese. Will Núñez use the scent of you to stir that madman into a helpless frenzy? Goat eyes rolling back toward his heaven, nostrils quivering with dragon-stench—the groin-thickening odour of Eve—his own scabby back the dragon's scales—

Flail, Jesuit, flail.

 Seven to eight, the longest hour of the day, the hour of attending to our special penances and mortifyings. First the evening bath, its fragrant joys for me, if not for her, bound up now in the agonies to follow.

What am I becoming?

She seems to have lost all sense of privacy. Lets me see everything. Is it because she feels all America watching? Lets me draw her bath, dry her back and minutes later watch it lacerated anew. And then cover it with poultices.

It's hard to admit this, harder still to write it, but for all the horror I feel at the spectacle—for all the nightmare rhythms I will later rap out in my sleep to the flail's evensong melodies—for all my UNSPEAK-ABLE DISMAY . . . the sight is now less pitiful to me than seeing the other sisters doing the same thing.

In all the panic and confusion and desperation of these last few days—so strange it feels to be saying it, another little betrayal—but I find the sight now almost calming.

So what kind of monster does this make me?

Her floggings are as severe as any of the others' here, if anything, harder. And harder by the day. The blood just as red, on that frail back. It's not that I'm not afraid for her. I am, I'm terrified. But unlike hers, and more heart-breaking—I don't know why—the light I see in their eyes is rapture, a rapture of the spirit, stoked by each stroke, each barbed cut.

Hers is a kind of cold fury, not rapture, a fire of will or reason that nothing of this world can dominate.

Her soul's rapture I've seen at other times—out in the gardens, and at night under the stars.

Why should I find hope in this?

Hardly sleeping, nocturnal, she sits at the window to await the sunset. And at the door to watch the moon rise smoothly away from the tower above the chapel dome.

And I, hovering a few feet back from her.

The last full day, *do something.* . . .

Morning. Shutters thrown back, warm breeze sifting through the cool rooms.

A dragonfly's high clicking like the snap of twigs, or pebbles against a window.

Noon. Through the trees, the slippery glimmer of fountains shaped like crosses, surface broken by the preening of noisy birds.

I can think of nothing to say. Nothing to do.

Dusk. Along the south wall at the main-floor windows, the level where the envied servants sleep, unannounced visitors slump against the bars . . . a lover's coaxing lean, cajoling fingers trace the black iron that bars him from the sister of his dreams.

Did you never once sleep down on the main floor, Juanita, before I came to live with you?

Guess. Please. I went farther this time. Out into the country for you.

Close your eyes. . . .

Lying on your back, looking at the sky . . . the instant when you wonder if it is the mountain drifting, not the clouds.

The hour spent registering all the fickle changes in the wind—pressure, direction, urgencies, temperatures, constancy.

A warm wind's soft worry as it eddies past the ear.

Smell of moss-cloyed clay, dense, a carpet.

Guess.

Waking from a nap to a faint thrumming, a pressure, the faintest snapping, like fingers calling a distant servant to attention—the hummingbird's reclining hover, shimmer of dawn like oil across green feathers. Head-dipping shift from hover to dart—

Aerial collision of the hummingbird with dragonfly daubed the same shimmering green, turquoise tail, green-chalk patina of its tiny skullcap. . . . Both aerialists stunned by the collision, alighting on adjacent flowers—one red, the other shell-pink.

Guess.

Report of a cannon shot like tight twine fraying along a jagged mountain face, then shredding, gutted, across a swaying treetop reef.

I look at you and see the years we've been together, all the vanished things rendered and surrendered . . . but, now, at least you're listening. Gently . . .

Guess.

The eager clamber of baby crocodiles towards a piece of meat.

One small bird's convulsive chirping, its song a hiccup, a wracking birth contraction. Head's ducking, knees' splayed flexions, pivoting on tiny brittle feet ninety degrees—a quadrant at a chirp. One whit fiercer would surely jerk it headlong from its perch. . . .

The fine, angular distinction between a cricket song and its echo, at dusk before the dewfall, and the cricket's coppery trill from the frog's croak of tin.

I've done everything I can, everything I know, everything to bring you back. To make your America sing back to you. All that's left now, all that remains, is to hear your echo's last receding. . . .

Guess.

In the instant before a clean incision begins to bleed, a pause, like a fallen child reading her mother's eyes for pain.

Guess.

Out of a darkened barn into the light a mosquito's ruby lumbering under the weight of blood drawn from my throat. Like an osprey hooked into a fish too large to raise. I can't let go, can't swim.

Guess.

The wobble of a whetted razor bumping slow across the ridges of the tongue.

The tongue's severed slap against a wetted granite trough.

It's just a game. Guess which, I ask holding out my closed hand to slip the answer in your palm. What have I brought for you, what have I seen? What's true, what's real? Guess for me. Please.

Your eyes welling at last, with too much of everything, hands cupped out before you as though to catch it all, you say to me:

All of it, 'Tonia, it's all real, you don't need me to make it real for you. Can you see?

Night. Humid dark like a large beast breathing. Cicada battery ribs the utter black.

Eyes snap wide. You are not beside me. Or sitting at the window or the doors. Body coated in nightsweat, I look for you. The stillness of a gathering rain. I look for you outside—patios, orchards, garden. Faithless I look for you even in the chapel. Running barefoot silently, desperately back to the room to see if you've come back—blank panic— have you run away without me? Left me? It can't be! *Please.* Tilting wildly out the windows into the cloud-blackened streets—west, south—volcano looming invisibly in the blackness to the east, are you going back home? I can't see anything!

First few drops of rain, bloated spatter against the dusty window ledge. Then a movement on the roof across the courtyard as the sky splits—a flash of lightning trailing sparks, lighting you, sweat-drenched, naked, running in the dark away from me. The roof!—your draftsman's drawings memorized, some walled passage or false ending—some secret way. *How long,* how long have you known, been free up there, how often, free of everything, of me? How many nights?

Núñez is coming TOMORROW.

You could have shown me! I'll make you still! One shout, one scream from me could betray you. Another flash—you stand now, gleaming body arched back like a viol, panting mouth to the sky. I bite my tongue—*bite hard down*—till the taste of iron fills my teeth and my face is slick with salted rain.

And suddenly, more certainly than I have ever known any other thing, I know you will never run up on that roof again.

I wake late. Air mocking bright . . . salt parchment stretched across my eyes.

Today is Sunday.

CODEX:
RENUN-
CIATION

SUNDAY BELLS' INCESSANT TOLLING from across the city. Each hour from the belfry topping the red-tiled dome of Saint Jerome, the chapel bell clangs hollowly from doom's brass throat.

She walks back to the cell, eyes blazing, from seeing Núñez. Once inside she strips to the waist—*in the middle of the day*, I think stupidly. It's the wrong time of day. . . .

I feel it going on and on forever with the whole convent listening, breathlessly . . . how long, how many strokes I can't say.

So in the end the record will be incomplete.

I walk out to the orchards, out to where she would normally be, and begin shearing branches indiscriminately, cropping flowers, plucking leaves.

And now something else is clear to me: I can't stay for this.

The past days' rhythms lie shredded to ribbons all about me. In the deepening dusk I pass by the convent prison—door ajar—just to look, at the cell reserved for me. Prison within a smaller prison, like the blacker shade inside us on the darkest night.

This is where I will end up if I run or if I stay. They expel nuns not slaves. Running away from my rightful owner is petty theft, even if it's theft of me.

 Carlos tries to make me see she's not really submitting to Núñez, she's defying him. But how?—*tell me*. See, Núñez would want moderation, control—he's already created enough *extáticos*. Nothing he despises more in all the world. Losing her to this, and losing her in death are what he really fears. These two threats he cannot walk away from, must answer for: death and rapture. Two grim levers. And she knows how to work them.

Is this supposed to comfort me?

Come away with me, Juanita, come out of here! I can't stay a second longer in this place. This stone boat is sinking—*Juana, please. I won't go down with it.*

Do I dare ask this? Do you know how it feels to watch these years of ours end? To watch him come to you instead? Can't you see how this makes me feel?

Come, Juanita, Carlos would welcome both of us.

But I already know what you'll say to me, if you'll say anything at all—the same words Carlos tells me you used with him twenty-five years ago:

Would you ask me to exchange the nun's vows against the housewife's: enclosure, poverty and chastity for enclosure, silence and servility?[2] *What kind of bargain is this?*

Carlos comes.

Antonia, I was serious about what I said yesterday. I'm not prepared to lose both of you. . . . You—we—have done everything we could. Now we've got to get you out of here.

And leave her alone in this place?

You know better than anyone she's been alone in here for a long time now.

But where would I go?

Of course you'd come to live with me.

The Bishop's whore?

You'll come as a houseservant. There'll be food enough for two. Your duties will be light. No, please, don't misunderstand me. I'm not a carnal man. My demons are not insistent.

Carlos, I don't need promises—the idea doesn't horrify me, you know. But I'm embarassing you. . . . We could keep things simple then, if you want.

We'll have to think on how to get you out. If you were a nun, it would be harder, but as an oblate . . . perhaps it would be enough to find the money to repay your dowry.

Carlos, I thought maybe you already knew. . . .

Knew?

I'm not here as an oblate. Not really.

I'm not sure I follow. . . .

Two days later, I have him meet me at the market, partly to see if he'll actually be seen walking with me through the streets. Only walking beside him today, away from here, do I understand how lonely I have been.

Carlos wants to buy me. He's asking you to sell me to him.

I never told him, 'Tonia. You know that, don't you?

I know. He wants me to come and live with him.

Toñita, sweet friend, Carlos is right, it's time for you to go now. You should have gone a long time ago. . . .

(that, signed with her blood, the Mother Juana Inés de la Cruz made of her faith and her love of God at the time of her abandoning worldly studies in order to proceed, relieved of this encumbrance, along the path of perfection.)

I, Juana Inés de la Cruz, protest for now and for all eternity that I believe in one sole, all-powerful God, Creator of Heaven and Earth and all things; and I believe the most august mystery of the most Holy Trinity, that are three distinct Persons and one true God; that of these three Persons, the second, who is the Divine Word, in order to redeem us, incarnated and made himself man in the virginal womb of Mary, most Saintly, still virgin and Our Lady; and that afterwards He suffered death and crucifixion and arose from among the dead on the third day and now sits at the right hand of God the Father. I believe also that on the final day he must come to judge all men, to reward or punish them according to their deeds. I believe that in the Sacrament of the Eucharist is the true Body of Christ Our Lord; and finally, I believe all that believes and professes the Holy Mother Catholic Church, our mother in whose obedience I wish to die and live without ever failing to obey whatever she may stipulate, giving up my life a thousand times before betraying or doubting anything she may bid us believe; in whose defence I am ready to spill blood and uphold at any risk the holy Faith that I profess, not only believing and adoring it with my heart but also professing it with my mouth at any time and at any cost. . . .

And it grieves me intimately to have offended God, because of who He is and for which I love Him above all things, in whose goodness I find hope that He might pardon my sins by his infinite Mercy, and by the most precious blood that He spilled to redeem us, and by the intercession of his Mother most pure. All of which I offer in repayment of my sins; and prostrate before the divine observances, and in the presence of all the creatures of Heaven and Earth, I submit this new protestation, reiteration and profession of the Holy Faith; and I beg to serve all the most Holy Trinity that It might accept my protest and permit me to fulfil its holy commandments, just as It gave me by its grace the joy of seeing and believing its truths.

JUANA INÉS
DE LA CRUZ

To this effect I reiterate the vow I have already made to believe and defend that the always Virgin Mary Our Lady was conceived without the stain of original sin in the first instant of her most pure being; and in this manner I believe that she herself has greater Grace and to her corresponds more glory than all the angels and saints together . . . and prostrate, heart and soul, in the presence of this divine Lady and of her glorious Spouse, Lord Saint Joseph, and of his most holy parents Joachim and Ana, I humbly implore them to receive me as their slave, and to whom I bind myself for all eternity.

And as a sign of how much I yearn to spill my blood in defense of these truths, I sign with it, this the fifth of March of the year one thousand six hundred and ninety-four.[3]

Phaëthon BOOK SIX

CONTENTS

17th day of February, in the Year of Our Lord 1695
FILLED WITH HOPE I come directly with the news, of Father Núñez's death early this morning. After an operation for cataracts the patient must lie absolutely still in a darkened room, avoiding the slightest strain or worry lest the eyes start oozing blood.

I hurry to bring her word, to be the first to tell her I stayed up all night crouched beneath his window, *whispering your name, Juanita,* so that he died, his ears filled with her, his eyes brimming blood.

After another night of heavy rain, the day dawns so calmly. In the morning chill, I pause at a street corner as a vast flight of swallows pulses overhead, like a liquid, seeping, blotting out the sky with their banking and wheeling—hysteria's emblem in the air.

But by the time I reach the convent of San Jerónimo, my ripe news of Núñez is half-forgotten. The streets are filling with the first whispers. People have gathered outside the convent of Jesús María, and again at the approaches to San Jerónimo—why do we come to the convents first?

The news is of a horrid pestilence that flared up on the coast a few weeks ago then disappeared, smouldering now in the Indian communities of Chalco and Xochimilco. Seemingly overnight, a grim market of tattered awnings and gnarled tent poles has sprouted in the shadow of each convent's walls. Stalls selling amulets to be worn as pendants: walnuts filled with quicksilver. Charms, poseys, and fragments of holy scripture copied out and tightly scrolled, to be placed beneath the tongue. Nosegays of spices and medicinal herbs. My eyes dart everywhere. I take note of everything, to make you explain it all to me. Talismans, crosses, images of Guadalupe. A row of copper palladiums engraved with the number 4. Xylographies in another row—small woodblocks inscribed with pious scenes—to be swallowed whole, the vendor tells me. At the next stall, an old woman sells phylacteries: pouches stuffed with sacred verses, or else the powdered flesh of scorpions, spiders and toads. Seeing my interest, she whispers that during the Black Plague in Italy, Catherine de Medici had her pouch made from the skin of a newborn infant girl. Only as I walk away do I think to ask the cause of death.

GOD'S WAR

A year after concluding his forty-day interrogation of Juana Inés de la Cruz, the Inquisition's chief censor is dead. Sor Juana's secretary, Antonia Mora, tries to persuade her to take up her work again.

At the *portería*, they open the gate for me without a word, as though I had only been away on one of my trips to the market. . . . I have been away a year. It feels like centuries.

As I come down the long corridor, the mood in the *gran patio* is sombre, the figures there strangely seized, like statuary—all across the patio, sisters stand in tense clusters of two or three, as if the muscles of a single torso straining at a block. Many of the faces are familiar.

But upstairs, she is different. After the interrogation, after a year, should I have expected any less? She seems not at all surprised to see me, as if she'd been waiting for me to arrive. Her wide black eyes are grave, and in them the barest flicker of what I choose to see as pleasure to find me standing at the door of her cell. What is it that has changed? I remember that awful inward gaze, the blaze of tremendous energies focussed on the wavering tip of a flame, as though to still it.

You have stilled it. Should I be happy for you?

On the outside, people keep saying she has taken a vow of silence. Others, that after forty days of interrogation she can no longer speak. But the silence came first.

And now as we are discussing the plague she speaks freely to me. What does it mean, doesn't it matter anymore—what has happened? I can no longer restrain myself. "When did you start . . . speaking again?" I ask, feeling cheated. She tells me she never stopped.

"You know what I mean." Now no answer—*is it only me she does this to?*

"Because Núñez is dead, Juana?—or because I've come . . . ?"

I don't really believe this, but give her the opportunity to be cruel to me. The one who abandoned her here.

"No." She says this gently.

She waits for me to press her for more but I know this is all the explanation I will get. It's a relief when she turns away from me those black eyes that see everything. For this one moment I do not have to pretend to be still angry with her. She looks out the window over the rooftops. . . . Her chin is so small—the wimple, I know, is what does this, and makes her neck look so long.

"The Church has known for two weeks. It's been an open secret here, but no one is sure if it's one disease or three. One strain produces buboes. Another they call the Dragon, which can kill in a week or as little as an hour. Those two we knew. But the third may be new here. *La Flojera,* some are calling it. *La Flojera* likes her prey half-digested before she sits down to eat. . . ."

She turns finally to look at me. "Don't think I don't know why you've come."

"Juana—we can start *again*, now that Núñez is dead."

"You didn't expect the news to bring me pleasure."

"You didn't expect me to conceal mine!" Our eyes lock, then in her eyes the shadow of a smile.

"No."

"Carlos says the Archbishop has weakened."

"How is Carlos?"

"He wants to see you. He believes you *could* start again. With the Archbishop's confessor gone. . . ."

"We hear His Grace has ordered the building of an amphitheatre."

"The carpenters have already started."

"In the Plaza del Volador, I imagine."

"Carlos says the Archbishop wants you to write carols for the inauguration."

Finally I have the satisfaction of seeing a glimmer of surprise in her eyes.

The Mother Prioress enters as we're sitting by the window and without even glancing at me begins.

"Sor Juana, I've come to remind you of our understanding. Present circumstances notwithstanding, you are to continue to keep your contact with the others to a strict minimum."

Only now do I notice how the Prioress has been withered by the years. Her watery blue eyes stare out from a net of wrinkles. Liver spots dot the patrician face. Her hands are unsteady, but the voice is firm.

"Over these next days it will be difficult to keep order. Your presence here, now more than ever is an incitement to . . ." She searches a moment for the word, then continues. "If you have recommendations to make, if there are measures to be taken against the contagion, which is in all likelihood already among us, then you will communicate them to me only. We have no need of any heroism from you. It has been hard enough over these past months to reverse the influence you have had here. Your martyrdom would be a calamity for the order and spiritual well-being of this convent. This affliction, as with all things, must pass.

And for the survivors, things will go back to being as they were. I hope I have made myself clear."

Without waiting for an answer, the old wraith turns on her heel and totters dizzily out.

Juana stares after her a long moment. "We'll see how long their good order lasts."

Before very long the news comes from down in the kitchens that Concepción is dead. Dear old friend.

She had just finished making lunch. Feeling a little tired, she had gone to lie down. Vanessa was trying not to disturb her. She reached over her for a jar of flour. It slipped and came crashing to the floor next to that dear, grey head. She did not wake. She will not, again.

It is among us.

I tell Juana I'm staying. She does not argue. There's work to do, I say. She does not argue.

I tell Carlos, who has come to wait for me down in the locutory.

"We've been over all this!"

A flush spreads up from his collar to his cheeks. I know he has allowed himself the hope that she herself might come down. "We lost her a long time ago, Antonia. There's nothing more to do here."

I try to tell him there is, but he does not hear. He tells me they don't need me for this, that suffering is their vocation—what can one more person add but more suffering? More gently he adds, "Anyway nothing can be done. You have not worked in a hospice, no one even pretends to have a cure for *this*. And even if there were you'd still be doing it for her, and she for God knows what—do you think I've nothing better to do than pass my days waiting in the locutories of this *maldito claustro*—for her, now you . . . ?"

His face is flushed. "I thought it was Juana who was always leading me into these little tantrums. . . ." He cocks his head as if scanning the room. He is getting so grey. It makes his brown eyes look even bigger through the thick lenses of his glasses. "Maybe it's something in the air in here."

21st of February

I divide my time between her and attending to the sick. She is ever more frustrated to be confined to her cell. Her questions about what is being done have come to sound like criticism.

I ask Carlos to bring more news so I have something else to tell her about. After a year I thought I'd be grateful for any words from her at all.

In the street tonight beneath her windows and hers alone, the neighbours hold a silent vigil. I recognize a few faces, eerily lit by the upcast shadows—a candle held at the height of each chest. Hollowed eyes, a nose's triangle of shadow across each forehead. The look of silent, haunted carollers.

"Is it the same at the other convents?" she asks, standing at the window.

"They expect the convents to do their suffering for them," I answer. "You taught me that."

23rd of February

Carlos brings word that the Bishop of Puebla has refused to take over as viceroy for the Count de Galve, who has been recalled to Madrid. After demonstrating to everyone his political genius during the grain crisis, after having betrayed his friend Sor Juana Inés de la Cruz and leaving her exposed to her enemies and inquisitors, Santa Cruz claims to have withdrawn from worldly affairs. He must feel he has done enough.

Juana says it's his insane vanity. By retiring now he's punishing all of New Spain for his humiliation at not having been named Archbishop— instead of Aguiar—by universal acclaim.

Carlos comes every day. One of New Spain's most famous men. I know it's as much for me as for her. He endured a lot to let me stay with him. The scandal among his family and colleagues and neighbours—that a woman should leave a convent for a bachelor's house. Even if she was just an oblate and not a nun. At least they didn't know about my past.

He comes in the afternoon and waits in the locutory, waits till end of day then goes away again, to put in another long night working at the hospice. These past few days I've not been able to go down to him for even a moment. Yesterday from her window I watched him walking home, bent into the dusk as though into a stiff wind.

More and more I seek comfort in the learning that seems to allow Carlos and Juana to remain calm while the hysteria simmers down below, in the streets and the convent patios. I tell Carlos about the vigil, he tells me how it is in the city. With no trace of irony New Spain's finest historian says he's glad to be able to perform this small service at least.

After dusk the streets are almost empty. Few want to risk the miasmal airs that rise at night to spread the plague. Many in the surrounding countryside see visions in the pre-dawn skies. Each morning there circulate fresh tales of a flaming sword hanging over the city, dragons, giant black hearses . . .

Fly early, return late, the rich say as their coaches whisk them to lengthy retreats in Cocoyóc, the thermal baths Moctezuma once reserved for his personal use. Carlos describes the melancholy lethargy these flights provoke among onlookers too poor to leave. It echoes on long after each carriage disappears.

"And all the superstitions of Europe," he says in disgust, "are being dusted off now and retailed here. From normally reliable sources I'm hearing fantastic accounts—I hope they're fantasy!—of naked virgins being made to plough furrows around villages in the dead of night. . . .

"Now this talk again of an Indian uprising. Today any fool can see the Indians are too busy dying to threaten anyone."

We are sitting in the locutory. It is the one Juana used to use. There was once a rosewood grille here, but the room is divided now by an iron grate with barely room to slip a book between the bars. Carlos gets up and goes to the window, tall, barred, not much wider than his narrow shoulders. He stands looking into the little strip of garden. I am sure he is thinking of her. With almost anyone else he can be very short-tempered, and is not a little feared. Yet he endured no end of teasing from her in this room. Some of it wounded him, I think, more than he let on. But he told me once he would exchange the Chair of Mathematics for the privilege of her teasing.

"They've started in on the Jews again. I wonder if Juana was right . . . if our fear of them didn't start up again during the first great plagues in Italy. Soon they'll have Jews drinking the blood of Christian babies once again." I know he is speaking to her through me.

Juana listens carefully as I repeat his words.

"They're saying Jews are spreading the sickness to our drinking water."

She says nothing, eyes like coals. I've said this to make her angry. The old game I used to play to get her to speak. What kind of monster does this make me, that I played it then, that I should resort to it now?

25th of February
This morning there are two new red crosses of quarantine in the street below. But these are not the only signs.

Almost everywhere are hastily daubed 4s, and symbols I ask Juana to explain. One is the Greek *tau* wreathed in serpents. Another is an Egyptian trigram representing the *Animus Mundi*, though I am still not sure what this is exactly. Carlos says one of these was found painted in red on the cathedral floor. Juana couldn't say, any more than could he, who might have done it—unless someone from within the Church itself. What did interest her was to learn it took two days for the trigram to be removed from the cathedral.

This and other half-hearted responses to the tide of superstition give us the feeling the authorities are losing conviction, as though they fear God might be revoking the Church's magisterium on earth. It's true, everyone knows it: the Archbishop has lost his nerve, which more than anything feeds the malaise in the streets. This week he has had the fountain in his courtyard stopped, the basin drained. His mind was never stable. Carlos's devotion to him has always hurt and mystified her. I know that he brings news of the Archbishop's unravelling now as a gesture.

I find her sitting the window, gazing absently out. She listens to the latest without turning her eyes from the street. "How His Grace must fear this liquid inquisition, 'Tonia, like a woman's own flesh."

Does the *sound of many waters* trouble him so? Is it *la Flojera*, as Juana believes, that terrifies him? The old fanatic faces now the end of a life spent buying clemency with the charity of others. He has tried to purchase Grace. Now he finds nothing to preserve his body from its corruption. The Archbishop's palace is a fortress—walls thicker than the span of an arm, ceilings three times the height of a man. How it must trouble him now, Juana says, that his palace rests on the ruins of Tezcatlipoca's temple—ancient god of sudden reversals of fortune. The first bishop of Mexico, according to her grandfather, had a Mexica inscription carved above the main palace doors. An inscription since removed: *I leave you to the one whom I have seated on this throne; through him I renew all things.*

She is still thinking of him as, with a little smile, she tells me that to each Mexica god there corresponds a disease. To cure a disease, the healer acts it out, becomes it, in the guise of its god. A theatre of disease.

Old man, act out thine affliction.

Plague crones and plague maidens bring in the sickness. They enter through unlocked windows and unbarred doors. They exit the cracked lips of the dying as a tiny blue flame. They renew themselves each night from the earth herself, in the miasmal breath rising up out of the corruption of her bowels.

The man who spills his seed on the earth exposes himself to mortal danger.

27th of February

From the beginning, the rumours have held a special quality of unstoppable horror. Unnamed villages left without a living soul. Villages gone mad, thresholds and pathways strewn with bloated and blackened bodies. A vulture paradise. Fresh bodies, still warm, still moaning, reduced, by *la Flojera*, to the consistency of stew. They say it has followed the slaves out from Africa.

The War of God, they're calling it.

It should have come on crying panic and calamity. It should have spread like a forest fire roaring disaster. Instead it came quietly, as on the feet of mice.

Bolder at other times
my mind denounced as height of cowardice
yielding the laurels without one attempt
to meet the challenge of the lists.
Then it would seize upon the brave example
set by that famous youth, high-minded
charioteer of the chariot of flame;
then courage would be fired
by his grand and bold, if hapless, impulse,
in which the spirit finds
not, like timidity, a chastening lesson
but a pathway summoning it to dare;
one treading this no punishment can deter
the spirit bent upon a fresh attempt
(I mean a thrust of new ambition).
Neither the nether pantheon—
cerulean tomb of his unhappy ashes–
nor the vengeful lightning bolt,
for all their warnings, ever will convince
the soaring spirit once resolved,
in lofty disregard of living,
to pluck from ruin an everlasting fame.
Rather, that youth is the very type, the model:
a most pernicious instance
(causing wings to sprout for further flights)
of that ambitious mettle,
which, finding in terror itself a spur
to prick up courage,
pieces together the name of glory
from letters spelling endless havoc . . .

JUANA INÉS
DE LA CRUZ

Alan Trueblood, trans.

SACRED
HEART

28th of February

THE PRIORESS takes to her bed with a fever.

The number begins to mount. Within two days the bodies are accumulating faster than they can be buried. Someone has the idea of dragging them into the cellars where it is cooler, but those of us bringing the bodies are more and more horrified by the swelling ranks of corpses in the semi-darkness. It was a terrible mistake to bring them there, compounded now several times a day. Soon no one is willing to go down. With a shudder, averting our faces now, we tip each litter's dead freight and send it thudding down the steps.

Then comes a night of terrible rain, and hailstones as large as fists. In the morning the cellars stand at least ankle-deep in a reeking broth.

4th of March

At mid-day, a minor earthquake, but strong enough to send a crack running up the column across from her cell door, and cause a minute or two of vertigo.

Over the past few years, such tremors seem more like a monthly occurrence. The conjunction of hail and comet and flood and quake should seem to us almost commonplace. Instead we're like children cringing before the next brutal cuff, a blow amplified by our fear.

It is said that in a town in Italy the plague was once averted by rounding up all the beggars, lepers, Jews and sodomites, then locking them in a big barn and setting it alight.

5th of March
Soon we'll all be saved.

In the Plaza del Volador the construction is nearly complete. The Archbishop's amphitheatre will hold twenty-five thousand. One of its chapels is dedicated to San Sebastián and another to San Roque, our intercessors against the plague. Open-air Masses have been ordered at the portals of the city, the five causeways across the half-drained marsh they say was once a lake.

Another order is circulated, that the head of each household must say prayers three times a day at the threshold of his house.

Barefoot processions wend their way through the city, as many as fourteen a day. Flagellants go dressed in sackcloth, nooses about their necks, lofting imprecations to the sky. Sometimes the Archbishop can be seen trudging ever more wearily in the vanguard, violating a health edict against public assembly that he himself helped promote.

In the first week after the outbreak, he was said to be everywhere—saying Masses, launching pilgrims, blessing statues of San Roque, erecting rough crosses carved with the buboes of plague. Few claim to have seen him lately.

At the Archbishop's command a belt of wax is being laid that will encircle the city and be lit as a barrier against the pestilence.

I ask her how any plague could possibly stand against all this.

Faith should be made of sterner stuff, her answer.

Still Juana does not leave her cell.

From passing sisters and especially the novices, reproachful looks rise up to me on the second storey where I stand just inside Juana's doorway. They do not know about the Prioress's orders forbidding her to come out.

8th of March

Nine more bodies to the cellars. Tumbled down the steps through the swelling stench.

Within these walls, the body count rises; without, rumours spread unchecked. Almost every village to the east and south of the capital is said to be burning up with plague.

Like the Archbishop's belt of wax, she says grimly. A firebreak.

10th of March

Violent sensations batter my heart. Before the rage takes over I must write—or I am afraid it will never loosen its hold. I begin with the light that comes into their hopeless faces in the courtyard below as Juana emerges from the seclusion of her cell.

What did I *want?*—in one breath I am begging her not to come out, reminding her of the Prioress's order—yet my heart bursts with pride as she steps past me. In not a single face does there now appear even a glimmer of the usual resentment or scandal at her disobedience.

We stand at the top of the cellar steps. The scene strikes the eye like a vision called Despair. She is afraid, I know, if she does not do this now she will not be able to. I follow her down. I follow only her.

In the cellars, on the slippery stairs, in fluid halfway to our knees, I fight not to add my vomit to the putrid soup we walk through. How I would have fought to withhold my tears if only she had been able to stop hers. I watch them stain the pale fold of cotton she has wound about her face, another around mine. Thin shield against the reek clawing at our heads, searing our eyes.

How can he let this happen to His brides? Fury dims my eyes—is it so dark, can He not see? Can He not feel? This sacred heart of His, why does it not break? This? This is His sacred mystery—*misery?*

That's not what I see. I see bloated bodies swelling in the murk—a jumbled pyramid of meat. At its periphery rat corpses float like bloated little barges. I see this hallowed earth soaked in vomit and blood and pus. Out in the patio as we drag the bodies up, one of us stands guard to drive the carrion birds off—are these your dark attendants, then, that we defend our sisters from? She accepts your silence. *I do not.*

Where has the light gone that once was in their eyes?

No one should ever have to touch what we touched, what our sisters have become. To feel unwilling fingers tearing through skin riven like sodden paper, sinking through the puttied, putrid flesh beneath, finding purchase only at the bone.

What have you done to us?

It's no use. There are no words to express the horror of those hours. There are no tongues for this.

Weeping, sliding, stumbling, we begin dragging the corpses from the cellars up into the light. She needed my strength, her lumbering Amazon. She needed my strength.

When I see how many have rushed to our aid—familiar faces, names for those hours erased—all my resentments for all the years of slights and spites and jealousies just fall away.

After, we stand together in the light . . . slimy, fly-blown, sick with horror. And tonight I swear by all I can still find holy that for a moment I felt, we felt *clean.*

But he did not wash me. His hands never touched me.

 The negroes in the sanitary detail sent by the city had been refusing— even on pain of imprisonment and excommunication, even under the lash—to enter those cellars. And no whip or cane or iron in the world could ever have forced me down there either. But now, out in the open, the bodies can be washed and blessed, taken away for burial.

A mass grave has been dug at the bottom of the orchard in ground greatly esteemed for its flesh-eating properties.

When night fell we rested in the darkness, unable to bear the world by torchlight. And while we rested, more died.

11th of March

I feel Juana jostling me awake at first light. Mind numb from a sleep like death, I still know, even before I open my eyes, yesterday was no nightmare, at least not one I will ever wake from. In every aching joint and muscle burns the memory of yesterday's heartsickening cargo. My back is a column of fire. As Juana's frail form precedes me through the dim passageway, I wonder how she can even walk.

Without a light, we make our way across the convent grounds towards the infirmary. At our approach a low droning fills the space between our footfalls, the space between my indrawn breaths. Just inside the door we pause as our eyes adjust to the room's near darkness. Two torches flicker weakly at the far end of the room. The drone resolves itself into the buzz of bottleflies and the low moaning of two rows of figures twisting in the gloom.

So many varieties of horror still to discover. Suddenly, that today might be worse than yesterday is no longer unthinkable. My pace slows as we make our way up the aisle between the rows. Juana has stopped a few paces short of a robed figure bent low over a bed, while above it, a novice I recognize holds a lantern over a woman's bare torso.

A blade flickers in swift descent to the woman's neck—darkness spurts from a swelling the size of an egg. As the robed figure straightens my blood runs cold—*is it all a nightmare after all?* A giant, beaked bird with glittering eyes turns and comes toward us. I hear a woman's strangled scream—the patient whose neck has been slashed?

Juana grips me by the shoulders.

The robed figure hastily removes the mask to reveal a young man's earnest face. "It takes some getting used to, I know," he begins, then falters as he recognizes who is with me. "Sor Juana? What you *did* yesterday . . . I cannot begin to express my admiration." The mask dangles from one hand like a hunting trophy. "I've been trying for the past two days to get that vile mess cleaned up, but couldn't get a soul . . ."

"There were several of us," Juana says. "Antonia, I imagine you've met our new chaplain, Father Medina?" By the way she says this I know she approves of him. The little gesture of an introduction amid the mounting misery makes me want to cry. I don't trust myself to speak.

"Our chaplain, as you see, is wearing the very latest in Italian fashion."

With a trace of embarrassment, he starts to explain. "Antonia, yes?— the robes here are of a waxed linen," he says, holding up the hem. "Quartz eyepieces. . . . The beak is stuffed with spices, to counteract the plague's miasmas."

"What they *may* counter," Juana puts in, "are the smells. Our next task should be to set out braziers to incense these rooms."

 As the ill come in ever faster, Juana brings me to a grim appreciation of the chaplain's system for clustering the sick according to their symptoms. Those with only fever are held apart in case their illness is not plague at all. Those with buboes, who are the most numerous and the slowest to die, are brought to the main hall. If the swellings can be brought to suppurate within a week, some of these patients may yet live, though their hearts will be seriously weakened, the doctor explains.

"As will all ours be," Juana says gently.

Those in the clutches of the Dragon or *la Flojera* are confined together in the room nearest the chapel. Neither group lives long enough to catch the other's disease. And no one survives. The doctor almost never enters here to face his never-ending defeat, undisguised.[1]

> . . . so that they might concoct a healthful brew—
> final goal of Apollonian science—
> a marvellous counterpoison,
> for thus at times from evil good arises . . . [2]

12th of March
Today amid all the torment and darkness I am happy to be at your side, to do this simple, hopeless work. Our years together have come down to this. We will end here.

So little we can do to stem this sea of suffering. The kind chaplain's treatments are not just inadequate but seem almost to substitute one sort of suffering for another: man's for God's. Purges. Cauterizations. Emetics to induce still more vomiting, blood-letting to further swell the tide of blood, caustic vesicants to further blister the patient's blotched and burning skin, treacles of herbs to bring the buboes beneath to suppurate. Pain as an antidote for pain.

Still, the chaplain's energy and scientific presence bring comfort to the women who lie dying all around us.

Juana and I discover the finest treatment of all: cool water trickled across blackened lips and furrowed brows.

15th of March

Of the priests still courageous enough to stay among us, one spends most of his time among the victims of *el Dragón* and *la Flojera*, administering last rites.

I admire this bald little man for his gentle cheer. That he still finds the strength at times to smile. Sometimes I hold a lantern for him and listen to last confessions gasped over blackened tongues, feel shadowy pulse-beats at the neck or wrist flutter and still. I have seen him weep.

I never learned his name.

17th of March

Under Juana's supervision a few of us feed the braziers with spices, recharge the lamps, fetch water, tend the fires beneath great vats simmering in the courtyard.

The dead we lift by the corners of the sheet she died upon. We have neither the strength nor sufficient hands any longer to dress the dead nuns in their bridal costumes and shroud. But on each nun's head we still place the crown of wildflowers she wore at her profession. From the grave in the orchard, the sheets come back to be placed in one vat for boiling. From another, boiling water is drawn and the empty bed and floor beneath it are swabbed with lime.

To this work there appears no end.

Juana can be seen now all over the convent, among the nuns and servants equally. Lancing buboes with a skill she learned in dissections, applying hot and cool compresses, bathing the bodies of the dead.

Comforting the dying is the hardest thing of all, smoothing their tortured brows. As death approaches, she's the one they ask for. Most often it falls to her to signal to a priest and assist him in the ceremony I've come to detest.

My daughters, on your knees, pray to Our Lord God so that He may extend His mercy and His Grace to this sick woman, while I, His servant, give to her the unction of the holy sacrament.

Taking the oil from Juana's hands, the priest approaches the dying sister and anoints her, tracing the sign of the cross, first over the eyes—*close them, I bid thee*—then over the ears—*unstop them*—over the nostrils—*draw breath*—across the mouth—*seal it*—across the hands—*open them*—along the shoulders—*lay them bare*.

And so Christ's brides arrive before Him, attentive, mute, blinded, barechested. Open-handed.

20th of March, Spring
In one room they die spread-eagled in agony, in the other they go quietly and quickly, blood rushing from their faces and secret openings. For many it begins with the mockery of a knotting pain low in the belly and the groin. What a black brood they are about to deliver.

Excruciating headaches, flashes of intense heat and chills. For some, the sudden gush of nosebleeds, a thin bloody fluid leaking from the eyes and ears. For most, the sinister rashes we call poseys, the wracking convulsions, the dry, black tongues. And the blood—vomiting blood, coughing blood, voiding bloody clay.

And the worse this madness gets, the harder it is to remember their names. They have names. We have names our fathers gave us. We have the names our mothers used.

We have names.

Tomasina, María, Asunción, Araceli, Candelaria, Concepción . . .

 More terrible even than the agony is the confusion in their faces.

The horror, the prostration too, but worst is this anxious confusion. Their eyes glow with the purest humanity we see in the face of a suffering beast.

Who will explain this mystery? Will He? Will I? Will she?

28th of March
The second priest comes to the infirmary only when sent for. Father Landa. Yet at least he comes, unlike so many others. I try to remind myself of this to lessen my dislike of him, to not see the shadow of gloating in his fat, clean-shaven face. With such a beard he must have to shave twice a day. But how can that be—when is there time, and where . . . ?

It is late evening. I see him on a stool next to a cot, rounded shoulders hunched over the Bible in his lap, rocking strangely. I draw near, though I am reluctant to. Over the prone figure before him, he is reciting something. It sounds like Revelations:

And the Harlot of Nineveh was drunk on the blood of saints and martyrs. So He poured His hatred into the vessels of his judgement: that the horns of the beast should score her vitals, should eat her flesh and burn her with fire . . .

Can this really be Revelations? He isn't even *reading*.

He sent seven angels to pour out the vials of his wrath upon the earth, which broke out in grievous sores, and on the sea, the rivers and fountains, which ran blood, and into the darkness where they gnawed their tongues for pain—

He's making this up. It isn't like this—

And He tracked the dragon through the wilderness, where she hid from him in the swamps. He drove his sickle into the foetid earth and twisted, delivering her of the child she harboured there—

"Are you trying to frighten her to death?" I cry grasping at his shoulder, glaring into his mad eyes. "Get away from her!—Juana!"

She hurries over. The small, neat form beneath him is cool and lifeless. She's been dead an hour. Thank God, I murmur.

Vanessa . . .

This face we know. This name I have no trouble remembering. Vanessa.

I will remember your bright eyes, your graces, your body: small and slender and strong. Your mastery in the kitchens, Juanita's birthday party . . . I will remember.

I feel Juana's arms encircle me.

The next day, the little bald priest comes to tell us our fat Father Landa has been called away to duties at some monastery or other.

Our little priest, the one for whom I have no name, turns back to his work. I see a glint of satisfaction in his kind eyes.

2nd of April

Although the Dragon is more terrible, *la Flojera* more horrifying, it is the buboes I come to loathe. The very word . . . knotting first into clusters like tiny garlic heads, then swelling flower bulbs, then, ripe and soft and seedy. Huge, rotting figs.

Many of the corpses awaiting burial are so blackened that all distinctions of race are now erased. And so we go forth, hand in hand, equal before our God, waiting on His grace.

I find Juana in the infirmary, holding an old woman's hand. Her *name* . . . her name is . . . Ana.

The end approaching, Ana turns her face to Juana, a question in her eyes, in her face a century. "Is there something I can bring for you, Mother?" Juana asks anxiously. "Is there something you need?"

"No, daughter. Only to die."

A minute or two later, the Prioress comes, roused from her own sickbed by the news of Ana's dying. Ana is the convent's most ancient nun, an old woman already when the Prioress first took her vows.

For a moment, Juana and the Prioress sit side by side. A moment of grace.

3rd of April

Juana tells me she too is losing the power to discriminate. At times the droning of a fly seems as loud as a scream, as terrible as a death rattle.

Sometimes, she says, I can think of no words as beautiful as *agua* . . . *gracias*.

5th of April

Carlos no longer comes every day, but when he can. His own hospice is filled to overflowing. With what time he has, he is experimenting with an idea Juana once had many years ago for making ice. To bring comfort to those with fevers. He has mounted a series of fans on a drum over shallow pans of water. If the rate of evaporation could be increased sufficiently . . . but he lacks the strength to turn the drum with enough speed. Perhaps something could be done with gears, he asks, beside a swift stream? Juana sends me back with the idea of driving the drum with steam. She tries to explain the mechanism to me, but I cannot follow.

6th of April

The chaplain has been urging the Prioress to permit that the corpses themselves be burned. Most of the bodies reach a sickening state of decomposition within hours, and there is little ground left in which to bury them. Juana agrees. But the Prioress cannot bring herself to issue the order.

"Burial in this convent's consecrated ground . . ." Mother Andrea de la Encarnación draws herself up and squarely faces him. Despite the strain in her face, her voice is calm. "This is not just a nun's most fervent dream, young man, it is her sacred *right*."

7th of April

A pause amid the carnage. Seeing the surgeon's young face filled with exhaustion and dismay, Juana teases him into a debate on disease transmission, a conversation he soon engages in with great absorption. Plague atoms, the reigning view, versus her champion Kircher's theory: living infective corpuscles he claims to have seen through a microscope in his laboratory in Rome.

"The waxing of our chaplain's linen, Antonia," she says turning to me, "is thought to keep the plague atom from attaching itself. A very sticky sort of atom, it seems. In my view, Doctor, the only thing those robes will keep out is fleas. . . ."

In a moment they will forget I'm even here.

We are sitting outside the infirmary toward the end of day. She and the surgeon had been discussing the possibility of laying the most feverish patients in a shallow water pan. But before he leaves they agree there are too many ill, too few hands.

A year ago I would have clung to my anger that she should speak so freely with the surgeon and have so little to say to me. But for the past quarter hour she has been talking swiftly, intently, only to me. And yet these stories of her childhood, which I would have been overjoyed to hear a year ago, I am suddenly afraid of.

" . . . I remember it so clearly, the day we arrived. There was such a light . . . Branches hung low over the road and the sun was setting red in the hollow beneath them. The *campesinos* were unloading the mule carts.

"How we loved the trees, Amanda and I. Once we spent a whole morning planting pines . . . in a churchyard—yes, *in Chimalhuacan*. I remember. How tall are they now, I wonder. . . ?"

Juana turns to me to explain, but I know who Amanda is. She has told me before, though only once. Has she forgotten this?

Here in the courtyard tonight the light is so soft. We could almost forget what is going on inside. We sit on a stone bench at the edge of the orchard. Her face is pale, her round black eyes are lustrous with that intensity that still sometimes startles even those of us who think we are used to it. Her wimple is pulled back. Her black hair has grown back thick and straight, and above where it tucks under her robes, flares out like a satin cowl, framing her face.

 At dawn from the colonnade above the courtyard I stare into the eastern sky. White smoke from Popocatepetl, though the mountain itself I cannot see. Is the entire world and heaven too now ablaze? Has your hero's bright chariot run wild, Juana, drying up the lakes and seas, scorching even heaven?

What was it in her stories yesterday that troubles me? Stone lovers cursed, demonic serpent children haunting mountain meadows, a lost tribe disappearing after the Conquest into an underworld, over whose entrance sits the smoking mountain . . .

The mountain is in each one.

I remember something in a poem. Evading another day of horror before me, I grasp at this glimmering . . . this sweet release of verse.

A poem of hers—the only one, she claimed, that ever really mattered to her. *First Dream.* I go to its hiding place in the archives, deserted these past weeks. I return to the cell with it, light a candle, find the passage.

> . . . Of a mountain next to which that very Atlas,
> which like a giant dominates all others,
> becomes a mere obedient dwarf . . .
> . . . of the loftiest volcano that from earth,
> a rearing giant, goads high heaven to war . . . [3]

I read page after page of these lines, the rhymes, the visions always too difficult for me to do anything but marvel at—and that in this prophetic Dream of hers she has seen so clearly, even down to the counterpoisons we have used against the plague. And suddenly I know why I am frightened by her stories. One after another with hardly a pause between. Not just that they should tumble out after almost two years of silence. It's how they come. They ramble. She has never been unclear in her life.

It is time to return to work.

I wake her.

8th of April

Some of the sisters have gone mad. Three run wildly about. I can barely bring myself to write. One stands outside the infirmary screaming in answer to each scream she hears inside. No one bothers to quiet her, what is one more scream?

The last shred of convent discipline unravels now, the vow of enclosure. Men everywhere coming and going. Here now in a convent, here in our dying, most know more easy freedom with men than ever while they lived. At last I have this to share with them.

And even as we still live, the last differences between us fall away. Old and young, poor and rich, learned and ignorant, sensuous and ascetic, talkative and silent. All engaged now in an unceasing inner dialogue of questions and silences. Look at these faces.

What have You done to their beauty?

If I could be granted the power to accomplish one thing, in this final hour, one single wish—O pardon me my wistfulness—*I would restore to them their beauty*. I would have them see themselves, some now for the first time ever in her life, as simply . . . beautiful.

Who dares call this a lie? This beauty of girls.

Does He—is our Eternal Author well satisfied with His creation now? With the grace of His loving union. . . .

> . . . utmost perfection of creation,
> utmost delight of its Eternal Author,
> with whom well pleased, well satisfied,
> His immense magnificence took His rest;
> creature of portentous fashioning
> who may stretch proud arms to heaven
> yet suffers the sealing of his mouth with dust;
> whose mysterious image might be found
> in the sacred vision seen in Patmos

by the evangelic eagle, that strange vision
which trod the stars and soil with equal step;
or else in that looming statue
with sumptuous lofty brow
made of the most prized metal,
who took his stance on flimsy feet
made of the material least regarded,
and subject to collapse at the slightest shudder.
In short, I speak of man, the greatest wonder
the human mind can ponder,
complete compendium
resembling angel, plant, and beast alike . . . 4

9th of April

A wind has been clawing all night at the shutters. In the morning I wake to a sky swept clean of smoke.

Late morning. "I shouldn't say this," the chaplain offers, "but there were only two new cases last night. With God's help, we may have this thing beaten."

"A few more victories like this . . ." Juana murmurs.

"And we're finished. Yes, Sor Juana, I know."

11th of April

It should have come in like a hurricane, smashing everything in its path. Instead it begins with a rash at her neck, a little cat's paw.

A mark I took no notice of. My mind would not open. All day long the thought of her marred throat I managed to escape, but not the foreboding.

One day soon now, someone will say that the marks on your body traced exactly the contours of the lake of Chalco. . . .

Thirteen hours we work without stopping, fed on green delusions and false hopes. Night finds us still in the main hall of the infirmary, sitting on stools, slumped against a grimy wall. A strange light in her eyes, face flushed, Juana begins telling another story. A picnic beside a spring high up on the WhiteLady. Cold *tamales con rajas*.

"I remember a cream made from honey, the women used to sell. We'd spread it all over our bodies by the hot spring. Remember, Amanda?" Her eyes are very bright and full as I look deeply into them and blush.

"All the wasps . . . ? How we stood naked, letting them land—then jumped into the brook to keep from getting stung! What is it, Antonia, what's wrong?"

"You called me Amanda just now."

The lantern guttering, rain falling into the hush beyond the windows, she starts to tell me about a sorcerer. A jaguar, whose friend is a bishop, or an Inquisitor. I wonder if it is a children's story. No, a story important to her grandfather, a story told to her the night he died. She wants me to take it down. He knows a bookbinder who conceals manuscripts by binding them into Bibles. Who does? *Carlos.* Write it?—write what, write which? She wants me to have Carlos bind it secretly under the cover of a Bible. It is a story that cannot be lost.

And so I write, but as usual only half understand what I am copying down. Other things I do not understand at all. Lies, false gods, twins of gods. Night, two prisons, three escapes. A jaguar vanishing, Night. The fulfilment of a prophecy—or else its reversal . . . a wheel, or a spiral . . . I cannot make it out, I copy it down. *Gaps will not be tolerated,* she says. Why does she say this to me? Do I not always *try?*

So I write it, to have it bound under the covers of Bibles. Gaps will not be tolerated, gaps must be filled. Under the covers of Bibles, between their contents and their covers. Her brow is damp, her smile strange. What did she mean? Juana, I don't understand. I write it anyway. Her copyist, her parrot. I write to fill the silences, between each breath. I write to save my own life.

Ever since I was little . . . the last honest man . . . the last sorcerer was . . .
Who?
We had the most wonderful time.
She is asleep.

I write this and feel my heart swelling within me, a grotesque thing that will no longer sit in my chest—sits *on* it, crushing the breath out of me.

> This dismal intermittent dirge
> of the fearful shadowy band
> insisted on attention less
> than it coaxed a listener asleep . . .

> . . . while Night, an index finger
> sealing her two dark lips—

silent Harpocrates—enjoined
silence on all things living . . . 5

. . . All was now bound in sleep,
all by silence occupied.
Even the thief was slumbering,
even the lover had closed his eyes . . .

Darkness. Silence. It is the middle of the night. Green hopes withered on the vine, I hold her head to my breast as she sleeps her restless sleep, full of dreams.

In the morning word flies through the streets that Sor Juana has fallen ill.

Several times that day, the Archbishop sends men to report back to him on her condition. On the advances in God's War on the children of the earth.

12th of April, 1695

BY FIRST LIGHT I KNOW: three days, five at most. We know the symptoms too well to waste a lie. She will not leave this cell again alive.

LAST
DREAM

Carlos demands to see her. With so many people coming and going now, I know he can get in if he insists.

"Antonia, please," she gasps, looking up at me, wide-eyed, "don't let him see me like this."

It should have come down like a comet, crying disaster, setting all the temples ablaze, like a sun summoned in the blackest night.

Instead it came quietly as on the feet of mice.

"Remember, NibbleTooth . . . ? Walking up towards the mountain, up through the pines . . ." She stops, shuddering with cold. The sheets and blankets are damp. She clutches at my arm as I turn to go for fresh bedding. "Antonia . . . ?" She makes an effort to concentrate.

"Find Amanda for me." Her teeth are chattering. "Ask Carlos if he will do this for me."

"But she's in a delirium half the time!"

"She knows what she's asking, Carlos."

"She is just sending me away. You just finished saying she doesn't want me to see—"

"She said you'd understand what this means to her."

"What if when I get back . . ."

"With a good horse you can be there and back in two, two and a half days." The coldness of the calculation shocks me. "There's still time."

"He agreed to go, even knowing . . . ?"

"Yes, he knew."

"When he returns, will you ask him one more favour?"

"Oh, Juanita . . ." *He would do anything for you.*

"It will keep his mind occupied."

She tells me what it is. Yes, it will keep his mind occupied.

So tell me, Juana, about Nyctimene, this daughter of Lesbos—*shame-faced Nyctimene who keeps watch by chinks in the sacred portals.* . . . What last role would you choose for me: to desecrate the holy lamps, or top them up that no one die in darkness?

But it's too late to ask you this.

13th of April
I will not record any more symptoms. There are lies and slanders even I will not record.

Flashes of her old self, her clearness and irony. Like when she asks to be cremated so as not to have to lie next to Concepción and listen to her gossip for all eternity.

Just now as she opens her eyes I have the unreal sensation, almost of luxury, that she's just woken up from sleeping late. *We never once had the chance to sleep in, you and I.*

I reach for anger, anger is the safest. How can she make *jokes*?

"The question is not when but how. We are all dying, 'Tonia. How would you have had me go—breaking my neck slipping on the stairs? No, it is better to make a little comedy than die in one."

The sisters too begin to keep a record. A kind of recipe book. All now compete for miracles. To build a case for her beatification.

Did you see how the touch of her fingers healed sister Elena's sores?

Yes and as she kissed one of the slaves on the forehead I saw the pestilence leave the woman's lips like a blue flame. Sor Juana had no fear for herself. . . .

They are half expecting the plague to lift when you die. And I cannot rouse myself to anger. Any day now someone will claim to have seen your breasts running with milk.

I pore over—pour through this, her great book of dreaming. I try to meet her in dreams, to follow her through mine. To make her see me again, where the light is clean, where there is no smoke, no cloud, no sun.

> The body in unbroken calm,
> a corpse with soul,
> is dead to living, living to the dead,
> the human clock attesting

by faintest signs of life
its vital wound-up state,
wound not by hand but by arterial concert:
by throbbings which give tiny measured signs
of its well-regulated movement . . . [6]

I wake startled, overcome with fear. In the darkness my fingertips find
the faintest throbbing at your throat.

I sleep.

14th of April
Today a letter. A nobleman from Perú has written that he would like to
come here, to make a life near her. A wealthy gentleman. He offers everything he has, without conditions, only that she might have the freedom
to write whatever she wishes, whenever it pleases her.

More dreams, day and night, hers and mine. The cell is awash in dreams.
It is all we have left to talk about. She tells me hers, still asks to hear mine.

I will not let anyone in. They bring fresh blankets, soup, oranges . . .
and leave them at the door.

In a confused muttering she speaks to me of guilt—all the things and
people sacrificed to feed her mind. Her hungers, her shame . . . something about a river, a face, or a hot spring called the Face. I cannot make
it out.

What storm-tossed end would you have chosen for yourself, Juana, what
tempest of the mind and soul?

> . . . against her will was forced
> to run ashore on the beach
> of the vast sea of knowing,
> with rudder broken, yardarms snapped,
> kissing each grain of sand
> with every splinter . . .

I check on her. Her eyes are open. For a moment I . . .

"I had a dream, Antonia . . ." She pauses, closes her eyes, and after a
breath opens them again. "There was a mountain spouting glyphs of smoke,

ancient signs. An old dream of mine," she says forcing her cracked lips into a smile. "Good that it should visit me once more. Your . . . turn . . . now."

I'm not sure she even hears me. I have to speak loudly now. Her ears are leaking fluid. I shouldn't write this, but I can't help it. There is nothing else.

> . . . no rapid surging flight could ever reach
> of eagle soaring to the very heavens,
> drinking in sunbeams and aspiring
> to build her nest amidst the sun's own lights,
> however hard she presses upward
> with great flappings of her feathered sails
> or combings of the air
> with open talons, as she strives,
> fashioning ladders out of atoms,
> to pierce the inviolate precincts of the peak . . .

It is not darkness she strives against but light, an all-conquering light.

"I was flying again," she murmurs weakly. "Before me the mountain . . . the sun at night. All human history stretched below, since before the Flood. . . . How we cling, each to our life." Her laugh is a gasp. "So real it seems, our little bit of clay. How stubborn we are."

She wakes, sleeps. One minute, two. She wakes, pauses an instant to swallow painfully.

"Just now, 'Tonia . . . I dreamt the whole of human history. From the first dawn down to our last day, last hour. How long have I been asleep—Antonia, are you there?

"How long would a dream of all eternity last?"

I watch her slip back into her dream of the sun at night, blood streaming from her eyes.

> At this almost limitless elevation,
> jubilant but perplexed,
> perplexed yet full of pride,
> and astonished although proud,
> the sovereign queen of the sublunary world

let the probing gaze, by lenses unencumbered,
of her beautiful intellectual eyes . . .

. . . .

The eyes were far less quick
to reel, contrite, from their bold purpose.
Instead, they overreached and tried
in vain to prove themselves
against an object which in excellence exceeds
all visual lines—
against the sun, I mean, the shining body
whose rays impose a punishment of fire . . .

How could it have taken me so long to see that she was going blind?

The plague has broken. Or having eaten its fill, has gone away to sleep.
It is only hunger wakes the dreamer.

16th of April, 1695
The day dawns bright, mocking us with its orderly distribution of the
gifts of light. There will be but one death today.

I can no longer keep her to myself. Fresh bedding, the braziers
charged with spices. . . . By late afternoon I've done what I can to scrub
the walls clean of their rust-red streaks, like a child's fingers run mad
with paint. In this stained nursery I am about to go insane. She has just
asked if the day is clear, if I can see the volcanoes. She has forgotten that
the new cell faces west, not east. I tell her yes. She asks about the flowers
blossoming in the trees.

The survivors gather about the bed. Someone asks if anyone smells
it, yes they all smell tangerines. . . . Is it only my own lies that can be
beautiful?

The Prioress comes in, unsteady, hesitant. I can see it in her face. This
final irony cuts even her, deeply: that the Archbishop has asked to see
you, has asked that you leave the convent for your protection. Or his.

The faintest hint of a smile caresses your dark lips. "Last night . . . just
now. I had the most beautiful dream." Your voice is a faint whisper. I bend
low and struggle to fill in the words. You feel my breath on your cheek,
the drop of a tear. "Ahh, Antonia, it's you. How good . . ."

Your eyes try to find me. "All my life I have been falling back to earth.

I would not look down, would not see. But hovering over me . . ." She tries to swallow, shakes her head slightly as I try to press a *cántaro* of water to her lips. ". . . broken on the earth I looked up to the face of Ammon. *This bright dream. . . .*"

"What did she say?" the Prioress asks. I do not answer. "I heard her say something," she demands, reddening.

"You must have heard her say Amen, Mother."

To be a liar can sometimes be a mercy.

At the end, in your beautiful blind eyes I saw a faint light turning in . . . as if to sleep. The light I'd first seen last night. As though in a dream, I watched the Phoenix leave her nest of burning spices and take flight. . . .

How long does the dream of all eternity last.

It should have come howling riot, crying havoc, on the thousand voices of the flood. Instead the end came quietly, as on the feet of mice.

Sor Juana Inés de la Cruz died an hour before the dawn, April seventeenth, in the year sixteen ninety-five.

IT SHOULD HAVE COME rising up, like the foul earth splitting, groaning chaos and ruin. Instead your death came quietly. To me.

Before the day was out, before the eyes had dried, the Archbishop came in person, to confiscate her savings from the convent accounts. I pitied the Prioress, then. She fought him like a lion.

I have asked to wash her body in the fountain. I have asked their permission, and they have not yet denied me.

I have asked your sisters leave to come down among them, though I have done nothing to earn their friendship, I know. I will take you to where the survivors are gathered murmuring down below. Let me be your Camilla once more.

Ahh, Juanita, how easily you lift.

See, see how light. I am not so strong. Will they give me leave to carry you down? Though I know it is dangerous . . . though the chapel is stacked with these like cordwood, who once floated in the cellars. Who once breathed with us.

And if the answer is yes, I will take you to the fountain's edge, under the trees and the black wedges wheeling in the smoke. And beneath the sun's dull glare, I will ask them if this is the woman they remember. Remember her—remember you? In the orchards and the classrooms, in the chapel and the choir. Do they remember you that day, striding through a pouring waterspout—just to make us laugh? Do you remember her, as I do? I will ask.

Then I will make our sisters listen.

Will you all give me leave to speak, to ask something difficult of you?

You all have pity, I will say to them, if you but look for it. This, no one can take away, it must be relinquished willingly.

You loved her too.

But the fathers and the doctors will tell us she was impudent. They must be right, it must be true. Seventeen centuries must make it so. She defied an imperium of light.

I may say her death was unjust. But I will confess before you that I wanted a saint too, if of a different kind, and I lied to make her one.

I killed her too.

And now that I have bathed her body and shown it to you, confessed to you my capital crime, I ask you finally: how then do you find her? *How do you find?*

These are only words, and lack the power to stir your hearts. But our souls—may they only speak when spoken to? For Grace, must we only stand and wait?

 Carlos arrives after nightfall. He has found Amanda's village, on the other side of the pass. But she had left the mountain thirty years ago. "The same year Juana came to the capital—she *must* have known. Even now she makes a fool of me!"

I know he does not mean this.

"She asked, Carlos, if you would deliver the eulogy."

His lean, weary face is stricken. I am sorry to have taken his anger from him. We cling to each other like children.

After a while he goes on. "The mother is dead now. She returned to the village a few years ago. Amanda, no one is sure about. Some say people have seen her in the South. Oaxaca or San Cristóbal, or even farther. . . . It's all I have. And this."

From a cloth bag, he takes a bundle of leather, sodden and stained, and begins to unwrap its layers of canvas and oilcloth, as though peeling a fruit, or unwrapping a jewel. And it is like a jewel, that which he holds up to me, luminous and bright, the size of an avocado pit.

He has brought down ice.

"Yesterday," he says, his face still streaked with road dust, "I could barely carry it."

I turn it in my hand. He sits quietly watching.

For an hour after he is gone, I run this cold jewel over her forehead, along her temples, across her lips. I know it cannot help, I know I cannot help it. So slowly now it melts.

 You would have made Him speak. In the silence of the night at the bottom of the sea, drowning in the suffocating sufficiency of His grace, you dreamt of calling to the sun . . . calling him to answer!

And you called this dream cowardice.

Do not leave me with this work, Juana. He will not answer.

Do not leave me. He will not answer for His work.

Don't leave.

18th day of April, 1695

There is a vault where the flowered crowns are kept. It is entered only for
a death. Inside, it is cool and dry. In the months of rain the walls are lined
with sacks of rice to absorb whatever humidity they can. Two hundred
bridal crowns from the day of vows. Once . . . Forty now. The scent of
ancient wildflowers is indescribable. I did not want to come, I never want
to leave.

The Prioress has walked me here. She lets me walk back alone now
with the crown.

As for the fountain, it is too dangerous. But I may have as much water
brought up as I need.

Carlos tells me I am exhausted. I do not feel it. I ask him about the bookbinder. Yes, he will ask him, he will try. But even the sacrilegious, he says,
have little appetite for sacrilege these days.

He tells me to rest a while and take some food. Tomorrow will be the
most difficult, the funeral in the morning, the interment that afternoon.
But there is one thing left to do, one last duty to perform.

I have cleared the room to do this work. And into the middle of this
empty cell I have dragged the desk where once you wrote and I have laid
you out upon it.

I will return your body to you. I defy them to deny me this. I will
restore you to your beauty.

How much water do I need for this?

I cloak your shoulders, replace your veil, fold your fingers against your
empty palms. Cradle out these cool entrails with my own hard hands,
pack your cavities with balm. And lift up your vitals in my hands and
spread them through the sky, like ribbons.

Carlos comes afterwards, to tell me what was said. They should have
come by the thousands, tearing their hair and rending their cloaks . . .
and in truth the ceremony was a splendid one. Though many did not
come.

But Carlos was there. He rose and came to stand before them. His
closing phrases I record:

There is no pen that can rise to the eminence that hers o'ertops. I should like to omit the esteem in which I regarded her, the veneration which she has won by her works, in order to make manifest to the world how much, in the encyclopaedic nature of her intelligence and universality of her letters, was contained in her genius, so that it may be seen that, in one single person, Mexico enjoyed what, in past centuries, the graces imparted to all the learned women who remain the great marvels of history. The name and fame of Sor Juana Inés de la Cruz will only end with the world. . . .

 There is a bird, born in Heliopolis, from a nest of burning spices, who lives but once every few hundred years. She is forged from fire in silence. She is the sun of night. To the first fire, does the firebird return. To the sun's first city, to Heliopolis.

And if you have a little time, together we will take her out across the plains and over the tortured hills, up through pines like bearded giants, where in the cold air her voice echoes still. Up and up across the snowy slopes to the cone's smoking brim.

I will make her long lived. I will make her live three hundred years. I will deliver her. From you, to you.

Here. I place the crown of wildflowers on her brow. There, now we start.

This ceremony begins with the heart.

In recognition of the inimitable plumes of Europe,
whose praise has so increased my work's worth

JUANA INÉS
DE LA CRUZ

　　When, divine Spirits,
gentlest Swans, when
did my carelessness
merit your cares?
　　Whence, to me, such elegies?
Whence, on me, such encomiums?
Can distance by so very much
have enhanced my likeness?
　　Of what stature have you made me?
What Colossus forged,
that so ignores the height
of the original it dwarfs?
　　I am not she whom you glimpsed in
the distance; rather you have given
me another self through your pens,
through your lips, another's breath.
　　And abstracted from myself,
among your quills, I err,
not as I am, but in her—
the one you sought to conjure. . . .

TIMELINE

1321	Dante's *The Divine Comedy* is written not in Latin but in an Italian dialect.
1325	The Aztec capital, Tenochtitlán, is founded on the site of present-day Mexico City.
1428*	The Aztec poet-emperor Nezahualcóyotl creates the Council of Music, for the study of art, astronomy, medicine, literature and history.
1440	Cosimo de Medici founds the Florentine Academy, for the study of antiquity and the patronage of the arts and sciences.
1478	Ferdinand and Isabela receive papal approval to establish the Spanish Inquisition.
1492	Columbus discovers India somewhere near the Bahamas.
1517	Bartolomeo de las Casas, first Spanish priest ordained in the New World, begins a campaign against the oppression of the American Indians.
1519	Cortés lands on the shores of the Aztec empire.
1520	A guest of the Aztec Emperor, Hernán Cortés takes his host prisoner.
1521	The Aztec capital is sacked after a siege and naval blockade.
1532	A guest of the Inca Emperor, Francisco Pizarro takes his host prisoner.
1543	In Mexico, the apostolic Inquisitor Juan de Zumárraga is relieved of his position, for excess of zeal.
1571	The Spanish conquest of the Philippines is consolidated; Spain is a dominant power on four continents.
1577	Catholic mystic and poet John of the Cross is imprisoned in Toledo, Spain; composes *Dark Night of the Soul* subsequent to his escape.
1583	Examined at length by the Inquisition, *The Interior Castle* by Saint Teresa of Ávila is published following her death.
1588	First performance of Christopher Marlowe's *Dr. Faustus*.
1588	The Spanish Armada is destroyed off the English coast.
1589*	The grandfather of Sor Juana Inés de la Cruz is born in Andalusía, Spain.
1600	Philosopher Giordano Bruno, author of *On the Infinite Universe and Worlds*, dies at the stake in Rome following an eight-year trial.
1600	Shakespeare writes *Julius Caesar* and *Hamlet*.
1615	Cervantes completes *Don Quixote*.
1618	Start of Thirty Years' War.
1624*	Sor Juana's grandfather leaves for the New World.
1630	Spanish playwright Tirso de Molina creates the character of Don Juan in *The Libertine of Seville and the Stone Guest*.
1633	The Holy Office of the Inquisition begins the trial of Galileo.
1634	An affair involving Cardinal Richelieu of France, the Ursuline convent of Loudun, demonic possession of nuns, priestly satyriasis and exorcisms, culminates in Pastor Urbain Grandier's being burned alive at the stake.

1648 Sor Juana is born Juana Inés Ramírez de Santillana y Asbaje in a mountain village near Mexico City.

1648 End of Thirty Years' War.

1649 Massive *auto de fe* conducted by the Inquisition in Mexico City.

1650 René Descartes dies at the palace of Queen Christina in Sweden.

1659 In Spain, the painter Velázquez is made Knight of the Order of Santiago.

1660 Peace of the Pyrenees: Louis XIV of France marries María Teresa, daughter of Spanish King Philip IV.

1661 Hunchbacked, mentally deficient Carlos, future King of Spain, is born to Philip IV and his niece, Queen Mariana.

1664 At the age of sixteen, the poetess Juana Inés Ramírez de Santillana enters the Viceroyal Palace in Mexico City as handmaiden to the new Vice-Queen.

1665 In the year of his death, Philip IV loses Portugal, his army reduced from 15,000 to 8,000 in eight hours of battle.

1665 A royal edict is issued forbidding unauthorized books to enter the Americas.

1666 Antonio Núñez, a Jesuit officer of the Inquisition, is appointed Juana's confessor.

1667 John Milton completes *Paradise Lost*.

1667 Juana Ramírez quits the palace for the convent of San José, and leaves three months later.

1669 Juana enters the convent of San Jerónimo, eventually choosing the religious name of Sor Juana Inés de la Cruz.

1680 Grandiose *auto da fe* in Madrid; the Queen Mother attends in the company of her dwarf Lucillo. Twelve burned alive.

1680 A comet, eventually to be named after Edmond Halley, appears over Europe and America.

1680 The celebrated poet Sor Juana Inés de la Cruz is commissioned to create *The Allegorical Neptune* in welcome to the incoming viceroy and vice-queen, an auspicious beginning to Sor Juana's most productive period.

1687 Isaac Newton publishes his *Principia Mathematica*.

1690 Sor Juana's published theological arguments attract the notice of the Inquisition.

1691 Inquisition proceedings are instituted against a priest defending Sor Juana.

1691 August 23rd, a total eclipse of the sun.

1692 Floods, crop infestations, famine in Mexico. In June, a revolt against Spanish authority.

1692 Salem witch-hunts. Nineteen women hanged.

1693 The Archbishop of Mexico publishes an edict condemning the scandal and disorder in the city's twenty-two convents. Sor Juana ceases all writing and study.

1694 Sor Juana's defender is condemned by the Inquisition. March 5th: Sor Juana signs a statement of contrition in blood.

1695 Plague enters Mexico City. Death of Sor Juana Inés de la Cruz, aged forty-six.

BOOK ONE

Notes

Echo BOOK ONE

1. Editor's note: the translations of B. Lismosneros take at times reckless liberties, and should, wherever possible, be checked against the work of other translators, and Sor Juana's own.

2. Sor Juana's own words, from her autobiographical *Response to Sor Filotea*, translated in part by Alan Trueblood in *A Sor Juana Anthology* (Harvard University Press, 1988).

3. Two famous seventeenth-century anagrams for the angelical salute 'Ave Maria, gratia plena, Dominus tecum.'

4. The anagram of a 'mightier cry' is the two words 'mercy' and 'right' plus a missing 'I.'

5. About a year after this chapter was written (as closely as this can be determined), an article appeared in the Mexico City daily *La Reforma*, on the potential discovery of Juana's earliest poem. Composed by her at the age of eight, it was a *loa* of some three hundred lines on the occasion of the Feast of Corpus Christi. Among its many interesting aspects are these two: first, that at so tender an age Juana should have been writing on the Eucharist; second, that the poem was bilingual, one line beginning in Castilian and ending in Nahuatl, the next line Nahuatl / Castilian. Until recently, it has widely been supposed by Sor Juana scholars that she had help with her verses in Nahuatl; only recently have Nahuatl experts such as Patrick Johansson begun to assert that Sor Juana's fluency in the Aztec language might have been superb, given that her verses over such a long period (even longer now, should the attribution of this new poem prove correct) are of such a high calibre.

6. Poems by Juana and Sor Juana in this manuscript fall into three categories: authenticated (most of these appear with her name in sections separate from the chapters); attributed (one or two poems are used whose authorship is contested); speculatively attributed. All of these will be identified in notes. This anagram poem falls into the third category.

7. The translation is by Margaret Sayers Peden, and is found in Paz's *Sor Juana, Or the Traps of Faith*.

8. Translation by Thelma Sullivan, *A Scattering of Jades* (Simon & Schuster, Touchstone, 1994).

9. Plutarch, *Conjugal Precepts*.

10. A paraphrase of Sor Juana's autobiographical account, in her *Reply to Sor Philothea*.

11. Speculatively attributed to Sor Juana.

12. A similar placard from a poetry tourney of 1683 is quoted by I.A. Leonard in *Baroque Times in Old Mexico* (University of Michigan, 1959).

13. Miguel de Cervantes, *Don Quixote*.

14. This following chapter derives its documentation from the accounts of the *auto grande* (the great *auto-da-fé*) of 1649 published by Solange Alberro in *Inquisición y sociedad en México 1571–1700* (Fondo de Cultura Económica, 1988), pp. 581–82; and a wondrously detailed chapter on that subject in José Toribio Medina's *Historia de la Inquisición en México* (Ediciones Fuente Cultural, 1905), pp. 196–208.

Isis BOOK TWO

1. From Chapman's translation of Homer's *Iliad*.

2. Also possibly an allusion to the Gallinero, a famed house of rare birds at Buen Retiro palace.

3. This is Augustine's phrase for a 'God who is remote, distant, and mysterious' yet one 'powerfully and unceasingly present in all times and places.' *Totus ubique*—'the whole of him everywhere.'

4. A reference to one of the great spiritual transports of *The Confessions*, Book 8, Chapter 12, "The Voice as of a Child."

5. Axolotl, 'waterdog' or 'waterdoll.' Among the *axolotl*'s mythological attributes (by way of its association with Xolotl, the Feathered Serpent's double, usually represented as a dog): regeneration, deformity, twinning, dirty feet, a swamp life in hiding, cowardice and flight from sacrifice, death, especially by execution, and, oddly, playfulness or gamesmanship.

6. See Roberto Calasso, *The Marriage of Cadmus and Harmony*.

7. The translation of the Hebrew Bible was, according to one Aristeas, the project of Ptolemy II Philadelphus, who wanted a Greek version for the library of Alexandria. Especially as concerns the specific number of translators (who were said to have been sent to an island, each to work in seclusion on his own version), the story may be apocryphal; but what is more certain is that the translation, considered highly skillful, was executed in Egypt during the reign of one of the early Ptolemies.

8. Translation of Nahuatl hearth poem by Thelma Sullivan, *A Scattering of Jades* (Simon & Schuster, Touchstone, 1994), p. 138.

9. From Canto I of *Cantar de mio Cid*.

10. Speculatively attributed to Sor Juana.

11. Aside from the mention of magic, the concepts in this paragraph are a direct borrowing—be it tribute or theft—from Octavio Paz's *Sor Juana*, cf. p. 80.

12. English translation appears in Miguel León-Portilla's *Fifteen Poets of the Aztec World* (University of Oklahoma Press, 1992).

13. The scholarly Lucero, with his retinue of feminine companions, watches with growing horror the unfolding mystery of the Nativity, detecting in it the outlines of his final defeat.

14. Much of the first part of this chapter draws exhaustively upon a section of *Giro del Mondo*, a seventeenth-century account of a journey around the world by an Italian gentleman adventurer, Gemelli Carerri. The three volumes in which Carerri chronicles his travels in the New World are rich in detail. Carreri was an acquaintance of don Carlos de Sigüenza y Góngora, and a good part of the Italian's information on Aztec lore and the Conquest very likely came from don Carlos himself.

15. Speculatively attributed to Sor Juana.

16. Translation by Alan Trueblood in *A Sor Juana Anthology* (Harvard University Press, 1988).

17. Adapted from a translation by Alan Trueblood.

18. Translation by Alan Trueblood.

19. Two rich sources on this topic: Mario Lavista, "Sor Juana, musicus," and Ricardo Miranda, "Sor Juana y la música: una lectura mas," in *Sor Juana Inés de la Cruz: memoria del coloquio internacional*. Instituto Mexiquense de Cultura.

20. The fresco painter Luca Giordano did come from Italy to Madrid, did praise *Las Meninas* as the theology of painting, only he came in 1692, and at no time before 1667. The Vicereine, therefore, could not have been there or known anyone who had, could not therefore have lied or exaggerated about it, or even have been referring to a similar incident, 'the theology of painting' being so specific. If the anachronism is deliberate, its purpose is not obvious. Sor Juana, I suppose, could have heard this phrase and misremembered who'd told her of it, but only if she were looking back on her days at the palace at a distance of some twenty-five years. . . . But then this, I suppose, could be the point.

21. For a detailed account of the *galanteos de Palacio*, the reader might begin with the Duke de Maura's *Vida y Reinado de Carlos II* (Madrid: Espasa Calpe, 1942), pp. 41–54. See also Deleito y Piñuela's *El rey se divierte*. Octavio Paz, in Chapter 7 of *Sor Juana*, admirably situates the *galanteos* in the context of the history of courtly love and analyzes their function in the sexual economy of palace life. Paz's image of a dance around a dying Sun King has been lifted with a minor, if significant, modification: that Philip IV was the Planet King, and what was dying was not just the King but geocentrism.

22. A likely source here is Little's brilliant essay in Josep M. Sola-Solé and George E. Gingras, eds., *Tirso's Don Juan: The Metamorphosis of a Theme* (Catholic University of America Press, 1988).

23. If da Vinci has been held above all else and all others as the model Renaissance Man, today there is a tendency to see him as the illustration of a failed ideal. Athanasius Kircher, born in 1602, might be considered the model Baroque Man. But few have heard

of him today. His reputation has suffered much more than the Renaissance da Vinci's, perhaps by becoming the unfortunate epitome of an age with an image problem, the Baroque. If anything, his reach was broader and more ambitious than da Vinci's. He proposed a system of universal knowledge, which was to become a powerful inspiration to Sor Juana, the poet of *Primero sueño*. Mystic, magus, humanist, geologist, linguist and (mis)interpreter of the Egyptian hieroglyphs, Kircher nevertheless found time to serve as one of the pre-eminent Jesuit theologians of his time even while becoming a encyclopaedist of music; he also designed magnetic toys and magic lanterns (and has often been credited with inventing the latter). None of his many scientific theories earned him the acclaim of a Newton or a Liebniz, though he did claim to have resurrected plants from their ashes. But over two hundred years before the discovery of the plague bacillus, Kircher's pioneering work with microscopes led him to formulate a theory that the bubonic plague was transmitted through invisible 'infective corpuscles. . . .'

24. This was no mere racist hysteria on the part of the Dominicans and others faced with explaining a much longer list of uncanny correspondences: notably the red and black crosses adorning the robes of Quetzalcóatl in the ancient codices; trials in the desert; a promised land; an Aztec network of monasteries and convents and an almost-Catholic priestly hierarchy; fasting and celibacy and moveable feasts; confession in confidentiality followed by prescribed acts of contrition; the association of baptism and naming . . .

25. The family of Nezahualcóyotl ('fasting coyote') would continue to be associated with dissent and self-sacrifice. For instance, in a manoeuvre devised to prevent the Snake Woman Tlacaelel, a brutal general, from acceding to the Tenochca throne of the Triple Alliance. Nezahualcóyotl pledged to make himself and his people forever subordinate to the Tenochcas, who were then free to make Tenochtitlán the new imperial capital. Similarly, even as the Aztecs were being consumed by their fetishes for idols and blood sacrifice, Nezahualcóyotl was resurrecting from the Toltec tradition the possibility of an unknowable, unseeable god everywhere present—simultaneously near and far—and instilling all with holiness. Nezahualpilli, the poet-emperor's son, would one day visit Moctezuma II in his brooding solitude and foretell the calamities that would soon befall the Aztecs. Nezahualpilli's son, don Carlos Ometochtzin Chichimecatecuhtli, in 1539 was judged and condemned to death by the Inquisition as an apostate, idolator, libertine and predicator of the ancient beliefs. *His* son and the father of the fictional Juan de Alva, Fernando de Alva Ixtlilxochitl, would make it his life's work to preserve and make known the poetry and philosophy of his great-grandfather and the literature of his people. In 1692 it was this distinguished family's land titles that Carlos Sigüenza rescued, at some risk to himself, from archives set alight by rioters in Mexico City's main square.

26. The principal sources for this section on Guadalupe and Aztec sacrifice are works by Clendinnen, Gillespie, Brundage, Carrasco, Lafaye and Neumann. Central here is Susan Gillespie's thesis of 'the women of discord,' whose violent deaths propel the Mexica toward their destiny.

27. In this connection the interested reader might profitably turn to Tzvetan Todorov's *The Conquest of America*, particularly the first chapter of a section devoted to the theme of love in the Conquest.

28. *Vino de obsidiana* or obsidian wine was not necessarily wine, or even a drink at all, but seems to have been a decoction administered to victims before sacrifice. The early Spanish sources believed its main function to be sedative. One of the effects ascribed to it was called "parrot dancing," a state given to imitative movements of some sort.

Sappho BOOK THREE

1. An introduction to the themes of science and exploration in Sor Juana's *Martyr of the Sacrament* can be found in an article by Héctor Azar, "Sor Juana y el descubrimiento de América."

2. As a reminder to the Queen, Sor Juana's use of *Plus Ultra* here might have been two-fold: when the first Hapsburg King of Spain, Charles I (1516–1556), sailed for Spain from the Netherlands to claim the throne, an armada of forty ships sailed with him. On his flagship was an image of the Pillars of Hercules and the young king's new motto, *Plus Ultra*, which came to represent Spain's ambition to rule both hemispheres and proved to be an ambition that outlasted the Hapsburgs. Philip V (formerly Philippe, duc d'Anjou), grandson of Louis XIV, and the first of the Spanish Bourbon kings, had the motto stamped onto the Spanish eight-*reales* coin.

3. Apparent reference to the twelve labours of Herakles. The eleventh was to retrieve the apples of the Hesperides, the golden fruit given to Hera by Mother Earth as a wedding gift. The retrieval was actually performed by the Titan Atlas freed from the eternal task that was his punishment: to bear the world (or the celestial sphere) upon his back, a burden that Herakles offered to shoulder, proposing as a respite that Atlas grapple instead with the hundred-headed dragon guarding the golden tree. The Titan, having successfully retrieved the apples, very nearly did not take his burden back, and was only tricked into it by a Heraklean bit of table-turning.

4. For excesses committed on the banks of the river Heracleius, Hera visited upon Herakles a fit of madness. In a god-sent delusion, he mistook six of his children and two of a friend's for enemies and in a berserk fury murdered them. Turning to the

Pythoness at Delphi for a way to expiate his blood crime, he was sentenced to twelve years of labour for King Eurystheus. The legendary twelve labours.

5. Robert Graves lists three *daughters* born of Neptune to Amphitrite, the Triple Moon-Goddess: Triton (since masculinized), Rhode and Benthesicyme—lucky new moon; full harvest moon; dangerous old moon.

6. One might infer that by 'Ocean' the poet means Amphitrite, Queen of the Oceans, but finds it indelicate to say this directly, having already linked Amphitrite to the Vice-Queen.

7. In the seventeenth century, the absolute monarch's divine right to rule was promoted as never before, precisely when more human claims to legitimacy were becoming ever more plainly incredible: inherent nobility, wisdom, courage in the field . . .

Baroque art, largely sponsored by monarchs and by princes of the Church, for the most part actively colluded in the promotion of its patron's claims to divinity or sanctity. The equation being: beauty = divinity/sanctity = the right to wealth and privilege. Much as the godlike beauty of actor-models in their Elysian settings serve today, countless examples of seventeenth-century art drew on the gods of pagan antiquity, already secularized by the later Greeks. Thus, even as the pope was God's Vicar, the king in the guise of Jupiter or Neptune might now be seen as His viceroy. So it was that Baroque theatre, painting and poetry made demi-gods of their patrons at a time when not a few were pushing the opposite threshold, of the sub-human.

Sor Juana participated in the norms of her time. As an artist dependent on her patrons she did at least her share of beautifying and sanctifying; nevertheless, as in so many areas, she diverts and subverts these norms to her own ends: she turns the canons and cameras of Baroque art, as it were, on herself. It is herself she beautifies, reifies and sanctifies, not so much for wealth (though she was not averse) or for power per se, but for the privilege to do as she wishes, for a woman's freedom of action and inquiry. As Paz points out, *Allegorical Neptune* is a riddle at the heart of which Sor Juana herself sits, on the throne of the goddess Isis, mother, widow, knowledge incarnadine, Man to the second power. Sophia, Ennoia, Athena (Wisdom, Thought, Mind) are all feminine for Sor Juana. This takes her at least to the threshold of Gnostic heresy.

8. Why Neptune? The incoming Vice-King was Marquis de la Laguna, Marquis of the Lake. Surrounded by floating gardens, Mexico was built on an island and was in need of protection from floods made worse every year by logging and soil erosion. Neptune was the Roman (and therefore less pagan) version of Poseidon, who turned Delos from a floating island into a stable one; was master of earthquakes and flood; built the walls of Troy; invented navigation and first tamed horses; fathered monsters but also water figures such as his granddaughters the Danaïdes. Sor Juana followed Pausanias in making him father of Athena, which is not completely far-fetched: Athena was

without dispute sired on the sea-nymph Metis, was born along the river Triton, and was raised by Triton, offspring of Neptune and Aphrodite. Next, with a little quick footwork of her own, Sor Juana made Neptune the son of Isis—Horus/Harpocrates, god of silence and of wise councils. Just as significantly, Sor Juana's verses of welcome made the incoming Vice-Queen Amphitrite, Neptune's consort, goddess of the sea, mother of all waters, of all life, creativity, wisdom; and alternatively Aphrodite/Venus, foam-born daughter of the sea, beauty embodied, morning star, Lucifer rising at dawn, antebellum and antibellum, as it were, to oppose the bellicose fires of the Apollonian Sun. In sum, it is perhaps in this rather more dangerous context that we are to read this strange if beautiful fragment of *Allegorical Neptune*, as it veers away from the rising sun of Christian patriarchy and in doing so, towards Gnostic heresy, or *plus ultra*.

9. In a footnote to his translation of Sor Juana's *First Dream*, Trueblood writes of Nyctimene: "For tricking her father into incest with her, this girl of Lesbos was changed into an owl, a bird believed to drink the oil of holy lamps in order to extinguish them." The oil, presumably, was olive oil, Athena's gift to Greece.

10. *Quise ayunar de tus noticias* . . . line from a Romance written for the Countess of Paredes.

11. *Discalza* was the word in the original, which has been replaced with 'barefoot' and this explanatory endnote: roughly speaking, convents fell into two categories, and the *discalzas* were those convents conforming to the most austere rules of 'death to the world' and penitence. One such was the convent of the Discalced Carmelites, which Sor Juana quickly left before coming to San Jerónimo.

12. Machiavelli.

13. The story is almost certainly that of Sor Juana's contemporary and compatriot Sor María de San José, a nun and mystic eventually known throughout New Spain.

14. Though Sor Juana and Sappho were each called the Tenth Muse, there are only one or two direct mentions of Sappho in all of Sor Juana's surviving works.

15. Transit to Venus's gardens,
organ of marble, your songster's
throat imprisons even the wind in
sweetest ecstasy.

   Tendrils of crystal and ice,
alabaster arms that bewitch
fasting Tantalus's pendant desire,
banquets of sweetest misery . . .

16. A wry allusion, perhaps, to one of the posts held by the painter Velázquez at the court of Philip IV.

17. Matins being the last prayer of the night, Lauds the first in the morning. Though

the Divine Office may vary widely, the hours at San Jerónimo may reasonably be supposed as follows: Lauds—daybreak. Prime—7 A.M. Terce—9 A.M. Sext—noon. Nones—3 P.M. Vespers—5 P.M. Compline—8 P.M. Matins varies the most, anywhere from 9 P.M. to, say, 1 A.M. at San Jerónimo, in particular.

18. Bénassy-Birling (p. 226) appears to have provided the basis for speculations about the Godinez affair.

19. Núñez writes these injunctions to nuns in his *Distribucion de las obras del dia*. Cited by Wissmer in *Coloquio Internacional: Sor Juana Inés de la Cruz y el pensamiento Novohispano*.

20. The Council of Trent was convened to formulate responses to the Protestant Reformation. Among the reforms introduced: strict enclosure of nuns; no preaching except by approved ministers, especially not by women; institution of Inquisition Index of banned works.

21. As Queen Christina's tutor, Descartes was called to answer questions at all hours of the night. Unused to the Swedish climate, Descartes caught cold one winter night and died shortly afterwards. Or so the legend goes.

22. The ontological distinction between the written and the oral in New Spain, as illustrated by the Conquest's *Requerimiento*, seems to be one first offered by Margo Glantz.

23. The discussion of Aristophanes and Aeschylus appears to entwine observations made separately by Alan H. Sommerstein (on Aristophanes) and Richard Lattimore (on Aeschylus).

24. In another translation, Aristophanes has Lysistrata refer to these as Milesian Six-Inch Ladies' Comforters and to lament the wartime constraints on the importation of leather phalluses from Miletus that cruelly increased the dissatisfaction of the women who waited. . . .

25. A discussion of Sor Juana's putative heretical quietism appears in Bénassy-Birling.

26. That Sor Juana was the first in her time to return to an ancient notion of Beauty as the Fourth Transcendental is the thesis of Tavard, fully developed in *Sor Juana and the Theology of Beauty*.

Phoenix BOOK FOUR

1. Sor Juana's frequent recourse to structuring her ironies in triangles was detected and discussed in detail using *romance* 43 by Alessandra Luiselli, "On the Dangerous Art of Throwing Down the Gauntlet: the Irony of Sor Juana toward the Viceregents de Galve," a close reading of Sor Juana's relations with the last Viceroy and Vicereine she was to know and serve before her death.

2. Margaret Sayers Peden's fine translation of Sor Juana's response runs to seventy-two pages in Penguin's bilingual paperback edition. It has been violently abridged here, with what remains only just sufficient to convey the flavour of a text that, as pointed out by Penguin, "predates, by almost a century and a half, serious writings on *any* continent about the position and education of women." One might add here that for roughly two centuries, say 1725 to 1940, the name of Sor Juana Inés de la Cruz went largely unmentioned.

3. "Several factors make Sor Juana's last years seem sadly 'modern.' The first is the theological—today we say ideological—nature of her personal difficulties and quarrels . . . Personal quarrels disguise themselves as clashes between ideas, and the true protagonists of our acts are not we but God or history. Reality is transformed into an enigmatic book we read with fear: as we turn the page we may find our condemnation. We are an argument with which a masked person challenges another, also masked; the subject of a polemic whose origins we are ignorant of and whose denouement we shall never know. Neither do we know the identity of the masked powers who debate and toy with our acts and our lives: where is God and where the Devil? Which is the good side of history and which the bad? . . . Another resemblance between our age and Sor Juana's is the complicity, through ideology, of the victim with his executioner. I have cited the case of Bukharin and others accused in the Moscow trials. Sor Juana's attitude—on a smaller scale—is similar; we have only to read the declarations she signed following her general confession in 1694. This is not surprising; her confessor and spiritual director was also a censor for the Inquisition. Political-religious orthodoxies strive not only to convince the victim of his guilt but to convince posterity as well. Falsification of history has been one of their specialties." Octavio Paz, *Sor Juana.*

4. As an option slightly less inelegant than inserting dozens of citations throughout the chapter, the editor elects to acknowledge the principal and most likely sources for the ideas developed here. Two articles discuss Sor Juana as one of the great musical theorists of her age: Mario Lavista's "Sor Juana *musicus,*" and Ricardo Miranda's "*Sor Juana y la música: una lectura más.*" Tavard in his *Sor Juana and the Theology of Beauty* presents Sor Juana as being the first thinker of her time to take up Saint Jerome's notions of beauty, treating it throughout her work as a fourth transcendental attribute of the divine, and in a sense the *plus ultra* of the other three.

5. Fisher of flocks,

Pastor of schools,

at times it is his crook

and shepherd's call we answer to,

at times his net that gathers us in . . .

6. The Persian mathematician in question might well have ventured an opinion on the Catholic Monarchs' expulsion of the Spanish Jews by edict and the Spanish Moors by force of arms. Of Christianity, Al-Biruni once wrote, "Upon my life, this is a noble philosophy, but the people of this world are not all philosophers. . . . And indeed, ever since Constantine the Victorious became a Christian, both sword and whip have been ever employed."

7. Sweet deity of the air, harmonious
suspension of the senses and the will,
in which the most turbulent awareness
finds itself so pleasurably enthralled.
And thus:
your art reduces to what surpasses even science,
to hold the soul entire suspended
by the thin thread of one sense alone . . .

8. Sweet-throated swan, suspend the measures of thy song:
Chorister behold, in thyself, the master before whom Delphi bows,
and for earthly panpipes changes heaven's lyre . . .

9. Verses by John of the Cross, something of a graveyard for translators, apparently, for encompassing Dante's depths and Sappho's intensities beneath a surface simplicity.

. . . Of peace and piety
it was the perfect science,
in profoundest solitude
the narrow way
was a thing so secret, yet understood,
that there I stood, stammering,
all sciences transcended . . .

10. This craft of knowing nothing
is of such exalted power—
even with all the sages arguing—
as never to be persuaded
that its own simplicity does not come
to encompass non-understanding . . .
all sciences transcending.

11. As mentioned briefly in Book Two, Susan Gillespie traces the theme of 'women of discord' through the Mexica histories and legends. Sacrificed, these women serve as catalyst—fuel, one would almost say.

12. Even the casual reader of Mexica histories is struck by the frequency with which themes and details recur in various narratives. Given that the storytellers and their

audiences were influenced by the idea of Time as having a cyclical or spiral structure, it is not surprising that they should look for patterns, and therefore find them. But it would also appear that, in addition, the chroniclers planted them there: that is, the Mexicas revised the ancient histories, in inscribing themselves within a cycle of stories predating their own by at least a millennium; in highlighting those elements of new events corresponding to the older pattern; and, conversely, in drafting a revisionist version in conformity with what was seen to be the mythic structure of reality. In a sense, then, much of Mexica divination was not of the future but of the past, history being a form of prophecy. (Curiously enough, Carlos II, the last Hapsburg King of the Spanish Empire, had adopted methods at least superficially like those used by Moctezuma II, the last Emperor of the Aztecs.)

13. Don Juan Sáenz del Cauri is a near perfect anagram for Sor Juana Inés de la Cruz.

14. This excerpt from the sentencing request of Prosectur Deza y Ulloa, and the later one from the verdict of Master Examiner Dorantes, are verbatim translations from Inquisition records now in the Mexican National Archives, quoted in Castorena, pp. 297–300.

15. John of the Cross. Roughly, " . . . *Living in darkest fear / And yet I hope and wait / dying because I do not die . . ."*

16. The Nahuatl phrase for 'Enemy of Both Sides' is not the only epithet used for Tezcatlipoca. Others: tenepantla motecaya, nezahualpilli (FastingPrince), tezcatlipoca, moyocoyatzin, chicoyaotl.

17. *La peor de todas,* 'the worst of all women,' 'the worst woman in the world.'

18. A more or less literal translation: *. . . and I stooped so low so low / as to fly so high so high / that at last I caught the prey . . .* The lines are from a poem on falconry *'a lo divino'* by John of the Cross. The theme, according to John Frederick Nims, is common in Medieval love poetry: the pursuit of the heron by the falcon was thought 'the noblest and most thrilling' form of falconry. The heron rises in steep almost helical rings, while the smaller, faster falcon gains slowly in a widening gyre.

19. This document, although undated (and perhaps incomplete), was undoubtedly written after Sor Juana's final poem, itself left unfinished. In all, three such petitions were written over the last two years of her life, constituting her last writings, and the only ones from this period. Depending on whether the "Plea before the Divine Tribunal" was the first or last of the three, it will have been composed not much earlier than February of 1693 and not much later than March of 1694.

20. *Prometheus Bound . . .* Aeschylus.

21. Emperor of the Two Faiths: Alfonso VI of Spain. Lord Instructor of the World: a divine epithet used by the Inca. Lord of the Two Horizons: Ra of Egypt. Sovereign of the Two Worlds: the final honorific accruing to the throne of the Spanish Empire.

22. *Prometheus Bound* . . . Aeschylus.

23. John of the Cross, "La Fonte," translated by John Frederick Nims as *Bounty of waters flooding from this well / invigorates all earth, high heaven, and hell / in dark of night.* The final stanza is translated by Willis Barnstone as *O living fountain that I crave / in bread of life I see her flame / in black of night.*

24. A term of endearment of particular warmth, even among the many such to be found in Mexican Spanish, in this case denoting a fraternal twin; but the connotation is perhaps soul-mate, soul-sister. (*Cuate* may or may not derive from Quetzalcóatl, or eagle, just as *cholo* might be from Xolotl, Quetzalcóatl's 'double.')

Horus BOOK FIVE

1. " . . . Catherine of Siena (1347–1380), ate only a handful of herbs each day and occasionally shoved twigs down her throat to bring up any other food she was forced to eat. Thirteenth-century figures such as Mary of Oignes and Beatrice of Nazareth vomited from the mere smell of meat, and their throats swelled shut in the presence of food . . . Somewhat later, in the seventeenth century, Saint Veronica ate nothing at all for three days at a time but on Fridays permitted herself to chew on five orange seeds, in memory of the five wounds of Jesus . . . Many medieval women spoke of their 'hunger' for God and their 'inebriation' with the holy wine. Many fasted in order to feast at the 'delicious banquet of God' . . . Angela of Fogligno . . . who drank pus from sores and ate scabs and lice from the bodies of the sick, spoke of the pus as being as 'sweet as the eucharist . . .'" From Joan Jacobs Brumberg, discussing *anorexia mirabilis* in *Fasting Girls* (Harvard University Press, 1988).

2. See Margo Glantz, *Sor Juana Inés de la Cruz: ¿hagiografía o autobiografía?*

3. The "Protesta" may have been the last thing written by Sor Juana Inés de la Cruz.

Phaëthon BOOK SIX

1. A debt is owing here, obviously, to Camus's *The Plague.*

2. Sor Juana's *First Dream.* All translations of *First Dream* are by Alan Trueblood.

3. Sor Juana once wrote that *First Dream* was the only poem she had composed for herself. An exaggeration, no doubt, but there is little doubt that it was different—from her other work and from anyone else's. Octavio Paz argues that it is without precedent in all of Spanish literature. Again Paz: "*First Dream*'s break with tradition . . . is a sign of her times. Something ends in that poem and something begins. This spiritual

departure implies a radical change in the relationship between the human being and the beyond. . . ." (Margaret Sayers Peden, trans.)

4. First Dream.

5. Harpocrates is sometimes identified as the Greek Horus, god of silence.

6. This verse and the three remaining verses to appear in the text are from *First Dream*.